THE VILLA OF MYSTERIES

'A beautifully structured and absorbing thriller . . .
The city of Rome, her cops, her bureaucrats and
criminals, shine hard and clear as sunlight bouncing
off the Trevi fountain. But they're a lot less pretty'
Crime Time

'A novel to savour – imagine the deceptively relaxed
atmosphere of Donna Leon's Brunetti novels mixed
with the darkness of Ian Rankin's Rebus sequence.
Excellent'
Ink

'A riveting tale of revenge brought to life by sharp
characterisation and powerful dynamics'
Good Book Guide

'A genuine page-turner that you never want to end.
Hewson is brilliant at conveying mood and atmosphere
and wraps the reader in the tense and terrifying pursuit
every step of the way. If you missed the first book,
A Season for the Dead, buy them both and savour
every twist and turn'
Newbury News

A SEASON FOR THE DEAD
and
THE VILLA OF MYSTERIES

David Hewson was born in Yorkshire in 1953. He worked as staff writer on *The Times* from 1978, and has written seven novels, as well as several travel books. He is now a weekly columnist for the *Sunday Times*. Following *A Season for the Dead*, *The Villa of Mysteries* is the second in the Italian crime series set in Rome and featuring Detective Nic Costa. The author lives in Kent.

www.davidhewson.com

DAVID HEWSON

A SEASON FOR THE DEAD
and
THE VILLA OF MYSTERIES

PAN BOOKS

A Season for the Dead first published 2003 by Macmillan
First published in paperback 2004 by Pan Books
The Villa of Mysteries first published 2003 by Macmillan
First published in paperback 2005 by Pan Books

This omnibus first published 2008 by Pan Books
an imprint of Pan Macmillan Ltd
Pan Macmillan, 20 New Wharf Road, London N1 9RR
Basingstoke and Oxford
Associated companies throughout the world
www.panmacmillan.com

ISBN 978-0-330-50795-0

1 3 5 7 9 8 6 4 2

A CIP catalogue record for this book is available from
the British Library.

Typeset by IntypeLibra, London Ltd
Printed in the UK by CPI Mackays, Chatham ME5 8TD

A SEASON FOR THE DEAD

One

The heat was palpable, alive. Sara Farnese sat at her desk in the Reading Room of the Vatican Library and stared out of the window, out into the small rectangular courtyard, struggling to concentrate. The fierce August afternoon placed a rippling, distorting mirage across her view. In the unreal haze, the grass was a yellow, arid mirror of the relentless sun. It was now two o'clock. Within an hour the temperature beyond the glass would hit forty degrees. She should have left like everyone else. Rome in August was an empty furnace echoing to the whispers of desiccated ghosts. The university corridors on the other side of the city rang to her lone footsteps that morning. It was one reason she decided to flee elsewhere. Half the shops and the restaurants were closed. The only life was in the parks and the museums, where stray groups of sweating tourists tried to find some meagre shade.

This was the worst of the summer. Yet she had decided to stay. She knew why and she wondered whether she was a fool. Hugh Fairchild was visiting from London. Handsome Hugh, clever Hugh, a man who could rattle off from memory the names of every early Christian codex lodged in the museums of Europe, and had probably read them too. If the plane was on time he would have arrived at Fiumicino at ten that morning and, by now, have checked into his suite at the Inghilterra. It was too early for him to stay with her, she knew that, and pushed from her head the idea that there could be other names in his address book, other candidates for his bed. He was an intensely busy man. He would be in Rome for five days, of which two nights alone were hers, then move on to a lawyers' conference in Istanbul.

It was, she thought, possible that he had other lovers. No, probable. He lived in London, after all. He had abandoned academia to become a successful career civil servant with the EU. Now he seemed to spend one week out of every four on the road, to Rome, to New York, to Tokyo. They met, at most, once a month. He was thirty-five, handsome in a way that was almost too perfect. He had a long, muscular, tanned body, a warm, aristocratic English face, always ready to break into a smile, and a wayward head of blond hair. It was unthinkable that he did not sleep with other women, perhaps at first meeting. That was, she recalled, with a slight sensation of guilt, what had happened to her at the convention on the preservation of historical artefacts in Amsterdam four months before.

Nor did it concern her. They were both single adults. He was meticulously safe in his lovemaking. Hugh Fairchild was a most *organized* man, one who entered her life and left it at irregular intervals which were to their mutual satisfaction. That night they would eat in her apartment close to the Vatican. They would cross the bridge by the Castel Sant'Angelo, walk the streets of the *centro storico* and take coffee somewhere. Then they would return to her home around midnight where he would stay until the morning, when meetings would occupy him for the next two days. This was, she thought, an ample provision of intellectual activity, pleasant company and physical fulfilment. Enough to keep her happy. Enough, a stray thought said, to quell the doubts.

She tried to focus on the priceless manuscript sitting on the mahogany desk by the window. This was a yellow volume quite unlike those Sara Farnese normally examined in the Vatican Reading Room: a tenth-century copy of *De Re Coquinaria*, the famed imperial Roman cookery book by Apicius from the first century AD. She would make him a true Roman meal: *isicia omentata*, small beef fritters with pine kernels, *pullus fiusilis*, chicken stuffed with herbed dough, and *tiropatinam*, a soufflé with honey. She would explain that they were eating in because it was August. All the best restaurants were shut. This was not an attempt to change the status of their relationship. It was purely practical and, furthermore, she enjoyed cooking. He would understand or, at the very least, not object.

'Apicius?' asked a voice from behind, so unexpected it made her shudder.

She turned to see Guido Fratelli smiling at her with his customary doggedness. She tried to return the gesture though she was not pleased to see him. The Swiss Guard always made for her whenever she visited. He knew – or had learned – enough of her work in the library to be able to strike up a conversation. He was about her own age, running to fat a little, and liked the blue, semi-medieval uniform and the black leather gun holster a little too much. As a quasi-cop he had no power beyond the Vatican, and only the quieter parts of that. The Rome police retained charge of St Peter's Square which was, in truth, the only place the law was usually needed. And they were a different breed, nothing like this quiet, somewhat timorous individual. Guido Fratelli would not last a day trying to hustle the drunks and addicts around the Termini Station.

'I didn't hear you come in,' Sara said, hoping he took this as a faint reproach. The Reading Room was empty apart from her. She appreciated the quiet; she did not want it broken by conversation.

'Sorry.' He patted the gun on his belt, an unconscious and annoying gesture. 'We're trained to be silent as a mouse. You never know.'

'Of course,' she replied. If Sara recalled correctly, there had been three murders in the Vatican in the course of almost two hundred years: in 1988, when the incoming commander of the Swiss Guard and his wife were shot dead by a guard corporal harbouring a grudge, and in 1848, when the Pope's prime minister was assassinated by a political opponent. With the city force taking care of the crowds in the square, the most Guido Fratelli had to worry about was an ambitious burglar.

'Not your usual stuff?' he asked.

'I've wide-ranging interests.'

'Me too.' He glanced at the page. The volume had come in its customary box, with the name in big, black letters on the front, which was how he knew what she was reading. Guido was always hunting for conversational footholds, however tenuous. Perhaps he thought that was a kind of detective work. 'I'm learning Greek, you know.'

'This is Latin. Look at the script.'

His face fell. 'Oh. I thought it was Greek you looked at. Normally.'

'Normally.' She could see the distress on his face and couldn't help being amused. He was thinking: *I have to try to learn both?*

'Maybe you could tell me how I'm doing some time?'

She tapped the notebook computer onto which she had transcribed half the recipes she wanted.

'Some time. But not now, Guido. I'm busy.'

The desk was at right angles to the window. She looked away from him, into the garden again, seeing his tall, dark form in the long window. Guido was not going to give up easily.

'OK,' he said to her reflection in the glass, then walked off, back down to the entrance. She heard laughter through the floor from the long gallery above. The tourists were in, those who had sufficient influence to win a ticket to these private quarters. Did they understand how lucky they were? Over the last few years, both as part of her role as a lecturer in early Christianity at the university and for purely personal pleasure, she had spent more and more time in the library, luxuriating in the astonishing richness of its collection. She had touched drawings and poems executed in Michelangelo's own hand. She had read Henry VIII's love letters to Anne Boleyn and a copy of the same king's *Assertio Septem Sacramentorum*, signed by the monarch, which had won Henry the title 'Defender of the Faith' and still failed to keep him in the Church.

From a professional point of view it was the early works – the priceless codices and incunabula – which were the focus of her constant attention. Even so, she was unable to prevent herself stealing a glance at the personal material from the Middle Ages on. In a sense, she felt she had listened to Petrarch and Thomas Aquinas in person.

Their voices remained, like dead echoes on the dry vellum and the ancient stain of ink they had left on the page. These traces made them human and, for all their wisdom, for all their skill with words, without their humanity they were nothing, though Hugh Fairchild would probably disagree.

There was a noise from the entrance, a half shout, not loud in itself but, given the context, disturbing. No one ever shouted in the Reading Room of the Vatican Library.

Sara raised her head and was surprised to see a familiar figure walking towards her. He moved briskly through the bands of sharp light that fell through the window, with a swift, determined intent that seemed out of place in these surroundings, wrong. The air-conditioning rose in volume. A chill blanket of air fell over her and she shivered. She looked again. Stefano Rinaldi, a fellow professor at the university, carried a large, bulging plastic bag and was crossing the empty Reading Room with a determined stride. There was an expression on his round, bearded face which she failed to recognize: anger or fear or a combination of both. He was wearing his customary black shirt and black trousers but they were dishevelled and there were what looked like wet stains on both. His eyes blazed at her.

For no reason, Sara Farnese felt frightened of this man whom she had known for some time.

'Stefano . . .' she said softly, perhaps so quietly he was unable to hear.

The commotion was growing behind him. She saw figures waving their arms, beginning to race after the figure in black with the strange, full supermarket bag dangling from his right hand. And from his left, she saw now, something even odder: what appeared to be a gun, a small black pistol. Stefano Rinaldi, a man she had never known to show anger, a man for whom she once felt a measure of attraction, was walking purposefully across the room in her direction holding a gun, and nothing she could imagine, no possible sequence of events, could begin to explain this.

She reached over, placed both hands on the far side of the desk and swung it round through ninety degrees. The old wood screeched on the marble floor like an animal in pain. She heaved at the thing until her back was against the glass and the desk was tight against her torso, not questioning the logic: that she must remain seated, that she must face this man, that this ancient desk, with a tenth-century copy of a Roman recipe book and a single notebook computer on it, would provide some protection against the unfathomable threat that was approaching her.

Then, much more quickly than she expected, he was there, gasping for breath above her, that crazy look more obvious than ever in his dark-brown eyes.

He sat down in the chair opposite and peered into her face. She felt her muscles relax, if only a little. At that moment, Sara was unafraid. He was not there to harm her. She understood that with an absolute certainty that defied explanation.

'Stefano . . .' she repeated.

There were shapes gathering behind him. She could see Guido Fratelli there. She wondered how good he was with his gun and whether, by some unfortunate seren-dipity, she might die that day from the stray bullet of an inexperienced Swiss Guard with a shaking hand that pointed the gun at a former lover of hers who had, for some reason, gone mad in the most venerated library in Rome.

Stefano's left arm, the one holding the weapon, swept the table, swept everything on it, the precious volume of Apicius, her expensive notebook computer, down to the hard marble floor with a clatter.

She was quiet, waiting, which was, his eyes seemed to say, what he wanted.

Then Stefano lifted up the bag to the height of the desk, turned it upside down, let the contents fall on to the table and said, in a loud, commanding voice that was half crazy, half dead, 'The blood of the martyrs is the seed of the Church.'

She looked at the thing in front of her. It had the consistency of damp new vellum, as if it had just been rinsed. Apicius would have written on something very like this once it was dry.

Still holding the gun with his left hand, Stefano began to unravel the pliable thing before her, stretching it, extending the strange fabric until it filled the broad mahogany top of the desk then flowed over the edges, taking as it did a shape that was both familiar and, in its present context, foreign.

Sara forced her eyes to remain open, forced herself to think hard about what she was seeing. The object which Stefano Rinaldi was unfolding, smoothing out carefully with the flat palm of his right hand as if it were a table-cloth perhaps, on show for sale, was the skin of a human being, a light skin somewhat tanned, and wet, as if it had been recently washed. It had been cut roughly from the body at the neck, genitals, ankles and wrist, with a final slash down the spine and the back of the legs in order to remove it as a whole piece and Sara had to fight to stop herself reaching out to touch the thing, just to make sure this was not some nightmare, just to *know*.

'What do you want?' she asked, as calmly as she could.

The brown eyes met hers then glanced away. Stefano was afraid of what he was doing, quite terrified, yet there was some determination there too. He was an intelligent man, not stubborn, simply single-minded in his work which was, she now recalled, centred around Tertullian, the early Christian theologian and polemicist whose famous diktat he had quoted.

'Who are the martyrs, Stefano?' she asked. 'What does this mean?'

He was sane at that moment. She could see this very clearly in his eyes, which had become calm. Stefano was thinking this through, looking for a solution.

He leaned forward. 'She's still there, Sara,' he said, in the tobacco-stained growl she recognized, but speaking very softly, as if he wished no one else to hear. 'You must go. Look at this.' He stared at the table and the skin on it. 'I daren't . . .' There was terror in his face though, in the context it seemed ridiculous. 'Think of Bartholomew. You must know.'

Then, in a much louder voice, one that had the craziness back inside it again, he repeated Tertullian, 'The blood of the martyrs is the seed of the Church.'

Stefano Rinaldi, his eyes now black and utterly lost, lifted the gun, raised it until the short, narrow barrel pointed at her face.

'Down!' the guard screamed. '*Down!*'

Guido was an idiot. Sara knew that instinctively, knew he could not be seeing this scene and reading it the way she did.

'No!' She insisted, raising a hand, to both men, and

saw, to her dismay, Stefano's gun move in front of her again, going higher. 'Both of you! Stop this!'

Guido screamed, gibberish that was both fear and anger. He was out of control. And Stefano simply stared at her, stared with those mournful, forsaken eyes, an expression that finally began to make her feel cold since it seemed to contain so much dead fatalism inside it.

He mouthed a single word, 'Hurry.'

'Don't,' she said, to both of them, knowing it was useless.

An explosion rang from Guido's gun. The room was enveloped by a sound that made her ears scream with pain. Stefano Rinaldi's scalp opened up and issued a livid burst of blood and tissue. Then Guido was dancing around the dead man, wishing he dared touch the corpse now slumping to the floor, letting the gun jerk in his hand as if it had some mind of its own.

She closed her eyes and listened to the sound of fire, heard the bullets whistling round the room, the quiet room, the place of many splendours she had grown to love.

When it was done, Sara Farnese opened her eyes. Stefano lay still on the floor. One of the attendants was close by, shrieking, his hands holding his stomach as if he dared not let go for fear of what might tumble out.

She looked at Stefano's head. It lay on the floor, resting on the ancient copy of Apicius, staining the page with thick, black blood.

Two

They stood in the shade of the colonnades in St Peter's Square, Luca Rossi wondering how badly the sun might have burned his bald head already that day. A couple of rocks were rumbling around his stomach from the previous night's beer and pizza feast. Then, to make matters worse, he had that very morning been given the kid as duty partner for the next four weeks. It was a kind of punishment, for both of them he guessed. Neither fitted in well with the Rome state police department at that moment, for very different reasons. His were distinct, directly attributable to an obvious and, for him, understandable, source. The kid just didn't look right, full stop. And never even knew.

He eyed his partner and groaned. 'OK. I know you want me to ask. So do the trick then.'

Nic Costa smiled and Rossi wished he didn't look so young. Sometimes they had to arrest the odd vicious type in the hallowed precincts of the square. He couldn't help but wonder how much use this slim, adolescent-looking character would be in those circumstances.

'It's not a trick.' They had never worked together before. They came from different stations. Rossi guessed the kid never even knew why some old, overweight cop had been made his new partner. He'd never asked. He just seemed to accept it, to accept everything. Still, Rossi knew something about him. They all did. Nic Costa was one of those cops the others couldn't quite believe. He didn't drink much. He didn't even eat meat. He kept fit and had quite a reputation as a marathon runner. And he was the son of that damned red the papers used to go on about, a man who had left Nic Costa with one very unusual habit. He was a painting freak, one particular painter too. He knew the whereabouts and the provenance of every last Caravaggio in Rome.

'Sounds like a trick to me.'

'It's knowledge,' Costa said, and for a moment looked more like his real age, which Rossi knew to be twenty-seven. Maybe, the older man thought, there was more to him than met the eye. 'No sleight of hand, big man. This is magic, the real thing.'

'Give me some magic then. Over there . . .' He nodded towards the walls of the Vatican. 'I guess they're full of the things.'

'No. Just the one. *The Deposition from the Cross* and they took that from its original location too. The Vatican never much cared for Caravaggio. They thought he was too revolutionary, too close to the poor. He painted people with dirty feet. He made the apostles look like ordinary mortals you might meet in the street.'

'So that's what you like about him? You get that from your old man, I suppose.'

'It's part of what I like. And I'm me, not someone else.'

'Sure.' Rossi remembered the father. He was a real trouble-maker. He never stood to one side for anything, never took a bribe either, which made him one very odd politician indeed. 'So where?'

The kid nodded towards the river. 'Six-minute walk over there. The Church of Sant'Agostino. You can call it *The Madonna of Loreto* or *The Madonna of the Pilgrims*. Either works.'

'It's good?'

'The feet are really dirty. The Vatican hated it. It's a wonderful piece of work but I know better.'

Rossi thought about this. 'I don't suppose you follow football, do you? It may give us more to talk about.'

Costa said nothing then turned on the radio scanner and plugged in the earpiece. Rossi sniffed the air.

'You smell those drains?' he grunted. 'They spend all this money building the biggest church on the planet. They got the Pope in residence just a little walk away. And still the drains stink like some backstreet in Trastevere. Maybe they just chop up bodies and flush them down the toilet or something. As if we'd get to know.'

Costa kept fiddling with the damned radio scanner. They both knew it was supposed to be banned.

'Hey,' he growled. 'Don't you think I get bored too? If Falcone hears you've been messing with that thing he'll kick your ass.'

Costa shrugged his narrow shoulders and smiled. 'I was trying to find some football for you. What's the problem?'

Rossi stuck up his big hands and laughed. 'OK. You got me there.'

They watched the thin crowds shuffle across the square in the enervating heat. It was too hot for the bag-snatchers, Rossi thought. The weather was doing more to reduce the Rome crime rate than anything a couple of cops could ever achieve. He could hardly blame Costa for playing with the scanner. None of them liked being told there were places in the city where they weren't welcome. Maybe Costa had some anti-clerical thing in his genes, however much he told everyone he was apolitical, the opposite of his father. And the Vatican *was* part of the city, whatever the politicians said. It was crazy to think some thieving little bastard could snatch a bag in front of them then scuttle off into the milling masses inside St Peter's and suddenly become untouchable, the property of the Pope's Swiss Guards in their funny blue uniforms and ankle socks.

Costa was never going to hear anything of import on his little pocket scanner. Too little went on in the Vatican for that. But just listening was a form of protest in itself. It said: *we're here*.

Rossi eyed a long crocodile of black nuns who followed a woman waving a little red pennant on a stick. He looked at his watch and wished the hands would move more quickly.

'Enough,' he announced, then, to his surprise, felt Costa's hand on his arm. The young detective was listening intently to a squealing racket in the earpiece of the radio.

'Someone's been shot,' Costa said, suddenly earnest. 'In the Library Reading Room. You know where that is?'

'Of course,' the older man said, nodding. 'Mongolia as far as we're concerned.'

Costa's sharp brown eyes pleaded with him. 'Somebody's been shot. We're not going to just stand here, are we?'

Rossi sighed. 'Say again after me, "The Vatican is another country." Falcone can put it more clearly for you if you want.' Falcone could, Rossi thought, put it very clearly indeed. He didn't even want to imagine what that conversation would be like. He'd been very glad that the last five years had been spent outside Falcone's reach. He only wished it could have been longer.

'Sure,' Costa agreed. 'That doesn't mean we can't look. I mean they never said we couldn't go in there. They just said we couldn't arrest people.'

Rossi thought about that. The kid was right, up to a point.

'That's all you heard? Someone's been shot?'

'Isn't that enough? Do you want to go back and tell Falcone we didn't even offer to help?'

Rossi patted his jacket, felt his gun there and watched Costa do the same. They looked down the Via di Porta Angelica towards the entrance to the private Vatican quarters. The Swiss Guards who were normally there checking visitors' papers were gone, doubtless called to the event. Two Roman cops could walk straight in without a single question being asked. It seemed like an invitation.

'I'm not running,' Rossi grunted. 'Not in this damned heat.'

'Your decision,' Costa answered and was off, out of the square, through the open gate, legs pumping.

'Kids . . .' Luca Rossi grunted and shook his head.

Three

By the time Rossi arrived at the library, some seven
minutes later, Nic Costa had quietly established that the
man who now lay on the floor, head ripped apart by at
least three bullets, was indeed dead. He had watched
the injured attendant being taken away by two scared-
looking medics. He had quietly, carefully made a few
enquiries. The room was in utter chaos, which suited
Costa just fine. The terrified Guido Fratelli had immediately assumed that Costa was some kind of Vatican
official, which was good enough for the three other Swiss
Guards who had come to the room, established there was
no imminent danger and now awaited further orders.
Costa had no early desire to disillusion any of them. He
had, in four years on the force, seen plenty of dead bodies
and even a couple of shootings. But finding a corpse and
the epidermis of another, and in the Vatican, was a new
experience, one he was unwilling to relinquish.

His mind was working overtime. He let it race. The
effort almost pushed the smell of the room from his
consciousness, making the stench of blood and the way it
mixed with the hot, arid air from the open windows just a
little less noticeable.

He let Fratelli babble out his story, unable, all the time, to take his eyes off the woman who sat on a chair, back to the wall, watching everything. She was something short of thirty, modestly dressed in a tight grey business suit. She had shoulder-length dark hair, expensively cut, large green eyes and a serious, classically proportioned face, like that from some medieval painting. Not Cara-vaggio, she was too beautiful for that. No one had that kind of radiance in his work, not even the Madonnas. It wasn't supposed to exist. She looked, too, as if she were holding everything that had happened inside her, trying not to let it explode.

When the guard was done she stood up and walked over to him. He noticed that her grey suit was spattered with blood. She seemed unworried by it. Delayed shock, he thought. Sometime soon she would realize how close she had come to being murdered, how a man had been shot to death in front of her after displaying this strange and gruesome trophy on the desk. The skin still sat there looking like the cast-off from some bad Halloween party. Nic Costa found it difficult to believe it had once belonged to a human being.

'You're city police?' she asked, in a voice which had some odd tinge of accent to it, as if she were half English or American.

'That's right.'

'I thought so.'

The Swiss Guards looked at each other and groaned but had yet to find the courage to argue. They were still waiting for someone.

Rossi, who had been content to let the kid do the talking, smiled at them. The big man was willing to stand back. It felt a touch weird but Costa had got there first.

He already seemed to be in control. All the same Luca Rossi felt a touch grey around the gills. Which he did more and more recently.

The woman said, trying to recover his attention, 'I think Stefano was trying to tell me something.'

'Stefano?' Costa asked. 'The man who was going to kill you?'

She shook her head and Nic Costa couldn't stop himself watching the way her hair moved from side to side. 'He didn't try to kill me. That idiot . . . ,' she indicated Guido Fratelli who went red at her words, '. . . didn't understand what was going on. Stefano wanted me to go with him somewhere. He didn't get the chance to explain.'

The guard muttered something in his own defence and then was silent.

'What was he trying to tell you?' Costa asked.

'He said . . .' She was trying hard to think. He could understand why it would be difficult. There was so much crammed into such a short period of time. 'He said she's still there. To think of Bartholomew. And that we should hurry.'

He watched her deliberate these points and Nic Costa revised his opinion of her. Perhaps it wasn't delayed shock. Perhaps she really was this cool, this detached from what had gone on.

'Hurry where?' he was about to ask when a thick-set man in a dark suit elbowed his way into the conversation, stabbed him hard in the shoulder with a fat index finger, and demanded, 'Who the hell are you?'

The newcomer was about his own size, well built and middle-aged. He wore a dark suit which stank of cigars.

'Police,' Costa said, deliberately cryptic.

'ID?'

He took out his wallet and showed the man his card.

'Out,' the suit ordered. 'Out now.'

Costa looked at his partner, who felt similarly incensed judging by the small amount of colour that came back into his cheeks.

Rossi bent down to the truculent newcomer and asked, 'And we are?'

He looked, Costa thought, like a boxer who had just found God: a big face with florid, pock-marked cheeks and a broken nose. He had a crucifix in the lapel of his black wool jacket which, as far as Costa was concerned, meant nothing.

'Hanrahan,' he grunted, and Costa tried again to place the accent: maybe there was some gruff Irish touch and a little American in there. 'Security. Now you boys just walk along, eh? Leave this to us.'

Costa tapped him on the shoulder and was amused by the anger in his grey eyes. 'You want to know what we found out? I mean, we were just here to help, Mr Hanrahan. This could have been one nasty thing. Someone shooting in the Vatican. Let's face it, you took a while to get here. We could've been stopping something pretty bad.'

The woman looked at the three men fiercely. Costa knew what she was thinking: *they lock horns at a time like this.* She was right too.

'This is a Vatican matter,' Hanrahan said. 'We'll look into it. If we need your help, we'll call.'

'No it's not,' Costa insisted. 'This is our business too.'

Hanrahan said just one word, 'Jurisdiction'.

'You mean,' Costa asked, 'your dumb guard here killed the man on your turf so that's it?'

Hanrahan glanced at Guido Fratelli. 'If that's what happened.'

Costa walked the couple of metres to the desk and picked up an edge of the skin. This had once covered an arm. It felt damp and cold. More human than he had expected.

'And what about this?' he asked.

Hanrahan stared at him. 'What's your point?'

'My point?' The man was not a cop, Costa realized. He wasn't even a Swiss Guard because they always wore some kind of uniform. Security maybe, but he was about defending things, not interested in the slow, careful process of discovery. 'My point is that somewhere there's got to be a body this fits. And for the life of me I don't think that's going to be here.'

'Detective . . .' the woman interrupted.

'Please. Bear with me. What I'm saying, Mr Hanrahan, is that we've got two murders here and if you're a betting man I'll give you good money one of them took place in *our* jurisdiction because we've got the people for this. And you . . .' he cast a withering glance at the miserable Guido Fratelli, now close to tears, 'you don't. Now we're co-operating, we're being nice. Do you think there's some small chance we might get the same in return?'

Hanrahan shook his head. 'You really do not know what you are dealing with.'

'Hey!' Costa's voice rose. He put a hand on Hanrahan's shoulder. 'Are we after the same thing or what?'

'No,' Hanrahan said instantly with a grimace. 'Not at all. Now . . .'

The woman pushed between them and looked Nic Costa in the face.

'Do you have a car?' she asked.

'Sure.'

'He said to go there quickly. Can we do that, please? Now?'

Costa was puzzled once again by how calm she was. All the time they had been arguing she had been thinking, trying to work out the riddle the dead man had left her.

'You know where?'

'I think so. It was stupid of me not to realize earlier. Now. Please?'

Nic Costa patted Hanrahan on the shoulder as they left and said, 'See? You just have to know how to ask.'

Four

Costa thought about the abbreviated story Sara Farnese told them in the car. It raised a host of questions. He wondered too about her reasoning. Maybe the woman was already in shock, only inwardly, and this was just some crazy wild-goose chase.

'Why Tiber Island?' he asked.

'I told you. We have to go to the church.'

Rossi, who was driving, cast him a chilly glance. Costa wondered if he was starting to get bad feelings about this whole thing. It was an odd decision. They should have waited for instructions maybe. But he had no evidence a crime had been committed on city territory. Besides, the woman was adamant: she wanted to get there quickly. Costa thought he could make out a good case in front of Falcone. He normally did.

'Do you mind if I ask why?'

She sighed, as if she were talking to a school child. 'Bartholomew. The saint was flayed alive. Skinned. Stefano worked in that field. He would have known. The church on Tiber Island is Bartholomew's. I can't think of anything else.'

'That's it?' Costa wondered, fast revising his hopes of keeping Falcone sweet.

'That's it,' she agreed testily. 'Unless you have a better idea.'

The two men looked at each other. The August traffic was light. They made their way along the Trastevere waterfront at speed then took a left turn onto the tiny island that sat in the middle of the river.

'This Stefano,' Rossi asked as they pulled into the piazza in front of the church. 'He was a friend of yours?'

She said nothing, and was stepping out of the door before they had come to a halt.

'One scary woman,' Rossi grunted just out of earshot, and shook his head. The two men followed her and looked at the church. It was hard to believe there could be anything wrong here. It was an old, unspoilt corner of the city, with a cobbled piazza where you could sit in the shade away from the murmur of traffic that ran along both banks of the river.

'You think we should call in?' Rossi asked.

Costa shrugged. 'What's the point? Let them hang us in their time, not ours.'

'Yeah,' the older man agreed. 'Let me see if I can find a warden. Get some keys.'

The woman was already at the door of the church.

'Hey,' Costa yelled. 'Wait.'

But she was gone. Costa swore and raced after her, shouting for Rossi to follow.

The place was empty. Costa stood in the nave, framed by the polished columns on either side, feeling the way he always did in churches: uncomfortable. It was a matter of upbringing, he guessed. The places just spooked him out sometimes.

They looked in the dimly lit side chapels. They tried a couple of doors that opened onto tiny storage rooms full of dust.

'There's nothing here,' she said.

They stood in the nave, Costa trying to think of other options. She was disappointed, anxious, as if this were some intellectual puzzle demanding a solution.

'It was worth a try,' he said. 'Don't blame yourself.'

'I blame myself already,' she said softly. 'There has to be more to it than this. We did some work here once. There was a temple, to Aesculapius, before the church. Maybe something underground.'

'Aescoo— who?'

'Aesculapius. He was the god of medicine.' She looked at him. 'That makes it appropriate too, don't you think?'

'Maybe.' He was out of his depth and knew it. There was more going on in the woman's head than he understood. He wondered how much she acknowledged herself.

Rossi returned waving a set of large, old keys. Costa felt awkward. Somehow he seemed to have taken the initiative which was surely Rossi's prerogative. He was older, more senior. He knew more.

'We've been everywhere,' Costa said. 'It's all open anyway. Nothing.'

'Best we call in then,' Rossi said, and seemed relieved at the idea someone else might have to pick up the pieces.

She was staring intently at a small door on the left, before the altar. 'Over there.'

'We tried it,' Costa said.

'No. There's a campanile here too. We didn't find the way into the tower.'

Costa led the way and threw open the door. The room was small and dark. He pulled out the little torch from his pocket and saw instantly why they had missed the exit earlier. The stairs were hidden in the dark far corner, behind an iron screen that was secured with a huge padlock. Rossi grunted then went to it, fumbled with the keys, found the right one and pushed through into the darkness, scrabbling up the stairs.

'Jesus! What was that?'

The big man's screech echoed up the stone staircase.

Costa's hand finally found a light switch. It illuminated the ground floor of the tower and the stone spiral leading upwards through a first floor of old, dry planking.

Rossi staggered down the stairs, still squealing. His bald head was now stained with blood. It ran down his temple, into his eyes. He squirmed trying to clean it, scrubbing at his head with a handkerchief, yelling all the time. For the first time in his police career Nic Costa felt bile rising in his throat. Now they were at the staircase there was a smell inside the hot enclosed oven that was the tower's interior. It stank of fresh meat starting to go sour. He flashed the torch upwards. From the wooden ceiling above the stairs there was a slow, steady drip of coagulating blood that Rossi had walked beneath the moment he put a foot on the first step.

'We need help,' Costa said grimly, pulling the radio from his pocket.

He looked at her, not believing his eyes. Sara Farnese was already on the stairs, squeezing past Rossi. 'Hey!' he yelled, seeing her slim form disappear completely out of view. 'Don't do that. Don't touch anything. Jesus . . .'

His partner was losing it. He was scratching at his face as if the blood there were poison, acid, ready to eat into his skin. Costa took the radio and made a short, urgent call. Then he told Rossi to stay downstairs and wait for him. He didn't like the look on the older man's face. There was something crazy there, something that said this was all travelling a little too far from home. Nic Costa felt the same way but she was gone, she was upstairs with whatever else lived there, and he couldn't accept the idea she might be there alone.

He heard the sound of a switch overhead. A dim, yellow light cast shadows down the stairs. Then Sara Farnese made a noise, something halfway between a gasp and a scream, the first real sign of emotion she had uttered since the carnage in the Vatican Library half an hour before.

'Shit,' Costa cursed and took the stairs two at a time.

She was slumped with her back to the wall. Her hands were over her mouth, her green eyes were wide open in shock and amazement. Costa followed the direction of her gaze. He saw the corpses in the full beam of the single bulb and fought to keep the contents of his stomach down.

There were two bodies in the room. The woman's was fully dressed in a dark skirt and red blouse. It was suspended from a beam by a makeshift noose. Close to the dangling legs was an old wooden chair which might have been kicked from beneath her – or, perhaps, had fallen away as she tried to keep herself upright. Costa did not look too closely at her face but she appeared to be in her mid-thirties, with streaky fair hair and thin, leathery skin.

Two metres away was a second figure, strapped upright to a supporting timber beam: a man with a striking shock of golden hair and a face contorted by the agonies of a terrible death, with a gag tied tightly across his mouth, raising the bloodless lips and perfect white teeth into an ironic smile. He hung by his arms which were tethered above his head to a blackened beam. His legs dangled free to the wooden floor. There was skin on his face, hands, feet and groin alone.

A buzzing cloud of flies hovered over the fleshy torso. Their noise filled the tiny circular room. Around the walls, painted time and time again in the dead man's blood, was the message Sara Farnese had first heard in the Vatican Library, written in rough capital letters: THE BLOOD OF THE MARTYRS IS THE SEED OF THE CHURCH. And, once only, a couplet in English, one Nic Costa could understand enough to realize it was even crazier. It was painted on the wall behind the body so the writing stood behind his head. The words read like the first two lines of a poem . . .

> *As I was going to St Ives*
> *I met a man with seven wives.*

Nic Costa felt his stomach give a single heave then looked at her. Sara Farnese was unable to take her eyes off the bloody, stripped corpse. She looked as if she were going crazy inside her own head.

He crossed the tiny room in two strides and knelt down, between her and the flayed corpse, touching her hands with his.

'You've got to get out of here. Now. Please.'

She tried to avoid the obstacle of his body, tried to see once more. Costa placed his hands on her cheeks and forced her to look into his face.

'This is not your doing. This is not something you should see. Please.'

Then, when she failed to move, he bent down and lifted her into his arms with as much care as he could muster, and walked down the circular stone stairs, feeling her weight in his hands, avoiding as best he could the diminishing drip of blood from the ceiling.

Rossi was outside the door. As they passed he looked back and muttered something about support being on the way. Costa carried her into the nave. At the front he placed her on the bench pew. She was staring at the altar. Her eyes shone with tears.

'I've got things to do,' he said. 'Will you wait here for me?'

She nodded.

Costa beckoned Rossi to stand by the woman's side, then took a deep breath and returned to the tower and the bloody room on the first floor, to sort through what he could. The woman was easily identified from an ID card in her handbag. The skinned man's clothes lay in a tangled pile near his body. In the jacket pocket was a UK passport and the stub of a ticket for a flight from London that morning.

Ten minutes later the teams began to arrive, clambering up the stairs, filling the tiny room: scene of crime, lab people, an army of men and women in white plastic suits who wanted him out of there, wanted to get on with their work. Teresa Lupo, Crazy Teresa, the woman pathologist the police admired in a distant, scared fashion, was leading the way. It made sense; he couldn't see Crazy Teresa passing up on a case like this. She must have known the big man was there too. Station gossip had it that something had been happening between them recently.

Leo Falcone walked in and considered the stripped

corpse as if it were an exhibit in a museum. The inspector was as well dressed as ever: pressed white shirt, red silk tie, light-brown patterned suit, shoes that picked up the full yellow light from the single bulb and still managed to shine like mirrors. He was a striking figure: completely bald, with a perfect walnut tan and a silver beard cut in a sharp, angular fashion, like that of an actor playing the Devil on stage. He stared at Costa and said, with what sounded like venom in his smoker's voice, 'I sent you out to catch bag-snatchers. What in God's name is this?'

Costa thought to himself that one day he would lose it in front of all these people. One day someone would push him just a little too far.

'The woman is Rinaldi's wife,' he said. 'I looked in her handbag. It's with the other one's pile of clothes.'

'And the other one?' Falcone demanded.

Nic Costa felt like screaming at him. He hadn't asked for this. He didn't want to come to this place. Most of all he didn't want to watch Sara Farnese going steadily crazy as she began to accept what had happened in front of her.

'Working on it,' he said and walked down the stairs, leaving them to get on with their business.

Rossi, to his disappointment, had not stayed with Sara Farnese. Costa located him outside trying to find some shade in the hot, cobbled square, sucking on a cigarette as if his life depended on it.

'Did she say anything?' Costa asked.

Rossi was quiet. The horror of the crime was bad enough but Costa knew there was more to his distress than mere shock. There was something about this big, complex man he failed to understand.

'Not a word.' Luca Rossi didn't look Costa in the eye. He frowned. It put a big double chin on his pale, flabby face. 'I was scared in there. I didn't dare go into that room. You could feel it. Bad . . .'

'It's enough to scare anyone.'

'Bullshit!' Rossi hissed. 'You walked in like it was just another day.' He motioned to the scene of crime people outside the church door, smoking just like him. 'They're the same.'

'Trust me. They're shaken. We're all shaken.'

'Shaken?' Rossi mocked him. 'Falcone looks like he could eat breakfast off that corpse.'

'Luca.' It was the first time he'd used the big man's Christian name. 'What's wrong? Why are we working together? Why did they move you here?'

The big man's watery eyes cast him an odd, sad glance. 'They never told you?'

'No.'

'Jesus.' He stubbed out the cigarette with a shaking hand and immediately fumbled for another. 'You want to know? I went to some road accident. Happens all the time, I know. This one wasn't so different. There was the father behind the wheel, dead drunk. And on the road his kid, who'd gone straight through the windscreen and was now in pieces. Dead. Very dead.' Rossi shook his oversized head. 'You know what bothered the father? Trying to wheedle his way out of the accident. Trying to convince me he wasn't drunk.'

'There are jerks in the world. So what's new?'

'What's new?' Rossi repeated. 'This. I picked the jerk up by the scruff of his neck and started throwing him around the place. A lot. If the traffic cop on the scene hadn't been there I would probably have killed the moron.'

Costa looked back inside the church, checking she

was still there. When he turned away Rossi's sad, liquid eyes were burning at him.

'They moved me as part of the deal to stop him suing. To be honest I don't really care, not any more. I'm forty-eight, unmarried, unsociable. I spend my nights watching TV, drinking beer and eating pizza and, right up till that moment, I didn't mind, I didn't care. Then something hits you out of the blue. Sometimes the scales just fall from your eyes for the stupidest of reasons. It happened to me. It'll happen to you one day too. Maybe you get tired, with some bright new kid snapping at your ankles, and then you just see this stuff for the shit it is. Maybe it's something worse. You finally realize this isn't just some game. People die, for no reason whatsoever. And one day it's you.'

'I never thought it was any other way,' Costa replied. There was some personal resentment towards him in Rossi's voice. Costa didn't like to hear it. 'Go home, Luca. Get some sleep. I'll deal with everything.'

'Like hell you will. You think I want Falcone busting my balls tomorrow?'

Costa put a hand inside the older man's jacket and pulled out the packet. It was almost empty. 'Well, in that case just get some serious smoking done. We can talk about this later.'

Rossi nodded at the church. 'You want to know something else too? I'll tell you now. I doubt you're going to listen.'

'What?'

'*She* scares me. That woman in there. A woman who could watch all that stuff and hold it tight inside her. What kind of person can do that? She almost died today. She saw whatever was up in that room – no, don't tell me.

I don't want people with no skins on them walking around inside my head at night. It's not healthy. You look at her and you could think she doesn't mind a damn. That might just be where they belong.'

Costa felt his hackles rise on Sara Farnese's behalf. 'You didn't see her there, Luca. You can't judge. You didn't stay long with her at that altar either from what I can work out. You didn't watch her, not knowing where to look, wanting to bawl her eyes out. It takes time with some people. You ought to know that.'

Luca Rossi prodded him in the chest, hard. 'You're right. I didn't see.'

Crazy Teresa came out into the bright sun too, saw them, came over and cajoled Rossi for a smoke. When he reluctantly agreed she climbed out of her white polyester suit and stood there, a heavily built woman in her thirties, with a long black ponytail. She looked like Rossi, a little wasted. She wore the baggiest pair of cheap jeans Costa had ever seen and a creased pink shirt. Crazy Teresa lit the cigarette, blew a cloud of tobacco fumes into the scorching afternoon air and said, with a beatific smile on her face, 'It's days like this that make it all worth while, boys. Don't you agree?'

Costa swore, then went back inside the nave, cursing himself for the way he handled that one.

She was still at the altar, on her knees, hands locked low on her blood-spattered dress, eyes wide open, praying. Costa waited a couple of minutes until she was finished. He knew what she was looking at. Ahead of her, behind a painting of the head of Christ, done in gold, like some Byzantine icon, was a bigger image on the wall. It was Bartholomew, about to die. He had his hands tied above his head, just as the corpse did in the tower. A grim-faced executioner stood next to him, holding the knife, looking into his eyes as if he just couldn't work out where to begin.

Finally, Sara Farnese got off the floor and joined him on the bench.

'We can do this some other time,' he said. 'It doesn't have to be now.'

'Ask what you want. I'd rather get this out of the way.'

'I understand that.'

She was calm again and he wondered about what Rossi had said. Sara Farnese was certainly a woman in control of herself.

'This Stefano Rinaldi,' he asked. 'What was he to you?'

She hesitated then said, 'He was a professor in my department. I had an affair with him. Is that what you wanted to hear? It was brief. It ended months ago.'

'OK. And the woman upstairs in the room. His wife.'

'Mary. She's English.'

'I got that from the papers in her bag. Did she know?'

Sara Farnese peered at him. 'You want all this now?'

Costa said, 'If that's fine with you. If not we can do this some other time. It's your decision.'

Sara Farnese looked at the painting behind the altar again. 'She found out. That was why it ended. I don't know why it began in the first place. It was a friendship that just spilled over into something else. Stefano and Mary's marriage was shaky in any case. I didn't make it that way.'

He pulled out a plastic bag from his jacket pocket. There was a sheet of paper on it, a message from an office notepad covered in handwriting. 'I was trying to work out what's happening here. Not sit in judgement on anyone. I found this in the other one's clothing. It's a note that was left for him at the airport this morning I guess. It says it's from you and asks him to meet you here, at the church, as soon as you can. Says it's really important. Did you send that?'

She shook her head. 'No.'

'How could Rinaldi know he was coming?'

'I've no idea. Perhaps I talked about it at work. I really don't know.'

'The other man was your lover?'

She winced at the word. 'We . . . met from time to time. His name is Hugh . . .'

'Fairchild. I know. He had his passport with him. You want to look?'

'Why?'

'Next of kin. It says he's married.'

'No,' she said coldly. 'I don't want to look.'

'You didn't know?'

'Does it matter?'

Costa wondered. Was he being prurient? And if so, why? 'Maybe not. There was that thing about blood and martyrs written on the wall. You saw that I guess. And that other stuff. Who's this St Ives? Is he another martyr or something?'

'No. It's a place in England.'

'And seven wives?'

'I didn't even know he had one,' she answered with some bitterness.

'So what do you think happened?'

Sara Farnese glowered at him, her green eyes full of resentment. 'You're the policeman. You tell me.'

He hated being rushed but this woman seemed to demand it. 'Anyone who looks at this will say one thing,'

Costa said with a shrug. 'Your old boyfriend found out about your new one and decided it was time to bring things to a close. For all of them, him and his wife included. Maybe you too.'

'I told you. Stefano didn't want to kill me. And they weren't "boyfriends". They were people I slept with from time to time. In Stefano's case months ago.'

Costa didn't get it. Even now, pale and shocked, with grey bags growing under her eyes, Sara Farnese was a beautiful woman. He couldn't understand why someone like her would want to lead such an empty life.

'People go crazy for all sorts of reasons,' he said. 'Not always the obvious ones.' Men walked up a set of stairs and found someone's blood dripping down their face. People you loved walked out in the morning and came home at night with a death sentence hanging around their necks.

'Perhaps.' She didn't look convinced.

'I'm sorry I had to ask these questions. You understand why?'

She didn't say anything. She was transfixed by the painting behind the altar: Bartholomew about to lose his skin.

'It's apocryphal,' she remarked in a matter-of-fact way.

'What?'

'The story of the skinning. He was martyred, certainly. But probably something more mundane. Beheading was the usual method. The early Church embroidered these stories to encourage the waverers. To make sure the movement didn't falter.'

'Hence "the blood of the martyrs is the seed of the Church"?'

She peered at him, surprised, he thought, that he had seen the point.

'Is there some family I can call?' he asked.

'No one, thanks.'

'No one? Parents?'

'My parents died a long time ago.'

'There are people we can get to help in situations like this. Counselling.'

'If I need it I'll let you know.'

He thought again of what Rossi had said. There was much more to this woman than met the eye.

'Don't you ever pray?' she asked unexpectedly.

Costa shrugged. 'Not a family habit. And I never knew what to ask.'

'You just ask the same old questions. Such as, if there's a God, why does he let bad things happen to good people?'

'They were good people? This Englishman? The one who killed him?'

She considered this, Costa noticed. 'They weren't bad people if that's what you mean.'

'Hey,' he added without thinking. 'You should think yourself lucky you're not a cop. We get to wonder that and the other one too: why do good things happen to bad people? Why are the rich so rich and the poor so poor? Why did Stalin die in his bed? My old man's a communist. I used to ask that one a lot when I was a kid and boy did I get whacked around the ear plenty.'

Nic Costa was amazed. There was the slightest flicker of a smile on her face and it made Sara Farnese look like a different person, someone younger, someone with a fragile, interior beauty nothing like the cold, icy elegance that was her normal face for the world. Against his own instincts he suddenly found himself understanding that a man could become obsessed by this woman.

'Families matter,' Costa said. 'They make you a team against the world. I don't envy anyone who has to stand up against all this crap alone.'

'I'd like to go now,' Sara Farnese said. She got up and walked towards the door where the sun was finally starting to lose some of its power and the day was starting to die.

Nic Costa followed her all the way.

Five

The following morning Costa and Rossi found themselves summoned into Falcone's office at eight. The
inspector looked grumpier than ever and uncannily alert,
his sharp-featured face set in a constant frown. No one
liked his temper. No one credited him with any great
management skills. But Falcone was a man of talent, and
there were insufficient of those in the higher levels of
the force. He'd solved some difficult cases, ones that had
made big space in the newspapers. He had influence,
beyond the police station. There was plenty of respect for
him in the Questura, and little in the way of affection.

He had the papers from the Rinaldi case on his desk,
complete with a set of grisly photographs.

Falcone waved the reports he had in their faces.
'Skimpy,' was all he said.

'Sir,' Costa answered, 'we're working on something
fuller now. You'll have it by ten.'

Rossi shifted uncomfortably on his seat. Falcone was
staring at him and both men knew what his look was
saying: *so the kid speaks for you now, does he?*

'You have anything on this Farnese woman?' Falcone
asked.

Costa shook his head. 'Like what? You mean records or something?'

'That's exactly what I mean.'

'She's clean,' Rossi said. 'I ran a name check last night. There's not so much as a speeding ticket.'

Falcone leaned forward and made sure Costa was looking at him. 'You have to check these things.'

'I know,' Costa agreed. 'I'm sorry.'

'So that's the story?' Falcone asked. 'The old boyfriend killed the new boyfriend and took his own wife along for the ride?'

'Looks like that,' Costa agreed.

Falcone shrugged. 'No arguing there. It does look like that. I talked to forensics this morning. They couldn't find a single trace of anyone else in that tower, ground floor or first. Clean as a whistle except for Rinaldi and the two dead people in there.'

'So what's the problem?' Costa wondered.

'The problem?' Falcone nodded at Rossi. 'Ask him.'

Costa looked at his partner. They still hadn't made up since the near-quarrel the day before. That had to happen, he knew. He respected the big man. He didn't want this coldness between them.

'Luca?' he asked.

Rossi frowned. 'The problem is: why? Rinaldi stopped seeing the Farnese woman, what, three, four months ago? Why now?'

'Maybe he only just found out about the Englishman,' Costa suggested. 'He heard her talking about how much she liked him and just went crazy.'

Falcone stabbed a finger at him. 'Do we know that? It's not in your report.'

Costa thought back to his conversations with her. 'No.'

'We're going to have to go back to that woman,' Falcone ordered. 'Get some detail in all this. Dates. Names. Reasons.'

'Fine,' Costa nodded. Rossi was looking out of the window now, reaching for a cigarette. They had had some conversation beforehand, Costa thought. There could be no other explanation.

'Why did he go to these lengths?' Falcone demanded. 'Why skin a man? Why go through this routine of putting his own wife on a chair as if he wanted the Farnese woman to find her alive? And this stuff he wrote on the wall . . .'

'He was crazy,' Costa said firmly. 'You'd have to be crazy to kill someone like that.'

Falcone snorted. 'Too easy. Besides, even if it's true, do you think there's no rationality behind craziness? It all just spews out for no reason? This man was a university professor. He was intelligent, organized. He was convincing enough for the Englishman to come to him from the airport thinking he was meeting the woman. He managed to get his wife into that tower and string her up. Then he killed the boyfriend, skinned him, went off to the library . . . Or maybe he did her first, in which case how come the Englishman let himself be strung up after seeing her? Can one person handle all those things? I guess so. But how? In what order? You tell me that. And this Fairchild. He was a big man. He didn't just hold up his hands and let Rinaldi tie him. What went on there?'

'I know that,' Rossi said. 'I talked to Crazy Teresa in the path lab just now. They think there's traces of some drug, some sedative maybe.'

'What sedative?' Falcone asked. 'How'd a university professor come to be walking around with medication to hand just when he feels like skinning someone? If it comes to that, how the hell does a man like that *know* how to skin someone? And – this is the biggest one for me, the one I keep coming back to – *why*? Why like this?'

'She's a professor in the same department,' Costa suggested. 'The quotation on the walls is from some early Christian theologian. Maybe it sounded appropriate.'

'*Appropriate*?' Falcone repeated, as if it was the most stupid thing he'd ever heard in his life. 'You mean he's saying to her, "We're all martyrs to you, bitch. And here's the proof"? I don't get it. What was he hoping to achieve? If he was going to kill her it would make more sense. But you claim that's not the case. He just wanted to get her to go, as quickly as possible, to the place he'd left his own wife, still alive. What's the point?'

Costa looked at Rossi for help. His partner was still staring out of the window, working on the cigarette. It was another hot, cloudless day out there. Nic Costa wondered exactly what it was that Falcone expected of him.

'And you're wrong,' Falcone continued. 'I checked. Rinaldi was in the same department but he didn't share the same speciality. His field was Roman law, the Curia, all that ancient stuff the Vatican still thinks we should be listening to today.'

'Is that relevant?' Rossi wondered.

'You tell me. I ran through the records. Four months ago Rinaldi was called as an expert witness for some government tribunal looking at the issue of diplomatic immunity for Vatican officials. They want more. We want less. Rinaldi came up with an expert opinion that said they were right, in law, very old law anyway. Where the hell do martyrs come into that?'

'Are you saying, sir, that you think my conclusion's wrong? That Rinaldi isn't responsible somehow?'

'Hell no,' Falcone answered immediately. 'It's difficult to see how it could have happened any other way.'

'Well, then what? Isn't it enough to know Rinaldi did these things? Sometimes we never know why. We just have to accept that.'

Falcone glowered at him. 'Not yet we don't. I'm an inquisitive bastard. It's what makes me tick. It's what makes every good cop tick. If you're not, you never get to know a thing. I want you to answer some of these questions that keep bugging me. I don't want detectives who think they're elves in Santa's workshop going out there, wrapping things up all nicely with all the right ribbons, all the right answers, dropping them on my desk, getting a pat on the head, then looking for some more toys to play with. This job isn't like that.'

'I know,' Costa replied. 'At least, I never felt the pat on the head.'

Rossi groaned, stabbed out the cigarette and immediately lit another.

Falcone was smiling again. He'd won a response and Costa cursed himself for being so stupid. 'You kids.' The inspector laughed. 'You're so *sensitive*. Listen. I think you've got the right answers. I just don't like the way you got there. Cutting too many corners.'

'Sir.' Costa scowled.

'And one more thing,' Falcone added. 'I'd like you to listen more. I know we're into this youth culture thing that says everyone over the age of thirty is a moron—'

'I'm twenty-seven, sir.'

'Yeah, yeah. I wish you looked it sometimes. The point I want to make to you, Costa, is the only way any of us really learns is by watching our elders and betters. Forget all that crap in the police college. All we do for a living is deal with human beings. Human beings who, for the most part, are trying to lie to us, trying to screw us around. This is a people business. You should talk less and listen more, son.'

Costa grimaced. 'Sir, I—'

'Shut up,' Falcone ordered. 'And here's another thing. That other stuff he wrote on the wall? St Ives?'

'Crazy,' Rossi said, starting to become interested.

'Maybe,' Falcone agreed. 'But I can tell you what it is. I got someone to look it up.'

He stared at a laser printout on the desk and read the words.

> *As I was going to St Ives*
> *I met a man with seven wives.*
> *Every wife had seven sacks,*
> *Every sack had seven cats,*
> *Every cat had seven kits.*
> *Kits, cats, sacks and wives,*
> *How many were going to St Ives?*

The two detectives stared at each other, dumbfounded. Costa grabbed the calculator on the desk and started punching.

Falcone grinned. 'It's a riddle. What's the answer?'

Costa scribbled some figures on his notepad. 'Seven wives. Forty-nine sacks. Three hundred and forty-three cats. Two thousand four hundred and one kittens. That adds up to two thousand eight hundred.' He thought of the tiny enclosed room in the tower and the remembered stink of meat. 'But what the hell does that mean?'

The inspector scowled. 'It means you don't understand riddles. And you just wasted a lot of effort not answering the question you were asked. "I met a man with seven wives . . ." They were all going in the opposite direction. There was just one person going to St Ives. The narrator. You were looking in the wrong place all along. The obvious isn't always the right answer.'

Nic Costa shook his head. 'That's the kind of game a crazy person would play.'

'And not finish the line?' Falcone asked. 'Why would a dead man set an incomplete riddle? Can you tell me that?'

There was no ready answer.

'I want you to go round to Rinaldi's home,' Falcone ordered. 'There's been some people there already but maybe they missed something. Try to work out what kind of man he was, whether there's anything to explain this. And try not to piss off Hanrahan again. He's been on the phone twice to me already. You certainly made an impression there.'

Costa failed to understand the relevance. 'Hanrahan? You know him?'

'Oh, we're just the best of friends.' Falcone was, Costa hoped, being sarcastic. Sometimes it was hard to tell. 'Now . . .'

He was out of his seat, standing in front of the window with his back to them, watching the traffic in the street, thinking, or so he wanted them to believe. Another Falcone ritual. The two detectives knew when their time was through.

Rossi led the way out of the room.

Six

The Rinaldis owned a large restored apartment in a late-nineteenth-century block on the Via Mecenate, a residential street by the park which led from the Via Merulana towards the Colosseum. The neighbourhood was on the cusp of acceptability. It was only a few minutes' walk to the smarter, older quarters of the Caelian Hill. Nero's Golden House lay beneath the parched summer grass a hundred metres from the entrance to the block. The apartment was well decorated in a lean, modern style, generously proportioned and quiet, since it gave out onto the vast internal courtyard of the building, not the street in front. Still, Nic Costa was unable to dispel the idea that the Rinaldis were not exactly rolling in money. The Via Merulana was not a place to wander with pleasure at night. It was only a little distance from the squalor of Termini Station. If he looked closely outside he would see the signs: needles in the gutter, used condoms in doorways. At night the park became a haunt for rent boys. A university professor would prefer to live somewhere else, Costa felt. It was one of those neighbourhoods that was always up and coming but never quite got there.

The apartment had been thoroughly searched already. Costa and Rossi studied the preliminary report: a small amount of cannabis, no messages on the answering machine, no incriminating letters, nothing on the cheap desktop computer that sat in the tiny study next to the bedroom. He wondered how Falcone expected them to come up with something new.

Rossi found the Rinaldis' bank statements tucked into a drawer of the computer desk. Costa's suspicions were correct. They maintained separate accounts and both were in the red, Stefano Rinaldi's to the tune of a quarter of a million euros. There were threatening letters from the bank too. Unless the Rinaldis cleared some of their debt, even the modest apartment in the Via Mecenate was in jeopardy of disappearing from beneath them.

Was this enough to turn someone like Stefano Rinaldi into a multiple killer? Falcone would never accept such a flimsy idea. Where was the evidence? Costa made a note to re-interview the neighbours. The preliminary report came up with so little. All the usual comments they got in domestic incidents, stories that painted the victims as a quiet, solitary couple, with few friends. No one had ever seen Mary Rinaldi with a bruised face. No one had heard her complain about the behaviour of her husband. They were, it seemed, a bland, childless everyday pair struggling to make ends meet. Falcone was right: there had to be more. The bank statements and the threats from the bank were symptoms, surely, of some larger malaise in the Rinaldis' life.

Something else bothered him. Mary Rinaldi didn't work, the report said. Even so, Rinaldi must have earned a decent package at the university. They should have been able to survive. Yet here they were with a sizeable debt outstanding on a mediocre home, fighting to keep their heads above water. Where was the money going? They went back to the bank statements and found the answer: cash. Stefano Rinaldi's salary from the university amounted to almost €6,000 a month after deductions. Even with a tidy mortgage that should have been enough to live on. The statements told a different story. Rinaldi immediately transferred a quarter into his wife's bank account, standing payments accounted for a further half, and the rest disappeared in credit card bills and some huge cash withdrawals, sometimes as much as €1,000 a week.

Nic Costa had been around long enough to understand there were only so many reasons why a man wanted ready money in his hand in this kind of quantity: women, booze and drugs being the main ones. Maybe Sara Farnese had been expensive to maintain, though somehow he doubted that. The woman seemed too independent to rely on someone like Rinaldi for money. Maybe there was someone else now in her place. But if that was the case, why was Rinaldi so furious with Sara that he wanted to kill her current boyfriend?

There was always a simpler answer. While Rossi ran through the answering machine he went into the bathroom which was small, covered in mirrors and had just a toilet, a washbasin with a plain cabinet above it and a shower in the corner. He opened the cabinet door and looked inside: a woman's razor, some headache pills, a packet of laxatives, and two neat rows of white plastic tablet containers from a health store. He read the names: evening primrose oil and ginseng, gingko biloba and selenium. There were eight different preparations in all. One or both of the Rinaldis must have rattled like a pill box when they went out of the apartment in the morning.

Costa picked up the biggest container, the one with evening primrose oil inside, opened it and looked at the round, shiny yellow capsules. There were only about ten left and they sat on a wad of cotton wool. Gelatine health pills nestled on a soft white bed of fluffiness. He hated cotton wool. It stuck to his fingernails. The feel of it gave him the same shivers some people get from running their nails up and down a blackboard. It seemed so pointless. They put cotton wool in pill containers only to stop things rattling around and breaking. A flexible gelatine capsule couldn't break, not easily. Costa turned the container upside down and emptied the visible contents into the sink. Then he righted it and, trying not to screech, gently pulled out the cotton wool from the base.

Beneath it was a small transparent plastic bag containing white powder. Costa swore at the incompetence of the squad who had made the first search. He hated getting people into trouble but, on this occasion, there really was no avoiding it. He took out the bag, unwrapped it, tasted the coke, confirming what it was. The source of the Rinaldis' cash problem was surely apparent. Perhaps dope would explain Stefano's excitable state. Except that the autopsy had so far failed to uncover any trace of drugs.

Costa swore again. It was still significant: it was the only thing he'd found so far that was.

He returned to the living room and showed the dope to Rossi, who commented, 'And these are supposed to be intelligent people? Why do they go around picking up gutter habits like that?'

'No family,' Costa said. It was astonishing how often

that factor cropped up in his line of work. Except every dopehead had a kind of family: the person who fulfilled his or her needs. In the case of the middle classes that was usually fixed, regular, like a visit to the doctor. Those steady withdrawals from the bank each week said as much. Somewhere in the city was the dealer who knew them, a person who, Costa understood, dealt only with professionals, never took risks, and was probably smart too, full of some quick philosophy to justify what he did.

The two of them spent an hour going through the address book in Mary Rinaldi's bag, phoning every number there, talking to hairdressers and doctors, distant friends and a couple of travel agencies. Any of them could be a supplier but it didn't feel right. Then they did the same with the names on Rinaldi's computer, printed off every one, forty in all, mainly academic contacts. The narcotics people could run through the list later and see if any rang a bell.

Rinaldi used the computer a lot. It was full of essays and letters, many to the bank. It was plugged into the phone line too. Costa clicked on the e-mail program expecting it to be protected by some kind of password. To his surprise it popped up and showed an inbox with three messages, each dated from two days before: one was junk mail, the other an invitation to an academic convention in Florida.

He opened the third and stared at it. The message said, simply, 'Money no problem. Be there ten am'. The sender's name and e-mail address were blank. But there was a Rome phone number at the bottom of the screen.

Rossi looked at him, staggered. 'They missed this? Falcone is going to go crazy.'

Costa picked up the phone on the desk and dialled. A woman answered. She said, 'Cardinal Denney's office.'

'Sorry. Wrong number.'

Rossi's long face wouldn't leave him alone. 'Well?'

'It was the office of someone called Cardinal Denney.'

The big man's watery eyes grew wide. 'Someone called Cardinal Denney?'

'The name means something?'

Rossi was making for the door. 'I need a drink. Before one more damn thing. A drink. Now.'

Seven

Costa insisted: if they were going to a bar on duty it would be somewhere he knew. Rossi now glowered at the modest wine glass which was half full of a liquid the colour of straw. He sniffed, tasted it, grimaced, then crammed a piece of cheese on some bread and nibbled artlessly, spilling crumbs everywhere. They sat on tiny stools around a low table in a wine bar Costa sometimes used. It was near his tiny home in the Campo dei Fiori. The place was quite empty apart from the two cops and a woman who had stopped mopping the floor to serve them.

'Why can't we go to a real place and drink beer like normal people?' Rossi moaned. 'Don't you know mathematics? Why do we have to pay twice the price to make our own sandwiches when I can get three times this quantity around the corner for half what it costs in this dump? And they do beer.'

Costa cautiously patted Rossi's colossal stomach. It was an act of some intimacy which the big man tentatively allowed, like a lion allowing its trainer to stroke its head.

'Beer makes you fat,' Costa said. 'Beer makes you fart. Trust me. A partner knows. Diet is important, Uncle

Luca. Particularly for a man of your age, in your . . . condition.'

'I'm happy where I am, thanks. And I'm not your fucking uncle.' Rossi grunted again. 'And what's with this fancy apartment in the Campo? Cops don't live in places like that. That's why I have to drink in a stuck-up *enoteca* . . .'

'It's not fancy. It's just where I like to live.'

'So you can screw the tourist girls when they've had too much to drink on a Saturday night?'

'No. Because I like it. That's all.'

'Inexplicable,' Rossi declared. 'So where's the nearest painting now, huh?'

'Too many to choose from,' Costa answered. The big man looked at him as if to say: *so now I know why you live here*.

'I didn't know about the accident, Luca. What happened there. I'm sorry.'

'I've seen worse,' Rossi grumbled. 'We both have. Yesterday. Sometimes it catches you like that. You just walk along thinking, it's not so bad, I can make it through the day. Then you just stumble round the corner and put your shoe into something that makes you realize the bad stuff was there all along and you just fooled yourself into thinking it could be any other way.'

'There's a painting near here. It's about that. I could show you if you like.'

Rossi almost laughed. 'Me? Look at a painting?'

'Sure. Why not?'

'You won't tell anyone? Some of those bastards take the piss.'

'It's a deal. But I want to hear about Cardinal Denney first.'

Rossi grabbed him by the arm. 'Keep your voice down, for Christ's sake.'

Costa raised an eyebrow. There was still just the woman in the place, mopping away, well out of earshot.

'You never know,' the big man said defensively.

'Know what?'

Rossi shook his head. 'You don't even get to hear the station gossip, do you?'

'Too busy doing a job.'

'Oh my,' the big man grumbled. 'The kid's a saint. Listen. You heard of the Banca Lombardia?'

'Sure.' He nodded. 'I read it was in trouble. Bad investments. Trouble with the authorities. There's supposed to be some mob money in it. Ours. The Americans.'

'Clever boy. Well, let me tell you something. Two partners ago I used to share the Fiat sofa with this grown-up guy who couldn't keep his trap shut. Probably yakked in his sleep, but the funny thing was . . . he was worth listening to. He'd done some secondment work with the spooky people in the Finance Ministry and, my, did he like to talk about all these secret stake-outs he did, and all the good-guy politicians that were really on the take. He knew all the names of the people who pulled the strings without anyone in the outside world seeing. You know what? One of them wore a red cap. Still could if he wanted. Goes by the name of Michael Denney and if it wasn't for the fact he could hide in that place of his we'd be throwing him in the cells right now.'

'The Vatican?'

'Where else?' Rossi waited, hoping for some enlightenment. 'Jesus. The bankers were just the front men. This was a private little operation that Denney spun out of some genuine Vatican venture without telling anyone.' He raised his glass, drained it in one. 'And now it's rapidly going bust. Liquidity problems. No one knows whether it's going to pull through or what. Remember?'

'Yeah,' Costa conceded. 'I think I read about that.'

'You read nothing. Listen to me, Nic. This Denney's been putting his holy hands into stuff no one ought to be messing with, least of all a priest. He had offshore funds in places that don't have offshore funds. Places anyone could put money and no one – not the tax people, not the intelligence agencies – would be any the wiser. There's a queue of people waiting to talk to him about that. Us. The Ministry of Justice. FBI. And probably the Mafia too from what I hear. They don't like it when the man from the Vatican does the laundry wrong. Lucky for him he can hide there trying to get the rest of us to agree that, if we let him walk out, he's covered by diplomatic immunity.' He paused. 'You remember what Falcone said? About Rinaldi?'

Costa did. The dead man had been called to give an expert opinion on the subject only a few months before.

'You think Denney was somehow paying him to come up on the right side?'

Rossi looked around him to make sure no one else came in. 'If he was it didn't work. Maybe that's why Denney got pissed off with him. He quit being a churchman years ago to work on the financial side. Should have filled in the right forms if he wanted to claim he was a diplomat. Too late to start whining when there's money gone missing. A whole lot of money too. I read the file.'

Costa was struggling to make sense of this. 'Why

would he steal it? Why would a man like that want money?'

'Runs in the family. Denney comes from some Irish-American family in Boston. Big in bootlegging in the early days, sidekicks to Joe Kennedy for a while. Moved into politics, finance, all that stuff. But they never could let everything go. It's in their blood, I guess. He was the kid they marked out for the Church while the rest stuck with the family business. Which was all Denney did for a while and pretty well too. Made a name for himself working the Irish ghettos in Boston. Man of the people. Didn't seem to be an act either. Then he hit the up escalator, came to Europe. By the time he's thirty he's in Rome. By the time he's forty-five he's wearing the red cap and suddenly it's no more listening to some local jerk confessing to playing fuck-thy-neighbour. He's gone business, running this bank and he's pumping the Pope's money all ways. Into IBM and General Motors. After a while into funnier places too, companies that are never going anywhere, ever, because that's not why they're there. Suddenly, it's no longer about the Pope's money. It's stuff coming from all over, laundered by God knows who.' Rossi stared at the empty glass. 'Why the hell am I telling you all this?'

'You're keeping me up to date on the gossip.'

'Right,' the big man grumbled. 'So according to this man of mine, along comes the new millennium and Denney's bank's doing like all the rest of them, not good. He's been betting on these dotcom morons. He's been hedging this by betting on the airlines and the telecom people too. In short he's losing his touch. One day in September he turns on the TV and sees a couple of planes fly into a couple of skyscrapers. And what do you know?

Bad turns awful. Bad turns fucking disastrous. Word is that if this bunch was out in the open Denney'd be bust and in the slammer facing some serious incarceration. Which is bad news for him and for all those mob guys who thought they were banking on something that had the Holy Writ on the cover. Now they are people who do not like to lose their money.'

'This man of yours knows a lot,' Costa observed.

'He was a knowledgeable guy. What do I mean "was"? Still is.'

'And he says it in such a memorable way too. Where's he working now?'

'Probably with some dumb smartass kid who doesn't believe a word he says. Do I make myself clear?'

'In a particularly obscure way. Did he get the chance to arrest someone?'

'Like who? Lombardia isn't officially bust yet. Just "suspended". All the money was passing through places like Liechtenstein and Grand Cayman. Try hunting that down. The finance people had one low-grade clerk in their sights, thought he might talk too if they offered him a deal. When they went to collect they found him floating face down in the bath in his apartment in Testaccio. "Heart attack". Very convenient. Who knows? Maybe Denney had him done. Maybe now he's got the taste he's offing a few more people who took the money and didn't come up with the goods.'

'Rinaldi did come up with the goods. He said the Vatican was right.'

'Didn't work though, did it? Remember, Denney has the contacts. To be honest, though, my guess is they're none too keen on him either these days. Which gives him plenty more reasons to stay behind those walls where no one can touch him. Not until the Vatican people themselves wash their hands of the black sheep and kick him out onto the pavement. Yeah. Like that's going to happen.'

Costa was baffled. 'Why not? Why would the Church tolerate any of this?'

It could have been Falcone looking at him. Rossi's expression said just one thing: *don't be so dumb, kid.* 'This isn't about the Church. It's about the Vatican. Another country. Like I said. Mongolia as far as we're concerned. Unless it's in their interests they won't give us anything. Maybe Denney's in some kind of purdah now they know what's been going on. Maybe not. Either way for us it's irrelevant. He daren't set foot outside the place. He knows we'd arrest him on the spot. He knows some of his shady friends might want a word too. They're too picky about their own in there to hang him out to dry. But my guess is he's not a happy little priest. This was a guy who used to hang around with presidents. The way things are going now he's just going to wind up a sad old man stuck in a nice comfy prison for the rest of his life. Unless he gets a fit of conscience, of course, and decides to tell us everything. Which I find somewhat unlikely, to be frank.'

Costa was adamant. 'We have to check it out.'

The big man wagged a finger at him. 'No! Didn't you hear Falcone clearly enough? I shouldn't even have told you any of this. You are not going back to that place. Understand?'

'You said it was gossip. I found out some place else.'

'What about the painting?' Rossi asked, trying to change the subject.

'Still want to see it?'

'My glass is empty. You're starting to scare the shit out of me. You bet I want to see it.'

Costa led him out of the bar, across the busy main road into the warren of streets that stretched between the Pantheon and Piazza Navona. Rossi followed as the kid ducked into a nondescript church in one of the side roads.

'Who'd put a masterpiece in a dump like this?' Rossi demanded in the gloomy interior. 'I've seen better churches in Naples.'

'This is San Luigi dei Francesi, big man. Here you've got two of the greatest works Caravaggio ever painted, exactly where he meant them to be, where he put them on the walls himself.'

'I get to see both?' He didn't sound enthusiastic.

'One at a time,' Costa said and walked forward to deposit some coins in the light meter. A set of bulbs came alive. Rossi blinked at the huge canvas in front of him. Most of it was set in shade: a group of men in medieval dress at a table, counting money. Three of them had turned to look at a pair of figures standing at the right of the scene. From behind came a shaft of revealing light. It burned brightly on the puzzled faces as they sat there, half-cowed, watching the newcomers.

'*The Vocation of Saint Matthew*,' Costa said. 'He's the one in the middle, pointing to himself, as if to say, "Who? Me?"'

'And the couple on the right?'

'Jesus, with his hand outstretched, indicating to Matthew he's been chosen as an apostle. And by his side Peter, who symbolizes the Church which will come to be built on Matthew's gospel.'

'So what's this got to do with me losing it in an accident? That *was* your point, wasn't it?'

Costa nodded. The big man wasn't slow. 'Look at the costumes. The men around the table are in what was, when it was painted, contemporary dress. Jesus and Peter look as if they've walked straight out of a biblical scene. Caravaggio was commissioned to record a specific scene but what he did was make a broader point. This is about a moment of revelation, a moment when, in Matthew's case, he realizes there's more to life than counting money on a table.'

'You sound like a priest,' Rossi grumbled.

'I'm sorry. I didn't mean to.'

'And this,' Rossi nodded at the painting, 'is where you get your kicks?'

'I wouldn't put it that way.' Costa thought about it. 'It's about looking for some meaning, looking for a reason to be alive. Not just working your way through the day and being glad you got to the other end.'

'That's fine as far as I'm concerned.'

'Sure,' Costa replied. 'Until you see something that says otherwise. And then you wind up working with me.'

Rossi sighed. He got the message. There was, Costa knew, no need to labour it.

'So you're a Catholic? In spite of everything they say about your old man?'

'No. Not at all. I just like to look for meanings. It's a hobby if you like.'

A couple of tourists turned on the light for an adjoining painting. It was brightness and shade again, Rossi noticed, but there was more action in this one. Some old guy was lying on the floor, dying, a madman over his body, holding a bloodied sword. There was something deeply disturbing about the work. It was dense, vivid, savage. It seemed poised on the very edge of sanity.

'*Matthew's Martyrdom*,' Costa said quietly. 'Another story. For another time.'

'I never did work out why a religion based around love and peace seemed to involve so much killing.' Rossi grunted. 'You know the answer to that? Or do you need to be a Catholic to understand?'

'It's about martyrdom. Sacrificing yourself for something bigger than one human being. Could be the Church. For my dad it could be the hammer and sickle.'

'Sounds the kind of thing dumb people do,' Rossi mumbled, then wiped his sleeve across his mouth.

Costa knew what it meant. He wanted a beer. He followed the big man outside, watched him working out where to go next.

'Listen.' Rossi's watery eyes hooded over. 'If you want to hear more about this I've an idea.'

'Really?'

'Yeah. We're having dinner with Crazy Teresa tonight. It could be useful.'

'We? *We* have a date with Crazy Teresa?'

Rossi eyed him as if to say: so what?

'We hardly know each other,' Costa objected.

'It's Crazy Teresa. Everybody knows her.'

'I meant *we* hardly know each other.'

Rossi seemed offended by that. 'Look. I know this relationship didn't get off to the greatest of starts. But I'm trying here, kid. I'm doing my best. And there is something in it too. She wants to talk. I know the rumours doing the rounds. There's a touch of truth in them but it's not gone as far as people think. I'm not eating with Crazy Teresa on my own, not tonight.'

Costa couldn't believe his ears. 'Jesus. Why should I be there?'

'She wants you. Don't ask me why. It's only polite. Interdepartmental relations and all that.'

'Wonderful.'

Costa couldn't work up much enthusiasm to complain. He had nothing else to do. Maybe Crazy Teresa off duty would be a different woman.

'Is that a yes?'

'Depends,' Costa said slyly. 'Are we still negotiating?'

Eight

Sara Farnese lived in the Borgo, the residential area that led from the river to the very walls of the Vatican. This was still Rome, still under the jurisdiction of the city. Yet it was impossible to ignore the proximity of the papal state up the hill. Her home was in Vicolo delle Palline, a narrow cobbled lane that ran between the Via dei Corridori and the Borgo Pio. *Il Pasette*, the elevated, fortified corridor which joined the Vatican with the Pope's former fortress, the Castel Sant'Angelo, abutted her medieval, ochre-coloured building. When parties of visiting luminaries were allowed to walk down the passage, treading in the footsteps of long-dead pontiffs sometimes fleeing for their lives, she could hear them through the wall and often listened to their idle chatter. The commercial bustle of St Peter's Square and the hectic tourist trade around it were only minutes away, but in the little street and the close, narrow lanes she favoured, people moved at a different pace. This was still a local quarter, residential, largely untouched by the modernization of the city. Homes were handed down from generation to generation – though not hers, which had been bought at a substantial price.

She had acquired the first-floor apartment four years before when she finally moved to Rome for good at the age of twenty-three, putting on the professional suit of a university lecturer and, shortly after, starting to look older, perhaps more serious, than she felt. College, in London and America, was now a fading memory. Her teenage years, spent in boarding schools throughout Europe and finally in the cold Swiss town of Montreux, seemed remote, as if they had happened to another person. She remembered boarding the steamer and meandering across the great shining expanse of Lake Geneva on her own, trying to escape the prying attention of her classmates, who found her distant, different. She would sit on deck for hours, overlooked by nothing except the towering crown of mountains bordering the eastern end of the glittering inland sea, peering down at her from high, like God from Heaven: some vast, omnipresent watcher over her life, detached from its emotionless daily tedium.

These were Sara Farnese's most vivid memories, ones of physical, geographical objects. The green at Harvard. The college quadrangles of Oxford. A handful of ancient streets behind the Blue Mosque in Istanbul where she could lose herself for hours, following the tangled history of Byzantium, imagining herself into its formative years under Constantine, realizing that the study of early Christianity, the subject she had chosen – or had it chosen her, she was unsure which – was one where she had a certain distinct talent.

There were few people stored in the dark vault hidden within her head. An exception lay in one of the oldest memories of all: Sister Annette, in the convent kindergarten in Paris, taking her to one side on a sunny June morning. This was twenty-two years ago. Yet, seated now in the apartment in the Borgo, she could still recall the nun's gaunt, worried face, framed by a starched white wimple, like a picture waiting to be hung on the wall.

They had gone to a small room she had never visited before. The bright sunlight filtered through a single stained-glass window depicting Jesus with a lamb in his arms. The plangent clatter of the bells of St Eustache drifted into the room, together with the racket of a reggae band busking outside Les Halles shopping complex. The place smelled of dust, as if it were little used, though it was as clean, and as simple, as every other corner of the convent. They sat next to each other on hard wooden chairs, with their hands joined together around an old, battered Bible.

Sister Annette was not as old as she looked, the child Sara thought. Sometimes she imagined the nun's face without the wrinkles, without the tension which seemed to come from some inwardly felt pain. Without the wimple and the habit too, dressed in normal clothes, like the people she saw on the street. When Sara did this, Sister Annette became a different person: full of life, vibrant, restless. Normal somehow. This imaginary person and the real sister who now sat next to her shared only one identical feature. They both had very bright, very intense blue eyes and, on this long-dead Paris day, the real Annette turned them on the infant Sara with a fierce, unbending power which gave the child no room for escape.

Memories were about generalities, not details. Even the child Sara had understood this and never tried to fix each word precisely in her head. It was the meaning which counted and in that, said the nun's eyes, there could be no room for mistakes.

They had spoken about the mysteries of God and how no one, not even the greatest human being who has ever lived, could begin to understand everything in his mind. Not Sister Annette. Not the kindly priest with the foreign accent who came into the convent from time to time, gave them talks she could not understand, then left, touching each child on the head as he walked to the front door and the bright world beyond.

Even the Holy Father himself was outside every last detail of God's great plan she said, which surprised the child Sara greatly since she had been given to understand that the distant white figure who lived in the Vatican was, in some unexplained way, part of Heaven itself.

On occasion God could appear cruel. There would be times when no one would comprehend his meaning. The innocent would suffer, perhaps more than the wicked. There would be pain where it was undeserved, grief which could appear so great it was impossible to believe one would ever escape its morbid clutches. One would ask – and this was quite normal, Sister Annette said, this happened to everyone – whether a loving God could allow such things to happen at all. This was the Devil talking, whispering in our ears at the moment of our greatest weakness. God's grace, though sometimes incomprehensible, was there to make us free. We made our own prisons. We – not him – sent ourselves to Hell. He loved us through our agonies and would, in the end, redeem us with his kindness. Once we had walked the path towards him. Once we had found our own particular path to Paradise.

Life was a mystery, she said, a gift. And like all gifts it

could be taken away. When that moment happened, the faithful didn't complain. They thanked God that the gift was there at all. They acceded to his greater wisdom. They loved him all the more and found, in that love, some solace.

Sara had looked up into the sharp blue eyes, trying to understand. She adored this woman with all her heart. For as long as she had been in the school – and that pre-dated even the haziest of distant memories – Sister Annette had been like a parent. Her own mother and father were infrequent visitors, tall, stern figures, not staying long when they did arrive. They were busy people. She felt fortunate they had the time to come at all. When they did they would kiss her on the cheek, leave endless gifts and promises. Sister Annette had agreed on this point too, and Sara knew she would never lie. This was not an absence of affection on their part. They lived in a different world, one where a quiet, five-year-old child who spoke so little, who spent her time in daydreams she never revealed to another living soul, would never be happy. They did this for her own good and she would one day be grateful.

'God works constantly,' the sister said, 'beyond our understanding.'

She hesitated. There was, the child thought, something wrong with her. A cold. Flu perhaps. Sister Annette was ill and the thought made Sara clasp the nun's hand to the Bible all the more tightly. It was impossible for the child to imagine a world without this woman in it.

'Sara,' the nun said finally. 'God has taken your mother and your father to him. Yesterday. In America. There was an accident.'

She recalled – would always recall – how this made her

mouth go dry, made something hard and painful begin to grow in her throat, like a cancer coming from nowhere.

'They live with God now. They're in his Heaven, where you'll see them one day too, provided you are a good girl, as you are now. God loves you, Sara. We all love you. We will love you every day till he calls us to go to him too and wait for you patiently there until we're reunited. Your parents. All of us.' Sister Annette paused. Her eyes were glassy. 'There's nothing for you to worry about,' she said in a voice that abruptly took on a practical tone. 'We'll look after you, for ever if you like. You can go out into the world too if you choose. You'll have the means to do whatever you want.'

At this point the nun hugged her. Sara could still remember the smell. The stink of death sat upon her, an old, dry stink, like something going off. Within the year, Annette would join God in Heaven. She would become part of the great procession to his door, willingly, smiling perhaps, as she died.

'Be sad,' Sister Annette said. 'But be happy and wise too. And be grateful. You've much to be grateful for.'

'I will,' the child answered, wondering if she had the courage to make good her promise.

The sister smiled. 'I know you will. You're a good girl, my little Sara. You always will be. And one day – on this earth – you'll be rewarded. One day you'll know some great joy in your life.'

Those last words were so fixed in Sara's memory she was convinced they were accurate, the very ones Sister Annette had used. Yet there was another memory too, an inexplicable flaw in the picture: that as the sister spoke there were tears, thick and salty, running down her cheeks, so slowly, so ponderously, she resembled the pale, static figure of Mary in the chapel whose face was stained with drops that were mother of pearl, not human at all.

Sara Farnese looked at her watch and wondered at the power of these memories. Sometimes they stood in the way of the present, she thought, easy crutches on which to lean as a substitute for decision and action. What would Sister Annette make of her present existence? She knew the answer and did not wish to dwell on it.

It was now 2.27 and the press were still making a noise beyond the windows. She was sick of the notes being pushed through the door of the apartment block. She had taken the phone off the hook. Still they waited. Still they haunted her.

She put on a pair of sunglasses and walked to the window. Outside, in the narrow lane, cameras flashed, voices rose, TV crews scrambled to take advantage of this rare appearance by the woman they all wanted to see. A woman the media was already painting as some kind of black temptress, the guilty party to an affair in which one lover – a married one at that – murdered his wife and his ex-mistress's partner in the most bloody of fashions.

People walking down the main road hesitated, stopping to stare at this commotion in the shadow of the Pope's thoroughfare. Would they be any more forgiving? Would they even wish to understand? She doubted it. The best she could hope for from the masses was a lack of interest, which was unrealistic given the curiosity the media was creating in the story.

At 2.29 Sara Farnese walked into her bedroom and unlocked the secure compartment in the small bedside cabinet. The phone still bore the sticker from the mobile operator in Monaco. Calls made using it were, he said, untraceable, unlike those from Italian models. He had one too. If they just used the pair of mobiles, at times they agreed beforehand, everything would be fine. No one need ever know.

She turned on the handset, waited and, sure enough, at half past it rang.

He wasn't angry with her, not this time. Sara Farnese felt grateful to hear his voice which was full of warmth and reassurance, telling her everything would be fine, just to keep calm, keep quiet and never say more than was necessary, particularly to the police.

She cried a little. It was impossible to halt the tears. She told him, too, about the animals on the doorstep and the way the thought of them kept invading her head.

'I'll send you a gift,' he said.

They spoke for no more than four minutes, four minutes in which she felt herself restored to the world, one which Sister Annette would have recognized, even if she found parts of it questionable.

Just after three she walked tentatively to the window, standing far enough back to be able to see without being seen. The street-cleaning vans had arrived in the Borgo Pio, a day before schedule, even though the place was still just dusty, free of litter, thanks to the cruel August weather which was chasing people from the city. Two vans were working their way along the road, spraying water everywhere, big circular brushes turning from beneath their bellies. Then they turned into Vicolo delle Palline, a place no cleaning truck had ever visited before, and made straight for the crowd beneath the window. The media mob scattered, clutching for their cameras, cursing as the vehicles ploughed slowly through their midst.

Sara Farnese watched from behind the curtain and

wished she could laugh. There had been more generous gifts but none so welcome or well timed. Nevertheless, this unwanted attention would return.

The crowd began to reassemble. Through it came two now familiar figures, one large, one smaller and slender. She recognized the policemen from the day before and began, very carefully, to assemble her thoughts.

Nine

Jay Gallo sat on the dry turf of the Esquiline Hill, not far from the Via Mecenate, eating calzone from the pizza rustica shop around the corner: zucchini flowers and salty anchovies wrapped inside mozzarella. The dig was in its fourth day and halted once again. He wondered how long it would be before some anxious producer in New York read the latest accountant's report and pulled the plug on the show, taking his meal ticket with it. Gallo desperately wanted out of this job. There was better money to be made running rich tourists around the city and spinning them rare and occasionally racy stories. He hated TV crews. He hated their dirigible-sized egos. He hated their organizational incompetence. But most of all, Jay Gallo hated their dishonesty. Once, before the drink and the dope took hold and sent his life swerving off in a different direction, Gallo had been a promising scholar at Harvard. He knew his subject: late imperial Rome, though it was now greatly expanded to embrace the needs of a hungry translator and tour guide. Watching this fake archaeology show dig up what may or may not have been an unimportant chunk of the Domus Aurea, Nero's Golden House, and imbue every shard of pottery, every rusting iron nail, with some dubious link to the past was agony. For all his personal deficiencies, Jay Gallo understood intellectual rigour and recognized when it was being tarnished for the sake of pecuniary gain.

Scipio Campion – even the name made his teeth grate – personified this sin completely. A minor Oxford professor with very little chin and an accent that could cut glass, he was born with the fake English academic poise American television adored. If the show were to be believed, Campion had – in one single season – found the camp from which Spartacus's army had surveyed Pompeii; uncovered the remains of a palace in Glastonbury, complete with wall paintings, which he was able to pass off as a possible site of Avalon; and, on the outskirts of modern Alexandria, revealed the tomb – and within it, to much excitement, the decapitated skeleton – of Caesarion, the son of Julius Caesar and Cleopatra. It was all so unseemly. Undeserved too. He had watched Campion go through the motions on camera. There was nothing to it. Jay Gallo knew he could do better if they gave him a chance. The bitch of a producer had laughed in his face when he just happened to mention it.

He finished the calzone and listened in silence to the latest argument between Campion, the producer and the camera crew, which seemed to focus largely on how the star should be lit.

'Morons,' Jay Gallo said miserably to no one, wishing he were not in such an evil mood. Business had been bad of late. He'd been reduced to playing errand boy for people he didn't like, delivering packages that contained God-knew-what to addresses he never wanted to see again. Being stuck on the set of some lousy TV show was better than jail. Just, he mused. Then his mobile phone vibrated in his shirt pocket and with a sweaty, tired hand he pulled it out, got up and walked away from the crew to make sure they didn't start yelling at him for talking on set.

'Mr Gallo? My name is Delgado. I work for a tour company in the Borgo. You won't have heard of us. I have an urgent problem. Are you busy?'

'Very.' It was a stock answer. There was always this ritual with the last-minute customers. You had to make them feel very grateful – and very generous.

'Ah. I'm sorry. Perhaps some other time then.'

'I didn't say I was unavailable,' Gallo snapped. 'Just busy.'

'But we need someone right now. I've been let down badly by one of the agencies. We have a party of very important people due to visit Ostia. I must find a translator for them within the hour.'

'What's the gig?'

'The what?'

'What kind of tour? What am I supposed to talk about?'

'Late imperial finds. The harbour. Nothing too detailed.'

Gallo smiled for the first time that day. 'Hey. I can go into as much detail as you want. I worked on that at Harvard.'

The man hesitated. 'So I heard. Then you're free?'

Gallo knew when a sap was rolling over. 'Let me be honest with you. I've got some personal business. If I'm going to cancel it's got to be double time. Six hundred dollars for the day.'

The voice on the end of the line hesitated. 'That's a lot of money.'

He could only say no, Gallo reasoned. There was just one more day of filming anyway. The crew had paid him in advance. He didn't normally jerk people around but on this occasion it would be a pleasure.

'Take it or leave it.'

'Can I pick you up in thirty minutes? Where will you be?'

'At the bar of the Osteria Capri. In Labicana, the Colosseum end.'

'Drinking coffee?'

'Drinking coffee,' he replied, puzzled. Had people been talking?

'I'll be there,' the man said and cut the call, before Gallo even had time to ask how they'd recognize each other.

He walked over to the crew. They were back to filming now. Campion was holding up a piece of broken pottery and speculating on whether it was an imperial wine goblet which Nero himself had once gripped.

Gallo stepped straight into the scene and prised the shard of unglazed brown ceramic from Campion's fingers.

'Let me interrupt this pile of fancy with a fact,' Gallo said, smiling for the camera. 'Nero lived here two, three years at most before he had his slave kill him to stop the Romans tearing him apart limb from limb. Emperors weren't into Mediterranean peasant chic. They ate off fancy plates. They drank from fancy glasses. This is stuff that never got out of the kitchen. This is stuff a slave would have been ashamed to own. You have excavated imperial Roman Tupperware, my man. Now don't you tell those good people out there otherwise.'

Jay Gallo felt good. Maybe he would fit in a quick beer before the agency man turned up. It could hardly do any harm.

The producer, a small woman with a malevolent dark face, stabbed him in the arm with a podgy finger. 'You're fired, mister,' she hissed.

'Oh calamitous day.' Gallo chuckled and set off down the hill, so happy he began to whistle.

There was time for two beers before the man arrived. Gallo had a pleasant smile on his face. He could do a good job when he felt like this. Everybody loved him.

They went outside and left in a long, black Mercedes. Gallo noticed when he climbed in that it had Vatican number plates, which seemed very odd indeed.

Ten

The mob of damp hacks clustered around the door looking grumpy, determined and somewhat ridiculous.

Luca Rossi scowled in their direction. 'I cannot believe I fell for this.'

'It was a deal. Remember?'

'The deal was I came here. Well, I've done that. Now you go in and talk to the woman on your own. She can't stand the sight of me anyway. You'll likely get more out of her.'

'You're going drinking again?'

'Ha, ha. There's one of these reporters I know. He's been useful in the past. We need to talk. Sometimes they know stuff that's never come anywhere near us. OK?'

Costa shrugged. He wondered if Rossi was being entirely honest with him. There had been times in the Rinaldis' apartment when the big man seemed to be engrossed, puzzled, though he never said a word afterwards. 'If that's what you want.'

'And then I'll make my own way back. Don't worry about me. We can talk again at dinner.'

Costa very much wished to get out of this arrangement. 'She's got the hots for you, Uncle Luca. There can be no other explanation. I'd just cramp your style.'

The big man seemed offended. 'Crazy Teresa's not so bad-looking. A man could do worse.'

'I just don't want to deflect attention away from you, me being young, slim and attractive and all.'

Rossi put out a big hand and patted him on the cheek, not so gently. 'It's a new place in Testaccio. Caligula. Thirteen Alberoni. Eight o'clock. Don't be late. I'm paying.'

'Great.'

Then Rossi was gone into the crowd, pushing his way through, exchanging a glance with one individual Costa thought he recognized. Soon there'd be a beer round the corner, he guessed. Maybe there was something to talk about. It still seemed a slim option. He remembered Falcone and thought: look for a simpler explanation. The big man just didn't want to see Sara Farnese. That was all.

The idea seemed even crazier when she let him into the first-floor apartment. She wore a dark-red cotton shirt and faded-blue designer jeans. Her hair was now tied back behind her neck. Her large and intelligent green eyes had a deep, shining lustre that was new to him. She was about his height and just as slender. She moved with a controlled grace as if she thought everything through first.

The apartment was decorated with a degree of taste Nic Costa associated with the wealthy middle-aged: reproduction wooden furniture, a polished dining table at the centre, and paintings everywhere, landscapes, medieval portraits and some more modern, abstract works that still seemed to fit. The walls were lined with the kind of heavy wallpaper you saw in expensive hotels.

And books, shelf upon shelf of books, all hardbacks, some leather-bound. There was no TV set, only a very pricey-looking stereo system and a pile of classical CDs next to it. None of this made sense to him. The designer jeans and her own magnetic looks apart, it was as if this woman – who could be no more than thirty – was living the life of a rich spinster in her fifties.

He indicated towards the crowd, now out of sight beyond the window.

'There are laws about harassment, you know. If you want me to do something I can call the municipal police.'

She sat down in a stylish high armchair that looked uncomfortable. 'They'll go away, won't they? I still don't understand what they want.'

They wanted a picture of her. He knew that. They wanted to splash her beauty all over the front pages and say: here's the woman some university professor went crazy over, killing himself, his wife and her boyfriend, all for some approximation of love.

He fell into a low sofa feeling awkward and out of place in these surroundings. 'They want your photograph. They want you.'

'Then they'll have a long wait. I'm getting my groceries delivered. The man downstairs brings them to me. I'm not going back to the university until this nonsense is over. They can camp out there for a week if they like. They'll still get nothing.'

That was easy to say, he thought. She didn't understand how soon you wore down under this constant attention, and how that was all part of their game.

'You never told me your name.'

'Costa. Nic Costa.'

'What do you want, Mr Costa?'

He pulled out a notebook. 'Just some simple, basic paperwork. If that's OK. Personal details.'

'Very well.'

In an efficient five minutes Sara Farnese told him all the bare facts. They shared the same age. She was twenty-seven, a little younger than he thought, held both Italian and English passports, thanks to the nationalities of her respective late parents, and was a middle-ranking professor at the university. Her affair with Rinaldi had lasted no more than a few weeks. She had not, as far as she was aware, mentioned Hugh Fairchild's visit in Rinaldi's earshot, though it was possible this had happened. Nor was she aware of Rinaldi's money or drug problems, both of which came as some – genuine, he thought – surprise to her.

She cited from memory the source of the quotation about the blood of the martyrs but was unsure what relevance it had. Just for interest, Costa read her back the full version of the doggerel about St Ives as Falcone had explained it that morning.

'So it's just a riddle?' she asked, bemused.

'You're not reaching for a calculator.'

'Why would I? Isn't the answer obvious? There's one man going to St Ives. The rest are going the other way.'

He began to understand Rossi's discomfiture in the presence of this woman. She was too smart, too cool, too distanced. She made him feel small and stupid, not by any deliberate act on her part but simply from her presence, her way of speaking. This was, he thought, accidental. Some curious air of loneliness hung around her too and it was evident in this antiseptic, overdecorated place she called home.

'Did Professor Rinaldi know many people in the Vatican?'

'He knew the ones we all knew. The academics. The people who controlled access to the library.'

'You need a ticket to get in there, surely? Something that gets you through the private gates without having to queue with the tourists?'

She opened a small blue leather handbag that sat by the chair, one that was, like everything else in the room, too mature for her. Sara Farnese sifted through the contents and pulled out a laminated card. It bore her name and a photograph.

'Of course. The library has more sources on early Christianity than anywhere else in the world. That's why I came to Rome.'

Costa looked closely at the card. 'But this is for access to the Vatican itself. Not the library.'

'Sometimes,' she said a little hesitantly, 'one needs to look at items that are stored elsewhere. This saves time.'

He didn't know anyone outside Vatican staff who owned one of these things. 'And Stefano had a card too?'

'I don't think so. He was waiting for it to come through. Perhaps that's why there was such a fuss when he forced his way in. If he'd had a card there would have been no problem.'

It made no sense. She had been at the university three years and owned one of these precious things. Rinaldi, who had been in the department for more than twenty, had to wait in line with the queues of Japanese.

'Why didn't he have one? If it was essential?'

'I don't know. I'm sorry. We worked in the same department but not on the same courses. Perhaps he felt it wasn't so necessary. You can get a lot of material online these days. I prefer to look at the source. It feels more proper somehow.'

'Why wouldn't he feel the same way?'

'I told you,' she replied a little testily. 'I don't know. I had a brief affair with the man. I wouldn't claim I knew him terribly well.'

Yet Stefano Rinaldi felt he knew her well enough to try to commit suicide in front of her and rely on this woman . . . to do what? To save his wife somehow, in return for the death of her current lover?

A snatch of their conversation from the previous day came back to him. 'Miss Farnese. You said that he spoke in two different voices to you.'

She had forgotten that part. It was obvious in her face, and the return of the memory puzzled her.

'That's correct. When he quoted Tertullian it was as if it were some kind of pronouncement, meant to be heard by everyone. It was loud, purposeful.' She thought carefully before going on. 'It was much quieter when he spoke about Mary. He was just talking to me then.'

Costa racked his head for what that might mean. 'Was there anyone else in the room that you knew? Apart from the guard who shot him?'

'No. They were all strangers.'

'But if he said one thing in a loud voice and the next more softly there had to be a reason. As if someone was watching, someone who needed to hear the first part, and to miss the second. Please. Try to think. Is that possible?'

She considered the idea. 'I'm sorry. The way I remember it, he entered the room in a rush. The first time he said those words from Tertullian he was well past everybody else. Even when he spoke loudly they wouldn't hear. The second time was different. But . . .'

Nic Costa thought about the kind of money the Vatican could spend on security and felt a sudden and urgent need to go back to the place where he had last seen Hugh Fairchild's skin lying on an old mahogany desk.

'I understand. I'm sorry. They must seem very stupid questions.'

'Not at all. They seem very intelligent ones. As intelligent as anyone could ask in the circumstances. I wish I could help more.'

Rossi had been right. It would have been awkward with him in the room. Sara Farnese was an odd mix of strength and timidity. The more she was surrounded by people, the less she would divulge.

He put his notebook in his pocket and got up.

'Would you like a coffee, Mr Costa?'

'Thanks,' he said, smiling. 'But I have another appointment.'

'Will there be another time?'

'I hope we can clear this all up by tomorrow. There shouldn't need to be another interview.'

He nodded towards the window and gave her his card, scribbling his home and mobile numbers on it. 'Remember what I said about harassment. Call any time and I'll get someone to talk to them.'

She looked at the card then placed it in her bag. 'Thanks. I'll bear that in mind.'

'Good. Oh . . .' It was an old trick but sometimes an effective one. 'I almost forgot. Do you know someone in the Vatican? Someone called Cardinal Denney?'

She shook her head and smiled, the fullest smile Costa had seen on her face. 'I'm sorry. I've never heard of anyone of that name.'

'No problem.'

Sara Farnese was looking out of the window again, wistfully.

'Are you sure you don't want to go outside for a little while?' Costa asked. 'A walk. You can't stay here for ever.'

She frowned at the world beyond the window. 'I'm not sure I can face that right now.'

He looked at her and said, 'Maybe . . .'

Eleven

Ten minutes later the door to the apartment block in Vicolo delle Palline opened and the mob outside went wild. In spite of the heat the woman coming out of the building was dressed in a long, full raincoat. Big sunglasses obscured her features and a headscarf covered her hair. She pushed away the forest of TV mikes that were thrust into her face. She said nothing, keeping her head down, trying to look as anonymous as possible in the scrum of reporters clamouring for her attention.

Cameras flashed. Arms and elbows jostled for position. A reporter from one of the tawdrier magazines fell to the floor winded by a sharp stab to the ribs. Another screeched as he was jostled out of position. One of the bigger hacks started to throw punches at a TV cameraman who was trying to push him out of the way. The slender figure at the centre of the mêlée was unable to avoid the photographers but remained silent throughout, pushing forward through the mass, dark glasses fixed firmly on the ground ahead.

Then the centre of gravity shifted. The raincoat forced its way through the final barrier of bodies and was free in the cobbled street. The mob's clamour diminished. This was not what was supposed to happen. Victims gave in eventually. They offered a sight of themselves or a few words in deference to the power of the pack. It was unknown for them to reject the mob's advances so completely, so successfully. One or two of the hacks wondered what to make of it, but then there was no time.

Sara Farnese began to run. The two arms of the raincoat started to pump. Her legs beat on the ground. The figure that eluded them now set up a pace, steady and deliberate, out beneath *Il Pasetto* into the broad tourist street beyond, inviting them to follow.

The herd howled and was after her, pausing only briefly to think about how odd this situation was. Close to an ice-cream stand in the Via dei Corridori they almost caught her. Then she picked up speed once more and was away, only just, until the pedestrian lights on the Piazza Pia turned red and a surging sea of cars rolled forward, horns hooting, drivers screaming at each other, a solid sea of metal blocking her way.

The figure turned and saw the mob on her heels, panting, unused to this kind of chase, determined to repay the effort by pinning her down in public, forcing her to remove the disguise, bellowing at her until she said something, anything to explain why three people died in her name, and in such crazy ways too.

The first hack, some way ahead of the rest, pounced, placing a firm hand on her shoulder. This was a mistake. A sharp fist stabbed him in the ribs, the breath went out of his body in an instant, and all he heard for his considerable pain was a low, half-obscene curse.

The traffic was gridlocked in the wide piazza, a mass of overheated vehicles sending out a choking cloud of pollution into the humid forty-degree air. She watched the rest of the pack come close then turned, jumped, mounted the bonnet of a Lexus next to the kerb and raced quickly across the road, leaping from car to car.

The mob watched in anguished amazement. The hacks were out of breath. The photographers scarcely had the energy to lift their cameras. The TV crews were still struggling up the street wondering what was going on. It was just possible for them to see the conclusion once she had navigated the bonnets, roofs and boots that filled the piazza.

Sara Farnese, who was, as far as they knew, a quiet, academic university professor, kicked hard on the pavement, like an athlete setting off for the race. She broke into her pace, a faster pace than she had used down the Via dei Corridori, one which was more natural to her. Then she disappeared past the squat rotund magnificence of the Castel Sant'Angelo sprinting like a pro, arms moving rhythmically, legs pounding the ground, with the raincoat flapping behind in the wind.

Five minutes later a skinny, scared-looking young woman from Kosovo, with a ten-month-old baby in her arms, sat outside the makeshift tent that was her home. It was on the wide footpath by the banks of the Tiber near the Ponte Cavour. She was astonished to see a man walking towards her, a slender man with a woman's raincoat flapping around him. He wore a broad, self-amused smile and was somewhat out of breath.

She held the child more tightly to her and retreated into the shade of the small, tattered tent. He was not a cop, surely, who would move her on again. Cops didn't wear women's raincoats. They didn't smile like this, a nice smile, she realized, one that came from some happiness inside.

He stopped and crouched next to her, looking at the child, breathing heavily. Then he took off the raincoat, bundled it up with a pair of expensive-looking sunglasses and a headscarf and gave them to her.

'Can you use these?' he asked.

She nodded.

The man reached into his pocket and pulled out a €50 note. It was a lot of money. She knew what that meant.

'What do you want?' she said in what she knew was bad Italian. 'I don't . . .' She didn't want to say any more. It was a lot of money.

'Don't worry. It's a family habit. My father told me to give something away twice every day,' he said, in a warm, calm voice. 'Maybe one day I'll be hoping someone does the same to me.'

She couldn't take her eyes off the note in her baby's tiny fingers. It was more cash than she had seen in two weeks. 'A lot of money,' she said again.

'I told you. Twice a day. I was busy this morning, I missed out. You're lucky. You get both.'

She smiled nervously. 'I like being lucky.'

Nic Costa wondered how old she was. Probably no more than seventeen.

'Promise me something,' he said, scribbling on a page ripped from his notebook.

'What?' she said, taking the paper from him.

'You'll go to this address. It's a hostel. They can help.'

'OK,' she replied mutedly, some suspicion in her voice.

'I don't come this way often,' he said. 'Remember that address.'

Then he walked off, back towards the steps that rose

up to road level, back towards the bridge that led on to the Vatican.

He was on the stone staircase when his mobile phone rang.

'I'm in your debt, Mr Costa,' said Sara Farnese, and he could hear the relief in her voice.

'The name's Nic. You're welcome. I lost your coat and things. Sorry.'

She laughed. It was the first time he had heard her make any sound of pleasure and this was, he thought, the real Sara Farnese, not the person she tried to portray to the world. 'It was worth it ten times over. Watching them, chasing you . . . Nic.'

'So you escaped?' he asked.

The line went quiet. It was a direct question, an understandable one in the circumstances. Perhaps she was wondering whether it was personal or professional. He was unsure himself. Nic Costa was curious about where she would go in the circumstances, and cursed his prurience: he wished, automatically, that he had arranged to have her followed.

'Call again, Nic. If you like,' she said, and was gone.

Twelve

The man wore a black suit and dark glasses. He was muscular and probably middle-aged, though he wore such heavy clothing, in spite of the heat, it was difficult to tell from what was on show. For the life of him, Gallo could not work out the accent. Southern? Sicilian maybe? He didn't want to try. There was something serious about him, something that said you just did your job, did it well, got your money, then walked away.

The car struggled through the traffic out to the motorway which led to Fiumicino airport and the coast. He had jazz playing on the music system: Weather Report, with Wayne Shorter's sax wailing like a banshee. Gallo knew Ostia well. He'd taken many parties around the old port area and the ruins of the imperial town.

'Who are they?' he asked.

'Who are who?' the man grunted.

'The people I'm supposed to entertain.'

'Visiting college professors. Not archaeologists themselves, but people with an interest. I hope you know what you're talking about.'

'No problem.'

The car turned off the motorway early. Gallo was puzzled.

'Aren't we going to the town?'

'Not first. There's another area that got cut off from the meander by a flood hundreds of years back. The *Fiume Morto*. The dead river. You know it?'

'No.' Gallo felt his mood starting to wane. No one ever went to the dead river except hardened diggers. It was just mud and mosquitoes. 'You might have told me.'

The black glasses looked at him. 'I heard you were a clever guy. You can make things up if you want. What does it matter? It's all show business. Don't worry. It won't take long. After that we go to the town. Then you run on autopilot, huh?'

'Yeah, right.' He scanned the flat land of the Tiber estuary. The stink of the flat marshes came in with the air-conditioning. It was chemical, lifeless and made the back of his throat turn dry and start to ache. There was nothing ahead, not a coach, not even a single car. Gallo looked at the man again. He was wearing black leather gloves. Odd in the heat.

The driver turned to him again. 'You've heard of Tertullian?'

Gallo laughed dryly. 'Oh wow. What a sweetheart that guy was. Really full of joy and light. What was that wonderful line about women? "Tu es ianua diaboli." You're the doorway of the devil. Boy, do the feminists love that one. What a twisted dude.'

The man at the wheel was watching him and, in spite of the sunglasses, Jay Gallo could tell there was something severe about him, something cold and immovable.

'I was thinking,' he said, 'of another saying.'

'What?'

' "The blood of the martyrs is the seed of the Church." '

Gallo turned to look at the man. Maybe he wasn't as old as he had first thought. He moved with the ease of someone about his own age. The glasses, the clothes seemed to be there to age him.

The travel business, Jay Gallo thought. What a way to earn a living. The mention of Tertullian had put Gallo in full flow. It was rare he got a chance to display his erudition with someone who might begin to appreciate it.

'These early Christians. You know what puzzles me? How did anybody sign up for this thing? What was the point?'

'You mean why did Tertullian call for people to be martyrs?'

'No! Why did the poor suckers take him at his word? Why die just for some . . . idea?'

The dark glasses thought about that. 'You've seen the Caravaggio in Santa Maria deli Popolo? *St Peter's Crucifixion?*'

Gallo knew the church as well as he wished. It was a minor star in the galaxy of Roman sights. A chapel by Raphael, a touch of Borgia history and two famous Caravaggios, all in the perfect Renaissance piazza the tourists loved because it sat at the end of the tawdry shopping street, the Corso.

'Yeah.' He recalled a striking, large canvas of the saint about to be crucified upside down. The cross was being pushed and pulled upright by three largely unseen workers who could have come straight out of any sixteenth-century tavern. Peter stared at the nail running through his left palm with a determination, almost pride, which Gallo never could understand.

'That tells you everything. Peter's executioners believe they're raising the means of his cruel death. In truth, with each inch they build higher the foundations of the Church, as the saint clearly realizes.'

Gallo waved a hand as if to say this was obvious. 'Yes, yes. He's a martyr . . .'

'Furthermore,' the man continued, 'he's bathed in the light of Grace, which even shines on his murderers. He goes to his death out of duty, and happily because he knows there is a better life awaiting him in Paradise. This is a transformation he seeks. He *knows* he goes to Heaven.'

'Crazy . . .' Gallo grunted, shaking his head.

The dark glasses stared at the empty horizon ahead.

Gallo smiled and thought of another Caravaggio, in the Borghese, and the story behind it, one that always went down well with the Americans. 'And anyway, Caravaggio didn't believe that crap himself. Look how he paints himself as the severed head of Goliath. When he did that, my friend, he was under sentence of death himself, for murdering a man during a game of real tennis. He painted his own head there to acknowledge the Pope's hold over him and beg forgiveness. He had good, practical reasons to be afraid. And he was. You don't see him expecting salvation there. Just the grave. And oblivion.'

'You're a cultured man,' the driver said to Gallo's obvious satisfaction. 'And what happened to the painter?'

'He got his pardon. Then died on the way back to Rome. Ironic, huh?'

'Possibly. Or apt. Perhaps that was his punishment.'

But Jay Gallo wasn't listening. There was something he had to say, something important. 'And here's another irony. Tertullian didn't even take his own advice. He was no martyr. He died in his bed at a hundred and two or something. Hypocrite.'

He remembered the Vatican number plate and added quickly, 'Not that I know the first damn thing about religion, of course.'

'Just history?'

'That's right.'

Jay Gallo looked around. They had parked by the low muddy waters of the river. There wasn't a soul in sight. Or anything to look at either. All the usual places to visit were a good kilometre or two away. He wished there was somewhere he could buy a beer or a good coffee with *grappa* in it. He wished the place didn't smell so badly of chemicals and pollution.

'They'll be here soon,' the man said, seeming to read his thoughts. The jazz album came to an end. He hit the button on the hi-fi, removed the CD and carefully put it away in a case he kept on the dashboard. It was an odd action. For some reason it made Gallo think the car wasn't his at all. 'We can still continue our interesting talk while we wait, can't we? You're right about Caravaggio, I think. He did have good, practical reasons to be afraid. But you shouldn't exclude him, or Tertullian, or any of us, you and me, from being agents of God's will. That would be presumptuous, surely, even for one who knows nothing about religion?'

'Really?'

'You don't think God just uses those who believe in him as his instruments? What about Pilate? What about Herod?'

It was only then that Jay Gallo considered his position seriously. He was sitting by a remote stretch of the Tiber with a man he didn't know, waiting for a tour group who wanted to see . . . what exactly? There wasn't a single archaeological artefact in the vicinity as far as he was aware. Maybe they'd turn out to be bird-spotters instead.

Maybe they were reviving that long-lost art-form, the snuff movie.

He looked at the man in the seat next to him. If it came to it, Gallo thought, they were evenly matched. The man was stockier but older, maybe, and he gave him something in height. What was more, Jay Gallo had been in plenty of bar-room brawls over the years. He knew how to look after himself.

'Are you jerking me around?' he asked the man in the dark glasses.

'Mr Gallo?'

'Is this some kind of a joke?'

The man thought about it. ' "The blood of the martyrs . . ." Does that sound like some kind of joke?'

Gallo swore under his breath. The man was starting to annoy him. 'Why do you keep saying that crap? What the fu—'

A black fist, hard as iron, came out at him, flying fast, and caught him full in the eye. Jay Gallo's head went back, his vision narrowed, tunnelling into blackness at the edges. There was little pain; more an absence of sensation altogether. Then, in the limited focus he possessed, something darted at him again. The solid leather shape connected with his nose, there was the sound and the sensation of bone breaking. A warm, salty trickle of blood began to run down his throat.

Thirteen

The official quarters of Cardinal Michael Denney overlooked the Cortile di San Damaso, the sprawling private courtyard hidden from the outside world by the curving western wall of St Peter's Square. The Vatican was never built as a residence. Denney's apartment was one of only two hundred or so created within the palace walls. On the far side of the square lay the residency of the Swiss Guard. In his own block senior Vatican officials jostled for position to get the best view of the open space. His neighbours included some of the most powerful figures in the Holy See. The *camerlengo*, the Pope's chamberlain, who would briefly oversee the interregnum in the event of the pontiff's death, was some way down the hall. They rarely spoke these days. Denney was aware he had become *persona non grata*, a prisoner in a glittering cell. Sometimes he spent hours staring at the reflection of the paintings, the Murano chandeliers and the wall-length ormolu mirrors, waiting for the most menial of civil servants to return his call. All this must, he knew, change. A man could go mad in these circumstances.

The agents of that change were now assembled around the walnut dining table that sat by the long, eighteenth-century windows looking out onto the court-yard. It had taken him many weeks to persuade these three men to come to Rome and sit down together. Between them they represented a powerful trinity of interests which could, with a little persuasion and the right inducements, resurrect something from the shattered shell of the Banca Lombardia and with it a little of Michael Denney's reputation. Sufficient, he hoped, to allow him to return home and live out the rest of his life in dignified obscurity.

Two of the men present he thought he could handle. Robert Aitcheson, the sour-faced American lawyer who oversaw corporate affairs for the bank out of a base in the Bahamas, had as much reason as Denney to clear this thing up. The Feds were already on Aitcheson's back, chasing up a hot money scam that came to light in the wake of the currency laundering checks introduced after September 11. He needed to get out of the heat. Arturo Crespi was in the same boat. Crespi was a diminutive pen-pushing banker who oversaw the movement of capital in and out of the web of funds that underpinned the bank. The Finance Ministry was asking too many questions of him already. Ostensibly, he was the bank president, though in everything he deferred to Denney, who had assembled the complex network of offshore trusts piece by piece over the years from what had once been a legit-imate, onshore financial enterprise. Crespi was weak and respectable. It had suited Denney at the time. He had been charged with getting an above average return on the money under his care. There had, he believed, been little choice, and, when they began, little in the way of legal obstruction either.

The third man stood by the window, peering down

into the courtyard, sniffing with a summer cold. Emilio Neri was over six feet tall, a giant of a man in his mid-sixties, now beginning to run to flab. He had grey, lifeless eyes, a long, jutting jaw and a head of perfectly groomed silver hair. Today, as always, he wore an expensive suit: thin, pale-coloured silk which now showed damp patches under the arms. He rarely smiled. He spoke only when he had something to say. Neri was, from outward appearances, a successful Roman entrepreneur. He owned a palatial penthouse in the Via Guilia, a pretty young wife, three country houses and an apartment in New York. His name adorned the board of the Fenice Opera House in Venice, where he helped raise funds for its rebuilding, and any number of charitable organizations working with the Catholic poor.

Only once had his image as a man beyond reproach been questioned. It was in the mid-1970s when a radical press untouched by conventional party politics had existed in the city. A scurrilous reporter on a short-lived underground rag had published a portrait of Neri culled from police gossip. It was a story many recognized but few wished to acknowledge. The article told of his upbringing in Sicily as the son of a local Mafia don, his apprenticeship in the racketeering world of black-market tobacco and prostitution and his eventual emergence as a key liaison figure in the continuing dialogue between corrupt government, Church officials and the criminal state that lived then, as now, beneath the mundane facade of Italian society. The piece had accused Neri of nothing criminal. In a way, it was intended as a tribute to the man, who had genuinely come to be something of an art lover, was seen at all the right exhibitions, was always there, in his private box, at the opera and the ballet.

Three weeks after the magazine article, the author was found in a car parked in a lane near Fiumicino airport. His eyes had been put out, probably by a man's thumbs. His tongue had been ripped from his mouth. Every finger and both thumbs had been severed at the first socket with a knife. He survived, blind, dumb and unable, or unwilling, to try to communicate. The street gossip, which Denney later discovered was entirely accurate, claimed that Neri had performed his revenge personally in a warehouse he owned on the perimeter of the airport. He'd then, in front of the tortured hack, changed into evening dress and flown by private plane to Venice to see Pavarotti in a new production of *Turandot*, after which he had attended the first-night party as an honoured guest.

Denney, once he had come to know the man, wondered why he had gone to all that trouble. Emilio Neri could have sucked the life out of another human being just by looking at him. Still, the papers wrote only about Neri's charitable activities after that.

Denney watched Neri's big back at the window, wondering what was going through his head. There was just one thing Neri wanted now: the return of the money he had placed in Denney's hands. If that happened, they would, once again, be on the best of terms.

The door into the room opened. Brendan Hanrahan walked in carrying a tray with coffee on it. Throwing a mint into his mouth, Neri turned to stare at him.

'Don't they provide you with servants any more, Michael?' Neri asked.

'Just helping out,' Hanrahan interjected. 'This is a

private meeting, gentlemen. None of you wants to advertise your presence, I imagine.'

'As if anything's secret in this place these days.' Neri sniffed. He cast a glance out of the window and then at Denney. 'I'm amazed you still have one of the best views in the place. The Church is going soft.'

'Shall we get down to business, gentlemen?' Aitcheson complained. 'I want to be on the ten o'clock plane out of here.'

'Agreed,' Crespi said.

Neri sat down at the table opposite the little banker, grinning at him. 'Have you managed to replace that clerk of yours yet, Crespi? The one who talked himself to death.'

The little banker went white. 'My people are trustworthy. Every one of them. I stake my word on it.'

'You're staking more than that, my friend,' Neri said. 'Enough. You know my position. You know my responsibilities. You people talk. Tell me why we're here.'

'To get ourselves out of a hole,' Hanrahan said and passed around copies of a single printed page.

Neri scanned the document. 'Doesn't say here when I get my money back.'

'Emilio,' Denney replied with as much pleasantry as he could muster. 'I can't work magic. We all want our money back. We can all get it, I think. But it doesn't come out of nowhere. We have to rebuild.'

Aitcheson hadn't been listening. His eyes were fixed on the paper. 'There's this much money still left? Why didn't I hear of this before?'

Crespi threw up his hands. 'We've been liquidating assets for eighteen months. Quietly. Privately. Sometimes . . . we didn't know if we'd get paid. I didn't want to raise anyone's hopes unnecessarily. This is all very complex, gentlemen. We ran away with ourselves. We had so many accounts. In so many places. I couldn't tell you about all of them, my friend. I would have bored you rigid. And for what? You wanted to know what the return was. Not where it was coming from.' He stole a glance at Neri. 'That was all anyone wanted. It's one reason we're in this mess in the first place.'

Neri now seemed interested in the paper. 'Who else knows about this money? Where is it exactly?'

'No one outside this room.' Hanrahan looked Neri in the face. 'No offence but we've been too lax with our secrets already. Where it is, that's my business.'

Some $3 billion had been seized by the US authorities alone, on the basis of tax evasion and money laundering. It infuriated Denney. Had that remained undiscovered he could have weathered the storm. Crespi's feverish bid to liquidate what assets he could find and shift the funds into new, undiscovered accounts had, at least, offered him a lifeline. If only Aitcheson and Neri could be persuaded to grasp this.

'So we're not paupers,' Neri said. 'I walk into this room thinking this was money down the drain. Now you tell me there's, what, sixty, seventy million dollars out there we can lay our hands on. How did this come about?'

'You don't want to know,' Hanrahan said with a scowl.

'We have,' added Denney, 'worked very hard. We've had to persuade people, induce them, get them to see our point of view. It's not been easy.'

Neri sniffed into his hand. 'I heard you'd been spending a lot of money. The price of a Rome whore's gone up ten per cent in the last six months, Michael. Was that your doing?'

'Don't be ridiculous.'

'And none of this for yourself? To get you safe passage out of this place, back to America?'

Denney's hand stole across the table and gripped Neri's arm. The large man stared balefully back.

'Emilio,' Michael Denney said. 'I did this for us. We can be back in business. We can put some new people in place. Let them talk to the banking authorities. Let them run the risks. We just stay behind the scenes and pull the strings, as we should have done all along. This has been a learning experience for all of us. We come out of it stronger. Richer. More powerful. And in the end, yes, I can walk out of here. I can go back to America a free man because we have a whole new field of people in our debt by this stage.'

Neri smiled and looked at Aitcheson. 'You hear this? We're building a new bank. And all it takes is sixty, seventy million dollars.'

'Not enough,' Aitcheson grumbled. 'You know that.'

They hadn't said no. They were interested. Denney could feel it. They had the light of greed in their eyes. 'So we raise more. We still have the contacts. They still have the need. Lombardia wasn't brought down by us. We were the victims of the markets and laws that didn't even exist when we first went into business. We wipe the slate clean, we start again, we stay one step ahead of the pack.'

Denney paused, to give what came next some theatrical effect. 'It requires some investment on our own part. Personally I'll throw every last cent I have into the pot. That's a lot of money. All my money. Whatever you want to come in with, that's your decision. We know this business, gentlemen. We're very good at it. The best. We're needed out there.'

Neri laughed, a big deep sound, and clapped Denney on the shoulder. 'You mean this, Michael? We're back in business. What a salesman. What a guy.'

'We're back in business,' Denney repeated.

Hanrahan's phone rang. He answered it. His face went dark. Then he made an excuse and left the room.

'What do you think?' Denney asked, unable to stop himself stealing a glance out of the window, thinking of the world beyond.

Fourteen

There were two possibilities, Nic Costa decided. Falcone would either love the idea or he would just go plain crazy, unless there were results. Given results, the severe, overdressed man he called inspector would, he thought, forgive almost anything.

The queue to the museums was still fifty metres long though the place would close in an hour. He used his police card to work his way to the front then put it discreetly away and paid for a ticket at the desk. He walked to the library, waved the police card at the dull attendant on the door and entered the Reading Room without waiting to be stopped.

The hard yellow light of the late afternoon streamed in from the courtyard onto a sea of empty desks. The place had a sharp antiseptic smell. Someone had been cleaning up. Costa went first to the old desk where, the day before, Hugh Fairchild's skin had sat like the involuntary cast-off from some giant lizard. He was aware that the attendant was on the phone already. The man's low voice echoed across the spotless, vacant interior. Only one book remained out. It sat on a desk, three along from the one Sara Farnese had occupied. He looked at it:

something incomprehensible in medieval script. This was a place for a certain kind of human being and it was closing now, going to rest for the weekend.

Costa walked through the aisles, examining everything. Sure enough, the library was littered with security cameras: tiny dull eyes glinting back at him from discreet metal housings on the ceiling, in corners, attached to windows. He was no academic but he understood why. The library was priceless. The only way to get access was by obtaining special permission, something even a long-term lecturer like Stefano Rinaldi seemed to find difficult. This was a priceless store of irreplaceable treasures and one that loaned them to a grateful, privileged few to hold in their hands, to touch, admire and then return. The risks required great care. Every entrance into the room, every loan, every moment a work was in the hands of a reader, all these occurrences would be recorded, day in, day out. Whoever kept the tapes would know what Stefano Rinaldi looked like, how he behaved, probably from the moment he entered the library itself on the floor above.

Was this why the man whispered? Or was there someone he feared in the room?

Either way the cameras surely held the key. Still, Falcone's question kept coming back: *why?* Logically, because Rinaldi wanted to set Sara the task of saving his wife, and feared this would be impossible if someone, either in the room or with access to the tape, witnessed what he was attempting. Could he have left his wife standing on the chair in the tower, knowing that if she stumbled she would hang herself? Was it possible that somewhere between Tiber Island and the Vatican he changed his mind and decided to beg Sara to rescue her?

This was extending the craziness theory too far. Nor did it provide a link between Rinaldi's supposed actions and his whispered instructions to Sara. Had he changed his mind Rinaldi could have returned himself and removed his wife from the noose. Costa began to understand Falcone's doubts. The rudimentary logic which reduced these events to some simple act of bloody revenge began to unravel when one thought about the details. There was, now Costa thought of it, only a single possibility that could explain everything, and it was one he found deeply disturbing.

What if Rinaldi was not the lone murderer but an accomplice in concert with another? Or even a victim himself? What if he had come to the Vatican desperate because someone else was in the tower, someone who had entrapped him, his wife and the unfortunate Fairchild? Someone who had used Rinaldi's debts to arrange the initial meeting, murdered the Englishman in front of their eyes, strung up Mary Rinaldi and told her husband that she would be dead unless he sent Sara Farnese back there immediately? Someone who sent the man out on this mission with Hugh Fairchild's skin in a supermarket bag, demanding he spread it out on the desk, say these crazy words, knowing, surely, that the armed guards would think they had some homicidal madman in their midst.

And one more thing too. Someone who, as far as Rinaldi was concerned, would know whether all these conditions had been met. Either because he had an accomplice there, or access somehow to the tapes *even before Rinaldi could return*. Costa rejected this last thought. It could only be practical if someone in the Vatican was in direct contact with the man in the tower.

This was surely a conspiracy too far. No, the conditions that were set – the gun, the bag with Fairchild's skin inside, the repeated and crazy declamations – were invitations to the armed guards of the Vatican to intervene with all possible force because of the nature of the threat they perceived. That must have been the intention – to ensure Rinaldi, and perhaps Sara Farnese too, died in the library.

It was a hypothesis Nic Costa was reluctant to embrace. His years in the police force had taught him that simple solutions were usually the correct ones. The tapes were the key, Costa repeated to himself, then felt a firm hand grip his shoulder. He turned and, as he had expected all along, found himself looking into the cold, rheumy eyes of the man called Hanrahan, still dressed in the same black suit, still with a crucifix in his lapel.

Costa smiled pleasantly. These were different circumstances. He could think more about this curious man who now stood in front of him, blocking his way to the door, not angry, more jaded, even curious perhaps.

'This is tiresome,' Hanrahan said finally. 'Don't you know anything of the protocols that govern how we're supposed to work?'

The voice was thick, rough-edged and familiar somehow. Then Nic Costa remembered. He had briefly played for the force rugby side, before deciding that the more solitary sport of running suited him better. There had been an Irishman who coached the team for a while. He spoke like this. He even had the same kind of coarse features.

'I realized I forgot to give you my details,' Costa said. He took out his wallet and handed Hanrahan the official police card. Then he pointed at his face and the broken nose. 'I know where you got that. You're a player, right? On the field. Rugby.'

Hanrahan read the card then put it in his pocket. 'When I was young. When I thought there was nothing in the world that could harm me.'

'I used to play a little too.'

Hanrahan eyed him, sceptical.

'Fly half,' Costa said. 'Pretty good, even if I say so myself.'

'Falcone told me you ran. He said it was one of your talents.'

Costa nodded.

'In fact,' the Irishman continued, 'I think he said it was your only talent.'

'Sounds like the man.'

'I can imagine you running, Mr Costa. I imagine you excel. But at some stage you have to turn and fight too. How good are you at that?'

Costa laughed. 'Probably not so hot, to be honest. It's a question of size.'

'No, it isn't,' Hanrahan said. 'What do you want?'

Costa nodded at the ceiling. 'A look at the tape. You must have our dead professor covered from the moment he walked into the library. I'd just like to see.'

Hanrahan shook his head, as if amazed. 'Who do you think you are?'

'Just a cop trying to understand why three people are dead. Who do you think you are?'

Hanrahan thought about this and pulled out his own card. 'I'm a consultant here, Mr Costa. I advise on security matters. I have no power to give you your tape . . .'

'Then introduce me to someone who has.'

'Why?'

Costa was starting to feel exasperated. 'Don't you think you're under any obligation to help us crack this thing? Three people dead, Hanrahan. I know none of them are Vatican citizens, but even so.'

The Irishman waved a half angry hand at him. 'Don't give me that crap, son. When you deal with us, you deal with another country. This isn't police work, it's diplomacy.' The sharp, liquid eyes narrowed. 'If I talk to the person who can give you that tape, what do you have to offer in return?'

He knew what Luca Rossi would say if he were here. You never do deals with these people. You never even think you can broker some kind of covenant because there's always a caveat, a get-out you never know about until it's too late.

But Rossi was somewhere else, contemplating dinner with Crazy Teresa. All the relevant information he could think of was here, locked inside this tiny country that just happened to live behind its own high walls in the heart of Rome. If he didn't cut some kind of deal it might never see the light of day.

Besides, some small, quiet voice told him, there was an opportunity here. A moment when you could throw a stone in a pool and wait to see the patterns the ripple would make once the stone hit the surface. Sometimes you had to take chances.

Nic Costa pulled out his notebook and copied the phone number he'd found on Stefano Rinaldi's computer that morning. He gave it to Hanrahan, who stared at the page with a stony expression.

'Someone from here, someone in the office of a

person called Cardinal Denney, was in contact with Rinaldi by phone. On the day he did this.'

Hanrahan seemed genuinely surprised. 'Do you know why?'

'Maybe I should ask Cardinal Denney.'

He was amazed. Hanrahan laughed, a big, hearty laugh, one that, had it lasted, might have brought tears to his eyes.

The Irishman's hand slapped his shoulder, hard.

'You're a funny man, Mr Costa,' he said. 'I just haven't the heart to call Falcone again. Not this time. Now just do me a favour will you?'

'What?'

'Get the fuck out of here. And go sign this thing off whatever way you want. We both know what happened. Some crazy, personal tragedy to do with a rather fine-looking young woman with lax personal morals. Don't turn over stones for the sake of it. Sometimes those little creatures underneath can bite.'

Fifteen

'What do I think? Michael, Michael.'

Neri couldn't stop laughing, couldn't stop slapping Denney on the shoulder.

'You make a good cardinal. Why'd you ever think you could make a good banker too?'

'It was what was asked of me,' Denney replied sharply. 'I know my duty.'

Neri's big face fell suddenly serious. 'And I know mine. You truly believe this money, this hidden crock of gold, is news to me.'

Denney turned to Crespi, astonished. The little man's face flushed. 'I said nothing,' he complained. 'He's making this up.'

'I don't lie,' Neri grunted. 'I'm too rich to have to lie these days. I told you. This place leaks like a sieve. I've known your little secret for weeks, Michael. I've had time to consider it. Carefully. To talk about it with my associates too. What I have to say to you now is painful, but say it I must.'

The door opened. Hanrahan walked in, making his excuses. Denney looked at him in despair. This was all

A SEASON FOR THE DEAD

going wrong. Neri had advance knowledge. He couldn't begin to guess how, or what this might mean.

'The choice before me,' Neri continued, 'is simple. Do I lose a friend? Or do I lose a fortune? Do I throw good money after bad for old times' sake? Or do I take what I can and be grateful for that?'

'This is a pittance,' Denney complained. 'It's a fraction of what we could earn if we go back in business. And you need a bank, Emilio. You can't live without that.'

'Banks, banks,' Neri snarled, waving a dismissive hand at Denney. 'You live in the past, Michael. It's the secret, small corporations that attract the interest of those cold-blooded lawyers in the first place. Why waste all our time and money on them when it's simpler just to go to someone more established and pay him for a mutual relationship? It's in the nature of the world we live in now that men like us may hide more easily in the light of day. Scurrying around in dark corners merely calls attention to ourselves. Sadly . . .' Neri seemed genuinely surprised by this insight, 'that's what seems to come naturally to a man like you. Perhaps it's in your background. Perhaps it comes from this place. If the latter, then more fool you, because they've abandoned you, Michael. Even if you don't know that yourself.'

'What?' Denney knew he was out of favour. But a renewal of his business interests, some clearing of debts, these were actions that would surely begin to clear his name.

'I want my cut of this money,' Aitcheson said. 'I want it now and I want it based on what we invested in the first place.'

'You'll walk away with pennies,' Denney repeated.

Aitcheson stabbed an angry finger at him. 'I'll walk

away with something. Listen to me well, Michael. I was on the phone to someone in the Justice Department only yesterday. This present state of limbo isn't going to last. They're closing Lombardia for good soon, not just suspending us. They're preparing the warrants. Your name's on the top. No one else's right now and as far as the rest of us are concerned that's the way it's going to stay.'

Denney glared at them. 'You knew this? All of you? You didn't think to tell me?'

Crespi stared at the table. Neri looked bored.

Aitcheson sighed. 'You've been living in la-la land these last six months, Michael, thinking you can bribe your way out of this mess. It isn't going to happen. Even if it were possible, Emilio's right. Letting you back into the game would just mean we open up a black hole again. You're finished. Face it. We have nothing left to discuss. I wash my hands of you.'

Neri glanced at Hanrahan then nodded at the ceiling. 'They do too. He doesn't know?'

Denney felt hot, confused. He looked into Hanrahan's eyes and saw the future begin to fall apart.

'You don't have a deal?' Hanrahan asked. 'After all this work? All this time?'

Neri shook his head. 'My dear Irish friend. Please don't act so surprised. Do we look like fools?' He paused, enjoying this. 'Well. Tell him . . .'

Hanrahan grimaced then pulled out his phone. Denney heard him calling the janitorial staff, asking them to send a couple of men round. 'If there's no deal,' he said, 'things are very different.'

'What are you doing?' Denney demanded. 'What the hell is going on here?'

Neri smiled at the apartment, appreciating the Murano glass, the mirrors, the paintings. 'Nice place,' he said. 'They'll be scratching each other's eyes out to see who gets it next.'

Sixteen

Teresa Lupo, Crazy Teresa to the Rome police department, sat in front of a varied collection of animal body parts: veal hearts, cartilage, pig thymus glands and a tangle of cow intestines with milk still inside. She was ecstatic and was joined in her joy by Luca Rossi who wore, for the occasion, a Lazio baseball cap, placed backwards on his balding head, and ate with noisy, open-mouthed enthusiasm. This was, it transpired, Rossi's favourite food, *cucina romana*, the traditional working-class fare of the city: the offal which, by tradition, the proletariat had been left after the clergy of the Vatican had picked from the best cuts of meat.

The restaurant was a cheaper clone of the flashy, expensive Checchino dal 1887 around the corner, the city temple to the eating of guts and glands. Its sixteen simple tables were fully booked and heaving with cooked organs which Nic Costa could not begin to identify even if he so wished. This was the big man's joke; to bring a vegetarian to a place where the consumption of arcane flesh was a religion. Or perhaps he didn't even think about it. Costa watched the way he looked at Crazy Teresa as they prodded and poked at some tripe and hoof jelly and wondered if there was the prospect of love in the air.

They made an odd pair. Rossi, with his big, sad face and sprawling body, looked like a man who would stay single all his life and had probably forgotten when he last slept with a woman. Crazy Teresa had run through endless affairs in the department, all of them short, all of them encounters which tended to leave the male party wan and glassy-eyed afterwards. A little taller than Nic Costa, powerfully built, with a handsome face that smiled constantly as it examined every last thing that fell under its gaze, she was an astonishingly skilled pathologist who had worked as a successful hospital surgeon before something – the craving for excitement was her excuse – drove her into the morgue. Costa never really swallowed that line. Her work wasn't exciting. She was so painstaking and exact she found herself working long, tiring hours just to extract every last shred of evidence. The bodies Teresa Lupo called her 'customers' were, in spite of her easy way with them, still the remains of human beings. Her relationship with them went beyond the forensic. At times she was able to offer the kinds of insight that failed the best of cops and that, he thought, was what drove her. She liked playing detective, and often was very good at it.

Rossi and the woman sat together opposite him, picking at the plates, guzzling the cheap house red and sucking at cigarettes when a gap between the delivery of the flesh and the booze allowed. Costa had arrived late, on purpose. He waited until the waitress, a surly looking girl with rings in her nose and ears, came up with a pad then ordered salad and a glass of Cala Viola, a young

Sardinian white which was the only wine he recognized on the list.

'Chicken salad?' the girl demanded.

'Just salad.'

'We don't *do* "just salad",' she snarled. 'You can take the chicken off if you like.'

Costa sighed, digging in his heels. 'Why don't *you* take the chicken off?'

'Hah! And have you moaning when it comes to paying the bill? Do I look that stupid?'

Rossi leaned forward and gave her the serious look. 'Hey. If it comes to it I'll take the chicken off. He's a vegetarian. OK?'

The nose ring twitched. She suddenly looked more sympathetic. 'Sorry,' she said sincerely.

'Me too. Jesus, are we in the wrong place or what?'

When the girl returned with a large plate of rocket and salad leaves and a decent glass of icy wine Crazy Teresa was midway through an explanation of the physical function of the mushy glands sitting in front of them, lightly cooked with garlic and celery.

'Can we not talk food tonight?' Nic Costa asked.

'You're squeamish?' Crazy Teresa enquired, amazed. 'You two, of all people. After what happened yesterday?'

Luca Rossi sided with his partner. 'Maybe it's because of what happened yesterday. I mean, I like eating this stuff. To be absolutely honest with you, I'd really rather not know what it is.'

'OK.' She shrugged. 'But you . . .' she pointed a strong, aggressive finger at Costa's face, 'need to watch this diet thing carefully. Medically, scientifically, vegetarianism is a fad. A dangerous one too. Unless you know how to balance the diet.'

Costa looked at the plate of unidentifiable meats, the pile of spent cigarettes and the near-empty flagon of wine in front of her and wondered who Crazy Teresa was to hand out lectures on eating habits.

'He can run faster than any man in the Questura,' Rossi said defensively. 'They say you should've seen him on the pitch.'

'I did see him on the pitch, before he took up this solitary running thing. He's fast but that doesn't mean he wouldn't be faster if he ate some meat now and again. Look at that guy who plays hooker.'

Teresa was a rugby groupie. That was another well-known fact.

'Lamponi?' Rossi asked, a little jealous perhaps.

'Yeah. Look at the pecs. Look at the thighs on that.' She stabbed a ribbon of tripe. 'That's what meat does for you. Gives a man a body.'

Luca Rossi exchanged a knowing look with his partner. 'He's gay,' he said.

'What?'

'Lamponi. He's gay,' Rossi repeated.

'Hell!'

'Perhaps,' Nic Costa suggested, 'it was something in his diet. Too many female hormones in all those glands he keeps eating.'

'Yeah,' Rossi agreed. 'Things start growing where they shouldn't. Stuff starts shrinking instead of . . .' He shrugged.

Crazy Teresa banged the empty carafe on the table to order a new one, lit a cigarette and glared at them. 'Bullshit merchants. You don't know what you're talking about.'

Nic Costa looked at his watch. It was his turn to go to

the house tonight. He didn't want to be late. 'What are we supposed to be talking about, Teresa? I gathered there was something on your mind.'

She pushed her fork around the remains on the plate. Costa realized he liked this woman. She was smart, fun too, but there was a serious side to her that underpinned everything.

'This skinning trick?' she asked slyly. 'You're happy with the way things have turned out? All nice and obvious like that?'

'It's not closed,' Costa said. 'Not by any means, though I didn't see anything in your report that raised any new issues.'

'To hell with the report. That's just about what I know. Sometimes there are things that grate, and maybe they're nothing at all, but you still ought to hear them.'

Rossi folded his arms and looked at her. 'We're listening.'

'The professor. Did he have any medical experience? Had he worked in an abattoir at some stage?'

Costa shrugged. 'Not that we know of. He was an academic. I can't see how he would have done either of those things. Why?'

Teresa Lupo was unhappy about something. 'I don't know. I may be wrong about this, but it's just a very odd thing to do. To skin someone like that and do it pretty well too at what I assume is his first attempt.'

Rossi's long face grew doubtful. 'Is it that hard? I had an uncle in the country. He used to do this trick when he killed a rabbit. He'd make some little nick in the back of the neck, sort of shake the thing up and down in some way he knew, and the whole skin came right off. Like a glove or something, inside out, clean as anything.'

Crazy Teresa was incredulous. 'You're comparing human beings with furry rodents? Are you serious? What you call "skin" is actually three separate, living organs. The epidermis, which is the outer part, the dermis underneath, the subcutis, the layer of fat below that. You can't make a nick somewhere, throw the corpse up in the air and have it come down stripped. This is complicated.'

She watched some food land on the neighbouring table courtesy of the pierced waitress.

'Wait here. I won't be a moment.'

Crazy Teresa walked into the kitchen. Rossi watched his partner warily from across the table.

'I'm paying,' he said.

'Oh, I know that, Uncle Luca.'

'She said it was important, Nic.'

And maybe it is, Costa thought. More important than Luca Rossi could begin to guess.

Crazy Teresa came back with a side of pork belly, uncooked, and a small kitchen knife. She dropped the meat in front of them and watched the raised eyebrows from the tables around.

'It's OK,' Teresa yelled back at them. 'We're not going to eat it just yet.'

Costa smiled at her. 'That's a relief.'

'Listen. The pig is a pretty close approximation to the human skin system in some ways, which is why it's used for grafts from time to time. You've got to remember, too, that some cannibal cultures call us the "long pig", and there's a reason for that. Physiology *and* taste. So here.'

She gave the short knife to Rossi.

'Try skinning it.'

He grunted then began to slice away at the fat

underneath the thick epidermis. Then he pulled, hoping to lift it away from the carcass. It was impossible, even for a strong man like Rossi.

'There's all that fat,' he complained. 'People aren't like that.'

Teresa eyed him. 'Not all people. You'd be amazed how much fat you can get on a corpse. You're right. It's not an exact match, but it's close. What I'm trying to say to you is there's no easy, quick solution. I looked up some of the classical images of this Bartholomew person on the web. Almost every one shows him about to be martyred and they all have the same idea. The person who wants to do it is staring at him, wondering how to do the job. It's not obvious.'

Costa thought of the painting in the church. This was exactly what it portrayed. Skinning a man required more than just strength and resolution. It surely needed some level of knowledge of the body as a starting point.

'So how'd he do it?' Costa asked.

Teresa took the knife off Rossi, stood up, went behind the big man and made him hold his arms up in the air.

'My guess is he went in behind the neck and circled there, feeling his way, getting an idea for how deep to cut, not trying to remove anything right then.'

Rossi took down his arms, feeling stupid. 'You mean he cut his throat?'

'Not enough to kill him,' Teresa noted. 'That's not the idea. All the reference works on skinning people emphasize how important it is for the victim to remain conscious for as long as possible. In some North American cultures they prided themselves on their ability to remove most of the skin intact and be able to show it to the victim before he died.'

'What happened then?' Costa asked.

'This is all conjecture,' Teresa warned. 'I've tried to come up with a way in which I can estimate the exact sequence of events but it's impossible. I guess he turned him sideways somehow, went down the back, all the way along the spine, lifting a little on each side, then gradually opened it out, up to the shoulder blades, out to the waist until most of the back was off.'

The party at the adjoining table stood up, mumbling, and went to the counter to pay.

'And he'd still be alive?' Rossi wondered.

She shrugged. This was all hypothesis. 'He might have blacked out from the agony, if he was lucky. But then he'd probably come to later. After the back, the knife would work round the groin, the arms, work round to the front. Just very slowly, until he could bring it all to the chest, like a sheath.'

Rossi pushed away the plate in front of him.

'How long?' Costa asked. 'From beginning to end?'

'An hour. Maybe more. And you don't just need a strong stomach for this. You need a lot of physical strength too. This Rinaldi man was in rotten shape. He ate terribly. He drank too much. He had the kind of liver you'd see on a French goose. I don't know . . . This may be all wrong.'

Costa and Rossi waited. Crazy Teresa was about to say what she had wanted to say all along.

She leaned over the table and spoke softly, so that no one beyond would hear. 'My feeling is this. The average surgeon wouldn't have the strength for that. Someone who worked in an abattoir maybe. Someone who had watched a procedure in a hospital could too. But a flabby, out-of-condition university professor? No. I can't give you any hard scientific fact to put down in a report. But I don't believe it. Not for one moment. Sorry . . . I know you thought you had this one fixed.'

The two men looked at each other.

'On the other hand,' she said, 'you're listening to Crazy Teresa. So maybe you should take that into account.'

Rossi put a hand on her arm, shocked. 'What do you mean? "Crazy Teresa"?'

She refilled her glass again. 'I gather that's a nickname some of them are using now.'

'Who?' Rossi demanded. 'You let me know! You give me the names!'

Costa said nothing and wished he didn't face the drive ahead, wished he could order another glass of the good wine.

'This is a professional organization,' Rossi continued. 'We don't countenance behaviour like that, do we?'

Nic Costa raised an empty glass to his partner.

'Sweet man,' Teresa said, flattered. 'Excuse me now. I need to go.'

They watched her large, happy frame squeeze through the restaurant and head for the corridor at the rear.

'I think you've found the perfect partner, Uncle Luca,' Costa said. 'One who can drink, smoke and eat at the same time.'

Rossi was offended. 'She's a good woman, Nic. Don't you say otherwise. And she's not crazy either.'

Nic Costa took the small knife and stabbed at the raw joint of pork on the table. It was tough. She had a point. The waitress returned and looked at it too.

'Are you done with this, sir?' she asked Rossi. 'Or

would you like a bag to take it home? I mean, it is going on your bill.'

Rossi sighed as she cleared the table. When she was gone he looked Costa in the eye.

'So what do you think?'

Costa frowned. 'I hope to God she's wrong.'

'Yeah,' Rossi nodded. 'All that work. All that nagging from Falcone.'

'That wasn't what I meant.'

'Well?'

This change in their relationship seemed permanent now. For some reason the big man seemed to look to him for a lead. Perhaps, in spite of his greater experience, he felt lost in these complexities.

'If it was someone else, Luca, we don't have a clue to his motivation. And if we don't know why he did it, we don't know why he shouldn't do it again.'

He hesitated before going further. Rossi's long face was beginning to droop towards the empty plate in front of him.

'All we have,' Nic Costa said carefully, 'is that number to the man in the Vatican.'

Teresa Lupo was coming back from the toilets, smiling, happy, ordering *grappa* from behind the bar. Rossi was right. She was a smart woman, not crazy at all. And she was correct in her analysis. He knew it instinctively.

Seventeen

When Jay Gallo came to it was night. Lying on his back on the hard sand he could see the lights of the planes descending into Fiumicino airport, hear the roar of their engines. It was the only sound around him. He awoke knowing full well where he was: by the banks of the dead river, with its stink of chemicals, and worse, miles from anywhere. It would be a long walk back to the road and, perhaps, a long time before any motorist would pick up a hitchhiker in his present state. Gallo's mouth was full of blood. His head felt as if it had been split open. His nose was shattered and his face ached like hell. But he was alive. His hands moved around his body, feeling for broken bones. He raised himself from the sand on a single arm. He could see only through one eye. He could taste the dead river in his mouth. The water seemed stagnant, poisonous with the scum of algae.

'Bastard,' Jay Gallo spat through broken teeth, wondering who, of the many people he had pissed off over the years, had arranged this particular lesson. It seemed rather pointless without that piece of information.

Gradually his senses began to return. His sight improved, enough to see the lights of the coast at Ostia.

He began to hear the shriek of sea gulls, the far-off sound of a dinghy's weak motor.

And, behind him, breathing.

'Oh, Jesus.' Gallo groaned and began to turn.

The man was still sitting there on the bank, looking as if he had been waiting patiently for hours. He no longer wore the dark glasses. He had removed the jacket to reveal a plain white shirt. There was a reason for this, Gallo thought. The night was desperately close, so hot it was hard to take in sufficient air in a single breath. Then he cursed his own stupidity. The man had shrugged off the jacket because it was part of some disguise, a way of concealing his identity when they had met, in the presence of others. Now that they were alone, and his intent was clear, it was no longer needed.

Gallo fixed his attention on the figure in front of him. He was much younger than he had first thought, possibly about his own age. He was muscular too, in a way that spoke of work-outs and gyms. Oddly, there was sympathy in his face, as if some part of him regretted what was happening.

It was a face that was familiar somehow, which both surprised and irritated him.

'Who the hell are you?' he croaked.

The seated figure looked closely at him. The hint of compassion was there. Gallo did not mistake the expression. 'Just a cog in the wheel,' he said. 'Just a part of the mechanism.'

'We've met.' His head hurt too much to think straight. But the memory was there. He'd done something with this man. Picked up a package maybe. Or delivered one.

'If I ever offended you in some way . . .' Gallo wanted

to plead with this odd, taut figure in the dark, though he knew it was useless. And there was another thought in his head, one that kept getting bigger. If the man intended to kill him – and Jay Gallo could think of no other reason why they had come to the dead river – why had he waited? Why had he sat for hours by his unconscious figure on the sand, risking discovery, just to see him wake? Was there something he wanted? Something Gallo could still provide, maybe barter with?

'You want to trade?' Gallo asked.

The seated man turned. His face came into the harsh moonlight. It was an exaggerated face, one that would turn from beauty to ugliness with a simple change of the light. He had dark, alert eyes glinting in the moonlight, pale skin and full cruel lips. The face of a bit player in a canvas by Caravaggio, Gallo thought randomly.

'What's there to trade?'

'You tell me.'

'Nothing.'

To Gallo's dismay he was rising to his feet.

Jay Gallo tried to struggle to join him but his head hurt too much, his mind was just too woozy.

'Hey,' he said, desperate for anything that could delay what was coming. 'Why did you wait like that? *Why?*'

The strange face was cut in half by the moonlight. It was shocked, offended by the question. 'You think I kill sleeping men?'

Gallo's hands went up in front of him, two out-stretched palms trying to ward off this big, black figure overhead.

'You think,' the man repeated, his voice beginning to rise, beginning to turn into a roar, 'I'd send you to glory without you knowing?'

'Don't,' Jay Gallo whimpered. 'I'll do anything.'

The black figure nodded. 'I know,' he said, calm once more.

The pale disc of the moon disappeared behind blackness. A stone-hard fist came down out of the high dark, punching. The meagre light began to fade, began to be subsumed by blood and shattered bone. He found himself moving, lifted by two strong arms above.

Then there was some final relief: he fell into something cold, something that stank rotten but woke him all the same.

Jay Gallo choked on the stagnant water, wondering whether it made him feel better or worse. Then, under the unrelenting pressure of the hands that gripped his shoulders, his head went below the surface, his eyes stared into black nothingness.

The cold poison began to fill his lungs, no matter how much he struggled against the fists that held him down, how often he tried to vomit out the dank water.

The chill left the dead river and raced into his mouth. Jay Gallo fought it for as long as he could but at some stage the body needs to breathe even if there's nothing out there to pass as oxygen. When he thought his lungs might break he coughed once, felt the coldness win some bitter victory in his chest, and then was still.

Eighteen

Five minutes after Teresa Lupo had returned Costa made his excuses. Rossi had been right. There was a practical reason for the three of them to meet that evening. Nevertheless there was an unspoken one too, one in which he was an unwanted witness. Rossi and the woman were beginning to get too close for him to watch.

He drove through the thick Saturday night traffic, down brightly lit streets into the darkness at the edge of the city. It was a clear, starlit evening with a full moon. Even with the windows down, the interior of the old Fiat was uncomfortably hot. The car swept round the illuminated hulk of the gate of San Sebastiano, out to the old Appian Way, travelled a mile down the narrow road and took the familiar turning to the house, following the rutted drive until he parked beneath the vines of the rough car shelter that leaned drunkenly against the wall. He stepped out of the car and breathed in the smell of the countryside: parched scrub and dust, with the distant fragrance of wild thyme somewhere underneath. Cicadas rattled in the dead grass at his feet. The black, darting outlines of bats, squeaking frantically, broke the perfect night sky.

The house was an old lone farmhouse in the dead land between the old Appian Way and the modern, busy thoroughfare of the Via Appia Nuova. He remembered what he had said to Sara Farnese in front of the altar in the church on Tiber Island. A family was a team against the world, a bulwark against the insanity. He could not imagine what it would be like to be denied its sanctity. He could not begin to understand how anyone could survive the day without some place like this, some safe, holy refuge in which joy and hope, fear and tragedy inter-mingled, became controllable through the mutual regard individuals felt for one another.

The light was still on in the front room. Marco Costa was asleep in an armchair. Pepe, the argumentative little terrier his father loved so much, sat at his feet, curled into a ball. Nic could remember the animal as a puppy, bought after his mother died, as if in compensation. He had been offended at the time, but his father had been right. The dog's ceaseless need for love and attention, and his instant return of the same, made those dark months bear-able. Now the years were taking their vengeance with the same, vicious brutality, for both of them.

Giulia, his sister, had left a note in the kitchen, where the old man could not find it. She had to go to Milan on business for a week. There had been a call from their elder brother in Washington, young Marco. It was hardest for him. The busy lawyer's life and the harsh working regime of America left little time for home visits. The slow process of dying was difficult enough to manage when one lived just a few kilometres from the old man; from the other side of the Atlantic it was impossible. During the coming week, however, some routine could be main-tained. Nic would stay during the evening whenever possible; Bea, Marco's former secretary, from his earliest days in politics, and still a firm friend, would come in for the daylight hours and any other time when work called Nic away. Giulia hated to leave him but she needed the time off too. He read the rest of the note. The old man had taken his pills with his usual bad grace. His mood was up and down. The doctors said . . .

Her writing had faltered as she spelled out the words: *perhaps weeks, not months now.*

He closed his eyes and wanted to scream. His father was sixty-one, half a head taller than him, and once a bull of a man, someone who had, on occasion, stood up to the toughest of Turin union hoods and won his bloody way. Now he was some flimsy human husk, being eaten away each day by this insidious, invisible disease. It was savagely unjust, whatever the doctors said about the old man's habits. To move, in the course of a single year, from such strength to such frailty was a cruel transformation, for Marco Costa and those who loved him. It was also implacable, beyond treatment, something his son still found hard to accept.

There was a sound from the kitchen. Bea came in with two glasses of wine for them. She was still a handsome woman, straight-backed, with short auburn hair, attentive blue eyes and a sharp tongue when it was deserved. As always, she wore bright clothes; on this occasion an orange silk shirt with cream trousers. Gold glittered at her tanned neck and on her slim wrists. She was a little younger than Marco, perhaps fifty-five now, and had been single throughout her life. The relationship puzzled him; there were memories from his childhood, uncertain ones, which suggested Bea had been more than merely a friend to Marco at one time. Seeing him through his illness was now a matter of duty, something she would not shirk. She waved at him to come back into the kitchen, out of earshot of his father.

'Don't believe everything you read,' she said, nodding at the note.

He put down the wine and poured himself some water. 'Bea, the doctors . . .'

'They're all a bunch of quacks and charlatans.'

'But . . .' He waved the piece of paper, feeling stupid.

'But nothing. My own father had the same kind of disease, and the same kind of head on his shoulders. Sure it kills them in the end. But I tell you this, Nic. A man like that dies when he chooses to let go, when he thinks there's no more reason for him to stay around.'

'Of course.'

She gave him a harsh look, with some cause: his answer had been too quick, too easy. 'You think I'm deluding myself? Listen. If Marco finds no reason to live he'll be in a casket tomorrow. If something holds him – and something does right now – he'll be sitting down with us at Christmas.'

Bea owned a tiny apartment in Trastevere which she always said she would sell one day, to return to her native Puglia. He had come to understand over the last few months when that day would be: once Marco was dead.

He took her hands which were still young, the fingers long and supple. 'I can't thank you enough for your kindness, Bea.'

'Then don't. Pay attention to him, Nic. This is a time that will be with you for the rest of your life. There are things that must be said or you'll always regret them. Perhaps things that must be done too. I don't know. A woman never understands the relationship between a man and his father. Still, most of them don't either. There . . .'

She picked up her bag and took out the car keys.

'Lecture's over. I'll be back as usual tomorrow.'

He watched her go, trying to recover those mental images of her when she was young. Bea was beautiful then: a glorious, colourful presence in the family's life. There was a time, perhaps when he was seven or eight, that he felt he was in love with her. The perfume she wore – the same invasive scent she still used – continued to prick his memory. She still had the same exotic air about her, one that his father never seemed to acknowledge. Bea was a mystery. She had never talked of a man, never seemed to need one. Marco Costa, and the cause, had been her life, and now one was dying and the other already dead.

He went back to the room where Marco still slept, undisturbed by the movement around him. It was late. Nic bent down and carefully placed his arms beneath his father, lifting him out of the chair, shocked by how light he had become.

Halfway to the bedroom, Marco's breathing changed. The old man's grey eyelids opened slowly. Nic Costa saw the glint of a welcome recognition in the familiar features which were now creased and wrinkled, like those of an eighty-year-old.

'You should be out chasing women,' his father said in a voice that carried the stain of a lifetime's tobacco.

Nic carried him to the bed and gently laid him on the clean white sheet, newly ironed by Bea. 'I have been.'

'Bullshit,' the old man whispered, then began to smile at some returning memory. 'People have been chasing you. I watch TV you know. I can recognize the way my own son runs even when he's wearing some woman's coat.'

It was the body that was failing him. Marco Costa's mind was as sharp as his son could ever remember.

'Did they know too?' he asked. 'Did the TV people realize it wasn't her?'

'No.' He laughed. 'Do you think I should call? Collect a little tip-off money? I don't understand where you get this theatrical streak. Not from me.'

Nic began to work on his clothes.

His father slapped gently at his hand. 'I can do that. I'm not a cripple. I keep telling Bea that.'

'No,' he agreed. 'You're not a cripple. Bea knows it.'

The old man gave him a curious glance. 'She knows everything, Nic. She's family now. In a way she always was though I was too stupid to tell her.'

'I think she knows. You treat her badly enough.'

'If you pamper me like an invalid I've a duty to be demanding.'

He never gave up, never let go. It was part of his charm and part of his problem too. 'Then you're doing your duty very well.'

Marco Costa's face grew serious. 'She *is* family. When the time comes, when you want to be near, I'd like her around. I say that now. I may not be able to say it when it happens.'

He nodded. 'Bea will be here,' he said, and walked away from the bed, feeling the familiar stinging in his eyes, hiding his reaction by tidying some stray papers on the desk.

The room had once been the family study, until Marco's illness and his inability to climb stairs made it the old man's bedroom. It was still alive with the memories of Nic's childhood, still decorated just as it had always been, with the striking communist posters, the bust of Gramsci, his father's hero, and the piece his mother had insisted upon, a classical head of a handsome man, turning, with an expression of determination on his face, as if to face some unseen enemy. Much of Nic's life was rooted in this room. It was here that all three Costa children had been educated, their parents refusing to tolerate the public schools because, at the time, they insisted Catholicism was the state religion, to be taught to every child. It was here that each in turn learned, and quietly rejected, their parents' own intense brand of politics, here that three studious children read classics and modern stories, Homer and Jack London. And later Marco's most cherished possession, a first edition of Gramsci's own *Letter from Prison* published in 1947, a decade after his death.

It was here too that Anna Costa had died, ten years before, refusing to go to hospital, as Marco would when it was his time. Nic Costa had found her, slumped at the desk as if reading, when he came back from a run. A left-wing magazine was spread out in front of her. Her grey hair, still as long as when she was young, had tumbled across the pages. He could still recall the sharp, painful sense of injustice he had felt. Perhaps it had somehow, illogically, propelled him into the police. It had taken a year before his father had forgiven himself for being absent; he was in Milan, addressing a conference. Nothing had been the same after that. Marco's career entered its decline; winter came into their lives. The bright, vivid joy of childhood – a childhood which Marco Costa had enjoyed alongside his children – was gone. The practical world beckoned and it was a cold place full of solitary people.

Marco Costa reached out with a scrawny arm and touched his son's cheek, smiling.

'So in between the cross-dressing and the athletics have you managed to oppress anyone today?'

'Not as many as I'd hoped. But there's always tomorrow.'

He laughed. 'Of course. There's always tomorrow.'

They had discussed the matter, just once, which was as much as Marco Costa desired. For the old man dying was an inconvenience, like a cab that arrived half an hour before it was due and honked its horn until you came struggling to the door. He was unafraid, more through practicality than courage. People died, he said, usually before they wished it. He hadn't achieved as much as he'd hoped, though he knew it was more than most. He had a good family too: two sons and a daughter whose chosen professions, in the police, in the law and as a professional painter, were so far removed from his own it was impossible for him to feel anything but pride. He did not fear the void that he knew lay ahead. He only regretted that it would disrupt unfinished business, work that would now fall to someone else, someone beyond the Costa clan.

His son felt differently. Even after a year of knowing its imminence, he still could not come to terms with the idea of a world which did not contain his father's considerable presence. This was the only secret he dared not share with the old man, and that made it all the harder to bear.

Nineteen

The phone rang just after he had served the old man breakfast: fresh fruit, orange juice straight from the squeezer, a cocktail of pills. His father watched him as he took the call.

'Don't worry about me,' he said the moment Nic Costa put down the phone. 'Bea will be here soon. I'm not helpless. I'll survive.'

'Thanks.'

'What is it?'

The old man never asked about his work. This was a pact between them. Nic Costa was surprised that was now changing.

'There's been another death.'

'So what? Are you the only cop they've got?'

'It's not that.' He was trying to clarify matters in his own head. 'It's connected somehow by the sound of it.' He had come part of the way to rejecting his earlier ideas already. It should have been no surprise. 'Maybe we've jumped to conclusions about what happened in the Vatican. Maybe . . .' The old man's tired eyes wouldn't leave him. Marco Costa knew when something was badly wrong. '. . . it's all a lot worse than we thought.'

'Tell me about it,' the old man ordered. 'If you want. When you get back. Now . . .' He picked up a bread roll from the table. 'You eat that in the car. No one can live off fruit alone. Not even you.'

Fifteen minutes later Nic Costa was parked outside the old, low church near the Colosseum, by the narrow road that led to the Lateran palace, the first St Peter's. This was a part of the city he never really understood. The Colosseum was two minutes' stroll away. The busy modern thoroughfare of Labicana set up a constant traffic roar to the north. A short walk would take him to the Rinaldis' lonely apartment in the Via Mecenate. There were high, late-nineteenth-century blocks towering over the narrow cobbled streets of the neighbourhood. A few stalls made up the tiny street market that had probably worked here for ten centuries or more. It was a quiet, residential area, one that the tourists rarely visited. And within it lay such odd, unexpected sights: churches and squares that seemed to go back to a different city.

Sara Farnese would, he felt sure, know this area well, would be able to point out a wall here, a crypt there and know its place in the Roman story. He felt lost, all the more so when he walked into the large, elegant courtyard that now bustled with people. The centre was occupied by rows of simple seats, perhaps three hundred of them, pointed towards a low wooden stage. The floor was still littered with cheaply printed programmes: Vivaldi and Corelli performed by a local semi-professional orchestra. An open-air concert had taken place here the night before. That made the morning's discovery even more odd. At 8.15 an Irish Dominican named Bernard Cromarty, a senior member of the order that had administered San Clemente for almost three hundred and fifty years, had opened the doors to the chapel to prepare for the morning service. What he found there led him to run, terrified, from the dark, enclosed interior, out into the hardening morning light, screaming for help.

Nic Costa studied the courtyard, noting how much had been left behind after the concert, took a deep breath and went inside. This was a grander, older church than the place on Tiber Island. It had a solemn, distinguished interior, with a quiet richness of decoration. The murmur of men's voices sounded like the whispering of monks rebounding off the walls. In the centre of the nave, flanked by two high, imposing pulpits, was an ancient choir leading up to a dimly lit altar, raised slightly above ground level. A group of recognizable figures was bent low around the far edge of the structure studying something out of sight. Falcone stood upright, in expensive jeans, their neat crease visible even from this distance, and a too-white shirt. It was Sunday. Perhaps he had been called away from a social engagement Costa could only guess at. He'd been married once but that had ended in divorce years ago. Now, the gossips had it, he played the field, in fancy company too.

The cold, bearded face was creased in concentration. Costa joined Luca Rossi by Falcone's side. The focal point of this part of the church was supposed to be the small casket which lay at the base of the altar, beneath a canopy supported by delicate columns. Now another object stole their attention. In front of the coffin, surrounded by flickering candles which were almost spent, was the figure of a naked man. He lay on his side. His knees were drawn up as if crouching, his arms were extended and bent upwards, with the hands placed together in an obvious position of prayer. His eyes were open, as was his mouth, giving him an expression of mute, dead surprise, as if he had chanced upon something in the night, something that had stolen the life out of him.

His fair hair was wet and plastered to his skull. His face showed signs of a severe beating: livid dark bruises, a swollen eye and several open wounds. Around his neck was a thick nautical rope which was attached to a small rusty anchor – of a size suitable for a pleasure dinghy – now lying flat on the mosaic floor behind his back.

Teresa Lupo busied herself around the corpse. With minute care she placed a gloved finger in the mouth, leaned forward and sniffed. She wrinkled her nose and, very gingerly, took a slender arm and tried to move it. There was obvious resistance.

'Well?' Falcone asked. Standing next to him was a priest, a severe-faced man of seventy or more with a wild shock of white hair and sad grey eyes. He watched them covetously, as if the church and everything inside it was his personal property.

'Brackish water,' the pathologist said. 'The salt's pretty strong. He wouldn't smell like this if he'd been in the Tiber. Must be somewhere else. Somewhere estuarial. I'll be able to tell you more once I've got him back to the office.'

Falcone stared at the dead man's face. 'How long?'

'Several hours,' she replied. 'There's obvious rigor. He must have been placed here in the evening or early this morning.'

Rossi stared gloomily at the corpse. 'How was that possible, Father? I thought there was a concert here last night. How could a dead man be brought into this place?'

'There was a concert,' the priest answered, warming

to the unexpected politeness in Rossi's question. 'Every last seat was sold. I was here myself until one in the morning, helping to clear up.'

'Then how?' Falcone demanded.

The priest shook his head and stared at the stone floor. Nic Costa nodded towards the sunlight behind them in the open courtyard. Something large, shiny and black leaned against the far wall. 'What's that doing there?' he asked. 'Why would a musician leave an instrument behind?'

Rossi grunted, walked out into the daylight, heaved the double bass case carefully under his arm, not touching the handle. From the way he carried it the thing weighed very little. He returned to the nave and placed it on the stone floor. Falcone bent down, took a nail file out from a leather case and gingerly worked his way around the perimeter, flipping up the clasps. When he was done he threw open the lid. The case was empty. The cheap red velvet lining was soaked with water. It had a sour, salty smell.

'I still don't see,' Falcone exclaimed. 'He couldn't have moved a naked body when you people were clearing up. And afterwards the church would be locked, surely.'

'Of course,' the priest agreed. 'There are many valuable items in here.'

'Cameras?' Costa asked hopefully. The man shook his head.

Teresa Lupo waved to her men at the door to come and retrieve the body. The interior echoed to the squealing of the gurney's wheels. She came and stood next to Rossi, staring at the empty well for the double bass.

'Well?' she asked.

'Well what?' Falcone demanded testily.

'Is no one going to ask me how he died?'

The detectives looked at each other. It had seemed so obvious.

'Poor bastard was beaten up, wasn't he?' Rossi asked.

'Sure,' she said. 'I don't think that killed him, though. I could be wrong. Ask me again after the autopsy.' She took off the plastic gloves and smiled at Rossi and Costa. 'You guys are quite something, you know. I just don't get this quality of material from anyone else.'

'Meaning?' Falcone thundered.

'He was drowned,' Teresa Lupo said. 'Forcibly, in shallow water, maybe less than a metre, which would explain the amount of muddy material in his mouth. I'll be able to be quite precise with that I think. The combination of salt water and mud . . . it can't be hard to track down where it came from. He was drowned and then, for some reason, the anchor was placed around his neck after he was put on the floor there, after the candles were lit. It couldn't have been any other way because that thing isn't heavy enough to hold down a man and the length of rope is too great to have been of any use in the sort of depth I'm talking about. That's just symbolic somehow. Part of the picture we're supposed to be appreciating.'

Costa couldn't take his eyes off the priest. The man's eyes were closed. He had crossed himself and was now quietly saying a prayer.

'Father?' he asked, when the man was done.

'What is it?' the priest replied grumpily.

Nic Costa waved at the interior of the church. 'There are anchors here already. I've seen them. Carved into the columns. In the paintings on the walls. What does it mean?'

'And none of you can even begin to guess at that?' the old priest asked sourly. 'Is that what it's come to?'

Falcone eyed him unpleasantly. 'If you have some information that could help us, Father . . .'

The old man tut-tutted. 'So many professional people. So little knowledge. This is the church of San Clemente. The fourth pope of Rome.' He pointed to the tomb beneath the altar, beyond the naked body surrounded by the guttering candles. 'His remains lie there, as they have done for almost two millennia. Do you know nothing? San Clemente was martyred by drowning. He was found with the anchor round his neck.'

The man waved at the corpse on the mosaic floor, a controlled fury in his face. 'This . . . abomination is a deliberate, a direct insult to his memory. The work of a madman.'

Nic Costa wondered at that. If it was a madman it was one with a very precise theological knowledge, a very definite purpose. And, more, there was something almost akin to reverence in the violence too.

'Have you any idea who the dead man is?' Falcone asked.

'None,' the priest grunted. Luca Rossi shrugged his broad, stooped shoulders. The others in the police team looked just as blank.

Falcone's fierce gaze turned on Nic Costa. 'We're not moving a damned thing. Call her. Bring her down here. Do it yourself if necessary.'

'What?'

'The Farnese woman. I want her to see this. Before

anything is moved. I want to know if she recognizes him. I want to know what she . . . *thinks*.'

'Sir . . .' Nic Costa objected and hunted in vain for the words. What Falcone said made sense. She would have to be shown a picture of the dead man. There were too many coincidences here. Still, there were easier, less painful ways of achieving these ends. There was, it seemed to him, no practical reason to drag Sara Farnese into this grim scene.

'Why don't I just bring her to the morgue? What difference does it make?'

'You heard,' Falcone said, walking out to the court-yard, reaching for his phone.

Then he was gone and there was just Luca Rossi staring into Costa's eyes, looking shifty.

'We fouled up, didn't we?' he grunted. 'We just leapt right in and thought what somebody wanted us to think.'

It was all there, Nic Costa thought. Just waiting for them in that stinking death-filled room on Tiber Island. *I met a man with seven wives . . .*

'I guess so.' He found it hard to shake off the thought that Rossi had been expecting this all along.

'You know what?' the big man said. 'We keep thinking we're looking for facts. And that's only half the job. The other half is looking for lies, seeing them for what they are.'

'I'll do this on my own,' Costa said. 'Tell Falcone to give me thirty minutes.'

Then he was out of the door, feeling the August heat starting to fall from the sky, wondering what he was going to tell her.

Twenty

'Why did you do that?'

Sara Farnese was wearing black: casual trousers and a cotton T-shirt. She looked younger and on her guard. The press mob had yet to arrive at San Clemente but the beggars, Kosovans and Africans, were always there. Without thinking Nic Costa had handed out some money to a young black boy with wide, haunted eyes, choosing him, as always, at random. She seemed surprised they had not simply barged through the small crowd, ignoring them.

'Family habit,' Costa said. 'Twice a day, every day. Just in case.'

'In case what?' she wondered.

'In case . . . it makes a difference, I guess.' He'd never thought about it much. They were modest sums of money. The idea had been ingrained into them at such an early age. For his father this was, he thought, an act of faith, one more proof, if Nic Costa needed it, that the old man's communism was a kind of religion in disguise.

He took her by the arm. They halted outside the gateway to the church. 'Let me say something. You don't have to go through with this, Sara. Not here. We could arrange an appointment at the morgue. It may be a waste of time anyway.'

Her green eyes watched him carefully. 'Then why was I asked to come here?'

'My boss,' he said instantly, not wanting to lie since he felt sure she would know. 'It was his idea. He thinks this is more complex. He thinks we don't know everything we ought to know.'

She understood Costa's point immediately. Sara Farnese acknowledged it in silence then peered inside at the courtyard of San Clemente.

'I've been here for concerts. Have you?'

'I'm not much of a one for music.'

'What are you for?'

'Looking at paintings. Running. Making sense of things. How many times have you been here before?'

'Three. Four.'

Costa nodded, taking in the information.

She sighed, exasperated. 'Is that supposed to be significant too? Are you listening to every word I say and wondering what it's worth?'

'Not at all. I don't think anyone understands what's going on here. Except that it's obvious there seems to be some link that leads back to you. Who did you come here with, Sara? We may need to know.'

'Really,' she murmured, then pointed up the narrow street of San Giovanni in Laterano. A small electric bus was navigating the cobble stones up the hill, towards the sprawling hospital at the summit. 'Have you heard of Pope Joan? The female pope?'

'I thought that was a myth.'

'Probably. The myth says she gave birth outside a house there, on her way to take the papal crown in the

Lateran. The mob killed her and the infant when it realized what she was. Still, myth or no myth, there was an image on a house nearby, until the sixteenth century, of a woman with her breast bared and a child in her arms. Until it was torn down by the Vatican, along with a portrait of her in Siena.'

'Why are you telling me this?' he asked.

She shrugged. 'I don't know. Perhaps because I thought you'd understand. Pope Joan isn't real. She never existed. Her story is as apocryphal as that of some of the early martyrs but it doesn't matter. It's about faith. It's about how something can be fiction and true too, after a fashion. In Joan's case it's a truth about the place women are supposed to have in the world. How we're meant to be harlots or heroines. Virgins or whores. It doesn't occur to you that there might be other permutations. Some middle way in which, perhaps, we're both, or neither. Or something else altogether.'

'You sound like my father,' he grumbled. 'I'm sorry, I wasn't trying to judge you. I just feel jumpy about everything. About what's in there and why this is all happening.'

'Show me,' she said and then they walked into the dark church interior, towards the group that stood around the body, now covered with a sheet.

Falcone watched her arrive. He looked hungry for information. The smell of tobacco hung around him. There was ash on his white shirt now. It was the grey, flecked colour of his beard. Luca Rossi shuffled awkwardly on his giant feet, accompanied by some detectives Costa didn't recognize. Teresa Lupo stood at the edge watching them all, taking in everything. Costa was beginning to appreciate her presence more and more. She was honest. She had some insight, too, that was lacking in the men.

'Miss Farnese,' Falcone said, coming towards her, extending a hand. 'I'm grateful you came. This won't take long.' He looked at the pathologist. 'Please . . .'

Teresa bent down to the body and carefully pulled back the sheet exposing the dead man's face. Sara Farnese's slim hand went to her mouth. She closed her eyes and exhaled a quiet, anguished gasp, then sat down heavily on one of the bench seats. Costa was unable to prevent himself glaring at Falcone. He was relishing this spectacle, as if her grief contained within it some precious intelligence only he could see. Costa was intrigued by some small element of theatricality in her reaction too; he found himself wondering whether she was not expecting to see some other body beneath the sheet. Whether he was, in fact, witnessing her relief.

He walked to the small office that led off the nave and came back with some water, sat next to her and gave her the cup. She accepted gratefully. Falcone and the other cops watched, curious.

'I'm sorry,' he said.

She opened her eyes and stared at him. It was impossible to know whether there was some personal bitterness in her gaze.

'Why are you apologizing? I know who he is. Wasn't that the point of bringing me here?'

Falcone took a step forward. 'Of course. His name, please?'

'Jay Gallo. He was an American tour guide.'

'Address?' Falcone asked, indicating to Costa to take a note.

'In the Via Trastevere. I don't know the number. It was a cheap little apartment above the supermarket.'

Falcone paused. 'And you knew him . . . how exactly?'

She sighed and looked at Costa, as if this proved some point. 'We were both at Harvard together for a while. When he moved to Rome we renewed our friendship.'

Falcone waited, in vain, for her to go further. Finally, he asked, 'Meaning what exactly?'

'Meaning,' she replied icily, 'that for a while, a few weeks, several months ago, we slept together. Is that what you wanted to know?'

'I want to know what's relevant,' Falcone said brusquely. 'There are four people dead now. Three of them were your lovers. Where did this Gallo character fit in? Would the others have known him?'

She considered this, appearing to regard it as a reasonable question. 'No. He'd no connection with the university. Stefano never met him. Hugh came a long time after.'

'But you would have mentioned him to other people?'

'Why?' she asked, puzzled. 'What was the point? I was with Jay for a couple of weeks and then we agreed to be friends, nothing more. I haven't seen him in months. He was an entertaining man but there was something lost about him. He drank too much. He was far too intelligent to be engaged in the work he did. He was failing himself and he knew it. However amusing he could be, that kind of thing wears off pretty quickly.'

Falcone gave Costa a significant glance as if to say: see the bitch, see what she's like. The moment she's bored, the moment she has doubts, she dumps them. And now one of the names on that list of rejections, maybe a long, long list, is fighting back.

'So what do you think is happening here, Miss Farnese?' Falcone asked.

She seemed taken aback. 'I've no idea. What do you mean?'

'Why are your former lovers being killed like this? As if they were martyrs somehow?'

'I can't begin to guess,' she insisted. 'This is as inexplicable to me as it is to you.'

'And yet,' Falcone continued, 'you must know the person responsible. This is someone who is familiar with the intimate details of your private life. You see my point?'

'Everybody sees your point.' It was Teresa Lupo who intervened, risking Falcone's wrath. 'It's the way you ask. May I suggest you get some women detectives in here? You need to strike a balance between duty and prurience.'

'Thanks,' Falcone hissed. 'You can take the body out of here now, Doctor. I want an autopsy report by this afternoon.'

The pathologist sighed and called for her team. The wheels squealed across the old, stone floor. Sara Farnese watched the covered corpse being lifted gently onto the gurney, watched in silence as it was pushed out into the sun-filled courtyard. They had removed the anchor and the rope which now lay on the ancient mosaic floor.

'San Clemente,' Sara said. 'Why didn't I realize? He had that anchor round his neck when they found him?'

'As if he was another martyr,' Costa said, watching her like a hawk.

'I told you,' she snapped. 'Mostly these stories are apocryphal. In the case of Clemente it certainly is. If the person who did this knows Tertullian – which I assume he does – he knows that too. Tertullian wrote about Clemente and never once mentioned any kind of martyrdom. It's a fairy tale that was never even told until the fourth century.'

Costa tried to understand the significance. 'Why would it matter? What difference does it make whether he knows this is a sham or not?'

Falcone interrupted, smiling. 'Because it's a question of belief. We look at these acts and think they must be the work of a man with some misplaced sense of religion. In fact . . .'

Teresa Lupo, now returned to the nave and glowering openly at Falcone, interrupted. 'In fact you don't have a clue. Spare us cops practising fake psychology, please. All any of us knows is this: a man who can skin another human being is not a suitable subject for some kind of cheap Freudian analysis, however hard you try. He can surely hold two entirely conflicting rationales in his head simultaneously and never hear them rub up against each other. I told you boys last night. I tell you now. This is a man who is strong, determined and powerful. A man who has some kind of medical knowledge, or has worked in a slaughterhouse. Forget what's in his head because it's got some impenetrable logic all of its own and you'd need to be as crazy as he is to understand it. Look for the physical facts.'

Costa watched Sara Farnese's face. 'Do you know anyone like that?'

'No,' she said, looking at the long-haired woman in the white coat, grateful for her support. 'But whoever he is he knows Tertullian too. You forgot that.'

'Quite,' the pathologist agreed. 'Seems like I've got the easy job around here.' She walked away, grabbing for the cigarettes beneath the enclosed suit.

'What else do you want?' Sara Farnese asked as Lupo's team left through the outside gate.

Falcone shuffled on his feet, thinking. 'The name and address of everyone you've had a relationship with since coming to Rome.'

She shook her head. 'That's not possible. You can't ask for someone's entire private life.'

Falcone leaned towards her, so close that their faces almost touched. 'Miss Farnese,' he said softly. 'Everyone you have slept with is a suspect. Everyone you have slept with is a potential victim. We need their names. For their sakes as much as ours. Surely you can see that?'

'Some of these are married men. This is ridiculous. How would you feel if it were you?'

Falcone gave her a disagreeable frown. 'Maybe I'd feel glad to be alive.'

She had no answer. Costa touched her arm gently, wondering again about this strange chasm there seemed to be in her life. 'Sara. It's important. We can get some women detectives you can talk to. Everything will remain confidential.'

'You honestly believe that? Please . . .'

He couldn't argue. They all knew that everything leaked from the department in the end. He couldn't begin to guess what names existed inside Sara Farnese's head but it would be impossible to promise them privacy once they entered the files in the Questura Centrale. There was too much media interest already and too much money riding on any scraps of information that could be secretly gleaned from the files.

'We require this for your sake too,' Falcone said forcefully. 'Whoever this man is, he knows everything about you. Perhaps he's trying to impress you with these acts.

Perhaps they are warnings. But one thing I'm sure of. At some stage he will realize they're not having the desired effect and he will hold you to blame. At that point his next victim will surely be you, the source of his sorrows.'

She stared at him. 'Whoever this is, I am not the source of his sorrows. This is not my doing.'

'As he sees it . . . I should have put it that way,' Falcone said, in the closest to an apology his pride would allow. 'Who do you know in the Vatican?' He threw the question at her idly, as if it were unimportant. Costa cursed himself. He had told Falcone of his concerns about what had happened in the library that morning. He had no idea his vague doubts would translate into direct questions so quickly.

'What?'

'There were phone calls, between Rinaldi and someone in the Vatican. There were indications that Rinaldi believed he was under some kind of surveillance when he entered the Reading Room, either electronically or from some person in the room. In your line of work you must know many people. It's important we have their names.'

'I've no special relationship with anyone in the Vatican.' Her face was pale and hard, a mask.

'Without some honesty . . .' Falcone shrugged. 'I fear this will go on. I can't see any reason why he should stop here. We need names. All of them.' He reached forward and looked intently into her eyes. 'We need to know everything about your life.'

'Go to hell,' she hissed.

Falcone smiled. Costa recognized the moment. He enjoyed breaking people. He believed this was the point of victory. 'Miss Farnese. I can insist on your cooperation.

I can take steps if it is not forthcoming. I can call you into protective custody.'

'Sir,' Costa interrupted, gaining the full blast of Falcone's furious gaze. 'This is happening too quickly. If we give Miss Farnese time. If I get one of the women detectives to help us back at the station.'

'If . . .' Falcone said sourly.

Costa took him to one side so she couldn't hear. 'Please. If you push her she'll say nothing. Let me talk to her somewhere else. Somewhere she can think it through.'

Falcone's hard features froze for a moment. Then he nodded at Costa. 'Maybe she needs one person she can trust. Maybe . . .'

He eyed Costa, wondering. 'There's a lot of reporters out there now. Take her out on your own. Go have a coffee somewhere and think about this. Bring her in by the back door in an hour.'

'OK.' Costa was puzzled. There was something else and Falcone was uncharacteristically reluctant to say it.

'Sir?'

'You're right,' he said, smiling. 'I've an idea. Act a little, kid. Those reporters think they've got some scarlet woman in their sights here. Let's play them along. When you go outside stay close to her. Make it look like . . . there's perhaps something between you.'

'You're asking me to . . .' Costa began to say, furious.

'I'm telling you to send out a message. I want this lunatic to see you and think he knows who's chasing her tail now. We could spend months following him around like this. It would make it a lot easier if he comes to us. Comes to *you*, to be precise.'

'Sir . . .'

'Don't worry, kid,' Falcone beamed. 'We'll be waiting. You do have faith in your own police force now, don't you?'

Nic Costa walked off without answering and beckoned Sara to follow him to the door. Outside the media had arrived in force. A mob five metres deep thronged the gateway into the courtyard, held back by uniformed men trying to keep the line intact. The moment they saw her the questions came: screamed out of the heaving mass, unintelligible in the babble of desperate voices. Nic Costa threw an arm around her and they braved the mob, moving through the cameras and the thrusting microphones, pushing forward, all the way to his small car.

She kept her face down to the ground. He held his arm tight round her shoulders and stared, unbending at the cameras, finding time to smile once or twice, time too to look at her, fondly, with an affection he didn't find hard to feign.

He remembered her story. About the female pope being torn to pieces not far from here, and how it was all untrue, and maybe that wasn't the point anyway. Nic Costa stomped his way through the pack with all the finesse he once used in a bad-tempered rugby match, holding her safe, feeling her slender, fragile body and, after a while, an arm clinging to his waist.

Then they reached the car, he made space with a few deftly aimed jabs of his elbow, and they were free.

He looked at her, pale and frightened in the passenger seat, and thought of the faces he had made into that sea of cameras, the way he had acquiesced so easily, so willingly, to Falcone's idea.

She turned to him, puzzled, hurt. 'What's happening, Nic? What's going on?'

'I don't know,' he said. 'But don't worry. I'll fix this. Somehow.'

She stared out of the window, out into the hot, airless day. Nic Costa watched and felt he was swimming in a sea of lies.

Twenty-one

Gino Fosse lived in a three-storey tower which belonged, he felt, in the pages of a Gothic fairy tale. The structure was built of honey-coloured bricks and situated on the Caelian Hill midway along the imperial thoroughfare of the Clivus Scauri. Opposite stood the sprawling hulk of the basilica of Santi Giovanni e Paolo, to which he was now loosely attached as one of the parish priests, though almost all his professional time was spent at the hospital of San Giovanni, a ten-minute walk away. It was not the same as working in the Vatican, but the Church knew best.

Fosse felt obliged to know some history of his surroundings. The tower which had been his home this last month was embedded in the Aurelian Wall, built in the third century AD and still, for the most part, an intact circle around the centre of the city. A pleasant run, one he sometimes made in a tracksuit which disguised his calling, was to follow its line unimpeded straight to the great gate of San Sebastian and onto the Appian Way.

Initially the structure had been a small Roman sentry point along the brick expanse of the defences. In the Middle Ages it had been enlarged to provide accommodation for the expanding ecclesiastical entourage of the large and powerful basilica across the square. Giovanni e Paolo, though little known to the average tourist, was, for Fosse, one of the most interesting churches in Rome. The visible shell was unremarkable, save for the Romanesque campanile which cast an afternoon shadow across his first-floor window. Beneath the church lay centuries of rich history, however, and a story which had bemused him from the moment he first encountered it.

The tale of the martyrs John and Paul was, for centuries, thought to be apocryphal by those who dared say as much. It concerned two Christian officers at the court of Constantine who, after the accession of Julian the Apostate in AD 360, refused to sacrifice to pagan gods. As a consequence, they were beheaded, along with a woman who came to comfort them, in their own house on the Caelian Hill which later became the site of the basilica.

Myth begat myth, church begat church. Centuries of building and rebuilding ensued, resulting in the formidable pile which now dominated the view from Fosse's tower. Yet, when the archaeologists – doubtless atheists to a man – came to explore the foundations of the present church they found, deep beneath it, the well-preserved remains of an ancient Roman house. And three Christian graves, with clear signs that they were the scene of much reverence from as early as the end of the fourth century AD.

Sometimes Fosse would take privileged visitors into the subterranean houses and show them the paintings on the wall. It was always a humbling experience, an unspoken sermon on the mystery that underpinned all human life, and the relentless unreliability of what the clever people in universities like to call 'facts'.

The former guard post had, since the fifteenth century, been given over to the more humble employees of the parish. The modest living quarters afforded him a sitting room, a bedroom and a tiny bathroom, all built into the first floor of the circular tower, with the ground floor used for storage. At the top was a small octagonal room which Fosse regarded as his private place, closed even to the occasional visitors who were, to his annoyance, granted entrance to the tower.

The composer di Cambio, who wrote a choral work described by the 'bad pope' Alexander VI as 'the sound that angels now make in Heaven', had lived and died in these quarters in the late fifteenth century. This obscure historical connection – which Fosse found baffling on the occasion he listened to the boring drone of the work when it was performed, on the anniversary of di Cambio's death, in Santi Giovanni e Paolo – meant the tower was on the list of ancient monuments for which permission to view could be gained by applying to the relevant office in the Vatican. Accordingly, every few weeks since his arrival he had been forced to allow some curious gaggle of sightseers, usually American, into his home, where they would bill and coo at the 'cuteness' of the place. They would then stare out of the four slitted medieval windows that gave onto the Clivus Scauri and begin, surreptitiously, to peek at their watches.

None had the wit to ask what was in the tiny space at the summit. Nor would they have gained admittance in any case; Fosse had established that this last room had no public right of view. This was part of the price of what he saw as his exile. The resulting privacy made it perfect for the purpose required when his new and urgent calling had become apparent.

It was now seven on a blazing Sunday morning. His collection of more than three hundred jazz CDs was scattered on the floor in the small octagonal tower. It was difficult sometimes to know what to play. Soon he would go to the hospital, to talk to the sick and the dying, to sit in on operations, gowned and gloved, and offer his support to the surgeons and nurses. Soon, too, he would be forced to think of other matters, of the names he had gathered, and how these lives might be taken.

While Gino Fosse sat listening to John Coltrane racing through 'Giant Steps', he felt a sense of wonder. On the walls were the photographs, the constant, nagging reminder of his duty. Here too were the tools of his new trade: the ropes; the drugs he had carefully smuggled out of the hospital for when his own considerable strength was insufficient; the nine-millimetre M9 Beretta automatic pistol he had stolen on a visit to the army hospital next to San Giovanni – he enjoyed the idea it should have virtually the same name as the cardinal's three-pointed hat; and the knives – large and small, slender and broad, all sharpened so delicately that he was able to believe there existed but a single atom at the edge of the blade, one that would slice through anything it encountered.

The hospital had need of him for the rest of the morning. But from lunchtime onwards he was free, and there was much to do.

Twenty-two

Publicity mattered. Alicia Vaccarini learned that two months after she had won the parliamentary deputy's seat for the Northern Alliance in Bologna. It took that long for one of the local rags to uncover the truth about her private life: that the former university professor was a lesbian with a string of lovers, some of whom were only too willing to talk in return for a little money. The Northern Alliance had a firm position about 'aberrant behaviour'. It did not approve. In a few brief, heady weeks Vaccarini had gone from being the fêted victor in a marginal seat to an outcast inside her own party.

When the central committee organizer had marched into her office to say she would not be chosen for re-election at the end of her term three years hence she'd complained, bitterly, 'Why didn't you ask?'

The cold, hard man had stared and said, simply, 'Why didn't you tell?'

She now had only a year left, a year before unemployment, obscurity, poverty perhaps, at the age of forty-eight. Yet Alicia Vaccarini was a clever woman, a lecturer in economics, a worker of the system. She knew how to get grants out of Brussels. She knew how to sit on

committees and wait until the right moment to intervene. She had worked to ensure her future, accepting
seats on a variety of bodies, judicial, municipal and even
one which had overseen some preliminary discussions
about the merging of the Carabinieri with the state
police. There had been opportunities, compromises, particularly when she found her decisions had some sway
with people of influence, interested parties seeking a
certain resolution. From time to time, there had been
arrangements which, under a strict reading of the law,
were illegal. But these, she reasoned, were the price of
political practicality. Whatever the Northern Alliance felt
about her now, she had been elected with a duty, to serve
those who voted for her in Bologna, and to further her
own career. These were not necessarily contradictory.
Vaccarini had been careful. None of the current corruption investigations came close to her, nor was it likely they
would. When she had intervened she had been careful to
ensure that the reward was never obvious: a favour here,
a simple, valuable gift or service, or a payment abroad.
She had cultivated new and unexpected friends, people
who would never have come close to her had she stayed
inside the cold, rigid embrace of the Alliance. And there
was the irony: some of them were from quarters she
would never have done business with before. On the
right. On the left. In the higher echelons of the police
and the security services. Even in the Vatican. The world
was full of people needing a little help, and willing to
offer something in return. It was pragmatic to accept
these visible flaws in the facade of society and, when
appropriate, to use them to one's own ends.

Still, unemployment beckoned. She had hoped for
a position in Brussels: perhaps even the job of minor

commissioner. Nothing had happened and the PR people she employed on a tiny retainer thought they knew why. It was the profile that was wrong. She remained, in the public eye, the lesbian from Bologna who had lied to get herself elected. True, she was bright, she knew how to navigate the system. She was, in many ways, a hard-working, dedicated Italian politician. Nevertheless the stain of her sexuality, and the way she had hidden her true self for personal gain, continued to taint perceptions. Without some more favourable press her hopes of a continued political career were unrealistic.

This was the reason, the only reason, why Alicia Vaccarini now sat at a table in a deserted Martelli's, the restaurant in the narrow alley around the corner from the Parliament building which, during the week, was the workers' dining hall for deputies, journalists and political hangers-on.

'I didn't even know this place opened on Sundays,' she said, lighting a cigarette.

The journalist said he was from *Time* magazine. Now she was here, Vaccarini realized she should have checked. There were some jokers out there. People with hidden tape recorders who tried to embarrass you into making stupid comments then selling them on to the TV and radio stations. This was an oversight on her part but an understandable one. The pranksters had low horizons; they always claimed to come from minor, regional papers, not the bigger ones in Rome and Milan where their false identities would be transparent. To say one was from *Time* was different; it was too bold a claim, surely, to be anything other than genuine. And now she was here Alicia Vaccarini could believe it too. The man was about thirty, well dressed in a casual, Sunday fashion, with a pale rose shirt and blue trousers. He had an anonymous face, handsome in a vapid if somewhat exaggerated way, with dark, intelligent eyes and a quick, slightly nervous smile. Only one thing stood out: he seemed too big for his clothes. His muscles bulged against his shirt sleeves, he held himself in an awkward, stiff fashion. He looked like someone who endured work-outs in spite of himself, endowing a body that was meant to be more slight with a physicality that didn't quite fit. And there was a smell too. Like some kind of liniment or a chemical that belonged in a hospital.

'It doesn't open normally,' he said in a measured, educated voice. 'You're witnessing the power of the American media, Deputy.'

She laughed and looked around. There was only one other couple dining on the far side of the room. 'I could almost believe that.'

'I thought you'd like privacy,' he said.

'Why?' she asked, heart sinking. 'I told you on the phone. If you're looking for some kind of dyke confession piece, if you think I'm going to pour my pink heart out in public, you've got the wrong person. That part of my story has been done to death and I'm very happy to leave it in the grave.'

He raised a glass of red wine. 'Me too.'

She joined him in the drink. It tasted good. Alicia Vaccarini realized she felt like some wine. There was nothing else to do in the city that afternoon. It was too hot to think straight. The Parliament was closed. The private work which had kept her in the city was finished. She could afford to be lazy.

'What I want is to talk about you. The real you. What

you believe. What you want to achieve. Where you see your life going after your term as deputy is over.'

'And this is going to make a story for *Time* magazine?' she asked.

He frowned and poured some more wine from the carafe. The waiter came and placed two plates of pasta on the table. 'You've got me there, Alicia. I'm a fraud. But only up to a point. Every story needs a tag. They want to do some piece about how being gay is no longer a bar to public office in Europe. I need some examples that show the real story. I need to ask the question: what would have happened to you if you'd been heterosexual? If you'd been married, with children, and put in the same kind of work you're doing now?'

'I see.'

He pulled out a small tape recorder and placed it on the table. Then he leaned over and placed his hand on hers. It was, she thought, a very powerful hand.

'Alicia. People like us have to stick together.'

Her eyes widened. 'You're telling me you're gay?'

'You're telling me you didn't know the moment you set eyes on me?'

'No. I mean yes.' She didn't know what she meant at that moment. He seemed a disconcerting person. When she thought about it she was able to think of him as gay. But it required effort and she couldn't help wondering whether this was not some trick on his part; whether he was, in truth, some kind of chameleon who could change his shape, alter his appearance at will.

He pressed the button on the tape recorder. She watched the little wheels whirl.

'Tell me about yourself. Only the things you want to

talk about. Tell me how you became who you are. What you believe in. About your religion.'

'My religion?'

'Everybody believes in something, Alicia. We just have different names for it. You came from a Catholic family. I read that in the files. You must have believed once.'

She nodded. The wine helped her remember. There had been a time when she was convinced by all those old stories, when they gave her some comfort in the lonely, dark nights of childhood.

'Of course. And then you get older.'

'Wiser?'

'I didn't say that.'

'And then you get older still, and sometimes it comes back.' He paused. 'Do you think that might happen to you?'

'Who knows?' she said lazily, feeling the wine go to her head, liking this strange young man, who was not really gay, she thought, simply very good at lulling an interviewee into believing whatever was appropriate for an easy conversation.

'Doubt is a virtue,' he said firmly as the meat course arrived: grilled lamb with artichokes. 'It's better to believe than to know.'

Alicia Vaccarini laughed. 'Quite. Are you really a journalist?'

'What else could I be?'

'A priest, I think. I could imagine you in black. Taking confession. Listening.'

He stopped eating and considered this. 'Perhaps I could be a priest. But not today. And I don't want to hear confessions, Alicia. Confessions are tiresome, whining things, surely.' He looked at her frankly. 'Confessions won't rebuild your career. Only the truth may do that.'

'Only the truth will set you free!' she said, deciding she would get a little drunk, because it was that kind of day.

'Precisely,' he said, suddenly very serious. 'Now talk, please. Of yourself. Of what you wish to become.'

The carafe was refilled. After the meat there was *zabaglione* and *grappa*, though she felt she drank more than he did. Alicia Vaccarini began to talk, more freely than she had recently with anyone, in the media or outside it, not caring what the little tape recorder heard. This odd young man, with his considerate, priestly manner, was excellent company, a sounding board who listened closely to everything she said, criticizing when he thought it appropriate, praising when he felt praise was due.

The afternoon disappeared in a whirl of one-sided conversation. When he paid the bill it was approaching four o'clock. She felt wonderful, elated, released of some unconscious burden that had been haunting her for years.

They walked outside. The heat of the day was beginning to fade. This part of the city was empty. The day was so hot it shuddered in front of her eyes. She was reluctant to return to the cramped, stuffy apartment in the Via Cavour that was her solitary home.

Her companion pointed down the narrow alley adjoining the restaurant.

'Alicia,' he said. 'It's such a lovely afternoon. I have my car here. Let's walk by the river for a while. Drink some coffee. Eat some ice cream. You're such excellent company. Would you like that? Please?'

She nodded, liking him all the more, and followed as he entered the shade of the alley, disappearing into the darkness. The alley grew dark and unexpectedly cold. There was the smell of damp in the air. Finally she saw him, standing by his vehicle. It was not a car but a small van, with windows in the back, the kind used by tradesmen. He was not smiling.

She walked up to him, wondering what accounted for the change in his face, which was now very serious, now looking at her in a way – was this distaste? – she did not recognize.

This stranger put his hand into his pocket and pulled something out: a plastic bag containing a piece of white material. There was that smell again, the one which seemed to belong in a hospital.

She wanted to run but she was too drunk. She wanted to shout but there was nothing to say, no one to hear it.

The white cloth came up to her face and the hospital smell filled her head. Alicia Vaccarini wondered stupidly why all the oxygen had just disappeared from the world then felt the blackness start to creep into her head, steadily, with a rushing, roaring sound, in from the corners of her vision, devouring her consciousness.

When she awoke, after an unfathomable period of time, she was in a small, brightly lit circular room, tied to a chair, surrounded by images: photographs and paintings, some so strange she refused to look at them, not daring to let their content enter her head. Music was playing from behind her: hard bop, fast and edgy. Someone was humming to the long complex solo, note for note.

A cloth gag was tied tightly around her mouth. Her hands were bound behind her back. Her ankles were secured firmly to the legs of her chair.

She tried to speak. The words came out as a pathetic

grunt. The figure emerged from behind her. In his right hand was a long butcher's knife. In his left a sharpening rod which he stroked quickly and professionally with the blade.

'You're awake,' he said, nodding to drive home his point. 'Good. We have much to discuss, and much to achieve.'

Twenty-three

Falcone glowered at the three names on the desk, names Nic Costa had provided in his report. He had assembled a team of sixteen for the investigation: all men. They sat in the briefing room smoking, drinking coffee, feeling uncomfortable. The air-conditioning was struggling to keep ahead of the heat. The atmosphere in the station was tense, unpleasant and desperate. They knew when they were grasping at straws.

'Is this all?' Falcone asked Costa.

'How many are there supposed to be?' Falcone had to learn that pressure wasn't the only option. There were other ways of getting what you wanted, Costa thought. Perhaps more efficient ones.

'I don't know,' Falcone grumbled. 'Do you think she's telling the truth?'

He thought about this. 'I don't think she's lying.' Sara had dictated the names very carefully over coffee, spelling out the addresses, giving a short rundown of the details of the relationships. Two of them were married. All were people she had met in some kind of professional capacity, as if she had no private life of her own at all. No relationship appeared to have lasted more than a few weeks. Most puzzling of all for Costa, she seemed non-plussed by this, as if it were normal to lead such an empty, two-dimensional existence.

'That wasn't what I asked,' Falcone complained.

'I know. What I was trying to say was that these people check out. We've spoken to them. They acknow-ledge what went on, even the married ones. They all have alibis for the period we can fix absolutely – those hours when he must have been in the church on Tiber Island. I'm not saying none of them is a suspect but they look more like possible victims to me. The way they leapt at the idea of protection certainly seems to suggest so.'

Falcone raised a heavy eyebrow at Rossi. 'Are you going along with that? He's doing a lot of the talking these days.'

'He's not saying anything I wouldn't,' the big man grunted. 'I go along with it all.'

Falcone looked at the list again. 'A judge. Some bureaucrat from the Finance Ministry. And this last one? It doesn't even say what he does.'

'Toni Ferrari,' Rossi said, reading from his notes. 'Creepy little stockbroker. Skinny string of piss. Believe me, he isn't up for this. Almost wet himself when I said he could be next in line.'

Falcone grimaced. 'What connects them? Why these men?'

'They asked her out,' Costa answered. 'She said yes.'

'Denney? Any connection there? These are just the kind of people he used to mix with.'

'Nothing that we can see or they admit to,' Costa replied. 'There's nothing like the link Rinaldi had. They've been near no judicial commission. As far as we can see they don't have any connection with the Banca Lombardia.'

'So that's it? She just meets these people, sleeps with them for a while and then it ends?'

Luca Rossi stabbed the air with his finger. 'At their insistence,' he said. 'Every one of them I talked to said that. It just got too freaky for them. She'd turn up on dates. She'd smile and talk all the way through. She'd sleep with them, and I get the impression that was no bad thing either. But it was as if there was something missing. Here. One of them said this . . .'

He searched through the notes. 'The Finance Ministry guy. He said, after a while it was like taking out some woman from an escort agency. Just impersonal. Even a man gets to tire of that eventually.'

'Guess he must have known what it was like though,' Falcone said. 'Could that be what she is? Some college professor who's a high-class hooker on the side?'

Costa groaned. 'Please. Why would she do that? The apartment's hers, bought with her own money, no mortgage, from the inheritance she got from her parents when she turned twenty-one. If she doesn't need the cash, what's the point? Because she likes it?'

'I've heard stranger things,' Luca Rossi said. 'Do you understand what's going on in her head?'

Costa said nothing.

'Check it out anyway. There are people out there who would know. What about one-night stands?' Falcone asked. 'Did she say anything about that?'

Costa hadn't pressed the point. She didn't want to go there; he didn't want to hear the answers. 'Nothing. I don't think they happened.'

'So what do we have?' Falcone wondered. 'A woman

who sleeps around casually. Nothing unusual there. A good-looking woman, someone people want to be seen with for a while. And then they get bored, or they get scared, and just fade into the background. Except one of them remains obsessed, one of them doesn't want this to end, or if he does he wants to make sure she remembers him. He'll do anything to make his point to her. Kill people. Do it in a way designed to make her sit up and take notice because it ties in with what she does. But . . .'

'She didn't finish with people,' Rossi said. 'They finished with her. All of them. Isn't that what she said?'

'Yes,' Costa admitted.

Falcone threw the sheaf of notes onto the far side of his desk. 'Then she's lying. She has to be. All of these men, the ones we know about, don't want to go near her. There has to be more. She's got to know. What about the apartment?'

Costa was lost. 'The apartment . . . ?'

Furillo, one of the men Falcone had brought in that morning at San Clemente, said, 'Nothing to go whoopee about.'

'You've searched her apartment? You did that while I was with her? That was the point?'

Falcone stared at him. 'This is turning into a serial murder investigation, kid. We don't have time for the niceties.'

'If you'd asked her . . .'

'She might have said no. And then we'd have got permission anyway. What makes you think we have time to wait around like that? Two days, four people dead. He could be back at work somewhere out there right now.'

Costa was silent. Falcone was right.

'One thing,' Furillo added. 'We found a mobile

hidden in a drawer in the bedroom. Not her normal phone. We called the number we had and checked. This thing didn't ring and it's locked by a code. Technical said they couldn't crack it. Doesn't store numbers either so we don't know who she's called or who's called her. Neat, if you want to make sure no one knows who you're talking to.'

Rossi was unimpressed. 'A phone in a drawer? Maybe it's just an old one she put away.'

'It's fully charged,' Furillo said. 'It's still got the sticker on the back saying it came from Monaco. Why would you have a phone from Monaco in your bedroom drawer?'

Falcone grimaced. 'That's it? Nothing else?'

'Nothing.'

Falcone watched them for a while and they knew what he wanted: suggestions. No one was willing to play the game. If Sara Farnese was keeping something from them there was precious little they could use to sweat it out of her.

'I'm taking her into protective custody,' Falcone announced eventually. 'Get some safe house somewhere. Not a nice one either. I don't want her comfortable.'

'It won't work,' Costa objected.

'Why?'

'Because . . .' He knew the answer. It was obvious. Falcone knew it too. 'Because she will only tell us when she wants to tell us. She won't break just because we pile on the pressure. She's not like that.'

Luca Rossi agreed. 'He's right. I've been watching that woman since we first saw her in the library. She holds it all inside and she's going to keep it there until she chooses to let it out. The tougher we make life for her, the harder it gets.'

'Then what?' Falcone demanded. 'She can't go back to that apartment. The media's camped out in the street. And she is, like it or not, potentially under threat.'

Costa thought of his father, how the old man's calm was perhaps what was needed. The house on the Appian Way had the room. There was privacy. It could be perfect.

'You're trying to drive this man to me, right?'

'The TV pictures I saw weren't wonderful,' Falcone moaned. 'Maybe they'll have something better on a different station. You could have got in a bit closer. You could have made it look more obvious.'

'Whatever. We can kill two birds with one stone. Let her stay at my father's place for a while. I can be there. If he's coming for her, he'll find out too. If you want to whet his appetite, what better way could there be? He could take his pick.'

'This is Red Marco, right?' Falcone said sourly. 'The commie with the big farm out in the country?'

'Most of which he rebuilt with his own hands if you want to know. Sir . . .' Costa was not taking that. He knew the real story behind the farm and it was nothing like the scurrilous gossip that the papers had made up.

Falcone smiled. It didn't make anyone in the room feel any happier. 'Oh, that could work. We can pump up the press with it. We can put you right in his sights. There's still time for the evening news. Is this place easy to cover? My guess is we'll get one chance with this lunatic and I don't want it thrown away.'

Costa thought of the untidy sprawl of farmland, enclosed by rickety fences. It wasn't ideal but it was manageable. 'We'll need plenty of people on the ground.'

'My, my,' Falcone said. 'I hope it's worth the expense.'

They waited.

'Do it,' he said. 'And you go break the news that she's going to be your house guest. If you're right, maybe she really will talk to one person and one person alone when she feels like it. Make sure it's you.'

'Sir,' he said.

'And Furillo?'

The detective nodded.

'Use this time productively. Go through that apartment of hers again. Go through it until you find something else. On with it!'

The team rose. Falcone looked at Costa and Rossi getting ready to leave. 'You two. We'll drop into my office on the way. There's one more thing.'

They walked down the corridor into the small, neat room where Falcone worked, Nic Costa wondering all the time how he would manage to sell this idea to her. Falcone closed the door and went to the desk. There he opened a drawer and took out a video cassette.

'This came in marked for your attention this morning, Costa. I took the liberty of opening it. Save you the trouble.'

Costa looked at the video. There was no label on it, nothing to indicate where it came from. Falcone handed it to him and nodded at the VCR in the corner. Then they watched the tape: three minutes of it, every second so gripping Costa couldn't took his eyes off the screen. When it was done he looked at Luca Rossi. The big man's face was deathly white. These were images the big man did not want to recall.

It was a composite of several scenes, culled from at

least four different cameras, and covered Stefano Rinaldi's time in the Vatican Library from the moment he walked through the main doors to the time of his bloody death, with the skin of Hugh Fairchild spread out on the desk before him. Sara had been right. He hadn't intended to kill her. The gun he held was going towards his own head. Rinaldi was trying to commit suicide on someone else's orders, someone he felt could see him through the security system and would, perhaps, let his own wife live in return. His eyes, dark, haunted eyes, caught the lens in every scene; in one, as he entered the Reading Room, he even nodded at the camera.

'So?' Falcone asked. 'What does that tell us?'

'That it was the video system he was trying to convince,' Costa said immediately. 'Not the people in the room. He checked the position of the video all the time. When he whispered to Sara he didn't even seem to notice them. He turned his back to the camera. It was deliberate.'

Falcone agreed. 'Exactly. So, rightly or wrongly, he believed someone who had access to that system would know whether he was doing the right thing or not. And?'

Costa's head was a blur. He couldn't think this through and Rossi wasn't helping. The big man was looking at him, horrified.

'Tell him,' Falcone barked at Rossi.

'Jesus, kid,' the big man moaned. 'Think about it. You've been stirring things in places we never want to go. Someone in the Vatican knows something. Furthermore, someone in the Vatican likes you. Likes you enough to send you this tape. Are they the same person? Or is it two different people working in opposite directions? What did you do after I left you yesterday?'

'I went and talked to Hanrahan,' Costa admitted. 'Why not? He knows stuff.'

'You leave this alone,' Falcone insisted. 'I talk to Mr Hanrahan. In my time. On my conditions. I don't want any more secret visits, you hear?'

Costa nodded and wondered how Falcone seemed to know, with such certainty, that he had returned to see Hanrahan again even before he admitted it.

Falcone walked to him and patted his arm. It was an oddly unfamiliar gesture. 'One step at a time, Nic,' he said. 'You've got enough on your plate with that woman. Talk to her. Make her feel at home. Make her feel you're her friend. She knows someone inside that place. Understand?'

'Yes,' Nic Costa grunted. But Falcone wasn't listening. He had turned the TV onto another news channel. It was coverage of Costa and Sara Farnese leaving the church that morning, with a voice-over story that was grossly lurid even for one of the Rome channels. The camera lingered on Sara, trying to catch her face as she ducked and turned from the pack. Then the picture turned shakily to him. Nic Costa was unable to place this moment. It must have happened accidentally. He had his arm around her, affectionately it seemed. She was clinging to his body. They looked like lovers.

In a moment that was quite foreign to him he smiled at the camera. A smile that was not his, an actor's smile, one that left little doubt as to its meaning. It was knowing, proprietorial. It said: *I own this troubled, dangerous woman, and I can do with her what I want.*

He watched himself on the TV and hated what he saw,

wondering what she would make of it, and how he could apologize sufficiently.

'Now that,' Falcone said, 'is good. That can change things.'

Twenty-four

He had given her some water and a piece of bread, allowed her to go to the bathroom, though strictly under his supervision, and he had watched, a little too closely she thought. Then he had led her back, kicked the chair across the room until it stood next to a black, upright beam, and tethered her tightly to the arms. Her hands remained bound throughout, with a loose rope around her ankles to prevent her trying to run. This was, in any case, not an option. They were in some strange medieval room, an upstairs octagonal chamber littered with rubbish: books and video tapes, CDs, clothes and, on the walls, photographs, everywhere, some of a woman she vaguely recognized.

The pictures continued to alarm her. Alicia Vaccarini refused to look too closely.

In the corner a narrow, circling staircase led to the room below, to the outside world and freedom. Some way distant, it had to be. As soon as he took off the gag she had screamed until her lungs hurt, bellowing for help, yelling murder, murder, murder. He just stood there, watching, not smiling, not angry. Waiting for the fury to subside. When she was done, when there was no more breath left in her body, he shook his head and said, 'No one can hear, Alicia.'

She had screamed again at that, until her voice went hoarse. He had hardly paid any attention, half watching the movie on the TV somewhere behind her head. She recognized the film from the soundtrack. It was Pasolini's *The Gospel According to Saint Matthew*, the arrival of the three wise men to the accompaniment of the old Negro spiritual 'Sometimes I Feel like a Motherless Child'. He seemed affected by it somehow; she wondered how to turn this to her advantage. How she might get out of the stuffy, airless tower alive.

Then he switched channels, over to one of the mainstream stations which was showing a soccer match. It was a deliberate act, one with a point. It said there was something to be done.

Gino Fosse picked up a low wooden stool, brought it in front of her, sat down and took her head in his strong, pale hands.

'You thought I was a priest, Alicia.'

She was too frightened to say anything, too confused to second-guess what he wanted.

'Well?' he insisted.

He waited. Perhaps her silence would make him angry.

'You looked like one,' she said. 'For a little while.'

'Then confess to me,' he said. 'Confess everything.'

'What do you want me to say?'

'The truth.'

He was crazy, she knew that. But there was some strong, linear logic in what he sought. If she found what that was, perhaps there could be some hope of survival.

'I have sinned, Father,' she said.

'*Don't call me "Father"!*' Gino Fosse's bellows echoed off the walls of the tiny, octagonal chamber. His face contorted with fury. She was silent. She waited, watching him make some purposeful effort to control his emotions.

'I'm sorry,' she said softly.

'Not your fault. My anger wasn't directed at you. Just talk to me, Alicia. Confess.'

The tears were starting to burn in her eyes. She racked her head trying to think of something that would satisfy him.

'I've committed unnatural acts.'

'Of course,' he said. 'And you'll be forgiven. But these are small things.'

It was impossible to know, she thought. No one was free of private vices, no one lacked a history he or she would not care to share with the world. 'Help me. Please.'

He nodded his head, understanding what she required. 'Four months ago,' he said, 'you sat on a judicial committee looking into the question of diplomatic immunity for certain people. You recall this?'

'Yes.'

'There were decisions made, votes taken. Were all of them based on fairness? Or did you seek, and get, some reward for some of your actions?'

'Denney,' she said, feeling cold.

'No names!'

'I didn't know the rest of them would vote against me. I thought . . . I was given to understand they'd received the same favours. They'd go the same way.'

His dark eyes regarded her coldly. 'Judges and deputies. Lawyers and "*public servants*".' Spittle flecked his lips when he said the last. Some deep, inner hatred surfaced within Gino Fosse and she knew, at that moment, this was hopeless. He would do whatever he planned to do because his mind was made up. The rest was an act, a show for his conscience, not hers.

'I did what I promised,' she insisted. 'I can't be held responsible for other people.'

'There was a price, Alicia. For you. And for those involved. What was that price?'

'Money,' she said. 'Don't ask how much. I can't remember. Not a lot, I don't think.'

'And?'

He knew. He had to have some prior knowledge. It was a wonder to her. She had believed this had been so private. She thought of the photographs on the wall. It was possible . . .

'I was provided with some personal entertainment.'

His dark eyebrows rose. ' "Personal entertainment"? Specify, please.'

'They sent me a woman for the night. She didn't mind. What's it to you?'

His hand came out from his side and slapped her hard across the cheek.

'What's it to me?' he demanded. 'I drove her there, Alicia. I was a party to that act. I thought I understood what was happening. I didn't. Just as you understand nothing, regret nothing, feel no sense of anguish for what you've done. This man you talk about. I still can't see him walking down the street. I still can't touch him, Alicia. There was such a great cost for your favours. You took so much and gave back nothing.'

'I'm sorry,' she said. 'I'm truly sorry. If there's some

way I can make amends. If it's a question of paying back the money.'

'Money.' He stared at her, his face full of pity. 'You think it's so important. You have no idea of how pathetic you are. Or how grateful you will be to me. And soon.'

Gino Fosse stood up and walked over to the bookshelf in the corner of the room, taking out two thick photographic volumes. He came back and placed them in front of her, opening the first at a double-page spread depicting a church courtyard.

'Santa Cecilia in Trastevere,' he said. 'Do you know it?'

She tried to catch his eye, pleading. 'Gino. Let me go. I won't tell anyone. I promise.'

He frowned. He had, she thought, an actor's face. It was so mobile, able to go from passivity to deep concentration in a second, able to change shape, from plainness to a kind of warped beauty with just the shift of an eyelid, a turn of the mouth.

'You must listen. This is important. Cecilia was a family woman. The wife of a nobleman who was converted to Christianity during the persecutions of Diocletian. Her house lay beneath this church. It was here . . .'

He glowered at her. 'You're not listening. I do all this for your benefit *and you're not listening*.'

Alicia Vaccarini was beginning to sob, was unable to stop the choking noise that kept rising in her throat.

He leaned forward to make his point plain. 'She was a martyr, Alicia. She will help wash your sins clean.' He pointed at the book. 'Here in the very place she died, in the very way she went to glory.'

His finger stabbed at the image there: a virginal woman, staring peacefully out from the page.

'First, since she was a high-born woman, they tried to suffocate her in the baths beneath the house, a noble death. When that failed, they were allowed three strokes of the axe. These still did not kill her. There's the miracle. There's the proof. The senators and the patricians came to see her lying in bed, wounded, singing hymns, turning to Christ as she died before them. Afterwards they made her the patron saint of musicians in recognition of her courage. Alicia . . .'

He opened the second book and thrust it in front of her face. She did not wish to look. His strong hand gripped her hair and turned her head to the page. It depicted a beautiful white statue of the prone corpse of a young woman wrapped in a shroud, face half turned away from the beholder.

'In the sixteenth century they opened her casket,' he said. 'Cecilia was incorrupt, perfect, still beautiful in her golden robe thirteen hundred years after her death. The marks of the axe were on her neck. An artist painted her, Alicia. A sculptor made this statue which still sits beneath the altar in her church, above her house.'

'Please,' she gasped. 'Gino . . .'

He took her hand. 'Don't fear. You'll be there tonight. You'll lie in front of her, give homage to her martyrdom. And in doing so you'll make amends, you'll help me put right these wrongs that you're a part of.'

'No . . .'

His face changed again, becoming hard and determined.

'It's time,' he said and went over to one of the windows, retrieved a large pillow from a storage box, returned with it and, very carefully, placed it over her mouth.

Alicia Vaccarini breathed in through the white fabric. It stank of damp and mould. She coughed, retching. He took it away, waiting until she recovered her breath.

'This is the first part.'

The pillow came back, covering her face. She felt something wind around it, something like a rope which fastened the thing behind her head, tightly, but not so hard she couldn't inhale. Not quite.

'Good,' said a voice from behind.

The fabric grew damp and sticky with her saliva. The passage of air seemed to diminish with every snatched effort of her lungs. She gagged, gasping, and felt him tighten the pillow further around her face.

There was one last push. The thing entered her mouth, its fibres stuck to the back of her throat. She threw up bitter bile into the fetid cotton, coughing. Then the rope relaxed, the smothering stopped. Gino Fosse withdrew the stinking, vile object from her face. She fought to get clean air into her lungs, hyperventilating rhythmically as she did so.

'Good,' he said. He now held a long sword in his hand. It was well polished, with a glittering silver blade, like something out of a military museum. With no perceptible effort, holding it in one hand, he raised it to her neck and cut the flesh there in a single, sweeping movement.

Alicia Vaccarini shrieked in agony. She could feel the blood starting to run down her neck, down onto the good, cotton shirt she had chosen to wear for the lunch at Martelli's. It was a painful wound, but a light one. He was testing himself. He stood over her now, wondering about the second blow: how hard, how deep it might be.

'I beg you,' she bawled. 'I'll do anything. Just don't kill me.'

She looked into his eyes. There was confusion there. Perhaps there was some hope. He was no longer focused on her, no longer wondering how deeply he might hack into her neck with the sharp, shiny weapon held in his hand.

Gino Fosse's attention now lay on the television set on the far side of the room, behind her. There was a newscast. She could hear it. There was talk of a murder and a woman, a scarlet woman who, the reporter said, seemed to bring death, a shocking death, to everyone she knew.

He was unable to take his eyes off the set. She heard him catch his breath when he saw whatever was on the screen. He put down the sword. Then he took out a clean, white handkerchief and wiped the blood off her neck.

'I apologize, Alicia,' he said. 'I'm distracted.'

'Untie me,' she pleaded. 'Let me go. I won't tell a soul.'

He looked at her and there was pity in his eyes. 'Tomorrow,' he said, 'I'll do you justice.'

Then he was gone from the room, leaving Alicia Vaccarini to her thoughts and the image from the book: a pale white corpse, wrapped in a delicate shroud, head obscured, waiting for resurrection.

Twenty-five

Sara had swiftly agreed to stay at the house once Falcone had outlined the alternative: protective custody in some safe house in one of the city's grimmer suburbs. At Nic Costa's insistence they had watched the TV news in the station before leaving. He didn't want her to find out accidentally. He also wanted her to understand that the media would follow them to the farm, where they would be carefully herded into a well-controlled position by Falcone's men.

She took in the TV clip, and the possessive way in which it portrayed him, with her customary passivity. Costa apologized. Sara said, simply, 'It's your job, isn't it? But I don't understand why you think he'll come. If there are so many police around and the press too. It would be stupid.'

'It's a gamble,' he replied, trying to convince himself. 'I guess we're hoping he can't resist taking a look.'

This was the best he could do. Falcone was, he judged, either clutching at straws or playing some deeper game altogether.

He'd told her about Marco in the car, withholding nothing. To his surprise she'd turned to stare at him and there was something new in her eyes, a different expression, of sympathy and perhaps something more: understanding.

'What do you want me to do? How do I talk to him?' she asked.

'I don't have an easy answer for that. At least I never found one myself. Treat him as if nothing's different. I think he likes that. He likes to amuse, too, and be amused.'

She was silent for the rest of the journey. Fifteen minutes later they left the city, entered the countryside off the Appian Way, and passed through the media posse at the front gate.

Bea was at the big barn-door entrance, waiting. She wore a gaudy floral shirt and cream trousers. Her tanned arms were crossed. She seemed ambivalent about welcoming a stranger into the house.

'How is he?' Nic asked. The inevitable question.

'Hungry. Or so he says. You kept him waiting.'

'Sorry.' He glanced at Sara. 'We have a visitor.'

'So I gather.' She held out her slim hand and examined Sara Farnese frankly. 'Don't let the old devil talk you into giving him wine. Or anything else for that matter. He's sick but he's not beyond mischief. And mind the dog. He's funny with women. It's a family trait.'

There was a scratching from behind the half-closed door. A paw worked its way around the woodwork and made the gap wide enough for a small body to squirm through. Pepe saw Bea and sat immediately, emitting a low growl.

'See what I mean?' Bea asked.

Sara reached down and touched the creature's head. It watched her warily then lifted its chin, deigning to be stroked. It had typical terrier colouring: white, brown and black, now tinged with the distinct grey of age.

'You seem to be accepted,' Bea said, surprised. 'It's a rare honour. I've known that beast for a decade or more and it's only in the last few months he's stopped trying to savage me.'

Sara smiled and stroked the dog more fondly. He closed his eyes, delighted. 'Dogs are easier than people,' she said.

'This is the Costa household,' Bea replied. ' "Easy" never comes into it. Am I right, Nic?'

'No argument there.' He kissed her cheek. 'Thanks, Bea. You can come tomorrow? I don't want to press you if it's awkward.'

'I don't want to be anywhere else,' she said, and Sara noticed how she failed to meet his eyes when she said this. 'It's just selfish, I know. You can't keep me out.'

'I wouldn't dream of trying. He needs you. We all do. We always have.'

'The ever loyal servant,' she said, with a measure of bitterness. 'I'm sorry. I . . .'

She walked briskly to her car, shaking her head. Sara watched her go. She was an intense person, she thought. But Bea needed the Costa family as much as they needed her.

The dog looked at her, barked once, then turned into the house. Sara followed him inside and walked straight to Marco Costa in his wheelchair, taking his hand, smiling, full of a level of small talk Nic had never expected. While he took her bags upstairs, Marco guided her around the ground floor, the dog following on faithfully behind in his tracks. His son then did the same for the rest of the sprawling house. She was staying in

Giulia's room on the first floor, one of six, at the far end from his own. It was private, with its own bath, and, like the house itself, secure. There was only the single barn door into the farm. Marco had insisted on the authentic, bucolic design for all its inconveniences. His son was satisfied that it was a good choice for the purpose he had outlined to Falcone and surprised too to find that he was looking at the place in a different way through Sara's enthusiastic eyes. When the tour was over she followed him downstairs looking more content than at any time since they had first met. This was, he realized from what she had told him about herself, something foreign to her: a home.

Marco Costa dressed for dinner: a white shirt, impeccably pressed by Bea, black trousers and a silk neck scarf which hid the scar of an operation. The old man had combed his thinning hair carefully. The spotlights in the farmhouse kitchen made his face seem cruelly cadaverous. Nic Costa had grown up seeing his father's round, caring, persistent features at every turn of his life. They were losing their form now under the punishment of the disease. The generous skin was sagging, as if something was removing the vitality that lay beneath the surface. And this was an entirely physical ailment. His father's personality, so warm when he wished it to be, and his quick intelligence were undiminished.

The three of them sat around the table eating pasta and salad and Nic Costa was astonished to find that he was the one feeling uncomfortable. Sara and his father seemed to have come to accept each other, as if they recognized some mutual trait.

'You've a beautiful house,' she said.

'We built it,' Marco boasted. 'Most of it, anyway. All

with local stone. There's masonry here that Seneca might have touched. Forget all the nonsense the press wrote about Red Marco and his country palace. When I bought this plot no one wanted to live here and it cost me next to nothing. I don't care what it's worth now. What you see is what we created, through our own labour, with no help from anyone.'

'Oh yes,' Nic agreed. 'No arguing there. I spent five years sleeping in a bedroom without heating, next to a bathroom with no running water. We were given a fine proletarian upbringing.'

'Quite right too,' his father declared.

'Except,' Nic objected, 'I seem to recall you grew up in a nice, comfortable council apartment . . .'

'Which is why I knew what was best for my own offspring. Look at this place, Nic. It's too familiar for you to see it properly but I can still remember how much we put into it. I can look at some of the brickwork and recall your mother laying in the mortar. I can touch something you plastered, and pretty well too, when you were thirteen. You could have made a builder. Instead it's his sister who's the artisan. I'll show you her paintings later. She gets that from her mother. Whatever *he* has comes from me, I guess.'

Sara raised a glass to them both. 'I don't think either of you have much to complain about.'

'No,' Marco replied, looking at his son with an obvious measure of pride. 'I don't believe we have.'

'Drink,' the old man added mournfully, watching the red wine in her glass. 'Lost pleasures.' He looked at her frankly. 'My son tells me you never had a home like this. Your parents died when you were young.'

She shrugged. It occurred to Nic that she was never

unwilling to talk about herself. What was missing, all too often, were the details, which had to be prised from her carefully, one at a time. 'I don't recall ever living at home with them. I was at a convent school in Paris in the early years. There was an accident.'

'I can't imagine what that would be like,' Marco said.

'The nuns were kind to me. I never lacked anything. Money least of all.'

'Money and happiness,' the old man declared, 'exist apart from each other. When I was in politics I met some of the richest and most miserable men in Italy. Five minutes' walk from that door I could take you to people who are dirt poor and wouldn't exchange their lives with anyone's.'

'Money *with* happiness,' Nic said. 'I think that's the goal.'

'Really?' His father looked disappointed. 'Why? Money's something you can strive for, something you can make yourself. Happiness, in my experience, only comes from others, when they decide to give it to you. You can't force people to do that, not even with money, though there's plenty out there who seem to think otherwise. It has to be earned and that's what makes it worthwhile.'

Sara finished her wine. Nic refilled the glass. She was dressed down tonight: a blue shirt with an exotic pattern, dark trousers. She looked young, naïve almost. She was relaxed too; the hard mask she wore so much of the time was gone. He wondered about her life; why no man had come to fill it properly, and, against his own instincts, could not help but wonder what was needed for that role. There would be pre-conditions. Honesty lay at the base of any relationship. He felt that strongly, so strongly it had ruined several of the liaisons he had enjoyed in the past. To love someone demanded more than physical attraction. There had to be some closeness, some pact of alliance against the cold, inexplicable vagaries of the world. Without those any affair was, it seemed to him, doomed to be a brief, shallow ghost of passion, something Sara Farnese seemed to know well.

'Is that what a family's for?' she asked. 'To give you that love?'

'Ideally,' Marco agreed. 'I hope we did that. Not perfectly perhaps, but then families aren't about perfection. They're about trying.' He stared at Nic. 'Any complaints?'

'You made me read Marx when I was ten.'

'And the Bible would have been worse?'

He thought about this. 'Probably not. I was ten. I wouldn't have taken much notice of either.'

'So there. Where's the harm? But don't think families are some kind of magic formula for happiness. They can cure you, they can kill you too when they go wrong.' The old man saw her reaction and grimaced. 'Sorry, I was being stupid.'

'Why?' Nic asked. 'It's true. You should see some of the families I meet.'

'But the alternative,' she said, 'is to walk down the middle. You know the highs. You know the lows. I don't really. It's like being . . . incomplete somehow. You're lucky. Both of you.'

The two men glanced uneasily at each other. It had not been the most comfortable of relationships at times and each bore equal weight of guilt and resentment for some of the arguments that had occurred in the past. In the present circumstances these seemed petty matters.

There was a reckoning coming, and certain things needed to be said.

'You're right, we're lucky,' Marco Costa said, watching her wine glass enviously. 'I'm a stubborn old man who always thought he knew what was best for the world. I don't imagine that made me an easy person at times.'

'You can say that again,' Nic agreed. 'But that was never the problem. It was the fact we always lived under your shadow. We were always the offspring of Red Marco, the man in the papers, the one who made the headlines. We were never individuals in our own right. We were parts of you. I know that wasn't your intention but it's what happened and it was hard. To have parents you loved so much you couldn't quite separate their identity from your own.'

The old man laughed. 'Now I understand! You see what this woman does? Tells us something we should all have seen years ago. I bring you three up as good revolutionaries. And what do you become? A cop, an American lawyer and an artist, and you do this in order to say, "We are ourselves." Good for you, son. More power to your elbow.'

Nic smiled. It was, he thought, the first time he had ever heard his father approve explicitly of his career.

Marco raised his glass to Sara. 'And thanks to you too. For extracting this from us. You grew up in a convent. Is this the Christian in you?'

'You mean do I believe?'

'Exactly!' It was as if no one had ever asked her.

'I suppose so,' she answered. 'I go to church some-times. I pray and it makes me feel better, though I'm not so sure I think there's a God. If there were, he would surely do something about the state of the world. That old excuse about free will isn't good enough. Still, as a way of explaining why we live, why we do what we do, it has a point. And they're very beautiful stories, some of them anyway. I always thought that as a child when they were read to me in the convent. Beauty counts. I don't know anything better.'

Marco stared out of the window, into the darkness, thinking. 'I suppose I'm meant to argue it's politics. Communism or social democracy. I don't think I have the energy any more.'

Nic felt a dark thought rising at the back of his head. 'You're kidding me?'

'No. Oh, it's not the sickness, Nic. It's just being realistic. What matters, I think, is that you believe in something, and something that's not too comfortable, something that keeps you awake at night from time to time. If that's religion, so be it. I never took you into that chapel down the road but you know the story, surely? That it was where Peter stopped while fleeing Rome, and Christ appeared to him. "Domine, Quo Vadis?" he asked. Lord, where are you going? And what did Jesus say? "To Rome to be crucified again." It's just a story, of course. That doesn't make it any the less powerful. The Church then wasn't what it is now. Peter would surely be horrified if he saw what's been built in his name in the Vatican. These people were revolutionaries. They were trying to change the entire Roman state, and the world after that. They weren't persecuted for no reason. Their beliefs were dangerous, treasonable. What the story of Quo Vadis is about is not giving up, not turning round when you're in trouble. Remembering that people have made sacrifices to get you where you are. Sometimes the biggest sacrifice of all.'

He closed his eyes briefly. Nic wondered if he was in pain. 'I haven't told you this before,' he said. 'But that was why I bought this plot of land. Because it was so close to that chapel. I thought it would serve as a reminder in the hard times, and it did. You know something else? If I'd been alive then I would have joined them. I would have been a Christian too. Maybe things will change sometime and people like me will take to it again. I don't know, but I do know we all need some kind of faith.'

'What's yours now?' Sara asked carefully. 'The same as you always believed?'

'That's a dead faith,' he answered. 'It killed itself before any of us ever had the chance to understand if it would work.'

He looked at his son. 'My faith rests in my children. This one in particular. One day Nic will find his calling. Perhaps in the police, where he'll cast out all those crooked bastards who give this country a bad name. Perhaps elsewhere. I don't know but I have faith it will happen, even if he doesn't believe it himself.'

There was a knock on the door.

'I'll get it,' Nic said. 'There are too many confessions for me tonight.'

They watched him go to the front of the house, take his police pistol out of the shoulder holster that lay on his carefully folded jacket, and gingerly open the door latch. There was an exchange of low, male voices.

He came back and said, 'Someone needs to see me. Outside. He doesn't want to come into the house. There's a guard by the door. Keep it locked. I'll let myself in. You don't have to wait up.'

Marco Costa nodded at the dog. 'Don't worry. We've got protection.'

Sara laughed. Nic looked at the two of them and the animal, its head cocked to one side, peering at him. He tried to understand why they should be so comfortable in each other's company. Then he mumbled an excuse and was gone.

'Did I make him feel awkward?' the old man asked, feeding the rest of his food to the dog.

'A little, I think,' she said. 'There's a conversation he needs to have with you. He can't do it with me around.'

Marco Costa's shoulders rose. A dry laugh emerged from his throat. 'Sara. Without you around we would never have spoken like that at all. That was the frankest talk we've had in years. You were the catalyst. We're both grateful.'

She was flattered by his compliment. 'I did nothing, but if that nothing helped I'm glad.'

He nodded at the bottle. 'Now I'll have some wine.'

She snatched it away from his grasping hand. 'No.'

'Whose house is this, girl?' he demanded. 'For pity's sake. You can't refuse a dying man a glass.'

'Convince your son of that, not me.' She started to clear the table of the plates, the glasses and the wine. 'If he doesn't want you drinking, he's got a reason.'

'I suppose a cigarette's out of the question then? It's medicinal.'

'Medicinal cigarettes?'

'These ones are. All the way from Morocco. Or Afghanistan if you prefer.'

She tut-tutted and loaded the dishwasher. 'Are you serious? Your son's a policeman.'

'It eases the pain. Really it does.'

'No!'

'Jesus,' Marco Costa moaned. 'Relax. There are no medicinal cigarettes. You know you're the first woman he's brought back that I can't wind around my little finger. What irony.'

Sara returned with a bottle of mineral water and poured some for both of them. 'I don't believe I quite fit that picture. I'm not here under the same circumstances, am I?'

The old man's face hardened in mock anger. 'So, there's something wrong with my son, is there? Not intellectual enough for the likes of you? You should hear him talk about painting. About Caravaggio. That's one legacy I left him. He knows a rebel when he sees one, and he knows a hell of a lot about him.'

She didn't blush. 'I'm not rising to the bait, Marco.'

'Ah. You're thinking he looks down on you for all this publicity.'

She sighed. 'And why shouldn't he? I thought I led a normal life. Now I'm painted like some . . . creature.'

'Pah! The press. If you listen to what they say you'll go crazy. You know what you are. He knows too.'

'Quite. It still shocks him. I see it on his face from time to time. Perhaps he's right.' She toyed with her glass. 'I like being on my own. I don't feel the need to be close to anyone. I can take men, I can leave them. It doesn't bother me.'

'Oh, please,' he groaned. 'The young. They think they invented everything. My dear, I grew up in the Sixties. Can you begin to imagine what our lives were like then? What you think of as promiscuity? Nothing. Nic's mother and I, we went through that in the first five years of our marriage. Talk to Bea about it if you like. She was there. I'm amazed the kids don't remember some of the things that went on.'

She thought of Bea, who said so much without uttering a word. Bea, who would not leave the old man's side. 'Perhaps they do and they're scared to show it.'

'Perhaps,' he acknowledged.

'Bea still loves you nevertheless. You do realize this?'

His face contorted in astonishment. 'What? You can see this? You, who has never met either of us until today? And saw her for, what, just a few minutes in any case?'

He had a point but she was certain of this. Even in the brief time they had met, Bea's devotion was obvious. 'Yes, I could see it. She loves you and regrets it was just a fleeting thing. And there you have the proof. The legacy of your infidelity. And that's nothing?'

'Defeated by your own argument,' he declared. 'I said Bea was there. I never said we were lovers. By the time Bea's feelings for me became apparent – men are deeply stupid on these matters as you doubtless appreciate – Nic's mother and I had realized that way of life was a waste. It had become unimportant to us. We were married, we were lovers but we were friends, allies too. All the other people were a distraction for us. We became monogamous because we wanted to, not through a need for propriety. Who's to say the same won't happen for you?'

'It won't,' she said with some certainty.

'If it does, it's in the future and none of us can see there, Sara. Not even a clever university professor. Mind you, I meant what I said about Nic. He has something in him if only he'd let it out. He has that anger, the same anger I felt, even if he keeps it well hidden.'

'He's afraid.'

'Of what?'

'Losing you.'

'All men fear their fathers' deaths. It's the moment you see your own mortality face to face. You witness a part of yourself dying with them.'

She went back to the counter and poured a glass of wine for herself, then one very small one for him.

'There's more to it than that, Marco.'

'Again? You know this?' he asked, a little angry. 'You, the convent girl who never had a family?'

'I can see what he feels. He's a transparent person in some ways. There's some part of him that's wounded already, in preparation, waiting for the real hurt.'

He grasped the glass of wine, took a tiny sip then pushed it away. 'Then it's time he grew up. We try to be their rock, you know, but even the rock goes in the end. You have to find your own.'

She listened. There were voices a long way off. One was Nic. He sounded angry.

'You know what I thought he would be?' Marco Costa asked. 'What I really feared him becoming when he grew up?'

'I've no idea.'

'A priest. It used to keep me awake at night. Not that he ever expressed any interest. There was just something in his manner. I was a politician. I tried to change big things, not help little people, individuals. You couldn't do both. And frankly I was no good at it. Nic has that gift. When he talks to you he sees you, no one else. He looks right into you, hears things you daren't even say to yourself. And here's another thing. You have that too. So I guess it's not a question of upbringing. Maybe you're both psychic. I don't know.'

Sara understood immediately that he was right. Nic had that talent. It was what had drawn her to him from the first. He seemed to possess the same internal emotional bruises.

'You're not drinking your wine,' she said.

His old eyes glittered and she saw a glimpse of a different Marco Costa then, a younger man, who was surely handsome in his prime, with a sharp, mischievous sense of humour. 'I didn't want the wine. I just wanted to see you pour it.'

A tea towel flew across the room and landed on his lap.

'Bea warned me. You're a wicked old man,' Sara Farnese declared.

Marco Costa laughed. They looked at each other, wary of the intimacy that had grown in a single night, an intimacy based on some unspoken, perhaps unrecognized, mutual need.

'Will you stay long?' the old man asked, trying not to sound as if he was pleading. She was a warm and human presence in the house, not least because she behaved as if there were nothing wrong with him at all. 'Bea is a friend, and a better one than I deserve. But the old require young people around them. We need to suck the vitality out of you like vampires.'

'As long as I'm welcome.' She had turned away from him so Marco Costa could not see her face. The old man watched this solitary woman and remembered what his son had said earlier in one of their brief conversations touching the case. There was a part of Sara Farnese that was beyond reach, a secret part that defined her. Nic believed it was there that the riddle of these bizarre deaths lay. Marco Costa had no way of knowing whether this was true. All he understood was that he did not envy the young any more, not Nic, not Sara Farnese. They had yet to place their hands into life's flames. They had yet to acknowledge their existence. Not Sara Farnese, though, the old man thought. She had been burned already, and in ways he could not begin to comprehend.

'Will you sit with me?' he asked. 'And listen to some music?'

'Of course,' she said, smiling warily.

Marco Costa pushed his wheelchair over to the hi-fi unit and found the CD. He put on Dylan, played loud, singing 'Idiot Wind' and was amazed that back in 1975, when he first heard this scream of rage and pain, he wondered what the hell it was all about.

Twenty-six

Luca Rossi's white face was miserable in the moonlight. The visitor he had brought along was refusing to come to the house. He wanted to meet Nic outside the farm, under the eye of the police team stationed there but out of earshot. Rossi explained this in a low, mournful voice as they walked.

'You should be asking yourself what a man like this is doing here, Nic,' Rossi said firmly. 'Why don't they leave us alone?'

He knew the answer and didn't want to say it. Falcone was right. Hanrahan was involved in some way, perhaps on behalf of the elusive figure of Cardinal Denney.

'What harm does it do to talk?' Nic asked.

Rossi grimaced as if to say: you never learn. The harm is you just don't know who you're talking to.

Hanrahan stood beyond the almond tree by the rickety wall that formed the perimeter of what once was a sheep field. He was half illuminated by the headlights of a black Mercedes with Vatican number plates parked some twenty metres away. Costa recognized it as one of the city's pool cars, familiar symbols of authority. An anonymous driver sat behind the wheel, the light of the radio reflecting on his wan face. Hanrahan wore a dark overcoat in spite of the heat and was smoking a cigar. The stocky Irishman stared at the cops around him until they dispersed, Rossi with them. Costa walked over and took the hand that was offered.

'Nice place,' Hanrahan said. 'All yours one day, I guess. A big house for a cop.'

'What do you want?'

Hanrahan stared at him. 'A little gratitude wouldn't go amiss. I took risks sending you that tape, Nic. There are people who'd be less than pleased if they knew what I'd done.'

'Thanks,' he said curtly. 'Is that good enough? It was all too late. We had another body by then. We knew Stefano Rinaldi wasn't the one.'

He shrugged. 'I was just offering a little something. I wasn't to know what would happen in the meantime.' Hanrahan pulled out a pack of cigars, took out a half-smoked stub, and offered him one. Costa shook his head.

'Clean-living boy,' the Irishman said cheerfully. 'That's what they all say about you. And now you've got that woman living in your house. How's that going? I saw her on the TV. She's an attractive piece of work. Quite a private life too. I saw that trick you played, pretending there was something special between the two of you. Do you really think anyone would fall for that? With all these cops around?'

'Who knows?' He didn't like Hanrahan. The man was too indirect. Talking to him was like juggling with eels.

'Perhaps you could take a shine to her. Anyone could, I imagine. Though I can't help wondering what would make an intelligent, attractive woman behave like that.

I'm a single man by choice. Young people. It's just laziness. All these empty lives. Why does it happen?'

Costa waved the stinking cigar smoke out of his face. 'I'm asking one more time before I go back in. What do you want?'

Hanrahan frowned. 'You don't like small talk, do you? It's a shame. You'll never make a diplomat. It's important to learn how to deal with people. Going straight to the point is not necessarily the best way. You have to learn about nuances. You have to be patient.'

Costa looked at his watch then glanced back at the house. Hanrahan waited, knowing he wouldn't walk away.

'I gave you something. It was a gift. The next one doesn't come for free.'

'The next one being what?'

Hanrahan threw the cigar on the ground and stubbed it out with his toe. 'A name. Maybe the name you're looking for. I don't know.'

Costa blinked back the fury rising in him. 'Let me make sure I understand,' he said slowly. 'This is a man who has killed four people and you know who he is? You think you can bargain for that? I could get you arrested right now for withholding information and throw you in jail until you talk. I could tell those reporters round the corner and let them sweat your ass off.'

'But why would you do that?' Hanrahan asked, bemused. 'I wouldn't say anything. To you. Or to the press. Where's the gain for any of us? And besides it's just a name. I don't know if it's useful or not. I just think it would be . . . productive if you talked to him.'

'Jesus, Hanrahan. What if someone else is killed?'

'It could be the wrong man. Who's to know?'

'You make me sick. Haggling over something like this.'

Hanrahan sighed. 'You're so young. I thought I was doing the right thing going to you, not through Falcone. Perhaps I made a mistake. Perhaps I should just let you go your own way. Whatever that may be.'

'I can get Falcone here in ten minutes if that's what you want.'

The Irishman scowled. 'No. I don't think so. You haven't even asked the obvious question. What's the point?'

Costa gripped the Irishman's dark coat in his right hand and pulled the man to him. 'I asked the question. It was the first thing I said. "What do you want?" Remember?'

Hanrahan released himself from Costa's fist and raised a conciliatory hand. 'Apologies. I forgot. You don't do small talk. Let's get straight to the point then. There's a man in the Vatican who needs his freedom and a particular kind of freedom at that. I require you to look the other way when I ask. Nothing more.'

'Denney? You're not serious. You think you can trade for that?'

Hanrahan looked surprised. 'You can trade for anything.'

'A cardinal of the Vatican? You don't need us. You can let Denney go yourself. There's a helipad behind those walls, isn't there? Get him out that way. Don't waste my time with this.'

'Nic.' Hanrahan looked disappointed. 'If it were that easy don't you think it would be done by now? Even if the cardinal were predisposed to leave like that, and he isn't, probably with good reason, we couldn't make it look as if the Vatican approved his departure. There are too many . . . strings attached. All he would require is discreet free passage to the airport, say. We could organize a private plane there. You'd just turn a blind eye for fifty minutes, no more.'

'Are you asking for this on his behalf? Did he send you here?'

'Not exactly. His life's going through a little turmoil too right now. People he thought were on his side are starting to desert him. He's an old man. Confused. A little scared. Don't believe everything you've heard about him. He was a good priest once. You should know what the press are like better than most. Do you think every word they wrote about your own father was true?'

Costa glanced back at the farmhouse, wondering what was going on there. 'My father isn't a crook. From what I hear Denney is.'

'So you know he's guilty? You're judge and jury in this too?'

'No. I'm a cop. I hand him over to people who make that decision.'

Hanrahan laughed. 'And you the Italian? Here, where nothing's ever black and white. Can you hear yourself talking?'

'I can. And one more thing. What if Denney has something to do with these murders? Maybe I'm letting go of a material witness. Or worse, someone who's involved.'

Hanrahan's bluff manner disappeared immediately. 'Nic, I swear to you. The cardinal has nothing to do with this. He doesn't even know I'm here. I'm just trying to grease a few wheels for all of us. You with your problem, me with mine.'

Kill two birds with one stone. The Irishman was so like Falcone. He tried to discern some unease on Hanrahan's rugged face. 'So Denney doesn't know Sara Farnese?'

'Why the hell should he?' Hanrahan answered, shrugging his stocky shoulders. 'You mean that call to the Vatican? Let me tell you. There are forty people working off that same switchboard, for lots of different officials. So someone answered, "Denney's office" by mistake. You ring again and you could get mine. It doesn't make him part of this any more than it does me or the other people who get their messages taken that way. But I've been looking at some of those we've had working there. And maybe – I don't promise this – but maybe there's something there for you. Nothing to lay at Michael Denney's door. Just a name, that's all.' Hanrahan caught him with a dark, intent eye. 'Maybe there's a little interesting history. But it doesn't come for free, my boy. I don't have to lift a damn finger to help you. Remember that.'

Nic Costa took a few steps away from him and looked down the dirt track. The other cops were smoking underneath the old carob tree that marked the farm boundary. They looked deeply bored. It was insane to think they could draw out anyone like this. Falcone was clutching at straws.

He came back and looked at Hanrahan. 'I'm not convinced.'

'To hell with it then. What else am I supposed to do?'

'Fix a meeting. Me and Denney. Inside the Vatican, naturally. Whenever, wherever he pleases.'

Hanrahan's eyes sparkled. 'Oh! Is that all?'

'That's all for now,' Costa said and turned to go.

'Hey.'

He felt a strong hand on his arm.

'Are you serious?' Hanrahan asked. 'You really want me to book an appointment between some junior Rome cop and a cardinal of the Catholic Church, a man you people can't wait to throw in jail? How do you think I'm going to sell that to him?'

'Tell him I want to talk about religion,' Costa said. 'Tell him I'm thinking of converting.'

Then he walked off to the farm without waiting for Hanrahan's answer.

Twenty-seven

She was sitting by the fireplace, next to the old man, who was asleep in his wheelchair. Sara put a finger to her lips and indicated to Costa to come to the foot of the stairs.

'You were gone a long time.'

'Sorry.'

'Was it worth while?'

'Possibly. I can't talk about it, Sara.'

She frowned, disappointed. 'I understand. I gave him the tablets he asked for. He was very animated for a while. And then . . .'

She looked down.

'Thanks for being so kind to him. He can be quite a handful at times.' He meant that. She had gone out of her way to amuse the old man, and in doing so revealed something about herself too.

'It was a pleasure,' she said. 'I mean that. Nic . . .' She seemed a different woman, he thought. Somehow his father had relaxed her, given her some perspective. 'He loves you deeply. He's worried about you. About how you'll cope.'

'*He*'s worried about *me*?'

'Of course. Why would he worry about himself? He knows what's going to happen. He accepts it.'

She was right. Sometimes he allowed himself to be led into blind alleys.

' "I met a man with seven wives . . ." '

'I'm sorry.'

In the low yellow light of the farm, dressed simply, unaffected by events outside, as if this place were a sanctuary, she was extraordinarily beautiful. He was grateful for her presence. But this was all a mistake. The man would never come to the farm, not with so many cops outside. And she, unconsciously perhaps, was beginning to work on him. He would be sleeping a few steps away from her tonight. Already he was wondering what she looked like in bed, how it would feel to touch her skin.

'Distractions,' Nic Costa said by way of explanation. 'Everywhere.'

She shook her head, not understanding. 'Goodnight,' she said and, before he could move, took his arms and kissed him gently on the cheek.

He watched her go up the stairs, then, for the first time in many a year, walked into the kitchen, took down the ageing bottle of *grappa* that sat there and poured himself a tumbler of the thick, colourless liquid.

Twenty-eight

Only thirteen hacks and TV people braved the night in the roped-off area which the police had set aside for the media. For a while they passed around beer and cigarettes, knowing there would be no action until daylight, and maybe not then either. The cops were keeping this woman to themselves. Maybe, the word went, one of them had good reason.

Just after midnight they were woken by a noise. A newcomer arrived, on foot it seemed. Denis Renard was wide awake; he wasn't drunk. The paparazzo from the French celebrity weekly had already decided he would be the first to get a decent photograph of Sara Farnese. In the darkness he glowered at this odd figure coming out of nowhere, asking questions, soliciting help as if he deserved it.

'Where you from, friend?' he asked.

The man shone a torch in his face. He wasn't big but he looked powerful in a way, not the sort to mess with.

'*Time* magazine,' the man said.

Denis Renard rolled over onto his front and swore into the dry grass. It was the ones who lied that you had to watch. *Time*. As if this was their kind of story. He knew a chancer when he saw one. This was a rival, maybe, with a little digital snap camera in his pocket, looking to fix something. He was trouble, to be watched.

The paparazzo set the alarm on his watch to 6.22: sunrise.

When it rang the man was gone. Denis Renard cursed himself. He was going to be first to get a picture of the woman. No one would stop him. Not even some faker from '*Time* magazine'.

Twenty-nine

Nic Costa rose at daybreak knowing he had to run. It was an addiction. When he ran he felt in control of himself. There was a stillness that came with the constant effort and the onset of exhaustion, a solitude which sometimes produced the most extraordinary insights. He had solved a case once, an awkward and violent domestic tragedy, one morning at six when he raced along the bank of the Tiber near his apartment, beneath the shadow of the Castel Sant'Angelo. It was a source of satisfaction, of consolation. Whatever Falcone might think of him leaving Sara briefly, he needed it now more than ever.

The house was still. The sun peeked above the eastern horizon intent on searing another August day. He wore shorts, a white T-shirt and the battered trainers that had survived the last two months, a record. Nic Costa quietly let himself out of the front door and walked down the drive to where the police cars were parked. The shift should have changed at midnight. He might not know the men who had now come to guard them. He steeled himself for an argument, then halted. Luca Rossi was in the first Fiat saloon glaring at him through the window.

Only one other cop in the adjoining cars was awake and he showed little interest in what was going on.

The big man got out, stretched, yawned and then said, 'You've got to be kidding me, Nic. Today of all days.'

'You should be home. Time for bed.'

'Yeah. And what's for me there? Too late to start drinking. I can sleep in cars. I've done it before.'

It was all a lie. Nic Costa understood what the big man was doing: staying there to look after him. He was touched and a little ashamed Rossi felt he needed the attention.

'Let me repeat myself,' Rossi said. 'You're not even thinking about this.'

'Team motto, Uncle Luca. Run or die.'

'You mean run *and* die? We're setting you up as a target here, kid. Don't make it too easy for him.'

Costa spread his arms wide, pointing down both sides of the narrow dirt track that led to the farm entrance. 'Oh, come on. Just up and down the track. Where's the harm? What's going to bite me? Mosquitoes?'

'Don't do it,' the big man pleaded. 'Just go back inside. Drink some coffee. Be patient.'

'Uncle Luca . . .'

The big man felt his heart sink. He knew it was pointless to argue. 'I am not your fu— Oh, hell, what's the point? Why do you do this to me?'

'I've got to run. I've got to get some space inside me.'

'Shit,' Luca Rossi sighed. 'How far? How long?'

'Just a little way. I won't even make it to the public road. I'll stick to the drive, that's all.'

'OK,' Rossi grunted. 'But I've got no one who can

keep up with you. And if you're not back here in ten minutes I start screaming. Understood?'

Nic Costa grinned and opened his arms wide.

'No hugging, no funny stuff,' the big man said forcefully. 'You got your own way, didn't you? Now let's have it done with.'

Costa laughed and was gone, down the track, kicking up dust, glad to feel the cool morning air in his face, glad that, for a few minutes at least, he could put the complex mix of problems in the farm into some kind of perspective. He thought of his father and how much the old man had enjoyed the previous night. He thought, too, of Sara Farnese. It had given her pleasure to be such good company. That seemed a rarity in her life. He could only speculate what she would be like if it happened more regularly.

He'd lied to Luca Rossi. The track wasn't long enough. He needed to pound the public road for a while too, as fast as his powerful legs could take him. The hard basalt stone that paved the surface of the ancient highway was part of his childhood. Once, when he was thirteen, after a row with his father, he had half jogged, half sprinted all day until he was ready to drop. Some fifty kilometres from home, exhausted, he had called the farm from a village bar. The old man had come cheerfully to fetch him and laughed off the whole thing as a grand adventure. They'd been closer after that. His efforts had somehow marked him out for the old man. Giulia was too scared to argue with him, Marco, being the eldest, too smart. Neither would have countenanced that kind of escape and Nic knew, from the moment the car arrived and his father had stepped out grinning from ear to ear, that this denoted some change in the nature of their relationship. It didn't become easier, just closer in some unspoken, mysterious way, as if they shared part of the same mind.

He spotted the press pack down the road, put his head down and sprinted past them. They scarcely gave him a second glance. It was early. All the associations were wrong too. They were looking for a beautiful woman and a smartly dressed cop, not a sweating runner in a tattered T-shirt and grubby trainers beating his way down the road. He allowed himself one look back to make sure no one was coming, then kicked hard and headed into the scrub. There was a narrow path of rock and dust that led behind the farm. He could take that, double-back around the house and surprise Luca Rossi by appearing out of nowhere.

The morning was turning out to be glorious, full of light and beauty. He put on some speed, dodged beneath a couple of olive trees, writhing and gnarled like old men, sprinted hard then stopped. The back of the farm was less than fifty metres away from this position. He could see into the windows. In the guest bedroom he could just about make out Sara moving around. She wore a scarlet shirt, nothing else. He felt guilty watching her like this but it was hard to stop. Every time they met, her actions had been shaped by the presence of others. Seen like this, she was, perhaps, the person that lived inside the hard, fragile shell she showed to the outside world. It worried him. He was becoming obsessed and not just by her beauty. There was something beneath the surface of Sara Farnese he wanted to see, to touch, and to know.

He breathed deeply, getting back his strength, leaned forward and placed his hands on his knees. It had been a good idea, whatever Uncle Luca thought.

A voice behind him, a hard voice, with a foreign accent, said suddenly, 'Smile.'

The sweat went cold on Nic Costa's skin. He turned. The man was skeletally thin and entirely bald, with a black shirt and trousers and staring blue eyes. He had a large SLR camera in his hands and was about to bring it up to his face.

'Who the hell are you?'

'Press.' He fired off a couple of shots then moved to improve the angle.

'This is private property. I want that film right now.'

'Fuck you,' the photographer hissed from behind the lens.

Nic Costa sighed. It was so obvious. He'd seen the trick many times. They'd try to make you mad just to get a better shot. A fist raised to the lens made the picture. Passive people didn't sell.

'OK,' he said. 'Fire away.'

He stood upright, folding his arms in front of him and smiled, a big, cheesy smile, like that of a teenager out for the day.

The photographer grunted. This wasn't what he wanted.

'Do I get paid?' Costa asked, then stopped. Someone else was coming. One of the team, he guessed, and about time too. They were supposed to be watching the perimeter. They should never have let the photographer get this far.

He peered at the figure walking rapidly up the track. He was about thirty, powerfully built, with a striking face and dark, straight hair. The check shirt and loose jeans didn't fit properly. The black spectacles he wore seemed out of place. Costa didn't recognize him. But the photographer did.

'Not you?' the paparazzo yelled. 'Hey. This is my find. You fuck off back where you belong. Back to . . .' He made a sarcastic quote mark gesture with his fingers. '*Time* magazine.'

The man in the checked shirt said nothing. He was staring beyond both of them, staring at the house. Costa said, 'You've both got to get out of here. Before there's trouble.'

Then he followed the gaze of the one in the checked shirt. His eyes were fixed on the window. Sara Farnese was there, watching this odd confrontation, as if she were trying to make sense of it.

There was a noise from the photographer, a gasp of surprise and hurt. The checked shirt had pulled a flick knife from somewhere and had stuck it into his ribs. The wounded man was stumbling to the ground, his hand clutching his chest as if he were trying to stop his life running out onto the dry, rocky ground.

Nic Costa watched him, watched the check shirt change his focus, away from the paparazzo, first to the distant figure of Sara and then to him.

Sometimes you fight. Sometimes you run.

'The blood of the martyrs . . .' the man said and took a swift step towards him.

Costa didn't move, finishing the sentence for him, 'Is the seed of the Church.'

The man stopped a couple of metres away, puzzled, watching. His eyes narrowed behind the ill-fitting glasses. This was not part of the plan.

'None of it's true,' Costa said. 'I never touched her. It was all a game. To get you here. And it worked.' He opened his hands, a calm, conciliatory gesture. 'Let's call it a day, huh? This place is crawling with police.'

The man looked around him, amused, as if to say: *really*? Something was wrong. They should have been here already. They should never have let him get this far.

He roared, coming forward with an unexpected turn of speed, the knife, now red, held firm in his right hand. Nic Costa feinted to one side, dodging the power of the attack, and began to sprint. There was no way he could reason with this man any more. He needed to get out of there, to distract him away from the wounded photographer, to bring in the rest of the team.

He dashed through the thorny scrub, feeling it rip his thighs, then breathed deeply, thought of nothing but the speed in his legs and leaned into the light morning wind. He'd taken no more than four long strides when something fiery and painful bit into his shoulder.

Nic Costa's foot struck a hard, solid object. He fell onto the dry, brown ground, slamming his head onto a rock, dragging at the thing in his back. The blade was lodged deep. He grasped the handle and felt like screaming, in pain and anger. He should have been able to pull it out and get back to running away from this deadly lunatic who seemed to have risen from the rocks of the parched scrubland.

He stumbled drowsily to his feet, anxiously scanning the dead farmland.

There was a figure on the shimmering horizon, approaching fast.

Sometimes you fight. Sometimes you run.

And sometimes, Nic Costa thought, his head reeling into concussion, you had no choice at all.

The dark shape grew larger. He wondered what else

the man carried in his armoury, wondered where the rest of the team were. A cop didn't deserve to die like a saint. It seemed inappropriate, somehow, almost profane.

Nic Costa slumped to his knees, feeling his consciousness begin to fade.

Then there were voices. Loud voices. Shouting. Two people only, and one of them familiar. One of them – the word came easily in his present state; he felt no shame in thinking it – cherished.

He lay prone on the hard, arid earth, feeling the darkness begin to swamp his mind, listening to Sara Farnese. It sounded as if she was begging for his life.

Thirty

Alicia Vaccarini spent the night tethered to the chair against the upright wooden beam in the curious octagonal chamber where Gino Fosse had left her. There had been a sound outside only once; the noise of a drunk going home, singing. She was gagged. She was tied. There was nothing she could do, nothing she could hope to achieve. He would return soon, she knew, and then there would be no more delays. This madman believed, in some strange way, that he was doing her a favour. The manner of his 'apology' left her full of dread. There was no avenue for persuasion, no prospect of clemency. He was set upon this path, and was distraught that something – something on the television – had disturbed his well-planned sequence of events.

She had slept, for how long she could only guess, and woke when daylight began to filter into the room through the narrow, slitted windows. There had to be people nearby. There had to be someone who would come, she believed. Even in August, when the heat had depleted the streets, this was still Rome. The city was alive beyond these crumbling medieval walls. The guards would soon be opening up offices in the parliament building. Secretaries would be delivering mail. Staff at the small neighbourhood café where she normally drank her morning *macchiato* would be wondering why she was absent. Alicia Vaccarini was a woman of habit. There would be those who noticed her absence. By lunchtime, she believed, someone would question it. She had been due to attend a reception for a visiting party of Brussels bureaucrats at ten. It was unknown for her to miss such events. She was diligent. She had nothing else to do.

So by two, three at the latest, there would be someone checking her apartment, discovering she had never returned home the previous day. The police would be involved. Questions would be asked, with no ready answers.

She tried to convince herself there was hope in this slow, muddled series of small discoveries. It was impossible. He would be back and when he did he would achieve what he wished. He would be anxious to be done with her and move on to whatever came next.

The book was still open on the floor. She refused to look at it. The patron saint of musicians deserved to be a brighter, happier figure, she thought. Not a white marble corpse lying in a shroud, with three visible wounds on her neck. Alicia Vaccarini had only one, and it was shallow and ceased to bleed soon after Fosse had raced from the room. One wound was enough, she believed, and closed her eyes, wondering if there was somewhere, within her, the ability to pray. It was a time for desperate measures.

Then there was a sound from downstairs. Her heart leapt in hope. She heard footsteps rising. Familiar ones: determined and heavy. She closed her eyes and wept.

When she opened them Gino Fosse was standing in front of her looking confused. He was wearing a checked shirt covered in dirt and torn at the front. His mouth hung open as he gasped for breath. She didn't know what to make of him, was unable to decide whether his odd appearance was good or bad. Then he started to speak, a rapid-fire babble of insane nonsense about the Church and the perfidy of women. The phone rang. It was on a sideboard next to the window opposite her. He walked over and picked it up. She listened intently. There was a shade of subservience in his voice. It was the first time she had ever noticed it. He seemed so confident, so capable of acting individually, most of the time.

He went quiet, his head fell down. This was bad news. She closed her eyes for a moment and prayed someone would come, that soon there would be the sound of the police beating down the doors to this odd monastic prison.

'No,' he said insistently down the phone. 'It's impossible. You can't ask that. Where will I go?'

He went quiet, listening. His shoulders hunched over and his face contorted with grief and fury. But he would do as he was told, she thought, and there, perhaps, lay salvation.

'*Shit!*' he yelled.

He threw the phone on the floor. He kicked it across the carpet. She watched as he dashed around the tiny, airless room, snatching at curtains, ornaments, anything he could lay his hands on, smashing these objects to the ground, screaming obscene nonsense.

They'll hear, she thought. Someone knows. Someone is coming. *And they will hear.*

He went behind her. She felt cold. Two clammy hands came around her neck and clasped her cheeks. He turned her head to look up at the disgusting, frightening photographs on the ceiling, photographs she had avoided up to that point. They were black and white. The women in them looked back, their faces immobile, as if they didn't care or wanted to wish themselves out of the frame.

'See what happens,' he murmured into her ear, half crying. 'See what's done and can't be undone.'

Her bladder failed and a warm stinging stream ran down her legs. The hands moved again. The gag relaxed. He untied the knot at the back of her head and let the gag fall from her. Alicia Vaccarini moaned, pleased she could breathe easily again.

Then he came back around her once more and she looked into his eyes. He'd changed again. This was a different person, one full of conviction and determination. His hand came up suddenly and slapped her across the face. She yelped. The hand swept backwards, his knuckles hard against her lips. She could taste blood. She could sense something new: an intense, personal hatred for her.

'Whore,' he hissed. 'You're all the same. The doorway of the devil. You know that?'

'Please . . .'

'Shut up!' His fist came up again, hesitated. She got the message. She was quiet.

He wiped his mouth with his hand, thinking. She watched him, silent. It was beyond protest, beyond pleading. The decision now was his, and he was crazy, violent one moment, repentant, or at least uncertain, the next.

'They're coming,' he said. '*Here!* To my home. *My* home.'

She spoke very quietly, very calmly. 'Don't make it any worse than it is.'

He stared at her, wondering. 'It could be worse? How?'

There was some light in his eyes. Some kind of doubt. There was room for her to work. 'I can help you,' she said. 'I have friends. I can tell the police you've been kind. That you didn't mean it. We all make mistakes.'

'We all burn in Hell.'

'No,' she said. 'That's an old story. Even the Church doesn't believe that any more.'

'Then they're stupid.' He sighed. 'I'm sorry. Truly, I'm sorry.'

She breathed deeply for the first time in hours, finding a flicker of hope in his apology.

'It's all right,' Alicia Vaccarini said. 'Everything will be all right.'

His face was so odd. In some light he would be handsome. In another, not hideous but exaggerated somehow, like a figure from a medieval painting.

'You don't understand, Alicia. I'm sorry because I can't do you justice. The church in Trastevere. The means of your death, a holy means. Something which could help wash away your sins. Save you perhaps. All of this is impossible now. They're coming to take away my home. They think they can trap me. They're very, very stupid.'

'It can work out. I can help.'

'Perhaps.' He was thinking. He was as rational now as he had appeared in the restaurant. Something occupied him. He went over to the pile of jazz CDs strewn on the floor, sifted quickly through them until he found what he wanted, then put it on the hi-fi. The sound of a high, sweeping electric violin filled the room. Then he came back to her.

'Have you ever watched a man smash a brick with his hand, Alicia? The martial arts place I go to. They show you how to do that. They teach you the secret.'

'No,' she answered quietly, not wishing to excite him.

'The secret is you don't try to hit the brick. What you aim at is something imaginary a little way behind it. That is what you're trying to destroy. You get the result you want by focusing on that hidden place, by making that your target. And in doing so you smash the brick. Do you understand?'

'I think so. Could you untie me, please? I'm very stiff. I need to go to the bathroom.'

He shook his head, annoyed she appeared to miss his point. 'This is important, Alicia. Our true goal's beyond. It's not something that we see. What we do along the way, what we touch, what we destroy, is irrelevant. It's the end point that matters. Being able to see it with your inner eye. To know you'll get there.'

She looked at him, not liking what she saw. 'They'll be here soon. It would look best if they didn't find me like this. You can understand that, can't you?'

'Of course,' he said and walked behind her. The earth began to shift. The chair moved through ninety degrees as Fosse tilted it forward until Alicia Vaccarini was on her knees, head hanging down, eyes fixed on the worn, stained carpet.

She waited for his touch, waited to feel him working on the rope. It never happened. Gino Fosse came back to stand in front of her again. This time he was holding the sword, the bright, glittering sword that had cut her once already.

'Jesus Christ.' She looked at the blade and felt the

breath disappearing from her lungs. 'Don't,' she whispered.

But Fosse wasn't even noticing. His eyes were on the chair to which she was tied and the space that lay beyond her neck.

He walked to one side of her. Only his ankles were visible: white socks in black trainers. She heard the sound of the sword cutting through the hot, dank air of the room and a strange memory came to her from a history course long ago: Anne Boleyn going to her death at the hands of the Calais swordsman, a bitter kindness on Henry VIII's part, to save her from the conventional executioner's axe. The man had been brought in for the occasion because of his reputation. The sword had a clean, deadly efficiency impossible with the axe. He'd hidden the blade beneath the straw, stood behind her, listened to her last words, then decapitated the disgraced queen with a single blow.

She could hear it: unseen, the silver blade dashing at her back as her executioner made his practice strokes. Then there was silence. She could picture him drawing it to his shoulders, turning in a deadly forceful arc.

Without thinking, she lifted her chin and forced her eyes shut. She didn't wish to see a thing. She didn't want to think of the blade missing her neck, smashing into the back of her skull.

In the curious practicality of the moment she recalled something further of the history lesson: Anne's last words, 'To Jesus Christ I commend my soul'.

It was impossible to say them. It would be an insult, she thought.

The music ended, then looped back on itself. The wailing violin began to dance again.

Thirty-one

San Giovanni, once a refuge for fourth-century pilgrims, was now a modern hospital that sprawled through countless buildings covering a vast parcel of the Caelian Hill. The complex stretched from the old narrow road that led to the church of San Clemente across to the traffic-choked modern highway that fed streams of cars, buses and trucks into the piazza from the south. Only minutes away too was the Clivus Scauri, where Falcone and his men were engaged in the discovery of a further victim and the disappearance of the priest who once, albeit briefly, worked the corridors of the place where Nic Costa now lay on a table in a small cubicle, his head hurting like hell.

Luca Rossi and Sara Farnese had only just argued their way into the room. They sat on the bench seat watching the nurse bandage him, watching the way he listened to the doctor talk about concussion and how, all things being equal, he ought to spend the day in a ward just to make sure there were no lingering after-effects. The knife wound was minor. The knock to his head when he fell and hit the rock had left a livid but compact blood-filled bruise on his right temple. Still, Nic Costa was alive and maddeningly ignorant of the reason for it. He waited for the doctor to go away, then turned to the big man.

'I don't like the look on your face, Uncle Luca. You took him?'

'We wish,' Rossi replied miserably.

Costa was wide-eyed with amazement. 'Christ. What more do you need?'

Sara Farnese looked at her feet. Rossi glowered at him from across the room. 'Hey, kid. Don't get precious with me.'

'There were how many men there?'

'*Enough!*' The big man's flabby white face turned an odd shade of half-angry pink. 'Eight. Maybe ten. Think about it. They were there to protect the farm. Which was where you were supposed to be. None of them knew you were running around doing this crazy stuff somewhere else. Falcone is going to tear the skin off my back for letting you go out there. Except, of course, it wasn't even where I thought you were going to be. Remember the deal? You stay in the drive? Where we could be close by?'

His head was painful, confused. He did remember now, and Luca Rossi was right. He'd no one to blame but himself. He remembered, too, the sight of Sara at the window and the terror on her face.

'I'm sorry, Luca. I was an idiot.'

'Yeah, well . . .' The big man cast a glance at Sara next to him. 'You survived. No thanks to us. And we've got a name. And another body. Enough there for Falcone to get happy about or crucify us with, depending on his mood.'

'I'll check myself out. I have to go there.'

'Nic, the doctors . . .' Sara began to say.

'This one's even less pretty than the others,' Rossi

grumbled, taking it as read that Costa would leave hospital. 'What can you do?'

He moved his shoulder and was pleased by the small amount of pain that resulted. 'It's not bad. Besides, Luca, you need me. I saw this man, remember?'

Rossi looked at the woman again. Costa couldn't work it out. There was something he disliked about Sara Farnese. It was so powerful he seemed to hate even sitting next to her in the hospital cubicle.

'Doesn't matter that you saw him, Nic. Weren't you listening? We've got his name. Miss Farnese here provided it once we'd got you into the ambulance. Seems she had it all along.'

His head hurt even more after that. She was staring at the white wall, intent on nothing. Her hair was tousled. It made her look different. Maybe there hadn't been time for her to do anything else. She'd just left the house with him, unable to put on the mask she normally wore to keep the world from touching her.

'I've got some calls to make,' Rossi said. 'Your father decided to stay at home once the ambulance people said you'd be fine. I'll let him know things are OK all the same. I'm outside when you want me. It's two minutes away, max. They can take her some place else. Falcone says the protective custody thing is still on. I guess you won't want her back at the farm so they're making other arrangements.'

He patted the pack of cigarettes in his pocket. 'Smoking time too.' Then he was gone from the room, out into the long corridor illuminated by cold fluorescent lights.

Nic Costa pushed himself upright off the hospital

table. The cut in his shoulder was minor. His head would get better. It was all a matter of time.

She still wouldn't look at him.

'Thanks,' he said finally.

Sara turned. Her eyes were scared, astonished too. 'What?'

'I don't know what happened out there, Sara. But you stopped him. Thanks.'

Her head moved from side to side, her long, unkempt hair shifting slowly around with the motion. 'I just saw him from the window, Nic. I knew something was wrong. When I got there he ran away. I imagine he was scared everyone else was turning up. He didn't want witnesses.'

That was a lie. He knew it for sure. He'd heard them talking.

'You spoke to him.'

'Of course I did! I screamed at him to stop. What do you expect?'

'No.' His memory was hazy yet there was something fixed there: he recalled the tenor of their conversation. 'You spoke to him. He answered back. It was more than that. You knew who he was.'

'Enough to know his name. He used to hang around the Vatican Library when I was there. We'd talk sometimes.'

'You didn't . . .' There was no easy way of asking.

'What?' she answered, furious. 'Sleep with him? No. There are men in Rome who've been denied that privilege. I hope that doesn't come as too much of a shock.'

'I'm sorry.'

'Oh, God.' She shook her head, eyes closed, miserable. 'I'm the one who's sorry. You don't know what you're saying. I saw him. I yelled at him until he went.

Then as soon as he was gone I yelled until the police came. For you and that photographer. He's worse than you, they say. He'll be in here for some time.'

It was possible she was right. He could have imagined the entire exchange.

'Someone else is dead?'

'So they say.'

'You know him?'

She picked up her bag and put it on her knee. 'I think I should leave. They want me to stay somewhere else. They say they're sending another police team to pick me up.'

Costa got up off the table and walked, a little shakily, across the room. He sat next to her on the bench, very close. He wanted to make a point: that she couldn't chase him away so easily.

'Do you know him?' he asked again.

The old Sara looked frankly at him, unafraid. 'It was a woman.'

He thought about the bold, unabashed way in which she said it.

'So did you know her?'

'I think I slept with her once. Is that what you want to hear?'

'You think?'

'No. I did. They showed me a picture. She was a politician apparently. I slept with her a few months ago. I can't be certain. I don't keep that kind of diary. I apologize. It happened once. It was her idea. Not my kind of thing really.'

He sighed. She could still shake him, even though he knew this was what she intended.

'I don't understand any of this, Sara. I don't

understand why you do it. I don't understand why you never gave us her name.'

She laughed, a dry, deliberate laugh, one that was supposed to make him hate her. 'You're so old-fashioned, Nic. You and your father. I love him. Really. I could talk to him for hours because it's like talking to someone from another time. But the world's not the way you two imagine it. Maybe it never was. You ask me why I never gave you her name? What makes you think I knew her name in the first place? This was just one night. That's all.'

It made no sense. It couldn't be the whole story. 'But why?'

'Because . . .' She had to hunt for the answer. 'You've your kind of love. I've mine. We're different. What happened satisfied me. Then it's gone, with nothing lingering, nothing to go stale. No awkward attachments. No bitterness, no pain.'

'So it's not a kind of love at all?' he said without thinking. 'And it isn't gone. Something stays behind. Something that may go wrong. Then people get screwed up. Sometimes horribly.'

Her eyes grew wide. 'So this is my fault?' she demanded angrily. 'You think I'm to blame for what's happened?'

It was a stupid thing to say in a way but she had misread his point. 'Not for a minute.'

He stood up, trying to convince himself he didn't feel too bad. His head was clearing rapidly.

'I knew you wouldn't stay here,' she said. 'Why can't you just leave it alone?'

He watched her get up and collect her bag, organize herself for whatever lay ahead.

'It's what they pay me for.'

'No they don't. No one pays you to risk your life.'

'Next time I'll be more careful.'

Sara Farnese stared into his face. Then she touched his cheek gently with two slender fingers. It was a deliberate act, one he could not mistake.

'Nic,' she said carefully. 'If you asked, would they take you off this case?'

The question threw him. 'I guess so. But why would I want to do that?'

'Because I want you to? This is about me. There may be things you'll find out that I don't want you to know. Things that will make you loathe me.'

'I'm a cop. They give you drugs to make you unshockable.'

'It's not a joke.'

'I know. Don't worry about it.'

She glanced at him, uneasy. 'Then you'll ask for something else?'

'Are you kidding? This is shaping up to be the biggest thing of my career. What would I look like if I backed out now? I don't give up on things. Not just because they might be hard or awkward or make me face decisions I'd rather avoid. That doesn't get you anywhere.'

'It makes life easy,' she said.

'It makes life dull and boring and . . . perhaps pointless even.'

She nodded. 'I thought you'd say that.'

'Thank you. Now, you face a decision. I have to go back to the team. You can stay in this safe house of Falcone's. Or I can make the case for you to go back to the farm. Not for my sake, you understand. It's my father. He enjoys your company. You seem to enjoy his.'

She didn't recoil from the idea. He was glad. 'Will he agree? This awful boss of yours? I don't like him. He's too . . . hard.'

'Falcone thinks that's what's required of him. If I ask him to let you stay I can't see why he'd object. Let's face it, your security can't be much at risk. You met this man. He didn't harm you. Did he?'

'No,' she said quietly. 'And your safety?'

He'd thought about that already. 'I'll be more careful. Besides, I don't think he'll come back somehow. It's as if he has an agenda. I wasn't really on it. Also I told him the truth. That we just set this up for him, the idea that something was going on between us. I told him it was all a lie.'

Was that the way a psychopath behaved, he wondered? Being so picky about who he killed? A chill, dark thought ran around Nic Costa's head. What if this lunatic had seen him there on the ground, spared his life, then wondered afterwards: what was the point? Would he make the same choice again? Or did you just let the innocent off the hook once and then, the next time, think . . . to hell with it?

There was a sound outside in the corridor. Luca Rossi poked his big white face around the door and looked pointedly at his watch. Costa waved at him for one minute more. She waited until the big man was gone, then said, 'You'll find him, won't you? He's sick. He needs help.'

'We'll find him.' He hesitated, wondering whether he dared ask. 'Sara?'

She didn't like the tone of his voice. She knew, he guessed, what was coming.

'Yes?'

'Are there more names we ought to know? Are there more people like this woman? People who aren't names, just faces?'

'A few. Not recently. I don't know who they are. I don't know how you could reach them.' She said it with such conviction. He wanted to believe her.

'There's a man in the Vatican. Cardinal Denney . . .'

'Nic!' She was the real Sara again. He could see the tears starting in her eyes. 'Is this you talking? Or the policeman? How am I supposed to know who I'm dealing with when you do this to me?'

'You mean the answer would be different depending on who I was?'

'Not at all,' she replied immediately. 'I mean that I want to understand what your interest is. Whether you're asking as a friend. Or because you think it's your job.'

'As a friend.'

'I don't know him,' she insisted. 'Whoever you are.'

Thirty-two

The apartment they gave him was on the third floor of a poky residential building adjoining the Vatican Library. It was unfit for a junior clerk, let alone a cardinal. That it was available at all was significant. Accommodation did not just materialize out of thin air in the Vatican. This was a pre-ordained punishment by the state, one that must have been planned weeks, if not months, before. The perfidy of Neri and Aitcheson was just part of the act. Perhaps Neri had worked in concert with someone on the political side. There was no way of knowing. Only one plain fact consoled Michael Denney: they could never abandon him altogether. If he was handed over to the Italian police or anyone else he could incriminate any number of men in Europe and America. Three present Italian cabinet ministers were deeply in his debt alone. The European Commission was full of his placements. He numbered Lloyd's names and syndicate members of the New York Stock Exchange among those who had, in the good times, been the grateful recipients of any number of generous gestures, from the provision of company for the night to a well-placed inside tip. These were all items he would willingly have traded over the past few months as he attempted to buy safe passage out of the Vatican by any number of different means. It was a disappointment that he had failed, but the power of these weapons remained undiminished. He was grateful, too, that he had declined Neri's whispered hints that the mob could find a way out for him. With hindsight, placing himself in the hands of Neri's friends could have proved the most dangerous option of all.

Now they would all wait, hoping he would die of boredom perhaps, or take a gun and put it to his temple, solving the problem for everybody. It was a poor reward for a lifetime's service. Nevertheless, Denney was a practical man. He could appreciate their reasoning. Trying to rebuild a new Banca Lombardia from the ashes was a desperate venture and one which, in all honesty, was designed more to elicit his own freedom than enrich anyone he could persuade to come along for the ride.

Denney had known the risks and the costs all along. Thirty years ago he had changed from being a loyal and caring servant of the Church to an agent of the Vatican state, part diplomat, part financier. The red, three-cornered biretta of his position soon began to gather dust in the closet. Someone had to do this, he reasoned. The Church was a family, but the Vatican was a nation. He knew from the start that it needed to be defended. Over the years, as he became more worldly, he came to appreciate, too, that it needed to safeguard its interests, to earn money, and, in the final analysis, to deal with the Devil when it suited him. He had come to believe that there was no room for sentiment or misplaced ethics. He never once asked himself whether the young Michael Denney would have thought otherwise. Secular matters made him a secular man. He was not unwise. When he guided Banca Lombardia by pulling Crespi's strings, he had never directed money straight into the coffers of crooks. There would always be a circuitous route, one which would allow him to feign ignorance of the ultimate destination. That, at least, was the idea. Now he knew better.

He had become a material man. He had taken up the reins of commerce and come to understand that there were, on occasion, grey lines between what was legitimate and what was not. He had discovered, too, another side to himself, that his spare, ascetic looks turned the heads of women who, from time to time, offered relief from the stresses of his chosen career.

If, in the end, the venture was a success any peccadilloes would soon be forgotten. When the numbers turned wrong, when scapegoats were sought, it was different. Had three key investments, two in Latin America and one with Russian partners in Spain, delivered the profits he expected, Cardinal Michael Denney knew he would now be a fêted member of the Vatican hierarchy, perhaps expecting further promotion. But the numbers were already looking sour on the day he watched, shell-shocked, as those two planes plummeted into the World Trade Center. The risks were cruelly balanced in the worst possible directions: technology, which was already suffering; some emerging East European economies; and the supposed safe haven of reinsurance. The markets and the staggering global economy cheated him of his prize. The small fish down the food chain began to complain. Lombardia was forced to suspend trading. Then the police and, eventually, the FBI began to take an interest, started to peer through the complex entanglement of financial records – shell companies, obscure trust funds, phoney bank accounts – that stretched around the world.

There were rumours about his personal life. No one regarded him as a priest any more, but the office of cardinal still belonged to the Church. The hint of affairs and the certain knowledge that he loved wine and fine restaurants were matters which bore little weight in the good times. When excuses were sought, they became ammunition in his downfall. Once, he received invitations to some of the most elite dining rooms in Rome where he was a welcome guest who would not always return to his own bed at the end of the evening. Once he was on first-name terms with the finance ministers of several Western nations. A nod from Denney, an expression of interest, could breathe life into a venture struggling to raise capital. He had power and influence and reputation. Then, in a short year, it was gone, accompanied by a whirlwind of vile rumour. Now he was a friendless prisoner trapped inside the tiny, close community of the Vatican, knowing his life would be in jeopardy if he stepped beyond its walls. From this point on it would be a struggle to get even the smallest favour – a meal sent in from a restaurant, a few cleaning trucks to sweep away the media mob from outside a friend's door.

The apartment had a single bedroom, a tiny living room, and a bathroom with a rusty cubicle shower. An ancient gas hob stood in the corner of the main room, perched above a miniature fridge. The place overlooked a dead, grey courtyard full of trash bins. The air-conditioning rattled and wheezed in the cruel August heat and still did little to ameliorate the temperature. Without asking, they had moved in some of his possessions: clothes, books, a handful of paintings. Perhaps Hanrahan hoped it would deaden the blow. The canvases seemed out of place inside these meagre quarters. Denney, who had once loved art, thought he might never look at them again. He was sixty-two and in reasonable health, though mentally he increasingly found himself prone to fits of doubt and depression. He should have known what was coming. No one, that week, had addressed him as 'Your Eminence', an honour to which he was still entitled. No one but Brendan Hanrahan and he found little comfort in that.

Denney knew the stocky Irishman only too well. Hanrahan belonged in the dock as much as any of them. Somehow he possessed the skill and foresight to see the storm clouds gathering long before Denny had – and failed to pass the message on. Hanrahan was a survivor and, in a way, still loyal to an extent, perhaps for the most basic, selfish reasons. It was in his interests to see that Michael Denney remained out of the hands of the police. That doubtless explained the private request for a meeting. Denney looked at his watch. A few minutes later there was a knock on the door.

On time, as ever, Hanrahan let himself in and bowed. 'Your Eminence.'

'I don't know why you bother with that, Brendan. No one else does any more.'

'That says more about them than it does about you.'

'Maybe.' Denney was a slender, fit man with not an ounce of flab. Now his once handsome face was lined by worry and age. He wore a grey suit with no ecclesiastical trappings. He had long ago given up hope of resuming a role in the Church in Italy. He would never wear the cloth again until he was free of Europe, anonymous, with a new name, somewhere near home in Boston perhaps, where a man might disappear for a while and learn how to make others forgive. There was no redemption for him in the Vatican. If he were to recover himself that would have to occur elsewhere, in the close Catholic neighbourhoods of his youth.

'Well, Brendan. These are interesting times. Is there news?'

The visitor sat down in the chair opposite the sofa. From outside the window came the noise of drilling. One of the workmen had told him why. They were improving these modest apartments, one by one. The work, and the racket, would go on for months.

'The woman politician. Vaccarini. The one who voted for you on the committee. She's been murdered.'

Denney's face fell. He looked grief-stricken. 'Good God, man. What are the police doing?'

'Looking for him. He tried to murder one of theirs. After that he killed her. At his home. The house we gave him, if you recall.'

The cardinal was aghast. 'Who?'

'Please,' Hanrahan said harshly. 'If I'm to help we must be frank with each other. There can be no mistake any more. I warned you. I said . . .'

'I know what you said!'

Hanrahan waited for him to recover his composure.

'I'm sorry,' Denney groaned after a while. 'You're absolutely sure of this?'

'It has to be. The police are in the place. Fosse is gone. They've no idea where. Neither have I. Do you?'

Denney leaned forward and folded his hands on his lap, rocking slowly on his chair – a habit he had more and more these days and one which emphasized his age. 'Of course not. Where can he be, for God's sake? He's not a man of the world, is he?'

Hanrahan considered his answer. 'I wouldn't say that. I took a very good look at Fosse's file. He did many interesting things before he worked here. He was attached to the Italian Olympic squad for a while and seems to have been a proficient athlete. He was chaplain to the National Theatre in Palermo and even persuaded them to let him appear in a Pirandello play while he was there. Not bad for a farm boy from Sicily.'

'So what?' Denney grumbled.

'So he sounds pretty resourceful to me. Educated beyond his standing too. And he seems to have a very clear idea of what he wants, what his plan is.'

Denney knew where this was leading. 'Which winds up with me? Is that what you're saying?'

Hanrahan frowned and looked around the apartment, as if he were noting how humble, how undesirable it was. 'I don't know. It's possible.'

'Why would he want to kill me, Brendan? Aren't there enough people with that in mind already? Do you have any reason for Fosse's interest in the matter?'

Hanrahan took a pack of cigars out of his pocket and lit one, letting the stink waft over into Denney's face. 'Something to do with the Farnese woman, perhaps? I don't expect you to give me details of your own personal life but I see the logs. I know who comes and goes in this building. Fosse has a grudge. He is, I think, a little like a tinder box. It takes very little to spark the flames and when they're alight, well . . .'

The Irishman waited for a response. None came.

'This is not, Your Eminence, a complete surprise now, is it? There was plenty of trouble before. He's quite a history. That matter here which necessitated his removal from your staff. What was it exactly? I was away at the time and the records are unclear.'

'Does it matter?'

'Perhaps.'

'He was overfond of the wrong kind of women, Brendan. He was warned many times. He ignored those warnings. It's not an uncommon fault.'

Hanrahan frowned. 'So we rewarded him with a rather fine home and a new job. Even though he did, I believe, threaten you publicly then. Your dismissal of him was, I hear, rather fierce.'

Denney's head rocked from side to side. 'I lost my temper. I'd put my trust in the young fool. He betrayed it. So he was upset at losing his post? He never mentioned Sara Farnese to me. Fosse was a troubled priest deserving of sympathy. I've no idea why he's behaving like this now.'

Hanrahan stared at his fingernails in silence.

'Do you think he could get in here?' Denney asked. 'Don't we pay you people for protection to save us from that kind of trouble?'

'Of course you do. And you get it. But Fosse is . . . different somehow. He's not an ordinary priest. He's not an ordinary murderer either. He has reasons, motivations, I can't begin to understand. Or rather ones which I lack the information to clarify.'

Hanrahan paused to give his revelation some weight. He had only just come off the phone with Falcone and even he was shocked by some of the detail. 'He beheaded Alicia Vaccarini. Quite extraordinary. I know for a fact he's seen files on everyone connected with your . . . ventures too. Names, addresses. Details of meetings. There were photographs in that place of his. Extraordinary photographs. You wonder about their purpose.'

Denney's sallow face turned the colour of granite. 'Why are you telling me this? Do you think I scare that easily?'

'No. But I think you need to know what kind of game we're in now. What we're up against. You've fallen from grace, Michael, and what's done is done. You can never go back. That charade you played this afternoon can never be repeated.'

Denney cast him an accusing glare. 'And you knew it wouldn't work all along?'

'I hoped against hope. One does in these circumstances. I try to help, Michael.'

'Then get me safe passage out of here. Fix it and I'll go.'

'To America? You think it's safe there? The FBI would meet you off the plane.'

'I've friends,' Denney grunted. 'People in Washington who can keep those hoods in their place. The FBI won't even call. Don't forget who I am, Brendan.'

'Who you were, Michael. These are changing times. I wish I could help. I've tried. Believe me.'

'Try harder.'

The Irishman held his big hands open. 'With what?'

Denney recognized the move. 'What are you asking for?'

'Leverage. Something I can bargain with.'

'Such as what?'

'The file on Fosse. Some information on his background. People he might turn to in Rome. I have most of that already though I'm sure there are some details you can add. He worked for you after all. They will want to know why you fired him. What happened after that.'

Denney grimaced. 'You think that's going to work? I've paid close to two million bucks out of my own pocket in bribes these last six months. I've sweetened politicians. I've done things I never thought I'd even consider to try to get my way out of here. Some of them make my skin crawl. None of it worked. You think they'll do this for a file?'

Hanrahan's blue eyes flashed in anger. 'Do you have a better idea? I'm looking for solutions. No one else is.'

'Sure, sure,' Denney grunted, trying to calm himself down. He didn't have many friends left. He needed this unfeeling, slippery Irishman.

'The truth is,' Hanrahan continued, 'I don't know of any other options right now. Let me make it clear, too, that even if this succeeds I doubt you'll get this open one-way ticket you fancy. The best we can hope for is that they'll turn aside just long enough to get you out to the airport. That's all I need.'

Denney stared at him, astonished. 'Are you serious? You think I can just hop into the nearest cab? You heard Neri. That psychopath would probably do the job himself. You know the kind of people out there. They make Gino Fosse look like an amateur. It's impossible. Get me some quiet escort all the way to the States. I don't intend to walk naked beyond those walls.'

Hanrahan acted offended. 'We'd have people to look after you to the airport. We're not complete incompetents.'

'I never suggested you were.'

'No? Well anyway. If you want the police to be your bodyguards then think again.' Hanrahan cast his eyes around the apartment again, pausing at the paintings, which seemed to amuse him. 'Consider your position, Michael. Think about what you've become. For that kind of treatment you need friends. You've none. Except me.'

'Thanks,' the cardinal said with bitterness.

'I was trying to put this into some perspective. Nothing more.'

'No friends? We'll see about that. Get Falcone in. He'll still talk to me.'

Hanrahan scowled. 'No. I've already spoken to Falcone. He won't deal any more, not in person. He won't come anywhere near you unless he has a set of handcuffs ready. All the favours have been called in. All the phone calls go unreturned. Everyone can smell failure on you, Michael. Maybe they can smell death. No one wants to be touched by that stink.'

Denney pointed a finger across the room. 'Don't try to make me the scapegoat here, Brendan. Don't let your masters try that trick either. I wasn't in this alone. I wouldn't be the only one to suffer if they throw me to the wolves.'

Hanrahan took a deep breath then issued a disappointed sigh. 'Now that, Your Eminence, is the kind of stupid talk I don't ever want to hear. That is the kind of talk that makes me think I'm wasting my time with you, Michael. That perhaps I'd be better off leaving you to rot in this dump, just waiting for the day you can't stand it any longer. Then what do you do? Put on an "I Love Rome" T-shirt and hope you can mingle with the tourists until you get to Fiumicino? Is that *really* what you think? Because if it is I have news. You'd be dead before you even got on the bus. Maybe it would be some of those people who think you owe them good money.

Maybe it would be Gino Fosse for whatever reasons he feels he has. Personally I'd prefer the former. It's just a gun, that's all. Gino . . . well, he's skinned a man, he's drowned a man, he's beheaded this woman you thought was in your pocket. What's he got saved for you, Michael? Is he going to nail you to a cross? Or has he been in that church just down the road from his apartment? You know, the round one with all those wonderful martyr-doms on the wall? He must have been there. Where else would he get these ideas?'

'From living,' he grumbled. 'From being a part of this nightmare.'

'Now that I don't believe,' Hanrahan said quietly. 'Or perhaps . . .' He considered the question carefully. 'Perhaps that's what Gino Fosse is trying to tell us. That by appreciating our mortality we inform these brief lives with a little perspective. It's an interesting intellectual point, I agree, but I'd rather avoid a direct involvement in the rhetoric. Fosse makes his case in a such a forceful way. Besides . . .' Hanrahan paused over his words, deter-mined to express himself precisely. 'Rain or shine, it's always a season for the dead, isn't it? Only a fool forgets that. I've no time for fools, Michael. Nor have you.'

Denney shivered in the stifling air of the tiny apart-ment. He was scared, Hanrahan could see that. But what the Irishman didn't know was that there were much bigger things to be frightened of. Denney was still a Catholic at heart. The faith had never deserted him entirely. There was a judgement coming, one in which his transgressions would no longer be hidden. He had to escape. In America it was possible he could find the courage to open his heart fully in the confessional. In America he could become another person.

'What do you want me to do?'

'Meet one of Falcone's colleagues. A junior one, who thinks very highly of himself, with only a little reason. Talk to him. Offer the files on Fosse. Then leave the rest to me. I will try to negotiate a price that gets you out of here. Then keep your head down and pray.'

He nodded. 'If that's what you want. I suppose I have no choice.'

'None,' Hanrahan agreed.

'Tell me, Brendan. How many more names are on his list?'

The question surprised Hanrahan. 'A few, or so I've heard. Sara Farnese seems to have been an active woman, if that's the right word. You won't see her again, will you? That would make my life too difficult. I can't protect you against yourself.'

'No,' he agreed softly. 'I won't.'

'Good. This is an opportunity. We mustn't waste it. I don't know if another will arise.'

Denney looked up at him, desperate. 'The police have these names from her? They'll warn them. The others. I don't want any more deaths on my conscience.'

Hanrahan glowered at him from the chair opposite. He made no effort to disguise his contempt.

'I've warned the ones who want to listen myself. For what it's worth.'

Denney felt like shrieking. 'It has to be worth something, Brendan. For pity's sake.'

Hanrahan got up, stretched lazily and cast him one last, backward glance. 'Spare me your concern, please. We both know this is about you. If you run, Michael, it all comes to an end in any case. Can't you see that's what he's doing? He's sending you a message. He's saying he'll go on killing until you flee and give him a chance to kill you. If he finds you on the way, then that's OK with him. If you manage to escape then it's finished anyway. He has no more reason to do what he's doing. Either the police catch him or he saves up for a fare to Boston or wherever you plan to run and hide. End of story. And no more corpses in Rome.'

Denney closed his eyes wishing he couldn't hear any of this.

'Don't talk to me about your conscience. Don't even dare.' Hanrahan's voice rang off the walls of the meagre apartment. There was a kind of judgement there, and one which Denney found hard to bear. 'This is not about conscience. It's about courage. It could be ended so easily. So would you care to take a walk with me now, Your Eminence? It's a fair day, a hot one, true, but I wouldn't be anywhere else except Rome on an August morning like this. There's not so many tourists. There's a breeze coming down the Tiber. We could get out from behind these walls. We could stand in the shadow of the castle. We could sit on the street and take coffee. I could buy you lunch in that old restaurant in Trastevere, the one where we used to sit in the garden, the one where the lamb's so good you just pick it up and eat it with your fingers. Then we could walk, anywhere we felt like and wait to see what happens.'

Denney heard the Irishman cross the room, felt his hand on his shoulder.

'Well, Michael.' Hanrahan demanded. 'Will you be coming out with me or won't you?'

'Get the hell out of here,' Denney hissed.

'I'll arrange for this kid to come at four.' He patted

Denney hard on the head. 'I take it you have no conflicting appointments?'

Denney said nothing.

'Good. And I'll call beforehand. You'll say what I tell
you to. Nothing more, nothing less. I'm putting in a lot
of work on your behalf, Your Eminence. I'd hate to see it
fucked up just because you can't remember your lines.'

Thirty-three

Nic Costa didn't know where to begin. Teresa Lupo was on her hands and knees carefully examining the sprawling blood stain which marked a good metre or more of the grubby carpet. Falcone and some detectives he only half recognized were on the far side of the octagonal chamber carefully going through the drawers of a small desk, scrutinizing every piece of paper it contained.

On the ceiling and upper walls were scores of black and white photographs, badly developed, roughly cut and taped to the crumbling plasterwork. Whatever other talents Gino Fosse possessed, he was a dedicated and skilful peeping Tom. The pictures were taken through half-open curtains, with a long, telephoto lens. They were grainy, squalid, intrusive. Most of the people in them were unknown to him. But Rinaldi was there, in three sets of shots, each with a different, unidentifiable woman. The other cast members were only half-seen: a woman, bent over the spread-eagled legs of a bored-looking hooker with blowsy hair, a fat, whale-like man whose mountain of white flesh tumbled onto the skin of the figure slumped beneath him. The pictures could have come from some porn magazine touted in the sex shops around Termini Station. The missionary position was largely absent. Several photos showed women gagged, hands bound behind their back, eyes staring blankly at the white shape heaving over them. Fosse had taken his time, photographing from every angle he could find.

Then he moved along the wall and saw what he knew, with some dread, was bound to be there. She was naked, on her back, legs wide open, waiting for a man who was only just visible, sliding towards her across the floor. It could have been the fat man in the other picture. He found it hard to judge. The location looked like an expensive apartment. A hotel maybe, since the bed had that clinical, just-made look that spoke of housemaids and room service. It was the first in a series. In others she was made to crouch in a vulgar sexual position, looking over her shoulder as if inviting the unseen viewer. There were grainy close-ups of her breasts and her abdomen: gross, intrusive pictures, almost clinical in their detail.

It was important, he thought, to scrutinize these images closely in order to understand what they had to say. There was no question of prurience. He found it impossible to look at them without feeling he was living on the edge of some waking nightmare, a world in which all the normal rules of human behaviour counted for nothing. He examined those in which her face was visible. She seemed detached, somehow, perhaps even drugged. Sara may have come here willingly but she did not wish to be a party to these games. Or was he being naïve? Her life was alien to him. Perhaps he really was, like his father, simply out of date. Perhaps it was not so unusual to meet a stranger, decide casually to have sex, and then play these bizarre, dark games in front of the prying camera. Terror and ecstasy sometimes walked hand in hand. Nic Costa was lost for answers.

He was still staring at the photographs when a hand touched his arm. It was Teresa Lupo, who looked a little less crazy each time he saw her. She was taking off her gloves. She seemed concerned.

'What do you say, Nic?'

'Nothing. It's beyond me. Rinaldi I recognize. The rest . . .'

She nodded at the body bag. 'The woman's over there. Most of her anyway. You know what I find most interesting? These aren't pictures of the protagonists. He's not trying to capture them at all. What he wants is the partner. The hooker. Or whatever they were.'

Teresa threw the gloves into a plastic bag, sniffed and let down her black hair which was tied in a rough, child-like pigtail. The act made Luca Rossi glance covetously at her from across the room.

'He kept plenty of souvenirs too.' She pointed at a couple of the photographs which showed Sara's clothes on the floor beside her naked body: flowered pants, a bra, and a loose, flowing dress. 'Look.'

She pointed to what was an untidy pile of underwear thrown into the corner of the room, so much it must have come from several different sources. 'He's a collector, I think. I just took a brief look but you can match some of those things with the photographs. This is a very tactile man. He needs some physical evidence to remind him of what he's been up to. Maybe he creeps in and steals them. Maybe he's best friends with some creep at the laundry.'

He couldn't stop looking at the photographs. 'He's crazy.'

'Never mind him. Think of the women. At least the

one woman we know. Look at the facts,' she said, pointing at a series of overlapping prints. They showed Sara
lying on the floor, neck uncomfortably upright, face to
the distant camera, staring towards the lens. The man was
scarcely in the frame. 'What do you see?'

'A naked woman in an uncomfortable position. I
don't get it. I don't understand what motivates Fosse.'

'It turns him on, I imagine. But look at the woman.
Some answers are there. What message is she sending
out?'

'She just seems . . . passive. As if it's happening to
someone else.'

Crazy Teresa groaned. 'Call yourself a detective. Are
there any signs of arousal? Are her nipples erect? Is she
opening her legs for whoever she's about to screw?'

He pulled down the clearest of the prints and peered
at it. 'No. Like I said, she looks passive.'

'You've got to extract as much as you can from this.
You get erect nipples for a variety of reasons. Arousal's
just one of them. Cold. Fear. Think about it. This woman
isn't feeling any of those. What does that mean?' She
waited. He said nothing. 'It means she's naked, possibly
with a stranger, and she's not that bothered. She's not
even half afraid. If I were a detective what would that
make me think? Why would a woman behave like that?
She knows this game. Maybe she's played it before. She's
practised.'

'That can't be true.'

'Look at it, Nic. Dispassionately.' She stared at the
pictures again. 'I could almost convince myself she knows
the camera's there. But I guess that's going too far.'

It was. It had to be. He was unconvinced by what she

said and that was not simply because he didn't want to believe it.

Teresa Lupo's big hand patted his good shoulder, hard. 'Alternatively, dear boy, she is very comfortable with strangers. I give up. Now excuse me. I need to write up some notes.'

Luca Rossi wandered over, discreetly touched her backside, then went to stand by Costa. 'How are you feeling, kid?'

'Fine.'

'I heard the woman's still going to stay with you. Is that wise?'

'Why should it be unwise?' Costa snapped.

'Hey. Will you stop biting my head off? Someone tried to kill you this morning because of her. In case you forgot.'

Costa cursed himself. It was unlike him to take out his unhappiness on others. 'Apologies again. But why shouldn't Sara stay with me? You people know how to guard the place now. I promise I won't play hooky any more. Besides, I think she's still got things to tell us. In her own time. When she feels she can trust someone.'

The big man grunted. 'I'll take your word on that.'

He nodded at the body bag. 'You hear who this is?'

Costa shook his head.

'Semi-famous lady. Alicia Vaccarini. Parliamentary deputy for Bologna. She hit the press when she turned out to be a dyke and the party bosses disowned her. Remember?'

'Vaguely,' he lied. Reading the papers was never one of his strong points.

Rossi eyed Falcone who was sifting through a pile of new photographs found under the desk. 'And he thinks he's got an idea why she was on the list too. Come on. Let's join the fun.'

Falcone shuffled through the set of prints someone had found in a tiny darkroom downstairs, built into an alcove. These weren't peeping Tom shots. They were taken in the tower, of women who'd received personal attention from Gino Fosse. In the pictures they were bound, exposed for the lens in a variety of sexual positions. Most looked scared, and two of them showed signs of violence: bruised eyes, cuts on the mouth and nose. None of them, however, was deemed worthy of display in the small octagonal room in the tower, which seemed odd. As if Fosse drew more inspiration from the snatched photos than the ones in which he was directly involved.

'He raped them,' Rossi observed.

'Really?' Falcone wondered. 'So why didn't any of them complain? We don't have anything on this man.'

'Who is he?' Costa asked.

One of the detectives he didn't know said, 'Gino Fosse. Priest at the hospital up the road for the last month. Before that he worked in the Vatican. This place is a Church property. They leased it to him at a peppercorn rent. That's as far as it goes. We're talking to the Diocese but they say they just got handed him by someone from on high. Got told to put him in here, look after him, get him a nice quiet job, keep him out of trouble.'

Falcone looked at the pictures. 'He had bad habits. Perhaps they were trying to hide him away for some reason. Perhaps he'd done this before.'

The detective shrugged. 'If he did I doubt we're going to find out about it. I've put in the calls. No one's ringing back. I'll tell you one thing though, he liked jazz.

The place is full of CDs. He had one track on loop when we turned up. Sense of humour, huh? It must have been on when he did it.'

The man held out the case: a picture of a dapper violinist sitting in a gorilla's open palm, and the title, *King Kong, Jean-Luc Ponty Plays the Music of Frank Zappa*.

'The track in particular,' he said, 'is called "How Would You Like to Have a Head Like That?"'

The morgue team heaved the body bag onto a gurney and lugged it to the narrow stairs. 'Alicia Vaccarini,' Falcone said. 'I met her once. She was on a couple of police committees. Cold bitch.' He glanced at Costa. 'Why her do you think?'

It couldn't be avoided. 'Sara Farnese slept with her. A one-night stand just like this Fosse character. Which is why she never mentioned either of them.'

Luca Rossi whistled. 'Jesus. How many other things has that woman got hidden inside her?'

'She says there were others like that. No names. She never knew them.'

Falcone put a hand to his silver beard and stared out of the slitted window. 'At least we know where Fosse is getting some of his information from. Peeping through windows, following her around.'

'Not just her,' Costa objected. 'There must be ten, twelve different women in these pictures.'

'Right. Let's show their pictures around. Specially to vice. See if anyone knows them. Let's see if we can identify any of the men too. They might appreciate the warning. Look for some link between Fosse and Denney too. It has to be there. Vaccarini certainly had one.'

She was, Falcone said, a player in political circles, with

no small amount of influence. Earlier in the year she was on the committee that looked at changing some of the diplomatic immunity rules for the Vatican. The same one that Rinaldi gave evidence to. Interesting or what? If that vote had gone the right way, Denney could have walked onto the first plane home unimpeded by the authorities, ready to disappear. Was this coincidence? Or was this the fundamental reason behind the deaths? In which case, how was Sara Farnese involved?

The men looked at each other. They knew when a case was slipping away from them. There were too many loose ends, too many roads to nowhere.

'This is turning bad,' Falcone said, glowering at Rossi. 'We missed our chance this morning. You . . .' He looked at Costa. 'You're fit to be here?'

'No problem.'

'Go back and see your friend Hanrahan. He's been on the phone hinting that maybe Denney will let you into his apartment for a talk. Could be they have something else to bargain with. And Sara Farnese. You still think she should stay at your father's house?'

'If that's what she wants.'

'To hell with what she wants,' Falcone snarled. 'Get something out of that woman. She's running rings around us, you in particular. Find out what the hell she's been dabbling in because this is more than just some nasty by-product of casual sex. She's been screwing the wrong people. Maybe someone with a cardinal's cap for all I know—'

'She denies knowing Denney,' Costa interjected, feeling weary with the man's relentless badgering.

Rossi wrinkled his fleshy nose in distaste. 'She denied

having any other lovers until one turned up without a head.'

'Just talk to her,' Falcone said. 'Don't stop until she says something. And here's a question for all of you. Just where does a runaway priest hide in Rome, for God's sake?'

'Somewhere we can't touch him,' Rossi said. '*That* place.'

'Don't be ridiculous,' Falcone sneered. 'This Fosse character is just like Denney now. They gave him some kind of chance. He threw it away. They won't want him near them. He's here. In the city. Someone knows. Someone can tell us. Get the papers onto it. Is there a photograph of him here?'

'Nothing,' someone said. 'We've got fingerprints. That's all.'

'Find some. Costa can give you a description for a photo-fit.'

Rossi scribbled out a note and gave it to one of the junior cops.

Teresa Lupo bumped into the gathering, gave them all a schoolgirl smile, fluttered her copious eyelids and said sweetly, 'I've got DNA. If anyone's interested.'

Falcone took one step back from her and said, 'What?'

There was one final package that hadn't gone on the gurney, a black plastic bag like a heavyweight super-market carrier. She had it in her grasp and, with gloved hands, opened the sealed top for a second look. The men watched as she withdrew the head of Alicia Vaccarini tenderly, held it by the severed neck and turned the dead politician's features around to face them. Luca Rossi breathed deeply and went to the window to stare out at the Clivus Scauri. A couple of the others joined him.

'Sorry, boys,' Teresa said with a grin. 'This is all for your benefit, you know.'

She held the short hair, allowing the head to dangle freely, then opened the mouth with a plastic prong, looking inside, peering into the throat. Even Costa, not the most squeamish of men, felt something churn in his stomach. Then she put the head back in the bag, called one of the team over and passed it to him.

'Well?' She beamed at the cops. 'Just making sure I don't say anything premature. Does anyone here want to know exactly how she died? Or am I just along for the ride and your charming company?'

Falcone lit a cigarette. The men were grateful, even Nic Costa. The head stank of meat and blood and the smell seemed amplified in the cramped, overheated room. 'We're listening,' he said.

'Listen well because there may be questions after,' she said, walking to the wooden pillar in the centre of the tower. 'You boys are causing so much work for me right now I'm going to have to call in extra budget. If I have to go through the inquisition to explain that, you can too.'

She walked to the window side of the beam, smiling as the men scuttled out of the way. 'You've seen the sword.'

'Oh yes,' Rossi agreed, his back still turned but listening to every word.

'Interesting weapon. Slim. Medium length. Not a stabbing sword. More the kind of thing used on horseback. Not what the hoi polloi would think of when it comes to decapitation but then, what do they know? They just think: head needs to come off, call for the axe. Stupid. Messy. Inefficient. You know how many times they get the whole thing off in one go? One out of ten maybe. Usually they're hacking at it like some dumb peasant trying to get a chicken ready for dinner.'

Without a word Rossi crossed the room and started to march down the stairs, fumbling at his cigarette pack all the time.

'A sword is the smart executioner's weapon,' she continued. 'This man knew his stuff. He'd done his research. There's a picture in the cathedral in Valetta, *The Beheading of John the Baptist*. Our young running friend here will know it, I guess. The work of Caravaggio on his travels, when he was avoiding the law. I'll be surprised if the main man here hasn't seen it too. You've got the Baptist on the floor already dead. His neck's almost entirely severed by a sword not dissimilar to this one. And over him stands the executioner, hiding, for some reason, a dagger behind the back. Which he needs for the final cut. The blade gets through the spinal cord, you see, but tends to leave behind a flap of skin that you have to snip through to get the whole thing off. Look . . .'

She pulled out a small package from the bags of evidence and opened it. There was a tagged knife there: a kitchen implement with a broad sharp blade which was stained black with dry blood.

'Exactly the same thing,' Teresa said with an undisguised note of triumph.

Even Falcone was lost for a suitable remark.

'The question is,' she continued, 'which saint was it that he was trying to emulate here? I mean, so many died by losing their heads. Is this really like the man we have come to know and love? Is this what he intended all along? Surely not. Otherwise why go to the trouble of San Clemente and skinning that poor bastard on Tiber

Island? This destroys his continuity somehow. And here's one more thing.'

She was mocking them, Costa thought. She was relishing every moment of it.

'Isn't anyone going to ask me the time?'

'Well?' Falcone demanded.

'Three, four hours ago. Couldn't be more. He did this *after* he tried to take out our small athletic friend here. And he did it in a hurry. Conclusion? Boys, boys! You're the detectives here. I'm just a butcher's girl with a postgrad degree. But to me that says: someone rang him. Someone said, do your worst then get your crazy butt out of there before the cops come down.'

They watched her stroll happily down the stairs. There was a look on Falcone's face that Costa recognized. He was thinking on his feet.

Falcone turned to one of Teresa's assistants, Di Capua, a tubby shapeless student-type face with long, lank hair. 'How many possible DNA samples do you have in all?'

'Here? You want me to count them?'

'And the rest?'

'Skin. Blood. Bone. We could keep the lab going for a week.'

'So what are you doing with it?'

'Right now? Keeping it cool. We just haven't had time.'

'Make time. Get samples from every one of those people we're guarding too. The ones the Farnese woman named. I want to know if any of them has been near these places. Understood?'

'You're the boss,' he said.

Then Falcone crossed the room and pointed at the

pile of spent women's clothes. 'Put these in too. Just for luck. I want to know who's been doing what with who here.'

Finally, he returned and took Costa to one side. 'When you meet Denney,' he said, 'there's something I need you to do. It may sound odd but just do as I say.'

'Sure,' Nic Costa agreed. And it was odd, very odd indeed.

Thirty-four

The address he'd been given was a couple of hundred metres from Termini Station, above a Chinese restaurant. It was the worst place Gino Fosse had ever occupied, worse even than the farm he dimly remembered from his childhood, before the church school in Palermo. They'd fixed it for him. They'd told him where to run and he did, so quickly he only just remembered to snatch a few CDs and the player along with some more important belongings. They'd told him too to keep quiet, stay inside for a few hours, until the police got less jumpy, less observant.

There was money waiting for him. There was someone to act as go-between: a red-haired foreign girl who could have been no more than nineteen. She said she worked tricks around the station back-alleys, took her clients into the adjoining bedroom, where he imagined her performing her work with a brutal, brief efficiency, and then sent them quickly back out onto the street. She'd fetch food for him. She'd act as a liaison with the people outside. At one on that stifling afternoon she sat down on the one spare chair in his bedroom and looked fetchingly at him. She was pretty after a fashion: big brown eyes, an alert, alluring face, a ready, open smile.

But her skin was flawed by pink blemishes and her teeth were crooked and discoloured, like two rows of pebbles from a grimy beach. She wore a skimpy red halter top and a glossy plastic miniskirt in fluorescent lavender. When she perched on the seat she opened her legs to show him there was nothing underneath. He thought of Tertullian and what might happen next. Then, when his head just got too full to think of anything else, he nodded at her, sat on the bed and let her come down on him, just daring to touch the back of her head as she went about her work, trying to force from his mind the picture of another scalp beneath his fingers that morning.

He wondered if she was familiar. When he was doing the cardinal's business, when he was ferrying women to and fro across Rome, using his camera at every possible opportunity, he met all sorts. She could have been one. Most of them were hookers. Most of them were classy. A few straddled the borderline. It depended, he guessed, on the taste of those that Denney was trying to please. And one fitted no such category. One was just beautiful, so beautiful that, on occasion, Denney would see her alone himself, leaving Gino Fosse to wait downstairs in the apartment block, like some miserable cab driver, imagining – there was no preventing it – what was going on in the bedroom above.

She never spoke when she was in the car. She never said anything after a visit, whether it was to Denney or someone on his list. She simply sat there as lovely and serene as a portrait in a church.

Then things got bad with Denney and Gino Fosse was only driving occasionally, when there was no one else for the job or the destination was too delicate.

A month ago, in disgrace for nothing more than a

rough encounter with a hooker, he'd been exiled to the place in the Clivus Scauri. They had given him the ridiculous and mind-numbing task of comforting the dying and the bereaved in the hospital at the top of the road.

And he'd begun to change, begun to understand that he was becoming something else. It started two weeks before, in the dark echoing belly of San Giovanni in Laterano, taking a break from the weary round of visits in the hospital. In front of him was the papal altar with its ornate Gothic baldacchino. Behind a curtain, the history books insisted, were the heads of Peter and Paul preserved in silver reliquaries. He stared at this hidden space wishing he could see into it. From his childhood in Sicily to his present unhappy state in Rome the Church had enfolded him constantly, warming his nights with its comforting promises, easing his mind when the demons – and demons there were, real ones with horns and gleaming teeth – came to him and forced his hand, made him mad and bold and violent. One needed imperfect people in the world. Without them the Church would lose its meaning. Everyone would go straight to God and learn nothing, feel nothing, along the way. Peter and Paul were no strangers to anger and deceit. One had denied the Lord not once but three times, the other was a persecutor of Christians, a supreme, cruel servant of the Roman state. And now they were saints. Now their mummified heads sat in silver caskets in a hidden partition of the canopy that stood before him.

Gino Fosse would recall this moment for the rest of his life. It was here, in the black maw of San Giovanni, that something wormed its way into his soul, wound itself around his neck and whispered in his ear what he already half suspected: *he was a fool and worse*. It spoke of what he had done on the sweaty bed in the medieval tower on the Clivus Scauri. It taunted him with the bright, vivid memories. It reminded him of the sinful ecstasies: the warmth of a woman panting on his neck, the feel of her flesh against his as he writhed and moaned above her. And it asked: where, in all this delight, is the sin? Where, in all this feverish, mindless conjoining of their bodies, was there room for the old, dead myths passed down by generations of men whose primary purpose was to serve themselves?

There were no heads in the canopy's space. Or if there were, they belonged to some hapless corpses which had been appropriated for the sake of the Church. Peter and Paul were distant shadows. If they lived, they may never have come to Rome. If they were martyred, their remains were now dust on the wind, particles inhaled and exhaled by black and white, young and old, Christian, Muslim and atheist, everywhere. They weren't hiding inside an ornate metal container in some vast, overweening basilica in Rome.

He was deceived. And if they tricked him about this, then what else was true?

He found himself sweating. His head ached. His eyes felt heavy. When he looked down at the ground, to make sure it was still there, it seemed to shift beneath his feet like water moving in a slow and relentless swell.

They lied. Every one of them.

He was amazed it had taken so long for him to see through their deceit. Gino Fosse burned with anger and shame at that moment and there was scarcely a waking second afterwards when these bitter, acrid sensations abated. Then, later, there was the ultimate revelation, in a smaller, darker place, with the Irishman's dank, tobacco-stained breath in his ear, bringing a new and terrible kind of sense and order with it.

It was in San Giovanni that he began to lose the faith of his childhood and that was worse than anything he could imagine, worse than going blind or becoming a cripple. In a few, terrifying moments he was transformed. He became an outsider, a man beyond the Church that had been a kind of parent to him for as long as he could recall. From this point on he would begin to live outside the normal bounds of humanity.

Yet a faith remained, hidden, silent, waiting for him to recognize it. Later, when that occurred, Gino Fosse would know he was not alone. In his soul there was a profound, inexplicable certainty. For all their trickery, there was a God, one Peter and Paul knew and the modern world had forgotten. Not the God of bureaucrats and basilicas. Not the God of love and reconciliation, the comforting face of Jesus hanging over a child's bed. The true God still lived on from the Old Testament, a supernatural deity, angry, vengeful and hungry, ready to punish those who betrayed him. This God would become a constant presence inside Gino Fosse's head, his one bulwark against a cruel and shallow world. From time to time he spoke, offering the promise of eventual redemption. He accompanied him when the work began, wakeful and watching in the church on Tiber Island, on the shore of the dead river, in the upstairs room where the sinning bitch Alicia Vaccarini would take her first step on the road to deliverance.

And he took them to his bosom, even the vilest. The bloody harvest served its purpose. They were, against their own instincts, snatched from the darkness to his side.

Fosse thought about this as the red hair bobbed beneath his hand. One day it would be his turn and he would go willingly, knowing his sins would be washed clean. This was a world of shadows, an unreal, transitory place of stinking bodies and vile physical couplings. He was a part of it, and a part of him too. The reconciliation of these two was under way.

She moved more rapidly. He felt the heat rise and pushed her away. She went to the sink. He listened to the sound of her there. It seemed an act as commonplace as brushing one's teeth. This woman's body had been subverted for a purpose. He was surprised by the realization that she was not to blame.

'What are you called?' he asked across the room.

She turned and looked at him, puzzled. 'You want to know my name?'

'Is that so odd?'

'You bet.' Her voice had an odd tinny quality, as if she struggled with the soft vowels of Italian.

'Well?' he insisted.

'Irena.'

'Where are you from?'

'Kosovo,' she answered, a little nervously.

'Orthodox? Or the other?'

'Neither,' she said sharply. 'Why do you want to know?'

'Just asking.'

'Where I come from you don't ask that. Good people don't. Just the ones looking for someone to kill.'

'I'm sorry.' There was a lifetime of fear and grief inside her. He could see it behind her pretty, blemished face.

'My name's Gino,' he said. 'I won't hurt you, Irena. I just want you to do something for me. Here . . .' He pulled out a sheaf of notes from his jacket pocket. She stared at them. It was big money for her, he guessed. They had been generous and he'd robbed Alicia Vaccarini's purse too. 'What do you make in a day?'

'A hundred and fifty. Two hundred sometimes. Maybe more.' She toyed with her hair. 'Don't get to keep it. I'm not what you'd call top-class goods.'

There was something else inside this damaged half-child. Something still young, still unspoiled in spite of everything. 'Looks don't matter. It's what's in here –' he patted his heart – 'that counts. And you don't look bad either.'

'Thanks.' The pebble teeth shone wanly in the afternoon sunlight streaming through the window.

'Here's three hundred. You get this every day you're with me. In return, you don't do any tricks. You just do what I say.'

She came over and took the money. There was a stupid, puzzled smile on her face.

'If I do some tricks we get more money.'

He took her arm, gently. 'No tricks.'

She smiled. 'OK. It's fine by me.'

'Now. Go get me a phone book. I want some wine too. Red. Sicilian. Some bread, cheese. Whatever food you like. I don't care.'

'Sure,' she said, grinning. 'And when I come back we'll have fun. I'll show you things. Things you don't get in Italy.'

A black angry look rose on his face. She took a step back. 'If you want . . .'

'If I want,' he repeated.

She scuttled out of the room quickly. It was almost two hours before she returned with what he asked for.

Surreptitiously he stood next to her, letting the smell enter his nostrils. He expected a stink to her, of sweat and something else he recognized, and a guilty look in her lost eyes. There was nothing. She looked at him, smiling, then, for no reason at all, kissed him on the cheek.

'What was that for?' he asked.

'Being kind.'

She lived in a lost world too, one in which an absence of cruelty counted as gentleness. She was a part of a greater mechanism, small, unimportant. She was, in a sense, very like him.

Thirty-five

Nic Costa and Luca Rossi stood in the Via di Porta Angelica, watching the Swiss Guards kicking their heels in the private entrance to the Vatican quarters opposite. Only three days before they had been in St Peter's Square routinely seeking out bag-snatchers. It seemed a lifetime ago. The city had turned strange and deadly since. Their own relationship had shifted towards sourness too and, it seemed to Costa, that stemmed from more than his new-found assertiveness. The big man was unhappy, deeply unhappy, and reluctant to explain why.

Rossi cast an evil glance at the blue uniforms across the street, then complained, 'If you hadn't had that damned scanner stuck to your ear none of this would have happened.'

'None of what?' Costa asked, dumbfounded. 'You mean those people would be alive? And all the world would be sweet and peaceful? All because I left the scanner at home?'

'Maybe,' he grumbled. 'Who's to know?'

'Right.'

'I'll tell you one thing, kid. You wouldn't have that hole in your shoulder and a face that looks like you've been head-butting the wall all day. And you wouldn't have that woman stuck in your father's house, messing up your imagination all the time.'

'That's crap, Rossi.' He heard the harshness of his own voice and how he used the big man's surname. It was all so foreign.

'Yeah, it's crap. Here's some more crap too. I talked to a couple of criminal friends of mine early today. Asked them if the name Cardinal Michael Denney meant anything. You know what? I was right. It's not just us that gets twitchy every time we hear about him. There are whole brigades of bad bastards out there itching to get their hands on him. Except they don't really want the conversation side of things. They just want to tear the heart out of his chest and leave it somewhere for the rats to gnaw on. He messed up some important people very badly and they don't take kindly to that sort of thing. Are you listening to what I'm saying? There's a bounty on him, kid. You could probably pick up fifty thousand dollars or more if you handed him over to a couple of thugs in dark glasses right now.'

Costa pointed to the gate. 'So why don't they just walk in and do it? We stay out because we have to. It's not like it's a fortress in there, except where the boss lives. They could go in if they wanted.'

'Get real.' Rossi was shaking his head, looking at him with contempt. 'You don't understand a damned thing, do you? These people who want him, they're all good Catholics to a man. Sure they kill. They maim. They steal. They sell people stuff that ruins their souls. But they think of themselves as honourable men. They've got rules. They don't even kill cops unless they have to, though judges, that's a different thing. They've got a code and it says that place in there's safe. As far as Denney's concerned he's living in some mink-lined sanctuary as long as he's behind those walls. He'd just better not step out, that's all. Or if he does, he'd better be gone from here real quickly and surface some place else looking nothing like he did before.'

Costa felt tired. His shoulder was aching. A vein was pumping through the bruise on his temple. 'So what?'

The big man leant down into his face. 'So we take care, Nic. We watch what we say, what we do, who we trust. This is a complicated world.'

'I'll bear that in mind.' Costa looked at his watch. 'Right now I have an appointment. I'll catch you tomorrow.'

'I can come along,' Rossi suddenly offered. 'No problem. I don't mind.'

Costa couldn't fathom it. 'You heard what Falcone said? He wanted me there, alone.'

'Yeah. I heard what Falcone said. I can still come. We're supposed to be partners, aren't we?'

But they weren't. Something had happened to open up a gulf of mistrust between them.

'I appreciate the offer, Uncle Luca. Don't get me wrong.'

The big man snorted as if he was expecting the rejection. 'Sure. Nice to be appreciated. Well, you just go do what Falcone wants, and make sure you do it to the letter. That's why we're here.'

'Luca? What's wrong?'

The flabby, bloodless face fell. Luca Rossi looked lost. 'Nothing. Everything. This stupid job. You. You more than anything, if you want the honest answer.'

Costa was silent. He felt hurt and responsible too somehow.

'When this is over, Nic, I want a change. Maybe they can give me a job pushing paper somewhere. I'm sorry. I lied. It's not just you. It's this line of work. It depresses me. It follows me everywhere. I want to sleep at night. I want to sit in a park and not notice the needles on the ground. I want to go for a walk and never wonder why some creep is standing by a car on the other side of the road, handing stuff out to kids who happen by. Most of all I want to meet women who talk about their clothes and where they shop, not about whom they dissected that morning and what they found in his gut.'

'If you date a pathologist . . .'

Luca Rossi sighed. 'Yeah. Point taken. I'm stupid. Sorry. Sure you don't want to reconsider my offer?'

'And get ourselves into deeper shit with Falcone?'

'Sometimes,' Rossi said, 'you have to be your own man.'

It sounded like the kind of thing his father would say.

Rossi waited until he saw there was going to be no answer. Then he turned on his heels and shambled off towards the metro station and the long journey back to his apartment in the suburbs. Nic Costa watched him go, asking himself what he could do to repair this breach. He wasn't ready to lose Luca Rossi just yet. He needed some pillars in his life. In the brief time they had known each other, he had become convinced this sad, big man could fit the bill somehow. Partly because they could, he thought, learn to lean on one another from time to time.

Disconsolate, he looked at the gate into the Vatican. Hanrahan was there, in a dark suit, watching him from across the road. Nic Costa remembered why he was here, threaded his way through the pedestrians, sweating in their shorts and T-shirts, wandering down to the piazza, and, for the third time in three days, found himself in a foreign country.

Thirty-six

They walked along a narrow road running parallel with the main public street to the south. The tall buildings on either side cast some welcome shadow on the pavement. The place was deserted. The crowds and the visitors were elsewhere, in St Peter's and the grand piazza outside. These were the administrative quarters of the Vatican state, with a few blocks set aside for residences.

Hanrahan looked him up and down. 'You've been in the wars.'

'Nothing to worry about.'

'I'm glad to hear that. I'm glad too that you took my offer of last night seriously. You'll find me a good friend, you know. I've a little influence beyond these walls. I know people that don't cross your path ordinarily. You never know when I might be able to help.'

Costa looked sceptical.

'Now, now,' Hanrahan continued. 'A friendship has to be based on some kind of exchange. Otherwise it's not friendship at all. It's just one person using another. This is the oldest kind of relationship in the world, Nic. I give you something. You give me something back.'

'Something you owe me by rights anyway, if I'm not mistaken.'

Hanrahan opened the door to a grey block that could have been an office building. 'But you are, Nic. I don't have to give you anything. Please remember that. It's most important.'

He walked inside. The Irishman followed. They were in a dark, narrow stairwell with simple stone steps leading up. Costa's surprise must have shown on his face.

'Now I know what you're thinking. You're thinking, what's a cardinal of the Catholic Church doing living in a dump like this? Do you know something? Our man here's asking himself the same question too.'

'And the answer?'

Hanrahan held his arms open wide. 'We all pay for our transgressions in the end. What more can I say?'

They went up to the third floor. Hanrahan rang the bell. Costa watched an eye glint at the spy hole, heard two sets of chains rattle, then saw the heavy wooden door fall back to reveal the slim form of Cardinal Michael Denney. He looked more like an old matinee star than a churchman. Denney had a fine, chiselled face that was still handsome in spite of the lined cheeks and the wrinkles at the corner of a straight and humourless mouth. His lips were grey and thin, his teeth when he briefly smiled were white and perfect. He had a full head of straight, silver hair cut unfashionably long so that it hung over his ears and his collar. He was a tall man with the slight stoop that came from perpetually looking down to the people he was addressing.

'Come in,' he said in an educated American accent.

Nic Costa walked through and found himself in a modest apartment, meagrely decorated save for a few expensive-looking paintings that were, he imagined, Denney's own. Then he looked more closely and saw one that was familiar: a copy of Caravaggio's *Martyrdom of Saint Matthew*, the same canvas that had caught Luca Rossi's attention as they left San Luigi dei Francesi. There was a threadbare three-piece suite, a low table in front of the sofa, and a small desk covered in papers. The two main windows were too small. Even on this bright, dazzling day Denney needed the extra illumination of a standard lamp to be able to work at the desk. The place was minuscule, smaller even than his own home. Denney had surely come down in the world.

'It's all a single man needs,' Denney said, watching the way Costa took in the room. 'Can I get you something to drink? A beer maybe?'

'Nothing.'

Denney picked up a bottle of Peroni and swigged from the neck. He was wearing a cheap grey sweatshirt and jeans. Costa found it hard to think of him as a churchman at all, least of all a cardinal. 'You don't mind if I do. Damned hot today. Don't worry about Hanrahan here either. Never seen him touch the stuff. Worried your guard might drop, eh, Brendan?'

The Irishman sat down in one of the chairs. He looked ready for business. 'Drink and work don't mix in my experience, Your Eminence. And I tasted enough of it when I was young, thank you very much.'

'See?' Denney said with a grin. 'The perfect servant of the Vatican. Brendan here's a true diplomat, son. Not a made-up priest like I was. He understands this place better than anyone.'

Hanrahan shot him a savage glance. 'May we get down to business now?'

'Sure.' Denney sat down heavily on the sofa, spreading his long legs wide in a way Costa associated with Americans. 'So, Mr Costa, what have you got to give me?'

'What do you want?'

'Safe passage,' Denney said instantly. 'Just a car to the airport with a blue light on the top, not flashing, I'd like some privacy. And a nice convoy back and front to keep any unwelcome spectators away. My colleagues here would rather I was gone. I think there are plenty of others outside these walls who feel the same way. To be frank with you, it would make me happy too. I've a fancy to go back home. There's some little places I knew back in Boston when I was a kid. There are some people who'll help me start anew if I ask them right. Thought I might change my name, get a life back. Not a lot to ask.'

Hanrahan was watching him avidly, as if judging every word, and making notes on a pad.

Costa wondered what there was to play with. 'Cardinal, I can tell you there are three judicial warrants in preparation for your arrest right now. The moment you step onto Italian soil any number of people, not just me but the Finance Ministry and the tax people too, have a duty to arrest you. I don't know how I can even begin to address that kind of demand.'

'So why are you here?' Hanrahan asked. 'If you've got nothing to offer, what's there to talk about?'

He thought about the long briefing he'd had from Falcone. It was precise and definite in its terms. 'What I'm authorized to say is this. If you cooperate with us on the Gino Fosse case, turning over every item of information you possess, I can guarantee that you will be placed somewhere secure, pre-trial and after, if there's a custodial sentence. You've plenty of friends.'

Denney snorted and looked out of the meagre windows, disgusted.

'No one wants to see you in jail,' Costa continued. 'Not least because I don't think we could guarantee your safety there. It would be somewhere comfortable. Somewhere you could have access to the people you want to see.'

'Jesus,' Denney snapped. 'Do you think I don't have that much here? I'd just be swapping one prison cell for another. Don't you understand? I don't want your protection. I don't want to talk to the judiciary. There's plenty of government people here wouldn't like that either. I just want to disappear back where I came from.'

Costa was unmoved. 'This isn't a parking ticket you're asking us to tear up.'

Hanrahan sighed and closed the notebook on his lap. 'I apologize, Your Eminence. I've wasted your time. I thought these people were serious. Clearly I was wrong.'

'No,' Costa insisted. 'We're serious about treating you fairly. About keeping you alive too and that may not be so easy. From what I hear I don't think you could just fade away into the back streets of Boston and lose these people. They're persistent. They're angry. They want your blood.'

Denney stared at his long thin hands. He had the fingers of a pianist. For all his dignity he was beginning to look like a broken man.

'Gino Fosse is dangerous, violent and unpredictable,' Costa continued. 'He's killed four people that we know of and caused the death of one more. He could be out there right now working out how to kill someone else. I can't bargain your freedom from justice against finding a man like this. You must understand that.'

'Justice?' Denney went over to the desk, opened a drawer and took out a file. It had Fosse's name on it and an official Vatican stamp on the cover. Hanrahan watched him, worried.

'Look,' he said. 'Fosse was some junior employee who worked for me. I fired him when he got out of hand. Everything anyone knows about him is here in his personal record. From the moment he went to school till last week when, as far as anyone knew, he was doing a routine job in the hospital. It's got the man in here. It's got his problems too. I never knew about them at the time we took him on. I swear that. But I've checked since. He was never someone we could be proud of. Still, the Church looks after its own. As much as it can. Everything's here. You're telling me that's not worth a bean?'

Costa eyed the blue folder anxiously. 'I didn't say that. I offered you preferential treatment. I offered you security. You wouldn't be getting that if you were some working-class hood from Testaccio. You still have to answer for what you've done. I can't avoid that.'

' "I can't avoid that"?' Denney repeated. 'You're sitting in judgement on me? Let me tell you something, son. I know what I've done. I know what others have done too. We all get judged sometime, and not by some bent and stupid judiciary either.'

Nic remembered Falcone's instructions. 'Can I have that beer now?'

Denney looked puzzled. He walked to the corner of the room, opened the fridge and came out with two fresh ones.

'*Salute*,' he said.

Costa waved the bottle in his face. '*Salute*. Oh, and go to hell. This man's killed. He'll kill again and go on killing until we stop him. How can you ask for something in return? Is that what it means being a Catholic these days? Is that where your conscience lies? In your own self-interest?'

It was worth a try. He was tired of Denney's tricks. He was sick of Hanrahan's silent, oppressive presence.

Denney said nothing and stared at his hands.

'See that picture,' Costa said, nodding at the painting on the wall. 'What's that doing here?'

Denney looked at the Caravaggio. It sparked some interest in his face, as if he had forgotten it existed and was grateful for the reminder. 'Old times' sake,' he said eventually and left it at that.

Costa wondered whether to take the risk. There was nothing to lose. It was a good copy, a third size or so. The figure of the murderer, sword in hand, half-naked, and bathed in the same light of Grace that fell on the dying Matthew, prone and bleeding on the ground, dominated the centre, raging at the martyr. Onlookers fled from the scene in terror. Only one face, half-hidden in the shadows, was still, and keenly curious, with that familiar, pained expression, one that Nic Costa had recognized and understood since his father first told him the story.

'Let me tell you something.' He stood up and beckoned for Denney to join him. 'You know who this is?'

He pointed to the bearded figure almost lost in the shadows.

Denney let out a low murmur of pleasure. 'Hey, I remember that now. What is this? A cop who knows art?'

'I'm curious. That's all. So who is it?'

'Caravaggio. It's his self-portrait, putting himself into the scene.'

'Why?' Costa asked.

'As a witness. As a sympathizer.'

'And as a participant too. Look at his face. Isn't he asking himself why he has to paint this scene? Why he's partaking of Matthew's blood as if it were some sacrament? And, most of all, why he's creating this drama out of his own head in the first place, since none of it has any historical authenticity. What he's saying is: we're all involved, we're all part of the story, whether we recognize it or not.'

'Nice sermon,' Denney said, nodding. 'You missed your calling.'

Then he went back to his chair and picked up the bottle of beer. Costa followed him, wondering whether he had made his point.

'I meant that,' Denney observed. 'You're an unusual young man. Do you get many cops in church these days?'

'I just go where the paintings are. There's nothing religious in it.'

'That may be true, I guess. Or at least you could think so. To be honest I haven't looked at that picture in years. You forget what's important sometimes. You take it for granted. I loved that place when I first came to Rome. It seemed to me to be what being a Catholic was all about, much more so than . . .' He waved a hand in the direction of St Peter's. 'Hey. I'd better watch my mouth. That right, Brendan?'

The Irishman shuffled uncomfortably on his seat.

'To hell with it,' Denney said suddenly. He threw the folder on the table. 'Take the thing. No price. No deal. Just tell your man Falcone I expect him to think about what that's worth. Think of the risks I'm running letting private Vatican files out of this place. Then, maybe, he should consider doing me a favour in return.'

Hanrahan leapt from his chair and tried to grab the file. Denney's slender fingers went down on the cover. 'No, Brendan,' he said firmly. 'My mind's made up.'

'Jesus, Michael,' Hanrahan pleaded. 'Give him that and we've got nothing left to bargain with.'

'I don't care. I don't want any more deaths on my conscience. Let them have it.'

Hanrahan swore, then returned to his chair. 'Well, that concludes our business, I think. Quite what else there might be to discuss is beyond me now.'

Costa looked Denney directly in the face. 'Do you know Sara Farnese?'

'Who?' He didn't even blink.

'The university lecturer in the papers. The one who seems to have sparked this.'

'Ah.' Some recognition rose in Denney's sallow face. 'I did read about her.' He shrugged.

'Is that a yes or a no?'

'You're an insistent little bastard, aren't you?' Denney observed dryly.

'Like I said. Just curious.'

He sniffed. 'Well, you don't need to be that curious to know I've had a taste for women in my time.'

'I was asking a specific question,' Costa insisted.

'Do you have a picture of her? The ones in the papers didn't jog my memory.'

'No. I gave you her name. Sara Farnese.'

'Names?' He smiled at Hanrahan. 'He thinks names are important, Brendan? What kind of people are the police recruiting these days? Liking art I can understand. But this *naïveté* . . .'

Hanrahan stared miserably at the folder and said nothing.

'Let me be honest with you, son. When a man like me wanted a woman, I got one sent. I can't afford affairs. Long-term relationships. All those things are just too messy if they go wrong. So if the mood took me, I'd get someone to place the call. Understand?'

'Does the mood still take you?'

Denney's head moved from side to side. 'You're getting personal. That's out of bounds.'

'So you're saying that if you met her it was because she was a hooker.'

'Your words not mine. *If* I met her. And that's an end to it.'

'OK,' Costa said. 'Do you mind? I need to go.'

He walked into the small bathroom and turned both taps on full. Falcone had suggested the toothbrush or a comb if there was no alternative, though it could have alerted Denney to what was going on. Instead, Costa rifled through the waste bin. There, beneath a spent shaving foam canister, was what he wanted: a paper tissue with a tiny blood stain, doubtless from shaving, on the edge. He picked it up and placed it inside a plastic bag, then hid the thing in his pocket.

The two men weren't even looking each other in the eye when he returned.

He picked up the folder, waved it at Denney and said, 'Thank you. I'll pass on what you said.'

Denney nodded. Then he and Hanrahan watched the young cop walk out of the door.

When they heard his footsteps die away on the stone staircase below, Denney turned to the Irishman. 'Well?'

'A good job, Michael,' Hanrahan said. 'I couldn't have done better myself. I'll have you safely out of here. And that I promise.'

Thirty-seven

By seven that Monday evening the case of Gino Fosse occupied most of the resources of the Rome state police. More than thirty officers were on duty guarding the men Sara Farnese had named as former lovers, all of whom had now been swabbed for DNA and the samples passed, along with that illicitly taken from Michael Denney, to the big police lab near the river. A team of four had been assigned to go through the personnel file from the Vatican which Nic Costa had brought back to the station.

Nothing looked promising. Fosse was raised in Sicily by peasant farmer parents. At six he had gone to board at a local Church school. His parents rarely visited. His record there was one of promising academic achievement and persistent, violent misbehaviour. Falcone pointed out a significant event: when Fosse was nine he'd been found torturing a young cat in a wood by the school play-ground. The inspector got one of the detectives to track down a retired teacher who knew the boy. The details were revealing: Fosse had skinned the animal alive then nailed the corpse to a tree. A year later there was another case. A stray dog was tethered to a set of railings, doused in petrol and set on fire. Fosse denied all knowledge.

No one believed him but, if they had proof, none came forward with it. He had, said the former teacher, an intense curiosity in one particular field of study: the lives and, most of all, the deaths of the early martyrs.

He grew older and discovered new interests. At the age of thirteen he was reported for a serious sexual assault on a schoolgirl. Two years later he was reported for an almost identical offence. Both cases were dropped, for no obvious reasons.

Five years later he entered the seminary. From that point on he had occupied a series of junior positions in Palermo, Naples, Turin and finally Rome until joining the administrative staff of the Vatican five years before. Falcone set men calling the cities where Fosse had worked before, talking to the local cops and any priests they could persuade to come to the phone. They soon picked up a picture, as much from what was not said as the details they gleaned from the reluctant parties on the other end of the line. Gino Fosse was constant trouble. In each job he'd been moved on for some misdemeanour. In Naples he had been accused of sleeping with prostitutes in his own parish. In Turin money had gone missing and he had become involved in a fist fight with the senior detective who had been assigned to investigate the loss. There were darker rumours too, all unproven, of sadistic sexual encounters. Yet he was never charged, never dismissed from his position. Fosse floated from post to post, falling apart after a few months, often with disastrous consequences. Still he made steady progress towards Rome, towards the Vatican and the pinnacle of Church bureaucracy. Finally he found himself in the job he had occupied until only a few weeks before, working on the clerical staff for Denney, typing, phoning, driving.

'So why does he keep on going up and up like this?' Falcone asked Costa.

'I don't know. Maybe they try to keep people in the fold.'

'Bullshit. Look . . .'

It was a single-page report someone had gleaned from the anti-Mafia squad: six years old and scarcely the stuff of scandal. It said that a young trainee priest, named as Gino Fosse, with the details of his parents' farm attached in parentheses, had stayed at the home of one of the city's most notorious Mafia bosses for three months while attending studies in a nearby college.

Falcone tapped the page. 'Friends. Look at that. He knows the people of old. He's a house guest of the biggest hood in Palermo.'

'And they could ease his way in the Church? They could get him off the hook when he walks into trouble?'

'Are you serious? How long have you been a cop, kid? These people can call the Quirinale Palace direct and ask if the president's at home. That's not the issue. The real question is, why? Why keep some farmer's punk out of jail? Why keep him groping up the slippery ladder like this? Do they really think he's cut out for better things?'

That was surely impossible. Fosse looked like a dangerous loser, a liability for anyone to have around.

Falcone dashed the folder on the desk. 'And I'm supposed to let that bastard in the Vatican go for this? Hanrahan honestly thinks he can trade for Denney's freedom with a bunch of personnel records?'

Costa had been thinking of Denney ever since he left the apartment. The man seemed desperate but defeated too, as if he were waiting for some unknown fate to overtake him. He wanted to escape the gloomy prison the authorities had made for him. Costa doubted there was much joy in the prospect either, or much hope of redemption. Even when he talked about home, about Boston, he seemed downcast, as if he knew it was a pipedream.

'Perhaps that's all they have. They're clutching at straws.'

'Now that,' Falcone replied, 'I do doubt. You must never take them at their word. Hanrahan least of all.'

'So you'll tell him there's no deal.'

'He can sweat until tomorrow. Then we'll see.'

Tomorrow, he nearly said, there could be another corpse. And Michael Denney still screaming to get out of that dismal apartment.

He tried to think straight and found his eyes closing, the drowsiness taking over. Falcone's hand on his good shoulder jolted him awake.

'It's been a long day for all of us, specially for you. Go home, Nic. Talk to that woman. Try to make more sense of this than I can. Come back in the morning and tell me how it all fits.'

'Are you sure?' The inspector's sudden amiable mood took him by surprise. He was dog-tired. All the same, there was so much happening. He hated being anywhere else.

Falcone looked him up and down, something not far from sympathy on his face. 'I'm sure you're no use to me here. And I don't want to be bawling you out for anything else today. It may just make me feel guilty. It was your own damn fault Fosse nearly killed you yesterday, no one else's. That doesn't stop me feeling bad about it. So no solitary running, mind. That partner of yours is pissed off enough as it is. As am I. Hey . . .' Falcone patted him on his good shoulder. 'On your way. You earned a break.'

Nic Costa looked outside the office door. Beyond the glass Luca Rossi was bent over the computer, stabbing awkwardly at the keyboard with a big index finger.

'Rossi wants out,' he said without thinking, then cursed himself. It was the big man's prerogative to break this news.

Falcone seemed unmoved by the idea. 'I know. He told me. People get like this in the middle of a bad case. Don't think anything of it. Don't take it personally.'

'But it is personal. There's something about me that bugs him.'

'Age. You're getting older. You're starting to want to be on top. He's just feeling everything winding down. His life's a pile of shit. He's got no future. He's looking for someone else to blame.'

Costa was incensed. 'That's unfair. Luca's a good cop. An honest cop. He'd do anything, for you, for me, anyone on the force.'

'Yeah. But he's *spent*, kid. Just a burnt-out case and I've got no room here for people like that. When this is done he can ship out and lick envelopes or something. Or take the pension and go drink himself to death in Rimini. Who's to care?'

'Me.'

Falcone's face turned sour again and creased with disgust. 'Then you're an idiot. One of these days you've got to decide whose side you're on. The winners or the losers.'

'You're going to say that when some young buck comes in and thinks you're a loser? Sir?'

'Not going to happen,' Falcone said emphatically. 'I

go when I choose to go. Look at him. Four years older than me. That's all. Do you think anyone could believe it? He's just run to seed. No use to anyone. He's no power over himself. A man has to possess that. If he doesn't, somebody else will take it from him or, worse, he just gives up on everything and blows with the wind. That's what your friend's doing and he doesn't even care much where it takes him.'

Costa stood up and walked out of the room not wishing to hear another word. He passed the big man at the desk and patted his huge shoulder gently. 'Goodnight, Uncle Luca.'

Two puzzled watery eyes looked up at him. 'What's wrong with you, junior?'

'I'm tired and I want to go to bed.'

He snorted. The sound was like a walrus choking on something. Costa was pleased. It was good to see he could still raise a laugh in the man.

Then Luca Rossi's face turned serious. 'Don't let her tuck you in, Nic. Not just yet, eh?'

He walked down two flights of steps, out into the open air. The night was humid and oppressive. There was scarcely anyone on the street. The usual bum was occupying his usual position by the café the cops used round the corner next to the station car park. He was hunched on the street, head between legs. He stank to high heaven.

The familiar, bearded face looked up as he walked by. Costa stopped and reached into his pocket.

'Why do you do this?' the bum snapped, half drunk already. 'Why the hell's it always you.'

'Does it matter?' he asked, surprised. 'It's just money.'

He had an ageless face. He could have been thirty or

twice that age. He was, Costa understood this, lost already. The money made no difference. It went on drink straight away, only hastening the inevitable. 'Not for you it isn't. For everyone else it's just small change. They don't notice me. I like that. Not you. With you I have to earn it. I have to talk. I have to act grateful. You know what I think?'

He felt dog-tired. His head hurt. 'Tell me.'

'This is for you. Not me at all. This is just a little ointment for your conscience, huh? A little something to help you sleep at night.'

Costa looked at the miserable figure on the ground. He held out a hundred-euro note: ten times the usual amount. The bum's eyes glinted in the gloom. 'Want it?'

The tramp held out his hand.

'Fuck you,' Nic Costa said, then put the money in his pocket and walked into the car park, only half hearing the slurred stream of curses directed at his back.

It was the first time in years he'd never made that second gift. Falcone had made his point.

Thirty-eight

Thirty minutes after an exhausted Nic Costa left the station Falcone looked up from his desk to see the familiar figure of Arturo Valena waddling towards him across the office. This was only the second time he had seen Valena in the flesh. The first was when the television presenter had been paid to MC a police awards ceremony, a job he had undertaken with a swift, efficient professionalism that almost merited the huge fee he pocketed with little grace afterwards.

Falcone had found the appearance of the man fascinating. He was one of the most familiar figures on Italian television. He interviewed everyone: politicians, film stars, entertainers. He had a big, handsome face and a gruff, booming voice that had a permanent question mark inside it, as if asking, perpetually, 'Really?' Officially he was forty-nine, though rumours suggested this was one of many myths surrounding the man. Valena had been born into dire poverty in Naples, probably at least fifty-five years before, working his way up through minor jobs in government and public relations until he was given his chance to try his hand at broadcasting. It was, Falcone now thought, the same kind of relentless progress Gino Fosse had made from his peasant farm in Sicily, perhaps aided by the same kind of friends. Once Valena had established his position as the leading commentator for one of the most successful private channels, he never hesitated to criticize government policy and, on occasion, question whether the fight against 'crime' did not infringe the rights of the individual. He had dabbled with politics himself, sitting on a variety of committees, and made no secret of his right-wing views. The one-time Naples gutter kid had become a mover and shaker in the higher echelons of social life in Rome, and had married a minor countess too, a severe-faced woman rolling in money who preferred to spend most of her time on the family estate in Perugia.

And it was all an act, one which could only be sustained on TV. The camera flattered his exaggerated features, the clever lighting hid his fast-expanding belly. The rigorous preparation for each interview, the ever-ready autocue and his cultured on-screen sensibility, which was more that of the actor than the journalist, all served to hide the real man from the public. Falcone had seen this at the awards ceremony, when Valena made the mistake to hang around long enough afterwards for people to talk to him and come away disappointed by what they found. Valena lived behind a mask and fought to keep everyone from peering round the sides. Close up, in unrehearsed conversation, he was exposed for the fraud he truly was: inarticulate, snappy, unconfident. And physically repellent. The man was a famous gourmand who had sponged his way around the city's finest dining rooms for years. Now he was paying the price. His waistline had expanded enormously, enough for the magazines to notice. In the last few months they had nicknamed him

'Arturo Balena' – 'Arthur Whale' – and started running a series of pictures to hammer home the point. There were snatched shots showing him at the table, with *foie gras* and worse on the plate, alone, eating like a pig. There was a series, too, of him around the swimming pool of a hotel in Capri, with an unidentified blonde. He lounged on a sun bed slowly cooking under the sun, his over-ample flesh turning an unattractive lobster colour. The spectacle had sold many, many magazines. Valena, unwisely, had complained to the authorities and pleaded for the editor of the rag to be prosecuted under the privacy laws. The result was predictable. He was now on the paparazzi's A-list of people to be photographed at every possible opportunity. They stalked him on scooters. They invaded the restaurants where he ate alone, in a single darkened table at the back. Arturo Valena had become fair game for a media sensing a figure on the brink of some spectacular, public downfall. The ratings for his nightly chat show were in decline. There were rumours that he might soon be dragged into an endless and messy civil court case about the misuse of state funds by bent officials who had bribed the media for favourable coverage. He was on the cusp of a cruel descent from the starry heights.

Falcone opened his desk drawer and took out a set of copies of the photos found in Fosse's room. There was a big, pale fat man in some of those. You never got to see his face but it could be the same man. He opened the door to the office and watched Valena collapse, sweating, into a chair.

The TV man looked terrified. His dull brown eyes were bleary and liquid. His chest heaved hard with laboured panting.

'I want protection,' Arturo Valena said, between

snatched gasps. 'You hear me? I only just got back from doing a show in Geneva. I read on the plane what this crazy bastard did to that poor bitch Vaccarini. He's after me next. You hear it?'

Falcone gave him a glass of water and smiled, hoping to calm him down. 'Please,' he said. 'From the beginning.'

'To hell with the beginning,' Valena spat back at him. 'I've got to be at the Brazilian Embassy in forty-five minutes. Can't avoid it. There's an exhibition opening and I need to be there. I want protection, you hear me? Or do I have to ring upstairs and get someone else to make you listen?'

Falcone pushed the phone across the desk. Valena glowered at him. 'What?'

'Call. Whoever you like. They'll just ask me to decide anyway. In case you hadn't heard, Mr Valena, we have every officer we've got on this case. Most of them are looking after people who have given us good reason to spend some time with them. You'll have to convince me you fit that category.'

'Idiot!' Valena yelled. He was sweating profusely. A bad smell, of perspiration and fear, was starting to permeate the little office.

He picked up the phone and started to make the calls. Falcone watched him, knowing what would happen. Arturo Valena understood he was on the slow drift downwards but had yet to appreciate how far he had already progressed. There would be no coming back. The future held only obscurity and perhaps some disgrace to fill it.

He tried six people, five of them senior men within the police department, the last, in desperation, a government minister. Every one of them was 'busy'.

After the final rejection he slammed the receiver back on the hook and buried his head in his hands. Falcone wondered if he was going to start to sob. Valena spared him that. The man was simply drained, left helpless by some inner terror.

'Mr Valena,' Falcone said calmly, in a pleasant, comforting voice. 'All you have to do is talk to me. I'm not saying we can't help. I'm just saying I need a reason why.'

The big, exaggerated face looked up at him. 'What do you want to know?'

'The Farnese woman? You're saying you had a relationship with her?'

'No,' Valena replied grimly. 'I wouldn't say that. I screwed her. That's all. And it wasn't a lot of fun either. At least when you got a real hooker they try to fake things a little. She didn't even make that effort. Lousy bitch. I don't know why she bothered.'

Falcone nodded. This was progress. 'You hired her? From an escort agency or something?'

'Are you serious? Did I come in here to be insulted? I'm Arturo Valena. I don't hire hookers. I don't have to.'

'I'm not hearing anything that helps me here,' Falcone said icily. 'Why don't you just go home, Mr Valena? You've got a big house here. You've got money. Hire yourself a guard if you're feeling scared.'

The man's face went white. 'A guard? With that lunatic out there?'

'I need more. How did you meet her? What happened?'

Valena closed his eyes. 'She was a gift. She was a reward. She was a prize. Call it anything you like. Someone wanted something. She was a few coins they left on the plate afterwards to try to tip my hand.'

'Who? What?'

'Huh?' Valena grunted. 'I've got one man out there wanting to kill me already. You honestly think I should make it two?'

Falcone shrugged. 'It only takes one though, doesn't it? I mean, what does it matter? If you tell me, I can put a couple of cops by your side. If you don't, you can walk out there right now on your own.' He paused, watching the man, noticing that there was something dead in his eyes. 'It's nothing to me either way, Valena. I hate your fucking programme. It stinks. You stink. And you're stupid enough to think you still carry some weight around here. The only weight's that tyre around your belly. Don't you get it?'

'Bastard,' Valena murmured. His head hung down once more. 'Bastard.'

'There,' Falcone said, smiling. 'Now that's out of the way. May we get down to business? Please?'

Thirty-nine

The police car had delivered her to the house late in the afternoon, where she was greeted by Bea, who left almost immediately, saying little, unwilling to look her in the eye. Something had changed at the farm, something between Marco and Bea. It was not simply the story on the news and her own direct involvement in it. Bea seemed nervous, somehow, as if expecting the slow, ordered life of the place to change.

Sara showered, slept for a while then changed into casual clothes to watch the television with the old man. When the latest bulletin came on he immediately switched channels. She insisted he go back to the newscast. He sat in his wheelchair, squirming, as the macabre details of Alicia Vaccarini's death were disclosed alongside stock footage of the deputy, smiling, looking happy at some public function. When it was over, Marco Costa said nothing.

She walked into the kitchen. Out back, close to where Gino Fosse had almost murdered Nic, a crow danced across the yellow scrub that led down to the Appian Way. Sara Farnese watched its black wings flapping over the dusty ground. There was a handful of police at the gate.

Marco Costa joined her and they sat around the table, drinking coffee. The city and its terrors seemed to exist in another world.

'Did you know her?' she asked eventually, desperate to break the silence that had come upon them.

'Who?'

'Alicia Vaccarini.'

'Ah.' It was an act. His mind never roamed, even when he was tired. 'We met once or twice. She seemed a pleasant woman. Vaccarini was after my time, you understand. One tries not to get personal in politics. I'd like to think I had friends across the spectrum, regardless of party. But the Northern Alliance . . . they never were my type. Those petty-minded bastards treated her very badly. So she liked the company of women? So what? Does anyone care these days?'

It was a pointed remark, designed to make her feel comfortable. 'You don't need to say that for my sake, Marco. It was a stupid thing to do. I didn't enjoy it. I never want to do it again.'

His lined, grey face peered at her. 'You mean that was all it was? Curiosity?'

'Yes,' she replied, knowing that he thought she was lying.

He shook his head. 'I never understood that idea. That you should try everything once. Where do you draw the line? Isn't there always something else untried along the way?'

'I said it was a mistake.'

'I was making a general point, not a personal one. You should never assume everything pertains to you, Sara. That's what children think. It's always seemed to me that life is about focus and depth. Something like your academic world perhaps. You presumably think it's better to know a lot about a little than the reverse?'

The university felt as distant as the city. So did the work, which seemed a part of another person, someone she no longer understood or even, perhaps, liked.

'Of course.'

'Then that's how I feel about most things,' Marco continued. 'I'd rather just make a good job of a few things and leave the rest to someone else. It makes sense, to me anyway.'

She looked around the kitchen, wondering if she should fill the silence by preparing a meal. There was good olive oil and balsamic vinegar for the dressing. He pushed his wheelchair forward and put his hand on hers, bidding her to stop.

'But that's easy for me,' he said. 'I was brought up that way. It was natural. For you . . .'

He put down the coffee cup, wondering whether it was correct to continue. 'I'm sorry, Sara. It's not my business. But I have to say it. I don't understand. Nic doesn't either. That doesn't make it wrong. It just makes it hard. No one's judging you. No one's thinking the worse of you for what happened. They're just . . . puzzled. That's all.'

'And you think you deserve an explanation?' she said coldly.

He retreated, feeling he had come too far. 'Not at all. You don't owe anybody anything. It's your life. To do with as you wish.'

'I know.'

'It's just that I find it hard to believe this makes you happy. You're so smart. You're good to be around.'

Her green eyes opened further. She was, he saw, surprised.

'And you don't know that, do you?'

She went to the fridge and poured herself a glass of Verdicchio dei Castelli di Jesi from the Marches. The wine was young and fragrant. Marco watched her taste it, his face a picture of envy.

'It's easy for you,' she said finally. 'It comes naturally. I can't just learn.'

'And why not?' he demanded. 'Are you the only person who ever grew up an orphan? I couldn't begin to understand how difficult that is. No one would wish it on another. But you should never think of yourself as some fixed, unchanging point in the universe. None of us is that. Not me. Not Nic. We're always changing, sometimes for the worse, sometimes for the better. The person you were when these things happened is not the person you are now, surely?'

'And you think that you know either of them?' She said it too harshly. There was disappointment on the old man's face and she was shocked to discover this made her feel guilty.

'I think I know one of them better than she might give me credit for,' he said.

She poured a second glass of wine and offered it to him. Marco Costa laughed and pushed it away from him.

'Now you're playing games with me,' he said. 'I don't want the wine, Sara. These drugs they give me they make everything seem the same. What I want is the old taste, the one I remember, and that's impossible. That will never happen. I can't get that back. So what would be the point?'

She poured the Verdicchio back into the bottle and gave him some water instead.

'Don't wait until it's too late,' he said. 'Regret's a small sour thing but it can poison you for years. You saw Bea when you left? How was she?'

'Confused, I thought.'

'Not surprised. I asked her back here for dinner with us this evening. What you said last night made me think it was the right thing to do. It's easy to take people for granted, all the more so when you've known them for a long time. We're lazy creatures, looking for the soft option.'

'So you asked Bea for her sake?' she said, half scolding.

Marco Costa smiled, accepting the rebuke. 'No. I admit it. Mine too. She's a beautiful woman. I can't believe I stopped noticing. I can't believe I forgot that life requires the occasional surprise. And this is a special occasion now I come to think of it.'

There was the sound of cars outside. She could hear the voices of the distant cops on the gate. Then the doorbell rang. The old man looked at her expectantly. She went to open the door and was, for a moment, made giddy by the perfume of flowers, bouquet upon bouquet, in the arms of two pleasant-looking middle-aged women chattering wildly, looking ready to go to work.

Forty

Rossi was three hours past the end of his shift when Falcone collared him. He could tell from the smile it wasn't good news.

'Overtime,' Falcone said.

'That's voluntary, I imagine?'

'You're going to be in the company of a star. You should be paying me.'

Rossi had seen Arturo Valena walk into Falcone's office. He couldn't stand the man. 'Jesus . . .' he groaned.

'Piece of cake. The guy needs taking to the Brazilian Embassy in the Piazza Navona. There for half an hour, no more, then you see him home. I'll send someone else to take over around eleven.'

'How kind. He's another one on the list? Another one she never told us about?'

'Seems so.'

Rossi shook his head. 'Such taste . . .'

Falcone scanned the office, looking at the men on duty. 'Shame Costa's gone home. I could call him back.'

Rossi knew what game he hoped to play, winding the kid up with another ex-lover she'd forgotten to mention.

He was having none of it. 'Are you serious? The kid's half dead.'

'True. But he needs to learn. You know that, don't you?'

'Learn what? All the old tricks we know and love so well? Maybe he thinks that's not such a good idea. Maybe he's right.' Rossi was tired of Falcone. He couldn't give a damn about the job any more.

'You don't fit in here, Rossi. Just three days and it's so obvious.'

'Now should I be offended by that? *Sir?*'

Falcone looked out of the window of his office, thinking, calm, as always, in these situations. 'It doesn't make much of a pension at your age. You should have stuck it out longer.'

'There's more to life than money. Can I ask you one thing?'

The silver beard nodded.

'Just take the kid off this case. It's beyond him and he doesn't realize it.'

'Seems to me,' Falcone said, 'he's done pretty damn well. Found out more than you, to be frank.'

'Yeah.' Rossi wondered how far he could go. 'Found out lots of things that just seemed to be sitting there waiting for him, huh? I just don't want to see him damaged. Do what you like to me. I won't have that. Understand?'

'Get the hell out of here. Take Cattaneo instead.'

Rossi groaned again. In three days he had already come to learn the dull little man from Bologna was the least popular detective in the division: slow-witted, boring and an incessant talker.

'The sooner you're gone, the sooner this all becomes someone else's problem.'

'And the kid?'

'I'll think on it.'

'Sir,' Rossi grunted and walked to Cattaneo's desk to break the news.

'Arturo Valena?' Cattaneo was in his mid-thirties, single and without vices. He bought his suits, shirts and shoes in threes from Standa because he got a discount that way and it removed the needless task of deciding whether to choose something different each day. His shift had started one hour before, which meant he was just bursting with energy to expend in useless conversation. 'You mean *the* Arturo Valena? The man on the box?'

'Just don't ask for an autograph,' Rossi said. 'I don't think I could take it.'

'Oh, come on,' Cattaneo complained. 'It wouldn't be for me, you understand. My brother's kid. He just loves the guy.'

'Your brother's kid is how old? Twelve?'

'Eleven.'

'And he watches Valena on TV?'

'We all do.'

'Sweet Jesus. The poor bastard's marked for life. Can you walk and talk at the same time?'

Cattaneo scowled, picked up his jacket and followed Rossi to the door, where they joined Valena and went downstairs to the car. The detective from Bologna talked every step of the way. Before they'd even left the building, Rossi could see from the TV man's eyes that he loathed Cattaneo too.

Forty-one

She was sleeping. It made Gino Fosse feel odd. She'd made love to him on and off for two hours, never asking what he wanted, always knowing somehow. Irena was now curled next to him on the cheap, hard bed. With her mouth half open she looked younger, almost a child. The red and blue neon signs outside the window flashed repeatedly and cast lurid beams across her head. He touched the marks they made. She had soft, clean hair. It was fragrant, enough to be noticeable amid the smells of sweat and sex that filled the room.

He'd never slept with a woman before, not like this. They always came and went. He'd not known what it was like to close your eyes and find them still there when you woke up. It was unreal somehow, like a scene from some dream that would be shaken from his head in an instant. Then she stirred, her eyes opened, she saw him and smiled.

Unasked, Irena leaned up to his face and kissed him softly on the lips.

'You're crazy,' he said.

'Why?'

'Acting like this. Like we're . . . together or something.'

She touched his dark hair, let her fingers curl against his cheek. 'What's wrong with that?'

'You're just a hooker. And I'm just . . . nothing.'

Her lips formed a pout and he was sure now: she could have been no more than seventeen or eighteen. 'Doesn't mean you can't love someone, does it? Where's it say that?'

Somewhere, he thought. In the books they wrote. It didn't come from God. Even the old God, the cruel, hard one, understood the imperfections in the clay he'd once shaped. They were part of the journey each individual had to take, one that was unavoidable though so many people tried to ignore it. She was right there: there was nothing to say either of them should be denied a thing.

'How much money have you got?' she asked.

'Why?'

'We could go. We could get out of this hole. We could go to the coast, Gino. Someone told me it was nice there. All clean and fresh and none of this crap to ruin us.'

He found himself laughing. 'You *are* crazy. And what do we do when we get there?'

'Screw.'

The neon painted its colours on her hair again. He couldn't stop himself laughing again for a moment.

'And then?'

Her small, perfect shoulders shrugged. She grinned this time. He didn't mind the bad teeth, he decided.

'Whatever. We just roll, Gino. We just take it as it comes . . . and *roll*.'

He thought about it. They gave her to him. She knew their faces. She would receive a visit from the police sometime. It wasn't difficult to guess what their solution would be.

'I never ran anywhere before. I never had that option.'

Her face lit up with surprise. 'You mean you just do as you told? They say this. They say that.'

'These are big people, Irena. I'm just so small.'

Her hand moved stealthily and took hold of his penis. It lay in her fingers, rising, hardening. 'I wouldn't say that.' Her fingers moved. 'Let's do it, Gino. Let's go. Anywhere.'

He felt his breath begin to catch. He wondered how many times they had made love. His head felt fuzzy, unfocused.

The phone rang. Gino Fosse pushed her away from him and turned to get it. She looked at the sheets sulkily as he spoke. It took a good three minutes. Someone was telling him what to do.

'Got to go,' he said when it was through. He started putting on his clothes. Then he looked in one of the bags he'd brought, a big one. She'd taken a peek when he was in the bathroom, wondering if there was money there. It was just junk. Theatrical make-up. Stage props. Crazy stuff. And something at the bottom. Something grey and metallic she didn't want to think about, didn't want to see.

Gino Fosse sat down on a thin wooden chair by the neon-lit window, thinking, not taking any notice of her. Then he got up, ordered her off the bed and snatched the crumpled, stained sheet off the mattress. She sat down on the bare divan and watched him.

'We could catch a train,' she said, half-pleading. 'We could go anywhere. We could be in France or Spain.'

He picked up a pair of scissors and began stabbing at

the sheet. When he was done he bent down and touched her hair. 'But we'd still be what we are now, Irena. You can't run away from yourself.'

'So you want me to go work some tricks while you're out?' she asked petulantly. 'Or do I sit here like some stupid girlfriend waiting on her man?'

He seemed shocked by her reaction. She wanted him to stay. Gino Fosse reached into his pocket and pulled out some money. 'Go buy some champagne. Tomorrow, I promise, will be a special day.'

Her face brightened. She was attractive, beautiful after a fashion. But she was stupid. This wasn't about him. It was about her finding some rock she could cling to, something that could improve things a little.

She kissed him on the cheek. He could smell her rotten teeth.

Gino Fosse walked out into the stifling night with the bag on his arm. The air was acrid with traffic fumes. He strolled down one of the grimy back alleys that led from the station, thinking. There were drunks and hookers and dope dealers.

And a small, dark van with a man by the side. He was in uniform. He looked as if he'd had a few drinks himself. Fosse walked towards the vehicle. He recognized what it was now. There was the sound of animals moving in the back. The dog catcher still had his pole, with the noose on the end, in one hand. He held a bottle of beer in the other and waved it unsteadily in Fosse's direction.

'What a job,' he said with a slur in his voice. 'What a stupid, boring job. You know how many times I got bitten by these miserable mutts today?'

He hadn't killed an innocent person before. But he knew now: there was no such creature. They all shared in the guilt. They all partook of the shame. It was weakness to exclude them.

'How many?' he asked.

The man held up three fingers.

'I'm sorry,' Gino Fosse said and took the knife from his pocket. The blade caught the moonlight. A shaft of silver flashed in the dog catcher's face. Abruptly sober, he took one look at the man in front of him, turned and ran with a sudden turn of speed. Fosse watched him race frantically down the street, debating whether to follow. There was a low whimper from inside the van. He peered through the barred window, open to the air at the rear. The vehicle stank of dog crap and urine. Several pairs of eyes stared back at him. The animals growled. It was too much effort to give chase, he thought. There were better, more profitable, avenues to pursue that evening.

Forty-two

When Nic Costa arrived home he thought, for a moment, that he had stepped back in time. The house was alive with voices: his father, Sara and a laughing Bea who, when he walked through the door, was playing with the dog as if some unexpected peace pact had just been signed. There were flowers throughout the downstairs rooms: roses and chrysanthemums, dahlias and sprays of lurid irises. The scent hung heavy everywhere. Sara and Bea drank champagne. Marco stuck to mineral water. In the kitchen two women, hired hands for the night, were putting the finishing touches to an extravagant cold buffet, the kind of meal his mother had once prepared so well. Plates of cold grilled vegetables, glistening with olive oil, were going on the dining table alongside scampi and lobster, *bresaola* and a variety of cheeses. He had to close his eyes for a moment to ensure this was not some dream. When he opened them again his father sat in front of him, in the wheelchair, still grey and cadaverous, but wearing the broadest smile Nic could recall for many months.

'Why're you looking so damn fed up, son?'

'I just . . .' he stuttered. 'Did I forget a birthday?'

Marco waved a hand at him, then motioned for one of the women to pour a glass of champagne. 'Do you always need a reason? Isn't it possible I was just bored with being miserable? It's so enervating after a while. And all this crap out there. Your work. Sara . . .' Marco cast a glance back at the women chatting in the living room, the dog at Bea's feet. 'Whatever the facts tell you, Nic, I think she's a good woman. She just doesn't realize it herself.'

'I know.' He hesitated. He didn't want to break the spell. 'That's what makes it so hard to understand.'

'Bullshit!' Marco declared. 'How can you understand someone until you get to know them? You fret about things too much. You want everything wrapped up all nice and tidy before you'll deign to touch it. Relax, Nic. Make the most of things while they're still there.'

He picked up a glass of champagne and raised it to his father. '*Salute!*'

'And to you, my son. There . . .' Marco cocked an ear. 'You know that sound?'

Women chattering. The dog yelping at their feet for attention. Voices ringing off the plain stone walls of the farmhouse. He knew what his father meant. 'Yes.'

'How many years since we heard that racket in here? Eight, since you were the last to leave home? A house needs the noise of people or it starts to die. That's what I've been missing all this time. I'm going to record you all secretly and play it back when you're gone. Do that and you could fool yourself into thinking you'll live for ever.'

Nic Costa was unable to take his eyes off the women in the other room. Sara looked so calm, so lovely. Bea, too, was transformed, as if being invited back to spend some social time with Marco was the greatest compliment she could receive.

'And Bea?' he asked.

'She deserved it. That's all. I'm an idiot, Nic. You should know that about your father. I was never good at seeing things in other people. That was your mother's talent. It's where you got it from.'

The four of them sat down as couples around the dining-room table and admired the feast. Then the two women from the agency lit the large, antique candles Marco had insisted be set up throughout the ground floor and turned down the electric lights. He paid them, with much thanks, and they were gone. The farmhouse was now lit like a canvas. There were deep shadows where the guttering flames failed to reach, and rich, natural colours, the ancient timber table, the subtle red of the curtains, the ochre of the walls, in the idle beam of the waxy light.

'A toast!' Marco declared. 'You were right, Nic. There is a birthday. But whose?'

He looked at Bea and Sara. They had no answers. 'I give up.'

Marco raised his glass to the dog. Baffled, Pepe placed his paws on the old man's knees and was rewarded with a slice of dried beef. 'To him, of course. We bought the dog three months after your mother died, when he was eight weeks old. By my reckoning, that makes him ten today and I shall brook no arguments. Least of all from him.'

'The dog!' Sara repeated. Nic did the same and enjoyed the hard cold taste of the wine in his mouth.

'And the wisdom of dogs,' Marco added. 'Which surpasses our own if only we knew it.'

Bea cast a doubtful eye over the creature staring lovingly into Marco's face. 'Now *that* requires an explanation.'

'Surely not. Think of us. Consumed by worry about events beyond our control. Forever watching the clock and wondering what tomorrow brings. What concerns a dog? The present, only. Will he be loved? Will he be fed? He's no concept of tomorrow, no idea that any of this comes to an end. All he cares about is the here and now and he cares about that passionately, more passionately than any of us could imagine.'

'That's a kind of wisdom?' Sara wondered.

'Absolutely,' Marco insisted. 'Not our kind, but one that serves a dog very well. There's a lesson for us too. You don't remember, Nic? That little scene after we got him?'

Nic toyed with some buffalo mozzarella and refilled the wine glasses. Marco was now taking a little alcohol. 'Don't embarrass me with childhood stories, please. That's the cruellest trick a parent can play.'

'Not this one. It's informative. A man should always be ready to be informed.'

He sighed. 'And it's about?'

'Life and death,' Marco replied, amused. 'What else is there?'

Forty-three

It was impossible to move for bodies. Every tourist in the city seemed to have migrated to the Piazza Navona. Rossi scanned the ocean of blank faces, grateful that Valena had been smart enough to dash straight into the embassy building and not linger to sign autographs or attract the attention of the paparazzi. The small-time crooks were out in force, attracted by the prospect of stray handbags and easy pickings among the crowds. Rossi recognized a couple in a single sweep of the square. He'd seen two uniformed cops on duty – no more. It was a disgrace. The hucksters were just working the hordes of visitors with the usual set of scams: cards and cheap gifts, invitations to 'night clubs' and simple, sly theft.

'I like it here,' Cattaneo said. 'This is what living in Rome's all about.'

The big man scowled at him. 'It's a dump. It's Disneyland.'

It wasn't really. He knew enough history for that. In daylight, when it was half empty, the place was beautiful. It still followed the oval outline of the old Roman stadium that preceded it. He could just about imagine chariots racing round the perimeter. There was the big

fountain of the four rivers by Bernini, who seemed to
have built half of Rome. The piazza didn't bug him. He
could almost like it. The people were the problem. They
were just too loose, too relaxed to help him keep his mind
on the job when he was this tired. If Gino Fosse wanted
to attack the jerk from the TV – if he felt like just walking
up to him on the steps of the embassy as he left and
pumping a gun in his face – there was no way two cops
could stop him. The one consolation, Rossi thought, was
that this wasn't the man's style. It was too plain, too
prosaic. Every time he killed someone Fosse made a statement about himself, one that said: *See me? I'm different,
I'm smart, and I can send you to Hell in ways you never
even dreamed of.*

'Will you look at that?' Cattaneo gasped in delight.

The fake statue artists were out in droves. Rossi could
see at least eight of them, each covered in make-up,
perched on an upturned crate with a few simple props,
trying to get a little cash out of the tourists. It was honest,
he guessed. The first time he'd seen the trick, years
before, it was quite amusing. Then they appeared everywhere and soon ran out of subject-matter. At that
moment there were two Statues of Liberty, one Mona
Lisa, one strange, fluorescent alien and any number of
classical Roman figures in togas, a couple with scrolls in
their hands, all standing stock still in the square trying
not to blink. The nearest, who was no more than three
metres away, had painted himself a powdery white,
splashed the same stuff on what looked like a grubby bed
sheet, thrown the cloth around his shoulders and was
now pretending to be Julius Caesar or somebody. No,
Rossi thought, that was wrong. He had a full head of hair
and a young, half-handsome face. Caesar had to be bald.

He needed a laurel wreath. This was just a chancer trying to make some quick money. Maybe he was supposed to be Brutus, though his hair seemed a little long for that. There was one other point Rossi had got wrong too, he realized. It was about more than just standing there not moving a muscle for minutes on end. At some point you had to drop the guard. You had to let the people in the crowd know it was part of the game – by winking or even touching them – because that was the trigger that made them reach into their pockets. If you never moved an inch they'd just walk on. This was meant to be entertainment, after all.

Rossi stared at Brutus. This moron didn't even get it. He really didn't move. The whole act was just plain shoddy, unconvincing. He'd be hustling for a metro ticket before long, hoping to turn his gauche inexperience into sympathy.

Cattaneo tapped his arm. 'Now that Mona Lisa. She's a looker. She'll get all the money.'

He watched the figure in the black dress, standing with her head in a gold-painted frame just a few metres along from Brutus. 'It's a man,' Rossi said. 'I arrested him for picking someone's pocket once.'

'You're kidding me?' Cattaneo gasped. 'You mean he's a queer?'

'No,' Rossi replied, exasperated. 'Don't be so damned literal. This is what he does. It doesn't make him queer.'

People always got that wrong, he thought. Appearances were deceptive. Sometimes they were meant to be that way. The idea nagged at him but he felt too tired to examine it any further.

He looked at his watch. 'Where the hell is the creep? An hour he said. It's been at least . . .'

Rossi couldn't remember when Valena had walked up the marble steps of the embassy into the reception. It just seemed a long time ago.

'It's been fifty-eight minutes,' Cattaneo said. 'He's not due yet.'

Rossi swore under his breath, hating the precise little bastard by his side. Then he looked at the door. Valena's fat frame was waddling through it, brushing aside anyone who stood in his way.

'Looks like his timing's as bad as mine,' the big man said. 'Tut, tut. He could have spent a hundred and twenty more seconds inside with the glitzy people.'

'Yeah,' Cattaneo agreed, and then found himself staring at Rossi's broad back as the older man walked over to greet Valena.

He stood on the steps, looking nervous. He had food stains down the front of his white shirt. He smelled of drink, champagne probably, Rossi guessed.

'What kind of service is this?' Valena demanded. 'You're supposed to be looking after me every second I'm outside.'

'Apologies,' Rossi said, noting that Cattaneo had caught up with him now. 'We didn't want to cramp your style.'

'Idiots!' Valena bellowed. His eyes looked a little too wild. Rossi wondered if there was just alcohol rolling around inside his fat frame. Maybe he'd added a little white powder in there to help things along.

'Your car awaits, sir,' Rossi said with a wave. The two men watched him roll along ahead then Rossi cursed himself, caught up with the man and walked by his right, as he was supposed to. His head wasn't working properly.

It was just plain exhaustion. Cattaneo did the same on the other side. They picked up pace towards the far side of the piazza where Rossi had left the car. Then Cattaneo put a hand on Valena's arm. The TV man stopped, his head revolving right and left. Really out of it, Rossi saw. There surely was something floating around his fat-filled veins.

'Do the honours,' Cattaneo barked.

'What?' Rossi thought he would hit the man one day. He was just too infuriating.

'Look. He's good. Give him something for Christ's sake. Here . . .'

He threw some coins in front of the astonished Valena. The living statue, the one who looked like Brutus but with hair that was too long, smiled and caught them in a cheap black hat. He was holding it, fingers over the rim which was held tight in his very large thumb, panning for money.

'For the love of God,' Rossi declared and still found himself reaching in his pocket for money, wondering about these instant reactions and why you never questioned them.

Brutus was still on his crate. He was smiling like a loon. He was terrible, Rossi recalled. It was a crime just to give him money.

The big man pulled out a few coins and dropped them in the hat. It was odd. The statue wouldn't stop smiling like that, as if this wasn't about money at all.

'Enough,' Rossi said, looking around for the uniformed men, discovering that once again they were never there when you needed them. 'You don't get a cent more. You just beat it now or I start to get mad.'

Brutus bowed his head, still smiling. Luca Rossi suddenly felt his spine go cold. There was something familiar about the face. He knew it somehow, not well, but enough to make him think it deserved attention.

Forty-four

'As I said,' Marco continued, 'we bought the dog in sad circumstances. I don't even recall what gave us the idea. We scarcely even spoke about it.'

Nic shuffled on his seat, feeling uncomfortable. These were memories he didn't want revived. The past was difficult, painful. From time to time it pricked his mind unbidden, it pointed the way to the future. Sara watched him, saw how he felt. Her fingers briefly touched the back of his hand.

'And there I was one day. Talking to this man with a dog for sale, spouting nonsense, not knowing what questions to ask, whether this was a good idea at all. He was an old farmer with a little smallholding down the road there, a surly bastard who looked at me as if I were an idiot. Which I was, in his eyes, I guess, but this was all new to me. All he kept repeating was, "It's a dog." As if that said everything.'

He shuffled in his wheelchair, thinking of what should come next. 'I brought him home in my jacket. He peed and crapped in it on the way. The first night he cried, constantly, and none of us slept.'

'That I do remember,' Nic interjected.

'And the second night he cried a little less. By the third he was sleeping, in the kitchen there, starting to make it his home. There was just Nic and Giulia with me then, you understand. Young Marco was at college already. We were three damaged, angry people, full of hurt about what the world had done to us. Full of some stupid, blind fury over a loss that made no sense. And here was a dog, demanding we keep him alive, we love him, we give him so much attention, night and day. And what did you do, Nic?'

'I gave him it,' he said. 'So did Giulia. So did you, less than the rest of us, if you want to know, though it was still you he always saw as the boss. Some things never change.'

Marco shook his head. 'It was just age. He loved you then. If he had the brains to remember, the strength to play those games all over again, he'd love you in the same way now.'

The old man was right there. Nic had spent hour after hour with the dog, on walks through summer fields full of flowers and the humming of bees. In these lovely, lonely places he would talk to the animal as if it were a human being. They were inseparable. Then he'd grown older, and so had the dog. Time had worked its cruel trick once more.

'One day,' Marco said, 'I came home. It was just before Nic left school for college and that worried him, I think. But there was something else too. You remember?'

He did and he wished he could stop the old man saying it.

'I remember. Is this really . . .'

'Nic was almost as upset as the day his mother had died and it was over this. He'd come to think about the dog, an animal which has a natural lifespan of – what? – ten, twelve, perhaps thirteen years? He'd come to realize that one day, a day not that far distant, Pepe would be gone. Not in a human lifetime, but in a canine one, which seems so short to us. And he thought what? Come, Sara. You're the psychic, you tell us.'

She looked at Nic, wondering if it would embarrass him. It was so obvious. It was understandable too. 'He thought it was pointless. Owning the dog. Growing to love him. Growing to adore having him around. Knowing all along that one day he would die, and so soon.'

Marco watched her closely. 'And is he right?'

'I don't think there's a right or wrong for a question like that,' she replied cautiously. 'I can see his point. I can appreciate why one would think that way.'

'There, Bea! Behold the young. What have we done to bring them up like this?'

The older woman stared at both of them, amazed. 'And you both think this? Sara? Nic? I'm no dog lover. Even that damned animal can see that. But you must take what joy you find, while it's there. Not go worrying about a tomorrow that might never come.'

'And that,' Marco said, banging his glass on the table, 'is the wisdom of dogs.'

'Which is ignorance!' Sara declared. 'Surely you can see that? A dog has no comprehension of time. Of seasons. As far as it is concerned life is like a light switch, either on or off.'

'And isn't it?' Marco demanded, teasingly.

'No.' She looked at Nic for support.

'I agree,' he said. 'It's a bad comparison.'

'What you mean is,' Bea suggested, 'they never read

Ecclesiastes. A time to be born, and a time to die; a time to plant, and a time to pluck up that which is planted.'

'A time to love,' Marco continued. 'And a time to hate; a time of war, and a time of peace. You're right, Sara. An animal knows nothing of the seasons and that's what defines him. Are we that different? It was the knowledge of our mortality that informed all those early Christians buried along that old road out there. Today we make death the uninvited guest who sits in the corner, in perpetual darkness. We pretend he doesn't exist until finally he proves us wrong and then we are shocked – we are offended! – by his presence.'

Nic waved a defensive hand at him. 'Point taken. I understand what you mean.'

'Not at all!' Marco insisted. 'That was aimed at me more than you, son. I've let this damned thing wear me down so much I took the opposite view. I thought there was nothing but death around me. A time to plant, a time to pluck up that which is planted. This is a farm, remember? Until this blasted disease we fed ourselves from those fields. We turned the land, we grew, we harvested. And look at it now. Bare, barren earth. And for what reason? Because I forgot. Because, like a child, I believed I was the world and without me nothing existed which is, I think, the greatest sin a man can commit.'

There was silence. The mood of the evening pivoted around Marco's confession, and each of them knew it could easily disintegrate. Then Sara asked, 'What was this like as a farm?'

'Wonderful,' Nic replied, smiling, grateful that she had chosen the moment. 'We could grow anything then. I remember . . .' His head filled with the recollection of artichoke heads nodding in the breeze, tall rows of tomatoes, verdant clumps of *zucchini*. 'I remember how green it was.'

'Why do you think he eats what he does?' Marco asked. 'He gave up meat when he was twelve. Said there was no point.'

'There wasn't. And what we grew was ours. It came from us.'

Marco wheeled himself to the front door. They followed, watching as he unlatched the huge slab of wood, threw it open and turned on the floodlights which illuminated the front of the farm. The cigarettes of the men at the gate winked back at them like tiny fireflies. The earth stood arid and solid under the harsh lamps.

'And the best part,' Marco said, 'was the unexpected.'

Around now, he said, they would plant the black Tuscan kale *cavolo nero* for the winter. Sara watched the way his eyes glittered when he spoke about how they were his favourites for the very reason most people would avoid them: their sluggish, steady growth, from seedlings at the waning of summer, through the lean, cold winter months, reviving again, to give nourishment, in the spring. This was a rebirth of a kind, a token that the world began anew each year, whatever happened. A seedling planted in the earth in July knew nothing of the future that would embrace it when the warmth returned the following Easter – that is, if it survived the winter. This was a peasant's faith, and one that Marco Costa loved, the fundamental belief that the seasons always returned and good husbandry would be repaid. It was inevitable that the chain would be broken. Some years the crop would fail. Some years the gardener would fail to return to tend the land. Nevertheless, it was the act itself which mattered: the planting, the nurturing, the tilling of the soil.

There had been no winter crop that year. Marco's faith had failed him, crushed by the disease.

She watched the old man eyeing the earth. 'I want to see things growing there again,' he said. 'Tomorrow . . . I'll send for help.'

Sara looked at Bea and the two women exchanged glances. 'What's wrong with us? We can dig. We can plant seeds.'

Marco laughed and waved a dismissive hand at them. 'This isn't work for women.' They screeched at him.

'Peace, peace,' Nic said. 'They can start in the morning. Later, when I've time, I'll do my part too. You can just sit and watch and bark orders.'

'It has to be done properly,' Marco insisted.

'It will be,' Nic replied. 'I promise.'

They looked at one another and fell silent. The storm never broke. Marco had made his point.

The old man sniffed the air. 'There's autumn inside that heat,' he said. 'You can smell September on the way. I love the autumn. The colours. Sitting round the fire, burning a few chestnuts. I wouldn't want to be anywhere else when the leaves start to fall.'

Nic walked behind him, placing a hand on his shoulder. Marco's fingers gripped his. Nic felt his eyes begin to sting and was grateful for this moment.

'Old reds like me don't believe in Hell,' Marco said. 'But if I did, do you know what it would be? A place where nothing grows. A place where no one knows the seasons. God save us all from that, if you'll pardon the expression.'

Forty-five

Rossi cursed himself. It was so obvious when he thought about it. They'd found just one blurry picture of Gino Fosse and here, he now knew, was the same face, covered in white powder trying to pretend to be a statue. He grappled inside his jacket, trying to get the gun out, yelling at Cattaneo, yelling at the TV jerk, telling them to get down, to keep out of the way because Brutus wasn't Brutus at all, he was some crazy, bloodthirsty priest who didn't know when to stop. At least Cattaneo seemed on the ball then. He dragged Valena into the massing crowd by the scruff of his neck. Rossi turned and watched the two of them tumble into the mass of bodies then fell back, trying to follow them.

His hand felt greasy. His mouth went dry. By the time his fingers reached the butt of the weapon Brutus had leaned forward on his crate. The hat had fallen from his hands, Luca Rossi's few coins were rolling on the ground making a precise, musical sound oddly audible over the animal racket of the crowd. Maybe the metallic chink of the coins was, the big man thought, the last thing he'd ever hear.

Then the swarm of people closed around him and

Rossi was fighting to clear his head. Shoulders jostled him. Tourists yelled abuse. He held up his gun, high above the mass, trying to make them see some sense. Not knowing why – not even understanding whether this was a conscious action – he fired a single shot into the air and sent some small slug of lead flying out of Bernini's piazza, spinning wildly towards the bright moon set in a black velvet sky.

Someone nearby screamed. He saw a woman's bulbous, gaudily made-up eyes and they reminded him of the look he once saw on a bull as it went into the slaughterhouse.

'Luca!' It was Cattaneo yelling. He held Rossi by the arm. Valena was firmly attached to the other. Luca Rossi felt like a jerk. He'd always hated Cattaneo. Always thought him a loser. And here they were, rolling around inside some steadily panicking mass of people, not knowing where they were going or what was on their trail.

Cattaneo was barking something into the radio. Rossi raised his hand again, let the gun pump upwards once more. It felt good. It felt like a statement, something even a warped priest with blood on his hands and a penchant for women's heads might begin to comprehend. Then a big figure in a Stars and Stripes T-shirt pushed hard into him. Rossi felt the breath disappear from his chest, a sharp pain rising underneath his ribs. The strength left him, just for an instant. It was enough for the gun to slip from his grip, out from his fingers, tugged down by the nagging force of gravity into the sea of stampeding legs at his feet.

Rossi bent over, gasping for air, noting as he did so that some space appeared to be growing around him.

When he had his senses back – as much as he could muster – he pulled himself upright. Brutus was there, smiling in front of him, with a semi-circle of scared tourists at his back. He looked like a bit-part actor suddenly thrust into the limelight. He had something in his hand, something small and light and deadly.

Luca Rossi stared at it, saw Cattaneo racing to his side. He said, simply, 'Shit.'

The weapon shrieked once, jerked back in Fosse's fingers, then changed direction, just as Rossi's sight was beginning to fail him and a thick, stupid pain started to cloud his ears.

The last sound was thunder repeating itself, a muffled, echoing roar through which Luca Rossi wished to make some final point, about living and dying and what ought and ought not to be accomplished. Except it was impossible. Something stole away his thoughts, left him helpless, unable to speak. There was a hand on his shoulder and he knew it was Cattaneo's. The idiot was dragging him down to the hard stone ground of the piazza. He fell with an extraordinary, irresistible momentum, down towards the red pool running into the cracks of the cobblestones like a sluggish river, growing, turning into a flood.

Gino Fosse stood back, wiped his mouth with the back of his hand and looked at the two stupid cops prone on the ground, not moving. The crowd was going wild. They were screaming, fighting to get away from this white figure, his fake toga now stained with the splashback of Luca Rossi's blood.

Only Arturo Valena didn't run. The fat TV presenter stood there, cowering, unable to move, alone in a circle being created by the fleeing bodies around him.

Fosse walked up and held the revolver tight against Valena's sweating temple.

'Come with me,' he said. 'Quickly, by my side. Right now.'

Valena nodded.

A minute later the dogs had company.

Forty-six

She stood outside the main door, beneath the vine veranda, marvelling at the evening. The heat of the day had dissipated. Fireflies now danced through the twisting shapes of the olive trees that crouched on the moonlit horizon. The champagne had been followed by white wine, then red. They were all quite drunk, even Marco. It was as if the house had infected them with its spirit, as if its rich, hidden memories had woken from some dream and come to inhabit them. The coming day would exorcize these happy ghosts. She knew that had to happen. Still, Sara Farnese was grateful for the fleeting gift they had each received at Marco's prompting. The timing was welcome. The nightmare of the city was still real. There were hardships and trials ahead but they were not insurmountable. There was hope. There was the possibility of redemption in the light which shone in all their faces that night.

Bea took Marco to his bedroom and did not emerge again. Nic, perhaps to cover his embarrassment, had dragged the sleepy, stiff Pepe out for a final walk around the grounds. Sara could hear him talking to the men at the end of the drive: slow, lazy chatter, not the whispered, feverish talk men had when things were going wrong. They all deserved a respite from Gino Fosse. It wouldn't last. That was impossible. Yet even the shortest break seemed like a miracle. It gave her space to think, to breathe. Here, beyond the grip of the city, safe in the cool darkness of the farmhouse, surrounded by people who didn't judge her, didn't look at her as if she were a different kind of creature, Sara felt briefly content in a way she did not wish to analyse.

Marco himself had said it: nothing stayed the same. The world was in flux, always. This was its gift; this was its burden too.

She stepped onto the dry, hard ground and kicked at it with her shoe. It was impossible to believe anything could grow in such conditions. She knew nothing about gardening. Bea was probably just as ignorant. But with Marco's guidance, which would, she felt sure, be exact and exacting, something would take root here. It would become fertile and one day bring forth produce, though she knew she would never be there to witness it.

Nic stepped out of the darkness, from behind one of the few living things near the house, an old, wizened almond tree. The leaves rustled lightly in the breeze. He looked happy. She was glad, for him and for Marco. Something had passed between them, some unspoken pact, that night. There was no news from the policemen at the gate. Perhaps the distant city was quiet. Perhaps Gino Fosse slept easy, the demons gone from his head, if only for a little while.

The dog stepped forward, cocked a leg and peed profusely on the trunk of the tree. They laughed.

'The wisdom of dogs,' Sara said.

Pepe came to sit tamely at their feet. 'Or the

ignorance,' Nic answered. 'He doesn't know what lies ahead. He doesn't understand what there is to anticipate.'

'And because we do that makes us wiser?'

'I think so. Not happier perhaps.'

The dog's eyes closed behind dry, wrinkled lids. He looked old like that, she thought. He looked like Marco: grey and wasting.

'It's not enough for them to be alive,' she said, patting the old fur. 'They need to live. Happy birthday, Pepe.'

The dog stared at them both then fixed its gaze on the door with a firm deliberation.

An awkward silence fell between them. Sara turned and let them in. The dog ambled across the threshold, found its bed in the kitchen and curled its frail body into a lazy apostrophe.

She watched the animal settle, knowing Nic couldn't take his eyes off her.

Forty-seven

The dog catcher's van was parked inconspicuously outside the church of San Lorenzo in Lucina in a small piazza north of the parliamentary area where Alicia Vaccarini had dined with Gino Fosse the day before. The site had been associated with the martyr Lorenzo since the fourth century though a temple, probably to Juno, had existed here long before, its columns, crowned by medieval capitals, re-used in the dark portico that gave onto the square. The delicate illumination of the piazza now outlined the plain triangular pediment and the Romanesque bell tower, much like the one on Tiber Island, behind. In spite of its location next to the Via del Corso, the church retained a modest, fetching dignity. Gino Fosse was unable to forget the place for entirely different reasons.

This was, he knew, where the cycle began, where the doubts which first rose in his head in the dark belly of San Giovanni hardened, became real and demanded action. One week ago to the day Brendan Hanrahan had phoned him, sounding amiable, sympathetic, wondering why Denney had reacted so ruthlessly to what was, in truth, a minor infraction. Hanrahan suggested they meet, take a short tour of the city, visit some places which would, he believed, intrigue him.

Thirty minutes later the Irishman pulled up outside the tower in the Clivus Scauri inside one of the black Mercedes Gino Fosse knew so well. Then, as a chauffeur drove them around the city, the Irishman introduced him to Lorenzo's tale. In the van with Arturo Valena screaming pointlessly to the howling of the dogs beside him, he could still recall the moment the poisonous worm locked its jaws hard into his soul. Perhaps Hanrahan had noticed it. The Irishman missed very little. Perhaps he had wanted it there, feasting.

It was a scalding, airless day, the first to give a hint of the heat wave that was to come. Hanrahan ordered the driver to take a circuitous route passing the Villa Celimontana, the public park close to the Clivus Scauri.

'The man has a terrible temper sometimes,' he confided. 'Denney, I mean. I imagine he blames it on the stress, Gino. But we're all under stress now, aren't we?'

He had dead eyes, a dead face. Gino Fosse knew why they used him to fix things. Nothing was beneath Hanrahan. He was relentless, patient, forever planning.

'Note the fountain,' Hanrahan indicated as they rounded the park entrance. He had admired the stone boat with its generous water spout, uncertain about Hanrahan's intentions.

'An old priest from Limerick took me on this tour when I first came to Rome. Now I wish to return the favour to you. To take you through an entire episode of our glorious history, Gino,' Hanrahan declared. 'I'm a bureaucrat, not a churchman, so pay attention and forgive any errors, though I think I know this story well enough to be true to it throughout.

'Let's imagine,' he said, in the manner of a teacher, 'that today is August the sixth in the year of our Lord 258. The emperor is Valerian, no friend to the Church at all. Lorenzo, a Spaniard and one of the six Christian deacons of Rome, is standing on the grass over there handing out money to the poor, money he has gained from selling some of the Church's gold. Valerian has heard of this, decided he wants to wet his beak too, and demanded that Lorenzo show him the remainder of the Church's rich treasures so that he may claim his imperial share.'

Fosse had not been sleeping soundly. The incident which led to his banishment from the Vatican continued to puzzle him. He had behaved no more badly before. Hanrahan was right. The punishment seemed out of kilter with the crime.

'For three days Lorenzo has assembled a crowd close to where the fountain now stands and is giving out alms. He's surrounded by the poverty-stricken and aided by supportive fellow Christians. When Valerian's soldiers come and ask him for the emperor's gold, he gives them not a penny. Instead, he points to the assembled crowd and declares, "See! Here is the treasure of the Church."'

'Sounds like he was asking for trouble,' Fosse observed.

'Quite,' Hanrahan agreed. 'And he got it.'

He pointed to the Palatine passing to their left, on the opposite side of the road. 'Had we time, we could still follow Lorenzo along every stage of his impending martyrdom. He was dragged through the Cryptoporticus passage, up there, which you may walk today, to a trial, the verdict of which was already decided. We could go to the church of San Lorenzo in Fonte, in the Via

Urbana, see the cell in which he was incarcerated and the fountain he used to baptize his fellow prisoners. After that we could visit San Lorenzo fuori le Mura, built over the humble chapel Constantine himself erected to mark the martyr's burial place. In San Lorenzo in Panisperna, close by, we could stand on the site of his death and admire a vivid fresco of him receiving the martyr's reward, though this is a work that's perhaps a little too realistic, I think, for a young man's taste.'

Hanrahan was wrong there. Gino Fosse found these strange depictions of martyrdoms fascinating. He had spent hours in the church of San Stefano Rotondo, not far from the Villa Celimontana, watching the workmen renovate the startling images on the walls there. These pictures spoke to him, saying something he could not quite understand. On the martyrs' lips, as they endured their agonies, there was some cryptic eternal secret they could share across the centuries if only he knew the key.

When they reached San Lorenzo in Lucina and fought their way through the lazy crowds of shoppers into the small church in the square, Hanrahan had stood him in front of Reni's *Crucifixion* and asked what he thought. Fosse was indifferent. It seemed, he said, somewhat romanticized, unreal. A man would not die on the cross quite so prettily. Hanrahan had grinned with pleasure and pointed out the monument marking the grave of a French artist Fosse barely knew, Poussin. 'Another romantic,' Hanrahan declared. 'You know Caravaggio?'

'Of course,' Fosse agreed. 'He's wonderful. He paints real people.'

'Quite,' Hanrahan continued. He kicked the Poussin monument. 'This idiot derided him for his "partiality for ugliness and vulgarity". By which he meant, of course,

Caravaggio's wilful attempt to portray humanity as it was, not as seen through a pair of rose-tinted spectacles. We mustn't fool ourselves into thinking we're more than we are, Gino. Caravaggio was a thug and a lunatic and he knew it too, just as well as he understood his genius.'

He had agreed and Hanrahan had led them into the Fonseca chapel where the Bernini busts sat like frozen decapitated heads on their plinths. They then returned and spent a few minutes in silence on the hard seats in the nave.

Finally, Gino Fosse asked the inevitable question. 'What happened to Lorenzo?'

'Dead, of course,' Hanrahan said with a mock mournfulness.

Fosse was in no mood for black jokes. He was mildly disturbed. He had been looking into a small side chapel which contained a strange, glinting object. An elderly man was on his knees in front of the iron railings which separated it from the nave. He seemed intent on the odd, metallic frame beyond the bars. Then something had moved there. A rat, he was sure of it. And, in the shadows, a half-visible figure too, dressed in a dark-red cardinal's robe, looking much like Michael Denney. A man who may, in some way Gino Fosse could not quite envisage at that moment, be some kind of martyr too.

'Of course he's dead,' he said. 'But what happened?'

Hanrahan stood up. Gino Fosse followed him to the bars of the side chapel, standing next to the praying man, his head hurting. There was no mistake now. A rat was moving underneath the altar, scampering in and out of the light. At least it appeared to be alone. The figure in red was gone and he knew it was simply some strange creation of his imagination.

'When Lorenzo failed to find any gold the authorities were very cross. All the normal punishments seemed somehow inapposite for a crime of this nature. So he was sentenced to be roasted to death over a slow fire while strapped to an iron grille so that he was, very gradually, cooked.'

Fosse watched the shining eyes of the rat gleam from the shadows.

'What?'

'You heard,' Hanrahan said. 'Think of Tertullian. The blood of the martyrs . . . Lorenzo was among the bravest, which is why he's named in the canon of the mass. Several senators converted on the basis of his courage alone, believing that God must have spared him the true agony of his martyrdom, since he was in good humour throughout the entire ordeal. The poet Prudentius later wrote that he laughed and joked for the duration, telling his torturers at one point, "I'm done on that side; turn me over, and eat." '

The kneeling man rose and walked away, cursing under his breath.

'The grille is preserved,' Hanrahan said with a sudden dramatic gesture. 'There. You may admire it.'

He followed the direction of the Irishman's arm and saw the cruel iron structure in its enclosure, finally realizing what it was.

Gino Fosse had checked out this story afterwards. Hanrahan was being truthful, after a fashion. The gridiron was, some believed, a later invention. Prudentius was not born until eighty years after the event. In all probability, Lorenzo had been beheaded like most of those who figured in the early, bloody history of the Church. Perhaps all the martyr stories he had heard in

Rome – Bartholomew carrying his skin, Lucy with her eyes on a plate, Sebastian shot full of arrows – were inventions too. There was no way of knowing and never would be; no archaeologist had dug up the evidence, as they had in Santi Giovanni e Paolo. Everything was conjecture, dependent on faith; without it Lorenzo became simply a character in a fairy story, a player in a fourth-century tale from Grimm designed to cow the gullible into submission.

Then Brendan Hanrahan leaned over and whispered in his ear, the close, hoarse whisper of a man in the confessional. The words burned in his head. The rat scuttered across the floor in front of the altar once more. In his mind's eye – and he knew this could not be real – Cardinal Michael Denney really did lie on the rack now, over a slow flame, like that of some country barbecue, grinning at them both and laughing through a dead mouth, asking, 'Am I done yet? Are any of us done yet? Will *she* be here soon? Is *she* getting hungry too?'

It had occurred to him that there were so many stories concerning instant conversions, from Paul onwards. The Church revelled in them. Yet there must be some counter-balance to these: events, sights, sounds, perhaps even an odour that destroyed a lifetime's faith in an instant. How many Catholics walked into Belsen and walked out atheists? How many, on a more mundane level, felt some darkness enter their soul while walking down the street, put one foot in front of the other and found their previously held beliefs were gone for ever? That they had lost twice over, spending half their life in ignorance and the rest in the solitary despair of knowing there was no salvation and never had been?

He looked again. There was no cardinal roasting

slowly on the rack. Only the rat, running on the iron bars, bright eyes glittering back at him in the darkness.

A rat could steal away the last few remnants of your faith, snatch it from your mouth, then shred it to pieces with its sharp, sharp teeth, slowly, silently in some dark, dusty corner away from the sight of man. It was always the small things, the unexpected things, which would kill you.

Recollecting all this with a grim precision Gino Fosse shook his head, wishing the memories would disappear for ever. They clouded his judgement. They stole from him his determination. There was no time for thinking, only action. He'd killed two cops, something he'd never envisaged when this began. There would be repercussions. This was, he thought, the precursor to the end. Events were circling around him like crows eyeing a coming meal. Within the next twenty-four hours everything could surely be accomplished. It was a welcoming thought. He was growing tired of the game. He was impatient for the inevitable resolution.

How quickly that happened depended on what he did next. Denney had proved himself a stubborn man, unwilling to run, to let himself be exposed to risk, in the face of the most severe provocation. There had to be a final exertion, a turn in the savagery none of them expected.

Gino Fosse had rubbed off the white make-up, as much as he could. He wore his old clothes again: jeans and a black T-shirt. He was sweating like a pig. The night was unbearably close. The city felt like an oven. He felt conspicuous, as if the darkness was full of eyes, glittering rodent eyes, greedy human ones, glancing feverishly in his direction. He stuck his head outside the van window.

The piazza was empty. A few lone figures wandered down the Corso, past the shuttered shops and the flashing neon signs in the windows.

He picked up the sack of keys he had stolen six days before from the administration office in the Vatican when he called to pick up the rest of his belongings. He sorted through them until he found the set marked for the church. He had reversed the van so that the rear door was tight against the locked entrance into the building. No one would see Arturo Valena being dragged inside. Behind those heavy wooden doors, in this deserted part of the city, no one would hear what then ensued.

Forty-eight

They stood in the corridor on the landing, unable to find the words. It was quiet downstairs now. The house was silent, filled with some strange happiness, an oasis of sanity hidden from the sight of the hard, bleak world beyond the gates. Sara thought of the other times; how she had allowed herself to be used, how her own desires were always secondary to theirs.

Then, gingerly, she walked up to him and looked into his eyes. Was there fear in them? Perhaps, but not doubt. He had stepped beyond its reach. Something had happened in the old farm that night, moving them all: Bea, in her search for love before it disappeared, Marco in his quest for some meaning in this fast-diminishing period of life which had been left to him. She, too, had been touched by their closeness, their frank questions and answers. This was so unlike the world she had inhabited before. Here no one asked for anything except her presence and understanding. This small, enclosed universe – and Nic Costa – now existed for her satisfaction, to do with as she wished.

Sara Farnese reached out, touched his hair, waiting, mouth tentatively open, for his kiss. He hesitated. She brought her lips up to his, felt his response, letting her tongue wander into his mouth, touch the wetness there, feeling the hard outline of his teeth. His hand came behind her back, strong, determined, and moved below to her thighs, gripping them. In a single powerful movement he lifted her from the ground. Her legs wound around his waist. She tore at his hair, kissed him hard and deep.

Then he carried her purposefully into the bedroom, let her legs slip to the floor and slowly, nervously, with no small wonder, they undressed each other, coming to stand naked by the bed, breathless, full of anticipation.

Again he hesitated.

'Nic,' she whispered.

His dark eyes tried to look inside her, beyond the surface he scarcely knew. 'And tomorrow?'

'Tomorrow I plant seeds for your father,' she said without a moment's hesitation.

She looked at the bathroom and the small marble shower in the corner.

'Here,' she said, taking him by the hand.

He followed her into the cubicle. She turned on the water, letting it run down on their heads, soaking their hair, stone cold at first, then lukewarm.

He laughed.

She took the liquid and began working it into his soft white skin. His head came down to her neck. His lips closed gently on a nipple. Her face arched upwards, teeth clenched, charged by a new and sudden determination in his grip. She felt his hardness, reached down, let her fingers run up and down its length and leaned back against the cold wet tiles, opening her legs, guiding him.

For a minute, no more, he entered her, making a few

measured strokes, shallow at first, then gradually deeper until she clung to him, hand tight in the back of his head, legs wrapped around his back.

She sighed, anguished, as he withdrew. Nic led her to the bed, watched as she spread herself across the white coverlet, beckoning. He was thinking about where to begin, what to consume first. His head went down, his teeth suckled briefly at her breasts and moved on to probe her navel. Her breath caught and shortened to brief snatches. This was new to her. In the past she had always been the one to serve, who sought to deliver satisfaction. Nic was determined to deliver that gift to her. His tongue licked lower, pressed beyond her hair, found her widening, warm crevice, entered fully, writhing inside with a powerful, muscular intent. She held his scalp, forced him down further into her, arching her back, wishing she could open herself so wide he might be consumed in the rich fleshy dampness of her sex. Then, with a certain, relentless rhythm, he began to work upon the smallest, sweetest part of her, raising its tumescence until her head had lost all reasoning, her mind knew nothing but the fiery delight he brought. And at this last gasping moment he revealed another secret too: his little finger sought another entry, pressed insistently from a second direction so that these secret, private doors to her ecstasy became a single coursing torrent of wild and shapeless pleasure.

When her shrieks gave way to panting he paused, rising from the bed to peer at the pale, lovely body on the sheets, as surprised by himself as he was by her. She laughed, wiped away the sweat from her brow with the back of her hand, then cupped his face with her hands. His fingers moved across her cheek. She sucked greedily on the tips, tasting herself on the skin and the nails. He moved onto her. She lifted her legs, placed her feet around his back, gripping him, tugging him, demanding more, taking him into her with anxious fingers.

He hesitated again, waiting in front of the unfolding entrance like an uninvited guest unsure of his welcome. Then she held him more tightly and the game ended. In the small bedroom of the farmhouse off the Appian Way, where Nic Costa turned from man to boy, where his personality was forged, through happiness and pain, the oldest ceremony of all was enacted with joy, enacted again and again until a sated exhaustion took them into a sleep undisturbed by dreams, untainted by the memory of a fallen world beyond the open window and the vine-twisted veranda.

Forty-nine

Arturo Valena stumbled out of the back of the van, grateful to leave the dogs behind. He sniffed the petrol-stained breeze from the Corso hopefully, then screeched in terror and pain as Fosse fetched him a hard blow on the side of the head with the butt of the gun.

That was a mistake. Fosse was shocked by his carelessness. He'd half hoped the fat man would fall to the floor unconscious, making what came next easier. It was stupid. He should have realized this before the attempt. Valena was too heavy to be manhandled around a quiet piazza just a few yards from a street that still had its stragglers, even after midnight.

Fosse watched the fat man reeling in pain, wondering whether to run perhaps, and forced himself to think. Then he hit him once again, in the same place on the head but with a little less force, waved the gun in his face and hissed at him to go to the church railings. He had the keys in the small shoulder bag he'd brought with him from the van. He knew the place: where the light switches were. And where to find the instruments for the rest of the artistry.

Valena complied, shambling the few metres to the

entrance. Fosse fumbled at the lock, opened the gate, and pushed the terrified man through into the gloom of the portico. In the space of a minute he had unlocked the door to the church, sent Valena in and set the lights to low.

They stood in the nave, Fosse unable to detach his attention from the small chapel on the right which Brendan Hanrahan had revealed to him. Somewhere beyond the low, glittering frame of the iron grille a tiny voice squeaked. Fosse wished he could see them, not just hear their scuttering in the dark corners: tiny feet running, going nowhere, just like him. In his mind's eye he could imagine their yellow rodent teeth, ready to snatch away his soul the moment he faltered. He could picture their bright eyes glittering, the colour of polished jet. In those black pupils stood another universe, a black one that went on for ever, in time, in every direction, an endless place that could swallow up an entire world and still leave space for millions more.

Valena was trembling, holding himself by a pew. His face was a waxy yellow under the lights and there was an unmistakable flicker of hope there. His abductor had hesitated. Something had spooked him. Perhaps there was a chance.

'What do you want?' he asked, his voice husky with pain. 'Money?'

'Just you,' Fosse said flatly.

Valena's piggy eyes glistened, damp and pathetic. 'I never did anything to you. I never hurt anyone.'

'It's the not doing that counts,' Fosse said. 'You can go to Hell just as easily for your omissions as your deeds. Didn't they tell you that? Didn't you even begin to suspect?'

Valena fell to his knees, put his hands together. 'I'm just a stupid old man,' he pleaded. 'What do you want with me?'

'Your life.'

'Please . . .' His voice rose with that, turning almost into a squeal. It sounded like a rat. It sounded like the end of everything.

'Don't pray to me. Pray to God. And pray for yourself.'

The fat man sobbed. His hands went more tightly together. He closed his eyes. His lips moved, fleshy, blubbery lips, a mouth that had once caressed Sara Farnese. Gino Fosse knew that. He'd been the driver that night. He'd taken the pictures. It was one more stain to erase, one more station of grief along the way.

He reached into the shoulder bag and took out the pack he'd stolen from the hospital. The hypodermic was ready. The liquid sat in the barrel. He walked behind the praying Valena and stabbed him hard in the upper arm. The fat man got up, screeching.

'What are you fucking doing?' His eyes were burning black coals, full of hatred and pain. 'For the love of God . . .'

'Be grateful,' Fosse said. 'Hope it lasts.'

They danced slowly around each other for a while. He wasn't letting the fat man make for the door. Eventually Valena's eyes started to turn dull.

'What?' He swayed once. Then his pupils rose, went upwards into his head. His large frame collapsed like a building that had suddenly lost its foundation. Gino Fosse looked at the pile of humanity that lay on the floor, no more than ten metres from Lorenzo's altar.

The drug was the easiest option. There was much

preparation to be done to achieve the required effect. This would be the last before the final deed. He knew that somehow.

He bent down over the unconscious Valena and began to tug at his clothing. Five minutes later the TV man was naked on the tiles of the church. He'd pissed himself at some stage. Fosse was disgusted but not surprised. Ordinary men feared death, failing to understand the need for the transformation. They lacked the sense and the courage to greet it smiling, welcoming its inevitable embrace.

He turned Valena to face the small altar in the chapel. With no small amount of effort he dragged the iron grille into the nave. It was cold and shiny to the touch, polished for centuries, a perfect instrument alive with its past. Perhaps the story of Lorenzo's death was apocryphal. To Gino Fosse it seemed irrelevant. So many people had come to believe in it that this elaborate construction of iron, with its curlicues and its flamboyant grating, became what they imagined: the gateway to Paradise, the ultimate redemption. Even Arturo Valena deserved that.

Gino Fosse fetched the kindling, the charcoal and the petrol and decided, at this point, that he must cease deluding himself. He'd learned enough in the hospital to understand how long the shot would keep Valena unconscious. It was fifteen minutes, perhaps twenty, no more. Arturo Valena would not sleep his way to judgement.

Fifty

A noise woke her: the sound of a dog barking from some distant farm. He stood at the window, with his back to her, staring out into the blackness of the night, silhouetted against the moon. She looked at the clock on the stand. It was nearly two.

'What's wrong?' she asked softly.

He didn't even turn round.

'Nic? Look at me.'

He sighed and returned to sit on the bed. In the cold light that fell through the window his face wore the same hard expression she had seen when they first met. This was serious Nic, tough Nic, a man who preferred duty over passion. A man who feared anything that might disrupt an ordered, logical world.

'I'm sorry,' she said. 'It was too soon. I should have stopped myself.'

He stared down at the sheets and said nothing.

She took his chin with her hand, made him look at her. 'Don't sit in judgement on me.'

He scowled. It wasn't a pleasant look. 'I'm not. It's me. I didn't want this to happen. I promised myself I wouldn't allow it.'

'And I made you? Is that it?'

'No. Of course not.' He meant what he said, though there was no comfort in his sincerity. 'But that doesn't make it right.'

'It felt right to me,' she replied icily.

That touched him. He reached out and held her hand. 'It felt right to me too. But Sara . . .'

The words ran dry. His reticence annoyed her. 'What?'

'I don't know you. Not really. Just a side of you. There's still something missing, something important in your life you don't want me to see.'

She withdrew from his grasp. 'Haven't you seen enough?'

'No. Because what I know doesn't add up and that just makes everything worse. I don't believe it's the real you. Maybe not even a real part of you either. There's something else. Something you won't disclose. Something you're keeping from me, still, and I can't bear the thought because without that piece of knowledge I feel I don't really know you at all. It just . . . tortures me.'

'Listen to the cop inside you talking. Am I supposed to be more frank after you've screwed me?'

'No!' His voice almost broke. She recognized the truth in what he said and despised herself for doubting him. Nic was honest, too honest perhaps.

She came closer to him, put her hand to his face, stared into his eyes. 'I'm sorry. That was just the fear in me talking. This is hard for me too, you know.'

There was doubt in his eyes. 'Is it? You've a capacity for keeping things inside. I never learnt that.'

'I asked if you'd come off this case for me. I begged. You still can.'

'It's impossible. This is my job. It's what I do.'

'Then maybe this is what I do too. Maybe this is who I am. Just someone who sleeps around and then goes on somewhere else, not remembering, not caring. What's wrong with that? Is it a sin just because you don't think that way?'

He shook his head. 'No, it's a sin because you don't. This person you're trying to paint for me is someone you created and I need to know why.'

'Trust me. You don't need that.'

He put his arms around her shoulders. He kissed her lightly on the mouth then stroked her soft hair. 'I woke up with the taste of you. I can smell you in my head. Don't take this lightly. It doesn't happen to me.'

The first sign of dampness appeared at the corner of her eye. He wiped it away with a finger and placed the tip in his own mouth, tasting the salt of her, as if it were some precious fluid.

She closed her eyes. The tears ran freely down her cheeks. He knew himself to be on the verge of some new discovery and felt disquiet at his own insistent curiosity.

'Tell me,' he murmured.

She wiped her face with her arm then gathered up the sheet around her, ready to leave the room.

'Tell you, Nic? I'll tell you. I promise. When Michael Denney is out of the Vatican and gone from Italy. There. Is that what you want to hear?'

It was the last response he was expecting. No words formed in his head, only thoughts and images of Sara with the old, grey man trapped behind those distant walls in the city.

'No,' he said finally, with a bitterness which surprised him.

She got up from the bed, clutching the sheet to her body. 'Then I'm sorry, but it's true. And you'll hear nothing more from me, not a word, until that's happened.'

He gripped her arm, refusing to let her go. She forced his fingers from her wrist. His head was working over-time, a whirl of ideas, connections.

'Is that all I am?' he spat, shocked at his own unfam-iliar fury. 'Just another random fuck in the night like the rest?'

There was the coldness in those green eyes again. Nic Costa knew he'd broken the spell with his own stupidity.

'You sound like you're back on duty,' she whispered.

He was furious. He wanted to strike her. 'Maybe I am. Maybe I should have stayed there all along.' The cop in him was waking. He took her by the arms and forced her into the bedside chair. 'Let's talk then. Like we're supposed to. Did you sleep with Rinaldi to get that expert opinion to go Denney's way? Did Denney ask you to do that?'

Her eyes were fixed on the dead, dull tiles.

'OK. Don't answer. Either way it doesn't matter. It explains something. And the American, Gallo. He never knew Denney at all. We found nothing to link them. What happened there?'

His mind raced in the silence. 'You used him. Denney needed something. A messenger perhaps. Someone to take a package some place, pay someone off maybe. You slept with Gallo to get him to do favours. Denney didn't even specify him by name. He just asked you to find the right person. Was that what happened with the Englishman too? He was something big with the EU. Did that make him useful to Denney as well?'

'Hugh Fairchild was my lover,' she hissed. 'He came to me for what I am. Don't judge me with your guesswork.'

'He was a married man looking for a warm bed in a strange town. I'm not guessing. I'm just working my way towards something that makes sense. I believe . . .'

'Believe what the hell you like.'

She got up, pushed brusquely past him. He watched her slim figure disappear through the doorway, into the corridor, towards the room at the end of the house, torn by his own warring emotions. He wanted to know; he didn't. She was right. This was all guesswork. It still left so many questions unanswered.

Nic Costa lay back on the crumpled bed clothes, still damp from their bodies, and closed his eyes, wondering if he could sleep. His head filled with such possibilities. His mind ran with images he never wished to imagine. Beyond the window, in the hot darkness, owls called through the night. He could hear, far off, the chatter of the men on the gate, their radios crackling in the darkness, alive with some news from beyond this small, cherished haven, safe from the depredation of the city. He felt a fool. He'd let Marco's magic, and her sudden gift of a startling, physical ecstasy, steal away his concentration. Gino Fosse would surely not be sleeping. There was a cycle in motion beyond this fleeting sanctuary his father had tried to create. It would not be broken yet.

He thought of Michael Denney again, pushing aside the insidious vile images that wanted to rise inside his imagination.

Then, after a fashion, he slept until the phone woke him with a start. He looked at the clock. It was now nearly six. Almost three hours had disappeared in some jumble of a half-waking nightmare.

He listened to the voice on the phone, Falcone's familiar cold monotone, and was immediately dragged from his anguished reverie, back to reality.

Fifty-one

The livid stain of a new dawn was breaking over Rome as Nic Costa drove along the deserted road, towards the looming, illuminated shape of the gate of San Sebastiano. There was scarcely a soul on the streets. The city seemed to have died in the dry August heat. It was hard to imagine life ever returning.

Then he pulled onto the main road that led through to the Lateran and on to the police station. As he did so the phone rang.

'Where are you?' Falcone barked.

'On my way to the Piazza Navona.'

'Don't bother. He's been busy again. Meet me in the Corso, the church on the little piazza, halfway along. You know it?'

'Yes.'

Falcone paused for a moment. Then he asked, 'Did you get anything out of her? Anything we can use?'

'What?'

'The woman. That was the idea. Remember?'

'No,' he said, wondering how much Falcone could hear inside his voice. 'Nothing.'

He heard the familiar bitter sigh.

'Oh well,' said the voice on the line. 'And me with two men dead. The bastard's going to pay for that. Nobody kills cops in this town. Not my men.'

He couldn't find the words. Falcone seemed more offended by the personal affront than the loss of Rossi and Cattaneo.

'He was my friend,' Costa said. 'He . . .' The words wouldn't come out. He had to fight to stop himself pulling into the side of the road and falling apart.

'I know,' Falcone acknowledged. 'He was a good guy underneath it all.'

Even at that point Falcone had to make some judgement. Costa wondered why he worked with the man, why he did as he was told.

'One more thing,' Falcone ordered. 'Don't eat breakfast. Even Crazy Teresa couldn't smile through this one.'

He thought about that, recalling the evening the three of them spent together in the restaurant in Testaccio, in what seemed like another lifetime. There were other reasons, ones Falcone couldn't imagine.

'Hey. A question,' Falcone added. 'You come from farming stock. How many brothers and sisters you got?'

'Two.'

'You ever meet another peasant family smaller than that?'

Costa was baffled by the question. 'I don't recall.'

'Think about it. Farmers breed kids like they breed livestock. They need them to make the whole thing work.'

'So?'

'So where's Gino Fosse's siblings, huh?'

He recalled the file. 'Fosse didn't have any. He was an

only child. Maybe the mother had a medical problem or something?'

Falcone's dry laugh echoed in his ear. 'We got someone to talk to the local doctor about that. You're right. According to him she was barren. So what happened there? A miracle?'

He was headed for the big junction in the Lateran square. Here the traffic was starting to get heavy: trucks and buses hustled each other for position at the lights. He felt his concentration fading.

'No such thing,' he said, then turned off the phone. He didn't want to hear Falcone any more. He didn't want to think about Gino Fosse's family background. There was a picture in his head: of Sara beneath him, naked, a half-musical sigh emerging from her lips. The taste of her returned, a physical entity in his mouth. Somehow, and this made him feel ashamed, it even obscured the image of Luca Rossi, the big man, who was now dead on some slab in the morgue.

Fifty-two

He stopped a little way off from the church and watched
the circus growing in the piazza. The media pack was out
in force beyond the railings. He couldn't blame them.
Valena was a celebrity, a fading one too, which, in some
strange way, made the story even better. He was beginning to recognize the reporters now. These were some of
the people who'd doorstepped the farm until the hunt
had moved on. One, a woman with one of the seedier
dailies, caught sight of him and walked over. She was
about thirty, pretty, with fiercely hennaed hair and a
determined face.

'How's the back?' she asked. 'I heard he cut you up
pretty badly.'

'You heard wrong,' he snapped.

'Look,' she said, unmoved by his aggression. 'It's just
a job. You're doing yours. I'm doing mine.'

'They don't match.'

'Really? How many hacks have you seen on corruption charges recently? Nothing personal but we're just
looking for some socially acceptable reasons to justify
felling a few trees. We tend to hunt as a pack and it's not
a pretty sight, I know. To be honest it's a little like

attending a meeting of gargoyles anonymous most days. We're not crooked. Neither are you from what I hear but you're not exactly standard issue.'

To her surprise he didn't take it badly.

'Greta Ricci,' she said, extending a hand. He shook it quickly. 'I'm sorry. Mornings are not my time. This is the big one, isn't it? Arturo Valena. What a way to go. And those two poor cops last night.'

'There's no point in asking me. You probably know more anyway.'

She lit a cigarette. He waved away the smoke. 'No problem. I wasn't after anything. It's all running away from me anyway. One of the TV bastards has got something up his sleeve. I can tell from the smug look on his face. One more fuck-up and they'll have me off crime altogether and writing make-up advice or some such shit. I have this anarchical idea that somehow reporting's all about digging stuff up. Whereas what you're really supposed to do is suck up to the big people, your people, the politicians, then take down notes when they feel like leaking something. If I'd wanted to be someone's secretary I'd have worn a shorter skirt and learned how to type properly.'

Costa was interested. 'What do you think he might have?'

'Search me. The way this story's been running it could be anything. Craziest job I've ever worked on. But I'll tell you this. There's something up with the Vatican. I heard him calling the media people there, all quietly so he thought none of us could hear. He's asking for something from them. God knows what. I mean, this Fosse guy was a priest, sure. All the same, you can't blame them for what he's done, can you?'

He shrugged. 'I can't imagine the connection.'

She sucked on the cigarette, stared at him, knowing he was lying, then handed over a card. 'Listen. If you ever feel like leaking something . . .'

He put it in his pocket. 'I thought you were against that.'

The woman looked him up and down. 'From you I think it would be different.'

He nodded and said, 'I have to go. *Ciao*.'

Then he crossed the piazza, pushed his way through the crowd, ignoring their questions, showed his ID to the uniformed men on the gate and walked into the church.

There was a stink there, an odd mixture of burnt wood and meat. The forensic team was gathered around a low metallic object upturned on the floor, next to a pile of ashes. A thin wisp of grey smoke still worked its way upwards from the embers in the middle of the nave. The body was gone. He was glad of that, after Falcone's warning. In the far corner of the church, penned in by two uniformed cops, stood a straggle of dogs undergoing slow and careful examination by another of the forensic team.

Teresa Lupo was on a bench not far from the metal grille, her back to him, hunched, miserable. Nic Costa walked over and sat by her side. She'd been weeping.

He took her hand. 'I'm sorry, Teresa. I should have been there.'

Her damp eyes turned on him, full of sorrow. 'Why? So you could die too? What's the point of that?'

'Maybe . . . I don't know.'

Her mood changed from grief to fury in a second. 'Maybe it would have been different? Is that what you mean? Don't fool yourself. I talked to people who were there. This . . . monster just popped them, as if he were putting down an animal. He'd have killed you. He'd have killed anyone who stood in his way. That's what he's like. It doesn't mean anything to him. None of this does. It's as if it's all a game. Or as if he's in hell already and thinks this is the way he's supposed to behave, like he's handing out punishment to anyone who deserves it.'

'Luca didn't deserve it. He was a good man. He was . . .' His own eyes began to sting. 'I could have learned a lot from him.'

She pummelled at her nose with a handkerchief then squeezed his hand. 'He's in the morgue right now. I've got to go back for the autopsy after this.'

This sudden practical turn shocked him. 'You don't have to do that. Get someone else.'

'What?' She looked surprised. 'Nic, this is my job. In any case what's on that slab isn't him. Not any more. I've dealt with enough bodies over the years to know that. When they're gone they live in just one place. Here . . .' She tapped her lank, dark hair with a strong finger. 'He'll be there a long time. I liked the stubborn old bastard.'

'He felt the same about you.'

'Yeah,' she said, with the hint of a smile. 'I think he did too. He didn't call me Crazy Teresa, did he? Not behind my back.'

'Never.'

'Liar.'

He grimaced. It was hard to shrink from the truth when she turned on the heat.

'It was just that you scared him sometimes. Not because of who you are but because of him. Because he didn't like . . .'

He fell silent.

'What?'

'He didn't like having those feelings. They disturbed him.'

'Seems to go with the job,' she replied, staring at him. 'Tell me. Is that why you all do this? To get the excuse you want?'

'I don't follow.'

'Oh, I think you do. You tell yourself you're like this because of what you do. But is it just faintly possible there's another reason? That you pick this stupid profession because it allows you to be what you are and never have to take the blame?'

'Yeah,' he grunted, thinking that she could have been talking to herself. Teresa was a quasi-cop. That much had become obvious over the past few days. What turned them on, turned her on too. 'That's right. You see through us all.'

Her hand touched his knee. The tears stood big in her eyes now. 'I'm sorry, Nic. I'm so sorry. I'm just lashing out because it feels good, except it doesn't. I didn't mean it.'

He folded his arms around her, felt her over-large body against his.

'Don't apologize,' he said. 'Anyway, you're right.'

She wiped her streaming nose with her sleeve. 'Maybe for Luca. You . . . I don't know. You want to do something, don't you?'

'Do I?' he asked mournfully, not wanting an answer. He nodded at the activity across the nave. 'What happened here?'

'Someone had a barbecue. Let the dogs in to clean up afterwards.'

'Jesus.'

'It was that TV creep, Valena. Ask your boss. Falcone's livid, which I guess ought to impress me, except that it's weird. You'd almost think this was about him, not two dead cops and God knows who else. Seems to think he knows all the answers too. When this is over, Nic, I'm taking a break. Maybe I'll go back to the university, teach for a while. I don't mind the work. Truth is it's the best there is. It's just the people. Falcone in particular. He's . . . I don't know. Luca loathed the man and I trust his judgement. Let's leave it at that.'

He said nothing. It was unwise to be drawn.

'How's she doing?' Teresa asked.

'Who?'

'Sara Farnese. She's still staying with you, isn't she?'

'She's fine,' he said automatically.

'Fine?'

He wilted under the ferocity of her gaze.

'Nic. Whatever she is, and I sometimes wonder if you're even mildly qualified to judge, she is not "fine". Look at what's happening here. Look at what someone's doing because of her.'

'You sound like Falcone. It doesn't mean it's her fault.'

She sighed, exasperated. 'I didn't mean it was, not for an instant. I meant that she knows this is to do with her. She feels responsible to some extent, however much she may try to hide it. She's not "fine". And one other thing. She slept with Valena apparently. She never told us about that.'

'She said there were some others. She just didn't know the names.'

The look on her face was just a couple inches short of contempt. 'She didn't know the name of Arturo Valena?

The moron was on the box every night. In the papers too. Where does she live, this woman of yours? In a convent? Except when she's out screwing?'

She waited for an answer. Nothing came. Then she watched the team working on the iron grille, watched the men examining the dogs for traces of Arturo Valena's flesh. It was all pointless. Everyone knew what happened. A lunatic stepped out of the dark and death followed in his shadow. No, that wasn't enough. There was a reason behind it all. There had to be.

'I've got work to do,' she muttered, and joined the team with the dogs.

Nic Costa felt as if his head would burst. He was exhausted. He was confused. Then he heard a commotion at the door. Falcone walked in, flanked by some cops he recognized only by sight. Costa knew the investigation was moving away from him. Now the big man was gone, now he was reduced to little more than a bodyguard for Sara, Falcone had brought in a larger, more experienced team. He wondered what could be left for him to do.

Falcone caught his eye and waved him over. He was carrying a briefcase and Teresa Lupo was right. He wasn't himself. His eyes refused to meet Nic Costa's at first. He looked lost, distraught, furious.

'How's she doing?' he asked. 'Crazy Teresa. I heard they were an item.'

'Pretty cut up.'

'Join the club. Jesus. How dare this asshole touch my men? Does he think there's some kind of equivalence between them and dirt bags like Valena? I'll put the fucker down myself if I get the chance.'

'Wouldn't help.'

Falcone glowered at him and there was a little of his old self in the expression, asking: *is that so?* He took Costa to one side. 'You watch TV?'

'Not a lot.'

'You should. It's good sometimes. Going to get better too now that fat jerk's not preaching at us every night.'

Falcone barked at the team to start questioning forensics and anyone they could find living in the vicinity. Then they walked outside, into the fast rising heat and Falcone opened the door of the police Mercedes, ushering him into the passenger side and sitting next to him.

'Where are we going?' Costa asked. 'Do you know where Fosse is?'

'No idea. Be patient.'

Costa nodded at the door of the church. 'No time for patience.'

Falcone shrugged. 'Show a little trust, kid, we're almost there. Remember what I asked you? About Gino Fosse's family?'

'Of course.'

'Yeah,' Falcone looked at his watch. It was just coming up to six. Then he flipped open the cover of the little LCD screen in the dashboard, switched off the navigation system and tuned into the TV channel. 'Well, watch. After that you can go and see Rossi's sister. Act sympathetic. We don't want to get sued.'

'His sister?' he asked, furious with himself that he didn't even know Rossi had a relative in the city.

Falcone read his reaction immediately. 'He didn't tell you? They lived together in some apartment out near Fiumicino. Go talk her down from whatever state she's in. Tell her I personally guarantee the bastard who did this is going down for good. After that . . . take the day off. Go spend some time with that father of yours. Go fishing. I don't care. You're not going to be around when Denney runs. I want people with some real time under their belts.'

He said nothing, hating himself for the way he took this. Then the news came on. They extended the newscast from five minutes to fifteen. Valena's dreadful death led the bulletin. Costa listened to the details they gave.

'Is that right?' he asked.

'Should be. I gave them the briefing myself,' Falcone replied.

'You didn't hold anything back?'

Falcone scowled. 'What's the point? We know who we want. I could put him in the dock today without a scrap more evidence.'

'But we don't know why.'

Falcone put a finger to his lips, gave him that cold smile, then pointed to the screen. There was a stock picture of Michael Denney there, and a recent photo of Gino Fosse too. He listened to the newscaster, amazed. Then he turned to Falcone.

'The DNA? That's why you wanted something from his apartment? To prove this?'

'The DNA report doesn't come back until this morning. That was the idea but I didn't need it anyway. A little bird behind those walls started to sing for me. I've got documents. I've got pieces of paper that are proof, just as much as some stupid lab test.' Falcone smiled. 'Gino Fosse is Denney's son. We still don't know who the real mother was. But he was taken from her at birth and given to that couple in Sicily. Denney's managed to hush it up for years.'

Nic found it impossible to think. Nothing made sense. 'Why leak it to the media? What does it mean anyway?'

'I want that crooked bastard. I want him out of that place where he's sitting pretty, looking out of his window, thinking nothing can touch him. If we let him run from there anything can happen. If we cut a deal I'll stick to it. As long as the rules stay the same. But if the son comes in, that's different. We get him too and take the father in for protection. Because that's what this is all about. That's what Gino Fosse is trying to say. That he keeps on killing until he gets the one he wants. His old man.'

It was wrong. It was impossible. 'But why? Because he was fired from his job?'

'Are you serious? Sara Farnese was the old man's woman. She slept with these people – Vaccarini, Valena, some of the others, because Denney told her to. It was her attempt to get him safe passage out of that prison of his. She slept with Rinaldi. He tried to fix the judicial commission. Vaccarini the same. She slept with Valena. Four months ago he came out on that show of his arguing for wider diplomatic immunity in the Vatican on the grounds – get this – that the Church needed protecting in a godless world. You think maybe Sara Farnese performed a few favours on the fat fucker afterwards? The Englishman . . . I don't know. Maybe he was trying to swing something for Denney with the EU.'

He remembered her insistent denial of just a single accusation. The Englishman was her lover, he realized. A liar and adulterer. But he was unlike the rest. That much, Nic Costa now believed, was true.

'Maybe he was just standing in the wrong place at the wrong time,' he said.

Falcone nodded, surprised that Costa agreed with him

so readily. 'It doesn't matter any more. If Denney runs, they're both out in the open. Maybe I'll let the cardinal get on the plane, maybe not. Doesn't matter. If he makes it to America we extradite him anyway.' He shook his head, as if the game was already won. 'And Gino Fosse, he stays here. He's ours the moment he steps out into the sun and if he so much as sneezes I'll shoot the bastard myself.'

Falcone waited for Costa's reaction. 'You're quiet. Aren't you going to tell me I've got her all wrong? That she didn't know Michael Denney? This can't be true?'

'I don't know anything any more.'

There was a pained grimace on the inspector's tanned face. 'Say that again. You should watch the eight o'clock news. Take a break. Buy yourself a coffee and enjoy the fun. You have to stage these things with the media. You don't give them it all in one chunk or it just goes to waste. Come eight they'll have another little item to add to the public's knowledge about His Eminence Cardinal Denney.'

The triumph in his voice was muted. There was a despairing note of bitterness behind it. Leo Falcone felt the loss of Rossi and Cattaneo, more deeply than Costa would have expected. 'What else?'

Falcone reached for his briefcase on the back seat of the car and took out an envelope. He opened it and thrust the contents onto Costa's knee. It was a black and white photograph of dubious quality, taken from some distance judging by the flatness and the grain of the picture. A telephoto lens from slightly above the subject, perhaps, shot through a window. It showed Denney in a grand apartment, the one, Costa guessed, he used to occupy by right, before they threw him into the rat hole where he sweated now.

Denney stood with his back half turned to the camera. He wore a white shirt and dark trousers. His grey hair was neatly groomed. Sara Farnese faced the lens, smiling, a wonderful, open smile, full of love, an expression he'd seen for himself the previous night. Her arms were around Denney. She was coming forward as if to kiss his cheek or his neck. Sara and Denney would soon be one, her body merged with his. She held him, tightly, in a way which brooked no mistake. It was impossible to fake. This was the two of them engaged in a loving, close embrace. A prelude to what? He looked again and knew. Denney's right hand was already reaching for the curtain at the apartment window. In a few seconds the two of them would be snatched from sight.

The photo had the same grainy quality as the ones they'd found in Fosse's flat. It wasn't hard to guess where it came from.

'Where are the rest of the pictures?' he asked.

'That's all I have,' Falcone replied. 'Look for yourself. He's getting himself a little privacy. This is the Vatican, after all. What do you want? To see them in bed?'

Something still nagged at him. 'Where did it come from?'

Falcone scowled and looked at his watch. 'Come on. You've figured that out, surely?'

He had. He just didn't want to admit it. 'Fosse took it. Just like he took the others. He kept the ones of Sara, of the other women, for his own purposes. Really he was there to provide backup. To make sure that if they didn't bend from the favour, they'd bend from a little blackmail.'

'Precisely,' Falcone said, pleased with Costa's analysis. 'Fosse drove for Denney. He was the chauffeur on these little night-time escapades. For the Farnese woman. For the more conventional hookers Denney used too. He hung around peeking through the curtains with his lens while they got on with their work.' He paused for effect. 'They knew what was going on. She knew.'

Costa thought of her face in the pictures in the Clivus Scauri. The way she was looking towards the lens. Falcone was right but Teresa Lupo had seen this first: Sara was party to the trick.

'She knew,' he agreed. 'And Denney thought this was all his doing. He never realized Fosse was working on the side for someone else too. Maybe giving them the same information. Spying on Denney as well.'

He looked Falcone in the eye. 'Who was that? Who's pulling the strings? Hanrahan?'

'Hanrahan's just a servant. Like me. What does it matter? We've got what we need. At eight o'clock these go public. Match that up with the news about Fosse and I don't see how the Vatican can continue to hold him. He's an embarrassment. He's a visible scab they'll want rid of.'

Costa put the photograph back into the envelope.

The older man took it and said, 'If you breathe a word of this to anyone before it appears I'll have your hide. And I mean her in particular. This is all beyond you now. I don't want any more accidents, understand? So you just talk to Rossi's sister then sit back, get some rest. You look like you need it.'

'Accidents?' he demanded, his voice rising, some red stub of anger beginning to fire in his head. 'I lost a partner to this lunatic. I want to be there when he's taken.'

Falcone looked offended. 'Hey. Gimme a break here. I got two dead cops squatting on my conscience. I don't want your skinny hide added to the pile.'

This was the limit, this was the moment. Costa reached into his jacket pocket and took out his police ID card.

'Fuck you,' he said and threw the thing into Falcone's lap, then got out of the car, out into the fast rising heat of the morning.

Fifty-three

She walked out to the gate at seven and spoke to one of the cops. It was easy to get what you wanted with a smile. The man took her money, looked a little puzzled, and drove off to the nearby nursery. It wouldn't be open yet but he was a cop. He'd bang on the door till they came.

Then she stayed near the lane, mutely watched by the other policemen, trying not to think, trying not to expect too much from the day to come, waiting. Half an hour later he returned with the plants housed in a battered cardboard box. There were three sets, each wrapped in damp newspaper. She looked at the seedlings of *cavolo nero*, little taller than an index finger. It was hard to believe they would grow through the coming harshness of winter, thriving in the cold and damp, becoming stronger each day until, in spring, they would be ready for harvest.

Sara walked back to the house and found Marco and Bea on the porch drinking coffee. He sat happily in his wheelchair, Bea at his side. She thought about the expression on his face. Marco finally looked at peace with himself. He'd lost the impatient energy, the need to make some kind of point at every opportunity which she had noticed since the moment she stepped into the farm-house. The internal, gnawing need to settle accounts had been resolved, for the time being at least. There had been a debt to be settled, she thought, and one he'd forgotten, which only made things worse. In a sense he looked older, wearier, more resigned. Perhaps these were steps along the way, stations of love, of insight, which needed to be passed. This was the luxury – and the agony – of a lingering death. It gave one the time to consider, to make decisions. It contained, too, sufficient space for both regret and, with a little luck, reconciliation.

Bea stood up and took the box from her, smiling at the slender green forms that lay inside.

'You remembered?' Marco said, amazed.

'Of course.'

He laughed. 'It was the wine. I didn't mean you to do this. You can't really want to get down on your hands and knees and plant these damned things. What for?'

Bea patted him on his grey head. 'I thought we'd agreed. Because it's a farm, silly man. Things should be growing here. It looks barren otherwise.'

Marco scanned the arid, yellow ground. He gazed at both of them. 'I'm a fool, aren't I?'

'You're a man,' Bea said.

'Well, at least I won't be grubbing around planting something no one's going to look after come the winter.'

'They'll grow,' Bea said. 'I promise.'

He harrumphed, though there was still an amused satisfaction in his eye neither of them could miss. 'What's happening to my life?' he asked, then shot Sara a glance. 'You heard from Nic?'

'He left early,' she said, not committing herself. She understood they knew where she had spent the night.

Perhaps Marco and Bea had heard them. She'd no idea how much noise they had made. Her time with him, in his arms, astride him, touching his hair, feeling him inside her, all this now seemed like a dream. They had parted on bad terms. It was her fault. She knew this and she regretted hurting him. Nevertheless there were boundaries that had to be established. She wondered whether she would ever see Nic Costa again. Whether he would even want to see her. The future rose ahead like a mist, full of so many formless possibilities.

'We should watch the news,' she said.

Sara saw the expression cross Marco Costa's lined face, followed the way he looked at Bea. It was something bad. It had to be.

'I did,' he said. 'While you were down at the gate.'

'I need to know . . .'

'No you don't. Not right now. All that would mean is that we'd have to watch you go through the agonies again, Sara. This is not about you. These people aren't your responsibility.'

'You know that?' she replied coldly.

'We know enough,' Marco answered.

'Please tell me.'

They glanced at each other. Bea nodded.

'He shot two cops dead last night,' Marco said grimly. 'One of them was Luca Rossi, Nic's partner.'

She closed her eyes.

'Then he killed someone else,' Marco continued. 'Arturo Valena, the man from the TV. They're saying . . .' He hesitated. 'They're saying all sorts of things, to tell you the truth. They're saying this priest they're looking for is the son of that cardinal the papers are writing about.'

'I need to see this . . .'

His hand went out and held her as she passed him. Marco was still strong. This surprised her.

'No,' he insisted. 'It's just there to drive you crazy. *There is nothing you can do.* Are you hearing me? Leave this to Nic and the rest of them. It's their job. Not yours.'

'I have to know.'

His old face examined hers. He was a clever man. She understood that. Nic must have found out at an early age what she knew now: it was impossible to keep a secret from him when those sharp, intelligent eyes turned on you.

'No you don't,' Marco said, and let the rest of the sentence hang in the air. She knew what he left unsaid: *you don't need to hear because you know already.* It was, she admitted to herself, this that interested her: finding out how much they had discovered, using that information for her own ends.

Marco picked up one of the sets of plants and examined it, touching the stalk, feeling the tender young leaves with his fingers.

'These are good,' he said, looking at her. 'They're a little late but never mind. It's just a matter of care and attention. Don't plant them together too tightly. You'll need to water them in well. Sara . . .'

She did what he wanted. She looked into his face.

'The tools are in the outhouse over there. You should dress down a little, both of you. I want this done with care. When you're finished, then we let the rest of the world in here again. But not before, please.'

He knew everything, or thought he did. She could see this in his face.

'And when Nic calls? When he comes round?' she

asked, aware that she was already thinking about how soon she could get away and make the phone call.

'I think Nic will be pretty busy today, to be honest with you.'

'When isn't he?'

Marco had the answer already: she wouldn't be there. She would never have to face the possibility.

'The ground needs a little preparation,' he said. 'I'll teach you how.'

Fifty-four

Michael Denney sat at the low coffee table in the little apartment, opposite Hanrahan, trying not to look at the TV. The picture of Sara, her bare-sleeved, comforting arms around him, filled the screen. It seemed even more fascinating for the news programmes than the images of Arturo Valena's body being taken from the church off the Corso. What irked Denney most was that he couldn't recall the moment. He'd seen so little of her recently. He missed the time they spent together. It infuriated him that someone could have spied on them and not left sufficient clues for him to place the occasion.

'Who the hell took it, Brendan? You?'

The Irishman's lugubrious features met his angry gaze. 'Chickens come home to roost. You sent Fosse out to take those bedroom snaps for you. Don't blame me if he didn't know when to stop.'

'I thought Fosse was working for me.'

Hanrahan sighed and said nothing. Denney thought hard. He hadn't seen her like this in more than a month. That meant they had decided to throw him to the wolves long before he had tried, and failed, to resurrect the bank.

'You're an ungrateful man, Michael,' Hanrahan said.

'I've watched your back in this place too long. I've risked my own reputation, perhaps more than that. And what do I get in return? Your misguided anger. Your lack of trust.'

'I'm sorry.' It was possible Hanrahan was offended by the suggestion. Or perhaps it was just part of a broader, more subtle act than Denney had appreciated. 'I'm not myself right now. It's just the thought of Fosse spying on us like that. Did they really think I deserved that?'

Hanrahan stabbed at the TV. '*Deserve?* Michael, I told you so many times she would be your nemesis. And there she is. Plastered all over the place. In every newspaper too when they get the chance. A cardinal of the Church and the woman they've been painting as some loose whore all week. What do you expect?'

'A little understanding,' Denney grumbled. There was no point in telling this icy Irishman about the need for love. It was inexplicable, incapable of being reduced to plain and logical analysis. Hanrahan didn't believe in mysteries. He wanted only hard, unbending facts around him. He never noticed, never felt, the holes these hard, inhuman certainties made in a man's life.

'Don't blame anyone else now,' Hanrahan warned. 'No one made you start seeing her. No one else forced you to use Gino Fosse as a bagman on these night errands of yours. This is your doing. Not mine nor anyone else's. If you must indulge in these black secrets – bribery, black-mail for God's sake – don't go blaming others when they creep out into the light of day.'

'And you think I don't know that?'

Hanrahan grimaced. Denney looked at his grey, emotionless face and knew there was more to come.

'Maybe. Maybe not. You're a man prone to whimsies,

Michael. It's odd, given the job you used to do. I would have expected a more practical nature.'

'Like yours,' Denney said without thinking.

'I like to think of myself as a reasonable man. One who helps keep the wheels turning.'

There was a time they had been together for a conference in Dubai. A financier had provided company for them both. It was a ritual, a gift it would have been impolite to refuse. He'd watched Hanrahan with the woman. She was beautiful, a tall Cypriot girl with perfect English and a ready smile. It was the only occasion on which he had seen the Irishman uncomfortable, incapable of controlling the world around him. He had left before the dinner was finished.

'And never being touched by anything, eh Brendan? Living on your own. Running other people's lives. You're not like me. You could get married. You could do what you like. Instead you just scheme and scheme. For me. For anyone that pays.'

Hanrahan's thick black eyebrows rose.

'I gave you good money to fix things, Brendan. You were supposed to help me put the Banca Lombardia back on track.'

Hanrahan scowled. 'I can't raise the dead. That idea didn't stand a hope in hell from the moment you first suggested it.'

'And you never thought of saying so.'

'I'm a servant. Have you forgotten?'

'Who doesn't know who his master is.'

'Oh, but I always remember that. You were the one who forgot. You were the one who overstepped the mark because you just couldn't resist, could you? It flattered your fulsome ego, dining with all these politicians.

Having these women at your beck and call. You lost sight of yourself and drowned in your own arrogance. Don't take your own faults out on others.'

Denney nodded. There was truth in Hanrahan's words.

'But at least I've lived, Brendan. I'm not convinced you can say the same. Do you really believe the world begins and ends at your fingertips, man? Or are you just frightened of it all? Scared to death that a little love might steal away your powers? That you might be like Samson and wake up one morning to find your hair on your pillow. And suddenly you're just the same as the rest of us: weak and dependent on others. Is that what scares you? That you might lose your strength and someone will come looking for revenge? Because if it is, I must tell you what you are. An emotional coward. A man who fears what's inside himself and takes that fear out on the world.'

There was hatred in Hanrahan's eyes. Denney knew he had hit the spot. It gave him no comfort.

'To be honest,' Hanrahan said very carefully, 'none of this matters any more, Michael.'

'It matters, Brendan. Tell me now. Do you think we'll be judged one day? All of us? Or is that just one more piece of whimsy?'

'I think there's plenty who would like to judge you now.'

'And who are they? I've wasted my time in this dump, fearing them. Fearing you. What can they do except steal away what little of my miserable life's left?'

Hanrahan shifted uncomfortably on his seat. 'I wouldn't value that too lightly, Michael. Think of what happened to Arturo Valena and the rest.'

Denney looked around the apartment. It seemed smaller, more dismal than ever. He was unable to believe he had allowed himself to be talked into being some voluntary kind of captive here.

'Terrible ends,' he agreed. 'But you know the problem with spending your days afraid of dying? What you really end up fearing is life itself. You wind up hoping no one knocks on the door, no one comes close. You die anyway, it's just that you don't notice it happened a long time before you stopped breathing.'

Hanrahan closed his eyes as if he weren't listening.

'Tell me, Brendan. Do you believe in anything?'

'I believe in keeping our little piece of the world in order. Protecting it from those who'd destroy it.'

'Isn't that what Pontius Pilate said?'

'You're talking like a churchman, Michael. That's something you're not.'

'Say it then,' Denney spat back. 'Let's hear what you came here for. Because it wasn't to pass the time.'

'You're out,' Hanrahan said flatly. 'Today. By noon, it must be, or they'll send someone in and throw you onto the pavement, I swear it. I've argued till I'm blue in the face but it's no good. What with these pictures. The proof that Gino Fosse is your boy. The woman. They're scared there's more to come, Michael. And let's face it . . .' Hanrahan's emotionless face fixed on Denney. 'There is.'

Denney felt trapped in the small, airless room, felt as if his head might explode. 'Meaning?'

'Meaning I've known a lot about you for a long time, Michael. It wasn't that hard. You cover your footsteps well, but you're still an amateur. Now it's beyond my powers. When they turn and say, "Is this all?" I won't lie for you any more. That time's past.'

Denney folded his arms and rested back on the chair, thinking. 'So who's casting the first stone then? Just for interest's sake. I'd like the names. I'd love to know how many people in this place would survive having someone spying on them night and day, seeing everything they do.'

Hanrahan pulled a half-smoked cigar from his jacket pocket and lit it. The strong, vile smoke began to fill the room.

'Think of someone. Put him on your list. I tried my best, but not with much conviction, to be honest. They're right. You're too much of an embarrassment now. We have to wash our hands of the stain of you before it leaves a mark on the rest of us. There'll be a private plane back to Boston. Someone can help you there if you need it. We can give you a new name. A place to live where they won't find you, with a touch of luck. But . . .' he waved his hand at the world beyond the walls of the apartment, 'this part of your life is past. You can't return to Rome. You can't be Cardinal Michael Denney any more. If you stay in Italy, even under a false name, someone will find you. Maybe the police. Maybe some people with other ideas. Either way, you don't want it and we don't want it.'

It was what he expected but still the words smarted. 'So I'm reborn. I become Joe Polack and work on some factory line in Detroit. Is that it?'

Hanrahan shrugged. 'If that's what you want.'

Denney's pale face became suffused with red. He wished he could keep the anger away. 'Damn it, Brendan. *I want what they owe me.*'

The Irishman laughed. The sound made Denney miserable; it emphasized how alone he truly was. 'Everyone wants what they're owed, Michael. That's the problem, isn't it? All these debts to be paid, and so many of them to people none of us would like to know.'

'You'll take me to the airport.' He tried to make it sound like an order, not a question, but the words failed to come out right.

Hanrahan scowled then slowly shook his head. 'No. We can't afford the publicity. In America things can be different. There we can be more subtle. But for now we need to make it plain. At eleven the press department plans to issue a statement. I can show you a copy if you like. It will say you've decided to resign your office for personal reasons and intend to take up a new life outside the Church, beyond Italy. No more than that. We will brief the press privately, of course, and set some clear water between the Vatican and yourself. That must be done. You're a pariah. We'll make it clear we've been concerned by your actions, by the rumours about your personal life, for years, but these last revelations, which were, of course, new to us, proved too much to bear. You'll become the prodigal son, Michael, one we must send out into the world to atone for his sins. Except you'll never return, naturally. We'll not meet again after today. You're making the rest of this journey on your own.'

Denney couldn't believe what he was hearing, couldn't comprehend how Hanrahan took such obvious pleasure in torturing him like this. 'And what am I supposed to do, exactly? Call a cab and wait for one of those crooks to join me in the back? Do I look suicidal,

Brendan? I'd rather walk straight to the nearest policeman and ask him to take me in.'

Hanrahan laughed again. 'And how long do you think you'd last in prison? If you got that far. Don't be naïve. The police can't save you. Maybe even we can't save you in the end. You've gone so far. You've offended so many people, given them such a wealth of ammunition to bring you down. Oh, to hell with it . . .'

He scanned the apartment, wrinkling his nose. 'Don't pack much, Michael. Tell us what, if anything, you wish to keep and I'll see it's done. Bear in mind, though, that most of your possessions are attached to the office you held until this moment and remain our property. Anything that is truly personal you may mark and I'll send on later.'

Denney nodded at the copy of the Caravaggio. 'The paintings are mine.'

'That I doubt. But you're an accomplished thief. I'll send them on, perhaps.'

Michael Denney wasn't listening. His eyes were fixed on the couple at the focus of the canvas: the dying Matthew and his assassin, both bathed in the compelling light of grace.

'Now you won't be thinking of yourself as the martyr in all this, Michael, surely?' Hanrahan asked lightly. 'That would be a little rich, I fancy.'

Denney hung his head and whispered, 'Christ, Brendan, don't enjoy it so much.'

He looked up. The Irishman's eyes now held him in a fixed, concentrated stare, full of contempt.

'You confuse pleasure with duty, Michael. You always have. It's the root of your problem. Don't hate me, man. I've performed one last favour, for old times' sake. Two men will meet you outside the gates at twelve. A couple of Rome cops. They'll take you to the airport. Off-duty as it were.'

'Two men?' Denney asked. 'Do you want me dead?'

'If I wanted that do you think I'd have gone to all this trouble on your behalf? Not that we haven't discussed it, you understand. There are those who thought it would have been the . . . cleanest solution.'

Michael Denney closed his eyes. He could picture them talking, somewhere else, in a private, secret room, somewhere in this tiny, insular state which had, in the space of thirty years, turned from a kind of heaven into a cruel, unbending prison. Perhaps they met weekly. Perhaps they had more information, more pictures, tapes. And they'd been planning, for how long? Wondering how to dispose of him, safely, cleanly, with the minimum of fuss. Wondering where they would find a trigger, the catalyst who could flush him out of his lair. Time and fate had finally provided that, but not by chance.

He pointed an accusing finger at Hanrahan. 'You told him, you bastard.'

The Irishman said nothing. His eyebrows rose a fraction.

'You told Fosse about us. You set him against me, thinking that would be a swift end to it. You never guessed what he'd do instead. All these other people, Brendan. Alicia Vaccarini. Valena. Those poor bastards Falcone sent out to watch over him. Don't you feel the slightest sense of guilt?'

Hanrahan drew himself up in the chair, preparing to go. 'You're rambling again, Michael. All wars have their casualties. The trick is making sure you're not among them. Do yourself a favour and focus on that.'

Denney rose quickly from his seat, crossed the room and brought his hands to the Irishman's throat. Age and agility were not on his side. Hanrahan was on his feet in an instant, knocking his arms away, standing there ready to fight if need be. He had big fists and they were now half raised. Denney tried to remember who he was, who he still would be in his own head, whatever they did to him.

'Anger's such a wasteful emotion,' Hanrahan said. 'You should have spent more time dealing with yours, Michael, and a little less beneath the sheets.'

'Get the hell out of here,' Denney hissed.

'Midday,' Hanrahan said. 'I'll come to make sure you're gone. Don't worry. The press will be elsewhere. You'll leave in privacy.'

He extended a hand, waited, then withdrew it. 'You must place a terribly low value on your life, Michael.'

'What makes you say that?'

'Because I've saved it so many times. Here I am saving it again. And not so much as a word of thanks.'

He looked at his watch. They had their arrangements. He'd no idea whether they still held. Michael Denney closed his eyes and prayed for the call.

It was two minutes late but it came.

Fifty-five

Costa rang the doorbell of the apartment. It was on the third floor of a modern block a couple of kilometres from the airport, just off the main road. You could hear the traffic constantly but it was still better than he'd expected. In the few days he'd known Rossi he'd built up a mental image of what the man was like beyond work: unkempt, disorganized, solitary. He thought he'd be living in some dump closer to town. Instead here was this neat apartment block with geraniums on the staircases and the smell of good home-cooking floating out of the windows of the adjoining homes. He wished he'd noticed more about the man. Teresa Lupo had seen something else there. His own detachment had prevented him noticing, though he couldn't help but ask himself whether this was what Rossi really wanted.

A slender middle-aged woman in a plain blue blouse and black skirt came to the door. Her hair was greying and cut severely short. She stared at him through a pair of black-rimmed glasses. He didn't feel welcome.

'I'm from the station. I was Luca's partner.'

'Really?'

'I came to say . . .' She didn't look as if she'd been

crying. If anything she was full of fury. '. . . how sorry we all are. We'll do what we can.'

'Too late for that, isn't it? Hell, I'm not his sister. Come in.'

She threw open the door and he followed her along a hall decorated with paintings of flowers. It led into a sunny living room. In the corner, seated in a plain wooden chair, was a stocky woman in her early thirties. She was dressed in a nylon housecoat. Her face was pale and flabby, recognizably similar to Rossi's. She had long black hair flowing down her back and shoulders, like a schoolgirl's.

The woman looked at him as he entered, opened her mouth and made an unintelligible noise. It sounded like the moan of a wounded animal.

'Nic Costa,' he said, extending a hand. 'I worked with Luca.'

She made the noises again, only this time they were more prolonged, more agonized.

'Maria's deaf and dumb,' the older woman said. 'I'm her care worker. I used to spend time here when Luca couldn't cope.'

She turned to Maria Rossi and began signing with a quick, ready fluency.

'I didn't know,' he said. 'I didn't even know he had a sister, let alone any of this. I can't believe we never got around to talking about it.'

'Don't be too hard on yourself,' she replied, and began signing again. The woman in the chair nodded and smiled at him. 'That was Luca for you. I offered your condolences by the way. I made some small talk.'

'Thanks.' This was all so unexpected. He had no idea what to ask, what to offer. 'How bad is she?'

'How bad does deaf and dumb get?' the woman snapped. Then she cursed herself and went to the window for a moment, staring out at the motorway. 'I'm sorry. Don't take it personally. I've been working with Maria for five years. Ever since Luca took her out of the home to try and look after her himself. After a while I came to realize you don't just end up caring for one person. It's both of them, and lately, to be honest, it was him. He was a complicated man. A good man. Not that it ever made him happy.'

'Why didn't he tell me? I wouldn't have let him work all those hours. Last night . . .' He couldn't say it. Rossi's presence in the Piazza Navona was coincidence. Falcone could have sent any of them on the same job. No one was to blame except the man who killed him.

'What do you think?' she asked. 'He was ashamed of her?'

'No.' That was impossible. 'Perhaps in some way he was ashamed of himself, for not being able to make things better. I only got to know him recently. There was something . . . Luca wasn't happy inside his own skin. Maybe that's part of the job.'

She looked at him, seeming to approve of his answers, then went over to Maria, sat down next to her, smiling, and put an arm around her shoulders. 'I think you're right. He told me one time he kept waking up in a fury, mad that he couldn't do anything else for her. I don't think he was making it up.'

A flurry of signs brought a brief smile from Rossi's sister and then half a sob.

'She can't lip-read. Always found it too difficult. It means it's easy for me to lie.'

Costa scribbled out his home phone number. 'If she

needs anything, call me any time. We can help with money. There's a pension. I know it's no comfort now but tell me what she needs and I'll see to it.'

The woman looked at the piece of paper and sighed. 'She needs her brother back.'

Costa's face fell. The woman closed her eyes, ashamed of herself.

'I'm sorry,' she said. 'There's nothing you can do. Maria has to go back in the home. She can't look after herself. That's the only place she can get full-time care.'

He understood how Rossi felt.

'It's OK,' the woman continued. 'She's not going to be worried about that. She has friends there. She used to visit anyway. It's just . . .' She had to wait until she could continue. 'She'll miss him. We all will.'

'I know.'

He looked at the small, tidy apartment. There were images of flowers everywhere.

'They're Maria's,' she said, noticing his interest. 'It's what she does. She's deaf and dumb. She's not stupid. Nor was he.'

Costa walked over and looked at a small oil painting of a single hyacinth bloom: vivid blue hues against a yellow background. She'd seen Van Gogh. The work was full of life and happiness. She'd found something that eluded her brother and had, perhaps, fought to share it with him.

'If you want,' the woman said, 'I can show you his room. Perhaps there's something there you'd like. To remind you of him. A photograph. I don't know. He had a lot of stuff.'

'I didn't know him that well. But I know someone who'd appreciate it.'

She led him down the corridor. Rossi's bedroom was small and looked out of the back onto a car park. The dead smell of stale cigarettes hung in the air. There was a single bed, neatly made, a desk with a few tidied papers, an office diary and a swan-neck lamp. A corkboard on the wall was covered in little yellow notes and photographs. Costa looked at them. They were dates for outings: trips to the sea at Ostia, meetings at the hospital, coach tours into the country. His sister was in every last photograph, smiling throughout, on the beach, at a fancy-dress party, eating at a country restaurant. Luca made her happy. That was his gift.

There was only one with Rossi in it. The two of them were pictured seated in a long open-topped Bugatti 57 in a vintage car museum somewhere. Rossi had his hands on the steering wheel. Maria laughed from the passenger seat. He looked like a different man, someone in control of himself.

'That was before he had the breakdown,' she explained.

'Was he always like that?'

'No,' she answered with a bitter laugh. 'He was always on the brink, to be honest. For as long as I knew him.'

He touched the photograph. 'I can't take this. It belongs to her. It's too precious.'

'It's my photograph. I was on the trip. I can get another made. Take it.' She looked around the little room. 'He hated me coming in here. It was his secret place, I think. Somewhere he liked to hide on occasion. Still had to be cleaned though. I'll leave you for a while.'

She walked out, closing the door. Nic Costa sat at the small, neat desk and looked out of the window, out at the rows of cars and the apartment blocks running away from the motorway. This was a life he could never have associated with Luca Rossi: an ordered existence with responsibilities no one in the department could have guessed at.

He opened the desk diary and immediately felt guilty, ashamed. It was apparent from the moment he looked at the page that this was where Rossi put the other side of himself: the black and gloomy side that always threatened to lead him to the edge. The writing was unbalanced: sloping and too small. There were doodles, tiny scribbles that could have been the faces of demons. And a small line of doggerel, one Costa knew by heart . . .

> *As I was going to St Ives*
> *I met a man with seven wives.*

He read more. This was the private place where Rossi took his inner fears for a walk and everyone was in there: Falcone, Teresa Lupo, Sara, everyone. No one was spared. No small detail went unrecorded. He wasn't surprised Rossi kept the care worker out of the room.

Costa read two more pages then tucked the diary under his jacket, went back into the living room, said a polite, curt goodbye and was gone.

Fifty-six

'You made a sound. When . . .' He was reluctant to finish the sentence.

She laughed at his embarrassment. It was midmorning. The traffic outside made a low roar. Gino Fosse had returned at eight, showered, slept a little, not disturbing her. Then she had woken him slowly, gently, touching his strong, naked body with keen fingers, arching over him, letting her breasts fall into his face until his teeth fastened on a nipple and she felt his growing interest stir against her legs.

'When you what?' she asked. They were still locked lazily together, she above him, rolling gently, feeling his physical presence subside.

'You know.' His eyes went dark for a moment. There was so much inside him she didn't understand. Where he went to all night. What he did. Robbing, she guessed. It wasn't such a bad thing. Needs must. But if all he did was steal, why would they want her to look after him like this? Why would they demand, so insistently, with threats only barely concealed, that she had to call them every time he left and tell them everything they'd discussed?

'Say it,' she ordered.

The pinkness in his cheeks, the result of their mutual exertions, flushed a little brighter. 'When I came. You felt it.'

'Of course.' She laughed. 'What do you think?'

She threw back her hair. Her teeth glinted dully in the fierce morning light. There was a sheen of sweat on her soft, young skin. 'Those others. I make them wear something. But you're special, Gino. You're safe. With you I want to feel when it happens. Not that I wouldn't know anyway. I'm good. Aren't I?'

'You're good,' he agreed. 'Why? Why me?'

She peered frankly straight into his eyes. 'Because you didn't expect anything. Because you were gentle.'

There were so many mysteries for him here. He'd never wanted Irena, not in the beginning. Then something had changed, in him, not her.

'What do you feel when it happens?'

She thought for a moment. No one had asked before. He saw this in her face and felt some small, warm surge of pride to think he was the first. 'That there's something of you just blooming inside me. Something that could stay if I wanted it to. Stay and grow. Become a child maybe.'

His face went white. Abruptly he withdrew from her, shrinking back under the damp sheet. She hated to see him like this, the sudden shock, the strange, internal grief that seemed to be masquerading as fury.

'I told you,' she said, stroking his matted hair. 'With the others I make them wear something.'

He refused to look at her. She wondered once again what he did, thought about the curious smell on him when he came back that morning. A stink that suggested he'd been near cooked meat.

'But it won't happen, Gino. It can't.'

He looked into her pale, young face, struggling to make sure she told the truth. 'I got pregnant once back home. You can go places. You can get rid of the problem before it arrives. They made a mess of it. I can't have kids, not ever. I just make them wear these things so I don't get their diseases. But I can dream. We can both dream if we want.'

He let her fingers run down his cheek, play with his lips. She bent down and kissed him, hard, in a dominant way.

'Families kill you,' Gino Fosse said. 'Families tear your life to shreds.'

'Sometimes,' she agreed. 'What else is there?'

He was unable to think of an answer.

She leaned into his ear, her breath hot, gasping the way she knew he liked. 'When you come inside me I feel something warm and alive, where it's supposed to be, as if you were bleeding out your life for me, Gino. I take your gift and it sits there, wondering, making me grateful.'

Not once, not in any of the brief, aggressive encounters he recalled from the past, had he considered the idea that this was a mutual event. The act had always been about his own efforts to achieve some brief, cathartic satisfaction. It had never occurred to him that there could be pleasure on the other side too. *You're the doorway of the devil.* That was what Tertullian had said and he'd always interpreted this literally, that a woman was the receptacle, an unfeeling, unresponsive place into which he could cast his lust.

He looked around the room. It was grubby. Their clothes lay on the floor. His bag, now depleted of most of his tricks, sat on the stained carpet. All that was left was the gun and some ammunition. It had to be enough.

'Tell me about yourself,' she said. 'Tell me about your family.'

He looked at her with those cold, dead eyes and she wished she could keep her mouth shut sometimes.

'Why? What do you want with them?'

'Nothing.' His anger could annoy her. It was a reasonable question, not the kind he ought to resent. 'I want to know about you. I want to hear what they did to make you this way.'

'I was this way without them,' Gino Fosse said. It was foolish, dishonest, to pretend anything else was to blame. No family, no colliding set of events had made him what he was. He recalled the fat TV man roasting on the grille, thought of the look of terror in his eyes. This was no one's doing but his. It was a conscious, deliberate act with a specific purpose in mind. Just like skinning a live cat had been twenty years or so before. The dark seed had been growing inside him all along. It just needed someone to nurture it.

Before the work began he'd stared for hours at those haunting, grisly depictions of martyrdoms in the churches, watching the saints meet their fate, wishing he could hear the words on their lips. But they were different. Arturo Valena screamed nothing but curses in his agonies. Alicia Vaccarini went weeping, unenlightened. He tried to remember the Englishman, losing his skin, tied to the beam in the church on Tiber Island, tried to decode the noises that issued from his gagged throat. And the Rinaldi woman, so stupid, so baffled by what was going on. These were now distant memories. What happened that day was not his doing alone. Hanrahan had set the arrangements. The Irishman had spread his net wide, culling so much information, from tapped phone calls, Fosse's own illicit photographs, stolen items perhaps. He knew names and dates. He was a constant voice in Fosse's ear. Even so, there was no blood on Hanrahan's hands. He may have suggested the means but it was Gino Fosse who used them.

Then there were the cops. Hanrahan would never have sanctioned that. He had his limits.

'What do you do?' she asked. 'When you go out of here? Who are you, Gino?'

He scowled at her. She should have known better. She was in enough danger as it was. 'Don't ask.'

'I want to know!' she pleaded.

He closed his eyes, wishing she wasn't there. The end was so close. This distraction was the last thing he needed. And this revelation too: that she felt him inside her, that two people could touch one another in such a strange and intimate fashion. This was, in its way, a momentary, mystical epiphany just as shocking as the glittering eyes behind the altar in San Lorenzo in Lucina. This threatened his resolve. This made the world seem a different place.

He stood up, went over to the bag and took out the gun, brought the weapon back to the bed and placed it in her hand. 'I bring deliverance,' he answered. 'To people who deserve it.'

Her pretty face cracked at that. Her fingers refused to grip the gun. She seemed terribly young again, and scared. It occurred to him that she knew what a gun could do. He thought of where she came from. Maybe she had personal experience.

'Why?' she asked, handing him back the weapon.

'I told you. Because they deserve it. Because their sins cry out for vengeance.'

Not the cops though. They got theirs for free.

She wiped her damp eyes with her forearm, like a child.

'Come with me,' she said. 'We could run away.'

'Where?'

'The coast somewhere. Rimini. They say it's nice.'

He thought of the sea, the endless sea, and the way the blue tide washed away everything.

'I'd like that,' he said.

He walked over to the bag and took out an envelope. It was full of notes. He counted out all but a handful and gave her the money. She stared at it. There was so much, more than she could ever have imagined.

'I'm not finished. I've one more piece of work to do. Irena . . .' He leaned forward and kissed her on the forehead, surprised by his own tenderness. 'You must leave, right now. In two days' time. Rimini. Be on the beach. I'll see you there.'

Her chin hung on her naked chest. He wanted to feel she lied, too, lied about feeling his warm, sparking presence inside her. *You're the doorway to the devil.* Tertullian was right. He had to believe that. If he didn't he could never be the Gino Fosse he knew, the one he understood, the one with a goal, a mission. This Gino had heard the rats chattering in San Lorenzo, had dared the anonymous, shrivelled heads in the Lateran to speak their true names.

There was no choice. He clasped her hand, making her fingers curl tightly around the money.

'Go,' he ordered and handed her the cheap champagne. 'Take this and we'll drink it together.'

Her eyes were wet. She didn't dare call him a liar.

He watched her pack her few things, waited as she walked out of the door, not looking back. Soon now, he knew, the phone would ring. Soon there would be a new deliverance.

Fifty-seven

The office was empty apart from a couple of cops shuffling papers at the far end, out of earshot. Falcone had gone on from San Lorenzo in Lucina to organize the cover for Denney's departure. He had teams throughout the city and more at the airport. Almost every man in the department was on the case, except Nic Costa, who now sat at Luca Rossi's old desk, drinking bad coffee from the machine, trying to clear his head. Throwing his ID card at Falcone had helped. No one asked for it at the station anyway. Now he thought of himself as a civilian again, a state he barely remembered, he was surprised and interested to discover his mind could go to places that some inner restraint prevented it visiting in the past.

There were footsteps across the big, bare office. Teresa Lupo was approaching, a folder in her hand. She looked dreadful, older than her years. He wondered if anyone would ever call her Crazy Teresa again.

'Thanks for coming,' he said.

'You caught me on the way out. Got some papers for Falcone. What do you want?'

'Just to talk.'

She took a good look at him, trying to judge his

mental state. 'I have to do the autopsy on Luca this afternoon. If you want to see him, it would be best now.'

'Seen enough dead people for a while.'

She sat down and put her folder on the desk. 'Me too. And I never thought I'd say that.' She was puzzled. 'What are you doing here, Nic? Falcone's throwing every man he's got onto the street.'

'I guess he doesn't want me around. I'm supposed to deal with the loose ends over Luca. Contact the pension people. Do whatever you do when a cop gets killed.'

She shook her head, baffled. 'There are civilians who do that for a living. He doesn't need the poor bastard's partner to get involved.'

'I don't mind. He had a sister. Did you know that? She's deaf and dumb. Luca took her out of the home and looked after her.'

He took the photo out of his pocket and passed it across the desk.

'What?' She sighed. 'He never mentioned a thing.' She ran her hand across the photo, as if there was some of his presence still there.

Then he threw across the book. 'Luca kept notes too.'

She opened it and stared at the contents. 'Who'd have thought a big man would write like that? It looks like a girl's hand or something. One screwed-up individual. And all these tiny doodles. Jesus. Poor fucked-up man.'

There were scribbled headings with dates and times. It was a kind of diary, but one driven by Luca Rossi's head more than actual events.

'It's what he was thinking,' Costa said. 'I just spent the best part of an hour inside his mind and I'm damned if I can get out again. It begins the day after that accident on the motorway, when he thought he was losing it.

It's . . .' he hunted to get the right words, 'a little insane, to begin with anyway. Some of it I just don't understand at all. Rossi really thought he might be going mad. Then you come into it. Then Falcone.' He stared at her. 'Then me. It wasn't meant for public consumption. You don't have to take it personally.'

She flicked through the pages. 'He thought I was sweet? No one uses that word about me. Never.' Then she turned the page and went quiet.

'It's OK,' he said. 'I'm not offended. Read it out. Maybe it will make more sense that way.'

' "Kid Costa".' She spoke softly, even though the office was as good as empty. ' "V. clever. V. naïve. Why the hell me?" What does that mean?'

'Go on,' he said. 'It doesn't end there.'

A few pages later Rossi returned to the subject and didn't mince words. She was surprised by the venom in the dead man's words. She didn't realize Rossi resented being Costa's partner so much. He seemed offended by Nic's innocence and, in particular, the way he had dealt with the Vatican.

'I don't want to look at this,' she said, putting the diary down on the desk. 'It doesn't do anyone any good. It's just Luca rambling. Doesn't mean a damn thing.'

'You think he was mad at me?'

'Maybe,' she admitted. 'Or mad at himself. I don't know.'

'You haven't read enough,' he suggested. 'He was mad with Falcone. He genuinely didn't understand why the man was leaning on me like that. Luca thought I was taking too much on myself and not asking enough questions. Maybe he was right.'

'Don't resent a dead man, Nic. Luca liked you. He

told me so himself and that means more than any crap in some stupid diary.'

'No! I don't resent him at all. I just kick myself for failing to see what he saw. He didn't understand why Falcone kept putting me at the front of everything. Letting Sara stay at the farm so readily. Pushing me to pretend we were having some kind of relationship. As if . . .'

It could be wrong to take this further. He was aware of her intense, concerned attention, aware too that he didn't want to involve someone else in his own troubles.

'I don't like what I'm hearing, Nic.'

'Then forget it once I've said it. But I have to ask, Teresa. Why me? Why not someone with more experience?'

'You did your best.'

'That's not the point. I did what I was told. I always do, without question. And I should have been asking more questions. I should have made Luca want to say all this to me direct instead of putting it down on some piece of paper he thought no one else would ever see.'

He took the diary and turned it to a page near the back. The tiny handwriting was even more extended here, as if Rossi was scribbling down his thoughts in a frantic rush. He stabbed his finger at the point in question. She took the diary and looked at the passage, trying to interpret the scribble.

' "Rinaldi: dope in the bathroom. And they missed it! Message on the computer, appointment with the killer. And they missed it! Are we lucky or what? And this: someone from the Vatican phoned that morning to make the date. Fosse? No. He was in exile. Who?" '

She looked at him and he wasn't wrong now. Teresa Lupo was scared.

'It was the obvious question and I can't believe I never asked it. Gino Fosse couldn't have made the arrangement to meet Rinaldi. He was banned from Denney's office more than a week earlier. The way Rinaldi behaved in the library, looking for the video cameras, suggested there was some accomplice. This surely confirmed it, and makes it look like someone with access to Denney's office. But we let our heads go somewhere else. We got taken up by events and never stopped to think about what was really happening.'

'You had a serial killer on your hands. You knew who he was. Nic? What else do you expect?'

'And something else,' he said, ignoring the question. 'I checked. Before Falcone sent us round to Rinaldi's apartment the place had been searched by six experienced men who know scene of crime inside out. You see what Rossi's asking himself here? How come they missed two such obvious and crucial pieces of evidence?'

'People screw up. It happens all the time.'

'No,' he insisted. 'Not like that. It's too convenient. Rossi knew all along.'

'So why didn't he say anything to someone?'

'Who to? Me? He tried to, I think. But I wouldn't listen and look what he says in the diary. He didn't think I could handle it directly. He thought that, if I suspected the truth, I'd take it too far, start screaming for justice instead of doing what he thought was right: keeping quiet, keeping my head down. He wanted to protect me as much as he could. Could he tell Falcone? Think about it. If Luca was right, the reason the search team found nothing in Rinaldi's apartment was because *there was nothing to find.* Someone, Hanrahan maybe, put it there later. And then Falcone sent us round to find it. What interpretation do you think Luca put on that?'

She was beginning to look around the room, making sure no one was eavesdropping. 'Too much. You've got to look for simple answers. They always tell you that.'

'You've got to look for answers that work. Do you believe Gino Fosse is doing all this on his own? Just ticking off a list of Sara Farnese's lovers for the hell of it? Surviving in the city without any help?'

She was silent. It was too much to accept. There had to be someone else.

'I'll take that as a no,' he went on. 'So let's move on to the next point. Do you believe this is even about Sara Farnese at all? If he's so pissed off with her, why didn't he kill her when he had the chance? The two of them spoke, remember, when I was lying half conscious on the ground. She somehow persuaded this lunatic to let us both live. Have you worked out how?'

'No.' Her face said it all. It was ridiculous that they should both have survived.

'There's only one answer. Because I didn't matter. Neither did she except as some kind of trigger for his actions. A trigger someone knew how to pull. How?'

'I don't know. He's psychotic, Nic. You saw those pictures. He's sexually obsessed with her.'

'That's it? No. Someone made him like that. Deliberately. And then they set us on his tail knowing the direction we would take because it was a direction they had already laid out in advance.'

It was the only explanation that made sense, but even so there were gaps. 'And that destination was Michael Denney, all along,' he continued, thinking about the man in the Vatican, with the Caravaggio copy on the wall of his poky little apartment, desperate for a life beyond those walls. 'I picked up the fake appointment with his phone number attached to it. I brought him into this case just like I was supposed to. Luca was trying to tell me all along the whole thing stank. Now Falcone has the man wriggling on the line. He's got the evidence that's forced the Vatican to eject him.'

His head was spinning, trying to comprehend the possibilities. 'And it can't just be Falcone.'

She reached out and touched his hand. 'You're going too far, Nic. Take some advice. The world isn't black and white. Sometimes you have to look the other way. Leave this alone.'

He stared at her. 'I don't like "looking the other way". It's not why I came here. Think of the people who want Denney dead. A few politicians. A few *mafiosi*. A few people who worked alongside him in the Vatican. They know each other anyway. Luca understood that. I was too stupid to listen. Fosse is loose in the city, a crazy priest who's never, as far as we know, had to fend for himself for one day of his life. Someone's looking after him. Someone's providing him with weapons and money presumably. Falcone couldn't do that. The risk would be too great. I doubt it would come from inside the Vatican either. But there's plenty of criminals who could help. We keep trying to fool ourselves this is just one lunatic working his way through a list. It's not like that at all. This is a concerted, organized campaign. Three distinct sets of people, each with their own agenda, working together to get Michael Denney on the run because that will suit them all. I just walked right in and did what they wanted. Now Luca and some other poor cop are dead and Falcone's walking round with something on his face you could just about mistake for guilt.'

She glowered at him. 'Don't judge people without the facts. Not yourself. Not Falcone either. It was Gino Fosse who murdered these people. Whatever took him there. All of this is conjecture. Luca just had doubts, that's all. There's no evidence. Just a lot of inconsistencies.'

'Inconsistencies,' he repeated. 'You're right. Here's the biggest. Why did Gino Fosse start in the first place? He was bad material, but there's nothing to suggest he was a killer before. What was the trigger?'

He recalled the picture on the TV: Sara Farnese with her arms around the old man. 'They were lovers, I guess,' he continued. 'Sara and Denney. I know she denied it but they were anyway. Gino Fosse knew her through his work in the Vatican. He knew she was sleeping around somehow but not with Denney, not to begin with. When he found out . . .'

He waited for her to interrupt, in vain. 'He what? Went "crazy"? That's all it ever comes down to and it isn't enough. Gino Fosse is crazy, I don't doubt it. Everything we know about these killings confirms that. But it still doesn't tell us why it began.'

He thought about Sara. She was an extraordinary woman. It was not just her beauty. There was some luminescent quality that made him need her, made him feel that her presence provided some form of completeness for his life. Gino Fosse could have felt this way. It would have been easy. Still, it wasn't enough to kill for.

'None of this makes sense,' he said. 'The way she slept with these people. Fosse's reaction.' He recalled the tiny tower on Tiber Island, with its smell of meat and blood.

And the cryptic message that was still running round in his head.

'I'm an idiot,' he said. 'Even Gino Fosse told us this wasn't all it seemed. That's why he wrote those lines on the wall. He was laughing at us all the time. He knew we'd look the wrong way. He was taunting us all along.'

She looked into his eyes, not liking what she saw there. 'You want some advice? Just go home. Pour yourself a drink. Read a book or something. Falcone's put you out of this for a reason. There's nothing more you can do.'

He reached inside his jacket, pulled out the service pistol and put it on the table. It was a Beretta 92FS semi-automatic, the matt black police workhorse they all carried. The fifteen-round clip was full. He'd fitted the extra sight aid on the end of the barrel to make it more accurate. Not that it made much difference. Nic Costa was a lousy shot and knew it.

'So you're going to take on the world with that?' she demanded.

'I went into this job for a reason.'

'They all do, Nic! Luca probably said the same thing when he joined. Falcone too. Then you see the world for what it is. You learn to bend, before you break.'

He touched the black metal. 'Bend enough to conspire in a judicial murder? Because, if I'm right, isn't that what's going on here? Falcone doesn't plan to arrest Michael Denney. He just wants to step aside when some hood moves out of the shadows and does the deed. What's the betting Fosse never makes it out alive either? What does that do for Falcone? One more feather in his cap. He gets to close all the options on the case, put a few corpses in the morgue he feels belong there, and probably pick up some money on the side. Is this the first time? Did Luca know that already? Am I the idiot around here? The only one who doesn't know what's going on?'

She didn't argue and that gave him his answer. Perhaps Luca Rossi had even spoken about it.

'The gun won't do you any good,' she said.

'I know. I was just going to hand it in. I quit. I threw my card at Falcone this morning. Enough's enough.'

'Wonderful,' she groaned. 'I imagine that really made an impact. How many men do that to him in a week do you think? He adores that kind of thing. You can take it all back, Nic. Think of it as part of the initiation.'

'Initiation?' he asked, astonished. 'Into what? A world of compromises? A world where you're willing to cut deals with crooks, of all kinds, because that's the easiest way to get what you want?'

'There are people who'd say that's just being pragmatic.'

'I know,' he said. 'Falcone. Our man in the Vatican. The people it suits to think that way. Not me.'

'So what do you think you can do?'

'Something. Maybe.' The words sounded lame as he said them. 'Try to make sure this crap doesn't happen again.'

'And if you're wrong?'

'Then I look a fool. So what's new?'

She closed her eyes. 'Is there anything I can do to dissuade you from this madness?'

'Doubt it,' he shrugged.

'You're a stubborn kid.'

'I'm twenty-seven years old. I'm not a kid. Not any more.'

She pulled out a pack of cigarettes and lit one. The

smoke curled out towards the open window, out into the smoggy heat of the morning. 'No,' she agreed. 'You're not. You know what worried Luca most about you? He didn't understand why you couldn't let things go. Why you just hung on like a terrier when any rational person would just say enough's enough. Luca knows what Falcone is. We all do. Listen to me well, Nic. That doesn't make him a bad cop. This has all gone wrong for him now but you don't think for a moment he would have countenanced any of this if he knew his own men would get killed, do you?'

'I don't know.'

'I do,' she said firmly. 'And he doesn't take money either. In his book, he's as honest as they come. He just happens to think the ends justified the means. When you think that way, sometimes it all goes horribly wrong.'

He thought about that. She was probably on the ball. He could see the pain etched into the inspector's bitter features. 'So what if you're right? Doesn't bring Luca back. Doesn't put me on his side either. Blame my old man. It must be in the genes.'

'Oh, God.' Teresa Lupo looked at him then picked up the folder in front of her. 'Hell, let's live dangerously together. Here . . .'

She took out two one-page reports and put them on the table, turned towards him.

'What's this?' he asked.

'You wanted a reason why Fosse did what he did. You wanted a trigger. There it is and it isn't anything any one of us could have guessed. Even Falcone I think, though someone else knows because they must surely have used it.'

He looked at the pages. They were both DNA analysis

reports from Fosse's home in the Clivus Scauri. It took him a little while to understand. When the revelation came it was, somehow, a relief too, a final and welcome piece of the puzzle falling into place.

He checked his watch. In ninety minutes Michael Denney would get into the car that would, surely, take him to his death. Then a memory entered his head: of the day he stood outside the church of San Clemente, with Jay Gallo's drowned corpse inside, listening to Sara tell the tale of the fake Pope Joan and how she was torn to shreds by the mob once they understood her true nature.

Teresa watched him, waiting for his response. 'We just assumed what they wanted us to assume all along,' he said. 'That she was Denney's mistress, sleeping with these people to try to help him. We never began to think there could be some other explanation.'

'No,' she said, with some regret. 'Not that one.'

He ran his fingers across the report. His head was fighting to get all this straight. There were so many answers here if he could put his finger on them. Explanations that tied up everything, and left Sara as much a victim as anyone. 'This couldn't be some mistake, Teresa?'

'DNA doesn't lie. Sara Farnese is Denney's daughter. Gino Fosse's sister. Non-identical twins. I checked their birthdays through the driving licence records. Same day. Him supposedly in Palermo, her in Paris. God knows where in reality, but they're twins. There's no other explanation.'

He remembered what she told him about growing up in a convent in Paris. While she was surrounded by nuns, Gino Fosse must have been fostered on two Sicilian peasants, then shipped off to Church school as soon as he was old enough, perhaps because his true nature was already apparent. All the while Michael Denney had kept tabs on them both. Somehow he had managed to bring both close to his side, never telling one about the other. Perhaps he judged Fosse was too unstable to handle that knowledge. Perhaps the old man just liked playing these games. Whatever. He wanted his family near. Nic Costa could only guess at the reasons.

'She's doing this because he's her father,' he said, seeing the pieces fall into place. 'She knows the trouble he's in. She knows he's frantic for a way out. So she's sleeping with anyone he tells her to, letting Fosse take the pictures, just to give him some hope, a chance maybe. And none of it works. In fact it just makes things worse because someone's been watching the games Gino Fosse has been playing. Someone with a reason to get Denney out of there. So this someone tells Gino who she really is, knowing this is the trigger. Gino realizes Denney's been . . . pimping his own sister and using him to make the delivery. Getting him to take pictures of her. Christ . . .'

'That would piss me off,' she said. 'And I'm halfway normal. Nic?'

She watched him, worried. Costa seemed lost in his own world of startled shock.

'Nic?'

'I can't just sit back and let this happen.'

He picked up the phone and dialled the farm. Marco answered. He sounded happy, almost young.

'Is Sara there?'

There was a pause on the line.

'What do you mean?' Marco asked. 'She said she called you and checked it was OK.'

'Checked what?'

'She wanted some things from her apartment. Bea drove her there half an hour ago. She said she'd make her own way back.'

He swore, then snatched the gun back from the table.

Fifty-eight

It was an hour before noon and the weather was starting to change. Clouds of tiny flies hung in the humid air, as if held there by some electrical charge from the angry grey sky. The pressure was rising. It gave Teresa Lupo a headache. Looking at the tense, absorbed faces on the street she knew she wasn't alone. She had pumped a couple of plain clothes men on the street. They disclosed that an unmarked police car with two detectives inside would draw up at a small rear gate of the Vatican, some way north of the public library entrance, and pick up Michael Denney at midday. The media had been thrown off the scent by one more carefully placed leak. They had stationed themselves in the Via di Porta Angelica, a ragged mass of reporters, photographers and TV cameramen, squabbling in the baking heat. Teresa Lupo had seen them as her car took her to Falcone's lair, a long, plain khaki van sprouting antennae which was now parked just off the large square of the Piazza del Risorgimento, close to the bus stops. From here, she guessed, Falcone could jump into a car and follow Denney all the way to the private jet at Ciampino, waiting for Fosse to emerge from the shadows and do what was expected of him.

She wondered where they would let the lunatic loose. Not at the gates of the Vatican, surely. If Denney died there, the outcry against the State and the Rome police would outweigh the gain from his death. Nor was the airport an obvious option. They could hardly ask a man who had once dined with presidents to walk alone across the runway, bag in hand, waiting for his fate to overtake him. Some other eventuality was in hand and she was determined to find it.

Falcone looked up from the row of radio operators stationed at the communications desk and asked, sourly, 'What the hell are you doing here? We've got no corpses for you. No customers at all.'

She held out the folder with the reports inside. 'I have the DNA results from the Fosse place. I thought you'd like to see them.'

He was watching a computer screen with a digital map of the city on it. A red marker winked from a street round the corner. It was, she guessed, some tag on the car that Denney would take.

'We know all we need to know.'

'No you don't.'

He glared at her, annoyed. 'You've something to tell me?'

'I'm just a lackey. I deliver messages.'

He looked at the offered papers, refusing to touch them. 'Well?'

'Gino Fosse is Denney's son all right. But Sara Farnese isn't Denney's lover. She's his daughter. She and Fosse are non-identical twins.'

He was astonished. 'That's impossible!'

'It was all there on the DNA from Fosse's place. They

found menstrual residue on that underwear. Hers. We could match it with the photographs.'

The tanned face wrinkled in disbelief. 'Are you sure?'

'Look at the reports. Look at the dates on the birth certificates. There's no other possibility.'

'Jesus.' He seemed genuinely shocked. 'That place is just full of secrets. Hanrahan should have told me. We will have words. On that and other matters.' His face was lined, his eyes dead. Falcone looked terrible, damaged by events.

'Does it make a difference?' she asked.

'Not that I can see,' he replied, shrugging. 'So Denney's an even bigger bastard than we thought. Whoring his own daughter to try to get himself out of that place. Imagine sending your own flesh and blood round to sleep with that fat creep Valena. And the rest of them . . .'

'Imagine being the kind of woman who'd agree to that.'

'Family,' he muttered. 'There's no comprehending those ties sometimes.'

Falcone seemed pensive for a moment. She felt like pushing it. 'Or imagine being Gino Fosse,' she continued. 'Discovering the woman you've been driving around on these engagements, the woman you've been photographing, staring at on your wall, this woman's your sister. Who told him that? Who pulled that trigger?'

The dead eyes held her. Falcone really didn't know, she realized. He'd been fooled as much as everyone. 'Search me. I don't care any more. It's irrelevant.'

'Irrelevant?' she asked, exasperated. 'Whoever did this is as culpable as Fosse himself.'

'Stick to forensics. Why are we having this conversation?'

'Prurience.'

'That's my job. Not yours. And as for this . . .' He picked up the folder and waved it at her. 'I don't want to see a word of this in the media. Not for as long as you can stop it leaking out of the station. I don't want anyone seen in some kind of sympathetic light. They're all losers. Understand? The story that the Farnese woman is his mistress stands.'

'But it's untrue. It paints her to be something she isn't.'

'Fine! So she just whores herself around to a handful of influential jerks who might be able to do her father a favour. That puts her in a more favourable light? Here . . .'

He snatched the report off the desk, glowered at the type on the page then tore the thing to shreds in front of her eyes, walked to an open window of the van and dumped the pieces out into the hard light beyond the glass.

She folded her arms and shook her head at him. 'My. I am so impressed.'

'Enough. I want no more of this. And no more of you.'

'I'd like to stay. I'd like to observe. That's an official request.'

'Refused. You . . .' He nodded at one of the plain-clothes men working the radio desk. 'Show Crazy Teresa to the door.'

She was just a little shorter than Falcone but she had some bulk on him. Teresa Lupo took one step towards him, leaned in, close to his face, and noted the way he drew back. Then she jabbed a finger into his chest.

'You should never piss off a pathologist,' she said carefully. 'You know why?'

He said nothing.

Because in your line of work, Falcone, being someone with your manners, your warped sense of integrity, and your kind of friends, it is just possible I will one day find you on my table. And for that . . .' she ran a finger down the side of his tanned cheek, pressing it like a scalpel into his flesh, 'I would be delighted to set aside a great deal of time indeed.'

The dark face turned a touch paler.

'Out,' he snapped.

She turned and left, stopping by the short metal external staircase, exchanging glances with the uniformed man there. He seemed vaguely familiar. They all did. Over the years she must have met almost every cop in Rome. She offered him a cigarette. He shook his head. He was bored. He was like all the uniforms, she guessed, just manpower for the day, a bunch of innocents who could be persuaded to check how shiny their shoes were when the time came.

'So you're going all the way to Ciampino?' she asked.

'Right,' he grunted. 'The long way round.'

'I'm sorry?'

'You didn't hear? The big man wants to make one final stop in the city. A sentimental journey. We go there. Then we take him to the plane.'

'Sentimental journey,' she repeated, and then they talked a little more.

Three minutes later she began to walk towards the

river, back towards the hulking shape of the Castel Sant'Angelo, frantically punching the buttons on her phone, wondering if she could get there before the sky broke and brought with it the mother of all storms.

Fifty-nine

Michael Denney packed his belongings into a small, expensive flight case covered in airline stickers: three shirts, three sets of trousers, a couple of jackets, some underclothes. Then all the money he could persuade the Vatican Finance Department to release from his bank account in cash: $50,000, another £30,000 in sterling and €5,000. It was interesting, he thought, to see how easily they relented once he started to make the right points. Though he'd hardly touched it these past two years, Denney remained a man of considerable wealth. A good half was inherited from family in New England. The rest came from more unusual sources: gifts, commissions, fees. Bribes, if he were being honest with himself. The people with their hands on the purse strings knew that as well as he did. When he pointed out the problems that could ensue were his money to remain inside the Vatican – awkward questions about hidden accounts, calls from the left for the sequestration of funds – they were quick to sign the release. The balance of his wealth, close to $12 million spread around various institutions, would be remitted to a variety of banks across the Atlantic according to his mandates. Redemption and comfort were not, he thought, incompatible. He was only reclaiming what was rightfully his and he felt happier looking into the misty times ahead with some hard cash in his pocket.

There were two passports in the case: one from the Vatican which would, they said, be confiscated once he arrived in Boston. The second had an old photograph, from the days when his hair was sleek and black, one which made him look like someone completely different. The battered dark-blue jacket wore the familiar silver eagle. It had been a long time since Michael Denney had felt like an American citizen. The passport was, technically, out of date but, as a precaution some months back, he had let a contact he knew work on it, changing a few details. Now it looked valid, which meant he would not have to throw himself on the mercy of the consular service, pleading like an illegal immigrant. It would take him a while to get used to the idea of being American again. There was much to be learned in the months and years to come. But with money, and a US passport, there would be opportunity.

He looked around the apartment, imprinting the picture of it on his mind. It was memories like these that could keep you alive in the black days, knowing that some of the humiliation lay behind. Then he checked his watch. He was due at the rear entrance in thirty-five minutes. It would take a good ten minutes to walk there, through the private gardens, praying that everything he had been told about security inside the walled state was true. Denney was inclined to believe them. It would be too embarrassing to have a mishap on their own territory. The real dangers lay outside.

Denney looked at the painting that dominated the

cramped main room. That was one belonging he hoped to see again. There were memories behind the original which he did not wish to lose. For a moment he was lost in the precise and savage detail, held by the monstrous, lunatic assassin raising his sword high, ready to deliver the final blow to the saint who lay dying on the floor, hand reaching upwards for the palm branch of martyrdom offered by the angel. And there, in the background, Caravaggio's concerned face. Denney had always fancied himself as a spectator, one who looked on, caring yet detached, though never ignorant of one's responsibilities. Both murderer and martyr were victims in this painting, he thought, and he had no great wish to fulfil either role in his life. Matthew had been chosen, had offered himself willingly. And his killer? He remembered the conversation that began it all thirty years ago. How he had talked with the pretty young nun when they met in the church. She had railed against the man's cruelty, the savage anger in his face, asking how he could commit such a deed. He had asked the question which came into his head from nowhere: how could Matthew be what he was without his nemesis? Didn't the murderer deserve some of the credit too for delivering to him his apostle's fate? Wasn't he just as much a part of God's will as Matthew? Wasn't Caravaggio's stricken face in the background there to implicate us all in the act, and the artist in particular for his brutal imagining of it? Just as the young cop had said . . .

This was a cruel world, one in which breath could be stripped from the living in an instant.

Recalling that moment now, he remained unable to define what prompted the thought. Yet the consequences were so profound. Everything that followed, public and personal, stemmed from that moment. It was to prove the instant the young Michael Denney was touched by the world beyond the Vatican. It was a turning point, a step along the great journey, towards sin and worldliness.

He accepted now that he could never return to what he was. He knew too he could never leave the city without seeing the original once more, touching those memories that meant so much.

The bell rang. Denney was dismayed to find the sound made him jump. He walked to the door and squinted through the spyhole. Hanrahan stood there alone.

'Come to say goodbye?' Denney said, with a degree of cheerfulness, as he let the dour Irishman into the room.

'If you like, Michael. I want to make sure you're gone, to be honest.'

Denney nodded at the canvas on the wall. 'When I'm settled, Brendan, I'll be on the phone to you. There are things of mine here. You'll send them on. I'll pay for storage. You'll put that in good care.'

Hanrahan looked at it and sniffed. 'You think it's worth it?'

'I believe so.'

'It's in this church of yours, Michael. Is that correct?'

'The first church I ever worked in in Rome. I never told that young policeman, but it's true. The place is full of memories.'

'And now you expect us to leave you there for a few minutes, on your way to the airport?'

Denney stared into Hanrahan's grey face. He would not be cowed by this man. 'I won't run, Brendan. You'll make sure of that.'

'Oh yes. But why?'

There was a light in Denney's eyes. Something Hanrahan hadn't seen in a long time. 'For my own sake.'

'It's the woman, I imagine,' Hanrahan answered. 'The nun from Paris, Sister Annette. I read the files. You followed her there for a little while. Just for some bedtime games. All for a nun at that?'

Denney hesitated before replying. Just the thought of her painted such pictures in his head. 'She was the most beautiful woman I ever met. We opened each other's eyes for a little while. Life requires a few mysteries. Otherwise why would we need a God at all?'

The Irishman scowled. 'Abelard and Héloïse is a pretty story, but what a price they paid.'

'Still, they were alive, Brendan. You can't begin to imagine how these things happen, can you? I pity you for that. It makes you a small man.'

Denney closed his eyes. The memories were so vivid he felt he could touch her still. 'I made love to her for the first time in that place. First time I made love to a woman at all. I was a late starter. It was in a small ante-room off the nave. You could lock the door, do whatever you wanted. No one ever knew. We'd go there five, six times a week, take off the clothes they made us wear, become something else. What we were meant to be.'

Hanrahan's chill stare said it all.

'Don't look at me like that, Brendan. This is something you can't understand, something you've never experienced. When we were in each other's arms there I swear we thought we were in Paradise. I felt closer to God than I've ever been in my life and there's no blasphemy in saying it. I never wanted that to end. Then . . .'

'Then you followed her to Paris and she fell pregnant. You could have left the Church, Michael. You could have been with her. The coward in you always comes out in the end.'

Denney refused to rise to the bait. 'I was a coward, but not in the way you think. I wanted to do just that. She couldn't face the ordeal we both knew that would entail. The wrath of our families. Being cast out as sinners. I was a coward because, when the Church found out, as they were bound to, I acceded to them without a fight. I let them rule us both.' A picture entered his head, of Annette naked, lying back on the old cushions of a battered sofa, removing the crucifix from her neck, a shaft of light cutting through stained glass into the dusty hot air of the storeroom, her lovely face full of anticipation and joy. 'What happened in that room was no sin, Brendan. It was a holy thing. It was what was supposed to happen. If only you could understand it.'

One memory followed another. His grey face winced at the remembered pain. 'They let her keep one child provided she pretended it belonged to someone else, someone who didn't care a damn. Imagine having to face that decision and I was nowhere in sight, I was banished. Do you take the girl? Do you take the boy? None of this was my doing. These are the cruel ways of the Church. Sometimes they make my sins seem like mere transgressions. And then . . .'

He recalled the last time he visited them both and the way the sickness was dragging the light from her eyes.

'My family had more influence. I was saved for greater things. They put my worldliness to other uses.' He took one last look at the apartment. 'Sometimes these past few days I've wondered how much are we born to be what we become and how much are we made that way? What would have happened if we'd said to hell with them and got married? Would I have made a loyal husband? A good father? Or would I have become what I am now in any case? A devious old fraud desperate to save his own skin? It's the former I know, which is the worst of it. You see, Brendan? I don't need you to judge me. I can do that for myself, better than any save one.' Denney noted the Irishman's embarrassment with amusement. 'And now I've made you my confessor. How very awkward for you.'

Hanrahan coughed into his hand. 'We've twenty minutes to wait, Michael. When the time comes I'll carry your bag and you can follow me.'

Denney stood his ground. 'And the painting?'

'I'll keep it till I hear.'

Sixty

He waited in front of the Pantheon watching the crowds of tourists struggling in vain to find some shelter from the heat inside its vast, shady belly. It felt as if there was a fire beneath the world. The fierce humid heat was working its way to some catharsis. The sky was darkening, turning the colour of lead. From somewhere in the east came a rippling roll of thunder. A speck of rain fell on his cheek with only the slightest touch of gravity, as if it had materialized out of the soaking air.

Gino Fosse had saved these clothes for the last moment. They were his own this time: the long white alb almost touching the ground which he'd worn when he took his first mass in Sicily. It was gathered at the waist with a cincture. In one deep pocket was a CD player and headphones. In the other rested the gun.

A tourist, a young girl, pretty, with long fair hair, asked for directions to the Colosseum.

'Buy a map,' he snapped and she wandered away, puzzled, a little frightened perhaps.

He looked at the looming, lowering sky. A storm was on the way, a bad one. The city streets would run deep with rain. The people would race for shelter in the cafés and bars. The short, humid summer would come to a sudden climax and still the city would not be washed clean in the flood that followed.

Man was born evil and waited for the events that purified him. There was no other way.

He pulled out the CD player, put on the headphones and listened to the music. It was Cannonball Adderley live playing 'Mercy, Mercy, Mercy' with Joe Zawinul on piano. It sounded like a spiritual, like a sinner praying for redemption.

Gino Fosse sang the refrain out loud as he walked: *Da-da-deedle – deedle-deedle-dee.*

By the time he reached the church the sky was black. He walked inside and took a bench in the darkness, watching the way the light was beginning to fail beyond the windows, waiting for a familiar shape to walk through the door.

Sixty-one

Greta Ricci stood with the rest of the pack outside the main Vatican gate, eyeing the Swiss Guards in their blue uniforms, steadily becoming more and more convinced someone was playing them for fools. The men on duty looked half bored, half amused. She couldn't believe for one moment that the event they were expecting – an event that would make the news bulletins throughout the world – was about to happen here, in front of two dumb-looking would-be cops. The Vatican surely had other plans. Maybe they were using the helipad at the back, unseen. Maybe they were taking him out of one of the small exits in the wall which led to the Viale Vaticano at the rear, or putting him on a private train at the Vatican Station, behind St Peter's.

She was with Toni, the dumb teenage photographer from Naples who had been attached to her side since the story began. He was never the most fragrant of youths at the best of times. Days and nights of constant door-stepping and itinerant sieges had given him the odour of a street bum. Which Greta Ricci believed she could have handled were it not for his manifest incompetence. Toni was six feet tall and extraordinarily well built. His strategy for getting the best picture comprised waiting for the moment then fighting his way to the front of the pack and elbowing himself into position for the shot. It lent, she was forced to admit, a certain graphic immediacy to his work which almost always appeared, with some justification, to have been taken from the inside of a brawl. But it made him useless as a journalistic colleague. He looked for nothing except the emergence of an opportunity. He had no flair for creativity beyond the raw muscle of the snatched shot, no talent for seeing that pictures must sometimes be made, not merely captured. He was a chimp with a rapid-fire Nikon, hoping that somewhere among the scores of frames he squeezed out of it a memorable image would emerge.

Her mobile phone rang. She scowled at Toni, eyes fixed straight ahead, staring at the two smirking guards at the gate.

'Don't,' she ordered, stabbing a finger into his back, 'look away for an instant. Understand?'

He nodded. He didn't have a sense of humour either.

'Ricci,' she said, walking away from the herd to get some peace and a little silence. Then she walked a little faster, a little further, when she heard who it was.

'Nic? Where are you?'

'Doesn't matter. Where are you?'

'At the main gate. Where they're telling us to be to get the best view. Not that I believe a word of it.'

'No.' He kept it short and direct and made sure she agreed, first, to the preconditions. Just her and a photographer. No other people in the media. He couldn't take the risk.

'You think I'd invite someone else along to my own party?' she asked, then hastily scribbled down the details that he gave her, looking all the while for the nearest cab rank.

When he rang off she walked back into the media pack and physically pulled Toni out from close to the front of it, ignoring his screeching objections all the time.

'Shut up!' she hissed when they were close to the edge.

'Why? What gives?'

She looked at the faces around them. Interested faces. They were hacks. They had the same instincts she had. They knew when someone was trying to pull a stunt of their own.

She dragged him into the shadow cast by the high Vatican wall.

'I got a tip-off. Somewhere we can get a picture of Denney, all to ourselves.'

'Where?' he asked suspiciously.

The cameramen liked to hunt in packs. It was safer that way. She knew he'd tell them somehow, just a little later so that he got first pickings.

'Never you mind. We just find a cab and get the hell out of here now.'

'What? And let those bastards loose on whatever happens next? You want to get me fired or something?'

'I want to get the story,' she hissed.

'Well you go off and get it. If everyone else is here, then here is where I stay. If you want to change that, you ring the picture desk and get them to tell me.'

'Moron,' she muttered. 'Give me that spare camera you carry.'

'No. It's company property.'

She stared up at him. 'Give me the camera, dimwit,

and I will, when they realize what a screw-up you've made of this, do my very best to let you keep your job.'

He thought about it. Maybe there was a little insurance there.

'It's idiot-proof,' he muttered, handing the compact over. 'So you should know how to use it.'

'Moron,' she repeated, and strode quickly off towards the Piazza del Risorgimento, looking for a cab, noting, as she did, the long khaki van covered in antennae close to the bus stops, wondering why she had failed to see it before.

Sixty-two

It was a black Mercedes with darkened windows in the rear. Michael Denney looked through the windscreen: two men in dark suits sat in the front, anonymous behind sunglasses.

'Do I tip them, Brendan?' he asked.

The Irishman carried the small case to the back of the car. Then he looked around. The street was empty. It seemed to meet with his approval.

'I can carry my own luggage,' Denney said, watching Hanrahan begin to open the boot.

'If you choose.' Both men looked at the case. It seemed so small, so insignificant.

'Have a good journey, Michael. Call me when you're settled.'

'Of course,' he said, and extended a hand. Hanrahan looked at it.

'Come on.' Denney laughed. 'I'm not a leper. And you've got what you want, haven't you? No embarrassing revelations. No more scandal.'

Hanrahan took his hand and pumped it in a summary fashion. 'Call.'

'Yeah,' Denney replied as he started to climb into the passenger seats, taking the case with him. 'If I don't just disappear into thin air.'

Sixty-three

He abandoned the car in the street and dashed through the thickening rain, looking for her, knowing she would be trying to hide. Nic Costa had no idea what was driving Michael Denney to the church but he felt sure his daughter would join him there. Teresa Lupo's news had cleared his head. He could begin to see a direct, linear connection linking her actions now. When he had time to sit down and think it all through he would see more. For now that was a luxury. The truth seemed apparent. She was intent on joining Denney in his flight from Rome, unaware of the fate Falcone had in mind for her father.

The crowds milled around the back streets of the Pantheon, trying to escape the slow, greasy rain. He pushed hard through them, ignoring the curses he got in return, praying she was not already inside. Then, in a narrow alley a minute from the church, he saw her. She wore a neck scarf over her hair and had the collar of her light raincoat up to her face. She was huddled in a doorway, avoiding the rain, avoiding a decision too, perhaps.

He ran across the cobblestones and faced her, holding out his arms, barring the way. Her green eyes were dark in the half-light of the coming storm. They refused to leave the pavement.

'Sara,' he said, gently taking her by the shoulders. 'I know.'

'Know what?' she murmured, pulling herself away from him.

'There's no need to pretend any more. I understand.'

She detached herself from his hands and leaned back against the damp, grimy wall. 'Don't, Nic. I'd rather not hear this.'

He hesitated. These were big ideas. There was so little time. 'The labs have been looking at evidence. About you. About Gino Fosse. You're Denney's daughter, not his lover.' He made sure to see the effect of what came next. 'Gino's your brother. Did you know that?'

She groaned. 'Can't you ever stop prying?'

'There are people dead, for God's sake. It's not done yet. Did you know about Gino?'

'Yes.' She sighed. 'Michael . . . my father told me some weeks ago. He thought it unwise to tell Gino as well. He couldn't handle himself. Michael wanted me to know for my own sake. He only told me he was my father last year. Before that I just thought he was a friend from the convent in Paris. Someone who administered the estate of the people I believed were my parents.' She turned her face towards the wall, fighting back the tears. 'You can't imagine the joy I felt when he told me that. There was a part of me alive, outside myself.'

'A year ago. Exactly when he began to realize he needed help to get out of that place.'

Her green eyes stared into his and he wondered what emotion was there: love, pity, hate? Or a little of all three.

'You only think you understand what's happening, Nic. Stay away from me.'

'No. There's more. Someone else knew what was going on. When they found out about Gino they had the weapon they needed.'

'What weapon? Gino is . . . what he is.'

'Perhaps. But he was primed. I know it. Pretty soon I may be able to prove it too.'

'What?' Her head went from side to side. Her eyes were wild. 'What are you talking about?'

'This was what they wanted all along. Your father dead. Everything began from that. Gino was just a tool they used to try to make him run. I know what he was doing for Denney. Driving you to those people. Taking pictures for blackmail if he needed it. Then handing them to Denney who used them to try to get his freedom. What Denney didn't know was that he was being watched all the time too. By someone who eventually told Gino who you really are. That was what drove him over the edge. He realized what Denney was doing to his own sister. That's what we've been chasing every step of the way.'

He was unable to guess what she was thinking. 'Who would tell him that? Why?'

'Denney's former friends. Crooks. Maybe some people in authority too. Maybe all three. Why? Think about it. He could put them all in jail. He's stolen from them. They want to feel safe. Maybe they want payback.'

'Nic!' she said, despairing. 'Don't make this worse than it is. He's leaving. It said so on the news. They're letting him go back to America. He'll be out of everyone's life there.' She paused. 'Including mine. I just want to see him before he goes. That's all. He's made this arrangement so that we can say goodbye.'

She looked at him in a way he'd forgotten. It was the expression she wore when they first met, the one full of suspicion and doubt. The one in which he was a cop, nothing more. 'I suppose you know that anyway.'

He held her hands, not knowing what to say, wanting to believe her.

'You know what I did for him?' she asked.

'Yes.'

'He's my *father*, Nic. I thought I could help. The person who did all that . . . it wasn't me.'

'I know. I knew all along. I just couldn't work it out.'

She wouldn't meet his eyes. It was, he thought, embarrassment. 'Was I supposed to say no? What wouldn't you do to save Marco?'

He didn't say a word. She understood his answer.

'You mean Marco would never have asked, would never have allowed such things to happen? You're right. The trouble is, most of us aren't trying to be perfect like you and your father. We accept we're flawed. We do our best to cope with that.'

He touched her face, gingerly. 'What's done is done. All I care about now is what's ahead.'

'I have to see him,' she insisted. 'Stay away, Nic. You don't have to do this for me.'

'If I stay away, he's dead. This isn't just about you either. I've lost a partner. I don't forget things like that.'

She looked down the alley. The rain was starting to fall steadily now. The crowds were dispersing into doorways. 'Leave me alone with him. Just for one minute. After that . . .'

'I can't. It's not safe.'

'What is?' she asked. 'Nic, this church is where he met my mother. *Our* mother.' She waited to see his response. 'It means something you can't begin to appreciate. Something that doesn't concern you.'

He turned away from her, scowling.

'Are you jealous of him?' she asked. 'That we're close in spite of everything?'

The words hit home. 'Maybe. Baffled too. I don't know how he could do this to you.'

'He was at his wits' end. He needed my help. He was dying behind those walls. You didn't see it.'

'This was about help?' he asked bitterly. 'He keeps his existence secret from you for years. He reveals it only when he needs you. Is that an act of love?'

'No, desperation. Sometimes love grows out of despair. He wasn't the only one who felt that way. I was alone. I've been alone all my life. I told you, Nic. We're not perfect people. We never will be. I didn't have a family around me like you. I knew when he told me about my mother, about the choice they were forced to make . . . I knew I'd do anything for him. Anything.'

'And you still will?'

She looked him frankly in the face. 'Do you think it was easy for me? Sleeping with these people? Knowing I was being watched . . . used.'

'Then why do it?' He couldn't keep the note of disapproval out of his voice.

'I'll never make you understand. We're too different. My father's a frightened, vulnerable man. He's wronged people. He's wronged me. In a way I can't explain that made it all simpler. I could either abandon him, or I could . . . do what he wanted and hope one day he'd be free. I did what I did for both of us. To set him free. To restore to my own life something that had been taken from me. Given the same choices again I'd make the same decision. What's one night with a stranger if it brings your own father back from the dead?'

'You're right there,' he admitted. 'I don't understand.'

'Don't do this to me. You're as frightened of a world on your own as I am. That's one thing we do have in common.'

He didn't argue. He didn't even want to think about it.

'I want him safe,' she insisted. 'And Gino too, whatever he's done. He doesn't deserve this.' She looked down the street. 'You think the church is where they . . .' She couldn't go on.

He scanned the street, looking for someone, anyone, he knew. There were just tourists, skulking in doorways. Perhaps they were there already. 'Falcone agreed he could go there. It's insane. In the circumstances. He wouldn't go along with the idea without a reason.'

'What can you do?'

'Something, maybe.' It wouldn't be easy. He was on his own. He'd no idea whether the calls he'd placed would work. Or whether they'd been intercepted. 'I don't know, Sara. If it's Falcone, some enemies he's made among his own people, some crooks from outside too . . .'

She was silent. It was impossible for him to guess what she was thinking.

'I've talked to some people I can trust,' he replied, trying to understand the situation himself. 'My father's spoken to some of his contacts too. I can't guarantee this will work. I know I can't just walk away. Luca's dead because of what they did. If they get away with killing your father they get away with everything.'

His mind was, she knew, made up. 'You don't have to be there.'

'I don't have a choice.'

It came so suddenly. She reached forward, took his face in her hands and kissed him. He tasted her mouth. It brought back such memories. For a moment Nic Costa's head was lost in recollections of delight.

'I wanted to tell you,' she whispered. 'I despised myself for not having the courage. Don't hate me for this. Please . . .'

When she looked at him like this Nic Costa knew he was lost, knew there was no point in protesting.

'When we get there, when it's safe, I want a minute with him, Nic. Alone. That's all. You have to give me that. You have to trust me.'

His fingers gripped her soft, fine hair. 'I could never hate you.'

'He's my father. He's all I have.'

She kissed him again, hard. He wanted to hold her for ever like this, locked tight against each other, perfect, safe, until all the world went quiet.

'You have me,' he said.

The taste of her filled his head. He was lost in her anguished beauty.

Sixty-four

The church was in a medieval lane that ran from the Corso Rinascimento, by the side of the Piazza Navona, into the square of the Pantheon. Years ago the city authorities had raised the pavement at each end and turned it into a dark, narrow corridor for scurrying pedestrians who walked in the shadow of the high Renaissance buildings on both sides.

The unmarked police car crossed the Tiber into the dawdling traffic of Vittorio Emanuele, the drivers arguing about where to park. Michael Denney sat in the rear and closed his eyes, listening, thinking. Then he turned in his seat and looked around him. It was impossible to judge, but somewhere in the snarl of traffic winding its way out of the Vatican there had to be others. For a moment he thought he glimpsed a Fiat saloon with the brown face and silver beard of Falcone in the rear. Then it flashed past, slipping away over the river in front of them.

He listened to the plain-clothes men getting nowhere nearer a conclusion then said, 'Just park in Rinascimento. It's closest. I won't be long. You're police. I guess you won't get a ticket.'

The two sets of sunglasses looked at each other. One

of them, the man in the passenger seat, turned and asked, 'You're sure you want to go to this place at all? We can take you straight to the airport if you want.'

The driver swore under his breath, hissing at his colleague. The bass roar of approaching thunder rattled down the river and shook the roof of the over-chilled car.

'I'm sure,' Denney said. 'This is my church. No one knows it better. And it's arranged, isn't it? I wouldn't want to get you boys into trouble.'

They were quiet after that. As they passed the Oratorio dei Filippini the sky suddenly darkened and thick black rain began to fall, slowly at first, as if uncertain of its intent, then in heavy, driving columns that rebounded from the pavement. The city looked like the bowl of some fantastic fountain designed by a drunken Bernini. The driver turned on his headlights. It was now as gloomy as night. He screwed up his eyes and looked for the turning. Denney patted him on the back, guiding, giving advice. The black Mercedes pulled in at the end of the lane, Denney looked along into the black cavern which led to the church, seeing nothing but people racing for shelter from the deluge.

He tugged his jacket around him, took hold of the suitcase below their line of sight, and said, 'Ten minutes. Are you coming?'

'We'll see you to the door,' the driver answered. 'They said to let you have some privacy inside. One way in, one way out of that place. So I guess we trust you. Let's face it.' The black glasses peered at him. 'Where are you going to go?'

His companion was silent, looking out at the downpour in the street. Neither of them seemed much minded to remove the sunglasses in spite of the weather.

'Where indeed?' Denney replied, patting the driver on the back before opening the door and stepping out into the rain, holding the case out of sight as best he could, hiding it with his body. The two cops followed and immediately dashed under the paltry shelter of a nearby building.

Michael Denney stood his ground for a moment. The rain left his grey hair drenched in seconds. He didn't care. He was free in Rome for the first time in over a year. It made his head feel light. It was a delight beyond anything he could ever have expected. He looked around him. He was the only human being not trying to escape the deluge from the gloomy sky above. It would be so easy to walk away, to try to escape. But the two cops were young. They could soon retake him. And, as they said, where would he go?

He walked along the lane, in the centre, not minding how wet he got. They dogged his footsteps from a distance, dashing from place to place to avoid the storm. Finally he reached the door to the church. Denney closed his eyes, remembering her, trying, too, to remember himself all those years ago. This was a time when he understood a little of the word 'love'. So much had been lost in the intervening years.

'Ten minutes,' he yelled through the rain. 'You're sure you won't join me?'

'Absolutely sure,' the one who'd been in the passenger seat bellowed back. The driver struggled with a cigarette. The flame of his lighter looked like a tiny beacon trying to hold back the night. Two successive claps of thunder burst over their heads, with a sudden torrent of rain. They pulled their jacket collars into their necks and leaned hard into the wall, staring at nothing but the black stonework with water streaming down its face.

Michael Denney smiled at both of them then stepped inside, turned hard left and walked into the small vestibule. It was, as he had hoped, empty, and just as he remembered it. Even the old sofa, where they'd made love so many times, was still there. He walked to it, touched the ancient, dry fabric, remembering the feel, the smell of her, all those years ago.

'I was a fool,' he said softly to himself. Even so, a small inner voice said, she was dying already. As they coupled with such ecstatic delight on the dusty, old sofa, the worm of sickness was beginning to turn somewhere inside her. Had they married, she would still be gone, in the same space of time, leaving him with two children to raise, no career, and an exile from his own family.

It would have been worth it, Michael Denney thought. Just for those few short years. Even so, a part of him said that what had happened was for the best. The route of his life forked in two possible directions in this place, and bitterness lay down both. At least there was a part of her still in his life now, though she was not undamaged, for which he was entirely to blame.

'I'm still a fool,' he said. He put the suitcase on a chair and opened it. Then he took off his jacket, removed the long priest's surplice and pulled it over his head, letting the black gown fall down towards his ankles. He went into the case again, came out with the hair colouring and carefully dabbed it on his silver head, rubbing in the dark dye, running it through his locks with his fingers, wiping his hand with a cloth when the job was done. He looked at himself in the mirror. His hair had an unnatural sheen to it. Apart from that and a few extra lines he could have been the priest he was more than thirty years before, working the poor, deprived Irish areas of Boston. An anonymous man. One who hardly merited a second glance.

He smiled at this image of himself. Then he looked up at the boxes on the wall which had, as he hoped, not changed in three decades. Methodically, working quickly, knowing there could be no delay, he began to turn off the lights in the church, one by one, leaving the circuit covering the vestibule till last. Finally he threw that switch too and San Luigi dei Francesi fell into darkness. From beyond the door he heard noises: cries of surprise in the interior, fear perhaps, and a loud report, like a bulb bursting. Or perhaps a gun. A few people made for the door immediately. The storm had gathered over the city by now, he guessed. There would be so little light. Caravaggio would have recognized the scene.

When he walked out into the nave it was illuminated only by the spare, warm candlelight of the offerings in the chapels. Something was happening. There was fear in the darkness. Then it occurred to Denney he had forgotten one thing. The circuit for the meters on the paintings was separate from the rest. He had left it turned on. Sure enough there was a round, rich sea of light on one of the canvases: *The Vocation of Saint Matthew.* It reflected on the image and threw back a waxy yellow tint onto the confused faces of the visitors who had gathered in a line to admire the work.

Then the ancient mechanism worked its way through the coin. The switch was thrown. Night consumed the belly of the church, only partly rent in places by the guttering flames of the votive candles.

From somewhere came a scream. He began to move, praying she would remember his brief and precise instructions.

Sixty-five

Gino Fosse had listened to Cannonball Adderley twice, all the while watching the people come in and out of the church. There were more than there should be. It wasn't that much of a tourist attraction. They had men there. Men pretending to look at the paintings on the walls, men pretending to pray. Michael Denney was nowhere to be seen. He knew him so well. He could recognize that distinguished silver head anywhere. It lived in his imagination twenty-four hours a day. He looked at his watch. It was ten minutes past midday. Torrential rain sounded like drumbeats on the roof. The light beyond the windows was now a dull, threatening grey. He let the music come to a stop and knew he couldn't listen to one more note. With a muttered curse he tore the headphones off and stuffed them back into the pocket of the white tunic along with the CD. Then he thought about the act, almost laughed, took the things out and put them on the pew beside him. There was no more need for them.

He removed the gun from his pocket and held it under the cover of the bench ahead. The metal was soon hot and clammy in his grip. 'Mercy, Mercy, Mercy.' The melody still ran through his head, sparking pictures in his mind: of Michael Denney dead. Of Sara, naked, staring mutely back at him as he thrashed over her, limbs spread-eagled in the shape of St Andrew's cross, one simple question in those sharp green eyes: *Why?*

'Because I thought you were like the rest,' he whispered, seeing her now, on the floor of the tower room in the Clivus Scauri, recalling the way she hardly fought, the shock in her expression. 'I didn't know.'

Not until Hanrahan whispered the truth in the darkness of San Lorenzo in Lucina, with the rats' eyes glittering from behind the iron rack. From that point on, everything seemed a swirling, unreal dream.

He thought of his own end: a crouched, huddled figure, the white alb stained with red, the gun still pointed at his own temple. This was one final deliverance. He wasn't waiting for them to get around to it.

'Where are you?' he said to himself in a low voice racked with tension.

The rain was bringing in too many people. They struggled through the door, most unaware of where they were, what they might see. The church was simply a refuge for them. He thought about that idea: it was what he'd always wanted it to be. He'd been cheated of that experience, by his father, by his own nature too.

'Where *are* you?'

Gino Fosse looked at the door and caught his breath. She was walking through the entrance, leading the little cop, the one he'd nearly killed a couple of days before. They were striding into the nave with no fear, no caution on their faces. It was impossible. He blinked to make certain this could be true. They were heading for the paintings now, over to where the small crowds had gathered. Were they looking for him? Or were they looking for Michael Denney? He racked his mind to try to find some answers.

One small certainty made sense. He rose from the bench, the gun tight in his hand. His voice rose to a roar. '*Sara!*'

Her eyes met his across the nave. The little cop watched him intently. He didn't even move a hand to his jacket. They shouldn't have been there, either of them.

Then the lights failed altogether. The electric bulbs died. He'd been staring straight at them, into the pool of light around the painting: the image of the naked madman murdering the prone Matthew on the ground, sword raised, ready to deliver the final blow.

'*Run!*' he bellowed, and raised the gun, firing a single shot into the black air.

There was still some light. A few bulbs remained lit in an adjoining alcove. People huddled there, terrified, waiting. He staggered towards them but before he could get there even that was snatched from him. The wan lights failed with a clatter as the meter swung the switch. The image of Matthew, in his medieval costume, staring at the biblical Christ, asking 'Why me?', faded to black.

Fosse loosed off two more shots into the air. A woman began screaming hysterically close by. As his eyes adjusted to the velvet gloom and the random sea of tiny candle flames that now shed the last illumination on the scene, something brushed past him, something black and fast-moving, a man who never spoke a word.

He swore and lunged to catch the fleeing figure. There was nothing there. Everything eluded his grasp. Everything was denied him. He stumbled forward again, colliding with terrified bodies in the darkness, yelling every last obscenity he could think of, screaming his father's name, begging the black maw of the nave to give up his body for vengeance.

He stumbled against a pillar, banged his face hard against the stone. A warm, sticky stream began to flow from his nose. He tasted blood on his tongue.

'Bastard!' he screamed and let off another shot.

Something else collided with him, taking away his breath, almost bringing him to his knees. He recognized what it was: the iron railing that ran in front of the altar, the same kind of worked metal on which Arturo Valena had died screaming. He felt his way along it, towards the tiny sea of candles. The dark, glittering eyes, human this time, looked back at him in their reflection, scared, scattering as he approached.

'Bastard!'

A hand came to his shoulder, turning him. Gino Fosse lashed out with the butt of the gun, missing, and found his arm thrust briskly aside.

The pool of light from a few guttering candles revealed the man's face. It was the little cop. He held Fosse's gun hand high above them. It wouldn't be hard to overcome him, Fosse thought. He didn't look right for the part he was trying to play. But then perhaps none of them did.

'I didn't come for you,' Fosse hissed. 'Get away. Take her with you.'

A face came out of the darkness. She looked at him, serene, controlled, unafraid, which was, he thought, stupid.

'You have to run,' he said. 'They'll kill you too.'

'Gino,' she answered, and a slim hand came and touched his face. He shrank back, unable to comprehend what was happening. 'Come with us,' she said. 'Don't do this.'

He needed her gone. He didn't want to face her. Her fingers moved against his skin.

'It's not your fault. You didn't know who I was. I should have told you.'

'Too late for that.' Gino Fosse shook his head, wishing he could get the pictures out of his mind. 'Too late!'

'I forgive you,' she said. She seemed so calm. He wanted to believe her.

The little cop's grip was relaxing somewhat. There were people moving nearby. He wanted to catch their faces. He needed to see that silver head running away in the darkness.

'It's what they want,' the cop said. 'They've been using you, Gino. Who gave you the names? Who told you where to go and when?'

He thought of Hanrahan, smiling in the darkness of San Lorenzo in Lucina. 'What does it matter?'

'Because they're just playing with you, Gino,' the cop insisted.

He laughed. 'You think I don't know that?'

Sara's face, compassionate, loving, stared at him. 'Then why do it?'

He waved the gun in front of her. 'Because this is what he deserves.'

'He's our father,' she said. 'He deserves our pity. Not our hate. If I can forgive you . . .'

The little cop seemed puzzled. Gino watched her face in the half-light. It could have been an image from a painting. She seemed so placid, so sure of herself. 'Please,' she said. 'We can belong to each other. We can heal ourselves if we want. Don't let them use your fury for their own ends. Don't give them that pleasure. Or they win.'

He listened hard in the dark space beyond them. They had to be there. The rats chattering away in the darkness, shredding what little was left of his soul. But all he could hear, deep inside his head, was the refrain of the music: Cannonball Adderley's alto chanting 'Mercy, Mercy, Mercy, Mercy' with an insistent lilting sadness, like a gospel singer praying for absolution.

'If you talk to people I know, Gino,' the little cop said, 'there can be justice for them all. Your father. For these people who led you to do these things.' The cop hesitated. He was hardly holding the gun now. 'Isn't that what you want?'

Fosse thought again of the Irishman, his hot breath in his ear, saying those hated words in San Lorenzo in Lucina. How it would be so easy to make things right if only Michael Denney could be persuaded to flee from behind the high walls of the Vatican. He would like to see Hanrahan face justice, he thought. There was, when he considered it, so much he could tell them.

The cop's hand went up and grasped the gun. Fosse let go, let him take it.

Nic Costa's eyes flashed at Sara. 'Try to find your father. He must be hiding somewhere while the lights are out. Keep him safe until I say so. I don't know if the right people are here or not.'

In another situation, Costa knew, she would have kissed him quickly on the cheek. But Gino Fosse was still on a knife edge. Neither of them wanted to push their luck. Her hand reached out and squeezed his, then she was gone, a fleeting figure vanishing into the black maw of the church.

Fosse stared after her, a wild animal look in his eyes, part fear, part rage. Nic Costa felt, for a moment, afraid. 'Where is she?' Fosse asked. 'Will she come back?'

'Sure, she'll come back,' he said, trying to sound confident.

'I didn't know,' Fosse said. 'I did it to the others because they were whores. That's what they were for. I didn't know . . .'

Fosse's black eyes stared into his. 'It haunts me. I don't want it in my head any longer.'

A part of Gino Fosse wasn't mad at all, Costa thought, and then he let his mind go blank, unable to countenance the possibilities that lay within what he'd just heard. There was no time. People were moving through the shadows, big, dark bodies, men in jackets, men with a purpose. Costa wondered who would get there first, who might be in the church already. He'd tried to cover as many options as possible.

Someone brushed past him. An arm reached down towards the altar rail, some coins fell in the box there and, in a sudden, aching flash, the lights of the canvas burst into life.

Costa blinked at the image on the wall. It looked alive. If he tried, he thought, he would hear the assassin's breathing, feel the strength of the light pouring out from the canvas, trying to shed its redeeming grace on them all.

Then a familiar face, half lit by the yellow electric lamps, pushed between them.

'Where the hell is he?' Falcone demanded, snatching

the gun away from him. 'Denney? What have you done with the bastard?'

The people he called should have been here now. He could hear someone else moving through the darkness. They needed more light than this single wan pool of yellow in one corner of the nave.

'I never saw him,' he replied honestly.

'One way in, one way out,' Falcone hissed. 'For Christ's sake. He knew this place like the back of his hand. He's gone. He must be gone.'

He said nothing, trying to think. One minute, she said. Just a little time to talk and to keep him safe. Though they must, he now realized, have spoken already that day. Was there really anything else left to say?

'And you . . .' Falcone's finger jabbed into his shoulder. 'You just can't stay away, can you?'

'I think, sir,' he replied, 'you should consider your position.' He looked into Falcone's cold, bleak face. 'You can't carry on with this now. It's bound to come out.'

Falcone shook his head. 'What do I care about my position? To hell with it!'

Without warning he snatched a pair of handcuffs from his pocket, slammed one end on Gino Fosse's wrist and locked the other to the iron railing. Costa looked into Fosse's eyes. He was scared.

Falcone took Costa by the arm, peered closely into his face. 'This bastard killed your partner. We're walking away, kid. We're done with this mess.'

The painting shone at him from the wall. He was unable to take his eyes off the figure in the background: Caravaggio himself, watching the murder which came from his own imagination, pitying the victim bleeding on the ground, pitying too the assassin led by fate to be the instrument of his death.

Falcone was dragging him now, by the arm, away from the scene. He struggled.

'Jesus!' Falcone threw Costa against a pillar, and snarled into his face, 'I want you out of harm's way, Nic. I don't want any more dead men sitting around in my head.'

'No,' Nic Costa said softly. 'I can't let this happen.'

There were more bodies moving. Maybe they were the people Falcone expected. Maybe someone else. He thought he heard Teresa Lupo's voice rising in the clamour. From somewhere a camera flashed. People were beginning to shout. On the far side of the church a set of lights suddenly came on. Banks of bulbs followed them, marching around the ceiling as someone found the switches.

Costa looked at Falcone. The inspector's bright eyes were darting around the church, trying to make sense of it all.

'This has got to stop,' Costa said, pushing himself out of Falcone's grip. He fought free with a sudden jab, then raced the few yards to Gino Fosse. They were there. Two men. He pushed in front as they closed in on Fosse, raising their hands, two barrels beginning to gleam in the wan light. He fought to take his eyes off the figures on the wall: the stricken man, his white tunic red with blood, the furious, naked attacker.

There was a noise that could have been the angry, leaden sky outside, a burning flash of bright light so intense it seared a raw, sharp pain somewhere behind his eyes. Nic Costa stared at the image on the wall: a young bearded man, watching in agony and amazement the bloody, vivid scene he had created. Then the face faded and with it the bright, life-giving light.

Sixty-six

Leo Falcone had two appointments in his diary that chill October day. One was mandatory. For the second he would be an uninvited, unwelcome guest.

Disciplinary proceedings always left him cold. This was his third appearance before the tribunal in twenty-five years with the force. He knew what was required: an admission of some limited form of guilt, a display of penitence, the silent acceptance of a formal token of reproof. Perhaps they would dock his pay or make him attend some course of 'retraining'. It was possible that he would be demoted, though he believed that unlikely. The Questura was scarcely overflowing with experienced officers to take his place.

Falcone's position was plain. Whatever else had gone wrong, Gino Fosse was dead and the city was rid of a vicious, psychotic killer. He had lost officers to this man. His team had worked day and night trying to bring him to justice. Denney may have escaped, along with his daughter. There was more bloodshed than anyone wanted, even, he privately believed, those who initiated Fosse's game and made its existence known to official quarters when it suited them.

But none of this could be easily laid at his door. The investigation they had ordered found no evidence of collusion between himself, the Vatican and the criminal parties who had gathered at San Luigi dei Francesi to kill the fleeing cardinal and his wayward son. There was talk in the wilder parts of the papers about a cover-up. The last, snatched pictures of the shooting in the church, taken by the woman journalist Nic Costa had sent there, continued to do the rounds. The gunmen had escaped. They would, he knew, never be found. So be it. This wasn't the first time the authorities had acquiesced in order to forestall a greater furore. Given the nature of Roman politics, he doubted it would be the last. And the media had short memories. Soon there would be another scandal to occupy them, another face to sell more papers.

The hearing lasted ninety minutes. He walked out with a reprimand. They had been persuaded by his argument that a conspiracy, if it existed, and he felt sure this was impossible, could only have begun over his head. They were moved by his genuine grief for his lost men. They were willing to give him the benefit of the doubt. This time, anyway.

At the end, after announcing a verdict which had clearly been decided before he entered the room, the commissioner led him to the door, taking his arm. 'None of us is untouchable these days, Leo,' he said. 'We live in changed times. Take care. I can't save you again.'

Falcone didn't want to look into his eyes. Maybe the man would see the bitter amusement lurking there. Had Falcone fallen, the commissioner would have followed not long after, and they both knew it.

'I understand, sir,' he replied and walked down the corridor, thinking of what lay ahead.

For the sake of form – to let them know he was still in harness, his power undiminished – he then spent an hour in his office, taking reports concerning the stabbing of a tourist who made the mistake of hustling for dope at the station. At midday Falcone put on his coat and left the station. He could not, in all conscience, avoid what came next.

The crematorium was off the Via Appia Nuova, not more than two kilometres from the Costa family home. He watched from his car. There were perhaps twenty mourners, mainly men, in dark suits. A tall woman in over-elegant mourning clothes was pushing the figure in the wheelchair. Falcone sat listening to the radio for thirty minutes, thinking about the ceremony inside. It was a myth, a ritual. As a young cop he'd been called to a fatal accident at a crematorium once and come to understand the way they worked. This was a mechanical process. Messy, imperfect. It could be anyone's ashes you walked away with. No one would know. No one, if they were honest enough to admit it, really cared about detail. This was a dumb show to ease the grief of those still alive. Details hardly mattered.

The distant doors opened and they came out again, leaving in a slow procession of black cars. He followed them back to the farmhouse, parking opposite the drive, just out of sight. It was three hours before the last had left. Falcone got out of his car and looked down the drive. There was just the woman now. And the figure in the wheelchair.

He swallowed hard and wished he didn't have to go through with this. Then he walked up the drive, where he was met halfway by the woman.

'He doesn't want to see you.' She was attractive in an

old-fashioned way. Her eyes were bright and intelligent. She'd been crying.

'He doesn't have a choice,' Falcone said and kept on walking.

There was a table by the wheelchair. On it sat a bottle of old Barolo, almost empty, and a couple of glasses. And a white alabaster urn, a small thing, so bright and shiny it could have been plastic.

Falcone poured himself some wine, looked at the man in the wheelchair and said, 'You're cultivating expensive tastes for an invalid, Nic. That meagre pension we're giving you won't buy many cases of this stuff.'

Costa looked terrible. He'd put on weight while confined to the wheelchair. His face had puffed out. There was a distinct red tinge to his cheeks. Falcone knew what men looked like when they sat on the edge of a pool of booze, wondering whether to dive in. It had happened to so many cops. It was part of the job for some. He'd never expected Nic Costa to be among them.

'Why are you here?' Costa asked. His eyes were bleary, his voice cracked.

Falcone pulled the envelope out of his pocket. 'I brought your mail. They've been intercepting it, in case you hadn't guessed. Nothing to do with me. I've been lying low in Sardinia for the last couple of weeks. Enforced vacation. You probably heard.'

Costa gazed at the long white airmail envelope. It had the farm's address on the front, written in a long, sloping, feminine hand. The letter had been scissored open at the top.

'You know where they are?'

Falcone glanced at the postmark. 'Says here this was posted in the Florida Keys. Guess they're long gone from there now. Somewhere in the States, I imagine. Not a clue in the letter. The way Denney and the woman got out of here in the first place is still beyond me. He'd plenty of money with him but that doesn't explain everything. Maybe he had more friends than we knew. The Americans say they're looking for him, on our behalf you understand. Lying bastards. They're holed up somewhere with new names, a new house, new lives, promising to keep their mouths shut. We won't see them again. That's my take on things anyway. I could be wrong. It happens.'

Costa looked at the letter. It couldn't contain anything important. They would never have passed it on if it did.

'Take it,' Falcone said, pushing the envelope across the table. 'It's for you. Personal. Like I said, this wasn't my decision. They had to do it, though.'

It contained a single page. On it, in the same elegant hand, just five words: 'I thought you were dead.'

Falcone watched him, trying to assess his reaction. 'Can't blame her,' he said. 'We all thought that at the time. We forgot you were such a stubborn little bastard.'

'Sorry to disappoint you.'

'Hey,' Falcone snapped. 'A word of advice. A man in a wheelchair should avoid self-pity. It's not becoming.'

Costa reached for the Barolo and refilled his glass.

Falcone calmed down a touch and took a seat at the table. 'A lot of people were pleased to see you pull through, Nic. And then . . . this. It's like you're dead again somehow.'

'Is this you talking? Or your friends? Or Hanrahan? Tell me that.'

'Just me,' Falcone said. 'No one knows I'm here. Hanrahan's skulking somewhere back in Ireland, keeping his head down. Won't last for ever, of course. He's too damn useful to them. Just for the record, he's not my friend. Never was. Never will be.'

Costa's eyes were fixed on the neatly tended garden with its rows and rows of tidy plants. Falcone wondered if he was still listening. 'I heard it on the radio,' he said. 'You got off with a reprimand. So no one pays for this. No one except Gino Fosse.'

'You could look at it that way, I guess.'

'There's some other way to see things?'

Falcone shrugged. He was getting tired of this.

'Why are you here?' Costa asked again.

'I don't want any more victims. I've got enough on my conscience as it is. Nic . . .' He was back staring into the wine glass as if all the answers lay beneath its thick meniscus. 'I'm sorry your father's dead. I never knew him. People who did, say he was a good and honest man. We could use more like that. But don't think you can take his place. You don't belong in that wheelchair. You haven't earned that yet.'

Costa said nothing and gulped at the wine.

Falcone pulled up his chair and got close to him. 'I talked to the doctors. They said this isn't a permanent disability. You could be out of that chair in three months, maybe less. You could be back to your old self in six. If you turned up for the physio sessions. If you wanted to.'

'Get out of here,' Costa snarled.

The woman had returned. She'd been eavesdropping. She was carrying a bottle of mineral water and a couple of glasses. She put them on the table and removed the wine. Costa avoided her eyes.

'Listen to him, Nic,' she said. 'Please.'

'Bea, you don't know who this man is.'

She gave Falcone a cold stare. 'I know. I read the papers. I still think you should listen to him.'

He scowled and took the glass of water all the same. Falcone looked at the woman. He was grateful. Then he nodded and she retreated once more.

'Here.' He reached into his jacket, took out something and placed it next to Costa's hand. It was his old ID card, the one he'd thrown into Falcone's face a lifetime before.

'I'm back at work on Monday. I've got a desk with your name on it. I've got work for you.'

'Work?'

'Yes! Work! Let's face it. What else are you going to do? Drink yourself stupid day in and day out and call on the housemaid every time you want to take a piss?'

'I'm a damned cripple,' Costa yelled at him.

'Then learn to walk!' Falcone bawled back. 'Jesus . . .' The older man stood up. 'Look. I'll say this once. I need you, Nic. You're a smart cop. We can't afford to lose you. There's something else too.' Falcone eyed the horizon sourly. 'You remind me of what happened. How I screwed up. Maybe it'll make me think twice in the future.'

Costa's interest was stirring, Falcone could feel it.

'Don't think for one moment this is sympathy. I'll ride you as hard as I always did. All the more so once you climb out of that damn chair.'

'Go to hell,' Costa spat.

Falcone smiled. He recognized the moment. 'Thank you. By the way, I went back to work a few weeks ago. They said I showed up too early. Sent me back to do a little more time.'

There was something different in Falcone's eyes. Self-doubt maybe. An empty, dead loneliness. Or just the mask of a clever actor.

'Monday,' Falcone repeated. 'I'm not asking you to like me. Just to keep me company. Stay off the drink this weekend. You need to sweat some of that shit out of your system. And if you've got any questions . . .' he nodded at the urn on the table, 'ask him, not me.'

Then he set off down the drive, a tall man, beautifully dressed in a dark suit, but stiff, uncomfortable with himself in some way Costa hadn't noticed before.

A light breeze was coming in from the north. The wind was gently tearing the last few leaves from the old almond tree in the drive. They scuttered around the departing Falcone's feet. Through the bare branches Costa could now see the distant roof of the austere old church on the Appian Way. 'Domine, Quo Vadis?' Lord, where are you going? His father's reason for rebuilding the old farmhouse, for making this place the Costa family's home.

He shivered in his thin jacket. The wine wasn't enough to keep him warm. He looked around for Bea. She had moved into the house before his father died, caring for them both. He took her for granted, he knew. There seemed no other way.

'Bea!' he yelled. '*Bea!*'

She didn't come. Maybe she was watching him from the house, thinking about what Falcone had said. Maybe she was wondering why a woman in her mid-fifties should be looking after a man almost thirty years younger, a cripple who refused his own chance of redemption. Maybe she was thinking Falcone was right.

'Bea,' he cried, one last time. There was no reply.

It was cold now. The light was fading. If he had one more drink he knew what would happen, where his mind would go. To the bedroom upstairs and the night, the single night, he spent with Sara Farnese.

This was important. Nic hoped Bea was watching.

He grasped the alabaster urn with his right hand then, with his left, took hold of the gnarled grape vine that wormed its way up the patio pillar. Struggling, short of breath, feeling a distant sensation run down his injured spine and press a little movement into his half-dead legs, he dragged himself upright and looked at the field.

It was immaculate. Bea had called in men to help her. The green heads of *cavolo nero* were rising in spite of the season, forcing themselves upright, working towards the sky.

His fingers shook as he fumbled at the lid. Then, with a single determined movement, he tipped the urn upside down. Grey ash and dust spilled out onto the rising wind, gathered in a fleeting grey cloud then vanished, scattering across the land a lifetime of memories, an abundance of love and shared grief, gone in the blink of a disbelieving eye.

He clung tightly to the vine, watching this mortal smoke disperse. It was nothing. It was everything. It was gone. It would never leave him.

Then the breeze stiffened. The page on the table, with its five words written in a firm, elegant hand, fluttered in the wind, rose and began to tumble through the air, flitting across the arid ground, turning and turning before it disappeared into the scrub by the road.

He watched it vanish, wishing he could run again.

Nic Costa felt no wiser. Just a little stronger, perhaps, and that, in the circumstances, was as much as he could bear.

THE VILLA OF MYSTERIES

LUPERCALIA

Bobby and Lianne Dexter were good people. They owned a brand new timber mansion on an acre plot cut into a vast green swathe of pines thirty miles outside Seattle. They put in long hours for Microsoft down the road, Bobby in marketing, Lianne in finance. They hiked every weekend and, once a year, made it to the summit of Mount Rainier. They worked out too, though Bobby still couldn't keep what he called the 'family tummy-pudge' coming through over the belt of his jeans. And that at just thirty-three.

The Dexters were quiet, comfortably wealthy middle-class Americans. Except for two weeks a year, in spring, when they went abroad on vacation. They'd reasoned this through. It was all a question of balance. Work hard for fifty weeks of the year. Party hard for the remaining two. Preferably somewhere the locals didn't know you, where different rules applied. Or maybe didn't apply at all. Which was why, on a chill February day, they were ten miles outside Rome, dead drunk on red wine and grappa, seated in a hired Renault Clio which Bobby was driving much too fast over the potholes of an unmarked lane that ran from a back road behind Fiumicino airport down towards the flat, grey line of the meandering Tiber.

Lianne glanced at her husband, making sure he didn't see the anxiety in her face. Bobby was still fuming. He'd had the metal detector out all morning, hunting around the outskirts of Ostia Antica, the excavated remains of imperial Rome's one-time coastal harbour. Just when he got a couple of beeps out of the thing a pair of fierce-looking archaeology types came out of the site and began screaming at them. Neither of them understood Italian but they got the drift. Either they packed up the metal detector and got out of there pronto or the Dexter annual vacation was likely to end in fisticuffs with a couple of punchy-looking spic students who were only too ready and eager for action.

Bobby and Lianne had retired hurt to a nearby road-side *osteria* where, to add insult to injury, the waiter, an unshaven lout in a grubby sweatshirt, had lectured both on how wrong it was to pronounce the word 'pasta' as 'pahstah', the American way.

Bobby had listened, his white, loose cheeks reddening with fury, then snapped, 'Just gimme a fucking steak then.' And added a litre of *rosso della casa* to the order just for good measure. Lianne said nothing. She knew when it was smart to acquiesce to Bobby's mood. If things got too bad drinkwise they could always dump the car at the airport and take a cab back into town. Not that Italians minded about drunk driving. They did it all the time, it seemed to her. Or at least she assumed they did. Italy was like that. Lax. She and Bobby were just behaving like the locals.

'I cannot believe these people,' Bobby complained as he rolled the Clio over a pile of dried mud that had caked neatly into a solid ridge after the recent winter rain. 'I mean like . . . don't they have enough of this fucking stuff as it is?'

Lianne knew what the problem was. The previous autumn the Jorgensens had returned from vacation in Greece with a gorgeous marble bust the size of a soccer ball. It was of a young man, maybe Alexander the Great they said, with a full head of hair and a pretty, slightly feminine face. They kept it quiet at first, just to get the effect right. Then, out of the blue, Tom Jorgensen had invited them over to their extended Scandinavian-style cabin just down the lane – which had three storeys, mind, and a good acre and a half out back – on the pretext of a social drink. Really it was all about the marble head. Jorgensen let it be known he'd 'found' it by hanging around the edge of some archaeological exca-vation outside Sparta, waiting till the diggers had gone home and then bribing one of the locals to take him to where the mother lode lay. Tom had talked a good deal about how he smuggled it out of the country as excess baggage. It was all, Lianne suspected, one of Tom's stories. Really he'd just bought it at the store like everyone else. The big, muscular bastard was always spin-ning a line about something or other. It was why he'd jumped over Bobby's head to get into all the sexy music and TV stuff the company was doing now, meeting rock stars and movie people while Bobby, who was just as bright, maybe brighter even, was still lumbered with the tedious geeks who came over horny about databases.

But Tom's little act had struck home. Two weeks later Bobby announced that their annual vacation the coming spring would be in Italy. He hadn't even asked her opinion. Lianne was quietly hoping for Aruba. All the same, she demurred. It was the best thing to do, and, as it turned out, Rome hadn't been a bad choice. In fact, she was starting to like the place. Then, that morning, it had all turned worse. Some creepy British academic type had given them a history lecture over buffet breakfast in the hotel. About how this was the day of the dead for the ancient Romans, a day when they would sacrifice a goat or a dog and wipe its blood on the foreheads of their kids, just to make sure they remembered their ancestors. The history link pushed Bobby's buttons. Fifteen minutes later he was tracking down a hire company, renting the metal detector.

So now they were in the middle of nowhere, dead drunk, clueless about what to do next. Lianne pined for Aruba and the pain was all the worse because she'd no idea what the place was like. Without letting Bobby see she put a hand on the steering wheel and turned the lurching Clio just far enough away from a boulder coming up at them from the right. The track was getting narrower all the time. There were still mud holes here and there from some recent rain. Maybe they'd get the car stuck and have to walk back to the road for help. She didn't like that idea. She hadn't brought the shoes.

'It's just pure greed, Bobby,' she said. 'What else can you say?'

'I mean . . . what does it matter? If I don't find the shit it stays right there in any case! It's not like you see any fucking Italians digging the crap out of the ground.'

He was wrong there. She'd seen digs all over the place, half of them looking abandoned, maybe because they just didn't have the bodies to do all that digging. All the same it was best to go along with his gut feeling.

'They don't need it, Bobby. They got more than they can cope with already. They got it coming out their ears.'

They had too. Her mind was still reeling from all the museums they'd visited these past two days. There was so much *stuff*. And unlike Bobby, she'd read the guide-books. She knew they'd only scratched the surface. The pair of them were spending an entire *week* in Rome and would still come away without seeing everything. It seemed excessive. Bad planning. Poor taste. Bobby was right. If they had any manners they'd share it around a little.

The car headed down into a crater, leapt out the other side, briefly became airborne then slammed onto the ground with a bang. It sounded to her as if something had come loose underneath. She scanned the view ahead. Beyond the funny-looking grass, which seemed more like the kind of plants you got in marshland or bogs than on the beach she was expecting, lay a grey, scummy ribbon of water. The road came to a dead end a little way short of the low bank. Bobby had to get out here, have his fun – or otherwise – and then they needed to take the car back to Avis and scuttle off into the city before anyone noticed the dents and worse she felt sure would be there.

'Don't you worry,' she said. 'You're going to find something here, Bobby. I just know it. You're going to find something and when you do that asshole Tom Jorgensen is going to be as jealous as hell. You—'

He kicked down hard on the brakes, bringing the little car to a sudden halt twenty yards short of the end of the lane. Her husband was now staring into her face with that cold, hard expression she only saw once or twice a year, and hated, more than anything, hated so much that sometimes she wondered whether marrying Bobby Dexter, tubby Bobby, the one all the other girls laughed at behind his back, had really been such a good idea at all.

'What?' Bobby asked in a flat, dead tone that was supposed to be full of meaning.

'I only, only, only—' She stuttered into silence.

He prodded her chest with a stubby finger. She could smell the booze on his breath.

'You really think this is all about Tom Fucking Jorgensen?'

'No!'

'You really think I have researched, booked, paid for this entire fucking vacation, taken you to all these beautiful places, brought you out here to this stinking backwater . . . all because of Tom Fucking Jorgensen and his shitty piece of marble?'

She paused before answering. In three years of marriage Bobby had reduced her to tears only once and that was in Cancun over a sexual demand she regarded as irrational, unnecessary and intrinsically unhygienic. The memory still smarted. She didn't understand why it wouldn't go away.

'I didn't. It just seemed. I don't know—' All the wrong words tumbled out of her mouth.

'Jesus!' Bobby roared. 'Jesus Christ!'

He gunned the accelerator, rammed the Clio into first and let go of the clutch. The little car lurched bravely forward with a gut-wrenching start, veered to one side and impaled itself on a small dried mud mountain which appeared, to Lianne anyway, to contain the stump of a fence post at its heart. They were now pitched up at an awkward, sickening angle. The front right wheel screamed impotently as the mud mountain levered the entire right front end of the Clio into thin air.

Bobby stared at Lianne accusingly. 'Fucking wonderful,' he grunted. 'Oh so fucking wonderful.'

She was crying, trying to choke back the sobs.

'Don't do this to me, Lianne. Not today. You're not in Cancun now. You can't go phone that animal you call a father and get him to come round and threaten to beat my brains to a pulp just 'cos you got a headache or something.'

Telling her old man had been a mistake. She knew that all along. But Bobby had asked for it. He crossed the line in Cancun. She needed to let him know.

'Bobby—' she blubbed.

He stared out of the window at the grey river and the sluggish movement of scum on its surface.

'Yeah?'

'I can smell gas,' she said, suddenly serious, the tears drying almost instantly under the rising presence of fear. 'Can't you?'

'Jesus,' he gasped and punched at her seat belt then stabbed open the passenger door. She smiled at him, glassy-eyed. He'd done it for her. Before he unfastened his own belt.

'Bobby—'

He pushed her out of the door. 'Get out for chrissake. Dumb stupid bitch—'

Bobby Dexter took one last look to make sure she was safe then turned round, flung a few things from the back seat out onto the ground and rolled out of the crazily skewed car himself. He was so drunk he did a quick one eighty and wound up on the cold, hard earth banging his elbows painfully. Bobby got in a good chunk of swearing about that.

He pushed himself upright with a weary hand, picked up his things, then checked she'd got herself well distant from the smell of gas. Lianne watched from the side of the road, a good ten yards from the dying Clio, her hands clasped behind her back looking like a schoolgirl waiting to be told what to do.

He walked over to join his wife.

'You OK?' he asked. He looked a little worried about how far this was going. That was something, she thought.

'Sure.' She'd stopped crying. He looked glad of that. It was something.

There was a sound from the car, a sort of breathy whoosh. They watched as a thin finger of flame flickered out from under the hood and worked its way up the windshield.

'Now that . . .' Bobby said, 'is what I like about rental vehicles. They can do this sort of shit in front of your eyes and you just get to stand back and enjoy the show. Wish I'd hired something bigger now.'

The low scuttering wind caught the flames, rolled them over the roof of the Clio, sent them swirling inside the window, eating up the seats where, just a minute or so before, Bobby and Lianne Dexter had sat arguing. Then, with a sudden roar and a puff of heat and smoke, the Renault was ablaze, devouring itself in a cloud of black smoke and flame.

Lianne clung to her husband's arm watching the spectacle. Bobby was right. This was Avis's problem. This was what they were for. Why they charged the kind of prices they did.

'What are we going to do now, Bobby?' she wondered. Then she looked at him and found, to her relief, Bobby Dexter was smiling, happy once more, for the first time in hours.

He held up one of the things he'd taken from the back seat of the car. The metal detector they'd hired that very morning somewhere near the hotel in Rome.

'What we came here for,' Bobby Dexter said. 'Daddy's going a-hunting.'

She ventured a laugh and wondered if it came out wrong. Maybe it did. Maybe not. It didn't matter anyway. Bobby Dexter wasn't listening. He was working his way down to the river, walking over the odd, boggy ground that felt as if it might give way beneath them at any moment. He had the headphones on, listening. And pretty soon Bobby Dexter was laughing too. Something must have been coming through loud and clear. Lianne walked to join him. They were just twenty yards short of the river now. There wasn't another soul around for miles. Anything they found here now was surely theirs.

'Hear that?'

She took the headphones from him and held one earpiece to her head. It was beeping like crazy, like a kid's game from years ago.

'Fucking Tom Jorgensen,' Bobby spat and she didn't dare look into his eyes when he was talking like this. 'I'll teach that big fat bastard. Get me the gear.'

He was skulking in the little coffee bar around the corner from the Questura when Barbara Martelli walked in, dressed in her immaculate black uniform, helmet in hand, her long, blonde tresses bouncing above her collar with each step.

'Nic,' she said, looking surprised. 'You're back at work?'

'First day,' he replied, glancing at his watch. 'When I decide to turn up.'

'Ah.'

'How are you, Barbara?'

'I'm fine. I'm always fine. And you?'

He drained the macchiato. 'Yeah.'

'In case you forgot, this isn't the café the cops use.'

'So why are you here?'

She laughed. Barbara Martelli was about his height, with the kind of figure that turned every head in the station and a shock of blonde curls that seemed too full to squeeze inside that small black helmet. Her face was wrong for a cop. Too attractive, too ready to break into a smile. She looked as if she ought to be on the TV, announcing the weather or introducing some show. Instead she just floated around Rome on her big bike, handing out tickets with such charm the word was some people simply started speeding the moment they realized she was on their tail.

Back in the old days, before the shooting that put him on his back, fighting demons, Nic Costa wondered sometimes whether she was sweet on him. A couple of the guys egged him on to ask her for a date . . . provided he told everything afterwards. It didn't happen. She was just too perfect. She topped every driving exam, behind the wheel and on the force motorbikes. She was a tidy shot too, a talent that got her into most diplomatic assignments. Barbara Martelli was just a little too perfect to touch.

'Sometimes you have to escape for a while, Nic. Is that what you're doing? If so it's a little early. You have to get back in the ring if you want to hear the bell.'

'I'm having a coffee,' he mumbled.

'How long has it been?'

'Six months.' Six long months of slow recovery from the shooting and the mental damage that followed. Sometimes he wondered if he'd ever make it, whether he wanted to at all.

She looked at him frankly. She was, the more he thought about it, very possibly the most attractive woman inside the Questura. He was amazed he'd never asked her out. Not that he wanted anything to happen. She was just good company to be around, someone who could make you feel special. He didn't really know her at all.

'You do want to come back, don't you? It's not just Falcone pushing you into this?'

'No. I mean. I can't think of anything else. Can you?'

'No.'

'We're all like that, aren't we?' he said. 'Short of a choice.'

He listened to his own voice and found himself disliking what he heard. What was there? Resentment? Self-pity? He was twenty-eight. He'd never talked like that before. He had been changed by what was now known as 'the Denney case', an unresolved mess of entanglements that had cost his partner, Luca Rossi, his life, and almost left Costa dead too. This new Nic Costa no longer ran every time he wanted to clear his head, pounding the pavements around the Campo dei Fiori, arms flailing like a madman. He'd sold his tiny apartment in the Vicolo del Bologna and moved into his late father's old home, the sprawling farmhouse off the Via Appia Antica where he grew up. Costa's physical wounds were, for the most part, healed; the internal ones still ached from time to time.

Nic Costa continued to miss Luca Rossi's taciturn wit and astute insight, wishing he'd learned to appreciate them more during their brief time working together. He knew, too, that he would return to work touched by the cold, sceptical hardness of the world. It had become necessary to embrace what Falcone, who had single-handedly talked him out of a wheelchair and back into the force, would call 'pragmatism'.

Falcone, the cold, single-minded inspector, regarded this transition as inevitable. Maybe he was right. Costa, who with his old self hated cynicism, the defeatism that said sometimes you had to make the best of a bad job because the alternative was to lose the fight completely, was still unsure. He didn't like the idea of trimming his principles to match the awkward, unyielding shape of brute reality. That much of his father − a stubborn, unbending Communist politician who made more enemies from his honesty than most men did through their deceit − remained.

Barbara Martelli downed the tiny coffee. She was thinking. She seemed briefly troubled, he thought, as if there was something she didn't want to say. 'I know what you mean.'

'You do?'

'About the choices.'

Something crossed her face then, some shadow of doubt, of unhappiness, and it struck him that Barbara Martelli's appearance wasn't always an advantage. It could be a burden too. This was how people judged her, on her looks, not the person beneath, who was somehow oddly remote.

'But, Nic. The best thing is just to accept that's how it is and get on with the job. Not . . .' She looked at his coffee cup. It had been empty for a long time and they both knew it. ' . . . not hide away in the corner somewhere. That's not like you. At least, as much as I think I know you.'

He was late already. If she hadn't walked in, he'd still be there, hesitating. And a moment would come, he knew it, when he'd turn round, go back to the farmhouse, maybe open a bottle of good wine, then undo everything he'd achieved these past few months, rebuilding his health, resurrecting what was left of his dignity and self-respect. There was a kind of glory in crashing out that way. If you could only prolong that feeling forever, it would be enough, would see you through an entire lifetime. The trouble was it didn't last. You always woke up. The real world poked its head around the door and said, 'Look.' There was no escape and that was for the simplest of reasons: what he was running from lay inside.

'Do I have to march you into that place or what?' she asked.

'I could call in sick.'

'No!' Her large, green eyes widened with anger.

They were flirting with each other. Not seriously, he realized. This was Barbara's way of getting him moving. She'd use it on anyone she felt needed it.

'This,' she declared, 'is what we do for a living. It's our chosen vocation and there are no halfway houses. You're either in. Or out. So which is it?'

A wild thought ran around his head then popped

out of his mouth without even letting him consider the consequences. 'Do you think we'll ever go out on a date, Barbara? Do you think that's possible?'

A gentle blush rose in her cheeks. Barbara Martelli got asked out a dozen times a day.

'Ask me tomorrow,' she said. 'On one condition.'

He waited, still embarrassed by the sudden intimacy.

She pointed a long, manicured finger in the direction of the station. 'You ask me in there.'

They did everything wrong in Italy. The cappuccinos had insufficient milk. The pasta didn't taste right. The pizzas were too thin. And the booze. Lianne Dexter couldn't work out what was wrong. Ordinarily the effects would be wearing off by now, two hours after lunch. But she felt just as drunk as when they left the *osteria* and it was starting to make her edgy. She and Bobby had finished the single bottle of Pellegrino mineral water from the rucksack he'd snatched from the car before it went up in flames. Now they had nothing to drink, nothing to eat and not a lot of money either. She didn't even want to think about the walk back along the rutted lane towards the main road. How did you flag down an Italian and get him to take you to Avis for a refund on the crappy car they rented you? And what about the stuff Bobby had found? So far a coin, what looked like a very old, very big nail and something the size of a kid's hand, semi-circular, encrusted with crud, which Bobby assured her was definitely an ancient Roman neckband or the like and would come up great once he cleaned off the crap. Which was great except they weren't supposed to be hunting for these things. The Italians would surely know. And maybe the 'necklace' was just a brake lining anyway. Lianne's father was a car mechanic. She knew about these things, a little anyway. It looked awfully like a brake lining to her.

She licked her lips. Her mouth was dreadfully dry. A cheap wine migraine was pumping at her temples. It was now approaching three in the afternoon and the light was fading. They needed to be moving. She didn't want to be stranded all night in this odd wilderness, with its queer smell and the planes from Fiumicino screaming overhead every two minutes or less.

'Bobby,' she whined.

He wasn't satisfied with the haul. Tom Jorgensen still had the marble head and it looked better than any of these things.

He tore off the headphones and barked, 'What?'

'Gonna get dark soon. We gotta go.'

He looked around at the grey sky and sniffed. 'Five more minutes.' Then he popped the headphones back on and wandered over towards the water's edge. It was bog here. Lianne knew that instinctively. It had that odd, acid smell she associated with the cranberry farms in Maine, one of the places they'd trashed on an earlier vacation.

'Peat,' she said, suddenly remembering. Bobby mouthed 'what the fuck now?' at her with the headphones still clamped to his skull. A 747 careered over them so low she felt the earth shake. She had to put her hands over her ears just to try to keep out the bellowing of the plane's engines.

'Nothing,' she whispered to herself in the plane's wake, wishing she was somewhere else. Back home even. The cranberry farms had been nice. Interesting. Run by people who spoke the same language she did and never made her feel out of place. Rome wasn't like that. She felt all the faces in the street were looking at her constantly, waiting for her to say the wrong thing, turn the wrong corner. It was all so *foreign*.

Then there was a new noise, an unexpected one. It was Bobby, whistling. He tore off the headphones and pointed to a patch of damp earth, covered in feeble grass, a few feet in front of him.

'One more thing, sweetheart. Then we're gone. Gimme the spade.'

She did as he asked. Bobby Dexter placed the shovel on the ground then jumped on it with both feet. The thing went straight in like a knife through hot butter. Bobby tumbled off the spade and hit the dirt once more.

'Peat,' she said again, watching Bobby writhe on the ground, cursing. 'It's soft, Bobby. You don't need to try so hard. Look—'

She picked up the trowel they'd brought and squatted down on the ground, next to where his spade had bitten the earth. Lianne had watched an archaeology programme on the Discovery Channel once. She knew how people did these things, though why they bothered, for six, maybe eight hours a day, was quite beyond her.

'You just do it gently,' she said and poked the end of the trowel into the soft earth. The acid reek came up and hit her in the face. It made her think of cranberries: all that sharp red juice mixed up with vodka. 'Look—'

She scraped the surface, trying not to breathe in the smell. And then the trowel stopped dead on something solid. Lianne Dexter gulped involuntarily and wondered whether her throat might seize up. She ran the trowel tentatively through the earth. It encountered the same solid object as far as she could push it.

Bobby lurched over the ground and took the trowel off her. He began working at the soil, a little too roughly she thought.

'What is it?' she asked.

An object was emerging. It was the colour of the peat, a dark, woody brown, and hard to the touch. Bobby scraped some more then the two of them took a deep breath and sat back. What lay before them, emerging gradually from the earth, appeared to be the carved representation of a human arm. A feminine one, probably, with the folds of a simple shift visible through the dirt, reproduced with an uncanny accuracy.

'It looks real,' Lianne said eventually.

'Hello!' Bobby bellowed sarcastically. 'Earth to Planet Lianne. It's a statue. It's supposed to look real.'

'Statues aren't that colour.'

'Lianne—' He was getting exasperated again. His eyes had an angry roll to them. 'This thing's been sitting in the shit for a couple of thousand years or so. What colour do you expect it to come up? Shiny white or something? You think they shrink-wrapped it before putting it there?'

She didn't answer. He had a point.

Bobby scraped some more. A hand emerged at the end of the arm: slender fingers clenched tightly shut around the shaft of something big. The two of them stood back for a moment and stared at the object in the mud. To Lianne the figure now looked very feminine and curiously familiar. Then her head lurched into gear and she realized what the connection was. This odd, dead thing in the ground resembled a cut-down version of the Statue of Liberty, trying to raise a big, stone torch, struggling to get it upright in the mud.

'It's not metal, Bobby,' she said with a degree of boldness that worried her a little. 'How come your machine picked it up? You thought of that?'

He glowered at her. 'You amaze me sometimes. I'm sitting here maybe discovering Tutankhamun's fucking tomb or something and all you can do is pick, pick, pick. Get off my back for a moment, will ya? I'm trying to think.'

He scraped down the other side, where the other arm might be. Sure enough it was there, only a few inches beneath the surface of the peat. Maybe the recent rain had washed away some of the crap that had been covering it. Bobby ran the trowel gently across the space in between the arms. The figure's chest emerged. She was wearing what looked like a classical gown, with a V-neck that went low enough to disclose the rising curve of her slight and very lifelike breasts. The surface of the statue, when Bobby pushed away as much dirt as possible, was quite curious. It was the colour of old leather and a little shiny. For one brief moment, as he pushed and prodded with the trowel, Lianne thought it gave a little in places but that must have been the booze.

Bobby shuffled on his knees then pushed aside no more than four inches of soil a couple of feet below the areas he'd already exposed. He'd guessed well. There were the outlines of two ankles, some way apart, perfect, naked this time, no sign of a carved dress or anything.

'It's life-size, Bobby,' Lianne said.

'I know!'

'So what are you going to do?'

'Jesus. If only I could see that fat fucker Jorgensen's face right now. You bring the camera?'

She shook her head. 'Forgot it.'

'Typical. Thanks a million.'

'Bobby!'

He looked at his wife. Lianne knew she was close to becoming downright argumentative just then. She didn't care. Something bad was happening here and maybe it was time to take a stand.

'What am I going to do?' he asked. 'What the fuck I like, Lianne. Whatever the fuck I like.'

'It's too big. You can't pack that as excess baggage. Also it's the colour of shit. And it smells. Can't you smell it?'

'It's been in a bog for a million fucking years. You want it to come out smelling of roses?'

She pulled back from the thing and crossed her arms across her chest, mutinous. 'I don't want it smelling like that. And quit swearing at me all the time. It's not nice.'

He cursed under his breath and went back up to the top end, where the head ought to be. Cautiously this time he brushed away at the soil there. She was hoping the head had gone. She was hoping all Bobby would find was the torso and a couple of legs sticking out of the bottom. And wouldn't Tom Jorgensen see the funny side of that?

But there was a head. A beautiful one maybe once someone washed off all the crap. As Bobby Dexter scraped away, whistling again, his wife was beginning to put the pieces together, beginning to understand what they'd found. It was a life-size Roman statue, maybe a couple of thousand years old. Stained like shit from all this time in the peat, maybe, but perfect apart from that.

She understood what Bobby would be thinking too. Who knew what they could do in a lab these days? Maybe get it right back to nice, white marble, like it had been when Julius Caesar or some other dead Italian first ordered it.

And there was the problem. It was just too big. The two of them couldn't even try and get it out of the ground. Five feet or so of stone was bound to weigh a ton. Even if they got someone in to help, there was no way they could ever bring the thing back to the USA.

'Let's just go, Bobby,' Lianne pleaded. 'We can call someone and tell them about it. Maybe they'd give us a reward. Maybe we'd be in the paper. You could stick that under Tom Jorgensen's nose and see how it felt.'

'Fucking reward,' he spat back at her. 'This is Italy, Lianne. They'd steal the thing for themselves and probably lock us up for messing around down here.'

'Then what are you going to do?'

She was defying him now and they both knew it. This was some kind of turning point in their marriage, one at which either life could go in one of two directions: to freedom or to servitude.

He got up and went for the spade, picked it up, felt the weight of the thing in his hands then stared avidly at the queer brown form half buried in the peat.

Lianne looked at him, a cold tangle of dread beginning to form in her stomach.

'Bobby?' she asked, half pleading. '*Bobby?*'

Nic Costa drove the unmarked police Fiat east along the city side of the main riverside drag. Gianni Peroni, the partner assigned to him that morning, was in the passenger seat filling his face with a panino leaking roast pork at the edges. He was a big, muscular man approaching fifty, with an unforgettable face. Somewhere along the line – and Costa just knew he was going to have to ask before long – Peroni's features had walked into a wall or something. His nose was crushed worse than any Costa had seen on a rugby player. His forehead sank low over a couple of bright, smart piggy eyes. A vicious scar ran diagonally across his right cheek. Just to complete the picture Peroni cut his grey hair as short as possible, a crew crop, like a US marine. In a neat dark suit and a crisp white shirt and tie, he looked like a thug dressed up for a wedding. It was station lore that the man had never once raised a fist to a customer in his career. He didn't need to, Costa thought. People took one look at him, gulped and came clean. It was one reason why Peroni was known far and wide as one of the most popular and respected inspectors in the force, the last man Nic Costa expected to be sharing his car with as an equal.

'I don't know how they dare call this *porchetta*?' Peroni grumbled. 'Where I come from . . . it's this little town near Siena. All farmers and stuff, too ordinary to get the tourists. Now there they do *porchetta*, every damn weekend. My uncle Fredo was a farmer. He showed me how. You'd kill the pig, you'd bone it. You'd take out the liver and soak it in grappa and stuff. Then you'd stay up all night roasting the thing. Fredo used to say that was the only night of the week he slept with a pig that didn't snore.'

Peroni watched him, waiting for a reaction. 'OK. Maybe you had to meet his missus to understand that one. Anyway *that* was *porchetta*. All hot and fresh and lots of crackling too. This shit's been sitting in the fridge for days. Want some?'

Costa eyed the pale dry meat. 'Not while I'm driving, thanks. Anyway, I don't eat meat.'

Peroni shrugged then wound down the window and ejected the greasy paper out into the rising temperature of a Roman spring morning. 'Oh yeah, I forgot. Your loss.'

Costa took his eyes off the busy riverside road for a second and looked at Peroni. 'That's littering. You don't do it from my car.'

'You mean, "That's littering, *Sir*." '

'No,' Costa insisted. 'I mean what I said. You're just another cop. You heard Falcone.'

Peroni's oddly stiff face suddenly became animated. 'Equal rank, equal rank. How can Leo do this to me? Jesus, the stuff he's got away with and no one busts his ass. Leo and I are meant to be buddies, for God's sake. What does friendship mean in this world?'

Costa had made up his mind the moment he knew Peroni was his new partner. He wasn't taking any crap. He wasn't behaving like a subordinate. Maybe that was why Falcone fixed this in the first place. It was a lesson, perhaps a kind of punishment, for both of them.

Gianni Peroni's crime was now well known throughout the Questura, told and retold with a certain awe, a fable about how even the brightest and the best could fall from grace, and for such small temptations too. For years he'd worked his way up through the vice squad, with never a taint of corruption to his name. As inspector he'd busted three of the biggest hooker rings in the city and managed to stem the infiltration of the prostitute trade by the vicious Albanian crooks who'd started to muscle in on territories elsewhere. He never went out of his way to make friends. He never hid the fact that, at heart, he remained a working-class farm boy from Tuscany who didn't feel comfortable mixing with the upper strata of the force. All the same, Peroni's name had been marked out for big things. If he didn't look so weird and scary maybe they'd have happened by now too. Then he blew everything, one night some weeks before, an occasion that rapidly made its way into the hands of a gleeful press.

It was meant to be a sting operation organized by the Direzione Investigativa Anti-Mafia, the civilian force outside police control specifically aimed at halting mob activity. The DIA had set up a fake brothel in Testaccio, manned by real hookers brought in from Bologna. In three weeks it had run up enough clientele to attract the attention of the big-time pimps who would, the DIA knew, soon be round asking for either a cut or the heads of the men creaming off the profits.

Three heavies did turn up one Thursday night. When the DIA pounced they took in the brothel's customers, just out of interest, and went through their wallets before handing them on to the police as a free gift. Gianni Peroni had the misfortune to be in the room of a blonde Czech girl when they walked through the door. No amount of talking on his part was able to extricate him from the mess. Word got back to the Questura. Peroni was first suspended then sent crashing back to earth as a lowly plain clothes detective. And he was supposed to feel lucky. Had it been anyone else, an entire career would have disappeared down the drain.

Demotion and the loss of salary were the least of Peroni's concerns if Questura gossip was anything to go by. He wasn't just admired for being a great cop. He was renowned throughout the building as a family man. His wife and his two teenage kids, one boy, one girl, were well known. Men and women on his squad dined regularly at the Peroni household. When they had problems, Peroni acted like a proxy father, offering advice, trying to keep them on track.

All that had been shattered on a chill January evening. Peroni didn't face prosecution. He'd broken no law. He'd just lost everything. His wife had gone back to Siena with both kids, demanding a swift divorce, shouting his betrayal from the rooftops. In a matter of weeks he'd gone from being an important cop, with a loving family, to a single, middle-aged man, alone, uncertain of his future career. And now Leo Falcone had put him in a car with Nic Costa, whose own position in the police appeared equally as uncertain and directionless. Costa had no clear idea how to handle this. But then, he guessed, neither did Gianni Peroni.

The two small Roman temples that sat beside the Piazza della Bocca della Verità were just beyond the window, a couple of perfect, circular shapes from a different, Arcadian world. It was a pleasant day with enough warmth in it to indicate spring was on the way. Nic Costa wished he could sit next to them for a while, thinking.

Peroni turned to stare at him. 'Shall we have the clearing of the air conversation now?'

Costa looked into that intense, battered face and wondered how long it would take him to get used to sharing a car with someone who looked like a cartoon villain. 'If you want.'

'Let me be candid. It's not so long since you went loony tunes. You did the drink thing too. Me, I just got caught with my pants down with a Czech hooker. For that I have to be the rehab warder. The way I see it is that if I can keep you straight for a month or so, and who knows maybe along the way we deal with a few criminals, I can get myself back in Leo's good books. I can start climbing the ladder to what I do best, which is running a team, not sitting in some stinking squad car playing nursemaid to junior and keeping him away from the bottle. This is important to me, kid. I'll do my best to keep Leo happy. But you have to help me. The sooner you do, the sooner you have me out of your hair and get someone normal. Understand?'

Costa nodded.

'And let me tell you something else. *I hate* the drink thing. I have watched too many men turn into boozed-up pieces of shit in my time. You do that to me and I will feel very cross indeed. You wouldn't like me when I'm cross. No one does.'

'I'll try to remember that. Do I get something in return? A promise you'll stay away from hookers?'

Peroni glared at him and Costa, in spite of himself, couldn't help feeling a little scared. 'Don't push it now. I know Leo's looking out for you. The stupid bastard feels guilty for what happened when you got shot. God knows why. From what I hear you got yourself into that mess.'

Costa refused to rise to the bait. 'No I mean it. I'm curious. Everyone thought they knew you. This stand-up, working-class guy with the perfect family, the perfect life. And now they think they got it wrong all along. And they wonder: was it them, or was it you? Who was doing the lying?'

'Me,' Peroni said immediately. 'But let me tell you.

Everyone's got that little dark spot inside them. Everyone wonders what it would be like to take it out for a walk once in a while. Even you. If you know what's good for you.'

'I thought that's what you didn't want to happen.'

'I was talking about the drink. People who go that way do it for one purpose. To kill something. Maybe it'd be better if they did let the dark side out instead. Just now and again.'

It was a kind of philosophy, Costa thought. Not one he expected from a cop, or the kind of cop Gianni Peroni was supposed to be.

'And you tell me something, kid. I saw you walking into the building today with Barbara Martelli. Isn't she the loveliest thing in the world? What if she just turned round one day, just when you were happily married and thought everything was stretching out neatly in front of you, just when you're feeling a little old too. What if she said: *Nic, I just wished I knew what it was like. Just the once. Where's the harm? Who's to know?*'

'I'm not married.'

'I *know*. I said, what if?' Peroni waited for an answer and realized it wasn't coming. 'You should ask that girl out. She's got something in her eyes when she looks at you. I notice these things.'

Costa laughed. 'Really?'

'Really. And let me tell you one more thing. I knew her old man. He was in vice too until a couple of years ago. One of the meanest, most miserable bastards you ever saw. How he ever spawned a woman like that is beyond me. There. You got a good reason not to date her. You'd have to meet that old sonofabitch.'

'Thanks.'

'You're welcome. You look like the sort of person who appreciates reasons for not doing things. Which is fine by me, until I talk myself out of this seat. Do we understand each other?'

Costa didn't get mad. In a way he felt relieved. At least he knew where he stood.

'Is that out of the way now?' he wondered. 'Can we just settle down to being old cop, young cop, cleaning up the streets of Rome?'

But the big man in the passenger seat was waving at him to be quiet. The radio was squealing their number. Peroni picked up the mike and answered. They listened to the call. Nic Costa gunned the car and headed straight for Piramide and the *autostrada* out to the coast and the airport, casually flicking on the blue light and the siren to get the cars out of the way.

'What a day,' Peroni groaned. 'First I get baby-sitting duties. Now we're the fire brigade. Hard to know which is worse.'

Bobby Dexter's determined expression was one Lianne recognized. It usually meant they were headed for trouble.

'I'll tell you what we're going to do,' he said. 'We're going to take back a head for Tom Jorgensen to look at. One that's a million times better than that piece of Greek shit of his.'

She gaped at him, outraged. 'What?'

Bobby raised the shovel to shoulder height, holding it like an axe, a little breathless already from the anticipation. 'Watch. Watch and learn.'

He brought the metal down hard; where the statue's

neck ought to be. Nothing much happened. Some dirt moved. But Lianne was yelling, louder than she'd ever done before.

'Bobby Dexter,' she screeched. 'What the hell are you doing? This thing's like a piece of art or something. It's history. You're just going to smash it to pieces so you can make out your dick's bigger than Tom Jorgensen's?'

He held the shovel high, swaying slightly. 'What do you know about the size of Jorgensen's dick?'

'It was a figure of speech, moron.'

Bobby Dexter blinked at her. He looked downright ugly. The light was failing now and the world was getting weird. He took one more swipe at the statue's neck and missed, sending up a shower of stinking earth that bounced straight back into his face. A few grains fell into his mouth. He spat out the dirt as if it were poison.

'If you break that statue, we're over, Bobby,' she said, dead serious. 'I mean it. I don't go talking to my father. I get a lawyer. The moment we get back to Seattle.'

He hesitated, staring at her as if wondering whether she really did mean it . . . 'You tell me that when we're back home with the best fucking piece of coffee table statuary in private ownership anywhere in Washington State. You'd be amazed what a nice piece of household ornamentation can do for dinner parties.'

'Bobby—' she yelled.

'Bullshit.' He took a final swing.

This one connected. The sharp side of the spade went deep into the neck. There should have been a sharp, cracking sound that indicated a good clean break, one that went right across the stone in a level line with just enough randomness in it to look convincing. She knew

Bobby well enough to understand what he was thinking. There were probably ideas in his head already.

But everything just went straight out of their heads a moment after the blade hit. Lianne Dexter realized right then that they'd been wrong, terribly wrong, both of them. They saw what they wanted to see. Not what *was*. Maybe there was a reason behind that. Because what *was* turned out to be the last thing they wanted to encounter anywhere on this planet, least of all on their own down a little lane, next to a stinking grey river in a country where their language skills extended only to ordering pizza, beer and wine.

The blade didn't strike hard stone. It met flesh, a kind of flesh anyway. Something that looked like leather, tanned, tough, but supple. The side of the spade cut straight through just where the neck met the shoulders, severing something that resembled a real human tendon, spattering both of them with a mixture of foul-smelling wet mud that seemed to have something distinctly organic, almost alive, inside it.

Lianne's face was covered with the peat gore that had spat back at them when he attacked the thing. She was spitting bits of it out of her mouth, sobbing, dry-retching as she did so.

She stopped for a moment and watched Bobby bend down to look closely at the thing, just a hint of reverence in his face.

On the ground in front of them, partly severed from the body by the spade, was the head of a young girl, sixteen, seventeen, no more, dressed in a classical gown, holding some large, ceremonial wand in her left hand. The force of the blow had removed most of the solid cake of peat that had sat on her features. What they saw now was her face which, beneath the crud, seemed beautiful. She had a high forehead and prominent cheekbones. There wasn't a wrinkle in sight on her flawless leather skin. Her eyes were closed. Her lips were partly open as if she were uttering a final, dying sigh. She had perfect teeth which were just closed together with a hint of pearly whiteness showing through the brown stain of the earth. Her long hair was tied back behind her neck and matted into solid strands. Her expression was one of utmost peace. She looked, Lianne Dexter thought, happy, which was, she knew, ridiculous in the circumstances.

And just in case they were in any doubt about the nature of this object before them there was the matter of the neck. When Bobby had come down hard with the shovel he'd done what he hoped: split through into the interior. Bobby and Lianne Dexter were now looking at the inside of another human being's throat and it was black and complicated and messy, with bones and sinews and passages that looked vaguely familiar from some distant school lesson in anatomy.

'Holy shit,' Bobby muttered and started shivering.

A 747 swooped low over them. They felt the heat of its breath. They inhaled the chemical stink of its fearsome engines. When the roar of its gross presence diminished Bobby Dexter became aware of another noise. It was his wife, screaming.

'No,' he pleaded. 'Not now, Lianne. I'm trying to think for chrissake.'

Then he gave up altogether. Two men, one short, one tall, were walking towards them, staring intently. Some way behind them there was something else: a red fire engine struggling down the lane trying to reach the charred and smoking remains of the Clio.

The men were waving badges. They didn't look sympathetic.

The older cop was a bull-necked gorilla with a disfigured, scowling face and piercing, aggressive eyes that looked as if they could see everything. The younger, shorter one was staring at the thing in the ground, the shit-coloured cadaver with the head all to one side where Bobby had lopped it with the shovel.

'This day just gets stranger,' Gianni Peroni murmured. 'Pinch me. Tell me I'm dreaming.'

'You're not dreaming,' Nic Costa replied. He couldn't stop looking at the object half-hidden in the mud. Not for the weeping woman who looked as if she'd thrown up and was now hunched in a ball down by the edge of the river. Or the man, who held a shovel uncertainly in his hands, his body swaying rhythmically.

A man who, for no reason at all, suddenly pointed the spade at both of them and, with a slow, effortful slur to his voice, said, 'Listen. Don't fuck with me. Don't even think about it. I'm an American citizen.'

THE IDES OF MARCH

'How long has she been lying there? Answer me that.'

Teresa Lupo stood next to the brown cadaver that lay at a stiff, awkward angle on the shiny steel table in the morgue. The pathologist looked even more proprietorial than usual about the corpse in her care, and immensely pleased with herself too. It was two weeks now since Nic Costa and Gianni Peroni had encountered the body and the screaming American couple by the muddy banks of the Tiber, just a couple of kilometres from the sea at Ostia. Bobby and Lianne Dexter were back home in Washington State, talking to lawyers about their divorce and who should have custody of the cats, still feeling lucky to have escaped Europe without facing a single charge (which proved, Lianne thought, exactly what kind of people they were over there anyway). Costa and Peroni had, in the mean time, become, if not quite a team, partners of a kind, able to get through the day with a sense of shared duty and the promise that soon their artificial relationship would be over.

The body had made international headlines for a few days. Somehow a photo had been smuggled to the media, showing the serene, frozen face that had emerged from the chemical-smelling peat. It was a genuine mystery. No one knew how old the body was. No one knew whether the girl had died of natural causes or was the victim of some obscure crime. There was wild speculation in some of the Italian tabloids, stories which talked about ancient cults that had killed followers who had somehow failed the entry ceremony.

Nic Costa hadn't taken any notice. It was pointless to speculate until Teresa Lupo had passed judgement. Now she had made up her mind. They had been summoned to the morgue for ten that morning. At noon Teresa planned to give a press conference outlining her findings. The very fact she'd arranged this herself without asking advance permission from Leo Falcone spoke volumes. It meant she was confident there was no criminal investigation on the way. He and Peroni had simply been invited along out of politeness. They found the specimen; they deserved to hear its secrets revealed. Costa wished Teresa had left them out of it. He was starting to get the feel for police business again, starting to like the idea he could be good at it. If this really was a closed case, he'd rather be somewhere else, dealing with a live one.

The three of them – Falcone, Peroni and Costa – sat on a cold, hard bench watching her make a few last-minute, fussy observations of the corpse. Costa understood what this was: a dry run for the press conference which would be part of her re-entry into police life. Teresa Lupo had briefly quit her job after the Denney case, vowing never to return. She had been close to Luca Rossi and felt the pain of his death as much as anyone in the station. More, perhaps, than Nic Costa. More certainly than Falcone who, while quietly racked by guilt over the loss of his man, was too obsessed by the job to be distracted for long.

Grief chased her from the tight, close embrace of the force. Grief brought her back to the fold. She was like the rest of them: hooked, incapable of staying away. She loved getting to know her customers, trying to understand their lives and what had brought them to her slab. Unravelling these mysteries fulfilled her and now she was starting to show it, Costa thought. She was carrying a little less weight. The ponytail had gone, replaced by a businesswoman's crop, black hair short and sculpted carefully to hide the outline of her heavy neck. She had a large, animated face and slightly bulbous blue eyes that darted around constantly. There was something a touch obsessive inside the woman, something that quickly chased away most men who tried to get close to her. Maybe that was what made her the pathologist the cops always wanted on their side, however fierce her temper, however sharp her tongue . . .

'Ten years. Twenty max,' Peroni suggested. 'But what do I know? I'm just a busted vice cop. You got to bear the responsibility for any screw-ups I make, Leo. I'm used to dealing with people I know are guilty from the outset. All this detection stuff . . . it's not my thing.'

Falcone put a hand to his ear. 'Excuse me?'

'Sir,' Peroni said meekly. 'You got to bear the responsibility, Sir.'

Falcone sat there in a grey suit that looked as if it were new that morning, letting his fingers run through his angular, sharp-pointed silver beard, staring at the body, thinking. He'd returned from a holiday somewhere hot only the day before. A deep walnut tan stained his face and his bald scalp. It was almost the colour of the corpse on the slab. The inspector seemed miles away. Maybe his head was still on the beach, or wherever he went for enjoyment. Maybe he'd been through the force disposition. There was a flu epidemic gripping the city. People were calling in sick from everywhere. The Questura had so many empty desks that morning it looked like Christmas Day.

Teresa was grinning. Peroni had said exactly what she wanted to hear. 'That's a good and sensible suggestion, even for a busted vice cop. Your basis for it being . . . ?'

He waved his hand at the table. 'Look at her. She's a touch messed up but she don't stink too bad. Nothing going mouldy. I'm sure you people have seen worse. Smelled much worse too probably.'

She nodded. 'The smell's from the treatment. She's been lying in a shower ever since we got her here. Fifteen per cent polyethylene glycol in distilled water. I've been doing a lot of research on this girl. Reading books. Talking to people. I'm in touch with some academics in England by e-mail who know exactly how to handle a body in this condition. After ten weeks or so maybe we'll need to get her freeze-dried to finish the job properly.'

'Don't we get to bury her in the end?' Costa wondered. 'Isn't that what you're supposed to do with dead people?'

She screwed up her big pale face in amazement. 'Are you kidding me? Do you think the university would allow it?'

'Since when did she belong to them?' he asked. 'However old she is, she was a human being. If this isn't going to become a crime investigation, what's the problem? When does a corpse turn into a specimen? Who decides?'

'I do,' Falcone said, coming out of the daydream abruptly. Costa peered at him. There was something odd going on. Falcone wasn't as cool, as self-composed as normal. He looked glum, which was unusual. It was rare that anyone was able to discern much sign of human emotion in him at all. Costa wondered who Falcone had been on holiday with. The dour inspector's marriage had ended years ago. There were rumours of occasional attachments since then but that could just be station gossip. When Leo Falcone was in the Questura nothing else seemed to exist except the force. When he was gone, he was out of it completely, never mixing with his colleagues, never wanting to be invited round for dinner. Maybe the inspector, who always seemed so calm, so in control when it came to other people's lives, had no hold whatsoever on his own. Maybe he went on holiday by himself, sitting on some sunny beach somewhere reading a book like a hermit, turning browner and browner, meaner and meaner.

'Hear me out,' Teresa pleaded. 'It'll all become clear, I promise. A couple of decades? Nice guess. But I have to tell you it's out. By a touch under two thousand years.'

Peroni snorted. 'Someone's been hitting the wacky baccy around here, Leo. Excuse me. *Sir*. How else can you come up with that kind of shit?'

'Wait for it, wait for it,' she demanded, waving a finger at him. 'I can't be precise, not yet, but I hope to give you something pretty accurate very soon. This body's been in peat all that time. From the moment you put a corpse in that kind of bog it starts getting preserved. Sort of a mixture between mummification and tanning, and completely unpredictable too. Plus, there's no end of industrial effluent getting poured into the river out there and God knows what that does. I got parts of her almost as hard as wood, other areas soft, almost pliable. Haven't even contemplated a conventional autopsy – for reasons that will shortly become obvious – so God knows what kind of state she's in internally. But I have a date. Peat plays havoc with normal radiocarbon dating techniques. I won't get technical on you. Let's just say the acid in the water depletes just about anything we can use for a radiocarbon test. There are things we can try, like getting some cholesterol out of her, since that's virtually immune to long-term soaking. But right now I'm working with some organic material from the dirt beneath her fingernails. And that's somewhere between 50 AD and 230 AD.'

They just stared at her.

'Is that really possible?' Falcone asked eventually.

She went over to the desk and picked up a large brown envelope next to the computer. 'You bet. None of this is new. The archaeologists have a term for it. "Peat bodies". They've been there for centuries but no one noticed until companies started digging up the bogs for the gardening business. The area behind Fiumicino was never big enough to work commercially. Mind you, there's been a lot of rain this winter. Maybe that took off some of the surface soil and made it easier to find.'

She crossed the room and passed them a set of colour photographs. They were of corpses, brown corpses, some contorted, half shrunken, half mummified, a little more exaggerated than the one now on the slab but recognizably similar all the same.

'See this one,' she said, pointing at the first picture. It was the head of a man, apparently turned to leather.

The features were almost perfectly preserved. He had a calm, composed face. His eyes were closed as if in sleep. He wore some kind of rough leather cap, the stitching still visible on the crude seams. 'Tollund, Denmark. Found in 1950. Don't be fooled by the expression. He had a rope around his neck. Executed for some reason. Some good radiocarbon material there. Puts his death somewhere over two thousand years ago. And this—'

The next picture was of a full corpse: a man, reclining on what looked like rock. He was more shrivelled this time, with his neck turned at an awkward angle and a head of matted red hair.

'Grauballe, also in Denmark, not far away, though he's even older, third century BC. This one had his throat cut ear to ear. They found traces of the ergot fungus – the magic mushroom – in his gut. It's not easy to re-create what went on but there's a common theme. These people died violently, maybe as part of some ritual. Drugs tended to be involved. Here—'

She began scattering pictures over their laps, corpse after mummified corpse, many crouched in that tortured, agonized position any cop who'd visited a modern murder scene already knew too well. 'Yde Girl, in Holland, stabbed and strangled. She was maybe sixteen. Lindow Man, England. Beaten, strangled then dumped in the bog. Daetgen Man, Germany. Beaten, stabbed and beheaded. Borremose Woman, found in Denmark, face caved in, probably by a hammer or a pickaxe. These were all people in primitive, pagan agrarian societies. Maybe they did something wrong. Maybe there was some kind of sacrificial rite. Peat bogs often had a kind of spiritual significance for these tribes. Perhaps these were offerings to the bog god or someone. I don't know.'

Falcone put down the photos. He seemed remarkably uninterested in them. 'I don't care what happened in Denmark a couple of millennia ago. What happened here? How, specifically, did she die?'

She didn't like that. Teresa Lupo had been expecting a little more credit for what she'd found out, Costa thought. She deserved it too.

'Listen,' she answered sharply. 'We have limited resources. Like Nic said, when do we have a body and when do we have a specimen? I can make that judgement for myself, thanks. This is a very old corpse. I'm a criminal pathologist, not a historian. There are people who can perform a full autopsy on this girl and the rest. It's not a job for us.'

'How did she die?' Falcone repeated.

She looked at the frozen, leathery face. Teresa Lupo always felt some sympathy for her customers. Even when they'd expired a couple of thousand years ago.

'Like the rest. Badly. Is that what you wanted to know?'

'Usually, it's the first thing we need to know,' Falcone said.

'Usually,' she agreed. Then she gestured at the cadaver on the shining table. 'Does this look usual to you?'

There were times when Emilio Neri thought himself a fool for hanging on to the house in the Via Giulia. He'd taken on the property thirty years before, in return for an unpaid debt from some dumb banker who'd got in over his head gambling. Neri, then a rising *capo* in the Rome mobs, reluctantly became the owner. He'd rather have driven the yo-yo into the countryside somewhere and put his eyes out before dropping him in a ditch. But this all happened at a time when his actions were circumscribed by others. It would be a further ten years before Neri became don in his own right, giving him the sway to order executions directly, and take a cut of every transaction running through the family's books. By then the banker was back in business and never made the mistake of getting into his debt again, much to Neri's disappointment.

In the 1970s the Via Giulia was still pretty much a local area for everyday Romans, not the chic street for rich foreigners and antique dealers it was to become. Created in the sixteenth century by Bramante for Pope Julius II, it ran parallel to the river, set some way below the level of the busy waterside road, and was originally intended to be a grand entrance to the Vatican, by the bridge to the Castel Sant'Angelo. The market of the Campo dei Fiori was no more than a two-minute walk away. Trastevere was maybe a minute more, crossing over the medieval footbridge of the Ponte Sisto. On a fine summer evening Neri used to make that walk regularly, pausing in the middle of the bridge to look along the river towards the vast, sunlit dome of St Peter's. He was never much interested in views but this one pleased him somehow. Perhaps that was why he held on to the house, although by now he could afford just about any property in Rome, and was beginning to acquire a portfolio that would include homes in New York, Tuscany, Colombia and two country estates in his native Sicily.

The walk to Trastevere took him out of himself for a

while. The restaurants were good too, which was something Neri could never resist. Until he was fifty he'd been relatively fit, a big, powerful, muscular man who could impose his will by force and brute physical violence if need be. Then the food and the wine took hold. Now he was sixty-five and carrying way too much weight. He looked at himself in the mirror sometimes and wondered whether there was anything to be done. Then he remembered who he was and knew it didn't matter. He had all the money a man could want. He had a beautiful young wife who did anything he pleased, and was smart enough to look the other way if he felt like the occasional distraction. Maybe he was fat. Maybe he wheezed now and again, and had halitosis so bad he popped mints into his large, grey-lipped mouth the way some of his underlings sucked on cigarettes. Who cared? He was Emilio Neri, a don to be feared in Rome and beyond. He had influence. He had hard cash pouring into his offshore accounts, from prostitution, drug trafficking, money laundering, arms and any number of semi-legitimate investments. He didn't care what he looked like, what he smelt like. That was their problems.

In all this pampered life there was just one minor sore and, to Neri's occasional annoyance, it lived downstairs, one floor above the six servants he employed needlessly, just to fill up the space and dust things before they ever got dusty. While he and Adele occupied the top two storeys of the house – and had sole use of the vast terrace, with its palm trees and fountains – his only son, Mickey, had, after three fraught years pissing off Neri's friends in the States, come home to stay. It was a temporary arrangement. Neri wanted to keep an eye on the boy just to make sure he didn't start messing up with dope again. Once he'd found some kind of even keel, Neri would cut him loose. Maybe find him an apartment somewhere else in the city, or move him on to Sicily where there were relatives who could keep him in check. Neri did this partly out of self-interest – Mickey had grown up inside the organization. He could cause some harm if he started blabbing to the wrong people. But there was a degree of paternal loyalty there too. Mickey was an asshole. Maybe he inherited this from his mother, an over-tanned American bit-part actress Neri had met through a crooked producer he knew when he was pumping hot money into a Fellini movie. The marriage had lasted five years, after which Neri knew he either had to divorce the bitch or kill her. She now basked in the permasun of Florida and doubtless bore a close physical resemblance to an iguana, a creature, Neri thought, which could probably out-think her in its sleep.

Mickey never wanted to be near mamma. Mickey wanted to hang around his old man. He thought he was a don in the making and never missed an opportunity to throw his weight around. He had problems with women too, just couldn't leave them alone, whether they were married or not. His one saving grace was that he worshipped his father. Everyone else, Adele included, did Neri's bidding out of fear. Mickey went along with everything his old man decreed for a simpler reason. Most kids idolized their fathers until they were seven or eight, and then started to see them for what they were. The scales had never fallen from Mickey's eyes. There was some undying adulation stuck fast in his genes and Emilio Neri found it strangely touching. It led him to do crazy things, such as letting the kid wander around the house whenever he felt like it, even though he and

Adele, who, at thirty-three, was just one year older, loathed the sight of one another. It led him to overlook the problems that came when Mickey got a little too close to the drugs and the booze, problems that were, on occasion, expensive to fix.

Sometimes Emilio wondered who was indulging whom. Since Mickey moved in, he'd begun to wonder that a lot.

It was now mid-morning and the two of them had been bitching at each other, on and off, since breakfast. Adele half reclined on the sofa, still in her mauve silk pyjamas, face in a fashion house catalogue. Emilio thought she looked gorgeous but he knew it was a matter of taste. She was sipping a *spremuta* of blood-red orange juice which was almost the colour of her expensively cut hair. She sent out one of the servants to buy these things by the kilo from the market then watched as Nadia, the sullen cook she'd picked herself, squeezed them in the kitchen. Adele almost lived off the stuff. It drove Mickey crazy. Maybe it was why she was so skinny, he said. He bugged his old man about that constantly. Why marry some redhead with the figure of a pencil when you could have just about any woman in Rome?

'I still can have just about any woman in Rome,' Emilio told him.

'Yeah. But why?'

'Because I don't want the same picture over the fireplace everyone else has. Leave it at that.'

'I don't get it.'

Emilio had thrown a big arm around the kid. Mickey inherited the physique of his mother. He was lean, muscular, good-looking too. It was a shame he always chose clothes too young for him, though. And that he'd dyed his shoulder-length hair an overpowering, unnatural blonde colour. 'You don't have to. Just don't snap at each other all the time. Not when I'm around anyway.'

'Sorry,' he'd replied, instantly deferential.

The old man never said as much but sometimes he didn't get it either. Adele was unlike any woman he'd ever slept with: cool, adventurous, always willing, whatever he wanted. Young as she was, she actually taught him a few new tricks. Maybe that clinched it. He knew for sure it wasn't her personality, which he didn't really understand beyond her basic need for money and security. She was an expensive pet, if he were honest with himself, a living ornament to add some beauty to his life.

'So,' Neri declared, looking in turn at the two of them. 'What does my family plan to do today?'

'Are we going out?' she asked. 'We could have lunch somewhere.'

'Why bother?' Mickey said, smirking. 'I could send someone down the Campo. Buy you a couple of lettuce leaves. They'd last all week.'

'Hey!' the old man bellowed. 'Cut it out! And quit sending servants out to buy stuff you can get yourself. I don't pay them to get you cigarettes.'

Mickey went back to the sports car magazine he was reading and said nothing. Neri knew what the kid was thinking: *so what do you pay them for?* Neri never liked the idea of servants in the house. Adele said their position demanded it. He was the boss. He was supposed to own people. It grated somehow. Emilio Neri grew up in a traditional Roman working-class family, fighting his way out of the Testaccio slums. He still felt embarrassed by these minions downstairs. A couple were made men, there for security. He had no problem with that. But a house was for family, not strangers.

'I got work to do,' Emilio said. 'People to see. I won't be back until this afternoon.'

'Then I'll go shopping,' she answered, with just a hint of hurt disappointment in her voice.

Mickey was shaking his blonde head in disbelief. Adele did a lot of shopping.

'You!'

'Yeah.' Mickey closed the magazine.

'Go see that louse Cozzi. Squeeze his grapes and ask for some accounts. The creep's screwing us somehow. I just know it. We should be taking more in one week than he hands over in a month.'

'What do you want me to do if I see something?'

'If you see something?' Neri walked over and ruffled Mickey's wayward hair. 'Don't play the tough guy. Leave those decisions to me.'

'But—'

'You heard.'

Neri looked at the pair of them. Adele was acting as if the kid didn't even exist. 'I wish you two could work up the energy to be civilized to each other once in a while. It would make my life a whole lot easier.' He watched. They didn't even exchange glances.

'Families,' Neri moaned, then phoned downstairs, telling them to get the Mercedes ready. He keyed in the security code that unlocked the big metal door. It felt like a prison sometimes, hiding behind the bodyguards, riding around in a car that had been discreetly filled with bullet-proof panelling. But that was the way of the world these days.

'Bye,' Emilio Neri grunted, and was gone, without even looking back.

Mickey waited a while, pretending to read the magazine. Finally he put it down and looked across at her. She'd finished the orange juice. She was lying back on the sofa in her perfect silk pyjamas, eyes closed, glossy red hair splayed out on the white leather. Pretending she was asleep. She wasn't really. They both knew that.

'Maybe he's right,' he said.

She opened her eyes and turned her head lazily, just enough to meet his gaze. She had very bright eyes, vivid green, never still. Not smart eyes, he thought. Just sufficiently expressionless to hide the odd lie.

'About what?'

'About us getting along a little better.'

She became alert, alarmed perhaps. She looked at the door. There was a hard cast in her face: *fear.*

Mickey got up, stretched his arms and yawned. He was wearing a thin tee-shirt and tight designer jeans. She watched him, worried. They heard the sound of the big main door to the street slamming shut three floors below, and then, directly after, the growl of the departing Mercedes.

Adele Neri got up from the sofa, went to the door and threw the bolt, walked across to her stepson, put a hand on his fly and ran the zip down, clutching at what was inside.

'You need to shop for new pyjamas,' Mickey said.

'What?'

He took hold of the neckline of her top and tugged hard with both hands, tearing at the silk. The fabric ripped wide open. Her meagre white breasts came under his fingers. He bent down, sucking at them briefly, then jerked down the pants, helping her shrug out of the things, running his palms everywhere, letting his tongue work briefly into her small, tight navel, then slide lower into the thatch of brown hair.

Mickey got up, cupped his hands around her thin, tight buttocks, gripped her thighs, lifting her into the air, pushing backwards until her shoulders were up against the door. The green eyes looked into his. Maybe there was an expression there. Need. Maybe not.

'Never much wanted to bang a skinny chick until you came along,' he mumbled. 'Now I don't want to bang nothing else.'

She was doing things with her hands, things that were sneaky and gentle and rough and unsubtle at the same time. He was hardening in her fingers. His jeans were round his ankles now. She hitched up her legs and straddled his waist, holding on tight, guiding him.

'If he ever finds out, Mickey—'

'We're dead,' he said, and felt his body meeting hers in all the right places.

Mickey Neri pushed himself forward, stabbing into her. It was the best feeling he'd ever known. She was squealing. She was going crazy, chewing on his neck, whispering filthy words into his ear, pulling his long hair. He pushed harder. He was in deep, as deep as it got.

'Worth it,' he panted, knowing already he'd have to work hard to prolong the pleasure. Maybe she knew some tricks there too. 'Worth every second.'

'OK,' Teresa Lupo said briskly. 'I spent many nights sweating over this but I'll try to compress it as much as I can. Look—'

They did as she wanted, and got up to stand over the cadaver. She seemed quite young, Costa thought, halfway between girl and woman. Perhaps seventeen, if that. Her face was disconcerting, still alive somehow and undoubtedly beautiful. Her features seemed Saxon or maybe Scandinavian. They had the precise, symmetrical perfection he associated with fair-haired northerners. Someone had washed part of her matted hair. It was now a kind of muddy blonde, tinted by the redness of the peat. The smell was pungent close up too.

'You will recall,' Teresa said, pointing at the cavity around the cadaver's throat, 'that our thoughtful American friend tried to remove her head believing it to be that of a statue. This wound was caused by the sharp end of his shovel. I'm amazed you people let the bastard go without doing a single thing to him, by the way, but that's your decision not mine.'

'Here, here,' Peroni agreed.

'We went through this, Gianni,' Costa said. 'What were we supposed to charge them with?'

'Drunk driving?' Peroni suggested.

'Couldn't hold them in the country until trial.'

The older man scowled. 'How about disrespect? Yeah, I know. It's not a crime. Maybe it ought to be.'

Teresa smiled at Peroni and said, 'I agree.' Then she took a pointer and indicated an area on the girl's neck, just above the deep gash made by Bobby Dexter's spade. 'You can still see what happened originally though. That shovel wasn't the first time someone struck a blow here. The girl's throat was cut. From behind too. From the wound you can see whoever did it worked from side to side. It doesn't work like that if they come in from the front. Then you just get a slash from the centre out. Here—'

There were more pictures on the desk. Careful blow-ups of the neck. 'There's the slice the bozo made. There's hardly any earth on the tissue. But here—'

They looked closely at the photos. Close up the second, older wound, clearly tinted by the brown, acid water over the years, was unmistakable.

'That didn't happen two weeks ago. That happened not long before she got put into the bog. That killed her.'

Falcone nodded at the pictures. 'Good work,' he said. 'That was all I wanted to know.'

'There's more,' she added, trying not to look too eager.

Falcone laughed. She found it disconcerting that she amused him. 'Don't tell me, doctor. You've solved the case. You have a motive. You know when. You know who did it.'

'That last part's beyond even me. The rest . . . be patient.'

The inspector smiled, amused, and waved her to go on.

There was a book on the desk. She picked it up, and held it up for them to see. It was entitled *Dionysus and the Villa of Mysteries*. The cover photograph was of an ancient painting: a woman in a dishevelled dress, holding her hand over her face in terror of some half-seen night creature with staring, demonic eyes which leered at her from the edges of the image. The shapes had been damaged over the years. The creature was largely unrecognizable. But they could see what was depicted here. It was some kind of ceremony, one in which the woman was, perhaps, assaulted. Or even sacrificed.

'This was written by a professor at the university here,' she said. 'I got put onto it by an academic at Yale who'd done some work on a bog body found in Germany, close to a Roman town.'

'This is relevant?' Falcone asked.

'I think so. Most of these deaths weren't accidental. There was some kind of ritual going on. The guy who wrote this is trying to work out what that might be.'

'Something to do with Dionysus?' Costa asked. 'I don't get it. That's Pompeii. We went there on a field trip when I was at school.'

'So did we,' Peroni added. 'First time I ever got drunk.'

'Jesus,' she said. 'What a pair you two make. Yes, Nic. The Villa of Mysteries is at Pompeii and, according to this guy, who is, I am reliably informed, the world's living expert on the Dionysian mysteries, it is important. But it wasn't the only one. Pompeii was the provinces. Suburbia if you like. It was small time compared to what went on elsewhere. In Rome in particular. Ask yourself. Who's got the biggest churches? Us or them?'

Falcone sighed. 'Point taken. And this book says what exactly?'

She waved the cover at them. Costa glanced at the terrified woman there. It seemed such a modern image. 'Dionysus was a cult imported from Greece. You probably know him better as Bacchus.'

'Booze?' Peroni wondered. 'You mean this is the result of a drunken orgy or something?'

She grimaced. 'You watch too many bad movies. Dionysus was about much more than drink. This was a secret cult, banned as a pagan one even before Christianity because of what went on. Not easy to stamp out either. There were Dionysian rituals going on in Sicily and Greece until a few centuries ago. Maybe they're still happening and we just don't know about them.'

Falcone stared pointedly at his watch. 'My jurisdiction ends at Rome.'

'OK, OK,' she conceded. 'Rome.'

Teresa Lupo opened the book at a page marked with a yellow sticky note. 'Here are some pictures, from a place in Ostia. Still suburbia, but around the time this girl was put in the bog this was Rome's harbour town and a sight bigger than Pompeii. Lots of rich people. Lots of substantial villas on the edge of town, including this one . . .'

She pointed at an outline on the map then turned the page. There was a series of photographs of an old, churchlike building, then some interior shots of wall paintings. One of the scenes was the image from the front of the book. The rest was a frieze of dancing figures, human and mythical, dancing, coupling.

'Pompeii has a much fuller set of wall paintings. What they seem to show – at least the book claims – is the initiation ceremony for the cult. Not that anyone much understands them these days. The point is that they were all over the place. At Ostia. In Rome too. Probably with the big one hidden somewhere not far from the centre. The holy of holies.'

'What he calls the Palace of Mysteries?' Costa asked.

'Exactly,' she said, nodding. 'Which is probably where this poor kid died. I took a good look at the dirt beneath her fingernails. It's not estuarial. It didn't come from Ostia. It could be from anywhere in central Rome.'

Peroni looked lost. 'You mean these were temples or something? And they kept them hidden?'

'Not quite. More like fun palaces in the dark they could use when the time came.'

Peroni put his finger on the page and traced over the paintings. 'Use to kill people?'

Teresa shrugged. 'I dunno. You read this book and sometimes you think the guy is sure of what he's saying, sometimes he's making it up. What he thinks is that there could be bad consequences if the initiation went wrong. There was some kind of mysterious act which had to be performed with a representative of the god. Sexual, probably. Everyone got doped up to the nines so I imagine most of the time they didn't have a problem getting their way with these kids. But if the initiate backed off . . .' She didn't need to say the rest.

'She a virgin?' Peroni asked.

'I told you. I put off performing a full autopsy until I could get some idea of the date. Now we know I can pass it on to the archaeology people at the university. They can try to find out. From what I've seen it's going to be impossible to tell. Sorry. Do you need to know?'

'Maybe not,' he admitted. 'Look. Like I said, I'm no detective. But it seems to me there's not a lot of meat here. Could be it's all coincidence. Also – and I hate to point this out – that dating stuff just dates the dirt beneath her fingernails. Don't date her.'

'I know, I know,' she said firmly. 'Stay with it. I'm building a case here. You see what's in her hand?'

The girl was holding some kind of wand or standard about a metre long, clutched to her side, the head disappearing under her arm. At the base was a protuberance of some kind, round and knobbly.

'This is exactly what the book describes, and that isn't conjecture. It's based on historical sources. I took samples. It's made from several bound stems of fennel. At the top there's a pine cone, wound into the staff. The thing's called a "thyrsus". It's standard issue for Dionysian rituals. Look—'

She turned the pages of the book. There was a picture of a female figure, half dressed, holding the same kind of object, waving it in the face of a satyr, half man, half goat, leering at her.

'It's used for protection. And purification.'

'Have you dated that?' Falcone asked.

'Radiocarbon costs,' she snapped. 'You want me to spend time and money on this instead of something fresh off the street?'

Falcone nodded at the book. 'Just asking. You've worked very hard, doctor. Congratulations.'

He still didn't seem that interested.

'There's one thing left,' she said quickly, as if she thought they might leave the room any moment.

'That is?'

'They found it with a metal detector, remember. How? There's nothing metallic on her body. No necklace. No rings. No armlet.'

She wanted them to come up with an answer. It didn't happen. Teresa Lupo went back to the desk and returned with an X-ray of the head. She placed it on the cadaver's stomach. 'See?'

It was a straight-on image of the girl's skull. There was a bright object there, quite small, in the lower third.

'A coin beneath the tongue,' she said. 'To pay Charon, the ferryman who took the dead across the Styx to the Underworld. Without it you never got there. I didn't need any book to tell me that. I loved mythology when I was a kid.'

To Nic Costa's surprise, Falcone was abruptly animated by this discovery.

'You've got it? The coin?'

'Not yet,' she said. 'I was waiting for you.'

'Please—'

'Hey! I have other work you know.'

They did know that. They also knew how much she liked to be right, and seen to be proved so.

She looked at the face, the half open mouth, the perfect stained teeth. Then she examined the X-ray again, wondering where to start.

Teresa Lupo picked up a scalpel and, with one careful, clean movement, made an incision in the girl's left cheek, level with her lower lip. She put the scalpel down then picked up a small pair of shiny steel forceps.

'They dated coins in those days. If this one's anywhere in the range I outlined I expect you gentlemen to buy me dinner, one by one, in a restaurant of my choosing.'

'It's a deal,' Falcone replied immediately.

'Ooh!' Teresa squealed with a fake girlish glee as she exercised the forceps, making sure they would do the job. 'Dinner with cops! Aren't I the lucky one? What will we talk about? Football? Sex? Experimental philosophy?'

The forceps entered the slice in the cheek. She turned the instrument deftly, probing, feeling, pushing. Then the arms clamped on something.

'Pass me one of those silver trays,' she said to Costa. 'This is going to cost you guys plenty.'

Slowly, she retrieved the forceps from the girl's mouth and placed an item in the dish. Then she poured some fluid into the pan and cleaned the thing gently with a tiny brush.

The object was a small coin which came up quite shiny. It was silver on the edges with a bronze centre, though both colours looked as if they were slowly transforming to copper through the stain of the peat. It was also familiar.

Teresa Lupo pulled over a large magnifying glass on a swan neck stand. The four of them crowded around the lens, peering at the thing. She turned it over. Twice. Just to make sure.

Peroni stood next to her, shaking his head. 'My boy used to collect coins until someone told him it was uncool,' he said. 'I helped him sort out his collection. Bought him one of those, mint condition. Dated the first year they issued it, 1982. Five hundred lire. You know something? It was the world's first bi-metallic coin. No one had made one that was silver on the outside and bronze in the centre before. One other thing. If you look at the obverse, above the picture of the Quirinale, you'll see the value written in Braille. That was unique too.'

No one was really listening. Peroni bristled. 'Hey. Stupid old cop is sharing information here. Are you taking notes or am I speaking for my own benefit?'

'Shit,' Teresa Lupo whispered, glaring at the coin. '*Shit.*'

'You mean the body's been in the peat for not much more than twenty years?' Costa asked.

'Not even that,' Falcone said.

They all turned to look at him. The inspector had returned to his briefcase and now had a folder in his hands. He opened it and took out a photograph. It was a portrait of a girl in her teens. She had long fair hair down to her shoulders. She was smiling for the camera.

He placed the photograph on the cadaver's chest, over the X-ray of the skull. The features were identical.

'You knew?' She couldn't believe this, couldn't contain her amazement and anger. Peroni was chuckling, his shoulders rising and falling as if they were plugged into the mains.

Falcone was bent over, examining something on the girl's left shoulder. A mark. A tattoo maybe.

'Just guessing to begin with. You have to remember, doctor. I didn't get back from holiday till yesterday. I hardly had the time to dig this . . .' he waved the case folder, ' . . . out of the vaults.'

'You *knew*?' she repeated.

He bent down and looked at the mark on the girl's skin. Costa did the same. It was a tattoo, circular, about the size of the coin: a howling, insane face with huge lips and long dreadlocks.

'It's supposed to be a mask from an imperial Roman comedy,' Falcone said. 'Dionysus was the god of theatre too. This was used by the Dionysian cults. You deserve that dinner, doctor. I'll honour the bet. You were almost there. Just a couple of millennia out.'

Teresa Lupo pointed a stubby index finger at the inspector's chest. 'You *knew*? Eat your fucking dinner on your own.'

'So be it,' he answered. They watched him. Falcone couldn't take his eyes off the tattoo. There was something going on inside the inspector's head, something he didn't seem much inclined to share.

'You'll cancel the press conference,' he said.

'You bet,' she grumbled mutely. 'But what should I say?'

'Make an excuse. Say you've got a headache. Tell them we don't have the people, what with this flu thing and all. It's the truth anyway.' He picked up the photograph from the dead girl's chest and put it back in the envelope. Costa couldn't help but notice Falcone hadn't even let them see a name.

'Sir?' Costa asked, puzzled.

'Mr Costa?' Falcone's sparkling eyes gave nothing away. 'It's so nice to have you back with us.'

'What do you want us to do?'

'Catch a few crooks I imagine. Go help out down the Campo. There's a lot of pickpockets there at the moment.'

'I meant about this.'

Falcone took a final look at the corpse. 'About this . . . nothing. The poor kid's been lying in the mud for sixteen years. A day or two won't make much difference.'

He rounded on all three of them. 'And let me make one thing clear. I don't want you breathing a word of what we have here to anyone. Not in this building. Not outside. I'll call you when I need you.'

They watched him walk purposefully out of the room. Teresa Lupo stared at the body, her big, pale face a picture of misery and disappointment.

'I had it all worked out,' she moaned. 'I knew exactly what happened. I talked to these academics and people. Jesus . . .'

'You heard him,' Costa said. 'You did well. He meant it.'

Teresa was running her fingers over the dead girl's mahogany skin. She didn't need Nic Costa's sympathy.

She was over her disappointment already. It had been displaced by something new, something potentially more interesting.

The cadaver on her dissecting table was no longer a historical artefact. It was a murder victim. It required her attention.

Costa looked at the silver scalpel in her hand then looked at Peroni.

'The Campo it is,' he said and the older man nodded back in agreement.

'I guess there really is no rush,' Peroni said in the car. 'I just wish Leo would talk to us some more. I hate getting left in the dark.'

Costa shrugged. He knew Falcone well enough not to let this bug him. 'In his own time. It's always like that.'

'I know. He'd be a disaster in vice. You got to take people with you all the way there.' Peroni must have watched Falcone work his way up the ranks. Their relationship was hard to fathom, half amiable, half suspicious. That was hardly unusual. Falcone was a smart, sound cop, one who trod a fine line sometimes when he felt a case merited it. He'd won plenty of respect for his talents. He was straight, unbending on occasion. But he didn't give a damn about popularity. Sometimes, Costa thought, Falcone actually liked the antipathy and near-hatred he generated. It made tough decisions easier to take.

Peroni lit a cigarette and blew the smoke out of the window. 'You asked Barbara Martelli out yet?'

Where did that one come from, Costa wondered. 'Haven't found the right occasion.'

Peroni stared at him with a face that said: *are you kidding me?*

'I'm not ready. OK?'

'At least that's honest. How long's it been since you went with a woman? You don't mind my asking. We have these conversations in vice all the time.'

'I guess in vice you measure it in hours,' Costa answered without thinking and immediately wished he could bite back his words. Peroni's face fell. He looked hurt.

'I'm sorry, Gianni. I didn't mean that. It just slipped out.'

'At least we're on first-name terms now. I guess that means we can say what we want to each other.'

'I didn't—'

'It's OK,' Peroni interrupted. 'Don't apologize. You have every right to tell me when I'm acting like a jerk.'

Peroni was more complicated than he liked to appear. That much Costa had come to understand. Some part of him wanted to talk about what had happened too, even if he felt he ought to make a play of avoiding the subject.

'Why did you do it, Gianni? I mean you got a family. Then you go with a hooker.'

'Oh come on! It happens every day. You think it's just single men get horny from time to time?'

'No. I just wouldn't have thought it of you.'

Peroni let out a deep sigh. 'Remember what I told you once? Everyone's got that dark spot.'

'Not everyone lets it out.'

The big, ugly head shook slowly. 'Wrong. One way

or another they do. Whether they know it or not. Why did I do it? Won't a simple answer do? The girl was damn beautiful. Slim and young and blonde. And young. Or did I mention that? Maybe she made me feel alive again. When you've been married twenty years you forget what that's like. Yeah, before you say it, so does your wife. Blame me twice over.'

Costa said nothing, worried he might cross the line and destroy the delicate bonds the two of them had managed to build over the last few weeks.

Peroni's damaged face wrinkled some more in puzzlement at his silence. 'Oh. I get it. You're thinking, "Who does this hideous bastard think he is? Casanova?" '

'You don't look like the great Latin Lover. That's all. If you don't mind me saying so.'

'Really?'

'Really.' Costa knew what was going on here. He wondered if he dared ask.

'Are you calling me ugly? That happens from time to time, Nic. I have to tell you I don't like it.'

'No . . .' Costa stuttered. He took a good look at that battered face. 'I was just wondering.'

'What?'

'What the hell happened?'

Gianni Peroni burst out laughing. 'You kill me. You really do. In all the time I've worked here you are the first person who's come out and asked that question direct. Can you believe that?'

'Yes,' Costa said hesitantly. 'I mean, it's a personal question. And most people wouldn't like the idea that you could take it the wrong way.'

He waved a huge friendly hand in Costa's face. 'What

the hell do you mean a personal question? You guys have to look at this ugly mug every day you come to work. I got to live with it. This . . .' he pointed a fat index finger at his face, ' . . . is just a fact of life.'

Costa felt he'd made progress of a kind anyway. 'So . . . ?'

Peroni chuckled again and shook his head. 'Unbelievable. Just between the two of us, OK? This goes no further? No one knows this. Most of the guys out there think I look like this through getting into a fight with a hood or something. They wonder what the other guy looks like too. I'm happy with things that way.'

Costa nodded his agreement.

'A cop did this to me,' Peroni said. 'I was twelve years old. He was the village cop. I was the village bastard. I mean that literally. My mamma worked for the couple who owned the lone bar in town and got knocked up after the fair some time. She always was a little naïve. So I spend twelve years being the village bastard, getting the village bastard treatment all those years. Spat on. Beaten up. Laughed at in school. Then one day the moronic kid in the same class who was my principal tormentor went just a touch too far. Said something about my mamma. And I kicked the living shit out of him. First time I ever did that. You want the truth? It's the *only* time I ever did that. Don't need to now. I just look at people and go, *Boo* . . .'

Costa thought about it. 'I can believe that.'

'Good. The stupid thing was, I forgot the moron I was beating up was the village cop's kid. So Daddy comes along, and Daddy's been drinking. One thing leads to another. He gets done with the strap and he's still not happy. So he goes and gets these metal things he carries, just for protection you understand, and he puts them on his fists.'

Peroni watched the cars go by out of the window. 'I woke up in hospital two days later, face like a pumpkin, Mamma by my side. I couldn't see a thing. The first thing she says is, don't even think of telling anyone. He's the village cop. Second thing she says is, don't look in the mirror for a while.'

Costa sighed. 'You could have told someone.'

Peroni gave him a frank look. 'You're a city kid, aren't you?'

'I guess so.'

'It shows. Anyway, a couple of weeks later I come out of hospital and I notice things are different. People look at me and suddenly their eyes are on their shoes. A couple cross the road when they see me walking down the street. You know the worst thing of all? I was helping my uncle Fredo sell those pigs at weekends then. I went back to it. What else could you do? After a while he comes to me, tears in his eyes, and fires me. No one buys food from someone with a face like this. That was the worst thing of all at the time. I didn't want to do anything else when I grew up except raise those pigs and sell them every weekend. Those guys . . . they all look *so* happy. But—'

He folded his arms, leaned back in the passenger seat, and glanced at Costa to make sure this point went in. 'That was not to be. I became a cop instead. What else do you do? Partly to spite that old bastard who beat me up. But mainly, if you want to know, to even things up a little. I've never laid a finger on anyone in this job.

Never would, not unless there was a very good reason and in more than twenty years I never found one. It's a question of balance.'

Costa didn't know how to respond. 'I'm sorry, Gianni.'

'Why? I got over it years ago. You, on the other hand, have spent the last six months going loopy inside a bottle of booze. I'm sorry for you, kid.'

Maybe he deserved that. 'Fine. We're even now.'

Peroni was peering at him with those sharp, all-seeing eyes. 'I will say this once, Nic. I am starting to like you. A part of me says that I will miss this time we're spending together. Not that I wish to prolong it you understand. But let me offer some sincere advice. Stop trying to fool yourself you're something special. You're not. There are millions of people out there trying to cope with fucked-up lives. We're just two in the crowd. And after that little lecture . . .' he said, stretching up in his seat as Costa parked the car in a tiny space off the road by the ghetto, ' . . . let me make a request.'

Peroni looked into his face, hopefully. 'Cover for me. I got something important to do. I'll meet you back here at two.'

Costa didn't know what to say. Bunking off for a couple of hours wasn't unknown. He just didn't think Peroni was the kind of cop to do it.

'Anything I should know about?' he asked.

'Just personal. It's my daughter's birthday tomorrow. I wanted to send her something that might make her think her father is not quite the jerk she's come to believe. You can cope with the Campo on your own. Just don't pick on any big bastards, OK?'

Leo Falcone was reading the file on his desk, trying to focus on the case. He didn't want to rush anything. Going public too quickly only alerted those he would wish to interview, though given how leaky the Questura had proved of late they probably knew by now anyway. The pause would also give him time to turn his mind back towards work after a solitary two weeks spent at a luxury beachside hotel in Sri Lanka. He had met no one of interest, and had scarcely sought the company of others. It was an unsatisfactory, tedious respite from routine that left him mildly disturbed. He was glad to be back at his desk and with a challenging case to tackle.

Even so, a rare note of self-doubt lurked at the back of his mind. Falcone had, to his surprise, been aware of his own loneliness during the long, drab holiday. It was now five years since his divorce. There had been women in that time, attractive, interesting women. Yet none had stimulated him sufficiently to take the relationship beyond the routine round of meals, the cinema, and the physical necessity of the bedroom. He'd come to realize the previous night – when, completely out of character, he'd consumed an entire bottle of a wonderful, deeply perfumed and expensive Brunello – that there had been only two real lovers in his life: his English wife Mary, who was now back in London, pursuing a legal career; and the woman who was the reason Mary left, Rachele D'Amato.

Here, in the light of day, obscured only slightly by the remains of a hangover, lay a curious coincidence. In Sri Lanka he had thought consciously about these two women for the first time in several years. When he returned to Italy, it was to find them ready to re-enter his life. Mary had written to invite him to her marriage, to another rich English lawyer, at a country house in Kent. He would find an excuse and decline. She would, he thought, expect this. The invitation came out of politeness, nothing more. His infidelity had wounded her deeply, and her abrupt departure, without the slightest attempt at reconciliation, hurt him more than he realized at the time. Or perhaps the pain came from Rachele D'Amato, who had abandoned him with the same degree of certainty Mary had shown, and rather less grace, the moment he became free.

He'd never forgiven himself for allowing these events to happen. He never forgave them either. And now Mary was getting married, while Rachele was a successful lawyer turned investigator, steadily working her way up the ranks of the DIA, an organization which, thanks to the case Teresa Lupo had placed before him, Falcone knew he must soon approach.

His feelings about the DIA went beyond the recent sting that had wrecked Gianni Peroni's career, an exercise that was more about public relations than the defeat of organized crime. They stretched back years. There was scarcely a cop in the Questura who didn't hear those three initials and feel a small sense of dread. He realized, the moment the dead girl's identity became plain, that there could be no avoiding them. Strictly speaking he should have acted already, as soon as he realized the kind of people he would have to interview.

Falcone stared at the pages and pages of reports and tried to remember what the case was like when it was fresh. Sixteen years before he'd just been a plain detective. The inspector in charge was Filippo Mosca, an old-fashioned Rome cop who walked both sides of the track and, like many a man of his generation, made little effort to hide his friendship with people who were best avoided.

Eleanor Jamieson was reported missing on 19 March, a full two days after her American stepfather last saw her. She had just turned sixteen and had been living in Vergil Wallis's rented villa on the Aventine hill since arriving from New York the previous Christmas. The girl was English. Her mother had left Wallis a year before, after a marriage that lasted just six months. Falcone never could find out why. Nor would he. The woman killed herself in New York ten days after the disappearance of her daughter.

It was, Falcone recalled, a maddening case. Wallis was a curious man: educated, almost scholarly, yet black and originally from the ghetto. He was in his mid-forties then, vague about his business and his antecedents, a reluctant witness, unforthcoming about the girl's movements, what friends she had made in the city, any motive she might have to run away. The man had no good reason to explain why it took two days to report her absence, simply pleading that meetings had called him out of Rome. He had even seemed reluctant to hand over the few photographs he possessed, which revealed a young, naïve-looking girl, very pretty, with shoulder-length blonde hair and a ready smile. And, on her shoulder, fully revealed in a picture taken a day before she vanished, the curious tattoo, for which Wallis had no explanation. It had fascinated Falcone from the moment he saw it. There was a craze for tattoos at the time. All the rock stars and the hotshots in the movie world were doing it. But they didn't have anything like this etched into their skin. The ancient hieroglyph looked wrong on the girl, more like a branding mark than some badge of fashion.

It seemed out of character too, as much as any of them could judge. According to Wallis, Eleanor had bummed around Italy for a while then spent two weeks on an intensive Italian course at a language school near the Campo. She was an intelligent girl, with good exam grades. There was talk of her going to study at an art college in Florence later that year. She had few acquaintances beyond the school and, if Wallis was to be believed, no boyfriend, current or ex. Nothing they could turn up explained why she should suddenly disappear. She had, her stepfather said, simply set out for school on her scooter around nine on the morning of 17 March and never arrived.

It only took a couple of days for Mosca's team to acquire the sickening sense of powerlessness that comes with abduction cases. No one had seen Eleanor on her way into the city. A re-creation of her supposed last movements on TV failed to elicit a single reliable response from the public. It was as if she had existed one moment and then been abruptly removed from the face of the earth.

All along Falcone wanted to scream foul. Because something stank to high heaven and pretty soon he had an inkling what it was. Mosca had taken him to one side on the third morning and told him, in confidence, what he'd heard the previous night from a friend in the Foreign Ministry. Vergil Wallis was not, as he claimed, a straight-forward businessman from LA who loved Rome so much he was thinking of buying a second home in the city. He was a high-up figure in the West Coast mob, a black fixer who'd risen through the ranks to live in

Italy half the year for his own crooked reasons. Interpol had been following Wallis for years and steadfastly failing to bring him to justice on a wide range of counts, from racketeering to murder. Nor had the carabinieri, who had been assigned to Wallis's case, fared much better.

This was shortly before the creation of the DIA. Then, as now, the civilian state police maintained an uneasy rivalry with the carabinieri, who were part of the military. The lines of responsibility were, at best, blurred and on occasion deliberately murky. Privately Falcone was in agreement with the growing number of critics calling for a single, unified state police force. It was a logical, inevitable solution. But this was judged a heresy by those in charge of both organizations, and one that could cost a man his job. He was careful never to make his views known. They were, in any case, irrelevant. Soon the DIA came along, adding another layer of complexity to the business of chasing the swelling tide of crime that seemed to grow stronger with every passing year.

And Vergil Wallis was still free. So much for progress.

Mosca quietly closed the case of Eleanor Jamieson, marking it unworthy of further investigation without new evidence. Wallis's relationship with the Italian mobsters was far from easy. Some stories, garnered at great expense and with no small risk to those who supplied them, placed him in the role of criminal diplomat, a go-between trying to ensure the interests of his own particular buddies meshed with those of the Sicilians. It made sense to Falcone. The West Coast mob that Wallis represented was only loosely connected to the Italian organizations in the USA. There was plenty of room for misunderstandings. The bosses had learned long ago that pacts and partnerships, even with those they hated, put more dollars in their bank accounts than ruthless competition and turf wars. Money was what mattered these days. No one went to the barricades over honour any more. These were practical times in which cash was king.

Falcone had been present at three different interviews with Wallis and still couldn't work out what to make of the man. The American was thoughtful and articulate, quite unlike any crook Falcone had ever met. He was well read. He knew more about ancient Roman history than some Italians. The word was that he'd been groomed for the role of diplomat for years, put through law college after rising through the black ranks in Watts. It wasn't hard to see him smoothing out the rough edges of a relationship which must always have hovered on the brink of disaster.

There was, however, one fundamental problem. If the street gossip was right, he had been given as his prime contact Emilio Neri, a brutal thug who had worked his way from the public housing slums of Testaccio to the pinnacle of the Rome mob through the vicious and heartless disposal of anyone who stood in his way. Neri now sat on the boards of opera houses in Italy and America. He lived in an elegant house in the Via Giulia, behind an army of servants and bodyguards. It was a place Falcone knew only too well from his many futile visits there. The old crook had a carefully cultivated outward appearance of elegance, a mask of deceit worn for the public. It only fooled those who were too stupid or too scared to realize the truth. Almost from the moment Falcone had joined the force he had followed Neri's career, and with good reason. The man habitually bribed any cop who would take his money, simply to put him on side. Falcone himself had turned down a thinly disguised offer of money from one of Neri's hoods in the middle of an investigation into a protection racket involving some of the smaller shops off the Corso, an assignment Filippo Mosca had closed down just when it was making progress. Three cops who were known to be on Neri's payroll had been jailed for corruption in the past decade. Not one named him as the source of the largesse found in their bank accounts. They preferred prison to the consequences of his fury.

What set Neri apart from his fellow hoods was the obsessive system of personal control he wielded over his own family. Most bosses of his stature had long since ceased to dirty their hands with the day-to-day business of running a crime organization. Neri never stepped back from the front line. It was in his blood from the old days in Testaccio. He liked it too much. Word had it he still enforced his rule in person from time to time, with the same harsh violence he'd employed as a young hood. Maybe he got one of his junior thugs to hold the poor bastard down while Neri went about his work. Falcone had looked into the old crook's dead, grey eyes often enough to understand the pleasure it would give him.

He read the last page of the report and, knowing the volatile and untrustworthy Neri as he did, understood every word. It said that Wallis and Neri had, initially, proved the best of friends. Their families had dined with each other. Six weeks before Eleanor Jamieson died, she and Wallis had spent some time on holiday with the Neri family on one of their vast estates in Sicily. Some undisclosed form of business had been done. The Americans were happy. So were the mob.

Then, around the time of the girl's disappearance, a coldness had entered the relationship. There had been reports that, while in Sicily, Wallis had gone over Neri's head to talk to some of the senior bosses there, something Neri would soon learn about. There was rumour of a drug deal that had gone wrong, leaving the Americans out of pocket and angry. Neri never could resist taking people to the limit. He skimmed every last dollar that went through his hands, even after his 'legitimate' cut.

Some huge row took place between the two men. One informer even said they came to blows. After that, they were both in trouble with their bosses. Neri was told bluntly he was losing the job of linkman with the Americans. Wallis got a dressing-down too, though he continued to live in Rome for half of the year, with precious little to do except save face. It was an uneasy truce. One of Wallis's lieutenants was murdered two months later, his throat cut in a car close to a Testaccio brothel. Not long after, a cop on Neri's payroll was found dead in what had been made to look like suicide. Falcone wondered, was there a link here? Would the semi-mummified body of a sixteen-year-old girl raise these old ghosts from their graves? And if it did, how different would the world be now, with the DIA peering inquisitively over his shoulder every step of the way?

Leo Falcone looked at his watch. It was just after twelve. He thought of all the careful protocols which surrounded cases involving known mobsters. Then he took out his diary and placed the call.

'Yes?'

Rachele D'Amato's cool, distanced voice still had the power to move him. Falcone wondered briefly whether he was phoning her for the sake of the job or for more personal reasons. Both, he thought. Both were legitimate too.

'I wondered whether you'd be there. Everyone else I call right now seems to be at home, sick in bed.'

She paused. 'I don't get to bed as much as I used to, Leo. Sick or not.'

There was a deliberate, slow certainty to her voice. Falcone understood what she was saying, or thought he did. No one else had filled her life after the affair ended. He knew that already. He'd checked from time to time.

'I was wondering if you had time for lunch,' he said. 'It's been too long.'

'Lunch!' She sounded pleased. 'What a surprise. When?'

'Today. The wine bar we used to go to. I was there the other evening. They have a new white from Tuscany. You should try it.'

'I don't take wine at lunchtimes. That's for cops. Besides, I have an appointment. I have to run. We've got people sick everywhere too.'

'Tonight then. After work.'

'Work stops for you in the evenings these days, Leo?' she sighed. 'What happened?'

'Nothing,' he said. 'I just thought . . .'

He felt tongue-tied, embarrassed. She'd always said it was the work that drove them apart after Mary left. It wasn't. It was him. His possessiveness. His passion for her, which was never quite returned.

'Don't apologize,' she said wryly. 'It doesn't stop for me either. Not any more.'

'I'm sorry.'

'There's no need,' she said, and there was a new note

in her voice. A serious, professional one. 'You have a body. Is it Wallis's girl?'

'Yes,' he sighed, inwardly livid, wondering immediately who had talked.

'Don't sound so cross, Leo. I have a job to do too.'

The corpse had been lying in the morgue for two weeks. Anyone could have seen the tattoo and put two and two together. It would be impossible to find out who had blabbed.

'Of course. You're very good these days, Rachele.'

'Thank you.'

He wondered why fate had made him fall in love with two lawyers. Why not women who were a little less curious? A little more forgiving?

'Then we'll meet,' she announced. 'I'll call you. I have to go now.'

She didn't even ask if it was convenient for him. Rachele never changed.

'Leo?'

He knew what she'd say. 'Yes.'

'This is professional. Nothing more. You do understand that?'

Leo Falcone understood, though it didn't stop him hoping.

Costa crossed the busy road and headed for the Campo dei Fiori, reminding himself he used to live here and there were memories, important ones, pieces of his personality stamped on the place. He missed the Campo from time to time. He was an innocent when he lived here, young and unbruised by the world. There'd been fleeting relationships, brief flings which Gianni Peroni probably wouldn't count as love affairs at all. There was the place too. The cobbled *piazza* was grubby at the best of times. The market attracted too many tourists. The prices were higher than elsewhere. Nevertheless, it was a genuine part of Rome, a living, human community that had never been dislodged from its natural home. As always, he got a small rush of pleasure when he walked along the Via dei Giubbonari and came out onto the square. The stalls were still doing good business, selling spring greens, chicory, calabrese and cavolo nero alongside vibrant oranges from Sicily, stored over the cold months and now fit for little more than juice. The mushroom stand was piled high with all kinds of funghi, fresh chiodini, dried porcini. The handful of fishmongers tucked into one corner had scallops and giant prawns, turbot and sacks of fresh mussels. He worked his way through, picking up an etto of wild rocket and the same of agretti for later. Then he added a chunk of parmesan from the lone alimentari van.

'We got good prosciutto, Mr Policeman,' the woman said, recognizing him. 'Here . . .'

She held out a pink strand, waving it in front of his face. If he ate meat, Nic Costa thought he'd be hard pressed to find much better in Rome. 'I'll pass.'

'Vegetarianism is an unnatural fad,' the woman declared. 'You come back here one day when you've got time and we'll go through this in some detail. You worry me.'

'Please,' Costa said. 'I have enough people worrying about me just now.'

'Means there's something wrong.'

He took the prosciutto anyway. When she was out of sight he gave it to the scruffy young boy belonging to the Kosovan who was always begging in the square, playing an ancient violin badly. Then he handed the father a ten-euro note. It was a ritual he'd forgotten somewhere along the line too: twice a day, every day, as his late father had always told him. Being back in the Campo reminded him why it was necessary. He'd been spending too much time on his own, closeted inside the farmhouse on the outskirts of the city, thinking. Sometimes you had to get out and let life happen to you.

He'd just pushed his way through the crowd at Il Forno and was taking a bite of pizzetta bianca, salty and straight from the oven, when he saw what was happening. Leo Falcone was right. The Campo attracted tourists, and with the tourists came trouble. Pickpockets. Conmen. Worse sometimes. The police always had people on duty there, in uniform and out. The carabinieri liked the place too, parking their bright shiny Alfas in the most awkward of places and then lounging on the bonnets, eyeing the crowds through expensive sunglasses, trying to look cool in their dark, well-pressed uniforms.

Costa made a point of avoiding the carabinieri as much as possible. There was enough rivalry inside the Questura itself without extending it to these soldiers masquerading as cops. The demarcation lines were dimly drawn between this branch of the army and the civilian police. They could arrest the same people he did, and in the same places. Most of the time it was simply a matter of who got there first. There was an old joke: the good-looking ones joined the carabinieri for the uniform and the women, the smart and the ugly ones went into the state police because that was all they could get. It wasn't all exaggeration either.

A couple of carabinieri were in the Campo now, standing stiffly upright by their vehicle as a slender blonde woman harangued them in mangled Italian, wagging her finger in their faces, holding a large, portrait-size photograph in her left hand.

'Don't get involved,' Costa said to himself, and wandered over towards them in any case. The woman was livid. She knew a few good Italian swear words too. Costa took a bite of his bread and eavesdropped on what was going on.

Then he looked at the photo in the woman's hand and something cold ran down his back, made him shiver so hard the pizzetta dropped straight from his fingers.

This was crazy. He knew it. The face in the photo reminded him of the picture Leo Falcone had thrown onto the strange corpse on Teresa Lupo's dissecting table that morning. He thought of what he had seen there: an old image of a blonde-haired girl looking distinctly like the face he saw now, still at the beginning of her adult life, thinking there was nothing in the future but love and joy.

And it ain't necessarily so, an old, old song sang at the back of his head.

The carabinieri were the pick of the crop. Prize assholes, more interested in keeping their Ray-Bans clean than working out what seemed to have happened in front of their very noses. He thought he recognized one. But maybe not. They all looked the same. These two sounded the same as well, with their middle-class nasal voices.

They were sneering at the woman in front of them, exuding boredom.

'Are you listening to me?' she yelled.

'Do we have a choice?' one of them, the older one, Costa guessed, replied. He couldn't have been more than thirty.

'This,' she said, pointing at the photograph, 'is my daughter. She just got abducted. You idiots watched it and yawned.'

The younger uniform shot Costa a warning glance that said: *don't even think about getting involved*. Nic Costa didn't move.

The talkative one leaned back on the Alfa, shuffled his serge-clad backside further up the shiny bonnet, took out a packet of gum and threw a stick past his perfect teeth.

She stood in front of them, hands on her hips, full of fury. Costa glanced at the photo she was holding. They could have been sisters, but ten or fifteen years apart. The woman was a touch heavier. Her hair was a shade darker, more fair than her daughter's bright, almost artificial, blonde, practical cut.

He walked over, watched her trying to get her breath back, then, struggling to remember his English, asked, 'Can I help?'

'No,' the senior uniform said immediately. 'You can just walk away and mind your own business.'

She looked up at Costa, relieved to be talking English at last. 'You can get me a real policeman. That would be helping.'

He pulled out the badge. 'I am a real policeman. Nic Costa.'

'Oh fuck,' the uniform with the working mouth muttered behind him.

He got up off the car and stood upright in front of Costa. He was a lot taller. 'Her teenage daughter ran off with a boyfriend on a motorbike here. She thinks that counts as abduction. We think that sounds like some young kid looking for fun.' The Ray-Bans cast the woman a dead, black look. 'We think that's understandable. If you people playing amateur hour think otherwise, please yourself. Take her as a present from me. But just take her. I beg you.'

Costa managed to grasp her arm lightly at the elbow as it moved towards the man. Otherwise, he thought, the moron in the dark uniform would have been in for a shock.

'You saw this?' he asked them.

The younger one found his voice. 'Yeah, we saw it. Hard to miss it. You'd think the kid wanted the whole world to watch. You have any idea what you see if you hang around the Campo day and night? Caught a couple hard at it a few days ago. In broad daylight. And she wants us to start jumping up and down just because her daughter's got on the back of some guy's bike.'

The woman shook her head, as if somehow angry with herself, then stared in the direction of the Corso, the way the bike had gone, Costa guessed.

'It's not like her,' she said. 'I can't believe this is happening. I can't believe you people won't even listen.'

She closed her eyes. Costa wondered if she were about to cry. He looked at his watch. Peroni would be back at the car in forty minutes. There was time.

'Let me buy you a coffee,' he said.

She hesitated then put the photo back in the envelope.

There was a stack of others there, Costa saw, and he wondered again: was he really letting his imagination run away with him? The girl looked so like the teenager in Falcone's picture.

'You really are the same as these people?' she asked.

'No,' he replied, and made sure they heard every word. 'I'm a civilian. It's complicated. Even for us sometimes.'

She dropped the envelope into her bag and slung it over her shoulder. 'Then I'll take that coffee.'

'Nice job,' Costa said and patted the senior uniform on his serge arm. 'I love to see the carabinieri do public relations. Makes our life so much easier.'

Then, ignoring the torrent of curses directed at his back, he took her arm and led her away from them. She was pleased to go. When her face lost its taut anxiety she looked different. She'd dressed down, in jeans and an old, bleached denim jacket. But it didn't fit somehow. It was almost a disguise. There was something alluring, almost elegant underneath, something he couldn't quite put his finger on.

Costa led her round the corner, to a tiny café in an alcove behind the square. There were pots of creamed coffee on the counter, with people ladling spoonfuls into their cups to beef up the caffeine. She leaned on the counter, looking as if she came into the place every day.

'My name's Miranda Julius,' she said. 'And this is crazy. Maybe *I'm* crazy. You'll regret ever asking me here.'

Costa listened as she told her story, slowly, methodically, with the kind of care and attention he wished he heard more often.

'What's the matter?' she asked when the story was finished.

'Nothing.'

She stared into his face with a frank curiosity. 'I don't think so.'

He thought about what she'd said. Maybe the girl really had just run away with a boyfriend her mother had never even met. Maybe it was all as innocent as that. Her misgivings were based on intuition, not fact. She just felt something was wrong. He could understand why the assholes from the carabinieri just wanted to send her on her way.

'You said she came back yesterday with a tattoo.'

'Stupid, stupid. Just another reason for an argument. It wasn't supposed to be like this. It wasn't why we came to Italy.' She shook her head and it annoyed him he couldn't stop watching her. Close up she was older than he first thought. There were stress lines at the corner of her bright, intelligent blue eyes. But they just added character to a face that, when she was young, must have been too perfectly pretty for its own good. She looked like a model who'd later taken up manual labour or something just to make life more interesting, just to get a few scars.

'What was it like?'

'The tattoo? Ridiculous. What do you expect from a sixteen-year-old? She had it done a couple of days ago apparently. It was only yesterday she plucked up the courage to tell me, when the scars had healed. She said it was his idea. Whoever *he* is. But she liked it, naturally. Do you want to see?'

'What?'

She reached into her bag and withdrew the folder of

photos. 'I took a picture, just for the record. I had the film developed this morning which is why I have all this stuff with me. Taking pictures is what I do, by the way. Call it an obsession.'

She sorted through a set of photos then threw one on the table. It was a close-up of the girl's shoulder. There was the dark black ink of a tattoo at the top of her arm, and the howling face.

'You know what that is?' he asked.

'She told me. A theatre mask or something. If it was the Grateful Dead I might have understood. She wasn't that pleased when I said I wanted a shot of it for the record.'

She stared into his eyes with a sudden, determined frankness. 'I wasn't taking no for an answer. A tattoo. Jesus, if I'd done that when I was her age.' She hesitated. 'Mr Costa?'

'Nic.'

'What's wrong?'

'I don't know. I need to call some people. Give me a minute.'

She was starting to look scared.

'It's probably nothing,' he said, and heard how lame the words sounded.

Miranda Julius rented an apartment on the top floor of the Teatro di Marcello, the sprawling, fortress-like complex in the shadow of the Capitol Hill. She'd taken the place over the internet, she said, because the owner offered a good deal for the couple of months they needed, and it came with history. Though much changed over the centuries, the theatre was begun by Julius

Caesar, finished by his adoptive son Augustus and used variously as a fortress and a private palace before it was converted into private accommodations. The apartment looked out towards the river and Tiber Island. The steady drone of traffic was audible through the thick, double-glazed windows. Nic Costa had walked past this building countless times and never seen inside. Now he was there he didn't envy anyone who owned such a fancy address. It was too noisy, too detached from the city. It was in Rome, but not a part of it.

He was worried, too, that he'd over-reacted. He'd called in Falcone without discussing the matter with Peroni, which was probably a mistake. His partner had turned up only to find events shaping around him. Costa had risked Falcone's wrath even further by inviting Teresa Lupo along to join them. It seemed important. Teresa had read the book she kept quoting at them in the morgue. If he was right, she was the only one with immediate access to the research and insight they needed. Now the four of them sat listening to Miranda Julius, each wondering whether this could be coincidence.

Miranda Julius and her daughter Suzi had arrived in Rome one week before from London. She was a news photographer based there but working on assignment anywhere the agency sent her. Suzi lived with her grandmother, and had for most of her life. She was studying art at a local college. Her mother had taken her out of class for two months on a kind of 'get-to-know-you' holiday in Rome. Suzi had enrolled at the language school in the Piazza della Cancelleria for Italian lessons – the same school that the dead Eleanor Jamieson had attended. The two of them had begun a round of the

Rome galleries in their spare time. After a few days Suzi had made a friend. Not at the school, but somewhere nearby. A boy, she said, and one who was reluctant, at the time, to meet her mother, for reasons Miranda could only guess.

'How old is she?' Falcone asked.

'She was sixteen in December.'

'And you?' Falcone persisted.

Teresa risked glaring at him. Falcone was always direct with women, direct to the point of bullying.

'I'm thirty-three, inspector,' Miranda said immediately. 'Yes, I'm sure you're doing your arithmetic already. I was at school when I got pregnant. The father was a jerk. He was gone before she was born.' She had an upper-class English accent which sat uneasily with her crumpled, laid-back appearance. There was money somewhere. The apartment must have cost her plenty.

'Is this relevant?' she asked. 'I don't mind answering these questions but I would like to know why.'

'When you have a missing teenager anything could be relevant,' Costa said.

She turned away from Falcone and stared out of the big windows, out at the traffic roar. 'If she is missing. Perhaps I am overreacting. She could walk right in that door any moment and then how am I going to feel?' She watched them. This was a show of false confidence, Costa thought. There was fear in her face although he couldn't help wondering how responsible he was for placing it there. 'Will you please tell me why you're suddenly taking this so seriously?'

Falcone ignored the question. 'The tattoo. Tell us about that.'

The point of the question was lost on her. 'What's

there to tell? I noticed she'd been wearing long sleeves all the time. Then yesterday she just comes out and announces it. *He* told her to get one. He even suggested what it should be like, took her down some stupid tattoo parlour he knew. Paid for the thing, would you believe.'

'Does he have a name?' Costa wondered. 'Did she say where he lived?'

She shook her head. 'Apparently she wasn't ready for him to meet me. Not just yet.'

'Why? Did she give a reason?'

'She's still a kid. Young even for her years. She's still at the stage where a parent's embarrassing. What was I supposed to do? It wasn't as if she was spending the night with him or anything. And that's what's really strange. Look, I'm never going to win mother of the year contest. Most of the time Suzi's been growing up I've been in some shit part of the world photographing dead people. But I know my daughter. We can talk to each other. She wasn't sleeping with this boy. Not yet. It was as if they were waiting for something. In fact . . .'

She hesitated, wondering whether this was going too far, ' . . . she's never slept with anyone. She's a virgin. Her decision. Perhaps she looked at me and realized where it could get you.'

'Waiting for what?' Falcone asked.

'If I knew that I'd tell you,' she snapped. 'But I'm sure of one thing. When. It happens in two days' time. March the 17th. I heard her talking on the phone. Making arrangements to meet him. She sounded excited. Not that she'd talk to me about it, of course.'

Costa thought about the date. There were too many coincidences. 'Can we take a look in her room?'

'Feel free. It's the tidy one at the end.'

Falcone nodded at Costa. Teresa got up and followed him without being asked. The two of them wandered down the corridor, listening to Falcone's persistent drone continue to wear at Miranda Julius behind them. Costa couldn't help glancing into what he assumed was Miranda Julius's bedroom. It wasn't the tidy one. There were clothes scattered everywhere, a couple of professional-looking cameras, and a notebook computer, open, ready for work.

'Jesus,' Teresa groaned, when they were out of earshot. 'That man has the manners of a warthog. Can you believe he ever got married? What are we looking for, Nic? Why am I here for God's sake? It's a missing kid, isn't it?'

'I'm sorry. I thought you might like the opportunity to do a little cop work.'

She came to a halt, giving him a filthy look. 'I've got a corpse half finished back in the morgue. One that looks two thousand years old but only went in the ground sixteen years ago. I've got scientific problems with names you couldn't even pronounce. And you think I might "like the opportunity"?'

He opened the door to the girl's room. 'You want to look or don't you?'

'Lemme in.' She barged through and stared at the contents. Then she carefully closed the door behind her, not wanting to hear Falcone's voice, needing the privacy herself too. 'This is a teenager's room? Hell, my place is worse than this. Come to that . . .' She was thinking on her feet. Costa always liked to watch this. ' . . . how come the mother looks like that? Like the kid's sister? She's just a year younger than me, for God's sake, and if you walked her through the Questura every last jack-ass in there would be clutching at his groin making those heavy breathing noises you like so much.'

'They'd do that for you if they thought you wouldn't hit them.'

She glared at him. 'You couldn't stop staring at her. I couldn't help noticing that.'

He ignored the remark and went over to the table by the girl's single bed. There was a portfolio of photographs, black and white, printed in large format. He flicked through them: images from every war that had made the headlines in the last decade, Afghanistan, Palestine, Rwanda, places in Africa he couldn't begin to identify. Teresa came to join him.

'Is that what she meant?' she asked. 'When she said she went around photographing dead people?'

'She's a war photographer apparently.'

Corpses lay still on the ground, broken, bloody. Lost children, their eyes like saucers, stared back at them from the prints. 'Makes my job look kind of normal,' Teresa said. 'What drives you to that kind of work? Particularly when you've got a kid waiting at home?'

'I don't know.' Were the photos in the daughter's room because Suzi liked them? Or because she kept asking herself that question too. There was something complicated going on here, he thought.

'If I had a mother who took photos like that I'd maybe think of running away myself,' Teresa said carefully. 'You understand what I'm saying?'

He'd done plenty of missing kid inquiries. He knew what they felt like. And it wasn't like this. 'Of course I do. Half the time the kids aren't running towards something; they're running from it. Do you really think that's what's happening here? They're on holiday, Teresa. I've dealt with more runaways than I can remember. I don't recall one of them ever being a foreign tourist.'

'Point taken,' she said quietly. 'All the same—'

There was a pile of family snaps on the bedside table. Miranda Julius did take them all the time. Most were of the girl, looking lovely, happy. A few were taken by someone else, a stranger perhaps, or a waiter. There they were outside the Villa Borghese, on the Spanish Steps, eating pizza, laughing. Nic Costa looked at them and felt a pang of guilt. If he was right, Suzi Julius could be in big trouble right now, trouble that would bring her mother pain and possibly grief, whatever the outcome. Pictures spoke, they told stories. These two were close. They loved each other.

Teresa was staring at them too. 'Nice photographs,' she said simply. 'Nice to know she doesn't just snap dead people.'

For a moment he wondered: was there a small, bitter note inside Teresa Lupo's voice, whispering: *Look on with envy, because you'll never know this, you'll never feel the joy or the pain?*

'Can you imagine the feeling of responsibility?' she asked. 'What it must be like? Knowing someone else depends on you that much?'

He thought of his own dead father. He did know it, but only from the point of view of the dependant.

'You can see it on her face,' she continued. 'Whatever happened, whether there was a row or not, she's just sitting in there asking herself, "Is there something I could have done?"'

'It's always like that,' he said by way of an explanation. 'You're a pathologist. It's just that you don't see it.'

She toyed with one of the best photos: the two of

them laughing in a pale winter sun on the Ponte Sisto. 'Just because it's always like that doesn't make it any easier.'

'No.' He wondered if the resemblance was just his memory playing tricks. It was hard to compare this living, breathing kid with the mahogany corpse on the silver table. 'Does she really look like the dead girl? Or is that my imagination? Could the resemblance have sparked something? Made whoever was responsible sixteen years ago suddenly get the itch again?'

Teresa shrugged. 'Pushing it a bit, isn't it? She's blonde, pretty and young, if that's what you mean. From the pictures I'd say she's a bit on the thin side for most Italians. The mother's more our size. I wish. Nic, there are skinny blonde kids in Rome all the time. Why would it take sixteen years for him to run across one again? Face it. She's probably just one more runaway kid.'

He looked at the scattering of disjointed facts that faced them. 'I don't think so. It feels wrong. What the hell does it all mean? What does it say in that book you read? What exactly happens? Where do they get their victims from?'

'They're not victims, Nic,' she insisted. 'If you think that you're misreading everything. What happened to them was a privilege, even if it didn't feel like it at the time.'

'Unless it went wrong,' he reminded her.

'Unless it went wrong. But that can't have happened often. These girls were gifts. Some of them were slaves handed over by their owners. Some were daughters led there by their own fathers. They went through the ritual. They came out changed. Acolytes of the god, remember. That must have meant something.'

'But what?' he muttered. 'I still think this feels wrong.'

'Don't ask me. I'm a pathologist. Not an archaeologist. Or a cop. Or a psychic for that matter. Listen to yourself. *It feels wrong.* Are you really going to go back out there and tell Falcone that?'

Yet he felt sure she had seen some kind of link too. He could recognize it in her face, the bright spark of intelligence mixed with the dread of what that new information could mean.

'You're the only person I have right now who's researched all this. Please—'

She sat down and sighed. 'Don't do this to me, Nic. Don't take what I say as gospel. I don't like being imprecise. I'm trained for the opposite.'

'Just point me somewhere. I'll check it out. I promise. Tell me more about this ritual.'

'All I know is what I read. The ceremony was about the initiation of chosen girls into adulthood. On one particular day: 17 March. Sounds familiar? This was party time. There'd be men there, for sure. Priests, hangers-on, hoping they could get in on the fun. They drank, they danced, they swallowed every ancient Roman narcotic they could find. Then they did tricks to each other that would make a bunch of Hell's Angels walk out of the room feeling things were going a little too far. But this was about the girls. It was about giving them something they could use in adulthood. An advantage, maybe. Or some kind of membership of a club they could use later on.'

Costa stared at her, expecting more. 'Look,' she said. 'The man who wrote the thing said himself it's all guess-work. No one really knows what happened. All they know is that it got out of hand sometimes. It got bad enough for the Romans to ban it after a while. Long before the Christians came along with peace and love. It was all too much for them. They just carted off the organizers, put them to death somewhere, then relaunched the thing as some toned-down happy-clappy ceremony called the Liberalia. The same kind of stunt they pulled off to wind up with Christmas, if you recall. What preceded it? Who knows?'

He tried to make sense of this. 'So maybe two thousand years later someone's playing the same tricks? Using the same rituals?'

'We don't know that. All you've got is a tattoo. A date—'

'And a dead body.'

She tried to look hopeful. 'Which has no connection whatsoever with this girl. Be honest with yourself. The mother's probably right. The kid'll walk back in with a certain smile on her face thinking, "Thank Christ I got that out of the way". Jesus, a virgin at sixteen. What kind of lives do these people lead?'

He wasn't listening. He was doing the cop thing – opening drawers, looking into the contents, only with a touch more respect than most of them had. Nic Costa didn't up-end the things and turn the stuff out onto the floor. He just sifted carefully, as if he felt he were intruding.

'Do you realize,' she said out of nowhere, 'that if I meet someone now and we have a kid, when that kid is Suzi Julius's age I will be turned fifty? My God, who's the virgin here?'

Costa opened the bottom drawer, slid his hand beneath a neatly folded nightdress and stared up at her.

'What?' she said.

He took out a couple of items: obscure things, hidden, wrong.

One was the stalk of some plant, dried. A pine cone was attached to the thinner end, clinging clumsily to the stump, held there with tape. It looked like a schoolkid's craft project.

'She was working out how to make it,' Teresa said glumly.

'The name again?' he asked.

'Thyrsus.' She took it from him and sniffed the stem, her face deadly serious all of a sudden. 'That's fennel. Just like the one from the peat.'

'And this?' It was a plastic bag, full of seeds. Costa smelled the contents. 'It's not dope.'

'Not ordinary dope.'

She looked inside the bag, deeply miserable.

'Teresa?'

'I found something similar in the dead girl's pockets. I'm waiting for the full lab report. From my limited culinary expertise I'd say it's a mixture of herb seeds. Cumin. Coriander. Fennel again. Something hallucinogenic too maybe. Something fungal. Magic mushroom in all probability.'

He waited, wondering how she knew.

'According to the book it was part of the ritual. A small gift from the god. A thank you for what he was about to get in return.'

'Which was?'

She was silent.

'Guess,' he said. 'Give me some female intuition.'

'If you got it right? Paradise. You lost your virginity, probably to some temple creep wearing that spooky mask from the tattoo just to look the part. This was about ecstasy. Physical ecstasy. Mental, spiritual—'

She screwed up her eyes, thinking, remembering. 'The book said that, in public, 17 March was the day Roman boys attained their manhood. In private the women achieved some special kind of status too. At least the ones who were hanging round the cult.'

'And if you got it wrong? If you said no . . . ?'

'Then I guess you met one very angry god.' She hesitated. 'You really believe this poor kid's a part of all this? And she thinks she's just playing some game?'

He looked at the home-made wand and the little bag of seeds. 'It's a possibility, surely? We can't ignore it.'

'There's not enough here to push any of Falcone's buttons.'

She was right. These were just coincidental wisps of smoke in some distant, hazy mirrors. There was nothing to suggest an answer to the biggest question of all: why her? Why an English kid who'd only been in Rome a week?

They returned to the living room. Miranda Julius was red-faced and puffy-eyed. Falcone must have been working her hard. She looked at them as they came in and read their faces instantly.

'What is it?' she asked.

Costa showed her the thyrsus and the packet of seeds. 'Have you seen these before? Do you know what they are?'

She looked at them and shook her head. 'I've no idea. Where did you find them?'

'In her bedroom,' Costa replied.

'What *are* they?' She could be crying again soon.

'It could be coincidence,' Costa said.

'It could be anything,' Falcone interjected. 'We'll log your daughter's disappearance, Mrs Julius. We'll circulate her description. Usually these cases end with the child coming home. Usually they'll call. Probably today.'

'Look,' Teresa interjected, 'there's time. There are a lot of loose ends to work on here. If . . .'

Falcone stood up, glowering at her. She knew when to shut up.

'Doctor,' he grunted. 'Here's the deal. I don't go around cutting up bodies. You don't go around interrogating potential witnesses.'

Costa thought, for one moment, she might hit him and wondered what would happen after that. Instead Teresa went over to Miranda Julius, sat next to her on the sofa and put an arm around her shoulders.

Falcone led Costa and Peroni away from the women.

'This is serious,' Costa said. 'I know it looks odd but—'

'Don't tell me my job,' Falcone said curtly. 'We've got one clear-cut case of murder and one missing teenager to add to the scores we get every week. There's nothing that links them. Nothing you can count on. Be honest, Nic. If there were . . .'

Costa looked at Falcone. He wished the inspector wouldn't play his cards so close to his chest so often. It was coincidence. But that didn't mean they should reject it.

'We could hand out her picture to the media,' Costa suggested.

'And say what?' Falcone asked. 'This is a girl who hasn't been seen by her mother since this morning? Do you want us to look like fools?'

'I don't care what we look like.'

Peroni patted Costa on the back. 'Think about it, Nic. What's there to go on?'

'Circulate the girl's picture internally,' Falcone ordered, walking for the door, watching Teresa Lupo glower at him from the sofa, her arms still round the mother. 'Make sure it gets seen all round. And pull out whatever CCTV footage we've got of the Campo. We can look at that later. You could be right, Nic. I just don't feel ready to jump straight in at the moment. Beside, we've got an appointment.' He scowled at Costa. 'And note that word "we". Keep your friend from the morgue out of this. She's got other work to do.'

These days when Emilio Neri went out on his rounds he left most of the muscle work to Bruno Bucci, a muscular thirty-year-old hood from Turin. Bucci had been on the payroll since he was a teenager running dope dealers around Termini Station. Neri liked him, as an employee and as a man. He was taciturn, loyal and dogged. He knew when to talk and when to shut up. He never came back until the job was done, whatever it took. If Neri felt like slapping someone around personally, Bucci didn't mind holding the yo-yo still, making sure he didn't get any stupid ideas just because the individual rearranging his face was pushing sixty-six and wheezing and croaking like a set of malodorous old bellows.

Sometimes Neri wondered why Mickey hadn't turned out this way. If that had happened, he'd feel a whole lot easier about what would become of his empire when he was too old to stay in the driving seat. Which could be sooner rather than later the way he was starting to feel.

It wasn't a question of age. Neri felt sure he could carry on for a good decade more without handing over the reins. Something else, boredom maybe, or a sense of being out of place, bothered him. The big house, the servants, even Adele lounging around like a pampered plaything . . . all these accoutrements of wealth and power now seemed unreal, almost improper, silky bars for a prison that threatened to drown him in luxury.

He ought to be thinking about the transition. He knew that. The problem was Mickey's character. The kid did as he was told, mostly, but he was always chasing something on the side too, pursuing private scams that he liked to keep to himself. Neri had found himself forced to clean up this kind of mess – dope, women, money – too often. Mickey never lied when confronted like that. Neri just had to know to ask the right questions. He could put up with that when Mickey was twenty. Now it was getting tedious. Maybe there was some kind of a trade-off he could work. Bucci got to run the business, Mickey could sit back and take his cut from the proceeds.

Neri thought about this from Bucci's point of view. He knew what any decent working-class hood with ambition would do in that position. Wait till the old man was out of the way then take the lot, leaving the spoilt brat to drive a cab or wake up dead one morning more likely. Maybe that was the way of the world, Neri reasoned. He'd have done the same. Families were imperfect entities. Nothing said they had to last forever.

They spent the morning chasing up debts around the city, Neri fuming all the time about the way Mickey and Adele squabbled in his presence, wondering whether he ought to punish them both. He couldn't get them out of his head and he couldn't figure out why. His mind wasn't as quick as it used to be. Was there something going on that he should have seen? Some new scheme of Mickey's? He sat back in the rear seat of the armoured Mercedes and closed his eyes, wishing to hell he didn't have to worry about those two constantly. The bitch ran up a small fortune on credit cards. He footed every penny of the gigantic bills that fell through the door each month. Mickey was no better. The kid seemed consumed with a desire to own anything that possessed an internal combustion engine. He'd been through four sports cars in as many months, dabbled with a plethora of two-wheeled vehicles and was only cut short from buying a four-seat Piper Comanche when the owner of the flying school discreetly rang Neri on his mobile to warn him of the deal his son was trying to nail down. Then there were the women. All shapes, all sizes. All colours, all backgrounds. The only thing they had in common was the money they consumed with a vengeance, and none of that was Mickey's.

In his own way, Neri loved them both. Or, more accurately he thought, enjoyed owning them, having them dependent upon him in every way. In return they were supposed to stick to the rules, and one of those was never to display their antipathy towards each other in his presence. But they just couldn't bring themselves to do that one small thing and the resentment he felt was growing by the minute, making it impossible for Neri to concentrate on the work in front of him. On one occasion he broke off from watching Bucci beat the shit out of some cheating Termini pimp to call Mickey and find out what the louse was doing to earn his keep. All he got was the recorded message from the mobile.

Later he'd got Bucci to pin down Toni Lucarelli, a Tras-tevere bar-keeper who was siphoning off the dough Neri was due in order to pay for some piece of Algerian skirt on the other side of town. Neri punched Lucarelli a few times in the face, not hard, because his heart wasn't in it. Lucarelli was a nice guy. He just wanted more fun than his wallet allowed.

Then the stupid bar-keeper spoiled everything by breaking down and blubbing instead of taking it like a man. Neri wanted to let the big guy from Turin loose on the jerk, crying like a baby there in the storeroom of his crummy little bar. But he couldn't get the picture of Adele out of his head: cold, heartless Adele, who knew more tricks than a woman of her age ought to, looking down on his son like he was nothing, so cold it was deliberate, as if she were laughing about something. He told Bucci to rough up Lucarelli just a little then called her and didn't get through there either. It was a great day. Life would be so simple if he didn't have to go around like this, with a bodyguard dogging his footsteps all the time. You couldn't be the boss and expect not to have enemies. All the same, sometimes it made life hell.

Neri didn't beat up anyone else after that. He just let them look at Bucci and ask themselves how it would feel. At lunchtime, when he'd had what was supposed to be his pleasure, he called in to see an old friend on the staff at the Vatican. They talked about a different side to Neri's business: offshore funds and tax havens, covert bank transfers and double taxation schemes. Then they ate lunch in a small *trattoria* around the corner, one run by a man Neri had once employed, so he never ever paid the bill. The man from the Vatican skulked off back to work after a single plate of spaghetti carbonara, worrying he'd been seen. Neri hung on for some lamb with chicory and then *zabaglione* and still he couldn't get Mickey and Adele out of his mind.

Then came the phone call about what was happening in the Questura. He tried to cast his mind back sixteen years. He made some notes on the little pad he kept inside his jacket pocket: names, events, people to call. Everything went into the book. He needed it all the time these days. His memory wasn't what it was.

'To hell with it,' he grunted, staring at the empty plates in front of him. 'It's history. I am too old and too rich to let this shit get me down.'

When he came out into the side street close to the Piazza del Risorgimento Bruno Bucci was sitting on the wall next to the black Mercedes looking odd. Neri finally worked out what it was. There was emotion on his large, featureless face. He was pissed off.

Neri walked over and sat next to him on the brick-work. It was a nice day. Spring was working its way into the world. There was some blue sky, a touch of heat. Pretty girls walked by in dresses that had some colour. Some of them had long, brown legs. They got fake tans these days, he guessed, or maybe their boyfriends took them to the Caribbean for some sun and plenty of bedroom stuff. There'd been a time when Emilio Neri felt sufficiently free of the shackles of labour to do the same himself.

'Car's fucked,' Bucci said. 'Won't start.'

Neri shook his head and stared at the big, black hunk of metal. 'All that money. And what does it get you? Why do I bother with this?'

'I phoned the garage. They said two hours. Tomorrow I'm going to go round. Explain a few things in person.'

Neri looked into Bucci's brown eyes. Most of the time they appeared dead but that was just an act. Bucci was a smart guy. He didn't miss a trick.

'You do that,' he said, patting one of his big knees. 'Tell you what. Life's too short for this crap. Take the afternoon off. We're done. It's spring. Go back and see that pimp. Tell him he should give you a little something extra, keep us sweet.'

Bucci twisted inside his tight grey suit. 'That's nice, boss. But I don't need that kind of thing. Not now. Not that I don't appreciate the offer.'

Neri looked at him and thought again of Mickey. 'You're some guy, Bruno. I like the fact you're working for me.'

'Me too. Let me find a cab. I'll bring it round here. Go back with you.'

'No!' Neri laughed. 'I meant what I said. It's spring. Wake up a little. Feel alive. I'm done chasing debts for the day. Bores me stupid sometimes. You go enjoy yourself. Take some chick out this evening. On me.'

'That's kind of you,' Bucci answered. His brown eyes were dead again. 'But I'm not supposed to leave you on your own.'

Neri's face fell into a scowl. 'What're you talking about? You make me sound like some old cripple or something? You think I can't look after myself?'

Bucci was worried. 'No, boss. It's just . . . you always said . . .'

'Fuck what I always said! I'm saying something different now. Who the hell's gonna try something on me here anyway? Also, the way I intend to go home—' Neri grinned. 'A man's gotta feel free sometimes, Bruno. You understand that?'

'How're you getting home?'

'A unique form of transport. I'm going to catch a bus from round that corner. I want to look in the eyes of a few strangers, try to see what makes them tick. Haven't done that in years. It's a mistake. You get isolated. You forget how to read people.'

'A bus?' Bucci repeated.

'Yeah. Why not?'

Neri hesitated. He hated throwing his personal problems onto other people. 'You mind if I ask you something?'

'No.'

'That stupid kid of mine, Mickey. And Adele. What do you think I should do about them, huh? They're driving me crazy.'

Bruno Bucci shuffled uncomfortably on the wall. Neri watched him, wondering at the discomfort a few simple words could cause, not quite sure he could believe the slight flush that was creeping up the cheeks of the man from Turin.

'Cat got your tongue? Did I ask the wrong question or something?'

'I'd like to help, boss,' Bucci said eventually. 'You know that. If there's ever anything I can do . . . you've just got to ask.'

'That *you* can do!' Neri laughed, still struggling to work out Bucci's reaction. 'What are you talking about, Bruno? I was asking your opinion. This is my problem. A son I love. A wife I love. And the two of them can't stand the sight of each other. You think I'm going to ask *you* to fix it. Jesus—'

'I don't have an opinion.'

He slapped Bucci's shoulder. 'Yeah. Right. You northern guys. You think you've got the answers to everything. Just don't want to say it, that's all.'

'Got me there,' Bruno Bucci replied, brown eyes staring into Neri's face with no visible emotion in them at all.

'Here.' Neri flashed him some big notes. 'You're right. It's my business. I never should have put you in that position. You go have fun. Whatever. I don't care. "You've just got to ask . . ." You guys kill me sometimes.'

Bruno Bucci pushed himself up and came off the wall, counting the notes.

'Thanks,' he said.

Neri watched his broad back disappear down the street. 'Humility,' he said to himself. 'That is what the world is lacking today.'

Then he walked round the corner into the square, wondering how long it was since he sat on a bus, trying to remember what it felt like to be young, trying to separate several conflicting strands of thought in his head.

The benign mood didn't last. There was a queue. There were foreigners, pushing and shoving and asking stupid questions. It took ten minutes for him to work his way inside the doors. By the time Emilio Neri was on the 64 his mind was back where he had left it an hour before, stuck inside a foul mood, thinking about his stupid family.

There were no seats either. Not until a man not far short of his own age, smartly dressed, constantly smiling, stood up and offered his own.

Neri looked into the stranger's face, wondering why

he'd been stupid enough to refuse Bucci's offer of a cab and climb on board this thing in the first place. 'Because you're an old fool,' he thought to himself. 'And maybe they're starting to know it.'

The man couldn't stop smiling. It was beyond Neri why anyone would smile on a stinking, overcrowded bus. He couldn't wait for the thing to lurch across the bridge and into the Via Arenula so he could waddle home along the Via Giulia.

'Use the seat yourself,' Neri growled. 'I don't need it. What makes you think I do?'

'Nothing,' the man said, still smiling. He looked like a confidence trickster or some two-bit actor in the Fellini films 'I just thought—'

'You thought wrong,' Neri snarled.

And so he clung to the strap, wishing all the way that he'd fallen into the seat and taken the weight off his sweating feet. There was some black teenager in it now, headphones clamped to his skull, a hissing noise emerging from them.

He got off at the Via Arenula, in a big jostling crowd. He had to wait almost five minutes to cross the busy road. When he got home he was out of breath and stank of sweat, Mickey and Adele's fighting still in his head, jostling for attention with the call from inside the Questura.

The house was empty. He wanted them there. When the phone rang he knew an ancient corpse really was rising, in a way he'd have to anticipate, couldn't hope to avoid.

*

Twenty minutes after leaving the Teatro di Marcello Nic Costa and Gianni Peroni followed Falcone's car into a narrow private lane off the Janiculum hill, the sprawling piece of parkland that rose up from behind Trastevere and overlooked the river.

Peroni downed the remains of his second *porchetta* panino of the day, brushed the crumbs off his jacket into the floorpan of the Fiat and said, 'You know, I like the way you drive, Nic. It's careful without being over-cautious, sensitive to circumstances and a little rash if required. When I'm restored to my true position I will offer you a job, my boy. You can drive me anywhere. Most of the guys I have spend their time bouncing off other vehicles which is a little unsettling for a sensitive man like me.'

Then he unwrapped a chocolate bar and took a single bite before sticking it in his pocket, half-eaten.

'You're going to put on weight eating like that,' Costa observed. 'It's not natural.'

'Been the same weight for fifteen years. I burn it up inside, what with my nervous tension and all. You just see the exterior me. Calm, unflustered, ever-vigilant, ugly as a horse's ass, just what I want you to see. But inside I'm a tortured cauldron of torn emotions. I've got traumas that can burn off any amount of carbohydrate and cholesterol I throw at it. You watch. You seen so much as an extra gram on me since we started this relationship?'

'No.'

'Also, you should be aware that meat – even the shit they sell under that name in Rome – and bread, they're the best antidote there is against this flu thing. Forget all that crap about fruit and vegetables. You ever seen a chimpanzee? Fucking things never stop sneezing. Or doing the other thing. Sometimes simultaneously.'

Costa thought about this. 'I've never seen a chimpanzee sneeze.'

'You need to develop your powers of observation. Now do you want me to come in and hold hands with you for this or can I just stay in the car and nap awhile? What with mummified bodies and Roman history lessons this has been a tiring day for a nocturnal animal like me.'

Peroni took the cigarette packet out, saw Costa's face and thought better of it. 'OK. OK. One concession a day is all you get. About the English kid, Nic. Falcone's doing all he can in the circumstances. Putting the picture around. Getting the CCTV. I mean, I'm no detective but what this mother says seems so *vague*.'

'Things often are. Isn't it that way in vice?'

He shook his head. 'Not really. We're law enforcement, not detection. We just try to keep a lid on everything, make sure no one truly innocent gets hurt and the dope stays out of the equation as much as possible. I'm not like you. I'm a kind of social worker if you want the honest truth. You got to remember. If it comes down to violence and worse it all comes out of our hands anyway. We're just licensed informers who hand on some gossip you people can use. A popular job, you'll agree.'

'And when you want some information?'

'I ask,' Peroni replied. 'Straight out front. I'm a good asker. No messing. It's the only way. So let me say this again? What's the problem? You want to spend a little more time around the mother? A man should always consider his sex life but I told you. Ask Barbara out. She's a nice girl.'

'Meaning?' Peroni could be too direct for his own good. Too observant too.

'Meaning I saw the way you looked at the English woman. Don't get me wrong. She's great-looking in a kind of second-hand way. Older than you, though that's not necessarily a bad thing. Not my type. Too much of something – booze maybe, and bad dreams – been through her head.'

'I just think there's more to it,' Costa replied. Peroni hadn't heard as much as he had. Or maybe he was uncharacteristically slow off the mark.

The older man put his hand on Costa's arm. 'Nic. You heard Falcone. He said you could be right. But think this through. You just got back on the job. There are people in the Questura who happen to believe Falcone's crazy to give you a second chance at all. You're *on probation*. Just like me.'

'And you think that if I push this I can ruin your chances along with my own?'

'If you want to look at it that way, yeah,' Peroni conceded. 'That's a part of it. But mainly I'm thinking about you. Honest. I got to know you a little these last couple of weeks. Sometimes you take things on yourself. Someone else's problem becomes yours.'

'Thanks for the compliment.'

'It's a back-handed one. The flip side is that's a great way to get screwed. Or screw yourself.'

'I won't screw up, Gianni. Forget about me. What about the missing girl? What if these two are connected? All that stuff about the rituals—'

Peroni sighed and shook his head. 'A piece of vegetable and some seeds? Look, they don't call her crazy Teresa for nothing. I love her as much as anyone, but you got to admit this is stretching things. Even if she has it half right about the corpse there's no way it can have anything to do with the Julius girl. They're sixteen years apart. They have absolutely nothing in common except the looks. What are you saying? Someone's still doing all this mumbo-jumbo? How come we heard nothing all this time? You think Rome hasn't seen a pretty teenage blonde since the girl in the peat?'

It was a good question. He'd thought about it too. 'Maybe it went all right before. Maybe someone only gets killed if there's a foul-up. If the girl suddenly doesn't want to play ball. I don't know.'

Peroni nodded. 'So all the Julius girl has to do is let this creep have his way with her? Then she gets free?'

More than that, Costa thought. He recalled what Teresa had said about the book. The girl gets *rewarded*. She gets a taste of paradise. She becomes an initiate, part of the club. And the next time round she sees the ritual from the inside. She watches someone else *become*.

'Maybe,' he said.

'Doesn't seem a big deal. Women have been getting on that way since we all crawled out of the slime.'

Gianni Peroni came from a different generation. Costa reminded himself to keep that in mind. 'In this century it's a big deal.'

Peroni gave him a sharp look. 'Sorry. Just the dinosaur in me talking. Let's forget it, huh? My advice is: we just keep our heads down and do as we're told. That is the way of progress in the modern police force.'

There was the rumble of a sports car. A black Alfa Romeo coupé drove up and parked close to Falcone's vehicle. Costa watched as an elegant woman in a serious dark jacket and tight skirt, cut to just above the knee, climbed out and, very gingerly, embraced Falcone, kissing him lightly on the cheek.

Peroni closed his eyes. 'Oh shit. There goes my nap. There really is no God after all. Or if there is he's a bastard. Behold, one more reason to listen to what the dinosaur's saying. Know who that is?'

Costa shook his head.

'The ice maiden from the DIA. Rachele D'Amato. Big number there these days too. Does things like setting up stings in brothels and you wouldn't tell anyone in vice first if you did that, would you? Listen. Never, ever do you mess with her, understand? Not until you make inspector class and even then I'd wear gloves. She's the woman Falcone was porking way back until his wife found out. What the hell is she doing here? Come to that, what the hell are *we* doing here? I am living in darkness with you people.'

Falcone and the woman were talking animatedly outside the gates. It was a professional conversation, from the woman's side anyway.

'Anything else I need to know about her?'

'Oh yes,' Peroni added. 'She hates cops. At least . . . let me be more precise. She has a thing about us. Maybe it comes from her experience with Falcone. We're all assholes. Crooked assholes too in all probability. Before stiffing me she took down two men from narcotics last year for receiving backhanders.'

'More fool them,' Costa scowled. He hated bent cops. He couldn't work out why anyone had any sympathy for them in the Questura.

'Oh, I forgot,' Peroni groaned. 'You're the one with a conscience. Let me tell you something, kid. These were good guys. They put a lot of people in jail who deserved to be there. Until you've worked that beat yourself I suggest you don't pre-judge people. In that line of work it's sometimes hard to be black and white, because if you are, no one talks to you at all.'

Costa stared at his partner. He wished he could understand Peroni better. Sometimes the man said things that disturbed him.

'Whatever,' Peroni continued. 'The bitch has balls, I'll say that for her. Word was someone put out a contract on her a year back. When she found out she drove round to his house, walked in on him and his old woman over breakfast and . . . reached an understanding.'

The DIA people did walk a dangerous line. Costa knew one who'd been badly injured in a bomb blast in Sicily. They weren't just cops in the force either. Some lawyers were in there too. Somehow that seemed to make them easier targets in the eyes of the mob.

'Is she still on the list?'

'She's alive, isn't she?'

Peroni climbed out of the car and walked to the gates, Costa dogging his footsteps. Rachele D'Amato was slim, in her thirties, a type Costa recognized: businesslike, serious, but not above turning on the attraction to get her way. She had plenty to work with. She was just a touch taller than Nic Costa, with the kind of figure other women hated to see. The suit emphasized her slender waist. Her jacket hung open to reveal a tight, cream silk shirt, cut revealingly low. She had a hard, beautiful face, with a phoney smile accented by deep-red lipstick, and immaculate, long brown hair, pulled back from her forehead and tied behind. Costa could imagine Falcone with her. They'd make a convincing couple. He just wondered how much mutual trust they'd ever manage to share.

'Not that I'm complaining but why's a civilian here?' Peroni wondered.

Rachele D'Amato turned and smiled. 'Oh. Let me remember the name. It's *Detective* Peroni. Right?'

'Yeah,' he grinned. 'And there was me thinking you wouldn't recognize me with my clothes on. You know, I don't recall you looking at my face for one moment that memorable evening. Ah well. Meet the DIA lady, Nic. Rachele D'Amato. She's just so cute, isn't she? Why don't we get them that pretty in the police?'

Costa smiled and said nothing.

'So,' Peroni continued. 'You just passing or something? No need to answer. Nice that you should stop by and say hello. This, by the way, is what we call police work. You're currently looking at the only three cops in Rome with clear nasal passages, though I cannot guarantee how long that will stay true for my veggie-eating partner here. Best you run along in case something nasty happens.'

Falcone gave him a filthy look then pressed the button on the videophone. 'Miss D'Amato is here because I asked for her help.'

Peroni wasn't about to give up. 'You mean this is a brothel too? Jeez. They show up in the strangest places these days. Oh, oh. Icy stare time. I got it wrong. This guy's some kind of hood? No! Don't recall any of them living in this part of town. Place looks like it ought to belong to some playboy or something.'

It was a shrewd observation. The main house lay a good hundred metres beyond the big secure gates. It resembled a reproduction imperial villa, a single-storey palace built around an open patio. An avenue of classical statues lined the pathway up to the house. At the end there was what looked like a fishpond and a fountain.

Rachele D'Amato looked Costa up and down while Peroni stood there, grinning. 'I don't know you. Leo made you his partner. You must have done something very bad.'

'Nic Costa,' he replied, and held out his hand. 'I like challenges.'

'Me too, kid,' Peroni growled.

'Well that's the formalities done,' she said. 'I'm here because you can't do this without me. Sorry, but that's the way it is these days. Wallis has antecedents. He doesn't worry me now but he's got a past. And he knows people who do worry me. Is that enough?'

Costa watched as a face filled the videophone screen: a middle-aged black man, handsome, speaking perfect Italian.

'Police,' Falcone said, holding up his card. 'We need to talk.'

'What do you want?' the man asked.

'It's about your stepdaughter, Mr Wallis. We've found a body. We need identification. Now please.'

Costa watched the head on the screen. Falcone's words gave the man pain.

'Come in,' Vergil Wallis murmured, and the lock on the gates began to buzz.

Silvio Di Capua had learned a lot in the three years since he became Teresa Lupo's deputy pathologist in the morgue. She'd taught him tricks of the autopsy trade they never told you in medical school. She'd shown him any number of smart-ass quips to make when cops fainted or threw up. She'd ingratiated him into the Questura too, introduced him to people so that he became her eyes and ears, the source of most of the hot gossip running through the station. Above all, though, Teresa had revealed to Di Capua – a good Catholic boy brought up by monks, a man who, at the age of twenty-seven, had still never been out with a member of the opposite sex – the unbridled joys of language when freed from the restraints of custom, taste and dignity.

Until she came along he'd been of the opinion that Italian was the structured, civilized tongue he knew from books and newspapers and conversation with fellow students in the monastery school. Teresa Lupo dispelled this myth within a matter of weeks, filling his head with all manner of slang and colloquialisms so colourful and bizarre that, for the naïve and awestruck Silvio Di Capua, it was as if he had entered some new and glorious world.

Even three years on he found listening to her in full, florid flow a thrilling experience, one that revealed arcane, hidden dimensions of profundity to a language transformed from that of his childhood. He swore like a trooper now too, not always appropriately and, he knew, without her masterful timing. On occasion he muffed his words, which had led to some awkward situations and, once, almost got him beaten up by a uniformed gorilla who misinterpreted a friendly jibe as some obscure hint at unnatural private practices.

Sometimes he wondered if he were in love with his boss. In his imagination this occurred in a wholesome, chaste and ethereal way, one that precluded physical sex, something Silvio Di Capua found as baffling and undesirable now as it was when first described to him in all its squalor fifteen years before in the school dormitory.

Nor would he dwell long on these thoughts. Di Capua accepted his failings. He was marginally shorter than Teresa. His thick black hair had begun to fall out when he was eighteen. Now it formed a priestly fringe around his bald skull, which, out of laziness, he allowed to grow lank and long. His voice was a scratchy falsetto that some found deeply annoying. He was chubby running to fat. His face was so blandly amorphous he had to reintroduce himself to people all the time. And he looked a good ten years younger than his true age. Silvio Di Capua's life was an incidental happening in the passing of human history and he knew it. Nevertheless, that didn't stop his admiring Teresa Lupo to the point of adoration, more with every new day of this warm spring.

There was, also, the matter of the nickname which had been inflicted on him the previous year by a garrulous traffic cop and stuck with a dogged and annoying persistence. No one dared call Teresa Lupo 'Crazy Teresa' to her face. Silvio Di Capua's standing within the morgue was less sure. He just had to learn to answer to it. On occasion even Teresa used the damn thing.

He'd just pushed the body from the bog back into what the morgue drones now called the shower when the thug from plain clothes appeared at the door. There was a dead junkie fresh on the slab awaiting Di Capua's attention. Teresa had done a little work on the corpse – the usual overdose pre-check, this time on a grubby hirsute man who'd been stripped for the examination – then passed it over to him with a few brief instructions before grabbing her coat and leaving. He was head down into the PC, logging some records, lost in thought.

'Hey, Monkboy,' the cop barked. 'Why don't you go to Google and type in "a life"? But before you do, tell me where Crazy Teresa is. Falcone says he wants that autopsy on his desk soonish and I, for one, don't wish to disappoint him.'

Di Capua looked up from the screen and scowled at the moron. '*Doctor* Lupo is away from her desk.'

The detective was messing with some of the specimen trays, picking up scalpels, touching stuff he was supposed to leave alone. He sniffed over the corpse and then, gingerly, with the end of a pair of forceps, flicked the dead man's grey, flaccid penis.

'Listen, sonny. Don't get snappy with me. It's bad enough dealing with her. What's with that woman? It's like the red flag's flying every day of the month. Don't tell me you got the same problem?'

Di Capua got up and walked in between the jerk and the cadaver, pushing the cop out of the way. 'You should never go near junkies unless you've had the right injections,' he said. 'There's a theory doing the rounds now that you can catch Aids just from the smell. Did you know that?'

The cop took one step back. 'You're kidding me.'

'Not at all. The early symptoms are very like this flu that's doing the rounds. Sore throat. Mucus.' He paused. 'And a nose so itchy you just can't stop scratching it.'

The cop sniffed then started dabbing at his face with a grubby handkerchief. Di Capua pointed at the sign that hung on the wall above the dissecting table. 'I don't suppose you happen to read Latin?'

The cop stared at the words. *Hic locus est ubi mors gaudet succurrere vitae.* 'Sure. It says, "You don't have to be crazy to work here but it helps." '

'Not quite. "This is the place where death rejoices to teach those who live." '

'What kind of crazy shit is that?'

Di Capua looked down at the corpse. The bloodless Y-incision Teresa had made earlier, from the shoulders to mid-chest then down to the pubic region, sat on the dead man's flesh as dark, narrow lines. The same feature ran across the scalp, which was now loose, ready to be reflected back to enable entry to the skull. Ordinarily, if they had the staff, he'd expect some assistance, But Teresa was gone and, what with the flu epidemic, there was no one else around. Except the cop.

'Pathologist shit,' he replied, and with a firm, sure hand took out the vibrating saw, turned back the loose scalp and began carefully to carve open the skull vault from the front.

The cop turned white then belched.

'Don't throw up in a morgue, please,' Di Capua cautioned him. 'It's bad luck.'

'*Shit*,' the man gasped, watching goggle-eyed the path the small electric saw was taking.

'The preliminary report's over there,' Di Capua said, nodding towards Teresa's desk and the folder that sat next to the PC. 'Note that word "preliminary". It's just a scant first look. And next time, for your information, the name is Silvio. Or Doctor Di Capua. You got that?'

'Yeah,' the cop answered with a burp.

He watched the idiot vacate the room, clutching the report with one hand and his mouth with the other.

'What *is* all the fuss?' Di Capua wondered out loud. 'It's just a body, for chrissake.'

There were bigger things to worry about. Teresa, for one thing. Where she'd gone, feeling so mad he didn't even dare question her wisdom. Why she was poking her nose into police work. Again. And, most of all, why she never noticed the way he felt.

'Do you know what month this is?' Vergil Wallis asked. 'The month of Mars. Do you know what that means?'

They sat in the main room of the fortified villa on the Janiculum hill. The place was odd: half oriental, half classical Roman. There were statues from imperial times, copies maybe, next to delicate porcelain vases covered in Japanese designs: chrysanthemums and country scenes sparsely populated with stick figures. A slight, pretty, oriental girl in a long, white smock served tea. Wallis scarcely noticed her presence.

In a brief conversation as they walked to the villa Rachele D'Amato had told them the man was long gone from the mob and now spent most of his time in Italy or Japan, source of his twin obsessions. In retirement he was a history freak: imperial Rome and the Edo Period. Wallis looked about fifty, a good ten years younger than his true age. He was tall, fit and strong. His dark hair was cropped short. He possessed an alert, fine-featured face dominated by large, intelligent eyes which were constantly active. Without the benefit of D'Amato's briefing, Costa would have said he had the dignified bearing of an intellectual or an artist. There was just one outward sign of his past that she'd warned him about. Before coming to Rome as an emissary for his bosses, Wallis had lived in Tokyo for several years, liaising with the *Sumiyoshi-gumi*, one of the three big Japanese yakuza families. Somewhere along the way the little finger of his left hand had gone missing in some kind of brotherhood ritual with the Japanese mob. Unlike most ex-yakuza

gangsters, he didn't try to disguise the loss with a pros-
thetic. Maybe Wallis seemed to think himself above that
kind of trick. Or past it, if they were to believe Rachele
D'Amato. It occurred to Costa, too, that this act was in
itself a ritual, one of belonging, in this case brotherhood.
If Teresa Lupo was right something similar had claimed
the life of his stepdaughter.

'War,' Costa said. 'Mars is the god of war.'

Wallis beckoned to the girl for more green tea. 'Right.
But he was much more than that. Indulge me. This is
how I amuse myself these days, for half the year anyway,
when I'm here.' His Italian was near perfect. If Nic
Costa closed his eyes he could have convinced himself
he was in the presence of a native. Wallis's soft, intelligent
tones sounded like those of a university professor. 'Mars
was the father of Romulus and Remus. In a sense he was
the very father of Rome. They worshipped him more for
that than his warlike aspect. The month of Mars was
about the health of the state, which for Romans meant
the health of the world. It was about rebirth and renewal
through the exercise of power and force.'

'And sacrifice?' Costa asked.

Wallis looked around him, considering his answer.
'Maybe. Who knows what you would have seen in the
spot two thousand years ago?' He scanned their baffled
faces. 'You don't know? Really. I thought the DIA knew
everything. I built this villa from scratch ten years ago,
on the site of an old temple. It filled my time. I have
plenty to fill. Some of the pieces you see here came
out of the ground. You won't tell the Soprintendenza
Archeological will you? I've left them to the city in my
will. It won't harm anyone if they spend a little time
with me, surely? You've got plenty else besides.'

'We're not here about statues,' Rachele D'Amato said.

Wallis stared at her and there was a note of icy disdain in his dark eyes. 'Listen to the Roman talking. You grow up in a place like this and walk around with your eyes closed. Still, people change. It was easier to handle the planning people a decade ago than it would be now. They were more . . . pliable. I would never have done this today, of course. They're different. So am I.' He waited. 'Signora. You're from the DIA. We've met before, of course. Twice is it? Three times?'

'Twice I believe.'

'Quite. I was generous with my time then. I don't feel that way any more. This doesn't require your presence. You know as well as anyone that I retired not long after my stepdaughter disappeared. You've no cause to be here now. I can understand why, in the present circumstances, the police have to call. But I've got nothing to say to you.'

Peroni caught Costa's eye, winked and held up a sly thumb.

'I know all this—' she said, taken aback by his frankness.

He interrupted her. 'Then why are you here?'

'Because of who you were.'

'Were,' he repeated. 'I try to take this lightly but you must understand. These are recollections of a double loss for me.'

'A double loss?' she asked.

'My wife died in New York not long after Eleanor disappeared.'

The memory broke her confidence. 'I forgot,' D'Amato stuttered. 'I apologize.'

'You forgot?' He seemed more perplexed than offend-ed. 'A detail like that?'

She was struggling to come up with something to keep this conversation alive.

'What happened?' Costa asked, trying to help.

'Ask her,' he nodded. 'Like I said. They're supposed to know everything.'

'I don't recall,' she murmured.

'No?' There was a brief hint of ironic victory on Wallis's handsome face. It gave Nic Costa pause for thought: something dark still lurked inside this man. 'Read the files. My wife and I separated a year before this happened. I rented an apartment for her on the fiftieth floor of a block near the Rockefeller Center. Shortly after Eleanor went missing she stepped off the balcony.'

The three men looked at each other. Costa knew what each of them was thinking: it was impossible to work out precisely how Wallis felt about this event.

'I'm sorry. Nevertheless,' D'Amato persisted, 'the protocols demand that the DIA are present if the police interview someone with your kind of record.'

Wallis smiled wanly. 'What record? No one's ever prosecuted me for a thing. I've never confessed to any crime. Perhaps I have never *committed* any crime.'

'Then I apologize but it's how it must be.'

Wallis shrugged. 'The Italian love of bureaucracy is one of the few things about this country I fail to under-stand. I don't wish to offend, Signora, but I will repeat myself: you are out of line. I don't see how I can refuse to speak to the police in these circumstances. You are different.' He pointed to the double doors that led outside to the patio. 'This is nothing personal. You must go. If you don't, I talk to no one. Please . . .'

'I . . .' she stuttered, looking at Falcone for support. The inspector shrugged his shoulders. Peroni uttered a low chuckle.

'This is wholly improper,' she hissed, rising from her seat. 'We . . .' she glared at Falcone, ' . . . will talk outside.'

Wallis smiled and watched her walk brusquely out of the door. 'There's a Japanese saying. "Yesterday's enemy is today's friend." Not always. A shame. She's a charming woman.'

'First time I heard her called that,' Peroni grumbled.

Wallis looked at him, just a hint of reproach in his eyes. 'You think you've found my stepdaughter. Are you sure?'

'We're sure,' Falcone said.

'So why the hell has it taken this long for you to tell me? It's two weeks since that body turned up.'

Falcone was off his guard. 'You knew we had a body?'

'Give me credit,' Wallis said pleasantly. 'Eleanor may not have been mine but I loved her anyway. She was a great kid. Bright, charming, interested. I loved her mother too, not that it was easy. I blame myself for most of that. But Eleanor . . .'

His eyes sparkled when he spoke of her. 'She took every good point her mother possessed and just made it bigger. Even at sixteen she was full of life, involved in everything. History. Language.' He waved his hands around the room. 'Let me tell you something I never told that woman from the DIA. Together Eleanor and her mother gave me . . . this.'

'How?' Costa wondered.

Some long-hidden pain flickered in his eyes. 'Because they made me realize it existed. They had the education. They opened the eyes of some kid from the ghetto who'd only dreamed about things up till then. The guys back home put me through a law degree. I got a taste for Latin through that. But until Eleanor and her mom came along I just didn't get it. The irony is that, if she were alive today, I wouldn't be what I am. It was her disappearance made me consider what I was. Her loss reshaped my life. It was a bum deal for her. I wish it had never happened.'

He looked at Falcone. 'Of course I knew there was a body. A parent who loses a child, even a stepparent, looks at the newspapers differently. We think: is this the end? Do we now *know?* Because that becomes the source of the pain. Not the loss itself. Not the images in your head about how she might have died. It's the absence of knowledge, the doubt that nags away at you, day and night.'

Wallis made a gesture with his hands. He had no more to say.

'You could have called us,' Costa said.

'Every time a girl's body is found in Italy? Do you have any idea how often I'd be on the phone? Do you know how soon people would start labelling me a crank?'

He was right. Nic Costa had seen enough missing person cases to know what happened when the investigation dwindled to nothing: no body, no leads, no clue as to how someone had disappeared. There was all too often an awkward juncture at which the grieving parents became a burden, one which ought to be supported by the counselling services rather than the police, since they were the only ones who, in truth, could help.

'You're sure?' Wallis asked again. 'You're absolutely sure?'

'Yes,' Falcone said.

'Yet the papers said something about the body being old?'

Falcone frowned. 'It was a mistake on the part of the pathologist. She'd been laid in peat. It made it hard to carry out the normal tests. Also, I was on holiday. There was no one around from the original investigation who could put two and two together.'

'Everyone makes mistakes,' Wallis said. 'What can you possibly want of me in these circumstances?'

'I need you to come to the Questura for formal identification.'

Wallis shook his head and almost smiled. 'What's the point in identifying a sixteen-year-old corpse? Besides, you said you knew it was her already.'

'It's not what you think,' Costa intervened.

'No. I know that. They printed a picture of her in the papers. I saw it at the time and thought . . . maybe. But what you've got isn't my stepdaughter. It's a corpse. I'll make arrangements with an undertaker for the burial. I'll see her then, when we're both ready.'

'No,' Falcone said firmly. 'That isn't possible. This is a case of murder, Signor Wallis. The body won't be released until I allow it. If we bring someone to court . . .'

They all heard the uncertainty in Falcone's voice.

Wallis stared at him. 'If —'

'I need you to think back to that time again. We

have to reopen the case. We have records but perhaps something else has occurred to you.'

'Nothing's occurred to me,' Wallis replied immediately. 'Nothing at all. I told you everything I knew back then. Now I remember less, and maybe that's for the best.'

'If you think about it,' Costa suggested.

'There's nothing to think about.'

'The girl was murdered,' Costa said. 'Brutally. Perhaps in some kind of ritual.'

Wallis blinked. 'Ritual?'

'An ancient Roman ritual. Dionysian perhaps,' Costa continued hopefully. 'There's a place in Pompeii. The Villa of Mysteries. A professor at the university wrote a book about how they might be interpreted. Have you read it?'

His cropped head turned sideways. Something in this idea intrigued Vergil Wallis. 'I read history not conjecture. I don't know anything about any Dionysian rituals.'

Costa glanced at Falcone. The villa was full of imperial Roman artefacts. It had been built on the site of an ancient temple. For all he knew, Wallis spent six months of the year pursuing only his private, historical interests. It was inconceivable that he was entirely ignorant of the subject.

'Signor Wallis,' Falcone said quietly. 'This may be coincidence, but another girl is missing. She ran away today with someone. It's possible, I put it no more strongly than that, that someone acted out these rituals when your stepdaughter was killed. It's possible the same person is re-enacting them now. Do you have any idea whether Eleanor was mixed up in some kind of cult?'

Wallis's passive face creased in surprise. 'What? Are

you guys kidding me? She was too smart to mess around with that kind of crap. Besides, I'd have noticed something, wouldn't I?'

'And you didn't?' Costa asked. 'The day she went missing was just like every other?'

Wallis scowled. 'I told you all this sixteen years ago. The day she went missing she climbed onto her scooter and rode off for the language school. I watched her go and you know something? I *was* worried. A kid like that riding a scooter through the middle of Rome. I was worried someone might knock her over. Shows how smart I was, huh?'

Falcone handed over one of the photos from Miranda Julius's apartment: Suzi, smiling happily outside in the Campo. The man's reaction was extraordinary. He seemed more shocked by this than anything else they had said or done. Wallis's face creased with the same pain Costa had seen on the videophone at the gate. He closed his eyes and was silent for almost a minute.

Then he looked at them all, one by one, peering into their faces. 'What is this shit? You think you can pull some kind of stunt on me?' Wallis shook his head, unable to go on.

'This is no stunt,' Costa said carefully. 'That's the girl who has just gone missing. She met someone. Someone who persuaded her to have the tattoo on her shoulder, the same one that Eleanor had. Someone who talked to her about these rituals, and told her something would happen. On 17 March, the same day Eleanor went missing. Do you know her?'

Wallis listened attentively. He took a final look at the photograph then handed it back to Falcone. 'No. I'm sorry. I shouldn't have lost my cool like that. The girl reminded me of Eleanor. Her hair . . . blonde like that. It's just the same, that's all. I suppose that's what you wanted.'

Falcone avoided the man's fierce gaze. 'I want the truth. That's why we're here. Nothing else.'

'This is the past for me. You must have some ideas.' Wallis seemed to be pleading for a way out.

'Nothing,' Falcone admitted bitterly. 'A corpse. A few coincidences.' He stared at Wallis. 'And you.'

'I'm no use to you, Inspector. I'm no use to anyone. Just an old man trying to find a little dignity out here on my own. My stepdaughter's long dead. I knew she had to be, years ago. You never really believe they just disappear like that, go marry, raise kids or something, and never call. Let me mourn her. This missing girl now . . . If there was anything I could do I would, I promise.'

Falcone was beginning to flounder. 'I need you to come to the station. I need you to identify the body. Go over the statements you made—'

'Statements I made sixteen years ago! There's nothing I can add to them now.'

'Sometimes, Sir,' Costa interjected, 'you remember more when you see things from a greater perspective. Small details that meant nothing to you then become important.'

'No,' Wallis said firmly. 'I had enough of this crap back then. Listen. Am I under suspicion or something? Do I need to consult a lawyer?'

'If that's what you want,' Falcone replied. 'You're not under suspicion as far as I'm concerned.'

'Then there's nothing you can do to force me to come with you. Don't forget, gentlemen. Way back when I did a law degree. Put through college by guys who needed legal people bad. Maybe this was American law but I still got the attitude if I want it. Don't pull any funny business. I won't allow it. This meeting is at an end. I'll appoint an undertaker to talk to you about the body. When you're ready for me, I'll bury the child.'

Wallis clapped his hands. The girl in the white smock came into the room, bending her head, awaiting her orders.

'The gentlemen have finished their business here, Akiko. You'll show them out, please.'

She bowed and looked pointedly at the door.

' "Here's the deal. I don't go around cutting up bodies. You don't go around interrogating potential witnesses." Who does Falcone think he is? If it wasn't for me he wouldn't even know half of what he does now. Gratitude, I know, is unreasonable. Just a little respect now and then wouldn't go amiss.'

Teresa Lupo was at the wheel of her cherry-red Seat Leon doing 160 km/h on the *autostrada* that led to the coast past Fiumicino airport. Her remarks were addressed to the grubby orange Garfield toy that dangled from the mirror, flaked with grey tobacco ash, like a polyester puppet caught up in the aftermath of Pompeii. The cat was her constant companion on the many solitary journeys she made. It was a good listener.

Falcone's remarks had stung her all the way back to the office. They burned in her head as she finished the preliminary report on the body from the bog, based on just a few exploratory procedures. They didn't, she hoped, cloud her judgement. On the face of things there was nothing more to be said about the corpse than they already knew. The girl had died because someone had cut her throat. The knife wound was, she now accepted, rather clean and tidy, more so, in all probability, than one might have expected in Roman times. Then there was the collection of grain and seeds which she'd sent off to a horticultural expert in Florence for analysis. These were the plain facts and, though a fuller autopsy would take place in the morning, Teresa Lupo knew from instinct there was precious little else to be extracted from the body. All the scraps of information that helped them in normal cases – fabric threads, paint, human hairs, traces of blood and, most of all, DNA – were either never there in the first place or got washed away by the brown acid waters that had worked on the poor kid's corpse.

What continued to bug her was the way Falcone was so cool about the cornerstone of her original theory. Maybe the girl had died only sixteen years before, not the couple of millennia she originally thought. Nevertheless, the idea she first came up with – that all this was somehow hooked into the obscure rites and rituals of Dionysus – still stood. When she held Miranda Julius's taut, nervous body in the apartment in the Teatro di Marcello she knew that Nic Costa was right. That part of the mystery – who had disappeared with Suzi and why? – still deserved an explanation. Maybe it was more important. Suzi was, as far as anyone knew, still alive.

Falcone was taking a cop's eye view of affairs. He could be right. He usually was. Still, she couldn't shake off the idea that there was an intellectual argument that needed resolving too. Come tomorrow, when Suzi Julius would surely still be missing, Falcone could, if he felt like it, throw people on the street looking high and low for her. He could give her picture to the TV channels and the newspapers and hope someone would recognize it. These actions were, she felt, good and proper. They just weren't happening soon enough. Falcone had missed a bigger question. With Eleanor Jamieson someone had acted out a ritual that was a couple of thousand years old. Why? What kind of people would behave that way? What motivated them? And – this seemed to her a very big question indeed – where did they get their ideas from? Was there an instruction manual, handed down from generation to generation? If so, by whom?

Teresa Lupo couldn't shake the picture of Miranda Julius from her head. She had no idea what it was like to be a mother. Instinct told her she never would. All the same she'd felt some extraordinary emotion burning inside the woman on the sofa in that plush, impersonal apartment, a place that already felt as if it belonged to one person alone. Maybe Miranda was a lousy parent. Maybe the kid was just wilful, playing some kind of game. It wouldn't be the first time they'd launched a missing person inquiry on the basis of what was nothing more than a childish prank. But none of that mattered. They were still under a duty to act as if this were the most serious possible crime imaginable, and keep on acting that way until Suzi Julius walked safely back into her mother's arms.

Or not.

This, she told herself, was why she was driving like a crazy woman, racing down the *autostrada* out to the coast and Ostia. This was why she was bending the rules so much they might fracture in a million different directions, any one of which could seriously damage her career. They needed to know more about the side of things that Falcone seemed least interested in: what happened with those ancient rituals, and why someone seemed to think they deserved resurrection.

There was, she knew, only one man to talk to. Professor Randolph Kirk of the University of Rome ought to hold the answers. His book refused to leave her imagination. It wasn't just that it was the single academic work on the subject she could find. It was also part academic, part speculation. Kirk almost sounded as if he knew every last answer to every last question and didn't want to let on. Maybe there was a sequel in there somewhere. Maybe she'd offer to proofread the manuscript when she got to the dig where, as she'd ascertained in a couple of phone calls, Randolph Kirk was working this very day.

She turned off the motorway and pulled into a side lane to check the map. This really wasn't very far from where the girl's body was found – two, maybe three kilometres. A random thought surfaced. She pushed it away. Five minutes later she found the place. It was on the edge of the established archaeological site of Ostia Antica, not far from the station on the slow line back to Rome. There was a wire fence around the property and modern walls to protect the dig. She kept her finger pressed on the bell at the gate, wondering if it was making a noise anywhere. Peering through the fence the only accommodation she could see appeared to be a couple of portable office buildings parked at the back.

After a while a lone figure came out. He was a balding man in his fifties with a scraggy grey and black beard, thick glasses, and absent-minded eyes. Randolph Kirk was about her height and running to seed a little. His cheeks were florid behind the beard. His nose looked like a rosy-red pincushion. Booze maybe. He walked with a funny, rolling gait, like someone who had hip problems. Instead of the safari suit she'd expected he wore very baggy, very cheap jeans and a faded-green windcheater. She couldn't help but be disappointed. She had been imagining an Indiana Jones kind of figure, unkempt but romantic. Maybe digging up old houses didn't attract that type.

Then he sneezed, an astonishing sneeze, a two-lungs-full sneeze, with a big hooting follow-through loud enough to wake the dead and decidedly liquid too. Automatically she closed her eyes, aware that the air around her was, for a good few seconds, misty with fluid. When she opened them Randolph Kirk was digging into that big, red bulbous nose as hard as he could with the scruffiest hankie she'd ever seen, one covered in dark curlicues that looked like alien hieroglyphics.

'Professor Kirk?' she asked, smiling as hard as she could and wishing she could stop the little refrain 'Booger Bill, Booger Bill' running round her head like a schoolyard chant.

'Yes?' He looked around. He was on his own, she guessed. Was a lone woman that frightening?

'Teresa Lupo. I called. About the book.'

She'd laid the praise on thick over the phone. People who wrote books always liked that.

'Oh, excuse me,' he gasped, attacking the padlock with some keys. 'I'm being so rude. Come in, please. You're most welcome.'

He spoke with that clipped, precise accent the educated English always used in Italy. The kind you got from Cambridge and Oxford academics who thought a touch of local slang and vernacular was beneath them.

He broke off for one more cataclysmic sneeze. 'Blasted cold. Hate these things.'

She circumnavigated him at a suitable distance. They walked past the excavated remains of an old villa, covered in scaffolding and tarpaulins, and on towards the bigger of the two portable blocks. There, Kirk led her to his office, which was a mess. Papers everywhere. Bits of rock. Photographs of paintings. And one small window that hardly let in any light. He slumped into an old leather chair that looked as if it had come out of the ark. She perched on a flimsy cane stool opposite that was, she guessed, meant for students. He offered her a warm can of Coke. She declined.

'You liked the book?'

'I loved it, Professor. It opened my eyes. You know I always thought that period of history was so interesting. You just lit up so many new corners for me.'

'My,' he sighed then popped a couple of pills in his mouth and washed them down with the Coke. 'Too kind. And you know I never did make any money out of it at all. Damned publisher paid me a pittance for the manuscript, printed a few copies then hid them in a garage on Romney Marsh somewhere. It's a miracle you found it.'

'Miracles happen.'

'They do,' he said smiling, toasting her with a can.

She looked outside. The place was deserted.

'Not digging today?'

'The rest of the team are on a field trip in Germany for a week. I just came in to do some paperwork.' He waved a hand at the pile of documents on his desk.

'Are you sure you should be at work? What with the flu and all?'

'It's needed,' he said then added, with no small measure of pomposity, 'I am a head of department you know.'

'Of course,' she said ruefully, unable to take her eyes off the hankie which was burrowing away again.

'Would you like to see it?'

'What?'

'Our Villa of Mysteries? What else? Normally we don't let people in without an appointment. And then we're pretty choosy. You wouldn't believe the amount of theft that goes on around here. Only a couple of weeks ago we had two Americans hunting around outside the gates with a metal detector, would you believe? Had to send a couple of lads to chase them off.'

'Quite. Later, perhaps.'

He seemed disappointed by her reaction. She should have looked more enthusiastic. 'It's not as famous as the one at Pompeii, of course. But that doesn't make it less interesting.'

'Is it as big?'

'Oh yes. Bigger probably, once we finish digging.'

'As big as they get? Temples like this?'

He looked briefly uncomfortable, as if this was a question he hadn't expected. 'Temple's not the right word. These places were more a private religious establishment. Temples tend to be more public.'

'Of course.' She thought about the dirt beneath the dead girl's nails. It couldn't have come from Ostia. It was Roman, no doubt about it. 'I just wondered . . . if you find something so fascinating in the suburbs. What would a place like this be like in Rome?'

He sniffed. 'Vast. Astonishing. It's out there somewhere I imagine. Waiting to be found. As I said in the book, it is the Palace of Mysteries. The wellhead of the cult. The place every acolyte wished to visit, perhaps, before they died. Not that anyone will give me the money to look for it, of course.' He stared sourly at the papers in front of him. 'Even if I had the time.'

He was a curious mix of arrogance and self-pity. He liked to tantalize, too. Perhaps that was all his book amounted to, a kind of historical tease. 'I would love to see around Professor,' she said. 'The thing is I have some important questions I need to ask you first.'

He suddenly looked worried, off-guard. 'You do?'

She folded her arms, placed her elbows on the desk and peered frankly into his beady eyes. Randolph Kirk didn't look well and it wasn't just the cold. He seemed tired, as if he hadn't been sleeping much lately. Nervous too. 'I've got to be honest with you. When I said I was a fellow academic who needed a little advice I wasn't being entirely frank.'

'You weren't?' he said quietly.

She pulled out her ID card. 'Professor, strictly speaking this is not official business. Actually no one back at the Questura even knows I'm here so there's no need to get worried or think this is a police thing in any way. I won't waste your time with the reasons.'

You wouldn't even believe them, she thought. You wouldn't credit how stupid cops can be when it comes to using academic, intellectual resources.

'The point is this. I'm a pathologist attached to the state police. I've got a corpse on my slab right now that, for the life of me, looks as if it came from one of the selfsame rituals you described so accurately in your book.

The corpse those same Americans who came here found. The papers wrote all about it.'

'They did?' he bleated. Randolph Kirk didn't look as if he read papers much or watched TV.

'She's got a tattoo on the shoulder. A mask. Screaming. She's clutching a thyrsus. Fennel with a pine cone on the end. There's grain in one of her pockets. Just the kind of thing you wrote about. The body was found not far from here. In peat, which preserved it and threw out conventional dating techniques, which confused me . . . us for a while.'

He shuffled in the old leather seat, making it swivel and squeak and squeal. 'Oh.'

She was starting to find him annoying. 'All that is just as you described in the book. She was sixteen, too. The right age. What's different is this. Her throat was cut. From behind. One move, sharp knife.'

Teresa Lupo made the gesture, arcing her arm as if she were wielding the blade. Kirk's florid cheeks went a shade paler and the hankie performed a double dance across his face.

'And it can't be what I thought. She's not a peat body from a couple of thousand years old, maybe sacrificed here and then buried in the bog. We know who she is. Or at least we think we do. And she died just sixteen years ago. They even put a coin in her mouth. A tip for the ferryman. Can you beat that?'

'No,' he whispered. 'I can't.'

'I just need to understand more about what motivated these people. What exactly did they hope to gain? Knowledge?'

He shook his head. 'Not knowledge.'

'What then? Some kind of personal advantage? Or was it just like joining a club or something?'

He thought about those ideas. 'A club,' he said. 'That's an interesting idea.'

Teresa was beginning to get exasperated. 'I was hoping, because you knew so much about all these rituals, you could maybe help me. You see there's another girl. She went missing today and somehow . . .' she struggled for the right words to describe this odd situation, ' . . . it all looks similar. It all looks as if something could happen the day after tomorrow, 17 March.'

'17 March?' He had another habit, too, when he wasn't poking at his adenoids. He kept moving his glasses up and down his red, pock-marked nose with the forefinger of his right hand. Thinking, she guessed.

'You're a police officer?'

'No,' she corrected him. 'I'm a pathologist working with the police.'

'You didn't tell them you were coming here. Why?'

'Because—' It was an odd question. The alarm bell that was beginning to sound somewhere at the back of her head was just plain stupid. It had to be. 'Can you help me, Professor?'

The glasses were going up and down his nose. He didn't look the physical type. He didn't look anything much at all.

'You must excuse me,' Professor Randolph Kirk said, suddenly getting out of his chair. 'I have a digestive problem. I really have to go.'

He paused at the door and looked back at her. 'One moment please. I may be a little while.'

Thirty minutes later, feeling more and more stupid, she got up and tried the handle. Randolph Kirk had locked it. She walked quickly to the window and took a good look at the frame. The ancient clasp for the latch had rusted long ago. It must have been years since anyone opened the thing.

'Shit,' she groaned. 'Shit, shit, shit and double shit.'

There was just the trace of a signal on her mobile phone. She wondered who to call, what to say. Falcone was going to go ballistic. As if that were the biggest of her worries.

'Don't sweat, girl. He's an academic. He's got a nose like a pineapple and flu bugs doing the Macarena in his veins. Unless he comes through that door wielding a pickaxe I've got no problem at all.'

All the same she looked around the room for something to use as a weapon. There was a small, short hammer on a filing cabinet, nothing more.

'Nic,' she murmured, starting to dial. 'Come save me, Nic. Oh crap—'

The number rang once and then went dead. There was a sound outside. It was a motorbike. A powerful one, judging by the low rumble of the engine.

She stopped dialling and listened hard. This could be important.

After a couple of seconds, Teresa Lupo couldn't hear a thing. Some unseen force, the pumping of her own blood in her ears maybe, was drowning out the sounds beyond the door and she felt she ought to be grateful. She was familiar with death, not with dying. Just then she was an outsider, overhearing some important dumb show happening in the shadows. Even when she was a real medical doctor and people died in hospital it was, somehow, appropriate. Nothing ever really came out of the blue, violently, as it did for so many of the customers on her shining silver table. But she knew nothing of what it was like to witness such an act.

And here it was, happening unseen just a few metres away, beyond the flimsy door of Professor Randolph Kirk's office. Over the beating of her heart, she could hear the drama being enacted, like a scene from a radio play leaking out from a neighbouring window. The voices, two, both high, one rising, one falling in grim fear.

Then the scream and the report of a gun, so loud it blocked out everything.

Her breathing stopped for a moment. Something had happened then. A void had opened in her head, a blank page of expectation, and into it walked some dark, shrouded certainty that a human being, Professor Randolph Kirk to be precise, had, at that instant, ceased to be. A living person was gone from the earth and the scariest thing of all was that Teresa Lupo, in her imagination felt as if something, his spirit perhaps, his departing shade, had stepped through her own body leaving a single word imprinted in her mind: *run*.

She couldn't think straight. She could hardly catch her breath. There were footsteps and she found herself frozen, looking at the door, hearing someone rattle a set of unfamiliar keys at the lock, searching for the right one.

'Turn that damned thing off,' Falcone barked. 'I want to think.'

They were in Falcone's office watching the clips of CCTV from the Campo when Costa's phone rang. It sounded once before he hit the power button. The mood wasn't good. Rachele D'Amato was nursing a tender ego and uninterested in pursuing any link with Suzi Julius. Falcone had scowled at a skimpy preliminary report on the Jamieson girl from Teresa Lupo. The video seemed predictable at first but it bothered Costa all the same.

The bike rider wore a shiny helmet with an opaque visor and a full-length leather black suit, just like a street punk out to do some bag-snatching. The girl had 'tourist' written all over her. Here she was, dashing through the dwindling crowd in the Campo, dressed in tee-shirt and black jeans, a small canvas bag over her shoulder, right in front of the two uniformed carabinieri men who stood by their car yawning, uninterested. Costa couldn't believe their lack of attention. Suzi seemed to be running from something, or so it seemed to him. It should have rung an alarm bell somewhere.

The rider's wrist flicked on the throttle. There was something odd going on with the girl. He couldn't work out whether she was laughing or crying. Then another figure came into view, sprinting: Miranda Julius fighting her way through the tangle of shoppers, yelling at her departing daughter's back.

Costa wondered whether he was reading this all the wrong way. Sometimes cops took too much upon themselves. They walked into domestic situations that were best left alone. They interpreted events mistakenly and wound up with egg on their faces. Suzi reached the big, powerful bike, kissed the side of the helmet quickly, then hopped on the back, wrapping her arms around the rider's waist. The machine bucked once as it went into gear. Then the two of them were off, bobbing and weaving through the crowds.

As the bike negotiated the corner of the square the

girl turned round, one hand still clinging to the rider's waist, looking for someone. Miranda halted then looked back at the carabinieri. She was panting, out of breath. Suzi brought her fingers to her lips and blew a farewell kiss across the Campo before the bike disappeared, out into the Corso.

Just a teenager running away with her boyfriend? Maybe, Costa thought. This was meant to look like some simple, domestic drama, almost enacted deliberately for public consumption. Maybe for the girl it was. But there was something wrong here. The bike didn't have a number plate. Even street hoods didn't favour black like that, with opaque visors. Nor did they like such big, powerful bikes. Little scooters were cheaper, more manoeuvrable. It was all too much of a giveaway.

'I don't like it,' he said when the clip came to an end. 'Why does the bike have no plate?'

Rachele D'Amato wriggled on her seat. 'Can we focus on the task in hand, please? I'm not here to chase runaway teenagers.'

'It could be linked,' Falcone said. 'Costa's right. There's something strange going on there.'

He got up and threw open the door of the office. The staff room was horribly depleted, no more than ten men at the desks, close to half the normal manning level thanks to the flu. Falcone looked at the officer nearest to the door.

'Bianchi. Who's hottest on this CCTV stuff around here?'

The man thought about this for a moment. 'You mean of the people who're in? Me. Ricci's the real expert but he's home sneezing his eyeballs out. I can call him, though. Get some tips. What do you want?'

'Get some footage in from the cameras in the Corso. Find out where that bike went afterwards.'

Bianchi hesitated. 'Er, that's some job, sir. You get no more than a hundred metres or so coverage from each camera. I've been through this before. All you can manage is about a kilometre a day, no more. If he's gone any distance we're talking a week, if we're lucky.'

Falcone scowled and scanned the office again. 'Give it a day. Maybe he didn't go far.'

'Sure,' Bianchi said.

'And get a couple of pictures out to the media. Keep it low key enough not to start a panic. Just say she's a missing girl and we're looking for information. Say there's no reason for concern just now but we'd like to hear from her, or someone who's seen her, all the same.'

'It's done, boss,' Bianchi said and picked up the phone.

Then Falcone went back to his desk, closing the door behind him and looked at D'Amato. 'So tell me something about Wallis I don't know.'

Her eyes widened. 'Are you serious? The position as I understand it is he won't talk to me at all. And when it comes to having a meaningful conversation, he won't talk to you either.'

'I don't think he's his own man in this,' Costa said. 'Not completely. It's as if he's looking behind him all the time. Why's that?'

She cast him a cold glance. She knew the answer. She wanted to make them work for it.

'Well?' Falcone demanded.

She swore quietly under her breath. 'Wallis fell out big time with the hood he was supposed to befriend. Emilio Neri.'

'We know that,' Falcone declared impatiently.

'Perhaps,' she snapped. 'But do you understand the implications? Both sides, the Americans and the Sicilians, had to come in and keep those two apart. Big people don't like that. Wallis's punishment was retirement. The punishment sticks. My guess is that if they think he's messing around again with things he shouldn't, even talking too freely to us, he's in big trouble.'

'And this Neri guy?' Peroni asked. 'I remember him from my beat. What was his punishment?'

'A slap on the wrist,' she said. 'Neri was on his home turf. He was bound to come out on top. Besides . . . Neri's a different kind of animal. Wallis is educated. He's got limits. He was in this for business reasons, not some personal vendetta. Neri would rob his grandmother's grave if he felt like it and go home to boast.'

None of this helped them understand what had happened to Wallis's stepdaughter, Costa thought. Or where Suzi Julius might be now.

'What if Neri was involved with the death of the girl?' he wondered. 'Maybe that was the way he punished Wallis?'

'Neri's a thug,' Falcone said. 'If he wanted to kill someone, he'd kill Wallis himself.'

He nodded at D'Amato. 'You're wrong if you think Neri doesn't have a code, by the way. Men like him still have some rules. They need them to maintain their position with their troops. Killing a teenage girl to punish another hood . . . It doesn't look proper. It would damage his standing. Besides, he'd have to let it be known he'd done it, otherwise why bother? If he'd taken responsibility we'd have heard.'

'There's still plenty of reasons to talk to him,' she suggested. 'No harm done.'

'I get it! I get it!' Peroni said, a little too loudly. 'That means, of course, the DIA still have to tag along because we got the mob in the loop. And if it's just a plain murder inquiry it's nothing to do with you.'

She shot him a savage glance. 'I'm trying to help! Will you people kindly stop treating me like I'm the enemy?'

Peroni looked out of the window and whistled.

'And the girl?' Costa wondered. 'Suzi Julius? Where does she fit in?'

Falcone looked at the image frozen on the TV screen, of the Campo, with Miranda Julius static, staring at the route the bike had taken from the square. 'I wish to hell I knew. Let's hope she's just another runaway kid. I don't see how we can treat this as anything else but a missing teenager inquiry until I see something that says different. If there's any indication this is something more – and I mean *any* – I want to know about it instantly. Until then . . .' he made sure Costa looked at him, ' . . . let's get our priorities straight. We have a murder case on our hands and that's what we focus on. It's the only thing we know for sure right now.'

'Suzi Julius is still alive—' He couldn't get the picture of the mother's face out of his head, all the pain there, and the fearful anticipation.

'I know that,' Falcone said firmly. 'We're doing all we can, Nic.'

'And we're in too?' D'Amato asked. 'You know the rules, Leo. This involves organized crime. Like it or not, the people you're talking about here have been up to their necks in it for years. Neri, for one, still is.'

'Yeah, yeah. You're in.' Falcone looked at his watch then looked at her. 'Provided it's share and share alike. Understood?'

She smiled. 'How could it be otherwise?'

Falcone rose from his chair and the three of them got ready to follow him. 'Let's talk to the harpy in the morgue about that body. This report is skimpy and she knows it.'

Costa punched his phone back on as they left the room. He didn't like losing the call. He didn't want to be out of touch with anything for a moment.

It came alive halfway down the corridor, ringing straight away. Teresa Lupo's voice was so loud it almost hurt his ear.

There was a single, snatched message then the line went dead.

Stupid things come naturally in some circumstances.

You think about throwing an ancient PC monitor through the jammed window of a dead academic's portable office, knowing all along the frame is too small for you to squeeze through even if you succeed.

You sit in a fake Roman villa on the Janiculum hill and try to remember what it was like in the days when you had to scheme to stay alive.

And, in the case of Emilio Neri, whose phone had burned long and hot that afternoon, you storm around your rich man's palace in the Via Giulia, amazed at the way the past can resurrect itself out of nowhere, cursing your errant son and your profligate wife, wondering where the hell they were when you needed to yell at them.

Fear and fury share the same ill-defined borders. Watching the door handle twist just an arm's length away from her, Teresa Lupo felt both mad and scared as she tried to force some sense and reason into her head. Then blunt instinct took over. She stood to one side, by the hinges, gripping the puny hammer with both hands, waiting.

It took no more than a moment. The lock turned, the door began to open, slowly. She held her breath, wondering what he was expecting: a figure cowering in the corner. That had to be it.

'I don't cower,' she whispered to herself, and waited until he'd pushed it to forty-five degrees, enough, she guessed, to get his body positioned in the potential vice between the door edge and the frame.

She had a pathologist's muscles. She was carrying some excess weight too. She snatched some air into her lungs, stepped back briefly, then lunged with her shoulder into the centre of the plywood slab. It closed on the rider's body. She bounced harder. Someone screamed: high-pitched, pained. Teresa Lupo darted round the edge of the door and saw him: a black figure in leather, face invisible behind the dark visor of the helmet. He was crouching, clutching his chest. Maybe she'd broken a couple of ribs. She hoped so. A long black pistol lay on the grubby office floor where he'd dropped it. She stabbed at the thing with her foot, was dismayed to see it slide only a metre or so away from him. Then she threw aside the hammer, grabbed the creep by the back of the helmet and yanked hard.

The biker fell into the room. He wasn't a big guy. If she'd gone to self-defence lessons as she'd always intended, Teresa Lupo reckoned she could have taken him on there and then. Beaten him up a touch. Tied him to a chair. Waved a magic wand over the gun just in case. Been Linda Hamilton out of *Terminator 2*, all muscles and vengeance. Or something. Her head was running away with itself. Dangerous. She kicked him hard out of the way, struggled through the door, was glad to see the dim light of a clear early evening sky drifting through the bigger windows here.

The old cheap wood slammed shut behind her. She turned the key in the lock then snatched the bunch and threw them across the room, gasping, short of breath, trying to think about what to do next.

You look.

Professor Randolph Kirk lay on the floor in a bloody bundle, face uppermost, dead eyes staring at the ceiling. There was a ragged black hole in his forehead leaking gore. Automatically, she began to think of the autopsy. All the incisions, all the organs she'd have to examine, just so that she could come up with the obvious con-clusion: *this man died because someone pumped a piece of metal into his brain. I see no sign of improvement in his condition. The likelihood is that this is a permanent affliction.*

With shaking fingers, Teresa Lupo dragged the phone out of her jacket pocket again, stabbing Nic Costa's number on the keys, struggling to get it right, praying, praying.

His voice crackled in the earpiece, surprised, and sounding very young.

'Nic, Nic!' she yelled. 'I'm in deep shit. Help me.'

There was silence on the line. She wondered whether that was really his breathing she could hear or just some digital static blowing in with the chemicals from the Mediterranean a kilometre away to the west.

'Just outside Ostia Antica,' she screeched. 'The place I told you about. Please—'

Then there was a sound behind her, a sound so loud it just had to go down the phone and convince Nic Costa this was indeed serious. A sound that reminded Teresa Lupo she really was stupid in these matters.

He still had the gun.

'Idiot,' she hissed at herself, and dashed out of the door, the blasts of the pistol, emptying its load into the lock, ringing behind her.

Three police Alfas sped past Piramide, sirens blaring, blue lights flashing. Falcone sat in the front vehicle, with Peroni driving down the middle of the road, pushing everything to one side. Costa held onto the dashboard, trying to make sense of things.

'Stupid bitch,' Falcone murmured. They'd talked to Monkboy who'd come clean about Teresa's destination once they scared him witless. 'Who does she think she is?'

'We should've talked to the man ourselves,' Costa volunteered.

Falcone leaned forward from the back seat and prodded his shoulder. 'It was on my list for tomorrow, smart-ass. We take things one step at a time.' The inspector leaned back in his seat and stared at the lines of grey suburban houses flashing past the window. A red, poisoned sun was setting through the smog in the distance. The city looked grim and dead. 'And we don't go anywhere on our own. In case you two hadn't noticed we're dealing with big boys here. I don't want any risks. I hate funerals.'

Rachele D'Amato was in the car behind. Falcone had organized it that way.

'At the risk of repeating myself,' Peroni ventured, 'do we really need the woman from the DIA along?'

'Who knows?' Falcone replied. 'Until we get there.'

'This is some university professor she went to see, right?' Peroni wondered. 'What's a man like that got to do with the Mafia?'

Falcone said nothing. Peroni braked hard to avoid a street-cleaning truck, then wound down the window and began yelling obscenities into the smoggy evening air.

She came back at five thirty, laden down with shopping bags bearing the names of all the best designer labels. She looked perfect. Adele always did. Her red hair was newly trimmed and a little less red somehow, with a blonde tint shining from beneath. Not a strand was out of place. She wore a trouser suit in crumpled white silk and a grey mink jacket. Neri couldn't work out whether they were new or not. She bought so many clothes he guessed she must throw half out each week just to make room for more.

He watched her go to the open kitchen and make herself a *spremuta*, topping up the juice with black Stolichnaya. 'Where the hell have you been? I tried getting you on the phone.'

'Battery went flat.'

'Then charge the fucking thing next time you go out. If there is a next time. Maybe I'm introducing a curfew around here.'

She walked over and kissed him on the cheek, taking care to let her loose hand idly stroke the front of his trousers. 'Bad day, sweetheart?'

'The worst. And where are my family when I need them?'

She blinked at him. She had long, very fine black eyelashes. He wondered how much they cost, how much of them was real.

'You need me?' Her hand went down again. He pushed it away.

'Don't have time for that shit.'

'What else do I do for you?' she asked plainly. 'What else is there?'

'You're supposed to be a wife. You're supposed to be here. Giving me some support. Instead I just got a couple of my own men and them stupid servants who piss around doing nothing downstairs.'

'Support? What kind of support do you want?'

He wished she'd just let this go. Normally she did. Lately, though, she'd been different. It began soon after Mickey had come to live with them. The kid was bad news, like a piece of grit getting inside an oyster, always rubbing away, making things worse, and no pearl at the end. Neri couldn't help wondering what scams he was running on the side too, and keeping it quiet whenever he got asked. The stupid clothes and the dyed blonde hair were beginning to bug him. And the way he and Adele just kept going at each other. A thought floated across his mind. Sometimes, Neri knew, you saw what you wanted to see, what you were supposed to see. You never saw the truth.

'Never mind. Was Mickey out with you? He should've been back here hours ago.'

'Out with me?' She looked at him as if he were crazy. 'Don't you think I see enough of him lounging around in here? He's your son. Not mine. You work out where he is, who he's fucking now.'

Neri couldn't believe his ears. She just didn't talk like this. He raised the back of his hand. 'Watch your mouth.'

Adele waved a long skinny finger in his face. 'Don't hit me, Emilio. Don't even think of going down that road.'

He balled his fingers into a fist, made as if to swipe her with it then stopped. There was too much going on to let distractions like this worm their way into his head. He could deal with Adele later. And Mickey if need be.

'Where is he?' Neri repeated.

'I haven't seen him since this morning. He went out before midday. Maybe he's out screwing some dumb hooker in his car. It's what he likes to do, isn't it?'

They'd argued about this before. Two months ago the police found Mickey shafting some cheap African whore in Neri's own vintage Alfa Spyder down a back street off the Via Veneto. The stupid kid didn't even know the law, which gave the cops the right to impound the car. It had taken all the powers of persuasion Neri possessed, and a substantial bribe, to get the thing back. Another expense. The cost of parenthood. Had Mickey learned? Probably not. The kid just didn't care.

'Listen,' Neri said, taking Adele by her slender, bony shoulders, shaking her just a little. 'Listen carefully.'

She pulled free, but she looked a little worried all the same. Maybe, Neri thought, she sensed the atmosphere was changing somehow, was wondering how it might affect her.

'In case you haven't noticed, this is not a good time

for me,' Neri said. 'That means it's not a good time for you either, if you could just get it into your scrawny fucking head. There are bad things happening I don't need at my age. Some of it of my own making maybe. Some of it because of other people who ought to know better. I just want you to understand.'

'Bad?' she asked, looking puzzled by his sudden frankness. 'How bad, Emilio?'

There was a noise outside: a couple of cars drawing up. They went to the window. It had started to rain now. Thin lines of drizzle came down silvery black through the night, drenching the steady traffic on the Lungotevere.

Neri watched her eyeballing the men who got out of the cars. She was no fool. She knew their type. Normally he didn't even allow them into the house.

'Why are they here?'

'You ever been in a war?' he asked, hating the word as he said it. Wars weren't supposed to happen. They cost money. They could get you into big trouble with people who thought those days were past.

'Of course not.'

'Start learning,' he murmured, as much to himself as her. 'These are what we call troops.'

'Four wheels good, two wheels bad,' Teresa Lupo chanted to herself as the Seat lurched along the rough, potholed lane leading from the dig, topping a hundred and twenty as it tackled the bumps. She'd just made it to the car in time to see him stumble out of the portable office, still with the helmet and black visor in place, looking like some deadly insect hunting its prey.

Bugman was riding a motorbike. She was in a car.

There had to be some advantage there. It was dark now too, with a little greasy rain falling from the sky. *Four wheels good . . .*

Except it didn't mean much right then. The bike rider seemed to possess his own special brand of gravity. The Leon breasted the hard shoulder of the main road, leapt briefly into the air, and turned, tyres screeching, towards the airport.

When she managed to get control of the car once more, seeing with some relief the lights of the main terminal a couple of kilometres off in the distance, she plucked up sufficient courage to glance in the mirror. He'd made up ground. He must be riding the Honda from hell. It seemed to stick to the greasy road in a way the Seat couldn't. They'd been a good three hundred metres apart when she approached the end of the track. Now half the gap she'd enjoyed had disappeared. The thing moved like crap off a hot shovel.

'Holy fuck,' she whispered idly and stared at the mobile phone on the seat. She didn't even dare try to call again. She needed both hands on the wheel. She needed her mind set on survival, nothing else.

The car dropped into fourth, she floored the accelerator and roared past a couple of slow-moving trucks, one of which was just lumbering into the outside lane to overtake. The mirror was briefly a mass of metal as the two leviathans leaned into each other for dominance. Then the bike came through between them, squeezing into a gap no more than a metre or so wide, speeding ahead.

'Jesus.' She stared into the mirror. 'What did I do? Where are the cops, for God's sake?'

The terminal didn't seem much closer just then. All

her ideas of safety in its bright lights were starting to disappear. And anyway, her mind told her, Mr Insect Head didn't care about bright lights. She could run in and march straight up to check in at the Alitalia First Class desk and he'd still follow, all the way on his bright and shiny machine, pausing only to pump a couple of bullets into her head before riding out of the doors again, because that's what men on motorbikes did.

Four wheels good . . .

The shape was getting closer all the time now. If he made a couple of flicks with his insect wrist he could draw right up at the driver's window, even tap on the glass.

'To hell with that,' she said, and dragged the wheel hard over to the left, braking all the time.

The bike rider caught on quickly. He wasn't going to plough straight into her side and pop his black frame right over the roof, thrown by the deadly weight of his own momentum. Instead he just put down a strong leather foot, slid the machine along the damp road, in control all the way, staring, staring.

'Point taken,' Teresa murmured, and hit the accelerator once more, straightened the Seat with a vicious lurch, and found herself heading straight for the no entry barrier over a side road in construction just a hundred metres or so ahead.

There were men in white jackets and yellow hard hats working there. She held her hand on the horn, watching them scatter. The Leon went into a long, lazy sideways skid. She found the wheel twitching in her hands like a wild creature with a mind of its own.

Instinctively, she turned into the slide, felt the car come back under her control. Something smashed into the window behind her and exited out of the front windscreen, taking with it her vision of the road ahead. A circle of opaque shattered glass now sat between her and the black emptiness that was the world racing up to greet her. She glanced at the dashboard. It read ninety. She couldn't hear a thing except the car screaming.

'Not a good day,' Teresa Lupo murmured, and was minded, for some reason, to take her hands off the wheel because there was something else demanding her attention.

A figure kept bobbing up at the driver's window: long and black and deadly. Its arm was extended. The insect looked ready to sting.

Knowing it was stupid, and doing this very suddenly, very deliberately, she released her hands, crouched down in the driver's seat, hands over her head, praying for protection, muttering over and over again that odd word they told you on the airplanes, 'Brace, brace, brace . . .'

The Leon bounced once. The universe turned turtle. She was aware, for one brief moment, that things were not as they should be and wondered whether this was the start of the great secret called 'death'. And then another unsettling thought, as the Leon rolled, and bounced through the air, making her feel giddy and sick.

'Not Monkboy,' she murmured. 'Let anybody do it but Monkboy.'

There was the noise of shrieking metal. A sharp pain stabbed at the top of her skull. She felt herself rolled around inside the dying Leon like a bean in a can.

Finally, the world stopped moving.

Teresa Lupo was upside down in the car. Something warm and sticky was dripping down her face: blood. She reached up and felt for the damage. Just a cut above her right temple.

'What fucking awful luck,' she gasped, and suppressed an urge to laugh.

There was a desperate, scrabbling sound at the driver's door which was now pointed at the black night sky. She heard voices and cowered in the front seat, wondering if the insect had bred. All the world seemed hostile at that moment. Logic and plain humanity had disappeared from the planet.

Then cold air blew into her face. Faces peered at her. Men said all the usual things they liked to say about women drivers in these situations.

'Can you move?' someone wearing a yellow hat asked, holding out a hand.

She tried lifting herself. It worked. Just bruises, that was all. And a little cut in the hairline.

He had to be gone, she thought. He wouldn't dare come into this mass of people, all of them extending their arms to her.

Teresa Lupo climbed out of the car, wondering whether she was about to burst into a fit of hysterical giggles. The Leon was on its side in what appeared to be the middle of a building site. A few metres away was a vast hole with concrete round the edges, a chasm cut into the earth big enough to take a train.

'Where's the bike?' she asked.

The man who'd helped her out looked into the dead mouth of the hole and pointed downwards. 'Not good,' he said. 'Boy was he moving.'

'How deep is it?'

'*Very* deep. We're doing some work on the metro.'

'Wow,' she said, and couldn't stop herself beaming, in spite of the bruises and what felt like a cracked rib.

There were sirens in the distance. The lights of police cars. She thought about Falcone and his temper. Then she thought about Randolph Kirk and a lost girl called Suzi Julius, who was the point of all this in the first place.

'We're getting a crane in,' the man said. He hesitated. 'Did you two argue or something? We called a doctor.'

Teresa Lupo nodded, smoothing down her clothes, trying to put on a professional face, wondering how she could even begin to square this with Falcone.

'A doctor?' she asked. 'Thanks, but I'm fine.'

The man gave her an odd look and nodded at the big black chasm in the ground. 'For him . . .'

'Oh?' She walked to the edge of the hole and peered into nothingness. Then Teresa Lupo picked up a big block of smashed concrete and launched it into the air, watching it tumble downwards and yelled, '*Impudent fucking bastard . . .*'

She came back and took the man by the arm. He flinched.

'I can deal with him,' she said with a smile. 'I'm a doctor. I'm with the police too. So go tell the rubber-neckers to run along now. Nothing to see here.'

Police tape ran around the site of Randolph Kirk's excavations. Floodlights stood over his portable office illuminating the bloodstains on the bare floor. Monkboy had been assigned the job of dealing with the body. Teresa Lupo had argued, with some justification, that she should be kept away through a conflict of interest. In truth, she wanted to be with the second team, watching the cranes lower a recovery section down into the big black hole near Fiumicino, waiting for them to come back with a corpse, desperate to see it transformed from the dark insect of her imagination into a real and dead human being.

Falcone had deferred to her judgement. He didn't even look mad. Maybe he was saving his fury for a time when she'd feel it more.

Nic Costa watched Monkboy and his men remove the corpse. Falcone stood to one side with Rachele D'Amato, deep in some private conversation, Peroni eyeing them, making grumpy noises all the time.

'She's here for the duration,' Costa said when he could stand no more. 'Best learn to live with it.'

'But why? This guy didn't work for the mob. He was a professor for God's sake.'

'We don't know,' Costa said. 'We know less than we did a couple of hours ago.'

Suzi Julius was somewhere, though, even if her name, and her mysterious disappearance, were now sinking deep into the squad's collective unconscious, despatched there by bigger, more pressing events. Maybe she was nearby. Here, even, dead already because all those well-laid plans for two days hence suddenly seemed impractical. He glanced around the site, at the other office and the low, hulking shape of the old Roman villa.

'I'm going walkabout,' he announced. 'Falcone won't miss me.'

There was nothing of any interest in the other office. The villa looked more promising. It could have been an old church or something: brick walls, loose, crumbly mortar. The darkness hid most of the detail but he guessed the building was that familiar pale honey colour he knew from the spent masonry on the Via Appia Antica where he'd grown up. The place was about forty metres square with an open courtyard at the front full of wrecked stones and, fenced off, a small mosaic, unidentifiable in the dark. The colonnaded entrance was open to the air. He walked in and found himself inside a cold, dank anteroom with two adjoining chambers on either side running back into the heart of the building. They were open too, and empty. The centre of the place must have been a windowless hall. The design was odd. This couldn't be a normal home. It didn't make sense.

There was an old wooden panelled door blocking the way to the interior, with a padlock on a rusty chain keeping it closed. He went back to the car and returned with a big torch and a crowbar. It took a minute to prise the rusty links from the lock. Then the torch made a bright arc into the pitch-black interior, illuminating the shadows on the walls. The place seemed empty: just a bare room. So why was there a padlock on the door? What was it protecting?

He made a careful circumnavigation of the small, windowless space: nothing. Then, just before he gave up, his foot stumbled on something. It was a wooden panel on the floor, built into the ancient brickwork. Modern, by the looks of it. And it had a padlock too, bright and shiny, hooked through a clasp.

Costa worked at it with the crowbar and forced the fastening free. When he removed the panel he exposed a series of narrow, shallow steps leading down into blackness, a subterranean cavern of some kind.

There were lights here too. Wires ran down one side of the steps, with a switch cut into the rough wall at the base of the stairs. A bare bulb, perhaps the first of several, dangled ahead in the darkness. Nic Costa didn't know anything about archaeology but that struck him as odd. Surely they would use portable floods? A string of bulbs seemed like normal lighting, the kind you got in a hall.

Costa checked himself. You were supposed to do these things in twos. It was possible there was someone else around. This could be a perfect place to hide, to stay out of sight until it was all over.

And then drag Suzi somewhere else. Or just leave a body on the mouldy earth.

'No time,' he said to himself. Besides, he was sick of the way they kept giving him that tired look whenever he mentioned the girl.

He took the gun out of its holster, hugged the wall, and walked down into the subterranean cavern, step by step. The temperature immediately seemed to fall a couple of degrees. The place had the dank, fungal smell of something rotten.

There wasn't a sound. At the bottom he flipped the switch on the wall and walked through a doorway so low he had to duck to get through.

The room was brightly lit. This must, he realized, have been restored somewhat. It was impossible that original wall paintings could have remained so bright and vivid for two thousand years. Or maybe they weren't original at all. Maybe someone had painted them there recently for some reason.

Nic Costa looked at them and thought: *here lie nightmares.* And maybe that was what they really were. Some desperate effort to take this poison out of the human mind, to exorcize it by transforming the living demons inside a man's head into images on some ancient, pagan wall.

They ran around the rectangular chamber in a series of frames, each with the same bright red background behind the detail. A figurative mosaic frieze of dolphins and sea monsters capped every scene. Painted columns divided one frame from the next. The pictures were designed, he understood, to be viewed as a series, a set of linked images which told a story. From what he recalled of Teresa's brief lecture that morning, it had to be that of an initiation into the Dionysian mysteries.

To his right, covering the short wall by the door, was what he assumed to be the beginning of the tale. An imposing male figure, the god himself perhaps, reclined lazily on a golden throne, with a horned satyr on each side, both peering into silver water bowls. At his feet lay a young woman, her face covered by a veil, holding a phallic object topped with a pine cone: Teresa's thyrsus. The long wall next to this contained three further frames. A naked child read out loud from a scroll. Three female dancers, hands clasped together, faces ecstatic, turned around an urn. An old crone in a dark robe, crouched on a decaying tree trunk, peered malevolently at a beautiful young woman seated in front of a mirror, toying with her hair.

The main wall opposite the entrance was occupied by a single work. The young woman was entering the presence of the god. Black slaves scourged her with whips. Satyrs played lutes in the background. There was terror on the initiate's face. The god leered hungrily at her from his throne.

Costa turned to face the left wall. Here were more rituals: scourging, drinking, dancing, coupling. The four frames depicted an orgy but one that sat at the edge of sanity, like something from the imagination of a Roman Hieronymus Bosch. In the corners of the images there were revellers who were unconscious or vomiting. A pregnant mother suckled a child on one breast and a goat on the other. Women lay on their backs embracing horses and lions. Two girls were engaged in a bloody fight, rolling on the floor, scratching at each other's eyes.

And in the last image an execution: one woman walked on, blindfolded towards the god. The second was killed, her throat cut from behind by a grinning satyr who pressed his groin against her buttocks.

He turned to face the final frame, the counterpart to the first, set on the other side of the door. The god still sat on his throne but now he wore a mask, the obscene screaming mask that was the source of the tattoo he'd seen on both the dead Eleanor Jamieson and the living Suzi Julius. They were poor imitations. In the god's face lay a blind, hungry fury that couldn't be reduced to a scrawl on flesh.

The initiate was naked, half standing over him, face forward, as he savaged her from behind, his hand reaching round to grip her left breast hard between his fingers. Her face was partially covered with a veil. Her mouth was wide open in a screaming rictus of agony. The shape of his massive erection was visible beneath her open legs. Satyrs and hangers-on watched avidly, with wild eyes and open, hungry mouths.

Was this the ordeal Wallis's stepdaughter had refused? Costa wondered. Perhaps in a room very much like this? And if she hadn't, where would she be now? Anywhere, he realized. If Teresa was right, this villa was just an outpost. Somewhere in Rome there stood the Villa of

Mysteries, the heart of the cult, a hidden temple, just like this one, buried beneath the earth.

It didn't add up. One man, surely, would not go to these strange lengths. Randolph Kirk couldn't have been the figure racing a bike across the Campo with Suzi Julius happy on the back. That was someone young, someone she knew.

Costa tried to think practical thoughts. This wasn't an active dig. There was no sign of recent excavation. Yet people did come here regularly. He could see the odd cigarette butt and a few sweet wrappers. The university maintained the site. They would use it for study, surely.

He walked around the corners, using the torch to illuminate the darker parts.

Something bright lurked close to the image of the god and the screaming initiate. He took a plastic envelope out of his pocket, bent down and picked it up. It was an elastic hair-band, bright red, green and yellow, Rastafarian colours, the kind a young girl would use. He searched the rest of the room as best he could. There was nothing else of obvious interest.

Then he walked back up the stairs, back to the portable office. It was getting late now. Falcone looked tired, gloomy. D'Amato stood silent by his side.

'The scene of crime people can take a look at the place once they're done here,' he said after listening to Costa's ideas. 'There's probably nothing left from sixteen years ago, Nic, if that's what you're thinking. Besides, Lupo already said she was probably killed somewhere in the city.'

'I know,' he answered and held up the hair-band. 'But this isn't sixteen years old.'

Rachele D'Amato peered at the plastic bag. 'It's the

kind of thing a child would wear,' she said. 'Did they let children in there on visits?'

He thought of the pictures on the walls. 'I can't imagine they'd allow that.'

Falcone raised a grey eyebrow. 'You think so? These are liberated days. Look, it's late. If you think there's something to chase here go and see the mother. On your own. We're a little short of men. If she recognizes it, try the lab. There must be millions like it. We need to know for sure. Then get some rest. We're all going to be working overtime tomorrow.'

'You can say that again,' she whispered.

Costa saw them exchange a glance. He wondered if something was going on between them and whether that could cloud the man's normally excellent judgement.

Then Falcone took him to one side, peered inquisitively into his face. 'How are you doing? You look dog-tired. You been drinking recently?'

'No,' Costa snapped. 'Are you my boss or my keeper?'

'A little of both. For now anyway.'

Falcone's phone rang. He listened then said, 'Wait for me.'

Costa hesitated, wanting to know the news.

'We'll follow you part of the way,' Falcone said. 'That was the crew at Fiumicino. They're about to bring up the body. It seems Crazy Teresa can't wait to get her hands on it.'

'Can you blame her?' D'Amato wondered.

'Damned right I can,' Falcone murmured, walking away so quickly they had to struggle to keep up.

*

The rain had stopped. The heart of Rome was growing silent. A generous moon now stared down at its own hard reflection in the black shiny waters of the Tiber. The day's warmth had fled, a reminder that winter was relinquishing its grip with a slowly dying reluctance.

Adele Neri lay alone in the bedroom. Her husband was still up, talking long and hard to the bleak, grey men he'd invited into their lives. Their voices crept beneath the closed door, intruding into her most private thoughts. Mickey was nowhere to be seen. Nor had he called. It was unusual, but not unexpected. He'd been crazier than normal recently. Some of it was due to the dope, which he was taking unseen by his father. Some of it was down to the deals on the side, and his terror that his father would find out about them. But most of it came from this sudden and fierce fixation for his stepmother, one she had no intention of discouraging. She liked the way he thought of her, the things she could do to him drove Mickey wild. Adele had some power over Emilio, but it was muted, fixed by boundaries, and always had been. Now it was waning too. Emilio was feeling his age, realizing that change would soon be inevitable.

Mickey was different. He'd do just about anything she asked. Anything. And he was young. He didn't thrash away for a couple of minutes then roll over and go to sleep, grunting, snoring. He gave her something back. Although, when she thought about it, Adele Neri realized those gifts no longer contained the attraction for her they once had. The physical world had limitations. With age came a realization that there were more intangible goals in life: power, control, security. The ability to shape one's own destiny.

Mickey wasn't the only one she held in thrall like this either. When she thought about it, she was amazed she'd got away with her secret lovers for so long. She'd been careful, discreet, and sure to choose those who knew better than to boast. All the same Emilio Neri was a curious and vengeful man. There was a look in his eye just now that she didn't like. He'd find out one day, and then she could only guess at what he'd do. There was, she thought, an inevitability to a life like hers: a period of infatuation, a time of spent satisfaction, then the final leg of the journey, *ennui*, sloth, disaster. Unless you planned. Unless you moved when the moment came. Emilio was getting slow and stupid. It was time, she thought, to think of the succession, before the hourglass ran dry and the empire crumbled to dust.

Nic Costa parked the car outside the looming bulk of the old Roman theatre, walked to the apartment and pressed the doorbell. He was still fighting to clear his head, to make some sense of what was happening. It was like untangling a skein of wool.

'Yes?' Her voice sounded anxious, expectant. He could hear the disappointment, fear perhaps, when he answered.

'It's just a small thing,' he said quickly. 'I have to check. I'm sorry.'

'Don't be,' she murmured and let him in.

Miranda Julius was alone in the living room which was still echoing to the buzz of traffic on the Lungotevere. She was wearing loose white-cotton pyjamas and a red dressing gown. Her fair hair was still damp and dark from the shower. She appeared younger somehow.

Maybe it was her eyes, which seemed wider than he recalled, and shone a bright, intense blue. The pain lent her face a delicate, stressed beauty. He couldn't start to imagine how she felt.

She took one look at him and said, 'There's no news, is there?'

'No. Sorry.'

She sighed. It was what she expected, he thought. 'Do you want a drink? Or is that out of bounds?'

She was clutching a glass of red. He remembered how many times he'd dived into that rich, fragrant lake since his father died, and the struggle required to get out and shake yourself dry. The longing never disappeared.

'Just a small one,' he said and straight away she went into the kitchen and came out with a bottle of Barolo, a good year, an expensive one.

'This all goes tonight. I couldn't sleep. I just keep wondering . . . Didn't *anyone* see her?'

He'd watched women in these situations before. Sometimes they went to pieces. Sometimes they just turned inside themselves. Miranda Julius was different. She seemed determined not to let the agony of her daughter's disappearance defeat her. He hoped this act of defiance would last.

'No,' he answered honestly. 'It's early. This isn't good or bad. It's just how it is. She could still just be another runaway for all we know. You'd be amazed how often that happens.'

She raised her glass. 'Thanks, Nic. Thanks for trying.'

Then she poured his, clumsily. Some of the purple liquid stained his jacket.

'Sorry,' she apologized, dabbing at the fabric with a tissue. 'Had a couple of glasses earlier. It helps.'

'Don't worry.'

He tried the wine. It tasted gorgeous: rich and full of subtle delights.

Costa pulled the plastic envelope out of his pocket. 'This is a very long shot but I have to ask. Do you recognize this? Did Suzi have something like it?'

She stared at the coloured hair-band. 'Yes . . . Yes, I think so. But they're not exactly rare.'

'I know. Is it still here?'

He followed her to the girl's bedroom. They sorted through the piles of clothes and the drawers. Everything was very tidy, he thought. There was a handful of bands in a bedside drawer. None in the same style.

'Where did you find it?' she asked.

'It could be anybody's. I'll get the lab to look. I need something of hers they can check it with. A hairbrush?'

There were two on the dressing table. She nodded. He took the biggest. It was full of stray blonde hair, soft and golden, a couple of shades lighter than her mother's.

The blue eyes shone at him, unyielding. 'Nic . . . *where*?'

'Someone was killed out near the airport this afternoon. A university professor who was working on an excavation. He could have been involved with some kind of cult. There was a villa there. It seems to have been used for some kind of ceremony, perhaps recently. We don't know.'

'Killed?'

'We don't know why. I doubt there's a connection at all. There's no evidence Suzi went there. We'll check the hair-band, of course.'

'Was there—?' She clutched the glass, her shoulders

hunched. 'This ceremony. Had someone else been hurt there too? Before?'

'We don't know that anything's happened to Suzi,' he said firmly.

'But you know something you're not telling me. This ritual. This isn't the first time, is it?'

'Maybe not,' he conceded.

'And someone died then?'

'Sixteen years ago. It's a long time.'

The blue eyes fixed on him. 'Who was she?'

'I can't tell you. In any case it's probably just coincidence.'

He could see she didn't believe him. Miranda Julius walked back into the living room and poured more wine, standing by the table, nervous, uncertain of herself. He followed, watching her. She was shivering. He put down his glass and, very gently, held her by the shoulders. 'I can get someone to come and stay here, Miranda. A policewoman. You don't have to be alone.'

There was an intensity about her at that moment, as if she were grasping for something important. Costa was suddenly aware that he felt attracted to this odd, damaged woman, against all his better judgement.

'You know the thing about kids?' she asked. 'They drive you mad. They keep you sane too. It took years to work out, that was why I stayed away from Suzi. If I lived with her she'd force me to be responsible. She'd make me try to become something I'm not. So I just dumped her, somewhere safe, somewhere invisible, and went wherever I felt like. Places that made sense to me because they were stupid and pointless and perhaps I could forget she even existed.'

'What changed?' he asked.

'You think something changed?'

'You're here. You came with her. From what you've said that wouldn't have happened a while ago.'

She seemed to appreciate this insight. He took away his hands. There were thoughts rising in Nic Costa's head he didn't want there.

'I wanted to do what was right for once,' she said. 'It was almost as if I'd forgotten about her. Forgotten about a part of me—'

She refilled their glasses quickly and gulped at the wine.

'She deserved better than that. So I went out and bought the tickets, booked this place. It was a last-minute thing. It seemed a good idea. Just get up and go somewhere. Together.'

'Why now?'

She didn't seem to want to think about this too much. There was pain there. He wondered why he wanted to know.

'Because I needed someone I guess. There was a gap in my life and, in my own selfish way, I thought perhaps it was time to fill it with family.'

She turned her head to one side, remembering. 'Last year, when I was still working, I was in yet another shitty hole in the Middle East, watching people shoot the crap out of each other. I had a man at the time. A reporter. French guy. He made me laugh. That was all. But it was enough. All I needed. Then one day he climbed into a jeep and—'

She put down the wine glass and came close to him, peering into his eyes, shaking her head. 'It was just a car crash. Can you believe it? All those years, both of us had been walking past bullets, driving over land mines. And then one day he's going down the road and the idiot behind the wheel turns right instead of left. Bang, they're over a cliff. Dead.'

'I'm sorry.'

'Why?' she asked severely. 'You didn't know him. You don't know me.'

Her breath smelled of wine, her body of something else. Expensive perfume.

'And I didn't love him. I liked him. Respected him. Before all this happened I'd promised myself I'd dump him. That ought to make it easier. Instead it makes it worse.'

She reached forward and splayed her fingers across his chest. Costa stepped back, put his hands up and said, 'Miranda. You're upset. Let me get a woman officer in here.'

'Don't want one.' Her voice was slurred but more through tiredness than drink he thought.

'Sorry,' she whispered. 'It's a habit I have when things start to go wrong. Sleeping with strangers. You know something?'

He didn't dare say a word. His head was racing to places he wanted to avoid.

'Sometimes it helps. Sometimes it's the best thing, the kindest thing, you can find.'

Gently, she placed her arms around him, let her damp head fall onto his chest. Nic Costa felt the warmth of her lips brush his neck.

'I don't want to be alone tonight. Please. Just hold me if that's what you want. But don't leave me. Please—'

He pulled himself away, and it was the hardest thing. 'I have to go. I'll call you in the morning. This will work out. I promise.'

There was a hungry, desperate look in her eyes.

'Of course,' she said, and it was impossible for him to read what she was thinking.

It was cold outside, with a little light rain falling gently as a veil in front of the moon. He walked to his car thinking how close he'd been to giving in, whether she was right, and whether it mattered at all.

Teresa Lupo was jerked awake by the bright lights of the crane swinging its burden out of the artificial cavern. The gurney swayed from side to side as if it were teasing her. She yawned and looked at her watch. It was close to midnight. The day seemed endless. Her bruised body hurt like hell. She needed sleep desperately. Yet a man had tried to kill her. This was a new experience. His corpse deserved her attention. For her own sake she needed to peer into his dead eyes and search for some meaning.

Falcone had been on the phone for almost an hour before she nodded off. After the brief factual account she gave of what happened in Randolph Kirk's office he'd hardly spoken to her. If that was as far as the punishment went, she would be lucky. Teresa Lupo had overstepped the mark several times over and she knew it. But if it helped, if it found Suzi Julius, if it began to unravel the riddle of Eleanor Jamieson's death, everything would be worth while. Perhaps everything would be forgiven.

Rachele D'Amato sat in her own car, talking to no one. The morgue crew, short-staffed because they had divided between Kirk's site and the airport, did their work mutely, knowing something was wrong. Here were three arms of the state, Teresa reflected: the police, the morgue and the DIA. And none of them talking to each other much. Private matters, bruised egos and past relationships had intruded into what should have been a professional, impersonal assignment. She was as much to blame as any of them.

'To hell with it,' she whispered to herself. 'If we find out just one more thing about the girl we're better off than we were.'

Falcone walked over with Peroni. D'Amato got out of the car and joined them. All three looked dog-tired. 'We've got a body,' the inspector grunted. 'I presume you want to see.'

'You bet.' She'd spent hours waiting for them to find a safe way of bringing it to the surface. They'd had to bring in extra machinery, longer cables, teams of men in white hats who disappeared into the ground looking grumpy and puzzled by why they were there. It wasn't a crime scene. It was a construction site.

Now the corpse was here, on the ground, strapped to a gurney that shone under the artificial sun of the crane lights, Teresa Lupo didn't feel as keen to see it face to face as she had earlier. The image of the black-headed insect trying to take away her life was one that would stay with her a long time.

'What do you want from me?' she asked as they walked towards the small team gathered by the trolley, on the side away from the pit.

'Identification would be useful,' Falcone said.

'I can take the helmet off. I can go through his pockets. What about the bike?'

'Checked that already,' Peroni replied. 'The number was false but we managed to ID it from the code on the frame. Stolen from Turin three weeks ago. They've been losing a lot of high-powered machines from there recently. They think it's some kind of organized ring.'

'It is,' D'Amato added. 'The Turin mob ship them here all the time. We've got intelligence. Neri's involved in that. He's not the only one. But—'

'Later,' Falcone said.

They stood over the corpse which lay face up on the gurney, limbs awry, pointing at crazy, unnatural angles, like a broken doll. The left arm was almost wrenched from its socket. Bare skin was visible next to bone and torn flesh from the shoulder joint. Teresa Lupo ordered them to turn off the big, bright lights of the crane. They were dazzling her. They had enough illumination of their own with the kit they'd brought along.

'He's smaller than I remember,' she said. Maybe that always happens, she thought. Normally she just saw dead people. She had no idea what they were like breathing, talking, being alive.

Falcone gazed at his watch and sighed.

'Patience,' she murmured and crouched down, wondering how she felt, whether she could draw up the customary amount of respect for the dead that she tried to bring to every autopsy.

The rider was probably gone the moment he hit the wall of the pit, before his shattered body fell to the bottom of the hole with the bike. His neck was broken, crushed down onto his right shoulder. The helmet had withstood the impact – just. A crazed pattern on the crown marked the impact. The black visor was covered in scratches and mud and dust.

'Poor bastard,' she whispered automatically, and scraped away at the fastening straps. Ordinarily she'd tell

Falcone to get lost. Tell him it was too awkward to try to remove the thing here, close to midnight, out in the freezing dead land by Fiumicino. He could wait till they got back to the morgue, with her tools and her easy tricks of the trade. But he didn't want to wait, and neither did she. The man was dead anyway. It wasn't going to be a pretty funeral whatever happened.

Teresa Lupo asked one of the morgue assistants to bring over a medical bag, took out a scalpel, carefully cut open the clasps then, as gently as she could, pulled the helmet back towards the top of the head. There was some initial resistance. She adjusted the position of the skull and found an easier path. The plastic moved under the pressure of her fingers, the wrecked corpse nodded forward, and slowly, with great caution, she tugged the fragmented casing free.

Matted yellow hair, coated in blood, fell beneath her fingers.

Peroni turned his back on them, swearing constantly. No one spoke for a minute.

Beneath the bright portable arc lights lay Barbara Martelli, the traffic cop most men in the Questura had, at some stage, fantasized about. Her blonde locks fell in spent and bloodied curls around a face that wore a pained, final sneer. Her dead eyes were half open. Her teeth, normally so bright and white and perfect betrayed the signs of her cruel death. Behind full, curled lips now turning pale, the gore had risen in her throat, staining them a dark, sticky black.

'For chrissake,' Peroni yelled at no one behind her. '*For chrissake.*'

Teresa Lupo reached down and unzipped the jacket, revealing beneath the torn leather the unmistakable

177

female form. Martelli still wore her uniform shirt. A wet, black stain was seeping through her chest, up towards her throat. She remembered the woman well. She looked so unlike any other female cop. Sometimes she'd watch her walk through the station, knowing every male pair of eyes was following her, and a good many female ones too. She'd wonder how it felt to be that attractive, how much maintenance you needed to do on a body that looked as if it just fell out of bed perfect every morning. She'd been jealous. It all seemed so petty now. Teresa Lupo was at a loss to put together any of these pieces. Why Barbara Martelli of all people should be the hitman – sorry, *hitperson* – deputed to despatch Randolph Kirk to hell. Whether Martelli had decided to extend these deadly privileges to the hapless pathologist locked in the next room from her own initiative, with a little on the spot improvisation. Or whether she was under orders. And whose? It was as if time were running backwards: with every passing minute they knew less and the world got murkier and more illogical.

'If you'd asked I'd have looked the other way,' she said softly to herself. 'I didn't even warm to Booger Bill.'

Then her eye caught something else and she couldn't work out whether the mist was clearing or had just become downright impenetrable.

She was shaken from this reverie by Falcone's hand on her shoulder, his sharp, sour face, with its silver pointed beard, staring into hers.

'Thanks, doctor,' he said.

'It's nothing.'

'No.' The inspector was making a point. She should have seen the signs. 'I meant thank you. Now I have a dead cop too.'

'What?'

Falcone was turning his back on her, starting to walk away. She couldn't believe it. Even Peroni seemed embarrassed.

'Hey!' she yelled.

He turned. She remembered a trick from when she'd briefly played women's rugby, before they threw her off the team for too many fouls.

Teresa Lupo lunged out with her foot at Falcone's falling leg, jerked him off balance, grabbed the arm of his jacket and had him down on the ground in one, letting his own weight do most of the work. Peroni was shaking his head, cursing again, looking at them as if they were beneath contempt. Rachele D'Amato watched this little drama in shocked silence. Teresa didn't want to think about what the morgue team were doing. Holding their heads in their hands in all probability.

'Fuck it,' she mouthed, and dragged Falcone down to the corpse; she let go of him, then pointed to the dead woman's shoulder, half ripped from its socket.

'See that?' she spat at him, forcing his head close up to the torn flesh. '*See that?*'

The inspector was breathless, struggling to regain some dignity.

'Yes,' he said and she believed she heard just a faint tinge of regret, apology even, in his cold reply.

It was small but distinct. Drawn with care into the flesh of Barbara Martelli's ruined limb was an inky black mark. A tattooed face surrounded by a head of snakelike hair, and a grinning mouth with bulbous lips, howling, howling, howling.

'You're welcome,' Teresa Lupo said softly to herself then barked at her men to load the body.

VENERDI

Spring was arriving with vigour. Emilio Neri had ordered the men to put some outside burners on the terrace. With them it was sufficiently warm for his family to eat their first breakfast of the year in the open air, overlooking the Via Giulia. It was eight in the morning. The house felt different. Neri had sent the servants away. He needed the room for his troops. The place was better without them. One of the foot soldiers had gone out to bring pastries and fruit from the Campo. Neri wasn't that keen to make a move himself, not until he'd thought this through. There was another reason for talking on the terrace, out in the open, high above the cobblestones of the Via Giulia. The scumbags in the DIA would stop at nothing to nail him. Sometimes he thought they were bugging the house, recording every word he said. Sometimes he wondered if he were getting paranoid in his old age. Either way he would feel more comfortable seated beneath the wan rays of the morning sun, with the growl of traffic from the Lungotevere murmuring away in the distance, overlooked by no one.

Or perhaps that was a distant hope too. They could have cameras trained on him from somewhere, helicopters hovering overhead. This was the way the modern world worked, peering into your private existence, sneaking around, asking stupid questions. And all the while real life just turned to shit and no one ever really noticed.

Adele and Mickey sat side by side opposite him. They seemed even more antagonistic towards one another this morning. The performance – the word seemed appropriate to Neri – just went on and on. His son had arrived home not long before midnight, in a foul, uncommunicative mood. Some date had failed to show maybe. Neri didn't know, and didn't want to know. The happiness or otherwise of the kid's dick was the last thing on his mind.

He had six soldiers downstairs, all equipped for the occasion should it arise. He'd called a few old *compari* from the past too, men who'd taken a back seat when they'd banked enough to keep them happy. He had called each one into his office separately, stared into their eyes looking for signs of disloyalty, finding none. Then he told them to keep the next few days free in case they were required. These were men who had reason to be grateful to him. They all knew some debts never got repaid in full. If there was to be a war, Neri would need every hand he could get. His was a Roman firm. He didn't have the rigid, militaristic structure the Sicilians liked so much. He had no *consigliere* to turn to for advice, to negotiate with the other mobs to keep them sweet. He didn't keep a bunch of *capi* running their soldiers beneath him. Just Bruno Bucci, who was a kind of skipper but never acted much in his own name.

Neri had always liked to do things himself. In the past there'd been time. Now, the more he thought about it, he was exposed by his own obsessive need for absolute control. Nothing could be delegated easily. There were insufficient troops on the ground. Rome hadn't seen an all-out mob war in more than two decades. The game should have moved on from those days. People were supposed to be more *civilized*. They'd been fools, Neri included. Human nature didn't change. It only went underground for a while. Now he had to adapt – and quickly.

Bucci walked up the metal stairs onto the terrace carrying breakfast on a tray: pastries, juice, coffee. Adele watched him place them on the table, nod respectfully to Neri then leave, and said, 'Would anyone care to tell me what's going on here? We've got a gorilla waiting on table. There's people down below who don't match the decorations. Why am I sharing my home with a bunch of zombies wearing black suits before I'm even out of pyjamas?'

Neri was going to have to say something about that. She was wandering around as if nothing had changed. She sat next to Mickey, beneath one of the burners, in a new silk outfit that looked like pure gold. There was nothing on underneath. She didn't bother buttoning the front that well. He couldn't help noticing. He didn't want the men getting a free look too. He guessed people did get ideas around Adele, then wondered again about the way Mickey wouldn't even look at her in his presence.

'You could try dressing a little earlier,' he said and gulped down some coffee, trying to think.

She sat there primly, one hand on the table, and gave Mickey an icy stare. 'You woke me. Coming home late like that. Can't you get hookers who work normal hours?'

Mickey smiled, his dyed blonde head lolling around stupidly. 'What hookers? I got busy. It took me a long time to chase down all those debts. I was working. How about you?'

He was lying there. Neri knew it. Mickey's brain lay behind his zip. Always had done. The kid was up to something, maybe some new private business on the side. Neri could see it in his face. 'So what happened to your phone? We seem to have a lot of phone problems in this family.'

He shrugged. He looked a little odd. There was sweat on his brow. His eyes rolled when he spoke. 'Gone wrong. I'm getting it fixed.'

'Do that,' Neri snarled. 'I got enough on my plate without having to worry about you two.'

The old man wondered how to phrase this. How much to tell them. Adele deserved to know for her own sake. Mickey probably thought it was owed him.

'We need to be careful,' he said. 'Maybe, just maybe, there's trouble.'

'From who? The Sicilians?' she asked immediately, and Neri wondered why the question came from her, not Mickey.

Neri waved an impatient hand at her. 'Nah. Listen to me. We've got nothing to worry about from our own people. We know each other. We go back years. Do you think I've spent half my life crawling around those peasants for no good reason? We're safe there, provided we let them suck a little blood now and then.'

'Who then?' she asked again and Neri couldn't take his eyes off Adele. She was holding a piece of pastry with her delicate, skinny hand and she couldn't stop herself yawning, didn't even try to stifle it or cover her face. This was all so distant from her life.

'We had,' Neri said calmly, 'a little problem way back when the boy was just a teenager. With some Americans.'

Mickey took a deep breath. 'That's over and done with.'

Neri smiled unpleasantly at his son across the table. 'Maybe someone thinks otherwise. Maybe someone thinks we're responsible.'

'Are we?' Adele stared at him with those wide open, guileless eyes. It was, Neri thought, perhaps the worst question anyone should ask in the circumstances.

'People have got short memories,' he said. 'Do you remember what you were doing sixteen years ago?'

'Sure,' she answered. 'Don't you? I was learning how to fuck. It seemed a useful skill to acquire.'

'Yeah, well not everything happens below the waist,' he snapped. Not always, Neri thought. 'What matters is that we take care. This is our town. Until everyone realizes that I want you two to stay here, where I can look after you.'

Adele shot Mickey a theatrical glance of pure distaste. 'You want me stuck here with him? Like a prisoner?'

Neri watched the two of them, thinking. 'Try to see it as therapy. A break from shopping.'

'Sometimes,' Adele murmured, 'I just can't stop laughing around this place.'

Mickey giggled. The kid looked odd. A touch red-faced. Maybe he was back on the dope again, Neri thought. That was all he needed.

'Me neither,' Neri grunted, then got up from the table and waddled downstairs to talk to the men. His family depressed him sometimes.

Adele watched him go. Mickey closed his eyes in delight. It was a beautiful morning. There were a couple of gulls screaming in the sky. A helicopter hovered somewhere overhead, maybe getting a good view of what was going on. Her fingers gripped him tightly, stroking, cajoling, running up and down with a certain, insistent rhythm, as they had throughout his father's tedious lecture. His dick sat upright, begging, in her hand beneath the table.

A finger crept close to the rim. Some insistent flood was moving, racing north. She lifted the tablecloth. Adele's head went down, dipping towards Mickey's groin. He felt her soft red hair fall beneath his hand. Her lips closed on the heat rising from inside him, her tongue performed two perfect circles of pleasure.

Mickey yelped, couldn't help it. When he opened his eyes she was back above the table, dabbing a napkin to one corner of her mouth, the tip of her scarlet tongue just visible.

'Did she do that for you, Mickey?' Adele asked when she was done. 'This slut of yours last night?'

'I told you,' he answered dreamily. 'I was working.'

'I hope that's true.' She was looking at him in an odd way. Adele had changed the last couple of days, he thought. There was something she wanted, something more than just the fucking.

'Did you listen to what he said?' she asked.

'Hard to pay attention to your old man when your stepmother's jerking you off under the table.' It was too. He was making a genuine point there, though it all came out like a wisecrack.

'Maybe I shouldn't do it any more. Maybe I should give this up altogether before he finds out.'

He blinked, unable to countenance the thought.

'Or maybe,' she continued, 'I should tell him you made me. You wouldn't leave me alone. I could just throw myself at his feet and beg for mercy. He'd listen, you know.'

He twitched and with it came the occasional stammer he had from time to time, when he was stressed. 'D-d-don't joke about stuff like that, Adele.'

Her hand gripped his arm. Her slim fingers bit into his flesh. 'We need to get serious, Mickey. You need to listen. He's old. He's out of his depth. He doesn't know what he wants to do. And the Sicilians . . . You know these people?'

'They're friends,' he explained, trying to give the words some conviction.

'They're associates. If they think he's weak or out of line they'll just walk in and hand all this to someone else. And you'll be dead in a car somewhere out in the stinking countryside, while I go back to doing tricks for any rich old jerk who can't get it up any more.'

'What are you saying?' She was starting to scare him. Mickey liked Adele. Maybe this was love even. Weird things happened in spring.

'I'm saying—' She hesitated, thinking. 'We need to be prepared.'

There was a sound beyond the balcony: cars, sirens. They went to the edge and looked down to the narrow street. Mickey took a deep breath then stepped back. He never did like heights. He didn't like what he saw down there either: a fleet of blue vehicles swarming across the cobblestones, blocking the narrow street completely. At their head, close to the church on the Tiber side of the road, a tall, distinguished-looking man had stepped out of an unmarked Alfa. With him was a woman: elegant, well-dressed, young.

'Shit,' he murmured, then pulled back from the edge, head swimming. On the floor below the bell rang repeatedly, insistent.

Costa got into the Questura early and took the hairband and the brush over to forensic. The surly-looking lab assistant in the white coat sniffed at the plastic envelopes.

'What case do I assign them to?'

'Excuse me?'

'We got some new cost management procedures sent down from above. You got to tell me the case so I can lay it against the right budget.'

Costa sighed. 'The missing teenager. Suzi Julius. I need to know if the hair on both of them match. By this afternoon.'

The man's eyebrows rose. He was about forty, short, skinny, with a long bloodless face. He held the plastic bag up to the light on the desk and took a good look at the contents.

'I can tell you right now, detective. They don't match.'

'What?'

'Take a look for yourself. The hair's a different colour.'

Costa snatched the bag off the man and stared at the contents. Maybe the man was right. There was a subtle difference in the hair colour. The sample on the hairband from the villa was darker. Perhaps it did come from someone else. Or maybe it had been stained by the ochre earth on the floor.

'Is a person's hair colour the same everywhere on the head?' he asked.

'Not unless they've done a very, very good dye job.'

'Then do me a favour,' Costa begged. 'Satisfy my curiosity. Check.'

The assistant grunted and made a note. 'This is gonna look good on the weekly audit. We're half down on manning right now 'cos of the stinking flu. I think I'm going down with it myself. Don't expect miracles.'

'So how long?'

'Three days minimum,' the man replied. 'It's the best I can do in the circumstances. Sorry.'

'Jesus . . .' Costa murmured and went back to the office to find Peroni slumped in a chair at his desk, eyes closed, face grey and downcast.

'Morning,' Costa said.

'You left out the word "good". I approve. You got a visitor. The Englishwoman's outside.'

Costa gave him a sharp look.

'Hey,' Peroni protested. 'Don't get grumpy with me. I offered to listen. Seems you're her main man. No Nic Costa, no talkie talkie.'

Costa went out to the reception area. Miranda Julius sat on a bench looking miserable. There were bags beneath her eyes.

He led her through to a reception room, past Teresa Lupo who scuttled along the corridor, head down.

Peroni followed and pulled up a chair at the desk, staring at her. 'What can we do for you, Mrs Julius?' he asked. It was, Costa guessed, a deliberate act, an attempt to make it clear they were a partnership, and she had to deal with both of them.

'Have you heard anything? Anything at all?'

Peroni frowned. 'We'll be in touch the moment we have some information. I promise.'

'So what are you doing?' she demanded. 'What about the hair-band you found? Do you know for sure if it's Suzi's or not?'

The two men looked at each other. 'Tell you what,' Peroni said. 'I'll just go ask about that outside.'

Costa watched him leave. 'It takes time,' he said. 'Everything takes time. You weren't sure about that hair-band yourself. It's probably just something left there by someone else. A school party.'

A school party out to study some Roman porn, he thought. Or a bunch from the university.

She leaned over the table and gripped his arm, peering into his face with that unavoidable intensity he was coming to know. 'Nic. My daughter is missing. I heard on the TV all that speculation about rituals. You found those stupid things of hers in the apartment. What if she's mixed up in this?'

He nodded. 'As of now, there's nothing to link Suzi directly with what happened in Ostia. Why should there be? Do you know either of these people on the news? The university professor? The policewoman?'

'No.'

Miranda Julius had the look he'd seen so often in these cases, a mixture of fear and self-loathing.

'Suzi ran away,' he said. 'Probably with some stupid kid she met when you weren't around. We're circulating her photo everywhere. Someone will see it. Someone will recognize her. That's if she doesn't call you first.'

She looked at her watch. 'I'm sorry. It's just that I feel so . . . helpless.'

'It's understandable. As I said, I can get someone to be with you if that's what you want.'

'No,' she replied immediately. 'There's no need.' She paused. 'I'm sorry. About last night. Embarrassing you like that. It was inexcusable.'

'Forget it.'

'No,' she said firmly. 'I won't forget it. Most men . . . well, I know what most men would have done. I guess . . . thanks.'

He didn't want to prolong this particular line of conversation. 'What are you going to do now?'

'Just walk around the place. Think. Hope. Just sitting in that stupid apartment on my own is driving me crazy. She's got my mobile if she needs it.'

He gave her his card. 'Call me. Any time. For any reason. Even if there's no news. If you just want to talk.'

She put the number in her bag. 'Don't take this the wrong way,' she said hesitantly. 'I didn't mean it last night when I said I had a habit of doing that. Sleeping with strangers. It wasn't strictly true. I don't want you to think . . . it was just automatic.' She glanced directly into his eyes for a moment.

Peroni saved him. He walked back into the room, shaking his head, saying there was no news from forensic, but they were still looking, they were starting to take phone calls from the public.

Then he sat down next to her, took off his jacket and placed it round the back of the chair, looking serious, businesslike. 'We're doing the best we can, Mrs Julius,' Peroni added. 'If there's anything you can think of that's occurred to you since yesterday . . .'

She clutched her arms tightly to her chest and nodded forward, a tense, nervous gesture. Her fair hair bobbed with the momentum of the sudden movement. 'Nothing.' Then she came to life briefly. 'No. I'm sorry. I'm not thinking straight. Last night, after you'd gone, I found one of those throwaway cameras in Suzi's room. I got it developed just now. There's nothing there. It's just . . . stuff. Places. A young man. It's just the usual holiday snapshots, though. No pictures of specific people, not that I can see. But you're welcome to it.'

'That could be incredibly useful,' Peroni said confidently. 'This is exactly the kind of help we need, Miranda.'

Costa looked at his partner and realized he was beginning to like him. A lot. They both knew there was nothing on the photos. Peroni was just helping her feel involved.

She reached into her canvas shoulder bag, took out an envelope of prints and handed them to Costa. He flicked through them: all the usual tourist jaunts. The Spanish Steps. The Trevi Fountain. The Colosseum. Suzi had done the rounds.

'We'll take a close look,' he promised.

They saw her out, watched her leave.

'I hate lying to people,' Peroni said when she was out of earshot. 'We've had three calls, and all them from the usual nutcases. I can't believe no one's seen the kid.'

'That's exactly what happened with the Jamieson girl.'

Peroni looked sceptical. 'Come on, Nic. I know enough about these things to understand this is what happens half the time. Let's not leap to conclusions. That poor woman knows we're doing that anyway and it's just scaring her stupid.'

Costa sighed. Peroni was right.

'The trouble is,' Peroni went on. 'I'm just like

everyone else here. I can't stop thinking about Barbara. It's driving me crazy. What the hell went wrong there? Her old man is an asshole. A crook and a cheat and a bully. Barbara seemed so different. I used to look at her and think: yeah, you can beat off all the crap you get in this world, so long as you try. And I was wrong, wasn't I? She'd got the poison just like the rest of us. Only worse. Why?'

Costa had seen Falcone briefly before he went to forensic. He knew where they were supposed to go next. 'You worked with her old man?'

'I had that privilege,' Peroni replied, suspicious all of a sudden. Then he looked Costa in the eye. 'Oh no. Don't tell me. Falcone wants you and me to go have a little talk with the bastard. Please, for God's sake tell me I'm wrong.'

Costa threw his hands open in exasperation. 'You *know* him, Gianni. It makes sense, doesn't it? The men who went round to talk to him last night came away with less than nothing.'

Peroni picked up his jacket from the chair and stood up, grimacing. 'Why does this have to happen to me? Let me ask you something, Nic. I've got a daughter too. She's just at that age where you start to see something adult beginning to emerge from all the kid stuff. So how'd you spot if they're going down that road? How'd you know they're not sucking some dark part out of you that you can't even see yourself?'

The big ugly face stared at Costa, full of bewilderment and something close to grief. 'If I couldn't spot that in Barbara Martelli, if she could take all of us in so easily, how are you supposed to know?'

Costa was only half listening. There wasn't time to

deal with Peroni's guilt. There was scarcely time to flick through the snaps again, seeing what he saw before, just familiar pieces of stone and crowds of people, tourists mainly. A sea of expressionless faces keeping all their secrets.

'I have no idea,' he said.

She had aches and pains from the car crash. A plaster was attached to part of her scalp where she'd headbutted the dashboard. Still, this should have been a good morning in the Rome city morgue, one full of interest. Two fresh bodies on the slab. A blank cheque to start running whatever tests she liked on the curiously mummified corpse of Eleanor Jamieson. The work had never been this promising, not in the eight years she'd worked there. Nevertheless, Teresa Lupo leaned against the exterior wall that linked her office to the Questura, hunched, deep in thought, puffing on the third cigarette of the day. Events were moving around her. Falcone had left with an entire team. Nic Costa and Peroni had nodded goodbye as they set off a few minutes later. And they were all, she suspected, headed in the wrong direction.

One obsessive thought had filled her head when she took the risk and drove to Ostia: a young girl called Suzi Julius was in big trouble and didn't know it. Somehow this kid had walked into the hands of a lunatic. An intelligent, careful lunatic, true, but a lunatic all the same. At best she might get off with being raped, and probably not in the missionary position either. At worst . . .

Teresa thought of the tanned, leathery body on the

slab and, for the first time in her career, began to wonder whether the job was finally beginning to get to her. Was it possible her fears for Suzi Julius were really just a manifestation of something else, a deep and growing malaise with the innate futility of what she did? She liked her work. Occasionally she came up with something that helped. She was good, better than average, which was why the authorities tolerated her behaviour. But whatever she did, however smart, however prescient, it always occurred after the event. You could comfort yourself with the thought that putting away some murdering creep could – just possibly – have prevented him killing someone else in the future. It still didn't bring back the ones who were already dead. She was, when push came to shove, just a prurient mourner at their funeral, offering tears and sympathy and nothing else. She helped, but it wasn't enough. Not in Teresa Lupo's eyes anyway.

And now she wasn't even doing that. When she'd gone to Ostia there'd been, at the back of her mind, the hope that she would find something to prove the bigger picture, to make it plain that some odd strand of recurring history linked Eleanor Jamieson's death with Suzi Julius's disappearance. It had to be that way. There was no longer any question of it in Teresa's head, even though she was unable to rationalize her certainties. Falcone was a good cop. Give him the evidence, give him the cards to play, and there could be no one better on the case. But she'd seen the look in his eyes when he sat in the apartment in the Teatro di Marcello the previous day. He already had one certain murder, albeit a crime that was sixteen years old. Next to this – and the gangland connections that were common knowledge around the station even before she left for Ostia – the wilful disappearance of a teenage girl seemed, if not unimportant, certainly minor.

The thyrsus, the dates, the curious collection of seeds . . . all the evidence she and Nic Costa had found in Suzi's bedroom carried insufficient weight. Maybe Suzi had been hooked on some Dionysian cult on the internet. There were plenty there. Teresa had checked that morning. Maybe the tattoo on the shoulder was just one of the things kids did. Still, she didn't really believe this for a moment. Falcone probably felt the same way. But without something stronger, something he could work on, he was lost.

Which was, she thought again, why she'd broken all the rules and driven out to see Professor Randolph Kirk, expecting to find Harrison Ford touting answers and bumping, instead, into Booger Bill who could only offer more complications and unfathomable mysteries. It was the worst possible decision in the world, and not just because it could end up getting her fired. With Kirk's death, Falcone got another real crime to get his teeth into, another spur to push Suzi Julius further to the back of his consciousness. When Teresa got chased by the helmeted beetle on a superbike, only to discover later it was an off-duty cop who was trying to whack her, and one whom most of the Questura lusted after daily, everything moved onto a different level altogether. A missing teenager became peripheral.

Teresa had sent Monkboy walkabout gathering gossip in the Questura that morning, before starting the autopsy on Barbara Martelli, a task she did not relish. Monkboy was good at this. The cops half pitied, half ridiculed him, and along the way he picked up all manner of information. He'd yet to report back. She knew, though, what he'd say. No one had seen Suzi Julius. Try as they might, no one had found any reason to believe this was anything more than the usual: a teenager trying to find out what adulthood was all about, not caring how shit-scared her mother might be in the mean time.

She'd taken a quick walk through the station herself too and seen the looks in their faces, understood what they'd have said if she raised the subject. *So there's this gorgeous traffic cop with hair the colour of gold and tits that never quite fit beneath her leather bike suit. One day this angel, this sex goddess with shades and a Ducati, whacks some university professor guy for no apparent reason. After which she tries similarly to off Rome's resident eccentric pathologist only to wind up dead herself down some stinking pit outside Fiumicino. And you're asking about a missing teenager who, when last seen, was smiling, waving a weirdly intense mamma goodbye as boyfriend number one drives her off in search of a suitable source of condoms? Does the word 'priority' have no meaning where you come from? Do you ever stop to wonder how that soubriquet 'crazy' came about?*

They had a point. A cop point. But she'd seen something else on their faces. When they looked at her it was as if they somehow felt she was to blame. If she'd never driven out to Ostia, Barbara Martelli and Randolph Kirk would still be alive, and we'd all be none the wiser about why one would, if a person was to press all the right/wrong buttons, render the other stone dead.

'Yeah, but—' she said out loud, stabbing a finger at an imaginary antagonist standing in front of her, arguing with the thin, fume-filled air of a Roman spring. 'Not knowing doesn't mean there wasn't something bad there all along. We just didn't understand what it was, or why it existed.'

And we don't now, she thought miserably. We know nothing.

'Could've happened anyway,' she mumbled to herself. 'Not my fault. Ignorance isn't bliss.'

The back door to the station opened. Monkboy stumbled out and shambled towards her, head down, not wanting to meet her eyes.

'Silvio,' she said cheerfully. 'My man. My eyes and ears. Tell me, darling. What are they saying about your beloved boss hereabouts? Am I up for Commissioner next? Or should I think of running for President instead?'

He leaned back on the wall next to her, accepted a cigarette, lit it with all the skill and precision of a nine-year-old, took one deep puff then had a coughing fit.

'You don't have to smoke for my sake,' Teresa observed. 'Frankly, Silvio, I'd prefer it if you didn't smoke at all. You don't look like a smoker. These things don't fit your face.'

Obediently, he threw the cigarette on the floor and stamped on it with his foot. 'They're all assholes. All cops. Every last one of them.'

She took his arm, leaned into his shoulder and, just for a second, twiddled girlishly with his lank, long hair. It required her to duck down a little. Silvio was not the tallest of men. 'Tell me something I don't know, dear heart. What about the Julius girl?'

'They've got nothing new.'

'So what *are* they doing?'

'Falcone's gone to see a hood or something. They sent Costa and the weird-looking guy with him to dig up Barbara Martelli's past. Try to work out why she'd want to kill the professor dude.'

'And me. Let's not forget that, Silvio. She tried to kill me too.'

'Yeah.' His eyes darted across the yard.

'And?' She wasn't letting him go just then. There was more to come.

'They're pissed off with you, Teresa. They are *really* pissed off.'

'That makes a change.'

'No.' His round, liquid eyes came to fall on her and for a moment she actually felt guilty for getting him this scared. 'You don't get it. I've never heard them talk like this before. It's as if—'

He didn't want to say any more.

'As if it's my fault?'

He stared at his shoes. 'Yeah.'

She thought of slapping him out of this state, then decided it might not be the best decision in the circumstances.

'But it isn't. Is it? Look at me, Silvio, for God's sake.'

He did. His mournful face wasn't a pretty sight.

'Say, "it's not your fault, Teresa." '

'It's not your fault, Teresa.'

'Good. So what is their . . . theory, if you can call it that.'

'They don't have one. They think there's some mob connection with the mummy girl from way back. They think – and this is something they do not want to face – that Barbara Martelli was getting paid by one side to keep tabs on things. Informing. Running errands.'

She couldn't get that black helmet bobbing at the car window out of her head. 'That was an errand?'

'They don't really know, Teresa. They're still in shock I think.'

'And Randolph Kirk? Where's he supposed to fit in?'

'When you started talking to him someone got worried he might blab about something or other and sent Barbara out to whack him and nip it all in the bud. They didn't want witnesses either so she went after you.'

'The Prof being in the mob too, then. I mean that's how most Mafiosi hide out from the cops these days, isn't it? By holding a chair in classical antiquities at the University of Rome or something?'

'Didn't get that far,' he mumbled. 'Didn't like to ask.'

'And they really think the Julius kid is just coincidence?'

'They don't know what to think. You know what they're like. They're primitive organisms. They don't multi-task. There's only so much they can handle at any one time. Also they got lots of staff off with this virus thing. Hell, so have we.'

She ran a hand through her hair. She hadn't been as careful as normal with it that morning. It was a mess, if she were honest with herself. Just like the old days. 'But, Silvio. Suzi Julius is still alive. At least until tomorrow, if I'm right. Doesn't anyone understand that?'

He muttered something about priorities and how it was unfair to throw all this at him, then looked helpless again. She hated herself for venting her anger on this hapless minion. It was cruel, unjustified. It was the kind of thing cops did.

'Sorry,' she whispered. 'It's not aimed at you. It's aimed at me if you want to know.'

He put his hand on her arm which was, all things considered, a little creepy. 'Let's just go back inside,

Teresa. We've got work to do and you and me are just about the only two people here right now who aren't sneezing up buckets. Let's keep our heads down and get on with things until it all blows over. They're paid to deal with this crap, not us. If we stay quiet, maybe it'll all go away. They'll find what they want and forget about the rest.'

Which was a nice idea, she thought, and one that had not a snowball in hell's chance of becoming reality.

'There's nothing in there you and the rest of the team can't handle,' she said abruptly. 'Let's face it. You don't need to be a genius to know how the beautiful Barbara and the professor died. And the bog girl's there more for the science than the criminology. We might as well admit it. We've got no answers for them. We should be trying to make sure Suzi Julius doesn't go into our in-tray instead.'

He took his hand away. He looked scared. 'That's what they get paid to do. We've got a big workload on. I can't cope on my own.'

'You can cope, Silvio,' she said. 'You can cope better than you know.'

'What if something else happens? What if—'

She took his arm again, smiling. 'Look. Statistics. How many violent deaths do we get in Rome? There's a week's quota lying on the slab right now. Nothing's going to happen today. Trust me. I need a break. I need to think.'

The pale, flabby face blushed off-pink. 'You're going somewhere,' he said accusingly. 'I know you. This is like yesterday all over again. You're going somewhere and it isn't good at all.'

'I just thought I'd—'

'No! *No!* Do *not* tell me because I don't want to hear. Two wrongs don't make a right—'

'I wasn't wrong! Stupid maybe. But two stupids just make you . . . stupid. And most of the jerks in there think that of me anyway. So where's the harm?'

'Please.' His little hands were together now, praying. 'I beg of you, Teresa. For my sake. Don't do this. Whatever it is.'

She kissed him lightly on the cheek and watched the blood make a big rush all the way from his jowls to his eye sockets. 'Nothing's going to happen, Silvio. Listen to your friend, Teresa. Just hold the fort for an hour and then I'll be back. And they're none the wiser.'

He looked wrecked. He looked terrified. 'An hour. Is that an earth hour? Or one of those special hours you have on that planet of yours?'

'Silvio, Silvio,' she sighed. 'Tell me. What could possibly go wrong?'

Beniamino Vercillo was a measured, organized man. He liked to start work early, at seven prompt each weekday morning, seated at his desk in the cellar of a block off the Via dei Serpenti in Monti. The place abutted a busy optician's on the street. It was a fixed-rent single room of just twenty-five square metres, with no windows, just a door to the iron steps leading down from the street. Space enough to house Vercillo and the female secretary who had been servicing him, in more ways than one, these last ten years. After the bus ride from the quiet suburb of Paroli near the Via Veneto he took breakfast – a cappuccino and a cornetto – every morning in the café across the road. Lunch was a piece of pizza rustica from one of the local shops. By six he was back home, work done for the day, ready for the life of a middle-aged Roman bachelor. Vercillo was now fifty-two. He preferred plain dark suits, pressed white shirts, dark ties and old, worn shoes. He was, it seemed to him, the most insignificant man to walk this busy little street that ran from the dull modern thoroughfare of Via Cavour over to the fashion shops in Via Nazionale.

This was, at least, the public image he wished to present, and for good reason. Vercillo was Emilio Neri's book-keeper. In his head lay every last detail of the big hood's Italian investments, legitimate and crooked. Those that could be written down sat stored on the single PC in Vercillo's office, ready to be transcribed for the annual tax forms, accurate down to the last cent. Vercillo was a good accountant. He knew what he could get away with and what would push the tax inspectors too far. Those items that were of a more delicate nature, Vercillo recorded differently. First to a prodigious memory, honed from the mathematical tricks he used to pull to impress the teachers when he was at school. Then written down, using a code Vercillo never revealed to anyone – least of all Emilio Neri – and kept in a safe, hidden in the walls of his subterranean office.

It was a satisfactory situation. Vercillo made the best part of half a million euros a year keeping Neri out of harm's way. And that secret code lent Vercillo some safety from the fat man's wrath should things go wrong. Vercillo knew only too well what fate befell accountants who served their mob bosses badly. Foul up and you might get away with a vicious beating. Steal and you were dead. But do the job well, keep yourself out of sight, and hold a little key in your head that no one else could share . . . then, Vercillo reasoned, everyone could be happy. The authorities stayed at a safe distance. Neri knew that if Vercillo stumbled up the stairs from his office and fell beneath the wheels of the little 117 tourist bus the secrets of his empire would remain secure, unintelligible to the taxman and the DIA even if they found them. For his part, Vercillo maintained a measure of security, a hold over Neri that both men recognized without having to state it. This was convenient. It meant that he rarely had to call Neri except for information, and the big, old hood hardly ever had to trouble him. This was the way it ought to be. He was an accountant. A money man. Not a foot soldier, out looking for trouble. He liked it that way.

Vercillo had given Sonia, the secretary, a day off to go out and see her sick mamma in Orvieto. She'd turned thirty now. She wasn't as much fun as she used to be. Soon he'd have to find a reason to fire her, get someone younger, someone more interesting, to take her place. He hated the thought. Vercillo always tried to steer away from confrontation. It was getting harder and harder these days. Neri's business empire grew and grew, sometimes into areas that gave Vercillo room for concern. When he was a bookish teenager in Rome in the Sixties, during the brief period of economic happiness they called 'Il Boom', Vercillo expected the world to improve on a constant, incremental basis, becoming happier, more prosperous, more peaceful year by year. Instead, the opposite happened. The Red Brigade came, then went, then came back again. There were bombs everywhere, and madness. He'd lost a cousin in Israel to a suicide attack. Vercillo scarcely thought of himself as a Jew these days but the idea that someone could die like that, just walking down the street, going into the wrong café, appalled him. There was a need for more order in people's lives. And some politeness too. Instead, all you got was this constant stream of bodies, foreigners pushing and shoving to get in front of everyone else. It had all gone wrong somewhere over the past forty years and, for the life of him, he couldn't understand how or when.

It was the tourists that got to him most. The English, drunk for every football game. The Japanese, constantly taking pictures, blundering into you on the street, not knowing a word of Italian. And the Americans, who thought they could do any damn thing they liked so long as they had a few dollars in their pockets. Rome would be better off without the lot of them. They intruded upon the native consciousness. They marred the place. Today especially. There was some kind of street theatre festival going on around the Colosseum down the road. They were setting up when he came to work. Commedia dell'Arte characters climbing into costumes. Africans. Orientals. And all the usual fraudsters pretending to be gladiators, trying to screw some cash out of the tourists for pictures.

Beniamino Vercillo looked up from the desk in his dark little pit feeling grumpy, tasting the sour bile of growing disappointment in his mouth, then wondered how much his thoughts were random, how much the product of what he was half seeing out of the corner of his eye.

In front of him, framed in the open doorway, was a figure from some stupid dream. It stood there like a crazy god wearing some kind of theatrical gown: a long red jacket, cheap brown sacking trousers. And a mask, one straight out of a nightmare, all crazy writhing hair, with a black gaping mouth, fixed in a lunatic grin.

The figure took one step forward, theatrically, like an actor making a point. He had to be from one of the street troupes Vercillo saw earlier.

'I don't give to charity,' the little accountant declared firmly.

The figure moved closer with two more of those stupid, histrionic strides. Vercillo's head started to work, remembering something from long ago.

'What is this shit?' Vercillo mumbled automatically. 'What do you want?'

'Neri,' the crazy god said in a calm, clear voice that floated out from behind the mask.

Vercillo shivered, wondering if this was all some hallucination. 'Who?'

The creature opened its jacket; its right hand reached down towards a leather scabbard on its belt. Vercillo watched aghast as it withdrew a short, fat sword that gleamed in the fluorescent lights.

The shining weapon rose, dashed through the air then dug deep into the desk in front of him, severing the phone cord, cutting straight through the sheaf of letters that sat in front of Vercillo.

'Books,' the crazy god said.

'No books here, no books here—'

He was quiet. The point of the blade was at his throat, pricking into his dewlap.

The crazy god shook his head. The blade pressed harder. Vercillo felt a sharp stab of pain, then a line of blood began to trickle down his neck.

'He'll kill me,' he murmured.

'*He'll* kill you?' It was impossible to guess what kind

of face lay behind the mask. A determined one. Vercillo didn't doubt that.

He threw up his hands and pointed to the edge of the desk. The sword went down a fraction. Vercillo hooked a finger into the drawer handle and gently pulled. With the slicing edge never more than a couple of centimetres from his throat, he gingerly drew out a set of keys.

'I need to get up,' he said, his voice cracking a little with the strain.

The mask nodded.

Beniamino Vercillo walked towards the wall of the office furthest away from the street. His hands trembling, the accountant turned the key in the security door of the safe then fumbled his way through the numbers on the lock. After a couple of attempts it swung open. He reached inside and withdrew something. The two of them returned to the table. Vercillo opened the large cardboard document box and stood back.

The crazy god's leather fingers dipped into the file and took out the pile of papers there. He threw them on the desk, not saying a word, anger leaking out invisibly from behind the static grin. These were just numbers. Numbers and numbers. Unintelligible.

Vercillo quivered, frightened, and wished to God he'd taken an office on the ground floor, with a window out onto the street. Not this stupid, cramped cave where anything could go on unseen by the busy world outside.

'Code,' the god said simply, pointing at the lines of letters on the pages in front of them.

He tried to think straight. He tried to imagine the consequences. It was impossible. There was only one consequence which mattered.

'If I tell you—?'

The lunatic head stared at him, no emotion in its features, nothing human there at all.

'If I tell you . . . I can go?'

He could run. Vercillo had some private money in places no one could ever find. He could go somewhere Neri's wrath would never find him. Australia maybe. Or Thailand, where the girls were young, and no one asked any questions. He looked around the drab little office, thought of his drab old clothes. Maybe this was fate doing him a favour. All his life he'd spent in the service of the fat hood, pretending to be something he wasn't. Lying, cheating, telling himself it was OK all along because, whatever Neri did to earn his money, none of the blood sat on his own fingers. He'd lied to himself there. Neri *touched* him. Always. It was one reason he started messing with girls. Neri offered him the chance, introduced him to that world. It was one way of keeping him in line.

The idea of retirement, of putting distance between him and this bleak existence built on nothing more than numbers, was suddenly appealing.

Besides, a stray thought wondered, what's the alternative? You're an accountant. Not a foot soldier.

'You can go,' the crazy god said, and again Vercillo found himself trying to place the accent, trying to imagine the human face behind it: young, undoubtedly, but not rough, not like Neri's henchmen.

Vercillo picked up the phone. The crazy god briefly raised the sword, forgetting, it seemed to Vercillo, that he'd already cut the cord. The omission cheered the little accountant. There was something human behind the mask after all.

'It's OK,' Vercillo explained. 'This is it. Watch.'

He set a page – a stream of unintelligible letters – next to the phone. 'It's simple. The person it refers to is identified by his phone number. Everything that comes after is a number too. What's owed. What the interest rate is. What's been paid.'

It felt stupidly exhilarating. In twenty-five years he'd never had this conversation with anyone.

The crazy god stared at the characters on the table, matching them off with the phone keypad using the point of the sword.

'It's clever,' Vercillo added. 'Just remember to use Q for zero and Z for one.' It was too. It meant you could encrypt the number '2' in any one of three ways – A, B or C – and anyone with a phone could still get the right answer in seconds. People assumed codes were designed to hide words, not numbers. As long as they kept to that idea the code was pretty much impossible to crack. It wouldn't fool the FBI, not in the end. But it could fool a lot of people. It would fool Emilio Neri and in some curious way that was all that mattered.

The crazy god laughed and there was something wrong inside the sound.

'Is that what you want?' Vercillo asked.

The mask didn't say a thing.

'I—' Vercillo wanted praise, or gratitude even. There was nothing. 'Maybe I could give you more.'

'Don't need more,' the crazy god murmured, beginning to move, beginning to lift the short, sharp blade higher.

'You said—' Then Vercillo fell silent. There was no point in talking to a sword. There was no point in anything at all. The world was mad. The world was a mask leering at him, getting bigger, crazier with every diminishing second.

Barbara Martelli had lived with her old man in a first-floor apartment on the Lateran Square. The communal front door faced the site of the first St Peter's built by Constantine. The place had five big rooms, a quiet view over the internal courtyard, and plenty of expensive furnishings with a personal, feminine touch. She must have bought them, Costa thought. Peroni had brought along the file from the previous night's visit which they'd read in the car outside. The old man had said little but the background was interesting. It contained more than either of them had expected. When they walked in Costa thought about some of the older papers, with their vague, unproven allegations, took one look at old man Martelli and knew straight away where the money came from.

He was in his mid-fifties and skeletally thin, hunched in a shiny wheelchair, staring back at them with cold, dead eyes. Still, Costa could imagine what he would have been like in his prime. Not that different from Peroni: fit, strong, dogmatic. He didn't look well now, and it wasn't just grief. Costa knew that kind of sickness, recognized the signs. The patchy hair from the chemotherapy. The dead, desiccated look in the eyes. And Martelli was still smoking like crazy too. The place reeked of stale tobacco.

Martelli stared at Gianni Peroni and shook his head. 'Jesus, talk about bad apples,' he snarled. 'I heard you got busted from vice. Didn't realize they busted you down this far. You enjoying it, huh?'

'Yeah,' Peroni said. 'Does a man good to get kicked in the teeth from time to time. This detective stuff's interesting too. We always used to think we had the short end of the stick in vice, Toni. We didn't. You know why?'

The sick old man just glared at him.

'In vice,' Peroni continued, 'we knew we were dealing with shit all along. The only question was how bad it was, and how much stuck to us along the way.' He waved a hand at Costa. 'These guys don't have that privilege. They try to assume everyone's innocent before they find out otherwise. Trust me. This really cramps your style. Fortunately, I haven't learnt that trick.'

'If you could've kept your pecker in your pants, you wouldn't be needing it,' Martelli retorted.

Peroni grimaced. He really didn't like this man. 'So I keep telling myself. Why are we talking like this, Toni? Me and the boy came round here to offer our condolences. We both knew Barbara. We loved that girl. We're in shock over what happened. So why are we making a fight out of things? You want some answers just the same as we do.'

Martelli started coughing like crazy, a cruel, rasping hack. It must have hurt. When he finished he took two gulps of snatched air then wheezed at them, 'I said everything I had to say last night. Can't you leave a father alone with his thoughts?'

Peroni pulled up a chair next to Martelli, sat down, gave Costa a look that said 'watch this' and lit a cigarette. 'I know, I know. It's that asshole Falcone. He just pushes and pushes.'

Martelli snorted. 'I remember him. He wasn't such

hot stuff. How come he made inspector? Don't they have any reliable men left these days?'

'Some,' Peroni replied. 'A few. How're you doing? People still ask after you.'

'Don't give me that shit. I hadn't seen a soul from the Questura in months till last night. Now I can't sleep for the doorbell ringing.'

Peroni shrugged and stared at the walls.

'Is it long since you retired, Signor Martelli?' Costa asked.

'Six years. The moron I was working with complained about my cough. Next thing you know they're doing X-rays, sending me down the hospital. Medical leave. Compulsory retirement.'

'He did you a favour,' Costa said. 'My father died of cancer. The sooner it's caught—'

'A favour.' Martelli's dark eyes stared back at him. 'That's what you call it?'

'Yes.'

'Well, here I am. Still coughing. Still feeling like shit. With my hair falling out and my guts with a mind of their own. Some favour. I could've worked a few more years. I could've done the job. Then what? Maybe they side me with some dumb kid who doesn't know his left hand from his right and gets me walking straight into one of them nice immigrant types we got working the Termini dope run these days. All knives and guns and shit we never had to deal with till they came along. Hell, I wasn't cut out for retirement.'

The man seemed consumed by his own self-pity. They'd come to talk about the death of his daughter. Instead it seemed Toni Martelli only had time to think about himself, how everything that happened affected his own fragile identity. Costa tried to recall Barbara more closely and found it impossible. There was, now he came to think of it, something fleeting about her, a kind of brittle anonymity masquerading as friendliness. Maybe that was all an act too, like the show she put on of being just another cop. There had to be some answers in this over-grand apartment and in the head of her father. He knew that nothing would be prised out into the light of day readily. Toni Martelli had crawled out from underneath some serious corruption allegations scot-free, and went on to take home a full pension. He wasn't the type to offer up the truth for nothing.

'So you and Barbara must have worked together?' Costa asked.

'Depends what you mean by "together". I worked vice and dope mainly. She was traffic. We met in the corridors. We said hello. We didn't talk about what we did if that's what you mean. A good cop leaves things in the office. Maybe you're not old enough to under-stand that.'

'Were you glad she joined the force?'

He shuffled, uncomfortable. 'Yeah. At the time. Why shouldn't I be?'

'Who gave her the job, Toni?' Peroni asked.

'Don't recall.'

Peroni scratched his crew-cut, thinking. 'One of those bent guys you liked, huh? What was the name of that big goon you were pally with? The one that did time for taking money from Neri a couple of years ago? Filippo Mosca wasn't it?'

'I don't have to take this shit,' Martelli wheezed.

Peroni smiled, leaned over and took hold of his

scrawny knee. 'That's the trouble, Toni. That's the worst thing of all. You do.'

'Where's her mother? Does she know?' Costa wondered.

'Back home in Sicily. Of course she knows.' Martelli's dead eyes glared at him. 'They got TV and papers in Sicily, haven't they? How couldn't she know?'

'You should have called her, Toni,' Peroni said. 'You got to bury these things sometimes.'

A skeletal finger cut through the air in front of Peroni's face. 'Don't fucking tell me what to do. Don't go places you don't belong. That woman walked out on me for no good reason. She can rot in hell for all I care.'

Peroni's face lit up at Martelli's reaction. 'She left right around the time Barbara joined up, didn't she? Any connection there?'

'Just get out of here.'

It wasn't grief that was eating the man up. It was hatred, and fear maybe.

'Is there something we can do?' Costa asked. 'Help make arrangements.'

Martelli's eyes fixed on the carpet. 'Nope.'

'Is there nothing at all you want to tell us?'

He didn't say a word.

Peroni leaned back and closed his eyes. 'This is such a nice apartment. I wish I could afford something like it. You know I could just sit here all day, smoking, thinking. You got anything to eat, Toni? You want me to send the boy out and fetch something in while we wait for you to get your voice back? Couple of beers? Some pizza?'

Martelli shook his head. 'She was thirty-two years old, for God's sake. A grown woman. You think she told me everything? It just makes no sense. She got here around three thirty after she came off duty. A little while later there's a call and next thing I know she's putting on that leather gear of hers, off for a ride. Hell, it was a nice day. I thought maybe she was doing it for fun. Maybe she was going to meet someone. I don't know.'

'She didn't say anything?' Costa asked.

Martelli turned to look at Peroni. 'Where did you get Junior? Is this one of them work experience things the schools do?' The bony finger jabbed at Costa from across the room. 'If she'd said anything I'd have mentioned it. I didn't do the job you think you're doing for more than thirty years without learning to put one foot in front of the other.'

'Of course,' Costa nodded and thought again: *where was the grief?* Was Toni Martelli just holding it all inside? Or was there something that overwhelmed even that? Fear? A sense that his own skin might be at risk now too?

'We could get someone round to talk to you. We could get you counselling.'

'Send round some grappa and a few packs of cigarettes. Counselling? And they wonder why the force has gone to pieces.'

'We could get you protection,' Costa suggested.

'Why would I need that?'

'I don't know. You tell me. Barbara had secrets. That much we do know. Maybe some people think she shared them with you.' Costa leaned forward. 'Maybe she did.'

'Don't try fishing with me, kid,' Martelli snapped. 'Ate up minnows like you for dinner in my time. You ask something sensible or you get the hell out of here. I was planning to watch some football.'

It was as if what had occurred was an everyday event. Or that Martelli refused to allow it to touch him, scared perhaps of the consequences. Costa couldn't begin to understand this strange old man at all.

Peroni looked at his watch then at Costa. They both knew they were getting nowhere.

Costa persisted. 'Tell me, Mr Martelli. Did Barbara have a boyfriend?'

The bleak, old eyes glared at him. 'Nothing special.'

'Any names? Did you ever meet them?'

'No.' He lit a cigarette, took a deep gulp then closed his eyes. 'None of my business. None of yours either.'

Peroni nudged him, smiling. 'It is now. We got to pry into Barbara's bedroom, Toni. We got to do that for her sake as well as ours. Did she always come home at night? Or did she stay with them?'

'You two getting off on this?' Martelli asked.

Costa was unmoved. 'Did she leave any phone numbers where you could contact her when she was out?'

The old man went silent again, staring at them sullenly. He was thinking, though. There was some kind of revelation going on inside his head.

'She didn't go for men,' he said. 'Don't get me wrong. She didn't go for women either. She wasn't interested. Not for a long while now. I . . .'

Just for a moment he looked pained. 'I wish she had fucked off with someone, got married, had kids. Instead of all this shit. All this lonely, lonely shit . . .'

'Why was she lonely?' Peroni asked. 'Barbara of all people? I mean she could have had any man she wanted. Why wouldn't she try a couple out just for size?'

'I dunno,' he grunted, recovering his composure. 'Why ask me? She never told me nothing.'

Nic Costa felt an intense dislike for this desiccated man. Peroni had hit on something too. Barbara never did go out with anyone, though she must have been asked all the time. Was she scared of men? Had something happened that made her incapable of maintaining an everyday relationship?

'I wasn't interested in you,' Costa said. 'Not directly. If it's at all possible, Mr Martelli, try to imagine yourself outside all this for a moment. I was asking about Barbara. We've only got three possibilities here. Either she did this of her own volition, just acting alone, for what reason none of us could begin to guess. Or she did it as a private favour. Or someone from one of the mobs kept her sweet over the years and used her to do jobs in her spare time. And paid her.'

Martelli sucked desperately on the cigarette and blew a cloud across the room. Costa waved away the smoke.

'You're her father,' Costa continued. 'You were a cop. Where'd you put your money?'

The cigarette burned brightly again.

'In fact,' Costa added, 'talking of money, where are Barbara's bank accounts? Where are yours for that matter?'

'They took them,' Martelli snapped. 'Last night. They're clean. Not a hint of anything bad. Do I look like an idiot?'

Costa stood up. 'You don't mind if we search the apartment again, Mr Martelli? In case they missed something?'

The old man turned his miserable gaze on Peroni.

'I've had enough of this shit. You've got no papers that give you the right to do this.'

Peroni shook his head. 'We're not going away empty-handed, Toni. There must be something. Something you remembered after they left last night. Otherwise we go out for the beer and pizza. I promise you.'

'Thanks,' Martelli said with a scowl. 'Tell them this. She was a good daughter. She cared for me. She always knew her family came first. I wish I'd appreciated that more. I wish—'

His voice broke. His eyes filled with tears.

Toni Martelli was crying for himself, Costa thought. None of this was supposed to happen. The company he kept had saved him from prosecution before. He must have thought himself untouchable, and believed, by implication, this sense of immunity applied to his daughter too.

'It would be a terrible thing to live with,' Costa said quietly. 'Knowing the events that led to your own child's death came from you.'

'Get the fuck out of here,' Martelli croaked. 'The pair of you. And don't come back.'

Costa thought of arguing. But there was no point. The old man felt protected. As long as he could stay inside the big empty apartment in the Lateran he could continue to fool himself into believing the world would never intrude upon his private hell. None of this could last, and he knew that as well as they did. It was just one of the reasons why he was steeped in such terror.

They didn't say anything as they left. The two men stumbled outside into the daylight. The morning was growing painfully bright under the strong sun. It hurt the eyes. It made the city harsh and two-dimensional.

'We need to work on this "good cop, bad cop" routine,' Peroni suggested as they walked to the car. 'I got confused about my role in there.'

'Really? What role did you want?'

'Good cop,' Peroni insisted. 'Maybe not with assholes like him. But temperamentally I'm much better at it. Whereas you . . . I think you could out-hardball Falcone if you wanted. Doesn't that worry you a little, Nic?'

'Not often these days.'

Peroni shot him a puzzled glance. 'I wish you wouldn't do this to me. Make me think like a detective. It hurts. It's not what I'm built for.'

'What are you thinking?'

He nodded back at the apartment block. 'Martelli was on the take. That we *know*. So Barbara must have got into it too. Or maybe her job was some kind of reward for something Martelli had done. She just inherited the crooked mantle.'

Peroni stared at his partner, half offended. 'What? Why are you looking at me like that?'

'You're imagining things,' Costa said with a smile. 'This is good. Maybe you could make detective.'

The older man laughed and pointed to the car. 'Hey, what I make next is inspector. And you get to drive for me. This is just a temporary hiatus, a blip in the natural order. Some things never change.'

But they do, Costa thought. The world was different already. Cops were killing people in their spare time, and getting killed in return. Something was loose, and random too, but that didn't make it any less powerful.

Costa got behind the wheel, waited for Peroni to strap himself in, then set off into the traffic struggling round the big, busy square, thinking about Miranda

Julius and her missing daughter, trying to work out if there was a way in which they might be unwitting parts of the shadowy, broader picture which had taken Barbara Martelli down to Ostia on a murderous mission less than twenty-four hours before.

'At least we've found out something,' he said.

'We have?'

'Whoever it was on the motorbike that picked up Suzi Julius yesterday, it wasn't Barbara Martelli. She was on duty. I'll check her movements but there's no way that could have been her in the Campo. She couldn't have changed uniform, changed bike, without someone noticing.'

Peroni nodded. 'That's right. Jesus, I should have seen that myself.'

'You're doing fine, Gianni. You just have to keep looking for the connections. Imagining what they might be.'

'I don't want to imagine,' Peroni objected, scowling. 'I wanna ask and get told. OK? And don't say I ain't a partner.' He started delving into Costa's jacket pocket as the Fiat sped down the hill towards the Colosseum.

'This is over-familiar,' Costa declared.

Peroni took out the envelope of holiday snaps Miranda Julius had given them and waved them in Costa's face. 'I can look, can't I? There's nothing private going on between you two? Not yet anyways?'

'Hah, hah.'

Peroni snorted. 'That's good. Get all the impertinence out of your system now, Nic. You won't be able to come out with all that stuff when I'm your boss. Firm but fair is my rule. I don't take any crap though and—'

He went quiet. Costa drew to a halt at the red light, tucked in behind a tram, watching in despair the way the tourists ignored every traffic signal on the road, risking their lives dodging between the cars.

'What is it?' he asked.

Peroni had four photos fanned out in front of him. Just crowd scenes outside the Trevi Fountain.

'Did you see our late professor friend out at Ostia?'

'No. I was busy looking around the place.'

'In that case you should have watched the TV this morning. They showed a mugshot of him. We've got the same guy. Here.' He pointed at a bland, middle-aged man in the crowd, staring back at the camera, interested.

'And here.' It was another shot at the fountain, probably just a minute or so later. The crowd had changed, but Randolph Kirk was still there, still staring intently.

'And here. And here.'

'Four shots,' Costa said, and didn't know whether to feel pleased or horrified.

'So was the creep stalking her?' Peroni wondered. 'Was he a distant admirer or something, and never took it any further? Or is this just coincidence?'

Costa glanced in the mirror, hit the pedal and pulled out into the oncoming stream of traffic, generating a furious howl of horns.

'I don't know about you,' he said, 'but I'm right out of coincidences.'

'It doesn't rhyme with "vagina". Try again. I have a rule about this. Kindly indulge me.'

Teresa Lupo was struggling for words. She'd expected

some boring university administrator, not this slender, middle-aged Scotswoman dressed in an elegant, black velvet dress, a string of pearls around her pale, flawless neck, and sitting bolt upright behind a gleaming teak desk. A large, imposing brass nameplate stood between them bearing the name Professor Regina Morrison, Director of Administration, followed by a string of academic letters. Teresa wasn't sure she knew how to cope. What was more, she was starting to feel sick. Her head hurt. Her throat was going dry, her eyes itchy.

'Excuse me?'

The woman adjusted a photograph of a small terrier on the desk so that the dog stared directly into Teresa Lupo's eyes with a fierce, unbending gaze. 'Reg-*een*-a Morrison. I'm not responsible for my own name. Sometimes I wonder if perhaps I ought to change it to something more usual. But then I think: *why?* Why bend to an ignorant world? Why not make it bend instead?'

'Reg-*een*-a.'

'There,' the woman beamed. She had a very neat, mannish haircut, her too-black locks clipped close to her scalp. 'That wasn't so hard, was it? Now tell me. You're a police officer?'

'Teresa Lupo. I'm from the police department.'

Regina Morrison leaned forward and put her hands together in the kind of gesture she must have used with recalcitrant students all the time. 'So you're *not* a police officer?'

There was, she thought, no point in trying to fox this woman. 'Not exactly. I'm a pathologist. This is Italy, Professor Morrison. Things get complicated.'

'In the six months I've worked here I must say I've noticed. Still, I imagine I should be grateful anyone's turned up at all. If this were Edinburgh I'd have no end of people trampling through my office asking all manner of stupid questions with half a dozen TV stations stumbling in their wake. It's almost a day now since Randolph was killed. And all I have is you. Should I be grateful? Or offended?'

'Ask me that when the real cops turn up,' Teresa observed wryly. 'My money's on grateful.'

The slender shoulders moved just a little. That seemed to amuse her. 'So why are you here and not them?'

'Because—' she shrugged. 'The woman who killed your man was a cop and that changes things somewhat. The focus shifts, to her, not him. For now anyway. I got a look at the report this morning. It said Kirk was something of a loner. He lived by himself. No relatives in Italy. Not many friends. Cops are just like . . .' she tried to think of a good analogy, ' . . . university administrators. They put their resources in the places where they think they'll get the best return. The woman who killed Professor Kirk is someone they all knew. I guess they think they'll get further, faster, by checking her first before driving round all day trying to track down any barflies Kirk drank with in his spare time.'

'Randolph Kirk drank alone, poor man,' Regina Morrison said with some firmness.

Then she opened a drawer and took out a half bottle of Glenmorangie malt and two small glasses.

'Cheers,' she said, pouring a couple of shots, picking one up and staring directly across the shining desk at her visitor.

'Sorry,' Teresa said. 'I'm on duty. I didn't mean anything by that. It was a figure of speech. If he was a friend of yours—'

'No,' the woman answered, with equal conviction, and downed the whisky in one go. 'He wasn't that either. Not at all. I'm just a mite put out to discover that he, and by implication the rest of us in the academic community . . . we're all somehow less interesting than this murderous colleague of yours.'

Teresa took Kirk's book out of her bag and waved it in the air. 'Not to me you're not. I was hoping he could clear up a few things that were bothering me. While I couldn't claim to have made much personal contact with him during our brief meeting yesterday, I have read his book. And that I find very interesting indeed. That, Professor Morrison, is why I'm here.'

'It was you?' she asked, intrigued. 'The woman who was with him when this happened?'

'Not with him. Locked in his office. He saved my life, I think. Not that he meant to.'

'Don't undersell yourself,' Regina Morrison said with some admiration.

Unconsciously, Teresa stroked the plaster sticking to her scalp. 'I'll try to remember that.'

'But I don't understand why you, of all people, are here. I'd have thought you had plenty of real work to occupy you.'

Regina Morrison had a way of coming to the point with a remarkable directness. It hit home too. When she thought about Monkboy being left to his own devices Teresa Lupo felt far from comfortable.

'I need to tie up some loose ends. You've read Kirk's book?'

'Oh yes,' she answered. 'I'm an administrator now but I'm a classicist at heart. One day I'm going back to teaching. Sooner rather than later if I lose another member of staff this suddenly. I got parachuted in here from Edinburgh last autumn so don't expect me to provide too many searing insights into Randolph Kirk's persona. But I read his book and admired it greatly. When I took the job I hoped he had another one on the cards and perhaps I'd get an early look-in. That was one reason I came.' She thought carefully about what to say next. 'Little did I know.'

'Know what?' Teresa asked impatiently.

'To be honest with you I thought I'd be telling all this to a real police officer.'

She couldn't wait that long, though. Regina Morrison was itching to get on with her tale.

'I'll pass it on. Promise.'

'I'm sure you will,' the woman chuckled. 'The truth is I was about to fire him. It's just one nasty job after another here at the moment. They brought me in from outside for a reason. No one local, and certainly no one Italian, was going to face up to the . . . difficulties that needed cleaning up. I may as well tell you. It's going to come out anyway one day. Maladministration. Fraud. Some exceedingly dubious academic projects. And Randolph Kirk. A wonderful scholar, one of the best of his generation at Cambridge apparently. But a lonely little man with a lonely little man's habits. He couldn't keep his hands to himself. Most academics move on once in a while. That's the way to get more money. Not Randolph. He stayed here for a reason, my dear. He had to. If he'd pulled some of his tricks anywhere else he'd be out of work for life, sued for every penny he owned, and possibly in jail too.'

For a moment, Teresa felt like a cop, standing on the

brink of some important discovery. It was a wonderful sensation. 'Tricks?'

'He molested young women. The younger the better. I don't know the full extent of what went on. Back home we're like the Americans. Girls scream sexual assault if someone says they're wearing a nice dress. Why Sigmund Freud settled in Vienna is beyond me. We're ten times more anal in Edinburgh. Here it's the opposite. Everyone keeps their mouths shut. Maybe they think it goes with the course. All the same, I had enough evidence to terminate him within six weeks of falling into this chair and had your gun-wielding colleague not intervened I would have done it very soon. Trust me.'

Teresa tapped the book. 'Was it connected with what he wrote?'

Regina Morrison smiled back at her across the desk. 'You and I think along the same lines. Remarkable. I read that a couple of years ago. Then when I turned up here and started hearing some stories about the real Randolph I read it again. You needed to meet the man to understand this. He wasn't just writing history. He was laying out the grounds for some kind of personal philosophy of his, one he thought he was copying from those rituals. You know what I think? He played it out. He persuaded some of those gullible girls. He convinced them what they were doing was worth a try somehow. I can't believe they were fooled by all his mumbo-jumbo, mind, but you know what girls are. Perhaps there was something in it for them. Whatever. My guess is he put on one of those masks he was always writing about, pretended he was the great god himself and had his fun. It didn't fool anyone else, of course. The kids knew why they were doing it. To get the right grades or something.

If old Randolph invited along a few visitors – and I suspect he did because he was a man who desperately needed to be told how clever he was every living second of the day – I don't imagine they bought into his fancy myths either. They were just having a little fun for free. I'm guessing there, which is something no academic should do, but I feel it's right anyway. I talked to a couple of ex-students. They're just too scared to tell, to be honest. I wonder why.'

Teresa's pulse was racing. There had to be evidence here. There had to be something Regina Morrison could give her.

'Do you have names? Places?'

The woman on the other side of the desk eyed her suspiciously. 'You could get me into big trouble. You think I haven't put enough noses out of joint around here already? They brought me in to sort things out. That kind of work never makes you popular. Once I'm finished firing then they fire me. That's the way it goes. But I don't want to give them any early excuses.'

'Regina,' she said, taking care to pronounce the name perfectly, 'this isn't an academic exercise. It's not about finding out why Randolph Kirk died. Not directly. There's a girl who's gone missing. Right now. Maybe she's been abducted. Maybe she went willingly, not knowing what she was in for. But I'm sure it's something to do with all this. There was evidence in her apartment. A thyrsus. Some other items. That's why I went to see him in the first place.'

Teresa Lupo looked at her watch. She needed to get back to the morgue. There were so many questions to ask this unusual, intelligent stranger, and so little time.

'But if Randolph's dead—' Regina Morrison wondered.

'Surely she's safe. You don't think he went around abducting these girls. He couldn't do that. Not—'

Regina Morrison hesitated.

'Not what?'

'Not on his own.' The Scotswoman's composure was broken for a second or two. Teresa could see she genuinely was worried. 'Look,' she said, toying with the photo of the dog in front of her. 'I've been sitting here all morning waiting for you people to turn up. Where have you been? Who are you to start shouting urgent now? When I heard what had happened to Randolph last night I came in here late and took a little look around his office. A raid you might say. I thought I'd get in there before you people did. I didn't understand your timekeeping habits then, you understand.'

'You broke into his office?' Teresa gasped, a little in awe.

Regina Morrison tapped her nameplate. 'That's what titles are for. I came up with something too, locked away in a drawer with some teeny little padlock on it. Randolph hadn't a clue, you know. The man was utterly unworldly. You don't seem the squeamish sort, Teresa. Am I right?'

'I'm a pathologist.'

'Sorry. I meant "prudish".'

'Me?'

Regina Morrison opened a drawer and passed over a manila folder. On the cover, written in a sloping, intelligent hand, was scrawled a single word: 'Maenads'. And a picture was glued there too, a print of a familiar ancient theatre mask, howling through an exaggerated mouth. Then she leaned across the desk and said, in a conspiratorial whisper, 'You know who they were, don't you? The Maenads?'

'Remind me,' Teresa hissed, snatching through the pages of typed text and photographs, breathless, head reeling.

'The followers of the god. Call him Dionysus. Call him Bacchus. Either works. The Maenads were his women. He or – by implication – his followers made them initiates through these mysteries of theirs.'

Teresa's fingers were racing through the documents. 'What happened exactly? At these mysteries?'

'Not even Randolph claimed to know that. Not exactly. From what we discussed I think he had a better idea than he put in that book, though. It was a ritual, Teresa. It's important you remember that.'

She paused over a page of incomprehensible text. 'Why?'

'Because rituals are formal. They have a structure. Nothing happens by accident. These girls weren't snatched from the street. Some of them volunteered. Some of them were gifts from their family.'

'What?' It seemed incomprehensible to her. 'Why would any mother or father do that?'

'Because they thought it was right. Why not? Plenty of girls get given to the Church today to become nuns. Is it that different?'

She thought of the book. 'Nuns don't get raped.'

'They're both offerings to their chosen god. The difference lies in the detail. Take out some of the weirder parts – the parts Randolph liked – it's not that different. Gifts or volunteers, they submitted to the ceremony. They became brides of the god. It's just that the Dionysians consummated that marriage, physically, in the shape of some hanger-on like Randolph I imagine.'

'And afterwards?'

'Afterwards they belonged to him. And the men who followed him. They worshipped him. Or them. Once a year he returned to meet his new brides and renew his gift for those who'd gone before. He gave them all that they wanted: ecstasy, frenzy. If Randolph was right, the nasty parts, the violence and the unbridled sexual encounters, occurred after the marriage, not during it. They enjoyed what we would call an orgy. Pure, mindless, dangerous, liberating. Then they went back to their homes and were good mothers for another year. Have you read *The Bacchae* or is Euripides not to your taste?'

'Not recently.'

Regina Morrison reached into the bookshelf behind her and took out a slim, blue leather-backed volume. 'Borrow it if you like. You can interpret the story in a number of ways. The liberal tradition says it's an analogy for the dual nature of humanity, the need to give our wild side an outlet now and then because if we don't it will surface anyway, when we least want it. The natural order breaks down. People get torn limb from limb by crazy women thirsty for blood just because someone broke the rules, unwittingly even.'

She leaned forward over the desk. 'Do you want to know what I think?'

Teresa Lupo wasn't sure she did but, all the same, found herself asking, 'What?'

'It's just about men and power and sex. How they can have it whenever they want, regardless of how a woman feels. And how we're supposed to be grateful however much we hate it because, well, let's face things, the god lives with them, not us, and the only way we get a taste is if we let them put a little bit of him inside us. Are you getting my drift?'

'Oh, I am, I am,' Teresa agreed.

'One doesn't wish to appear the puritan, Teresa. As a Scotswoman I am all too aware of that. There's nothing wrong with – what was it that American woman called it? – the "zipless fuck". Everyone likes some mindless carnality from time to time. Half an hour of pleasure and nothing to think of afterwards. You must have done the same?'

Teresa Lupo looked at the staid, elegant woman opposite her and after a while could still only think of one thing to say. 'Yes.'

'But a quick fuck in the dark's not the same, is it? Old Randolph *planned* all this. It's all just so damnably male.'

'Agreed. We must have dated the same men over the years, Regina, believe me.'

'I don't date men any more,' Regina Morrison said very sweetly. 'Where's the hunt? Where's the challenge? When you know they're panting for it anyway, with whomever or whatever they can find, what's the point? Here. Let me give you my card. My mobile's on there.'

'Right,' she replied, cursing her own stupidity, taking the item from the woman's slim hand in any case.

'It's a question of timing,' Regina Morrison said. 'Everything is.'

Teresa looked again at the file. There were pages and pages. And photographs. Lots of photographs.

'What is?' she asked idly.

'Finding this girl is your idea, isn't it? That's why

you're here on your own. The police don't think there's any connection.'

Teresa stared at her. The woman had been two steps ahead all along. It was disquieting. 'They're not sure.'

'You'd best hope they're right and you're wrong, my dear. Think about the dates.'

'The dates?'

'You read the book. Tomorrow is Liberalia. The day for making new Maenads. And the day the old ones come out to play.'

'Yes. I know that.' She thought of Nic Costa. *'We know that.'*

Regina Morrison smiled at her, bemused. 'You seem somewhat . . . distracted.'

Teresa Lupo took out one photo from the folder and placed it on the desk. Then she stifled a sneeze with a lone finger.

It was an old picture, shot secretly like the rest, in poor interior light using a cheap camera. Home-developed probably, which explained the thin, washed-out colours. That and its age. She could just about make out the images on the walls in the background. They were almost the same as the dancing fauns and leering satyrs in Kirk's book, from the place that seemed to double as his strange, private playground at Ostia. But not quite. This was somewhere different. The paintings looked even older, and more sinister somehow. The place looked larger too. Perhaps he'd found Rome's Villa of Mysteries and kept it for this one particular purpose.

Barbara Martelli was in the centre of the shot. She wore a plain white tee-shirt and jeans. She looked so young, just a teenage kid, so sweet it almost hurt. Teresa Lupo's head hurt trying to reconcile these conflicting

images into some sane, comprehensible whole: innocence on the verge of being spoiled, of entering the
long path that would transform this lovely kid into a
murderous black-helmeted insect. Was the beast in her
already, a cocoon of hate and death just waiting, growing
over the years?

She didn't want to look too closely at the figure next
to Barbara. It was Eleanor Jamieson. That much was
quite clear. But seeing the girl like this – alive, full of
spark and expectation – was almost more than Teresa
Lupo's pained, congested head could bear. She'd come
to think of her as a mummified corpse on a shining
silver table. This image made her something else, a real,
looming presence haunting Teresa's head, and emphasized, almost to breaking point, the enormity of her
death. This was all *before*. The god hadn't visited them
yet. Maybe they never even knew he was on the way.

And one more thing, one crazy, nagging idea that
couldn't be dismissed. Teresa was unable to forget the
pictures of Suzi Julius she'd seen. She and Eleanor were
so alike they could almost have been sisters, smiling
teenage siblings from the same template of classic blonde
beauty. The thyrsus, the tattoo, the seeds . . . all these
coincidences paled next to the physical resemblance they
bore to one another, and it was this, she knew, that had
triggered Suzi's disappearance, this alone that made her
reach the bottom of some long, dark narrow street and
get called into the shadows. Someone who knew what
had happened sixteen years ago found his memory
jogged when he saw this lovely young stranger walking
down the street. The wheel turned. The ritual was in
motion.

'Teresa?' Regina Morrison looked worried. 'Are you OK?'

'I'm fine,' she said softly, then coughed and felt the mucus move painfully inside her temples. 'I need to take these documents.'

Regina Morrison nodded. 'Of course. Sure you're all right? You look as if you could use that drink.'

'No. I'm fine.'

She was lying. Her eyes had started itching again, stinging cruelly.

She looked into Eleanor's face. It had never happened like this before. They were always dead, truly dead, long dead, dead and gone forever, when they fell beneath her knife. A switch had been turned: life went from on to off, with nothing in between and nothing after.

She remembered cowering in Randolph Kirk's scruffy little office, remembered what happened when she heard the shots, how something appeared to pass through her with a sudden resigned rush, like the last gasp of a departing persona.

When she stared at Eleanor Jamieson she felt the same sensation, the same lack of certainty about herself and what she did for a living. Just to pay the bills, to feed the prurient maw of the state. And now Suzi Julius was out there, walking in these same shadows, towards the same destination, with no one in the Questura paying sufficient attention because Teresa Lupo, Crazy Teresa, had taken matters into her own hands, pretended she was something she wasn't and made it all worse.

'Teresa,' Regina Morrison said. 'Here's a tissue. Take it.'

'Thanks,' she said, and put down the page, her hand trembling, her vision awash with tears, gulping at the whisky, gulping at another too when Regina Morrison briskly refilled the glass.

Falcone cast an interested eye at the bunch of men lurking on the first floor of Neri's house. Then the fat old hood hurriedly ushered him and Rachele D'Amato upstairs.

'I didn't realize you had guests,' Falcone said. 'And you answer the door yourself these days. Servants getting too expensive?'

'I don't need any damn servants,' Neri retorted. 'Don't give me any shit, Falcone. I could've turned you back at the door. You got no papers that give you the right to walk into a man's home like this. And her—'

Neri looked right through D'Amato. 'So you two are on speaking terms these days? I heard that ended when the sheets started to get cold.'

'This is business,' she said briskly, then followed Neri into a large living room furnished expensively with a minimum of taste: modern leather sofas and armchairs, reproduction paintings on the plain cream walls, and a big glass table at the centre.

Two people sat on the couch: a slim attractive woman in her thirties, with fiery reddish gold hair and striking, angry features, and a slightly younger man, slim, nervous, with dark, shifty eyes and a bad bleach job.

'I don't have a lawyer on the premises,' Neri said. 'So you can talk in front of my family. That way if you invent stuff I've got witnesses.'

Falcone nodded.

'You didn't introduce us,' the woman said. 'I'm Adele. His wife.'

'Current wife,' Neri added.

'True,' she agreed. 'This is Mickey. My stepson. Say hello to the nice policeman, Mickey. And stop twitching like that. It pisses me off. Quit gawping at the lady too.'

Mickey ceased fiddling with his fingers and muttered, 'Pleasure.'

Neri fell into a large, fat armchair next to them and waved Falcone and D'Amato to the table. 'I'd offer you coffee but fuck it. Why are you here? What am I supposed to have done now?'

'Nothing,' Falcone said. 'Just a social visit.'

Neri's big chest heaved with a dry laugh.

'When we decide you've done something, Emilio, it won't be just the two of us who turn up,' Rachele D'Amato said, amused by the way Mickey was still staring at her. 'We'll have lots and lots of people. And the TV crews, the newspapers too. I just know they're going to hear of it.'

'Not gonna happen,' Neri muttered. 'Never. There's no reason for it.'

She nodded at his son. 'Do we take him in too? Is he part of the family firm now?'

'You tell me. You DIA scum never give up spying on me. What do you think?'

She smiled at Mickey. He blushed a little and stared at his feet.

'I think he doesn't look like you. Maybe he doesn't act like you. I don't know.'

'No,' Neri agreed. 'You don't know. Tell you what. If you want someone to keep your statistics up you can take him now. Take her too if you feel like it, so long as . . .' He took a good look at them when he said this. ' . . . they get to share the same cell. She's got more brains than him though. You might find it harder fitting her up.'

Falcone smiled. 'Happy families. Don't you love to see them?'

'My patience is wearing thin. Get to the point.'

'The point,' Falcone said immediately, 'is that I want to know what you were doing sixteen years ago. I want you to tell me about Vergil Wallis and what happened to his stepdaughter.'

Neri's bleak, reptilian eyes narrowed. 'You're kidding me. You want me to try to remember all that way back? Who're you talking about?'

'Vergil Wallis,' D'Amato repeated. 'He was your contact with the West Coast mob. Don't try to deny it. There are intelligence photos of you two together. We know you had dealings.'

'I'm a sociable man,' Neri protested. 'I meet a lot of people. You expect me to remember every one?'

'You remember this one,' Falcone said. 'He nearly got you on the wrong side of the Sicilians. You screwed him over some deal. Is there still bad feeling between you? Have you spoken recently?'

'*What?*' Neri's feigned outrage was unconvincing. He meant it that way. 'Look, if you want to throw these kinds of questions at me it's best we do it some other time, in the company of a lawyer. Not now.'

D'Amato ran her fingers through her perfect brown hair, just for Mickey's benefit. 'You don't need a lawyer, Emilio. No one's accusing you of anything. We just want to know what you can recall. You did meet this man. We all know that. That's not why we're here. His step-daughter was murdered. Sixteen years ago. The body turned up recently.'

'You think I don't read the papers? You think I don't hear things?'

'So?' Falcone persisted.

Neri nodded at Mickey. 'You remember some black guy way back then? Rings a bell for me. Not much more.'

'Sure,' Mickey agreed, looking more nervous than ever. 'He and some kid were with us on vacation for a while. They were both history freaks or something. Couldn't stop talking about all that crap. Museums and stuff. Turned me off.'

'And you remember his stepdaughter?' D'Amato asked.

'A little,' Mickey conceded. 'I thought she was his, if you get my meaning. A black guy with a skinny blonde thing around them. What would you think?'

Falcone considered this. 'Are you saying there was some relationship between Wallis and the girl?'

'No,' he replied defensively, looking at his father for guidance. 'I dunno.'

'He was some jumped-up piece of work,' Neri added. 'Who the fuck knew what was going on? I'll say this, though. Met a few like him in my time. They come here, think they can do business, never have to pay nothing in the way of an entrance fee just because of who they are. Yeah, and one more thing. You ever seen a black guy with a blonde in tow he wasn't fucking?'

D'Amato shook her head, unhappy with this idea. 'She was his stepdaughter.'

'Oh right,' Neri sneered. 'That makes a difference. Tell me. If you found some rich Italian guy shacked up with a teenager, smiling at her all the time like he owned her, you'd say that about him, huh? You don't think

240

maybe there are some double standards here? Men like that can't keep their hands still. Can you imagine what it'd be like to get a couple at the same time? Mother and daughter? You go ask him about that. Not me.'

He had a point. Falcone understood that. Maybe Wallis was just a great actor. Maybe this show of grief was just that, a show.

'What about you, Mickey?' D'Amato asked suddenly.

'What about me?' he stuttered.

'Did you like the look of her? Was she your type?'

He glanced nervously, first at Adele, then at his father. 'Nah. Too skinny. Too stuck up. She talked all the history shit he did. What's someone like that gonna do with someone like me?'

Rachele D'Amato smiled. 'So you remember her well?'

'Not much,' he murmured.

Neri waved his big arm, 'Fuck this. Why are we talking about some kid who went missing ages ago? What's this got to do with us?'

They said nothing.

'Right,' Neri continued. 'Now that's out of the way maybe you can go. This place is starting to smell bad. I want some fresh air in here.'

Rachele D'Amato smiled at Mickey. 'What about Barbara Martelli, Mickey? Was she your kind of woman? Not skinny at all. Got a good job as a cop too.'

His eyes went round and round, flitting between his stepmother and Neri. 'Who? Who? Dunno what the hell you're talking about. Who?'

'The woman who was in the papers, dummy,' Neri snarled. 'The cop who got killed yesterday. They say she offed someone. That right? What is it with the police force today? How's a man supposed to trust anyone?'

'I ask the questions,' Falcone said. 'Where were you yesterday, Mickey? Give me your movements, morning to night.'

'He was here with me all day,' Adele Neri insisted. 'All day. And in the evening too.'

'We were all here together,' Neri added. 'Apart from a little lunch outing I had with one of my employees. He can vouch for me. We can vouch for one another. You got any reason to think otherwise?'

Rachele D'Amato took two photographs out of her briefcase: Barbara Martelli in uniform and one of her old man, back in the days when he was on the force. 'Her father was a cop. He was on your payroll.'

'Me?' Neri whined. 'Pay cops? Don't you think I pay enough already what with the taxes round here?'

'When did you last talk to Martelli?' Falcone asked. 'When did you last speak to his daughter?'

'Don't recall ever making their acquaintance. And I'm speaking for us all now. Understand? If you've got something that says otherwise you go show it to a lawyer. Except you don't have anything. Otherwise we wouldn't be talking like this now, would we?'

She put the photos back in her bag. 'Those men downstairs,' she said.

'We were thinking of having a card game later. They're good guys.'

'Make it last,' Falcone ordered. 'Make it last a long time. I don't want to see them on the streets. You got that?'

The big old hood was shaking his head. 'So Romans don't get to walk their own town now? Is that what you're saying? Jesus. Here I am taking this shit. Here I am listening to your dumb threats and all this crap about things you don't know. And that American bastard's just walking round doing what he likes. No one's asking him whether he was screwing that girl. No one's asking him if he's been paying off dumb cops to get what he wants.' He waved a fat hand at them. 'You tell me. Why's that? Are you people just plain stupid or what?'

Falcone stood up. Rachele D'Amato followed suit.

'Nice seeing you again,' Neri barked. 'Don't feel the need to rush back.'

'Do you know what tomorrow is?' Falcone asked.

'Saturday. Do I get a prize?'

'Liberalia.'

Neri screwed up his slack face in an expression of distaste. 'What? This some new European holiday they're pressing on us now? Don't mean a thing to me.'

'It does,' Falcone said. 'It means that if you know what's good for you, you stay right here. You don't get in my way.'

'Wow,' Neri sneered. 'This is what cops do now. Make a few empty threats.'

'It's good advice. I remember you. Years ago, when I was just a detective. I watched you, I *know* you.'

'Yeah? You think so?'

'And the thing is, you've changed. You're older. You look weaker somehow. Let me tell you something. You're not the man you were.'

'Bullshit!' Neri yelled, getting onto his feet, waving his big arms in the air. 'Get the fuck out of here before I throw you down the stairs, cop or no cop.'

Falcone wasn't listening. He had his phone to his ear and was engrossed in the call. There was something in his face that made them all go quiet and wait for what came next.

'I'll be straight there,' Falcone murmured.

'Leo?' D'Amato asked. 'Is something wrong?'

He looked at Emilio Neri. 'Maybe. Does the name Beniamino Vercillo mean anything to you?'

'All these stupid questions—' the old man grumbled.

'Well?'

'Not a damn thing. Why d'you ask?'

'Nothing,' Falcone replied with a shrug. 'He's a stranger. Why worry? Watch the news. Pay some bent cop to tell you first. Who cares? I'll let myself out.'

'Mickey!'

Neri pointed at the two of them. Mickey led Falcone and Rachele D'Amato downstairs, going first so that he got a chance to turn round now and again and get a good look at her long, lithe legs moving out from underneath the short skirt.

The visitors were sitting around a table in the big room on the first floor, reading papers, smoking, playing cards.

'I recognize a few familiar faces,' Falcone said. 'Is this the kind of company you keep, Mickey?'

'Don't know what you mean.' Mickey Neri continued on to the big front door, with its security cameras and multiple electronic locks.

Rachele D'Amato ducked out of the way of the lens and smiled at him. 'You should be smart, Mickey. It's important to be smart in a situation like this.'

'A situation like what?'

'Change,' she said and handed him her card. 'Can't you just feel it in the air? That's my private number. Call if you want to talk. I could keep you out of jail. If things turn bad, I could even keep you alive.'

He glanced upstairs to make sure no one was listening. 'G-g-get out of here,' Mickey Neri mumbled.

The scene of crime men pulled on their white bunny suits then clambered down the iron staircase into the basement office off the Via dei Serpenti. Falcone watched them, mentally trying to work out the manpower disposition inside the Questura. With the officers already inside that brought the total contingent on the murder scene to six. It wasn't enough. The Questura was getting desperately stretched. He'd already got people trying to persuade the sick to rise from their beds. Even with the few who complied, he was still struggling to keep every thread of the investigation – Randolph Kirk, Barbara Martelli, Eleanor Jamieson and, just possibly, the Julius girl – fully staffed. It was the spring holiday season. A quiet time of the year, or so everyone supposed. The gaps were already starting to appear. He wished he had more people to despatch to watch Neri and Wallis, make sure they didn't develop any stupid ideas. He wished, too, he had time to think about Suzi Julius. Falcone shared some of Costa's fears, though he was reluctant to act in the present circumstances until some hard facts emerged to link her directly to the Jamieson case. There was still no evidence to suggest this was anything other than a wayward teenager out for some fun. He couldn't afford to waste the men he had on hypothetical crimes when there were real ones demanding his attention.

Rachele D'Amato's black Alfa pulled up on the pavement and he watched her get out, watched the way she angled her slender legs carefully so that the tight red skirt she was wearing didn't ride up too much. For a brief moment Falcone let other thoughts dominate his mind. She was thirty minutes behind him. She'd had to call in at the DIA office on the way. He really had no idea what was going on there behind closed doors.

'She doesn't need to be here,' he reminded himself, then managed to work up a smile. 'Not at all.'

She walked up, eyeing him. 'Leo?'

'I don't recall issuing an invitation, Rachele. This isn't an open house. You don't get to walk into every investigation we have.'

She nodded at the door. A couple of the bunny suits were coming out again, taking off their helmets to light cigarettes. The path was clear for the rest of them to go in. 'Don't I get to take a look? You really believed Neri then? You think this guy was a complete stranger?'

'According to what we know Beniamino Vercillo was an accountant. We don't have a thing on him. He was just a little man. Lived in Paroli on his own. The safe's open. It's probably robbery or something.'

She eyed the men by the iron staircase, not believing a word. Falcone resented the idea she always seemed one step ahead of him. 'Is that so? I listened on the radio. I gather you have a witness.'

'You shouldn't go near our radios,' he said. 'That's not part of the deal.'

'I'm saving time. For all of us. What happened?'

He sighed. 'A girl in the optician's saw a character in a kind of costume going in. Something theatrical. With a mask. There's a street theatre troupe performing down at the Colosseum so she didn't think too much of it. We checked. They're performing Euripides. *The Bacchae.*

One of their costumes is missing. I've got men interviewing every last one of them. The trouble is they were
rehearsing at the time. Either they're all liars or it's
someone else who stole the costume. No one saw a soul
coming out. It's—'

Everything was going wrong, heading off in different
directions. It denied him the time to think, the opportunity to focus on what mattered. 'It's the last damn
thing I need right now.'

D'Amato didn't look impressed.

'Are you going to tell me or do I have to guess?'
Falcone sighed. 'We really aren't working together on
this one, are we? Am I the problem? Do you want to
liaise with someone else instead?'

Her hand went to his arm. Slim, delicate fingers. He
recalled their touch. 'I'm sorry, Leo. It's not you. It's
me. You're right. This is all . . . out of synch somehow.
The DIA's no different to you, really. We expect things
to happen the way they always did. None of this fits a
template.'

'You can say that again. So Vercillo wasn't some
boring little accountant?'

She laughed and it reminded him of how she once
was: young, carefree. And how much that used to affect
him. 'You didn't really think that, did you, Leo?'

'No.' He'd put on a bunny suit himself for a while
and been inside. He'd seen what was there. He couldn't
get the idea of that damned mask out of his head. 'I just
don't like jumping to conclusions.'

'We could never pin anything on him,' she went on.
'Vercillo was smart. He needed to be. He kept books
for Neri. Of that I'm pretty sure. Not that you'll ever
find a sheet of paper to prove it.'

A piece of the puzzle fell into place in his head. Falcone thought of the scene inside the dead man's office and knew she was wrong for a change, though he kept the news to himself.

'Why would someone murder Neri's accountant? Has he been taking from the boss?'

She'd considered that already. 'It's hard to imagine. He'd know what the result would be if he got found out. I don't think Neri would send round a man in a mask either. Vercillo would just be there one moment and gone for good the next.'

'Then what?' he wondered.

'We had some intelligence,' she said eventually. 'Early yesterday evening four, maybe five suspicious Americans flew in to Fiumicino. Separate airlines, separate classes for a couple. As if they didn't know each other. It could be Wallis beefing up his army.'

Falcone stroked his pointed beard. He hated the way she seemed to know so much about the mob, how she seemed to understand their movements instinctively. The DIA were supposed to do that. All the same it left him feeling cheated. 'What army? You said he was retired.'

'He is but that doesn't mean he's stupid. You saw the security on that place of his. Vergil Wallis doesn't let his guard slip, any more than Neri does. Men like that have to be careful, retired or not.'

Falcone wondered: could this be Wallis's first act of vengeance? Then there was a bustle down the street. It was Monkboy and the rest of the path team – except Teresa Lupo – arriving, unusually late.

'What took you?' Falcone barked at them. Silvio Di Capua just put his head down and stumbled onto the staircase. He looked scared.

'You're saying these men have been summoned?' Falcone asked her.

'Maybe.'

He thought back to the cool way Wallis had greeted them. 'It could make sense I guess. If he thinks there's a war on the way. He didn't look like a man getting ready for war to me.'

She gave him a sideways glance, as if she thought he were being naïve. 'You should never take these people at face value, Leo. Not even Neri. That was a performance this morning too, though not one I understand. Perhaps Vergil Wallis just feels he has no choice but to get some muscle around him.'

Falcone grimaced and started walking for the door. She raced to keep up with him.

The bunny suits had their helmets off. They were busy, dusting, poking, peering into corners, putting things into envelopes. Falcone glowered at Monkboy trembling over the corpse. Beniamino Vercillo was pinned to his old leather chair by a curving sword through the chest. His body had fallen forward a fraction. It was plain to see that the blade had been thrust up through the ribcage, exiting to the right of the spine and impaling itself into the back of the chair.

Vercillo was a thin man. Falcone wondered how much force such a blow would take. Crazy Teresa would know. She always did know this kind of thing. But she wasn't there and Monkboy looked out of his depth, surrounded by a bunch of junior morgue assistants waiting to be told what to do.

'Where is she?' Falcone demanded.

'Who?'

'Who the hell do you think? Your boss?'

'Had to go out,' Silvio Di Capua stuttered. 'She'll be here soon.'

Falcone was astonished she would have the nerve to play these games twice in twenty-four hours. 'Go out where?' he bellowed.

Di Capua shrugged, looking miserable and scared.

'Get her here,' Falcone barked. 'Now. And where the hell are Peroni and Costa? Didn't anyone call them like I asked?'

'On their way,' one of the bunny suits mumbled. 'They went back to the Questura. Didn't know you were out. They got something they said.'

'Jesus,' Falcone cursed. 'It's about time someone got something. What's going on around here?'

Then he stopped. Rachele D'Amato was standing by the late accountant's body, looking at the table, smiling. There were papers everywhere, printouts from computers, pages from a typewriter that seemed to pre-date these. Even a couple written in a careful, childlike hand.

They were just letters, a sea of letters, spilling everywhere. Apart from a single sheet with text on it, scrawled in a different style of writing, using a black felt-tip pen left by the paper. The ink looked fresh. The page depicted a phone keypad and beneath it a selection of numbers copied from the typed page next to it. The relevant section was ringed on the original page. Falcone had realized almost immediately what it was: the key to a code. A date. A phone number. An amount. And then some more codes that were impenetrable, because they probably related to the kind of transaction involved. Maybe, with more work, they could crack them too. This was a rich and generous gift. A deliberate escalation of the odds.

She reached for the papers, elated. He stopped her.

'We haven't gone over those yet,' he cautioned. 'Afterwards, you'll get to see them. I promise.'

'Do you know what this is?'

'I didn't. From what you've said, I think I do now.'

She was ecstatic, triumphant. He wished he could share her elation. 'These go back years. We can put Emilio Neri away for good. We may be able to nail anyone who did business with him. Have you thought of that, Leo?'

'Right now I'm thinking about a murder,' he answered. Then he wondered: was that the direction you were supposed to take in the circumstances? Did this bloody dumb show exist in order to make you miss a larger though more subtle point? He couldn't work up any enthusiasm for the information that lay on the table. However useful it was, something about its provenance troubled him. This wasn't the way the mobs normally went to war, killing underlings, leaving damning information on their enemies for the police. Not without some pay-off anyway.

For a fleeting moment he wished he'd never left that beach in Sri Lanka, never caught the plane home to these complexities. He'd felt old recently. The renewed, chaste presence of Rachele D'Amato did his mental state no good at all. The pressure was something he could take. It was the doubts that bothered him. He wanted certainties in his life, not shadows and ghosts.

'Where the hell is everyone?' he scowled, and felt, for the first time in many a month, the edges of his temper beginning to fray.

*

The moment Teresa Lupo left Regina Morrison's office Monkboy was on the line, screaming for all he was worth, making it dead plain that Falcone was possibly in the foulest mood in history and wanted her on the scene *now*. She drove through the choked streets, thinking about what she had heard, not wondering for a moment how she would explain her absence or the fact that, for the second time in two days, she'd wilfully trodden on cop territory.

Dead people didn't run away. There was nothing she could do for this new corpse that Silvio Di Capua couldn't. All the hard work came later. Falcone would surely realize that. Most of all, *she had a result*. She didn't expect him to be grateful. She didn't expect to get bawled out either. While the rest of them were stumbling around in the dark, grasping at cobwebs, she'd found something concrete: the photograph of Barbara Martelli and Eleanor Jamieson in the private files of Professor Randolph Kirk, a man the lovely Barbara had despatched so efficiently the day before.

'Shithead,' she mouthed, with precious little enthusiasm, at a white van blocking the street. Some Chinese guy was unloading boxes out of the back and, very slowly, running them into a little gift shop. She looked into the window. It was full of the crap cheap Chinese gift shops sold: bright pink pyjamas, plastic back-scratchers, calendars with dragons on them. It all seemed so *irrelevant*.

She opened the window and yelled, 'Hey. Move it.'

The man put down the box he was carrying, turned and said something which sounded very like, 'Fluck you.'

Red mist swirled in front of her eyes. She pulled out her ID card, hoping the state police seal would do the trick, waved it in his direction and screeched, 'No, ass-hole, fluck *you*.'

He hissed something underneath his breath that made her glad she didn't understand Cantonese, then slowly climbed into the van and started to clunk it through the gears.

The riddle still hung in front of her, grey, shapeless. Was her own presence at the site merely a rotten coinci-dence? Did Barbara decide to off the professor anyway – maybe through some recurring bad dreams – then add the one and only witness to the list? Had Kirk called her to say someone was around asking awkward questions, in such a panic that she decided to shut him up for good? Was that what a Maenad did? Dispose of the god if he lost his sparkle? Or did Kirk phone someone else, someone who knew Barbara Martelli, understood she'd become a Maenad somewhere along the way and just given her the job: *out you go girl, it's whacking time, and don't forget to clear up any prying pathologists who happen to walk into the firing line*.

They'd never know. The first thing the cops had checked was the phone records. She'd asked that morning. They hadn't a clue whom Kirk had called. There was no redial button on Kirk's ancient handset. The phone company didn't log local calls.

She was starting to think like a cop now and it scared her. All these possibilities lay in the dark, limitless recesses of the imagination, a place she was trained to avoid. A place that, if she were honest with herself, had begun to scare her. That was why she started blubbing in front of a complete stranger, why it took her a good fifteen minutes to recover sufficient composure to get on with the day. That and the shitty virus fighting it out with two quick shots of Glenmorangie in her bloodstream. Life would be so much easier if the dead could come back and talk, just for a little while. She'd drive over to the morgue, stare at the mummified cadaver that had once been Eleanor Jamieson, and murmur, *Tell Teresa all about it, sweetie. Get it off your mahogany chest.*

Still, that corpse had spoken to someone. It had said: *not everything dies.* And Suzi Julius, with her fateful blonde looks, had sparked something too. Cause and effect didn't respect mortality.

The white van lumbered off the pavement and rolled down towards the low shape of the Colosseum at the end of the street. Teresa Lupo's new yellow Fiat, provided by the insurance company and already sporting a couple of fresh dents, sat stationary in the road. The horns behind her began to yell.

She wound down the window and yelled back at the creep in the Alfa on her tail. 'Can't you see I am *thinking*, you crapulent piece of pus?'

Then she put the car gently into gear and drove down the Via dei Serpenti, at a measured, steady pace, trying to put her thoughts in order.

When she walked into Beniamino Vercillo's cellar she felt like putting her hands over her ears, like running away from everything and finding some oblivion in a long, cold drink. She'd seen this so many times before, the path team hanging round the corpse, waiting to be told what to do, the scene of crime men in their white bunny suits combing the place for shards of information. And Falcone, this time with the woman from the DIA, standing at the back, watching everything like a hawk, throwing questions at Nic Costa and Peroni, unhappy, uncommunicative.

The tall inspector broke off from barking at his men. 'And where've you been? In case you haven't noticed there's work to be done.'

She held up both hands in deference. 'Sorry,' she answered meekly. 'Don't feel the need to ask how I am. I get people trying to kill me most days.'

Falcone demurred slightly. 'We need you.'

'I'll take that as an apology though a simple sorry would have sufficed. How's it going with the missing girl by the way?'

'What?'

'The girl?'

Falcone scowled at her. 'Leave the live ones to us.'

She looked at the body behind the desk. There'd been so many over the years, it was like being on a factory line. Now something was different. When Teresa Lupo looked at this corpse, the professional, unconscious side of her already assessing what she saw, a low, rebel voice started sounding in her head, getting louder and louder and louder, until it drowned out everything else, the blood, the questions, the tension and the fears.

'I can't do this any more,' she murmured, and wondered who was speaking: her or the rebel voice. And whether they were, perhaps, one and the same.

Monkboy hovered over the body, watching her, waiting for a lead.

The voice got louder. It was her voice.

'Is anybody *listening* here?' she yelled, and even the forensic people dusting down the office furniture became still.

'I can't do this any more,' Teresa Lupo said again, more quietly. 'He's dead. That's all there is to say.

There's a girl out there still breathing and here we are, like undertakers or something, staring at a corpse.'

She felt a hand on her arm. It was Costa.

'Don't try that one,' she murmured. Her hands were shaking. Her head felt as if it might explode. She could hardly open the bag, hardly get her hands around the file Regina Morrison had given her, find the strength to take out the pictures. 'I trained as a doctor. I learned how to distinguish the symptoms from the disease. This is irrelevant. This is a symptom, nothing else. This—'

She scattered several of the photos on the table, over the sheets of numbers, obliterating them. She made sure the most important one, Barbara and Eleanor *before*, was on the top.

'This is the disease.'

Falcone, Costa, Peroni and Rachele D'Amato had to push their way through the men in bunny suits to get a good look. Someone swore softly in amazement. The girls looked even more beautiful now, Teresa thought. And it was so easy to imagine Suzi Julius just walking into the frame, shaking hands with them, not knowing they were both dead, sixteen years apart, but dead is dead, dead is a place where the years don't matter.

'Where did you get these?' Falcone asked, furious.

'Randolph Kirk's office. This morning.'

'What?' he roared.

'Don't rupture something,' she said quietly. 'You didn't look there. You weren't even interested.'

'I didn't have the damn time!'

His long brown nose was sniffing at her. She thought of the drinks Regina Morrison had given her. The bastard never missed a thing.

'Jesus Christ, woman,' he snapped. 'You've been drinking. This is the end. Because of you—'

He didn't finish the sentence. He was too livid.

'Because of me what?' she yelled back. '*What?* Your beautiful traffic cop is dead? Is that what you think?' She stared at the men in the room. 'Is that what you *all* think? May I remind you of one fact? Your beautiful traffic cop was a cold-blooded murderer. Maybe she did it for herself. Maybe she did it because someone told her to. But she killed someone. She'd have killed me too if I'd let her. I didn't cause any of this. It was just there waiting to happen and if it had been somebody else maybe there'd be two victims, more even, lying in the morgue right now, not one. Hell, maybe there are, maybe there have been more over the years. And we wouldn't know. Because Barbara Martelli would still be riding that bike of hers, smiling sweetly all the time to fire up all your wet dreams, because none of you, not one, could possibly believe what she really was. Thanks to me you found out. Sorry—' She said this last very slowly, just to make sure the point went in. 'I apologize. That's the trouble with the truth. Sometimes it hurts.'

'You have damaged this investigation,' Falcone said wearily. 'You have overstepped your position.'

'There's a missing girl out there!'

'We *know* there's a missing girl out there,' Falcone replied, and threw the four photos Peroni had given him onto the table to join the others. 'We *know* she's been abducted. We know, too, that somehow these things are all linked. This is a murder inquiry and an abduction inquiry and I will allot what precious resources I have in my power to try and ensure no one else gets killed.'

'Oh,' she said softly, staring at the pictures. 'I'm

sorry.' She was shaking her head. She looked utterly lost. 'I don't know what's wrong with me. I've got the flu I think. What a pathetic excuse.'

Costa took her arm again and this time she didn't resist. 'Go home,' he said. 'You shouldn't be working anyway. Not after what happened yesterday.'

'What happened yesterday is *why* I'm working. Don't you understand?'

'Teresa,' Silvio Di Capua bleated. 'We need you.'

'You heard the man,' she whispered, knowing the tears were standing in her eyes again, starting to roll, starting to be obvious to them all, like a sign saying, *Look at Crazy Teresa, she really is crazy now.* 'I'm sorry, Silvio. I can't do this . . . shit any more.'

The place stank of blood and the sweat of men. She walked to the door, wanting to be outside, wanting to feel fresh air in her lungs, knowing it wasn't there anyway, that all she'd inhale was the traffic smog of Rome, waiting to poison her from the inside out.

And she was thinking all the time: what was it the crazy god offered Barbara Martelli and Eleanor Jamieson really? Freedom from all this crap? A small dark private place where you were what you were and no one else looked, no one else judged, where duty and routine and the dead, dull round of daily life were all a million miles away because in this new place, just for a moment, you could persuade yourself you had a part of some god inside you too? Could that have been the gift? And if it was, could anyone in the world have turned it down?

Emilio Neri refused to skulk around like a criminal, hiding from everything, a fugitive for no good reason at all. But even without an unwelcome visit from the cops and the DIA he could read the signs, digest the intelligence coming in through the channels he'd created over the years. He had to face decisions, make choices, and for the first time in his life he found that difficult. This was a new, an unprecedented situation. Until he made up his mind how to proceed he felt he had little choice but to hole up in the house, trying not to let Adele and Mickey's endless bickering get on his nerves. It was time to stop pretending he could lead from the front, as he had twenty years before, when he moved from *capo* to boss. Now he had to act his age, directing his troops, being the general, keeping their trust. He was getting too old for the tough stuff. He needed others to do the work.

There were risks too. He wondered what they thought in the ranks. When he was with the men he had them tight in his hand. Now he was in danger of seeming aloof, his grip less sure. Adele and Mickey didn't help either. A man who couldn't control his own family could hardly demand respect from the ranks. He'd asked Bruno Bucci to keep an ear open to listen for any whispered remarks that might be the first indication of revolt. These were hazardous times, and not just from the obvious direction. Whatever he said in private, he had to make sure the Sicilians remained happy. He had to convince the foot soldiers it was in their interests to keep their hats in the ring with him too. Money only went so far. He needed to cement their respect, to continue to be their boss.

Then Bucci came in with more news about Beniamino Vercillo. The cops were trying to keep things quiet but Neri's mob had good sources. They mentioned the oddest part of the case: that the killer had been wearing some kind of ancient theatrical costume. This was, it seemed to Neri, a message, surely. The situation was more serious than he had foreseen. For a while, he was dumbstruck, floundering in his own doubts with no one to turn to. He blamed himself. As soon as he'd known a war could be on the way – as soon as those reports of American hoods coming in through Fiumicino reached him – he should have acted. If conflict was inevitable, the advantage always lay with the party that struck first. The Americans understood that lesson instinctively. Instead, he'd hesitated, and now they'd punished him in the most brutal and unexpected of ways.

Vercillo was a civilian. If they'd wanted to make a hit in order to prove a point, there were plenty of accepted targets they could nail: neighbourhood capi, underlings, street men, pimps. Instead they picked a skinny little accountant. It made no sense. It was *offensive*. Neri had no time for Vercillo personally. He wasn't even a real employee. It had never occurred to Neri to warn the man to stay at home for a while, to keep his head down until the air cleared. However bitter a war got, it just didn't involve people that far down the ladder. This was an unwritten rule, a line you never crossed.

Like killing someone's relative, a wife or a daughter, Neri thought.

Bucci watched him, impassive, stolid, waiting for instructions.

'Boss?' he said finally.

'Give me a chance,' Neri replied with a scowl. 'You got to think your way through these things.'

The big tough hood from Turin was silent after that.

Neri was glad of his presence. He needed a man of substance in his trust.

'How are the boys feeling?' Neri asked.

'About anything in particular?'

'The mood. *Morale.*'

Bucci squirmed a little. Neri recognized the signs. They weren't good. 'They get bored easy, boss. Men do in situations like this. They get hyped up like something's going to happen. When it doesn't they get to feel awkward. Like they're wasting their time.'

'I'm paying them well to waste their time,' Neri grunted.

'Yeah. But you know their kind. It's about more than money. Besides, one of them's cousin to that poor bastard Vercillo. He's got a score to settle.'

'So you're saying what, Bruno?'

Bucci considered his answer carefully. 'I'm saying that maybe it's not a good idea to sit here waiting for the next thing to happen to us. They're good guys but I don't want to push them too far.'

Neri's cold gaze didn't leave Bucci for a second. 'Are they loyal?'

'Sure. As loyal as anyone gets these days. But you got to recognize their self-interest. You got to massage their egos too. These are made men. They don't like thinking they're just doing security work or something. It'd help me no end if we saw a little action. Let these assholes know where they stand.'

'I was thinking the same thing,' Neri lied. Something else was bugging him. How had they known about Vercillo? He was a backroom guy. From the outside he looked straight. How did Wallis find him? Maybe Vercillo was less discreet than Neri expected. Maybe he'd been selling information on the side, and found out how dangerous that game can be. 'You got any information about who's doing this? Names? Addresses?'

'Not yet. The street's not talking much out there at the moment. Hell, if it's some people the American brought in for the job, our people probably don't know them anyway. If you want my honest opinion—' Bucci dried up.

'Well?'

'We're not going to get any more information than we have right now. People are bound to be sitting back on the sidelines, watching. They want to see who comes out on top. No one's going to want to do you any favours, not unless they're in with us deep already. It doesn't make sense.'

Neri said nothing.

'You don't mind me being frank,' Bucci said carefully.

'No,' Neri moaned, 'it's what I need. Jesus, these are people who've been sucking my blood for years!'

'Look, boss. You got plenty of respect with the guys here. Provided they don't get pushed too far. Outside—' He didn't say any more. He didn't have to.

'Respect,' Neri grumbled, his face like thunder. 'Tell the truth. Do they think I'm too old or what?'

Bucci hesitated.

'They don't think that,' the man from Turin said eventually. 'But they think about what comes next. You got to expect it. Anyone would in the same circumstances. Also, there's rumours.'

'Rumours?' Neri wondered.

'The people I got in the cops are being real secret about this. Falcone isn't letting anyone near except those close to him. And the DIA.'

Neri shook his head in disbelief. 'The DIA? What the fuck has this got to do with them?'

'They think they got our books from Vercillo.'

Neri laughed. 'Sure they got our books! Can't do a thing with them. The little guy put a code on them or something. He was good with numbers. That was his thing. He told me. They could work on it for years and they'd never get nowhere.'

'They got the code. The DIA's trying to work it all out now.'

'*What?*' It was impossible to work out what this all meant. Vercillo had been doing the books for almost twenty years. He was a meticulous man. He logged everything. Emilio Neri understood instantly that if the DIA and the cops managed to peer into that black hive of past misdeeds they could throw all manner of shit in his direction: fraud, tax evasion. Worse.

'Are you sure?' Neri asked in desperation.

'I'm sure,' Bucci replied. 'Also they want to nail you over this dead girl. They seem to think they got something there. This dead professor guy left some photos or something. There's this other girl, the one that's missing now. They think she's down to us too.'

Neri was outraged. 'Do I look like the kind that goes around snatching teenagers off the street? Why'd I need to do that?'

'They think . . . it points in our direction,' Bucci said carefully.

Neri understood what he was saying. 'And does it?'

'Not with anyone under me, boss.'

Neri raised an eyebrow, waiting.

'But I don't get to control everyone. Mickey, for

example. He's just a loose cannon. God knows what he gets up to when none of us are around.'

'Such as?'

'We know about the hookers. I think maybe he's back on the dope too. Maybe he's been doing other stuff.' Bucci paused, reluctant to continue. 'I don't know where he is half the time. Do you?'

'No,' Neri grunted.

'And this thing years ago with the dead girl. It was before my time. But they seem to think he was there.'

Neri shook his head. 'I don't want to talk about that.'

'I understand. Look, boss. I don't feel right saying this kind of thing. It's between you and him. It's just that . . . Mickey affects the way the guys are thinking right now.'

'And you?' Neri asked. 'I got this American asshole fitting me up for the cops and the DIA. I got a dumb son who can't keep his dick quiet. What do you think should come next?'

'Whatever you want. This is your organization. You get to say what happens. It's just . . .'

Bucci didn't go on. Neri couldn't work it out.

'Well?' he asked.

'It's Mickey. He don't help. Not with him and Adele.'

'Yeah,' Neri said, waving a hand, 'I know, I know . . . it pisses me off too.'

He looked at Bruno Bucci. The man appeared deeply uncomfortable. He'd seen him less nervous than this when they were about bad business. It didn't add up. Then Neri wondered about this idea that had been nagging him for a day or more. It was crazy. It was the kind of thing old men got into their heads for no reason whatsoever and that made fools of them if they blurted it out into the light of day. Which always happened anyway, even if they knew as much, because it was the kind of idea you couldn't keep inside forever.

Neri put an arm around Bucci's shoulder and said, 'You wouldn't lie to an old man, would you, Bruno? I always thought you were a bad liar. It was one of your limitations.'

'No.' Bucci's eyes never left the floor.

The old man's hand squeezed, hard. 'You've been in the house a lot recently. When I'm not here. Tell me, Bruno. Mickey's fucking her, right? That's what's really going on, huh? All this bad feeling between them. That's just for my benefit? Right?'

Bruno Bucci let out a long sigh and struggled to say something.

'No problem,' Neri said, slapping him on the shoulder. 'It just adds another job to the list. Now sit down. I want to talk.'

Falcone looked up from the scattered piles of photographs on the table in his office.

'Close the door,' he said quietly. 'We don't have much time. I want this Julius girl found. I want that to be the focus of what we do from now on. Understood?'

'Sure,' Costa nodded.

Falcone looked beyond the glass partition, out into the office. He'd managed to fill most of the desks. The men and women out there were busy, following up calls, chasing the couple of possible sightings they'd had. 'I'm stepping up the media on this. We're telling them we think she's in real danger, not that I'm saying why. We've as many people as I can afford on the case. But we need to go back over what's gone before. Someone's collecting the mother. When she gets here, you can talk to her, Nic. Just you. Too many people will make her clam up. Tell her what we know so far. Just the broad details. And go over everything with her again, every place she and the girl visited since they arrived here. There's got to be something she remembers that's of use.'

'Details?' Peroni asked. 'We've got details? I'm missing them. What is it we're supposed to think has happened here?'

Falcone didn't look too confident. 'We've got Kirk on her camera. That's enough for me. Kirk has to have been involved in taking her. If that's the case, we have to assume she's where he left her for safe keeping. We *have* to find where that it is. Not Ostia for sure. I've got a team rechecking that now. She's not there.'

The three men looked at each other. No one liked to think of a kidnap victim being left stranded, trapped in some hole, unable to call for help.

Peroni wasn't happy. 'I buy that but some of these things still don't add up. Kirk was just a dirty old man. The mother said Suzi went off willingly. We've got it on CCTV. The boyfriend riding that motorbike wasn't some man in his fifties.'

'I know,' Falcone agreed. 'I've got men looking into Kirk's background. Trying to work out if he had any close friends. Nothing so far.'

'And Neri?' Costa asked. 'Wallis?'

'All we have on them are some rumours from the past,' Peroni suggested. 'Why put a fire under some old feud after all this time? Why start playing these games all over again?'

Costa thought of the mummified body in the morgue next door. 'Perhaps because we found Eleanor Jamieson. Because that reminded someone of . . . the possibilities.'

'Let's stick with the facts,' Falcone said firmly.

'Which are?' Peroni asked.

Falcone stared at the pictures. 'These.'

Neither of them argued. The pictures were all home-developed. A search of Randolph Kirk's house off the Via Merulana had revealed a darkroom in the cellar. A couple seemed innocent: young girls, clothed, smiling with older men. But most looked as if they were taken later, when the party began. When the rules disappeared.

Falcone glanced at Peroni. 'Gianni. This is more your field than ours. What do you make of it?'

He shrugged. 'Pretty obvious, isn't it? We have a phrase for this kind of thing in vice. We call it a fuck-club. Sorry. The language isn't so great where I come from. What happens is you get some guys. You get some willing girls. Young girls in this case. Then you put them together and, without telling anyone, stick a camera up in the corner of the room, probably on a remote operated from somewhere else.'

Falcone turned over one of the prints. On the back, scribbled in pencil, was the date: 17 March, sixteen years before.

Peroni nodded. 'These days they've got remote controls. Even things that let you see through the viewfinder from another room. Back then they didn't have the technology to do this kind of shot too well. They just pressed the remote shutter and got whatever was there at the time. Hence all these heaving butts, all these shots where you can't really see who's doing what to who.

You wouldn't get that nowadays. Now it'd come back on DVD or something.'

'Why is it we just have the year the Jamieson girl went missing?' Falcone wondered. 'Why would he just keep the one set?'

'Search me,' Peroni replied, flipping through the prints. 'Maybe he only took pictures the once. Maybe they still had some value. Or it just happened on that scale once. Who's to know? I'll tell you something though. This is not the work of anyone on our books. These kids look like amateurs. Not hookers. Not that I recognize anyway. And the clientele? This is the fanciest fuck-club I've ever seen. Where is this place? On the Via Veneto? Next door to Harry's Bar or something? Hell, they *do* have some value. I could pick up the phone and do business with these today.'

Costa scanned the men in the photos. It was a little before his time but he still recognized plenty of faces.

'You got TV people,' Peroni went on. 'You got newspaper people. Couple of bankers I dealt with in the past. And politicians too. They're bound to be there. You know what puzzles me? Only one cop. What kind of club is it that has just one cop on board? And him that penpusher Mosca guy too? Can we go talk to him?'

'Dead,' Falcone said. 'Died in prison. Knifed.'

'Shame. He's in almost all of them. Seems he got pretty friendly with Barbara. I guess that tells you everything.'

'It does?' Costa wondered.

'Sure, Nic. Like I said. This is not just some gentleman's evening. *It's a sting*. Why else would they leave the likes of us out? If this was just a plain party for the boys we'd have a few more people there. You agree, Leo?'

Falcone nodded and left it at that.

'So,' Peroni continued, 'it was a sting. When this was over and done with, when these morons had gone back to their wives and moaned about how late the trains were getting these days, they got a phone call. Maybe a photo of their heaving butt. News of an account to settle. Or a favour to be called in some time in the future. And my, what favours? You ever seen a cast list like this, Leo?'

'No.'

Peroni smiled. 'Embarrassing, huh? Couple of these guys are still jerking our chains now, aren't they? Are we going to ask them if they saw the Jamieson girl before she died?'

'All in good time,' Falcone said. He sorted the photos in front of them, and pulled out a single shot: a beaming Filippo Mosca and Barbara naked, locked together on a thin mattress on the stone floor.

'Nice,' Peroni said.

Falcone threw another picture on the table. 'This one's even nicer.'

Peroni swore under his breath. The final shot almost looked posed: Barbara and Eleanor, dressed, standing around holding wine glasses, looking nervous, as if they didn't know what came next but thought it might not be too great. They were wearing some kind of costume: a thin sackcloth shift, the one Eleanor Jamieson had on when she was placed in the peat. Next to them stood Randolph Kirk, Beniamino Vercillo and Toni Martelli, looking at each other expectantly, grinning guiltily.

'Jesus,' Peroni said. 'So Mosca wasn't the only one

playing this game? Can you believe it? That sonofabitch Martelli was pimping his own daughter and getting off too? Look at the expression on those guys' faces. "Aren't we the lucky ones?" Assholes.'

'But they're not,' Costa pointed out, 'lucky I mean. Three of them are dead. Martelli doesn't look as if he'll be around much longer either.'

Peroni picked up the picture. 'Let me take this and ram it down the bastard's throat. He'll start squealing then.'

'Later,' Falcone said. 'Martelli's been out of the picture for years. Like I said. We've got to focus.'

'On what?'

'Where this happened,' Falcone said. 'We've checked out the backgrounds. We know it wasn't Ostia.'

Peroni's eyes lit up. 'Excuse me for pointing this out but Toni Martelli surely *knows* where.'

Falcone glanced at the table. 'Do you want to spend the rest of the day sitting with him in an interview room listening to nothing? I spoke to him a few minutes ago. I offered him a deal. He's not doing a damn thing. You've talked to him. We can't afford the time.'

'A deal?' Peroni looked amazed. 'You offer someone who could do this kind of thing to his own daughter a deal?'

'Yes!' Falcone snapped. 'Do you want to argue with the Julius girl's mother about this? Do you want to tell her it's wrong?'

Peroni stared at the photos. 'And I thought I had a conflict of morality on vice. So what *do* we do?'

Falcone had already made up his mind. 'We let the DIA handle the mob stuff. Watching Wallis. Going through the accounts from Vercillo's office. We let them see what they can turn up on the Vercillo killing too. It's theirs by right anyway and I'm happy to unload whatever I can. And we try for the girl. Gianni—'

He looked desperate, Costa thought. It wasn't like the Falcone they knew.

'What do you want us to do?' Peroni asked.

'Nic can get a room ready for the mother. For God's sake see if she can remember something. There has to be a face, a name, anything. I want you to get a couple of spare men out there and run through everything we have on the Julius girl so far. See if we've missed anything.'

'OK,' Costa said, and headed for the door. The two older men watched him go.

'It's a good idea, letting him talk to her on his own,' Peroni said after he'd gone. 'She's an attractive woman. He's noticed that already. Hell, I noticed that. Not you, Leo? Just eyes for the one, huh?'

'Don't start—' Falcone was staring at the pictures on the desk. 'And don't make assumptions either. I don't live in the past any more than you.'

'No,' Peroni said, sounding unconvinced, watching Falcone pore over the photos. 'You can ask if you like. I'm menial class for the time being. You've got the right to ask anything you want.'

Falcone turned over another set of prints, revealing another set of familiar faces. 'What the hell do I do with these things?'

'This lot . . .' Peroni pushed the last pile of pictures, with Barbara and Eleanor in them, to one side, ' . . . you guard with your life, because they may be all we've got between that Julius kid and the grave.'

'I know that,' Falcone replied testily.

·'Oh.' Peroni placed his index finger gently on the others. 'You mean these?'

He pulled away his hand and took a good look at them. 'You know, I hate to place your ego in jeopardy, Leo, but it is possible for other men of your rank to come and dip their beak here. You've now got three murders under your belt and an abduction. Maybe there's been some blackmail going on here too. It's a lot for one man. Pass the goods around a little.'

'They're linked,' Falcone insisted. 'I've had this argument upstairs already. If I'd wanted to split these inquiries off into different teams I'd have done that. My view – *their* view too – is that it would be counter-productive. We don't have the time or the resources and we could end up missing some connections too. I know it's stretching things but we really have no option.'

'No option?' Peroni grinned. 'Give me a break. I'm hearing ambition here, Leo. You bored with being inspector? After a commissar's badge? Or is it higher than that?'

'I want this girl found,' Falcone snapped. 'Don't judge everyone by your own standards.'

'So why are you worried about the photos? Just put them in a drawer. Wait and see if they ever become useful.'

'Useful—'

Peroni laughed. 'Leo, Leo. You're not cut out for this, are you? You can go upstairs and hard-ball your way through anything. Except—' He glanced at the photos. 'This kind of stuff. It embarrasses you, doesn't it?'

Falcone sighed. 'We should be playing to our strengths here. You ought to learn from what we're trying to do, which is make some connections. That's why I don't want this split up any more than it is. In return I'm asking for your advice. This must have happened to you plenty. You go in somewhere. You find the wrong people inside. What do you do?'

Peroni thought about it. 'Sorry. I shouldn't have taken a pop at you like that. You're right. I've got a lot to learn from you people. I just wonder what the point is because, believe me, I am not staying in this asylum for long.'

Falcone stared at him frankly. 'You seem very sure of that. If we screw up on this case . . .'

'You mean if *you* screw up. Look, here's my advice. There's no easy answer, Leo. It depends on the circumstances. But I'll tell you one thing you *don't* do.'

He picked up the bigger pile of pictures and flicked through them, shaking his head.

'You don't sleep on it. Either you walk upstairs with these things now or you let it drop forever. Hesitate and you become something they hate. An unknown quantity, with a little time bomb sitting in his desk drawer. If you're going to lay all the rest of this on them you've got to do it this very moment. If not—'

He picked up one of the prints and walked over to the shredder that stood by Falcone's office printer. Then he fed the photo into the plastic jaws and watched as it sprang to life, devoured the picture, tearing it into a million tiny, irretrievable pieces.

'Ambition's an interesting thing,' Peroni said. 'I had it once. I thought nothing could touch me. And look what happened? Tell me, Leo. If you'd been on that DIA bust, if you'd walked in and found me there with my pants down. Nothing going on except the usual. What would you have done? Looked the other way?'

Falcone didn't even give it a moment's thought. 'No. Because there'd have to be something going on. Why else would you be there?'

'She was beautiful.' Peroni looked at him and almost pitied the man. 'You really don't get that, do you? It just couldn't be enough?'

'No. And I still don't believe it was enough for you.'

'You're a bad judge of character. Is that because you don't have the same feelings the rest of us have? Or you're just scared of them? We've all got to let go sometimes. Even you.'

Falcone nodded at the pictures. '*This* is letting go?'

'Probably all it is. Listen, Leo. Unless you've got the stomach for it, don't complicate things. There's something really bad about this whole thing. Why don't we just get that girl out from wherever she is then close the door and let the dead stay dead?'

Falcone stared at the pile of photographs. 'There could be any amount of information in here. They could be invaluable.'

'Hand those over to the people upstairs and they'll smile, say thanks and hate you forever because you just made their lives hell.'

'If I gave them to the DIA—'

'If you gave them to the DIA they'd be all over you, telling you how wonderful you are, and what a credit to the police. Maybe you'd even get the D'Amato woman back in your bed. Then you know what? In six months your career would be dead. You'd be running traffic, cutting up credit cards 'cos you can't afford them any more. And the DIA wouldn't want to know you. Nor would she. No one likes a man who passes the buck, particularly one as dirty as this. You know that already if you're honest with yourself.'

Falcone took one last look at the pictures then turned his back on them. 'Do it,' he ordered.

Peroni laughed, picked them up and pressed them into Falcone's hands.

'No, Sir,' he said, then walked out of the room, closing the door behind him, and paused for a moment, listening. It didn't take long. Soon there was the whir of distant electric teeth.

Rachele D'Amato was walking down the corridor towards him, smiling, looking as if she owned the place.

'You moved in?' Peroni wondered.

She didn't answer, just gave him a cold look that said it all.

Peroni pointed at the door. 'You go easy with our boy in here. Some of us have fond feelings for him even if he doesn't feel that way about himself. We don't like the idea he might get hurt twice.'

'You have absolutely no worries on that front.'

'Yeah. Just joking.' He grinned. 'I know. Really. I *know*. Nothing could bring you two back together, could it?'

'I got a call asking me to come. You people should talk to each other more often.' She pointed towards an open door at the end of the corridor. 'There.'

Vergil Wallis sat stiff-backed, eyes closed, waiting patiently.

When Bucci opened up it was hard to stop him. Neri listened until he'd heard enough then motioned for him to shut up. 'You could have told me, Bruno. You owed me that.'

'I didn't—' Bucci looked scared. He was hunting for the right words. 'I talked with Mickey about it. Once. He said you knew. It was part of the deal.'

Neri's big shoulders heaved in a humourless laugh. 'Part of the deal?'

'Yeah,' Bucci replied coolly. 'Pretty stupid of me, huh? The thing is . . . I don't like the idea of you getting fucked around.' He flashed a cold stare at Neri. 'But it's not easy telling a man his wife's cheating on him. With his son. I don't know how to handle that kind of thing. I guess I knew Mickey was lying. To be honest though, I wondered how grateful you'd be if I came running with the news.'

Now Neri thought about it Bucci had been acting a little odd for the past few weeks. He was a good man, a loyal lieutenant. Neri could understand his point of view too. Mickey's perfidy was outside the box. He couldn't expect a street hood like Bucci to get involved in that kind of family betrayal.

'It's Mickey, you know,' Bucci said suddenly. 'Not her. I'm not saying you shouldn't blame her, but I don't think she wants it. Not really. You don't see Mickey the way the rest of us do. He just doesn't give up. He just goes on and on until you give him what he wants.'

Neri thought about that. 'But she's got other men, right?'

'I don't think so. You want my honest opinion? It's just boredom. Nothing more.'

Boredom. Neri could understand that one all right.

'I'm sorry, boss,' Bucci said softly. 'If you want me

to ship out or something when this is done I'll understand. I don't like letting you down.'

Neri's grey eyes shone with amusement. It was a good show of contrition. 'You let me down? Come on, Bruno. Let's not play games with each other.'

'All the same—'

Neri stared at him and Bucci fell silent. 'All the same nothing. Let me tell you a little secret. I've been getting bored too. Been thinking about that for a while. I got a little house in Colombia. Way away from all the trouble. No one can touch me there.' He nodded upstairs, in the direction of Adele and Mickey. 'And I could leave some excess baggage behind too.'

'Sure,' Bucci nodded.

'Would you run things for me when I'm gone? All straight and honest? This shit with the DIA won't come close to you, I promise. There's just my name in those files. I'd be wanting to give a few people some leaving presents, you understand. Something to remember me by. I owe them that. But you get a clear run. Nothing touches your name.'

Bucci shuffled awkwardly on the chair. 'You want me to act like I'm the boss?'

'No. I want you to *be* the boss. I can't do this forever. Someone's got to take over. I'd rather it was a man of my choosing, not some bastard from outside.'

'I could do it,' Bucci said. 'I don't think Mickey would be too keen.'

'Mickey, Mickey. Leaving this Adele crap to one side . . . what do you think of him? Be honest. Say I could straighten him out. Would it be worth it? Is he ever going to make something?'

'I don't know,' Bucci said carefully. 'I don't feel

qualified to make that judgement. There's things he's been doing I don't understand.'

'What things?'

Bucci rolled open his big hands in a gesture of despair. 'I dunno. Things he don't want any of us to hear about. And I'll tell you this, boss. He's good at that. Keeping stuff quiet.'

Neri wondered about all the crap that had come out into the open these past couple of days. Falcone wasn't going to leave them alone. It was only a matter of time before he came back, maybe with papers, turning the place upside down. 'We're going to have to hole up here for a couple of hours. There'll be cops swarming front and back. You get busy, Bruno. Find out how long we've got before they come calling again. Find out where they got people waiting out there, who needs to be paid to make those guys look the other way for a while. When we can crawl out from under their noses, we go out to play.'

'To play?'

Neri laughed. 'Yeah. If I'm going into retirement I want one last piece of fun first. I got some evening-up to do, all round. When that's done I'm gone. You call someone. Make sure I can get the hell out of here come tomorrow night, some way nice and discreet. The Albanian boys can do something. They owe me favours.'

Bucci blinked. 'Tomorrow night?'

'That too soon for you?' Neri cast an eye around the room. 'I got to tell you, Bruno, I can't wait to be out of this dump.'

Bucci didn't seem too happy.

'What's up?' Neri asked. 'I'm offering you your own empire on a plate.'

'Don't get me wrong. I'm grateful. I'll see you right. But there's . . . stuff I can't control.'

It was obvious what he meant. 'You're still worried about Mickey?'

Bucci shrugged. He was too polite, too respectful to push it. Neri looked at Bruno Bucci and wondered why he never got a son like that. Bucci was the one guy he could rely on. And if he wanted to fuck with Mickey when the time came, what the hell? To his surprise, it wasn't the news about him and Adele that made him feel that way. He just wasn't particularly warm to his own flesh and blood at that moment. They messed up his life. They leeched off him and gave nothing back in return. This wasn't what family was supposed to be about. As he got older, as he felt less need for the physical pleasures that Adele could deliver with her own particular skill, he was, he realized, beginning to feel happier in the company of men. He knew where he stood with them. So long as he kept to his part of the deal – being a good, fair, profitable boss – they would stick by him.

The old man smiled. 'The kid's right. It's time he got tested. Go get him. Tell him to meet me, up on the terrace.'

'The terrace?' Bucci asked.

Neri was already walking towards the stairs. 'You heard,' he said.

There were pictures of Suzi Julius everywhere. Blow-ups from Miranda's original snaps carpeted the whiteboard on the main wall of the operations room. Smaller colour copies were pinned to people's PCs, scattered across desks. Costa walked Miranda Julius through the twenty-strong team, introducing her to a couple of people along the way, making sure she understood how important the case had become to them. Then they went along the corridor to a smaller room where a further group of officers, most of them female, were manning the phones set up to handle any calls that came in from the public appeals. Suzi's picture was on the TV now. More photos would soon be in the papers. They had an anonymous hotline into the station ready for anyone who answered their plea for even a hint of a sighting. The full-scale hunt for Suzi was under way. But like every other case of its kind that Costa had worked on there was, at the onset, a frustrating lack of information. No one had seen her since she was driven out of the Campo dei Fiori the day before. Not a single clue to her movements had appeared in the three hours since Falcone gave the green light to turn the Julius case into an abduction inquiry.

He led her into a small interview room overlooking the courtyard behind the Questura. She sat down immediately and said, 'I know you're looking, Nic. You don't have to prove that to me.'

'I just wanted you to see it for yourself.'

The stress was starting to show. The impression Nic Costa had first had of her – as a model who'd gone into something manual just to prove she was more than she looked – came back to him. She sat on the other side of the table, hunched inside a plain black bomber jacket, snatching anxiously at a cigarette, trying to blow the smoke out of the half open window. Her sharp, intelligent eyes never left him.

'Do you have any idea where she is?'

Costa was careful with his answer. 'It takes time.'

She stared out of the window, squinting at the bright, late afternoon sun. 'I ought to say it again. I'm sorry. About last night. It must have been very embarrassing for you.'

The sudden close contact they shared continued to bother him. He could, he knew, have gone along with her so easily. 'Forget it. I have.'

For a moment an odd look, almost like anger, crossed her face. He wondered if he'd said the right thing.

'Sometimes I drink,' she said. 'Not to blot things out. It's just that events can make more sense that way. Or it appears they do. I don't imagine you understand what I'm talking about.'

He'd never forget the lost days after his father died, when he would sit alone in the old man's wheelchair for hours on end, talking to the bottle, trying to gauge how much of the hurt was physical, from his wounds, how much existed in his head alone. And how easy it would be to drown both in booze.

'I understand. Will you promise me something?'

'I don't like making easy promises,' she answered quickly. 'You disappoint people if it turns out you can't keep them.'

'It's just this. We need you, Miranda. We need you to think about anything we find. Possibly to react to it. I just don't know. But when that moment happens, it's important for all of us, Suzi most of all, that you're not—' He let the sentence drift off into nowhere.

'Drunk?' she wondered. 'Don't worry. That won't happen.'

'It's not a great idea being on your own. Isn't there someone from home who can come? You mentioned your mother.'

'She's on holiday at the moment. In California. I spoke to her this morning. What with the time difference, changing tickets ... she can't be here until Sunday.' She gave him a sudden intense glance. 'By then ... We'll know, won't we?'

There was no avoiding an honest answer. 'I think so. All the same ... I could arrange for a woman officer to be with you.'

'I'll be fine,' she said firmly. 'I don't need to be treated like a victim. Suzi's the victim here. She's the one I want to help. You just do your job and I'll try my best. Any way I can.'

'Good,' he said, then reached for the tape recorder button, dictated the standard header to the interview – date, time, subject, interviewee, officer – and tried to think of the right questions, the ones that would unlock something hidden, something lost inside Miranda Julius's complex, hurting head.

'Is there anything new that's occurred to you?'

'Not really.' She shook her head, as if she hated herself for being like this. 'I keep trying to think of something. There's nothing that stands out I haven't mentioned already.'

'The people you've met here—'

'They're just people. People in shops. People in cafés. People in restaurants. We've talked to them. Of course we have. But nothing stands out. It never went beyond just being polite.'

He placed one of the photos from Suzi's camera on the table. Randolph Kirk was there at the edge of the crowd by the Trevi Fountain, staring directly into the camera with an odd, focused expression.

'Do you recognize him?'

She peered at the picture. 'No. I've never seen him before. Not until I saw the paper this morning. My Italian's not great but I get the message. He was the man killed out at this archaeological place, wasn't he?'

'Yes.'

She came directly to the point. 'You think he had something to do with this other murder too? The girl from sixteen years ago?'

'There's evidence that he used young girls for his own . . . entertainment. With others.'

She swore under her breath. 'So what happens now? Where *is* she, Nic? Just locked up somewhere this monster's left her? Waiting to be found? It could take forever. God—' She closed her eyes for a moment. 'I can't bear to think of her like that. It's just so horrible.'

'We're circulating her picture everywhere. Someone must have seen her.'

'None of this makes sense. Suzi wouldn't just disappear with a man like that. It's preposterous. He's old. Look at him. What could he possibly offer her? You don't think he was on that motorbike, do you?'

'No,' he admitted. 'Maybe he just found her. Someone else did the rest.'

'But why Suzi? Why her?'

'Bad luck,' he said with a shrug. 'Coincidence. These cases are sometimes just that. Kirk seemed to have a fondness for blondes. Maybe she reminded him of someone else.'

She knew immediately what he was talking about. 'The dead girl you found? I saw pictures of her. They do look similar I suppose.'

'It's just a theory. We have two avenues to work on here. We can do all the usual things. Make sure as many people as possible see her picture. Monitor the calls we get from that. And we can work to try to understand what really happened. Why Kirk played these games. Who with, and where.'

'It could be anywhere, couldn't it?' she asked.

'No.' There was an important point here somewhere, he thought. This was a ritual. It didn't take place at the Villa of Mysteries in Ostia. Teresa's careful forensic work had proved that much already. Kirk had to have another location, larger, more important. In the city most probably. Perhaps Suzi was there now, trapped, waiting. But for whom?

'I need you to look at some more pictures,' he said, and reached for the files.

Miranda Julius stared at a standard police ID photo of Barbara Martelli. 'I saw her picture in the papers too,' she said. 'Blonde. She was another one of his women? The police officer?'

'We think so.'

'Was that why she killed him?'

'We've no idea,' he admitted. 'Have you seen her before, Miranda? Please. Think. Is it possible you or Suzi met her somewhere? Anywhere.'

She sighed. 'We've asked the police for directions a few times, I suppose. Maybe we talked to her. I don't know. I don't think I'd remember one way or another.'

'OK. Point taken. How about him?'

He placed a photo of Vergil Wallis on the table.

'No,' she said immediately. 'Is he Italian?'

'American. Have you talked to any Americans since you arrived?'

She couldn't understand the point of the question. 'I don't think so. I think I'd remember someone as distinctive as that. What's the meaning of this, Nic? Why would an American be involved in this kind of thing?'

'Bear with me,' he said. 'We have to keep trying. Do you know this man?'

She looked at a photo of Beniamino Vercillo. 'No.'

'Him?' Emilio Neri's big, ugly face glared up at her from the table.

She shook her head. 'He looks like a crook. He looks . . . horrible. Are these the kind of people you think could have Suzi? She'd never go away with someone like that. She's not stupid.'

Costa shuffled through the pile of pictures. 'That was taken in the Questura, when we were interviewing him about something. He doesn't always look like that. People have different faces for different occasions. You have to try to think beyond what you see sometimes.'

'Thanks for the advice,' she said icily.

'Look.'

This was a new set of pictures, ones they'd bought in from a photographer covering a social evening at the opera. Neri was there in his other guise, as an art-loving businessman, his wife at his side. They were both dressed to the nines, Neri in a dinner suit, Adele wearing a long, tight-fitting silk gown.

'He does look different,' she conceded.

She stared at the picture. 'Is that his wife?'

Costa nodded.

'She looks very young for him. He's that kind of man?'

Costa didn't answer.

'Nic? The kind who likes young girls?'

'She's not as young as she looks. Not Suzi's age

anyway. He likes lots of things. Maybe he was involved in Kirk's games. Maybe it's more complicated than that.'

She peered at the picture again. 'She doesn't look happy. She looks like a possession or something. Someone he owns.'

'You read a lot into pictures.'

She nodded in agreement. 'You forget. I take pictures for a living. It's like trying to tell a story. You want people to see it and get some sense of what's happening. What the people there are like. Otherwise it's just a snapshot. There's no meaning. No drama. No humanity. Just shapes on a sheet of paper. It's the back story that makes it work.'

She flicked through the set of photos from the opera. 'These are quite good. Whoever he is, whoever his wife is, they make interesting subjects. There's a lot going on there between them and I don't think it's nice. I could imagine photographing them myself. I could—'

Miranda Julius stopped at one picture. She separated the photo from the rest and stared at it in silence, thinking.

'You remember something about him?' Costa asked when he couldn't wait any longer.

'No. I don't know him from Adam. But *him*—'

She turned the photo round and stabbed at a figure at the edge of the photo. Younger, dressed in an evening suit, looking bored.

'I *have* seen him somewhere.' She stopped, trying to order her thoughts. 'It was just after we arrived. We were in the Campo, having coffee outside. He was at the next table. I went to the loo. When I came back he'd been pestering Suzi. Asking for her phone number. Trying to chat her up.'

Costa looked at the photo and felt a sharp stab of excitement.

'What happened?'

'Nothing. I think. He wasn't . . . very nice. He was so persistent. His English wasn't that great either. I didn't like him, Nic. I *really* didn't like him now I come to think of it. He was creepy. Just the kind of pushy young jerk I thought we'd be dealing with in Rome all the time.'

'But he could have given Suzi his number?'

'I'm trying to think—'

There was something here. Costa could feel it.

Miranda Julius looked into his face, her eyes wide open, worried. 'Oh my God. I do remember. Suzi was odd afterwards for a while. Almost shifty. We nearly had an argument. It wasn't like her.'

'So he could have passed her something? A phone number? She might have taken it.'

'Possibly. I don't know, Nic. I don't . . . It was days ago.'

'And she wouldn't have told you?'

He didn't like seeing the pain when she answered. 'I suppose not. Kids of that age do stupid things and don't want to admit it. I know I did. She *was* shifty about something. I should have known—'

Her eyes became misty.

' . . . Jesus, what an idiot I am. Thinking a girl of her age would be happy spending an entire holiday with her mother, never seeing anyone else. As if I'm good enough company for her. For Christ's sake. I haven't even been around for most of her life. Why should she want to be with me? How arrogant can you get?'

Then firmly, with absolute conviction, she said, 'I

remember I told her what an utter creep I thought he was. Exactly the sort of Italian man you get warned about. And she looked at me as if I was talking crap. As if I was *old*. Then we just didn't talk about anything for a while. We just let it blow over.'

He was anxiously gathering up the pictures, keen to end this.

'Except it didn't, did it?' she asked.

'This could really help us.'

'How? You know who this man is?'

Costa wondered how much to reveal. He reached over the table and took her arm. 'Miranda,' he said. 'We have rules about how much we can say in the middle of an investigation.'

'To hell with the rules. I'm her mother. I'm the reason she's in this mess.'

His voice rose. 'You're *not* the reason. Suzi's sixteen years old. She's not a child you can care for twenty-four hours a day.'

She was shaking her head. 'You don't know her. You don't know me. Don't make these judgements.'

It wasn't self-pity, he thought. More self-hate. 'I know enough. You're doing everything anyone could in the circumstances. Don't start blaming yourself before—'

The word just slipped out. She stared at the bright dusty window, blinking back sudden tears. 'Before what? Before there's a reason?'

He shook his head. 'I didn't mean that.'

She paused, trying to let the temperature fall a little.

'Who is he?' she asked. 'You can at least tell me that.'

'He's the old man's son. His name is Neri. Mickey Neri.'

Nic Costa got up, thinking about the possibilities,

what Falcone could do when he got the news. Outside the afternoon was dying. It would soon be dark. These operations were never easy at night. They had to move. There was so little time.

She was by his side, a shadow of hope in her face. 'What kind of man is he? Mickey?'

'The best kind,' Costa said smiling. 'For us anyway. Not a university professor. Not some anonymous figure in a suit. Mickey Neri's a crook, from a family of crooks, not a smart one either. We know him. We know where he lives. We know how to get what we want from him. Miranda—'

They just needed the warrants, and her ID of Mickey in the photo would surely put that straight in Falcone's hands. Then they could storm the big house in the Via Giulia, take Mickey in for questioning, and start to tear apart the whole Neri empire along the way.

Costa rested his hands on her shoulders and wished he could make her feel the same rising sense of anticipation he was beginning to recognize within himself. 'We'll find her. I promise.'

She stepped back from him, doubt still in her eyes.

'Promises,' she said.

The day was dying. Emilio Neri stood on the terrace, leaning on the handrail, looking down into the street, breathing in the smog from the Lungotevere. When he was a kid Rome was cleaner. More whole somehow. It had gone wrong, like most of the world, over the years. Back when he was young people would walk around the *centro storico* on a night like this, arm in arm, just looking in the shops, stopping for a drink before supper. Now they rushed everywhere, or tried to if the traffic would let them. They stood around whispering into mobile phones instead of talking to people directly. Rome wasn't the worst place either. When he went to Milan or London it seemed they spent their entire lives locked in solitary conversations with lumps of plastic. At least his native city maintained a stubborn streak of humanity at its heart. He could still walk across the Ponte Sisto and feel a kick of sentiment.

Except there wasn't time. There never would be time. That part of his life was past. Now he had to consolidate the future, and the reputation he'd leave behind.

He turned to see Mickey clamber up the stairs. The kid stood by the pots of anaemic palms that were still suffering from the winter. He was now wearing a different set of stupid clothes, too young for him as usual: flared jeans, a thin black sweater one size too small. He was thirty-two. He ought to stop trying to look like a teenager. He was shivering too.

Neri waved him over. They stood together by the iron balcony. He put an arm around his son's shoulder and looked over the edge. 'You never liked heights, Mickey. Why's that?'

Mickey shot a fleeting glance down at the street and tried to take one step back. His father's huge arm stopped him. 'Dunno.'

'You remember what happened to Wallis's wife? When she couldn't handle it any more – at least I guess that's what happened – she walked straight out of some apartment block in New York, fifty floors up. One minute she's weeping at the window. Next they're scraping her off the street. You wonder what could make someone do that? Guilt maybe? Or just plain stupidity.'

Neri's arm propelled Mickey straight onto the iron railing. Hard. The kid tried to push back but Neri had him trapped.

'You know,' Neri said, 'sometimes just one simple thing clears up so many problems. The cops get a body. They look at that mess down there on the pavement and come up with a story to fit. It can work out for everyone.'

'Pop—' Mickey gasped, struggling in vain to get free.

'Shut up. You want to know why you hate heights? I'll tell you. One day when you were real young you and your mamma were pissing me off no end. It was summer. We were up here on the terrace. I didn't allow no servants in the house in those days. That was all Adele's idea. Adele gets lots of ideas but I guess you know that. So there's you and your mamma, and you no more than three or four and you're shouting and screaming at her 'cos she ain't got the right toy or something. And I'm lying there on the old wicker sofa we used to have before all this fancy stuff got bought. And I'm thinking: fuck this. I work all day. I keep you parasites alive. And all you can do in return is shout and scream and moan.'

Neri squeezed Mickey's shoulder. The old man stared his son straight in the eye. 'You don't remember, do you?'

'N-n-no—' Mickey stuttered.

'Except you do. A part of you does anyway. It's just stuck deep . . .' He took his arm away for a moment and prodded Mickey in the right temple with a finger, ' . . . in there, along with all the other shit you've got.'

'I don't—' Mickey was saying, and then the old man moved. Two big strong hands took Mickey by the scruff of his neck, bounced him painfully against the railing, propelling him half over the edge, balanced over the tiny cobblestones that, from this height, looked like the pattern on a dead butterfly's wing.

Emilio Neri upended Mickey's legs with a brutal jerk of the knee, dangling his son over the street, letting the kid cling to his arm just as he'd done more than a quarter of a century before. The old man felt just as strong as he had back then, more so maybe. And just as in control. His face was up close to Mickey's this time round though and both of them were starting to sweat like pigs.

'You remember now?' the old man demanded.

Tears were starting to fill Mickey's eyes, his feet kept scrambling against nothing, looking for some kind of hold. Neri could smell fresh piss coming from the crotch of the flared jeans. 'Please—' he croaked.

'I heard a story, Mickey. Just a little fairy tale running up and down the stairs, in and out of the bedrooms of this stinking place. I heard you've been fucking Adele behind my back. People have seen you. People have heard you. Plus there's all manner of other stuff you think I don't know about. Don't you see this from my point of view? Don't you see how nice and easy it would be for me to let you go wipe your face on the cobble-stones down there and bite down the blame with your broken teeth?'

Mickey made an unintelligible squeak. Nothing more.

'You're not saying anything, son. You're not telling me I got it wrong.'

The kid scrunched his eyes shut then opened them again, blinking as if he hoped this were all some dream. 'You got—'

Neri pushed down with his arm, just for a second. Mickey's head bobbed down on the wrong side of the railing. The kid let out a terrified screech and went quiet: his father was holding him again.

'You mustn't lie to me, Mickey. If I think you're doing that I just let go. What use is a son I can't trust?'

Mickey sobbed and said nothing.

'So tell me,' Neri said calmly. 'Think about what you're going to say. This story about you and Adele. Is it true?'

The kid's head went from side to side.

'Say something,' Neri ordered.

'It's a lie. *It's a lie.*'

Neri gazed into his son's terrified face, thinking. Then heaved him back over the railing. Mickey sent a couple of plant pots tumbling down to the street as he scrambled back to safety. Neri watched them shatter on the cobblestones. Down the road a man in a dark suit jumped at the noise and looked up at the rooftops.

'You should be more careful,' Neri said and offered his son a handkerchief. 'People could get hurt that way.'

Tears were streaming down Mickey's face. His breath was coming in short sobs. He looked at his father and asked, 'Why? Why'd you do that?'

Neri shrugged. 'A father deserves the truth. If you'd told me different you'd be down there now. You do know that, don't you?'

'Yeah,' he whispered, and Emilio Neri had to fight to stop himself laughing. The kid really did think he'd got away with it.

'I've been a bad father,' he said. 'I tried to protect you instead of letting you get tough from all the shit that people like us have to deal with. I hear you want in on the action.'

'Yeah,' Mickey mumbled uncertainly. Even through

the tears he still had the teenage pout. Got that straight from his mother, Neri thought.

'Good. It's time.' Neri opened his jacket and took out a gun. It was a small, black Beretta. Mickey just looked at it, wide-eyed, speechless. Neri pushed it into his hands.

'Take it. The thing won't bite. It's one of mine. I know it works.'

'W-w-what—?' Mickey asked.

'You know the rules. You only go so far in these circles without whacking someone. You never did that, son. You just beat up a few people from time to time. It's not the same, is it? Be honest with me.'

'No,' Mickey moaned.

Neri patted him on the back. 'So look happy. It's whacking time. Nothing complicated. All nice and simple. You walk in, you don't say nothing, you put the gun to his head and you pull the trigger. You can manage that?'

'On my own?'

'That a problem?'

'No,' he stuttered. 'Who?'

Neri looked at his watch. His mind was already elsewhere. 'Just some cop. Sorry. That's the best I can do right now. Next time round I'll try to find you a real human being.'

Vergil Wallis wore a black suit with a crisp white shirt and black tie. He looked ready for a funeral.

'I'd like to see Eleanor's body.'

'You're in mourning,' Falcone replied. 'Who for? Yesterday you seemed to think there wasn't much point.'

D'Amato glowered at him. Maybe it was rude to talk to retired mobsters like this. Falcone wasn't sure he cared any more.

'You took me by surprise yesterday. I wasn't thinking straight. I hope you never know what it's like, Inspector. You spend all those years praying you'll discover the truth. Then, when you do, you wish you'd never wanted it so badly. You wonder if you somehow brought it down on your own head.'

'We don't know the truth,' Falcone observed. 'We're not even halfway there. There aren't many people helping us either.'

Wallis nodded, conceding the point, and said nothing.

'If we agree to let you see the body, we get to talk afterwards,' D'Amato demanded. '*Both* of us.' The impassive black head nodded. 'Not that I think you're in much of a position to bargain. Do you want me to call a lawyer?'

'You don't need a lawyer,' Falcone said. 'Not yet.'

He led the way downstairs, out to the morgue in the adjoining building. There was one assistant on duty, a short, dark man with a ponytail. Falcone had never seen him before and didn't feel too impressed. Silvio Di Capua and the rest of the path crew were still at Vercillo's, trying to pick up the pieces without Teresa Lupo. It wasn't going to be easy. Too few people, too little talent.

The morgue official nodded when he heard the name. 'We've got a place for that one. Teresa says it needs special treatment. She's gone loopy or something? Is that true?'

'Just show us,' Falcone snapped.

The ponytail headed for a corridor, moaning

constantly. 'Jesus are we in trouble now. They're not going to let Monkboy loose on the shop, are they? Don't get me wrong. He's a nice guy. Knows his stuff. But managerially . . . You should see his locker.'

They entered a side room. Eleanor Jamieson's mahogany corpse lay on a surgical table surrounded by a panoply of technical equipment that looked like a life support system arriving too late. Silver tripods sprouted from the floor, transparent plastic tubing wound around them feeding a network of tiny pipes and nozzles. These sprayed a fine mist directly onto the body, giving it a bright, leathery sheen in the harsh light of the room. The place had a chemical stink from whatever solution was being used to preserve the body. It made Falcone's throat ache.

'Don't ask me what to do when the stuff runs out,' the assistant said. 'Teresa fixed all this up. Says some academic in England e-mailed her the recipe. Told her it was the best way to stop the thing shrivelling up like a pair of old shoes.'

'Out,' Falcone barked, and the ponytail disappeared back into the morgue.

Wallis had taken a seat in the corner of the room. His eyes were fixed on the body. Eleanor still wore most of the sackcloth shift. The autopsy proper hadn't even begun. Falcone understood too that she would remain untouched for the foreseeable future. This strange, half-mummified corpse was beyond Silvio Di Capua. They would surely have to call in help from outside or persuade Teresa Lupo to come back to work. He wasn't sure which was more preferable. The woman was a loose cannon. Only her considerable skill had kept her in the job in the first place. But it would be faster, if they were spared more interruptions.

D'Amato took a seat on one side of Wallis. Falcone fell into a chair on the other. The room overlooked the street. The sounds of everyday Roman life drifted in through the tiny window: cars and human voices, stray music and the angry honking of horns. In spite of countless murder inquiries, Falcone never felt entirely comfortable in the morgue. It wasn't the grim presence of the cadaver that bothered him. It was the way death sat so easily, so effortlessly in the midst of life, just behind the curtain, unnoticed except by the few people it immediately affected.

He looked at Rachele D'Amato, nodding at her to start, wishing he could find more answers to all the questions that were bothering him. She'd brought the DIA into the case with a consummate skill. It was made easier by the fact that she and her colleagues seemed to know so much more than the police did. Someone was leaking, too, and she assumed, all along, it was the police. Maybe she was right. Everyone knew the Questura had its share of compromised cops. But it bothered Falcone that no one ever asked any hard questions of the DIA. Did she ever wonder whether the tip-offs could be coming from within her own ranks? If she did, would she let on to a mere cop? This was a one-way relationship. Just like the personal one they'd enjoyed for a while. He was, once again, at a disadvantage, and it bothered him deeply.

'Mr Wallis,' she said. 'We're in the dark on almost everything here. A motive. A precise time. Perhaps even a place. What do you think happened?'

Wallis shook his head. 'Why ask me? You said yourself I was not under suspicion.'

'You must have some idea.'

'Really?' Wallis asked. 'Why does that necessarily follow?'

'Was Emilio Neri involved?' D'Amato asked. 'How well did he know Eleanor?'

'Neri?' He hesitated. 'The name rings a bell. You should put that question to him, surely.'

'You went on vacation together,' she said. 'To Sicily. Please don't play games with us. Neri was there, and his son. Who else?'

Wallis nodded, conceding the point. 'Hell. It was a long time ago. I don't remember.'

Falcone sighed. 'I was hoping you could help us somehow. I told you yesterday. There's another girl missing now, in very similar circumstances. We're certain she's in danger.'

Wallis thought for a moment then said, 'What you say doesn't make sense. You told me at the outset you didn't know the circumstances of Eleanor's death. Now you say this other girl is in the same position. I don't understand. Which is it?'

'This isn't a time for playing games,' Falcone snapped. 'We need your help.'

Wallis's gaze was fixed on the corpse, bright and glossy beneath the artificial shower of stinking fluid. 'I don't know anything about this other girl.'

Very carefully, watching his reaction, D'Amato said, 'What about Eleanor's mother?' He flinched, just a little. 'Your wife. Wouldn't you want some justice for her?'

'Her mother took her own life,' he replied. 'No one did that for her.'

'You feel no sense of regret?' she asked. 'No . . . responsibility?'

'She died because she wanted to.' The words came out with difficulty. D'Amato was touching a nerve here.

'My question wasn't about her. I wondered what you felt.'

The man looked at his watch, his eyes glassy. 'This isn't something I want to discuss.'

Falcone watched Rachele D'Amato's face harden. There was such resolve there. It was good for the job. It was what they needed. Surely she'd changed over the years, though. The woman he remembered, the woman he had, perhaps, once loved, was not this detached from her feelings. 'Did you love them?' she asked. 'Eleanor wasn't yours. Your wife had left you already. Did you love them at that point? When the marriage appeared over?'

Wallis bridled at the question. 'You're a very persistent woman. Let me say this once and for all. They changed me. Before, I was what I was. They saw something in me that I didn't see myself. In return I learned to love them, and resent them too. A man like me isn't made to change. It's not good business. It makes for an uneasy relationship with one's masters.'

Falcone glanced at the body. 'Could your masters have done this?'

There was a sudden burst of anger on his face. 'What kind of people do you think I mix with? She was a child, for heaven's sake. What possible reason—?' He stopped, his voice breaking. 'This is a personal matter. I'm not talking about it any more. It's no business of yours. *I have nothing to tell you.*'

'Where were you this morning?' Falcone asked directly.

'At home,' he said immediately. 'With my house-keeper.'

'And your associates?' D'Amato demanded.

'Associates?'

She pulled out her notepad and read off some names. 'We have a list of them. Men you know. Men with the same kind of background. They arrived in Rome yesterday.'

'Sure!'

They waited.

'Golf!' Wallis declared. 'Do you think everything's bad news around here? We meet once a year in spring. I've booked a round at Castelgandolfo for Sunday, then dinner. Phone them if you like, and check. They can tell you. We've done this for years. Since I first came to Rome. It's an annual event for old men. Old soldiers if you like. Retired soldiers. Do you play golf, Inspector?'

'No.'

'A shame.' He paused to give his words some weight. 'I thought the cops were fond of clubs. You get to meet people that way.'

'Not all of us,' Falcone replied. 'You didn't ask.'

'Ask what?'

'Why I wanted to know where you were this morning.'

Wallis shifted on his chair. He didn't like being caught out. It was, Falcone thought, the most promising sign he'd seen of an opening in the man's guard.

'I assumed you'd tell me,' Wallis said lamely.

'Neri's book-keeper, a man named Vercillo, was murdered.'

He didn't even blink. The sombre, expressionless face stared at him and Falcone appreciated, for the first time, how Wallis must once have been a powerful, imposing presence. 'Inspector, do I look like the kind of person who goes around killing book-keepers? If I engaged in that kind of behaviour, do you honestly think that is where I'd start?'

'No wars,' Falcone warned. 'You hear me. I don't want any of that crap on our streets. If you people want to fight it out for some reason, you do it somewhere else and make sure no one else suffers.'

'War?' Wallis answered, amused. 'Who's talking about war?'

'I'm just saying,' Falcone said and heard how lame he sounded.

'Saying what?' The American took his arm. Falcone could smell something sweet on his breath. 'Nothing but the obvious. You've got to know, Inspector, you of all people. War's the natural state of humanity. It's peace and harmony that are foreign to us, which is why it's so damned hard to create them out of all this shit. Wars aren't part of my world, not any longer. Not here. Not anywhere. Others . . .' He opened his hands in a gesture of regret, ' . . . they may feel differently. That's none of my business.'

'And if they start to make war on you?' D'Amato asked.

He smiled. 'Then I'll expect the police to earn their keep.'

There was, Falcone thought, only one way to tackle the next question. Directly. 'I've already spoken to Emilio Neri. He suggested we ask you about what happened to

Eleanor. He seems to think your relationship was . . . not simply that of a stepfather and daughter.'

Wallis closed his eyes briefly and uttered a low, unintelligible sound.

'He suggests you had a sexual relationship with her. I have to ask, Mr Wallis. Did you?'

'You're going to believe scum like him?' Wallis asked quietly. 'You think a man like that would tell you the truth, even if he knew how?'

'I think he knows more than he's telling me. I think the same about you.'

'I can't help what you think about me.'

Falcone took a photograph out of the folder he'd brought with him: Eleanor and Barbara Martelli, with their little coterie of admirers. They were dressed, Eleanor apparently unaware of what was to happen next.

Wallis stared at it. 'What's this?'

'We think it was taken shortly before Eleanor was killed.'

'Where did you get it?'

'I can't discuss that,' Falcone said. 'This is evidence. Do you know these men? Do you know what kind of . . . event this is?'

'No,' he replied immediately.

'The other woman. Do you know her?'

'No.'

Falcone glanced at Rachele D'Amato. There was too much hard work here. Wallis's response was all wrong. He should have been asking questions.

'Does this photograph mean *anything* to you?' he demanded. 'If we're right, it preceded her death probably by no more than a few hours. One of these men may have killed her. You really know none of them?'

He pointed at one figure. 'I know him. So do you. He was your colleague. Mosca, wasn't it?'

'How did you know him?' D'Amato asked.

He shrugged. 'A social event, if I remember right. Nothing more.'

Falcone held up the photo. 'A social event like this? You understand where Eleanor spent her last few hours? You understand what went on?'

He took out more photos. From later. Barbara and Mosca, rolling on the floor, naked.

'This is not how I spend my time,' Wallis said coldly. 'Nor was it then. *Nor* do I believe Eleanor would have gone to something like this willingly, knowing what was involved. Do you have pictures of her like this, Inspector?'

'No,' Falcone conceded. 'Which is interesting in itself. But you see my problem? The idea that Eleanor just walked out of your house one day and disappeared, was abducted in some random way by a complete stranger. It's not true. This was where she was before she died. In the company of men who moved in circles you knew. Crime. The police. As if she were . . .' He paused, determined this would hit home, ' . . . a gift perhaps.'

Wallis nodded, considering this. 'An interesting idea. But it presupposes that the men to whom she was given had something to offer in return. To whom? Not me. So who could that be?'

'We may have DNA evidence from the autopsy,' Falcone said. 'I can only request this at the moment but it would help us if you were to provide a sample. Our forensics people can do what is necessary now. It won't take a moment. It's just a mouth swab. Or a piece of hair if you'd prefer.'

'DNA?' He didn't flinch. 'You're telling me that's some use after all these years?'

'Possibly. Is that a problem?'

'Tell me what you need.' Wallis was staring at the body. It was, they understood, a final act. He would not return. 'I've seen enough. I don't want to answer any more questions. You'll let me know when I can make the burial arrangements?'

Falcone called the lab assistant over and told him to organize the sample. They watched the two of them leave the room.

'DNA,' she said when Wallis was gone. 'There's an interesting thought. Wallis asked the right question straight away, though. Is it possible? I thought the pathologist said there'd be nothing useful because of the peat.'

'I've no idea,' he admitted. 'I just wanted to see if he'd refuse.'

'And the fact that he doesn't?'

'It leaves us in the dark. He could have been there. He could be thinking we wouldn't find out anyway. Maybe we just don't have the photo.'

'Without a real sample it doesn't matter, Leo.'

'No. What about the material I gave you from Vercillo's office? When will you be in a position to get a warrant to raid Neri? I want to be in there as soon as I can.'

She was putting on the diplomatic smile again, the one that said: *no way*. She was so wrapped up in all this. It consumed her more than he'd appreciated earlier. She wanted to own this case. She wanted it to own her too. There was, he thought, nothing else in her life right then. All the glamorous clothes, all the semi-flirtatious, teasing behaviour . . . these were simply the tools of her current trade.

'That'll take a week at least,' she said firmly. 'I can't risk screwing up a case like this out of haste. We're writhing in regulations when it comes to privacy these days. All that information is about fraud, financial misdeeds, tax evasion. We have to know for sure what we're dealing with before I can go before a judge. It's easier for you. A murder investigation. An abduction. You'll get a warrant. Just ask.'

He grimaced. 'I talked to legal. They won't countenance it on what we have. I need more.'

'I can't help there.'

She was thinking. Perhaps she really was trying to help. 'You know, Leo, your life would be so much easier if you could get some physical evidence out of Eleanor's body. The trouble is you've lost the best pathologist you have. You could call her. This is bigger than your ego.'

He groaned. 'This is *nothing* to do with my ego. That woman is the bane of my life. Also, she's sick.'

'She would crawl out of her death bed to work on this if she thought she could help. If you could convince her of that—'

'Possibly.'

He moved over into Wallis's empty chair and peered into her face. It wasn't a professional look. This was just him now, trying to be what he once was, trying to test the water. 'Do you ever wonder about what-ifs?' he asked. 'What would have happened if you'd turned left at the corner instead of turning right.'

'What's the point?' she asked warily.

'None I imagine. I just do it anyway. For example, what if you'd said yes to me when I invited you out to lunch yesterday? When all we had here was an ancient corpse? Costa would have talked to that woman and called in whoever else happened to be on duty. We'd have walked back here, got in a car, gone to see Wallis feeling entirely different about everything.'

She didn't like this conversation. 'It would have come your way eventually, Leo. It was on my desk anyway.'

'I know. But maybe we'd have had the chance to put things straight between us before all the crap began to happen. I would have liked that.'

She smoothed down her skirt. 'Things are straight, aren't they? Do I need to spell it out?'

'Not really. After you turned me down I made one more call. When you'd gone. Just to see if anyone knew what meeting you were in. There wasn't a meeting, was there? There's someone else.'

Her cheeks flushed. 'You checked on me?'

He shrugged. 'I'm a cop. What do you expect?'

'Jesus,' she hissed, then stabbed him in the chest with a long, slender finger. 'Understand this, Leo. I have a life. It is nothing to do with you. And it never will be. You keep your nose out of my business. You don't even peek through the door when you're passing.'

'I guess he's not a cop, then. Or a lawyer. We'd all know about it.'

'If I were you I'd be focusing on what's in front of you. Not my personal life. Call the Lupo woman. Apologize and try to get her back here. You need her, Leo.'

He nodded. 'I will. I'm sorry. I shouldn't have done it. It was just—'

But she wasn't listening. Nic Costa was walking down the corridor towards them and, from the look on his face, Leo Falcone realized he wouldn't be thinking about Rachele D'Amato for a while.

It was six forty-five. Emilio Neri was wearing a long grey overcoat, feeling content and, with a fat Cohiba smoking between his fingers, reflective. It was cold on the terrace of the house in the Via Giulia but he wanted to watch the last scrap of sunlight die in the smog and haze to the west. This was part of the ritual, an element in the growing rite of passage. Rituals . . . sixteen years before another one had touched him. He'd been dubious at the time, cynical even. The professor from the university was a nut, just a lonely man looking for some easy company. Neri had gone along with the idea because it suited him and he could see some profit from the photographs. He'd never believed what he heard. He was like the others, just along for the ride and whatever it offered him. Older now, touched by time, he wondered if he'd been wrong. He'd never forgotten what Randolph Kirk had told him. How it was a cycle, one that underpinned the whole of life: the hunting, the courtship. Then the marriage, the consummation. And finally the madness, the frenzy that was, perhaps, the real point of it all, because inside that brief bout of insanity lay some arcane secret about human nature, the simple truth that there was a beast beneath the skin, always was, always would be. When the moment came you had to acknowledge its presence then watch it slink, sated, back into the cage. There was, he now understood, no alternative. Randolph Kirk called it ritual. For Emilio Neri it was human nature, plain and simple. If he'd been smarter all those years before perhaps they could have avoided this mess. Perhaps now he would make better choices.

Neri was not a man to dwell on his regrets. Within the coming frenzy lay an opportunity, the chance to rebuild his life, shape it in his own image. He could throw away the pretence that had consumed him for twenty years. He need never waste his time at the opera again, or sit through interminable meetings for charities he didn't understand, fighting to stay awake. The money, the power, and the control they gave him over men outside his normal circles, had all blinded him to what he truly was. Apart from that brief time sixteen years ago the beast had never been free of the cage, and even then its journey was constrained by circumstances. Now it was time to put things straight, let the world remember him as it should, then flee to a comfortable retirement somewhere on the far side of the Atlantic, some place where he'd be untouchable.

Bucci and the three soldiers he'd hand-picked now stood on the far side of the terrace, waiting for orders. Neri didn't know any of them too well. He trusted Bucci's judgement all the same. The man had too much to gain to get this wrong. This was a night the city would remember. This was a time that would go down in the annals of mob history. A moment when a man of the old guard made his stand, pointed out what belonged to him and how he'd decided to bequeath it.

He recalled some of the crap Vergil Wallis used to spout years before. About history and duty and how this was ingrained into the true Roman soul, how these qualities would always come out, whatever the cost or the risk. Maybe the American wasn't that stupid after all. Surveying the city like this, for one last time from the home he knew he could never see again, Emilio Neri felt like a man moved by destiny, shaped by what had gone before him, determined now to leave his mark.

He returned to the four men with him on the terrace. 'You're all straight about this? You know what's got to be done?'

Bucci nodded.

'No doubts?' Neri said. 'No more questions? When we leave here, it's a one-way trip. You don't get to change your minds. None of us do. You wake up tomorrow morning and this is a different world. You wake up the day after and you're talking to Bruno here. He's your boss and he'll be a good man. Plus you know what you get from me in the way of gratitude. You'll be happy guys. Rich guys. You got opportunities. This city's yours. Understand?'

They were sound men. They wouldn't let him down.

'You gotta understand this too,' Neri added. 'No fuck-ups. We got no room for them. Any one of you fucks up it reflects on everyone else. So everyone else gets to pass judgement on you. That clear?'

'They got that, boss,' Bucci said.

'I hope so,' Neri muttered then sucked on the dying cigar and threw the stub over the railings, watching the red light flare as it fell. 'You know when the cops are coming?'

'Soon. Maybe half an hour.'

'And you think we can get out of here clean?'

'Piece of cake,' Bucci said confidently. 'We get your car up front really quickly. Franco here bundles inside. Then he's gone like he's running for his life. Stupid bastards will be after him straight away. We got some more cars out back. We just crawl off through the Campo. They'll never see us.'

Neri stared at him. 'You *know* that? You paid your dues to these bastards?'

'Yeah.'

'See?' Neri said, stabbing a finger at Bucci. 'You got a guy here who knows how to handle himself. You look after me. Then he looks after you. That's how it works. Now you wait for me downstairs. I want to talk to the family. Bruno, you send Mickey up. I want things straight with him.'

They left without saying another word. Neri sat down at the big table. Crumbs from breakfast were still on it. There was a noise at the door then Mickey stumbled in, looking lost, scared.

He got up and walked over to the kid, took him in his arms, kissed him on both cheeks.

'Mickey, Mickey. Son. Why are you looking so fucking miserable? This is what you wanted all along isn't it? To become a made man?'

'Yeah,' he mumbled.

Neri tweaked his cheek. 'You're still mad at me? Over our little falling-out earlier? Mickey. If I hear stuff like that I got to ask. You understand that, don't you?'

Mickey stared at the floor. 'That was asking?'

'Yeah,' Neri laughed. 'So your old man's a bastard. Why d'you think you live in a place like this? Why d'you think you never went short of a damn thing? That little scene is behind us now. I'm giving you the present I should have given you years ago. This is your coming of age, son. You got to go through with it. I blame myself for not letting you get on with it earlier. I've pampered you, Mickey, and that was wrong. A father wants to shield his boy from all the shit you get in the world. Can't blame him for that. But it don't work. Not forever. Every man's got to prove himself some time. Now's your chance.'

He embraced him again, squeezing hard.

'You're not scared, are you?' Neri whispered. 'Tell me. You can be frank with your own father.'

'No.' He looked terrible. He was back on the dope again, Neri guessed. 'It's just—'

'There's nothing wrong with being scared, Mickey. It clears your head sometimes. First time I killed a man I was real terrified. He was some old asshole who was pimping out in Monti. Wouldn't pay his dues. Thought he was bigger than he was. I stood outside that pit of his with a shotgun underneath my coat for ten minutes, wondering if I'd got the guts to go inside. Then you know what?'

'What?' Mickey wondered. His blonde hair looked more stupid than ever. Neri wondered if he'd been piling on the dye that evening, as if it might protect him from something.

'I realized. If I didn't kill him, some fucker would come along and kill me. That's the way it works in this business. Sometimes you don't get choices. You just go out and do your job. And . . .' Neri drew Mickey close, whispered in his ear, ' . . . you want to know something else? It gets easier. The first time, you got doubts, you wonder what it's like when the light goes out in some poor bastard's eyes. You'll be thinking that, won't you?'

'Maybe.'

'No. For sure. You wouldn't be human if you didn't. The point is . . . second time it ain't so bad. Third time out, you're curious. You're watching, wondering what's going on in his head. You're looking into his face and thinking, hey, maybe I'm doing the moron a favour! He gets to know some big secret quicker than me. Huh?'

He grinned and slapped the kid on the shoulder. 'Except there is no big secret. Fourth time out you know that for sure. They're just breathing one moment and gone the next. Which is as it should be. So after that you don't even think about it at all. If it's some scumbag you hate you even get some pleasure out of it too. Trust your old man. It's in your blood, Mickey. Once you get the feel it just comes natural.'

He didn't look convinced. He didn't look as if he were all there. 'Why a cop?'

'Because that's what I need. Does that worry you?'

'No one likes it when a cop gets killed.'

Neri wrinkled his nose, not liking what he was hearing. 'Depends on the cop.' He nodded downstairs. 'You got to make your mark. You're the boss's son. Don't ever forget it. You'll never get to lead them if they think you're on the same level. Understand?'

Mickey nodded. Neri leaned forward and took the gun from his son's jacket. He examined it carefully, checking the magazine, ensuring it was fully loaded.

'Killing someone's the easiest thing in the world, provided you do it right. Just walk up, pop the bastard quick in the head, and it's done. Work on it, Mickey. It's a talent you're going to need. On your way now.'

'And afterwards?'

A shifty look crossed Neri's face. 'Didn't I mention that? Afterwards things get a little hot for all of us around here. Best we don't hang around this place for a while. We're going to be flexible for the next few days. You just keep that phone of yours switched on.'

'What? Where am I supposed to go?'

He was so slow. Sometimes Neri wondered whether he really was the kid's father at all.

He handed the gun back. 'I'll call. Trust your old man. He's got your best interests at heart.'

Mickey shoved the pistol back into his jacket. 'OK,' he murmured listlessly.

'And when you see Adele tell her to come up here. I want to talk to her.'

Neri had been thinking about this side of things. Maybe there was another way of dealing with it. But that would have been indulgent. That could have wider repercussions. He didn't want to complicate matters any more than necessary. 'You know, now I come to think about it, I never should have swallowed that story about you and her. I always did believe the bad stuff about you and that's unfair. I owe you an apology, son. You never did get on with Adele, did you? You and her just rub each other up the wrong way.'

'Never did,' the kid said, not quite able to meet Neri's eyes.

Costa was walking down the corridor to the big conference room for Falcone's briefing when she came round the corner.

'You look terrible,' Teresa Lupo croaked.

He stopped and squinted at her, trying to work out what was going on. 'I do?'

'No. I just wanted to say it first.'

Then she coughed into a fistful of tissues and stared at him with pink, watery eyes.

'Actually,' he said, 'you don't look bad at all. It's amazing what drugs can do.'

'Lying cop bastard—' she mumbled.

'Ah, ah, ah. You're feverish. You have to try to keep the temperature down.'

'I ought to be in bed feeling sorry for myself. But then that asshole Falcone did the worst thing. Unbelievable.' She looked hurt for a moment. 'He apologized. Can you believe that?'

Costa thought about this. 'No. Do you have it on tape?'

'I wish. I doubt I shall hear its like again.'

'I doubt any of us will. So what are you doing?'

'Oh, just came in to fill in an expenses form. Pick up my mail. Scratch my ass. Doesn't seem much for the likes of me to do around here. Or did I get that wrong?'

'Teresa—' he said, and took a step towards her.

'Don't stand too close. Germs. If I start infecting his men he'll just get mad at me again.'

'Are you OK?'

'No,' she shrugged. 'But I'm back to being as bad as I was before. I'm sorry, Nic. I don't know what came over me. It was the thought of that poor kid being out there somewhere, abandoned, all because of me. And with you guys thinking about nothing but the lovely Barbara. Having people try to kill you is somewhat unsettling I find.'

'I'd go along with that.'

'Of course!' She brightened a little. 'Finally, we do have something in common. We could discuss it over dinner. Nightmares we have known.'

'Not till this is over,' he said. 'Which it will be. Soon, I hope.'

She nodded towards the room. Officers were steadily filtering through the door. A lot of them. Most of the Questura's denuded complement by the looks of things.

'You have that look about you, I must say. Is it promising?'

He tried to look confident. 'I think so.'

She sniffed again and didn't look too convinced. 'That's good. So what am I supposed to do if you smart-asses have it all wrapped up? Why is boss man practising his apology routine on me?'

'You could deal with the autopsy queue perhaps. Your deputy looks ready to crack up.'

'Silvio always looks ready to crack up. You have to give these people some room from time to time, Nic. Can't mother them every waking moment of the day.'

'Point taken. How about this? Take a look at Eleanor Jamieson. See if there's any DNA we can use?'

Her pink eyes grew bigger. 'DNA? As I keep pointing out to people around here she's been in a peat swamp for sixteen years. What do you think I am? A miracle worker?'

'Yeah. That's what Falcone wants anyway. And while you're at it, we'd really love to know who Kirk phoned while he had you locked in that office.'

She put a finger to her cheek. 'Oh, let me think now. Can I remember the ring tones? Beep, beep, fucking beep. No you just lost me there.'

'You asked. I answered. Now I've got to go. Bad guys to catch. Missing girls to find.'

She was dabbing at her nose again, looking a little happier for the conversation anyway. 'Have you talked to the university woman since I stormed in there? Regina Morrison?'

He shook his head. 'Not that I'm aware of. Why should we?'

'Regina was Kirk's new boss. Somewhere in those files of hers she must have a list of every archaeological dig he's ever worked on. Him being dead and what, I can't check this out for sure. But where do you think a man like that would hide someone?'

Costa nodded. 'Where did that thought come from?'

'I was putting myself in your shoes. Or at least I was trying to imagine what it was like being a cop.'

Teresa didn't say it this time but he got the message. They should have thought of it themselves. They would have, if there'd been the time and the people to manage the workload.

'Thanks,' he said, and walked down the corridor, the last man to enter the room.

Adele Neri didn't bother to put on a jacket when she went outside. Maybe she hadn't expected to be there long.

'You're shivering. Here.' Neri shrugged off his overcoat, walked behind her, and placed it on her bare, slim shoulders.

'You're thoughtful tonight,' she said. 'What's wrong?'

'That tongue of yours is getting too sharp, Adele. It never used to be like that.'

He sat down at the table, making a point of brushing away the crumbs. She joined him there, in the seat directly opposite, looking uncomfortable, looking as if she were struggling to read his mood.

'We're just at that stage of being married,' she said. 'Where some of the sheen's come off.'

He scowled. It was a lame suggestion. 'Is that right? I don't recall it being like this with anyone else. Not with Mickey's mother. We were working. Then we weren't working. Couldn't keep our hands off each other one moment. Couldn't stand the sight of each other the next. It doesn't feel like that now. Not for me. For you . . . I dunno. You're young. Tell me, Adele. Does the sight of me turn you over? Thinking about how old I am and that?'

There was a flash of edginess in her bright green eyes. 'Don't be ridiculous, darling. Why would you even think such a thing?'

'Why? Because I'm an ugly old man. Fat too. And you. Look at you. You can't walk down the street without some kid giving you the eye.'

'Kids never interest me. You know that.'

'And I did interest you?'

'You *do*.'

'Maybe,' he said with a shrug. 'Maybe it's just the money. I don't know any longer, Adele. The thing is, we got to spend a little time apart. That's a practical matter. All this trouble I've got now. There's no reason to fuck up your life too. It's none of your business.'

She gave him an acid glance. Maybe she thought he was fishing for sympathy. 'I'm your wife. Your problems are my problems. If—'

'No, no, no,' he interrupted. 'You don't need to give me that shit. You don't have to pretend. We don't have time. Let me put it another way. I don't want you involved in what's going down right now. That's for selfish reasons too. It's men's stuff. We got things to do a woman shouldn't have to know about. You'd complicate matters.'

He looked at her from across the table and felt no feelings for her. 'Maybe some people are going to get hurt. If I have you close it might give the wrong impression. As if you're part of it or something. Some of these southern families . . . you'd think the women are running them sometimes. Don't work like that here. I want you separate from me because I don't want to have to wonder what that mouth of yours is saying. Understood?'

She bridled at his suggestion. 'I wouldn't talk out of turn.'

'Who knows what anyone would do once those bastards from the DIA come calling? The cops I can deal with. These others—'

He looked at his watch. 'The point is I'm going now and I don't know when I'll be back. *If* I'll be back. We need some time apart.'

She nodded. Neri was unsure whether she was upset or not. 'Where will you be?'

He gave her a glassy, dead-eyed look and said nothing.

'How will I contact you, Emilio? I'm your wife.'

He stifled a laugh. 'Don't worry. There's money in the bank. You can pay bills. Buy stuff. Do whatever you like. Give me a couple of months. Then I'll be in touch. Maybe we'll have a second honeymoon. Maybe we'll be ready for that by then. If you feel otherwise, I'll call the lawyers. It'd be best to do it friendly if we can.'

'And now?' She looked as if she wanted to scream at him for behaving like this. She just didn't dare. 'What do I do now?'

He waved an arm around the terrace. 'Stay here. You got a beautiful house. You can bring back all those servants you love. I know how much you hate cleaning up yourself. I could never stand the idea of servants myself. I gave you your head on that one. Maybe I was wrong. Who'd want strangers in their own home? But hell, when I'm gone I don't *care* what you do.' He made sure this last point came across clearly. 'I don't care who you see. I don't care how you spend your time.'

She got up and took off his coat, laying it on his lap.

'You'll be needing this,' she said.

'Yeah. Tell me one thing, Adele.'

'What?'

'You ever been unfaithful to me? Not that it matters any more. I don't care right now. I got bigger things to think about.'

'Why would I do that? she asked.

'I dunno. For the sex. For the hell of it. Or maybe—' It occurred to him that neither of these would really move a woman like Adele. 'Because it suited you.'

'Those are little reasons. Too small to get yourself killed for.'

He laughed. 'Yeah. You're right. You're a smart girl. That's what impressed me most about you in the beginning. I never liked stupid women.'

'Thanks,' she muttered.

'Just remember this. Things have got to come out in balance at the end. Some American creep kills one of my men. I do something in return. Someone screws with me. I screw with them. Except I do it better. Bigger. I make it final. I win because that's how the balance is, that's my place. This is serious stuff, Adele. You don't want to go pushing your pretty face into it. Believe me.'

He stood up, walked over to her, kissed her on the cheek. Just one short kiss.

'You just stay here. Watch TV. Make yourself a drink.

And when the cops come, you tell them nothing. Say I went fishing. OK?'

Outside a familiar engine was gunning hard. Tyres were burning along the cobblestones of the Via Giulia. Emilio Neri knew what this meant. The first part of the deception was under way.

'Ciao,' he said, and waddled towards the stairs.

It was a cold, clear night, bright with stars and the silver disc of a waxing moon. The police convoy, a marked car at its head, blue light flashing, siren screaming, cut straight through the evening rush hour. Falcone rode with Costa and Peroni just ahead of the heavily manned riot van that was the last in the line. The radio was hot with chatter and none of it sounded good. The plain-clothes men stationed outside Neri's had reported the sudden departure of his car just fifteen minutes before. One team had detached itself to give chase but lost the vehicle somewhere over the river. The second saw two more vehicles scream away from a rear alley and were left standing in the street, with no chance of pursuit.

'What are we going to do?' Costa wondered. 'Go after him?'

Falcone shook his head. 'Go after what? We only have a number for Neri's own car, and what's the money on him being in that? Let's see who's still in the house. It's the son I want to talk to first. Wherever he is. Jesus, the timing. How the hell did Neri know?'

Costa and Peroni looked at each other. Falcone had ordered a big operation: ten vehicles, half of them marked. The DIA had two other cars along for the ride, with Rachele D'Amato at the head. It wasn't going to be easy keeping something of this size quiet.

They turned into the narrow lane of the Via Giulia, rattling across the cobblestones, and saw the flash of cameras, the lights of the TV men, a full-scale media mob waiting on Neri's doorstep.

Falcone went rigid with fury at the sight of them. He recalled Rachele D'Amato's promise to Neri that morning. One way or another, she said, his fall from grace would be a very public event. He swore under his breath, peered ahead and saw her car, saw her slim figure getting out and slipping through the pack of hacks, towards the house.

'Stop here,' he ordered. 'We don't want that mob on our backs. And I'd rather not have her getting into the place before us.'

Costa pulled into the side of the road, next to a medieval fountain, and all three of them watched, with rising trepidation, the melee happening in the street. Broadcast crew fought with press journalists, jostling to be close to the action. The first marked police car had arrived and men were leaping out. D'Amato and some of her team stood by as a bunch of burly uniformed officers went through the motions of waiting to be let in then, in the space of a couple of seconds, began attacking the expensive polished wood door with sledge-hammers. There wasn't much room. A small van marked with the logo of one of the minor cable channels was parked directly outside, its back end almost up against the building. The hammer men had to squeeze behind it to tackle their target. The vehicle cramped their action, made it impossible to get the swing they needed.

Then one of them climbed onto the bonnet and took

a hefty lunge at the woodwork. The door crumpled. Hands shot through to tackle the locks inside. Rachele D'Amato was over the door first, a couple of DIA men on her heels as the cops stood back, open-mouthed, wondering.

'Shit,' Falcone hissed and started running towards the mob followed closely by Costa and Peroni. When they got there the uniforms were stuck outside the shattered door, looking for direction.

'Next time wait for me,' Falcone barked at them. 'Don't let anyone else in. Don't let anyone out without my permission.'

Falcone in the lead, they went up the stairs. The DIA crew had a good start on them. The first-floor room, where they'd seen Neri's hoods that morning, was empty. The butt of a cigarette still smoked in an ashtray. There was a half-full coffee cup on the low table.

Peroni picked it up. 'Still warm. They really did cut this fine.'

'They knew what they were doing,' Falcone murmured then stopped. The DIA team were clattering downstairs, arguing among each other until a female voice told them to clam up. Rachele D'Amato walked into the room with her team, stood in front of Falcone and his men and folded her arms, furious.

'There's not a soul in the house, Leo. Is the Questura leaking again or what?'

'Don't start,' Falcone snapped back at her. 'Who the hell do you think you are, jumping in ahead of us? And this joke out on the street? You had the nerve to call the media? This is a police investigation. Not yours. The DIA don't even have warrants—'

She reached into her bag and pulled out a sheaf of papers. 'You want to read them?'

He glowered at the documents. 'You said—'

'I changed my mind. The information we got from the accountant's office this morning is like gold dust. We can lock this fat creep away for years, and scores of others too.'

'If you can find him . . . What do you think the media will make of that?'

'Leo!' she screeched. 'I didn't call the media. No one inside the DIA did. This was as secret as we get. Don't look to me.'

Falcone stared at her. 'No. You people are all so clean, aren't you?'

'*Leo*—?'

Costa was on the phone, talking to the ops room. He finished the call. 'They've found Neri's car. It just had a couple of his hoods in it. They were riding around, no destination in particular, down in Testaccio. It was just a blind.'

'Where the hell are they?' Falcone demanded. 'The son? The wife? He didn't pack for a family holiday. What's he doing?'

'Getting ready for a war maybe,' D'Amato suggested. 'We still have the house. We've got free run of it. We can tear the place apart. It's a gift.'

Peroni gingerly placed a hand on her slender shoulder. 'We appear to have a conflict of interest, lady. We're looking for a missing girl, in case you forgot. Right now we don't care about finding Mr Neri's cooked books. They can wait for another day.'

'We need the son,' Falcone said, then walked over to the long window and gazed down into the street. The hubbub was dying. The media crews were starting to pack their bags. They'd been cheated too. There was a story for them. A failed raid on a city hoodlum. But there was no real action, nothing to splash over the front pages and the newscasts. A bunch of cops hammering down a door in the Via Giulia was second division news. Whoever tipped them off surely knew they would be disappointed, which pointed the finger at Neri himself, though Falcone couldn't begin to fathom the reason.

He looked at Rachele D'Amato. 'You can do what you like here. If you find something that has a material bearing on the Julius case, call me. That isn't a request. If you delay what we're doing by a single second *I'll* be talking to the media about why we've been hampered unnecessarily. We've got to look for Mickey Neri and that girl. We've got to find someone to talk to.'

She wagged a long, elegant finger at him. 'No, no, no, Leo. Don't try and pass that responsibility on to me. We do DIA business, not yours. Leave some men if you want that.'

'*I don't have the damned men,*' Falcone yelled at her, so loud even the cops outside stopped talking for a moment. 'Don't you get it? We've a day to find that girl. Maybe less. We haven't a clue where she might be. We don't even know where to begin looking. But it isn't here. It's not in your damned books. It's wherever Mickey Neri is.'

Maybe, he thought. Leo Falcone didn't know any more. All he understood was that it was important to cling on to the human side of the investigation. You only got results by finding the right people and making them talk.

'Leo? *Leo!*'

Her voice dogged them halfway down the stairs, arguing all the way. Then she turned back to join her team, to get on with the job. *Her* job. Falcone didn't get it. Rachele D'Amato had won what she wanted. Neri was on the run. She had a *carte blanche* to investigate every last aspect of the old crook's empire. What was it to her to repay a little of the debt? Why was this vendetta the DIA had with Neri more important than the life of a teenage girl?

They stormed out of the house, out into the street, pushing past the TV van which was still backed up against the ruined door. The media mob was almost gone now. There were just a handful of cops, in uniform and out, waiting outside, looking uncomfortable, guilty that they'd overheard the argument.

'You can stand down,' Falcone told them. 'This is a DIA deal for the time being. Let's get back to the Questura. See what's happening with the phones.'

The men nodded. They'd caught the atmosphere.

'Stupid, stupid, stupid,' Falcone repeated as they walked to the car.

'They just got their priorities, Leo,' Peroni observed and got a cold, hard glance for his pains. 'Sorry, *Sir*. You can't expect anything else. The kid and me could go back in there and watch for a while.'

'No point,' Falcone said. 'She'll let us know if she finds something. How would it look otherwise? Besides—' He needed to get this clear in his own head too. 'There can't be a damn thing there that's any use to us. Neri had this planned, right down to the last detail. He's making monkeys of us. He'd love it if we stayed in that place, peeking under the carpet, scraping through dust.'

'Yeah,' Peroni agreed. 'I can see that. Sorry, I still find it hard trying to think like you people. It's all so damn *sneaky.*'

Costa's phone rang. He stepped aside so that he could hear the anxious voice on the other end.

'Why did Neri set this up?' Falcone wondered. It was all too small. It just caused the police some embarrassment and Neri had to be above that. The media didn't even hang around once they realized there was no big arrest coming, no sign of the fat old hood being led out in handcuffs, bundled into a car, head down for the cameras. They'd disappeared altogether.

Apart from the van.

'Boss,' Costa said anxiously. 'I think we've got something. An anonymous call just came in. Someone looking just like Suzi. No more than half an hour ago.'

'Where?' Falcone asked, still thinking about what had just happened, trying to make some connections.

'Somewhere along Cerchi. Didn't get an exact position.'

'Quite some road,' Peroni said. 'We could spend all night going up and down there.'

Cerchi ran the length of the Circus Maximus, now an empty, stadium-shaped field behind the Palatine hill, overlooked by the ruins of Augustus's palaces.

Costa remembered what Teresa had said about Regina Morrison. 'Kirk and Mickey could have used old archaeological digs if they wanted to. We can talk to his boss at the university. She should have a list of everywhere he worked.'

'Get her,' Falcone ordered. He reached the car, put his hand on the door, still thinking. 'Chase it, Nic. Let's go there straight away. This place is dead.'

He looked back at the street. They were parked a good fifty metres from Neri's door. There wasn't a TV crew in sight. The van was still there, up at an angle over the pavement.

'See the vehicle at the front door?' Falcone asked. 'Either of you notice someone using it? Any of those TV bastards go near at all?'

'Not me,' Peroni answered, puzzled.

Falcone looked at Costa, his mind full of possibilities.

'Me neither,' Costa replied. 'What do you think—'

He didn't finish the sentence. The earth began to tremble beneath their feet, cobblestones shaking as if hit by an earthquake. Then came a roar so loud it was unreal, a physical wall of audible fury burying itself deep in their heads.

A fierce, fiery tongue leapt out of the rear end of the van. The vehicle rose off the ground as if tugged towards the sky by an invisible force. For a brief moment the world stood still, then a cacophony of furious noise hit them, followed by a vicious, punishing force as hard as a fist.

When it ended Costa was on the cold hard ground, holding his hands to his ears, stunned, panting too. Peroni leaned against the car, mouth open, looking shell-shocked, gasping for air. And Falcone was running, frantically, as fast as he could, back towards Neri's house where a firestorm now raged out of the blackened, torn tangle of wreckage that was the van, flames licking greedily up into the shattered remains of the building.

Costa staggered in his footsteps, Peroni behind him. The air stank of smoke and the chemical smell of spent explosive. Car alarms, triggered by the shock wave of the blast, sounded all around. A man was screaming in the gutter, clutching at his stomach. Two others lay still on the ground. A team of uniformed officers materialized from a riot van around the corner, wondering where to begin.

It was impossible to think. Nic Costa looked at the faces of the men around him, faces locked hard in shock, and found it impossible to recognize any of them. In this sudden burst of insanity the world had become anonymous, simply a receptacle for its victims.

The blast had taken out two floors of the building. As the dust and debris cleared Costa could see, in the dim street lights, entire rooms in Neri's house now laid open to the elements: tables and chairs, a TV set, a kitchen cut in half by the savagery of the explosion. Flames raged in and out of the severed quarters. Somewhere on the second floor a dark figure danced crazily, as if trying to dodge the blaze that engulfed him, until he fell to the floor, rolled right off the edge and into the dust storm milling around the van.

Leo Falcone was fighting at the mountain of rubble which occupied the spot that, moments before, had been Emilio Neri's front door, clawing at the bricks, snatching them out of his way one by one.

There was a broken body in front of him, poised at an impossible angle, a slender arm, bloodied, blackened by the blast, quite still in the smoking debris.

A small, calm voice spoke at the back of Nic Costa's head and it said: *think*.

As the ambulances arrived, as a screaming fire engine bathed in blue light wove through the cars thrown into the road by the bomb, Nic Costa scanned his notes, found the number, then walked into the relative quiet of an antique shop doorway to place the call.

'Miss Morrison,' he said when he heard the clipped female voice answer. 'You don't know me but I'm a friend of Teresa Lupo's, a detective. I really need to talk—'

There was live football on the TV: Roma versus Lazio. The big local derby. Roma were beating the crap out of their neighbours. Again. Toni Martelli could hear people yelling with delight in the neighbouring apartments. He was a Lazio man himself. For him Roma were still the team of the lower classes, the rabble, the people who ran things these days. Not that Martelli had been to a game in years. Now he was out of the force he'd lost all the favours. With Barbara gone, he couldn't even sponge a few off her.

Falcone had been on the phone ealier saying he could probably release the body for cremation within a week. Sooner if Martelli had something to say. Martelli had told him where he could shove his offer. The girl was dead. What else was there to talk about?

Then came another call with news he half expected to hear. And so he locked himself in the over-large apartment, snuggling up to some cigarettes and a bottle of grappa he'd had sent round from the bar on the corner, waiting, watching the game on the TV, war disguised as sport, brute humanity pretending it was something else, something noble and elegant, like a savage trying to dance ballet.

The key started to turn in the door just after ten, rattling around clumsily as someone fumbled trying to get in.

'Cowboys,' Martelli sniffed. 'They don't even have the decency to send a real man.'

He turned off the TV and the light by his side, making the room appear the way he had planned. He now sat in his wheelchair in the dark. It was not easy to see. He'd angled the two big standard lamps in the living room so they shone towards the door at the end of the corridor. The man would have to walk straight into the light, maybe shade his eyes a little. Toni Martelli had thought this through. He half-guessed what the outcome would be but he didn't plan on making it easy.

A figure blundered down the corridor, too scared to hit the lights. Martelli had the remote control the social people had given him. You had to work your advantages when you were a cripple. He waited for the figure in the shadows to get close to the door, then he hit the corridor light. Three big bulbs running the length of the long passageway came on in tandem. Mickey Neri stood there, dressed in black, hands empty, waving stupidly in front of him.

'I got a gun, asshole,' Martelli grunted from the pool of darkness in the corner of the living room. 'I got a big shotgun. You want to see me use it?'

Mickey turned round, ready to run. Martelli pumped the twelve-bore noisily, ramming one of the four remaining cartridges he owned into the chamber.

'Sit down, sonny,' he bawled. 'Let me take a good look at you.'

Mickey Neri moved cautiously into the room and fell into the chair Martelli had nodded towards.

'Mickey,' Martelli sighed. 'Your old man sent you? That right?'

'Yeah.' There was a pathetic snarl beneath the fear. 'We met before?'

'A long time ago. When we were all up to things we hoped were dead and buried. I'm offended you don't remember. I seem to think—' Martelli started coughing, couldn't help it, and the fit went on and on until he fought back the phlegm. When it was over, he said, simply, 'I seem to recall that, when I gave my daughter up for you and your pop, not quite knowing what was on the cards, you were one of those who got to taste the goods.'

'Like you said,' Mickey grumbled, face screwed up, looking as if it were a struggle to remember. 'It was a long time ago. Lots of people got confused memories about what happened then.'

'Not me.'

Mickey nodded. He was staring frankly at Martelli who knew exactly what he was wondering. How sick was this frail old man really? 'Also,' he added, 'I don't recall you pulling out of what you got *Mr* Martelli. I seem to think you had your fun too. All you old guys . . . You just wanted to get into something fresh and young. You were as greedy as the rest of them.'

Martelli waved the barrel then coughed again, not quite so bad this time. 'You kids are all the same. No respect.'

Then he jerked the barrel and fired. The shotgun exploded a metre or so to the right of the terrified Mickey Neri, blowing a huge tear in the dining room table. And Toni Martelli started counting. This was an apartment block. Someone would hear. Someone would call the cops.

'You fucking madman!' Mickey whined. 'You—'

'Shut up. We got a deal, your old man and me. Not that he told you, naturally. If you walk out of here alive, then everything's square with you. If you're a piece of meat on the floor by the time the cops come, then I'm just sweet. I killed some creep who was trying to rob my apartment. I got Emilio Neri in my debt. And I took his scummy little kid out too. What d'ya think, Mickey? Is your old man pissed off with you or what? Where's your money going?'

'You believe that?' Mickey yelled, bright eyes bulging, terrified. 'Are you telling the truth? 'Cos if you are we're both dead, mister.'

'I'm dead already, moron.' Martelli coughed. And coughed some more. Then it was as if something had come alive inside him, as if the cancer had got scared by all this noise and violence too. A big, black pain rose up from inside his guts, freezing what little sensation remained in his spine, making his mind go blank with the agony.

'*Eeeeeeeeeeee*—' Toni Martelli screeched, rocking from side to side in the chair, trying to keep hold of the shotgun in his arms, which had a life of its own now, wanted to call time on this craziness and go for a walk somewhere else.

There was morphine somewhere. Barbara kept it safe for him. He'd not needed it since she died. Something seemed to kill the needling agony the sickness inflicted on him from time to time. Now it was back, with a vengeance, clouding his vision, dimming his thoughts.

Martelli couldn't stand it any longer. He let go of the rifle, let it fall on his lap and, with his free hand, started spinning the wheelchair, as hard and as fast as he could, fumbling for where he left the ammunition. Two cartridges made their way into the chamber, and for the life of him he couldn't remember willing them there. Two explosions rocked the room. The first blew out the big window looking onto the courtyard. Through the shattered glass came the sound of the football match, a wild, insane roar, blaring out of the neighbouring sitting rooms, where another noise, the lowing, frightened murmur of people, was growing too.

The second went in the opposite direction, somewhere towards the figure of Mickey Neri, who'd now thrown himself off the chair, trying to find cover.

Martelli's head cleared a little and the pain diminished. The chair stopped going round and round. The stupid screeching noise died in his throat. And at that moment Toni Martelli knew this was the end, one way or another. Neri's offer was meaningless. A bigger, blacker fate was rising up to grip him now, and all the hoodlums in the world couldn't keep it from his throat.

Mickey Neri was writhing around on the floor. Martelli heard his desperate shrieks, wondered how badly he'd hit the kid, and shook his head.

'Listen to the little rabbit,' he croaked. 'What makes him squeal? The pain? Or knowing what's gonna end it? You got no balls, boy?'

'You crazy old fucker,' Mickey whispered from somewhere beyond Martelli's receding vision. 'I could give you something. We could both walk out of this.'

'You got nothing for me,' Martelli said simply. 'No one's got a damn thing I can use any more.' He raised the gun, knowing there was just the one cartridge left and this had to count, because if it didn't Mickey Neri would somehow walk out of this place alive, and that, surely, was a crime.

Then he coughed some more, coughed and coughed, until the sound of his own breathing entered his ears, grew and grew.

Toni Martelli was choking on his own blood, wondering where this had come from, why the doctors never told him it would end this way. The shotgun still lay on his lap but he hadn't the strength to touch it. And Mickey Neri had stopped wriggling around on the ground. He was half out in the open now, looking up, a little hope in his eyes. The little jerk wasn't even hurt.

'What the fuck—' Martelli tried to mumble, but it all came out wrong because his mouth was full of stuff, his head was all over the place.

And the pain . . .

Different this time.

He looked down at the gun. It was covered in blood. His own. It came out of his chest somehow, poured down the front of his shirt.

He wanted to get angry. He wanted to kill someone.

A woman walked into view from the door. A skinny woman with red hair and a face that made him feel fear.

'Who the fu—?' Toni Martelli began to say.

She had a gun in her hand. She held the weapon purposefully, the way you were supposed to.

Mickey Neri crawled to his knees and looked up as if the light of God was shining out of her bright, glittering eyes.

The woman shook her head, disappointed. The red hair moved slowly in the light of the old apartment.

'You do it like this,' she said, then walked up to Toni Martelli, smiled briefly, coldly into his face, and put a bullet into his brain.

*

There was only so much a man could do with his hands. Brick and glass and rubble tore at Peroni's fingertips. The coarse, choking dust filled his mouth, solidified in his eyes. Every time he and Falcone tried to snatch something away from Rachele D'Amato's torn, unconscious body, another piece of debris seemed to fall around them to fill its place. Neri's house was losing its solidity, just like the world itself. The ancient structure was on the point of collapse, a huge hole rent in its belly. There was so little time. Falcone was grappling with an ancient timber beam that had shattered like an over-long, rotten tooth and now lay across her chest. It refused to move and it occurred to Peroni that maybe this was for the best. In the dark it was impossible to see what part of the wrecked building depended on the rest for support. If they shifted the wrong thing, the fragile remnants of wall around them could so easily topple down too.

He put a hand on Falcone's arm. 'Leo,' he gasped, snatching for breath. 'This is crazy. We could bring the whole thing down on her.'

The tall inspector continued to claw at the rubble and brick. Peroni grabbed him roughly by the shoulder. '*Leo!*'

Falcone stopped. He looked lost just then. Peroni had never seen him this way. It was unnerving. They needed Falcone to keep his cool. The shaky department was beginning to pivot around him. There was no one else. 'The rescue people are here. They know what they're doing. This is their job. Let's stick to ours, huh?'

Vehicles were arriving all around, fire trucks with shifting gear, their officers moving quietly among the carnage of the blast, trying to assess how best to proceed, paramedics in vivid yellow jackets, wondering where to start.

'She's breathing,' Falcone murmured. 'I can see it—'

Rachele D'Amato was alive, just. Peroni nodded at a bunch of paramedics placing black plastic sheets over several unmistakable forms. 'She's lucky. We got at least three dead already.'

Peroni knew it could have been even worse. If the riot men around the corner had been standing outside their van instead of sitting inside it. If the media animals had bothered to stick around to see what this was really about. It was too much for his head to handle right then. This was premeditated slaughter on a scale the city had never known, a calculated act of murder.

Two firemen elbowed past, took a good look at Rachele D'Amato, then yelled at Falcone and Peroni to get out of the way.

'We were trying to help,' Peroni shouted back.

'Nice of you,' the lead fireman retorted, dragging some gear behind them, calling for a back-up team to bring some lifting equipment. 'Now give us some room.'

Falcone closed his eyes for a moment, trying to quell the fury. He gripped the man by the shoulder.

'I'm the officer in charge here—' he began to say. Something in the man's eyes made him stop.

'I don't care who the hell you are,' the fireman bellowed back. 'We're here to get these people out, mister. If you stand in my way God help you.'

'OK, OK,' Peroni said softly, putting a hand on Falcone, gently guiding him away.

The firemen weren't even listening. The two of them were on the ground, carefully scraping rubble away from her body, yelling for more gear and paramedics.

Falcone watched them, his face a picture of misery. 'Gianni? You got any cigarettes? I was trying to give up.'

Peroni brushed some of the dust off his sleeves, then did the same for Falcone. The two men were filthy and they'd hardly even noticed. 'When it comes to cigarettes, I'm always prepared. Walk with me. I'm flattered, by the way, to hear you using my first name again. I thought, perhaps, we'd never get back to that.'

Falcone followed him to the far side of the road, putting just enough distance between them and the wreck of Neri's house to be out of the immediate stench of smoke and dust. Three more ambulances tore down the cobblestones and screeched to a halt next to the emergency rescue unit. New teams of paramedics burst out of their brightly lit interiors and started to work the scene. A short line of black cars arrived behind them. Both Falcone and Peroni knew what that meant. The big guys were coming in to pass judgement: men from the security service, the bureaucrats, the hierarchy of the DIA. This was no longer a simple crime investigation. It bordered on terrorism, and that changed the name of the game.

Peroni used his sleeve to wipe some debris off the bonnet of a Renault saloon and they sat down. He lit a cigarette and passed it over. Falcone's slim, tanned hands were shaking. He took a couple of drags at the thing then cursed and threw it to the ground.

'You know how much those things cost?' Peroni asked. 'I'm the only man in the Questura who buys them straight and honest. No black market stuff for this boy.'

'Yeah,' Falcone grunted. 'You and your cock-eyed ideas about honesty. I don't get it. You were the one man in vice I thought we could trust. Then you go and ruin it all over a woman. What for?'

Peroni cast a sideways glance at Falcone. He was a handsome man, in a hard, emotionless way. This inability to address the real seat of his fears – his apparent concern for Rachele D'Amato – was a rare weakness, one that made him briefly more human. 'She was a *beautiful* woman, may I remind you. A hooker, true, but let's not leave out all the salient facts. People make fools of themselves from time to time, Leo. There's a crazy gene in all of us. You convince yourself otherwise. You say to yourself, nah, the job's bigger than this. Or the marriage. Or the kids. You think: I can just push these thoughts back into the dark where they belong. Then one day, just when you're least expecting it, the crazy gene wakes up and you know it's pointless trying to fight. For a while anyway. Because fighting could be even worse. You're just beating up on yourself. But I think you already know that.'

Falcone glanced back at the chaos across the road. 'A bomb, a bomb. What the hell is Neri thinking?'

Peroni's mind had been working along the same lines. 'You think it has to be him? He had enemies. The American for one.'

Falcone stared dolefully at the firemen working to free Rachele D'Amato. 'Why would any of them bomb an empty building? No one's that stupid. Neri knew we were coming. The bastard left us this as a present and—'

Falcone was struggling to tie the ends together in his head. Peroni hated seeing him filled with doubt like this. 'And it doesn't make sense. This is so final. He can't talk his way out of this one. He can't pick up the phone and bribe some politician, some cop to look the other way.'

That was true, Peroni thought. This was the end of
Neri's career. There was no other possibility. Or, to be
more precise, it was the act which Neri was using to
announce the closure of his time in Rome. Something,
the papers on the dead accountant's desk, some threat
they failed to understand, must have convinced him there
could be no turning back. He had to flee, to seek anonymous sanctuary somewhere he hoped the Italian state
could no longer reach him.

Peroni thought of the body, the brown, shining body
in Teresa Lupo's morgue. Everything led back to that
first corpse. Every event that followed stemmed from its
discovery, and still they had no idea why, no clue to
explain the strange and deadly demons that flew out of
the ground once that small patch of peat near Fiumicino
was exposed to the light of day.

Falcone turned a sudden, sharp gaze on him, the one
that said: *don't lie, don't even think of it.* 'Tell me the
truth. Do you think I'm losing it? Is this getting too
much for me?'

'What?' Peroni stared at him, almost lost for words.
'Since when did you get to be super-human? This is too
much for all of us. This . . .' he waved a hand at the
scene across the road, ' . . . is the world gone mad. Not
just that bastard Neri.'

There was a sound from the house. The lifting gear
around Rachele D'Amato was being cranked into action.
The firemen were shouting to each other. Timbers were
moving. Walls were starting to shake. And there was
more light now. The bright, unforgiving light of the TV
cameras, back to see what they were supposed to witness
all along.

Falcone stood up and shook the dirt and dust off

himself, getting ready to go back. Peroni was with him instantly, a hand on his arm.

'Leo,' he said. 'There's nothing you can do. And whatever state that woman's in you can't change it. Furthermore, if she does wake up, she'll be livid to find you sitting by the bed like some dumbstruck husband.'

'Really?' Falcone gave him a familiar, cold look. 'You know her well enough to say that?'

'I know she's just as married to the job as you are. And when she does get conscious the first thing she'll ask is what you've done to get the sons of bitches who did this. You offer a bunch of flowers and you'll get it straight back into your face. Now am I right?'

Falcone glanced at him and Peroni wondered if he had read everything the wrong way. 'You think that's what this is about, Gianni? Me and her?'

'I dunno,' he mumbled, and Peroni realized that at that moment he really didn't. There was more going on in Falcone's head than he appreciated.

'She's got another man,' Falcone said flatly. 'She told me so.'

'Gimme a break,' Peroni answered immediately. 'Does she look like a woman with a man in tow? She's just playing with you, Leo. Women are like that.'

'Maybe.'

Falcone was focused on the meeting going on across the road. The men from the black cars were engaged in an impromptu conference near the sight of the blast. He knew, surely, he ought to go and join them. He ought to answer their questions, try to keep them happy.

Peroni looked at the shattered building and sighed. 'For God's sake, Leo. It's times like this people look to you. If you're riddled with self-doubt, how the hell do you expect them to go on? Here—'

He lit another cigarette and offered it. Falcone accepted reluctantly.

'Listen to your friend Gianni, please. Because he's just got a stupid vice cop brain in his skull and this primitive organ doesn't have a clue what's going on here. All these crazy genes bouncing around tonight. Where'd they come from, Leo? What the hell for? Who flipped that switch and why?'

Falcone scratched his chin and said nothing.

'This is good,' Peroni said carefully. 'This is indicative of cerebral activity. Come on. Reel off some options.'

Falcone shook his head miserably and threw the cigarette away.

'You are costing me big time, man,' Peroni groaned. 'OK, let me change the subject. How about this? You can bawl me out. Some time over the past half hour – don't ask when exactly because I can't tell you – Costa went off on his own, chasing this wild goose story about some blonde girl over in Cerchi. He didn't want to. Or rather, he did but he didn't want to let it show. So I told him to get his ass on the road anyway. Who knows? Anyway, it was me giving orders. So bust my ass.'

There was a flicker of interest in Falcone's face. Peroni was glad even that much was there.

'It was just a report of a blonde girl?' Falcone asked. 'Just that she looked like Suzi Julius?'

'Nothing more,' Peroni agreed. 'You seemed to think – this was just before the big bang event took place – it was worthy of attention, I believe.'

'It was. Hell, it *is*.' Falcone wasn't looking across the

street now. His mind was getting back into gear. 'Or maybe—'

'Maybe what?'

The old Falcone was lurking there somewhere. The one who didn't let go. And the men in black across the road were starting to look around them, wondering why no one had seen fit to acknowledge their presence.

'I'm not messing with you now, Leo. Either you pull yourself together or someone at the Questura's going to be sending you back on leave and finding some young smart-ass to warm your seat. Probably for good.'

'Yeah, yeah,' Falcone conceded. 'Maybe it's what Rachele said all along. A war. And somehow the Julius girl—' He waved his hand at the mess across the street, 'All these people, they're just, what do they call it? Collateral damage. Bodies caught in the crossfire. It's a *war*. Neri against Wallis. Or Neri against us, the world, everything. I don't know.'

Peroni didn't feel convinced. 'Don't wars need something to start them?'

'The girl. Wallis's stepdaughter. Neri or maybe his son did something to her. Wallis wants payback. This is Neri getting his revenge in first. Against all of us.'

'You people do live in a complicated universe. How'd you get there?'

'It's not "there". It's not even part way "there".'

'So what do we do? What *are* cops supposed to do in a war?'

Falcone gave him a withering look. 'Do we have men outside Wallis's place?'

'No. The DIA took that one, remember?'

'Yeah,' Falcone nodded, thinking. 'You remember what Wallis said?'

'Every word. But remind me.'

' "War is the natural state of humanity." '

'Bullshit,' Peroni protested. 'Lethargy's the natural state of humanity. Look at this mess! What's natural about that?'

'Nothing,' Falcone said, looking at his watch. 'Everything, if you've got the "crazy gene". We're seeing this all wrong, Gianni. We're trying to rationalize something that's not rational.'

Peroni patted his shoulder. 'Hey! See! You can still sound like the old Leo when you want to. Can we go out and do cop stuff now, please? This isn't a place for the likes of us. You can phone the hospital later. We got work to do. Furthermore—' He pointed to the men across the street, who were starting to look thoroughly pissed off. 'I believe your presence is required.'

Falcone nodded and walked over to talk to them. Peroni sat on the bonnet of the car and lit another cigarette, trying to think his way around what he had just heard. From across the road the inspector's sombre voice rose in the darkness. He was yelling at these anonymous men, arguing his case, refusing to back down, and it was music to Peroni's ears. Falcone really didn't give a damn. It made him unique. It made him invaluable. It was the reason his men followed him everywhere, even though half the time they couldn't stand him.

In the harsh artificial moon of the TV lights across the road a stretcher moved out from the rubble. Rachele D'Amato was headed for an ambulance, a team of men around her, one of them holding a drip. Peroni could just about make out her face. She was unconscious. If he were honest with himself, she looked dead. He thought again about what Falcone had said, and the distinct impression he'd had that it was curiosity, not jealousy, that lay behind his interest. She didn't look like someone with a man in tow. She was, surely, just saying: *back off, Leo*. Nothing more than that. It was a measure of Falcone's awkwardness in these matters that he just couldn't see this.

And now he was watching the stretcher too, still talking to the men in dark suits, his face impassive. Then he murmured one quiet oath and stomped off, to stand by the doors to the ambulance.

Peroni walked over to his side. 'Leo. She's in good hands.'

'I know.'

Falcone's mind was turning somewhere else. Peroni didn't know whether to feel pleased or sorry. 'So what'd they say?'

The cold grey eyes just stared at him.

'OK, OK,' Peroni conceded. 'Stupid question. They said: "go fix this shit". I get the message.'

Falcone scowled at the suits getting back into their cars. 'Never mind what they said. I want the Julius girl. Have you heard from Costa?'

'Not yet.'

'Get him.'

So Peroni called. And called again, getting madder and madder because of so many things: the dead ring at the end of the line, Falcone's cagy diffidence, his own confused state of mind. Then he phoned the control room asking if Nic Costa had checked in.

The woman handler couldn't believe her ears. 'Do you know what's going down in this city tonight, detective? I got bombs. I got people screaming blue murder about some shooting in San Giovanni. And you want me to find out which bar your partner fell into?'

'He don't drink!' Peroni barked down the phone.

Except maybe he did now. Maybe they all ought to. Maybe something made sense if you saw it through a musky mist of red wine.

'Yeah right,' the handler snarled. 'Maybe he's gone to choir practice.'

Then the line went dead and Gianni Peroni still didn't know what to do. He thought about what the handler had said and felt his mind starting to turn again.

'Shit,' Peroni murmured.

'Where the hell is he?' Falcone wondered, taking his eyes off the ambulance screaming away down the narrow road, lights flashing, klaxon screaming.

'I dunno,' he replied. 'But there's trouble in San Giovanni now too. That address ring a bell?'

Cerchi ran beneath the overhanging escarpment of the Palatine hill, all the way from the Tarpean cliff behind the Capitol to the busy modern street of San Gregorio that led to the Colosseum. Nic Costa had parked next to the open space that was once the Circus Maximus, wishing the tip-off had led him somewhere else. At night this was a seedy part of town, a haunt of down-and-outs and drug dealers who lurked in unlit corners, out of sight of the authorities.

He'd been to all five sites which Regina Morrison's records suggested were linked to Randolph Kirk. They were complex places, with multiple entrances, not all of them obvious. It took time but every last one seemed boarded up, abandoned long ago. He'd shown Suzi's photo to some of the stragglers in the area. Most were too scared or too doped up to talk any sense, and the few that had their wits about them were unwilling to help a lone cop. Peroni was right: Cerchi was a big street.

He thought about his partner and the rest of the team who'd been close to the blast outside Neri's house. Costa felt guilty about leaving them, but Peroni was insistent. One more pair of hands would make no difference, and they had a duty to Suzi Julius too. They had, in all truth, neglected her. Miranda knew that just as well as they did. The knowledge lay in her intelligent, all-seeing eyes. And it was a neglect that could be hard to rectify.

So what do you do? Costa wondered.

Go home, a weary inner voice said. *Sleep.*

He walked back towards his car, realizing how dog-tired he was, and how welcoming it would be to fall into the big, empty double bed in the old house off the Appian Way and listen to the comforting rustle of ghostly voices down the corridor. At that moment he remembered how important family, that tight, near-perfect bulwark against the cruelties of the world, was to him.

Even a family torn apart by tragedy.

The thought pricked his conscience. His father's premature death still haunted him. Nic Costa wouldn't wish that pain on anyone. It was now nearly midnight. If they were right, sixteen years before Eleanor Jamieson had been butchered, victim of some obscure ceremony involving . . . who? The family of a Rome hood? A bunch of sleazy hangers-on out for fun and unaware that Neri's cameras were filming their tricks? Suzi Julius could face a similar fate at any time over the next twenty-four hours, for no reason but bad luck, the misfortune of her looks, of turning the wrong corner at the wrong moment. And no one had the slightest idea of where she might be. Neri and his son had disappeared leaving a bloody trail of destruction behind them. Vergil Wallis, this time round anyway, seemed to be out of the loop. They had no real lead, just chaos and anarchy and violence.

He took one last look around him and narrowed his eyes at a pool of half shade along the street. Twenty metres or more away something had moved, dashing into the shadow of the great Palatine cliff. A head of bright blonde hair disappearing into the darkness, with another shape, that of a man, moving close behind. It could just be a pair of lovers. It could just be the break they'd been praying for.

Costa patted his jacket, feeling the Beretta safe in its holster, and walked towards the shadows, listening to the sounds of the night: the chatter of sleepy pigeons, the low rumble of traffic speeding past the grassy stadium, the scuttering of rats among the crumbling rock face that sat beneath the remains of the imperial palaces.

A distant voice, just recognizable as female, pleading, echoed out from the cavern mouth, now more visible in the leaking radiance of a bright yellow light within.

Nic Costa took out his phone and knew what he'd see. He was directly under the lee of the Palatine's rock face. The signal was blocked by the stone. The sensible thing to do would be to walk back out into the street, make contact with Falcone, call in help. But he had to keep the girl within his reach. Besides, this could just be a couple of secretive lovers. He didn't like heroics, but this time, there seemed no alternative. So he crept into the shadows, letting his back fall against the dusty rock wall, edging his way forward towards the light, towards the sound which was the voice of a man now, talking so low Costa couldn't make out the words.

He aimed for the sound and it wasn't easy. The place was a complex of dimly lit chambers, interlinked, set in a chain from the entrance which was, Costa suspected, just one of many, eaten into the hill like giant rat holes. The site should have been on Randolph Kirk's list. Maybe it was and Regina Morrison just hadn't got to hear of it. Or perhaps, if it was Kirk's most private sanctum, his holy of holies, he kept it private for his own good reasons.

Costa passed through four small chambers, each barely lit by a single bulb dangling from a wire in the centre, just like at Ostia. In the shadows he could make out more rooms and corridors, stretching into the gloom. The place was a subterranean labyrinth, an ancient maze cut into the rock. He wished now he'd waited for back-up. He wished he could hear what the man in the darkness was saying.

He tried to picture what lay ahead of him but it was impossible. When he thought he was heading for the sound, he would turn a corner and find himself floundering in an impenetrable darkness. After a while he couldn't work out which way was forward, which back. His legs dragged across the rough stone floor. His head hurt. More than once he tripped, and was aware of the noise he made. The distant voices rolled incomprehensibly around him from every direction.

Then he ducked to stumble through a low opening and found himself dazzled by the intensity of what lay beyond.

Three bulbs dangled from this ceiling, burning like

miniature yellow suns. On the rock walls around him, plastered everywhere, covering each other like an overlapping skin of living images, were colour photographs, all of the same two faces in the same two poses: Suzi Julius, happy and smiling, bright blonde hair waving around her face, and Eleanor Jamieson, this photo slightly faded from the years, still shocking in its similarity. They could have been sisters, he thought, not for the first time. No wonder Kirk saw her and began to remember.

He turned around, feeling giddy, wondering where to look next, where to go, clutching for the gun instinctively, feeling his hand wander to the wrong places.

'Oh, Jesus,' said a frightened, female voice floating out of the darkness. Then the breathy words faded, were replaced by the sound of something sweeping through the air.

Nic Costa felt an agonizing pain crash into the back of his skull. He was aware of falling, still dazzled by the bright intensity of the room. Then darkness.

LIBERALIA

Something stirred at the back of Teresa Lupo's mind, rumbling around the darker corners of her sleep, buzzing, shifting position, now near, now far. She swore, felt her heavy eyelids start to stir, then rolled awake at her desk in the morgue, just in time to see an equally sleepy honey bee lurch through the air then head off back to the open window.

It was morning. A warm spring morning, just after seven. The city was already alive beyond the window, cars and people, sounds so familiar, so normal that it took her a moment to remember this was no ordinary day.

She'd called in help, from the carabinieri and the health department, from anywhere she could think of, old, retired colleagues, med students looking for some experience. For the moment it had been a question of coping rather than discovering, filing material as she thought of it. Then, some time after three, she'd placed her head on the desk and fallen fast asleep. Silvio Di Capua had had similar ideas. He was still curled up in a crumpled, foetal heap on the floor in the corner of the morgue. A couple of admin people, only one of whom she recognized, were busy with paperwork. A bunch of medic types were working at the tables: the little accountant had just reached his place in the queue. Barbara Martelli's father was next.

'Any more signed up for the ride?' she asked the admin men.

'No.'

'Thank God for that.' She wasn't sure she could cope with another damned corpse. She wasn't sure she could cope with the ones she'd got. Her nose felt as if someone had jammed a couple of wads of leaky cotton wool up each nostril. Her throat was like sandpaper. Sweat soaked her hair. Teresa Lupo looked a mess. She knew it and she didn't care.

Then a figure came through the door, Gianni Peroni so fresh and alert it was unnatural.

He walked over and peered into her eyes, curious, a little judgemental perhaps.

'What drugs are you on that make you so bright and chirpy?' she asked. 'And do you have any for me?'

'Let me buy you a coffee. Outside this place. By the way, have you seen Nic?'

'No . . .' The question puzzled her. She'd almost forgotten she belonged to a world beyond those shining tables.

'Come,' he said, and took her weary arm then led her down the corridor, out into the waking morning.

It was the beginning of a beautiful day. She could even hear birdsong. Or perhaps, she thought, her mind had some preternatural acuity after the recent shocks. Her head didn't feel right. It hadn't for a while. Something was different after the sleep, though. She felt exhausted, drained, physically and mentally. But there was a measure of control inside this state too, and that was welcome.

Peroni led her to the café around the corner, ordered two big black coffees, stirred some sugar sludge from the glass on the counter into his cup, then did the same for hers.

'When you work vice,' he said, 'you come to know about getting through the night. You get to like it after a while. The world's more honest then somehow. People don't have to look you in the face when they're lying. You get to know about the value of coffee too. Here . . .'

He held up his cup and, instinctively, she clipped it with hers.

'What do you want?' she asked.

'Tidings of joy. Information. Enlightenment. For one thing, I'd like to know who Professor Randolph Kirk phoned to start all this crap.'

'Nic asked me that too,' she said. 'Tell you what. I'll ask old Randolph when I get back.'

'You do that. Any further gems for me?'

'Stand in the queue. It's a long one. How's Falcone doing? How's that woman of his?'

He made a tilting motion with his hand. 'She's still in intensive. She'll pull through. That woman's made of stone. As for Leo, I dunno. He's not looking lovelorn any more. Maybe that pisses him off too. Who cares? We got work to do. Big work, Teresa, maybe bigger than even we can handle. We need to get somewhere fast. So you see why I'm here? We need all the help we can get.'

She found herself thinking seriously about Gianni Peroni for the first time. He wasn't the arrogant, bent vice creep she first thought. Underneath that curiously ugly exterior he possessed some stiff, unbending spine of integrity that made his disgrace all the more poignant, all the less understandable. Falcone and Nic Costa were lucky to have him around, although she wondered how much the older man appreciated that.

'When are you going back to your old job?'

Peroni winked. It was a comic gesture. She almost found the energy to laugh. 'Between you and me? As soon as this shit is over. I bumped into my old boss in the corridor during the night. They drafted him in too. Nice guy. Understanding guy. He had some warm words for old Gianni. Thank Christ. This detective stuff is not my scene. It brings you into contact with the wrong sort of people.'

She waited a moment to make sure she understood that last statement correctly. 'And vice doesn't?'

'In vice you just meet people who want to mess with your body. These guys are forever hanging around those who just can't wait to mess with your head.' She didn't say anything. 'But then I think you know that already.'

'Possibly,' she conceded. 'So tell me what you want me to do.'

'Me?' Peroni replied. 'Hell, I don't know. None of us has a clue where to begin here. We haven't had a gang war in Rome in living memory. If that's what it is—'

'What else could it be?'

'Search me. But if it is a gang war it's a pretty one-sided affair, don't you think? Somehow from behind his iron gates, with no troops whatsoever except a few golf buddies, the American whacks Neri's accountant and lays out all those documents that mean Neri has to take to his heels. At least I guess that's how he feels. Then the fat man goes ballistic and puts a little leaving present outside his own house for us.'

She knew what he meant. 'It's a funny kind of war.'

'Sort of unbalanced, don't you think? And Wallis. He's just sitting there in that big house of his, twiddling his thumbs, looking as if butter wouldn't melt in his mouth. The DIA's bugging his phones. Bugging him direct too I suspect because they just love playing with those toys of theirs. He's not retaliating. He's not doing a damn thing as far as we can work out.'

Teresa sat up straight. She could talk cop again, and she liked that. She smoothed down the crumpled front of her blue shirt, wondered if it wasn't time to lose a little weight from the old frame. She was big-boned. That was what her mamma always said. But she could get fit if she wanted. She could meet these men at their own game. 'What about Barbara Martelli's old man? You're telling me Wallis didn't do that?'

'Now there,' he said, with a sudden assurance, 'we do know something. Wallis had nothing to do with it. Not unless he's running Neri's family for him. We got a good ID from a man who was seen leaving the building. The guy saw someone go in before Martelli got shot. It was Neri's own son did that one. Dumb bastard left prints too. Makes sense. I guess Neri thought Martelli might tell us what was really going on in that fuck club of theirs. So he sent his boy round. Still doesn't add up to a war. Not in my book.'

'Unless it's over already,' she suggested. 'The American's thrown in the towel.'

Peroni didn't look convinced. 'Maybe. A part of me hopes that's so. The trouble is I can't help thinking that if that is the case we'll never get to the bottom of anything. We never get to understand why poor Barbara whacked the professor and then drove into that big hole chasing you.'

This repetitive refrain was beginning to piss her off. 'Poor Barbara . . . Why's she always "poor Barbara"?'

He seemed surprised by the question. 'Because she's dead, Teresa. And whatever happened, whatever she tried to do to you, it wasn't *her*. It was something else. Something that affected her. Surely you can see that?'

She could, but she didn't want to face it just then. She'd come close to the edge herself at times. There was craziness in the air.

'What about poor Suzi Julius?'

He shrugged and looked abruptly despondent. 'We thought we had a sighting last night. Just before the bangy thing went off. Nic went over there to chase it.' Peroni hesitated, reluctant to go on.

'Well?' she wondered.

'Haven't heard a word from him since. His phone's dead. No sign of him in the street. Never went home.'

It always happened with bad news. A picture of the person involved just flew into her head. Teresa Lupo had, maybe unwittingly, got very close to Costa over the last year. He had qualities she didn't see in abundance around the Questura: persistence, compassion and a dogged sense of justice. And he never caught the cynicism bug either, which, perhaps more than anything, made him stand out from the crowd. 'Oh crap. What the hell can have happened?'

'We have no idea,' Peroni said honestly. 'But I like that young man, Teresa. He is going to be driving me around when I go back to my old job. No one's taking that privilege away from me.'

He flexed those big shoulders and she began to understand something else about Peroni. He wasn't a man to give up easily.

'You could have told me about Nic earlier.'

'I didn't want to worry you.'

'So what do you want from me?' she asked again.

'Look, I'm not telling you how to do your job. Nor is this a request from Falcone or anything. To be honest with you, everyone back there's clutching at straws anyway. I just want to say this. We're all short on resources right now. We all have to think about priorities. You're a good pathologist, you know the rules, you stick by them, mostly—'

She finished the coffee, looked him in the eye and said, 'Cut the crap.'

'OK, OK. I just can't help thinking that somewhere in that workload of yours there's something that can help us. And it's not going to be in the obvious places, or the most recent ones. I know you got to do it on all those poor bastards. I was just hoping you wouldn't kind of focus on the easy ones first. I mean, Toni Martelli, the accountant guy. Those people from outside Neri's house. We *know* how they died. We need forensic, sure, but I don't think our answer's going to come from looking at those corpses. Whereas—'

He left it at that, hoping she'd pick up the bait.

'Whereas—?' she wondered.

'Oh God. Do I have to say this? You were right all along. Whatever prompted this shit began with that kid we dug out of the bog. If we could work out what the hell happened to her, and where, then maybe we'd get some better perspective on what's going on.'

She looked across at the skinny bartender playing with his ponytail and said, 'After you've washed your hands you can make me another coffee.' The youth slunk off to the kitchen then returned and started working the espresso machine.

Peroni eyed her, just a hint of admiration in his face. 'You're direct, Teresa. I like that in a woman.'

'This Mickey Neri. He killed Barbara's old man. The Julius woman identified him hanging around her daughter too.'

'Yeah?'

'And if I recall correctly,' she continued, 'this same Mickey Neri met Eleanor Jamieson. I saw the notes. They said Wallis and she took a family holiday in Sicily with the Neris six weeks or so before she died.'

'Stands to reason—'

'Oh yes.' She swallowed half the cup of coffee and felt the caffeine and sugar buzz start to hit the back of her head.

'You want to be careful with that stuff,' he said. 'It can give you nightmares.'

'I don't need coffee for that. Do you?'

Peroni glanced at his watch. 'Well?'

'We haven't touched any of yesterday's,' she said. 'Well hardly anyway. I spent most of last night trying to complete the autopsy on Eleanor Jamieson. I did try to come up and talk to you people about this. Around two thirty. If I recall correctly, you were all too busy.'

His mouth hung open, hungry for information. Quite deliberately she slowly finished the coffee then wiped out the dregs with her index finger and sucked it, making little squeaks of pleasure all the time.

'Please—' he begged.

'I got it wrong, twice over, big time. She wasn't some virgin sacrifice. Or to be more accurate, she may have been a sacrifice but she wasn't a virgin. I was wrong too that you couldn't get any DNA out of a body that's been sitting in all that acid peat for sixteen years. There's one circumstance that allows this.' She looked at him. 'You want to guess?'

'No!'

'If there's a foetus. Even a tiny one. Eleanor Jamieson was pregnant. Six weeks or so I'd say. Probably just at the stage she was starting to notice, starting to wonder whether she dare tell the father.'

Peroni's eyes were shining with hope and outright joy. 'Jesus, you beautiful woman.'

'I said to cut the crap. The point is that she's pregnant six weeks or so after she met Mickey Neri, who's now been hanging around her look-alike, a sixteen-year-old kid who happens to have disappeared.'

It came so suddenly she wished she'd had the time and the strength to react. Gianni Peroni stepped forward, grabbed her face with both hands, then kissed her rapidly on the lips. She sat, transfixed. The pony-tailed waiter was staring at the pair of them.

'Don't ever do that again,' she whispered. Then added, 'Not without asking first.'

'Give me more.'

'I don't *have* any more,' she objected. 'Not until the lab get back on the DNA.' She smiled. 'We've Mickey Neri on file already. He was accused of rape two years ago. Somehow the thing never got to court. It could be waiting on my desk right now.'

'Oh sweet Jesus.'

Gianni Peroni was beaming. 'Don't even think of kissing me again,' she warned. 'Too early in the morning. Just go and find Nic, will you?'

'Yeah,' he agreed, nodding. 'You bet.'

He stopped and stared out into the road. A tall dark figure was walking across the road, towards the Questura. It was Vergil Wallis, leather coat flapping around his shins, striding deliberately like a man with a mission.

'Two miracles in a minute,' Peroni murmured. 'Maybe there is a God.'

Nic Costa woke up on a large, old double bed in an enclosed chamber that stank of damp. A single yellow bulb cast a pool of waxy light into the cold, dusty room. His head hurt. He ran his fingers gingerly over the faint, tender bump on the back of his scalp then sat upright, legs over the side of the bed, trying to think. His jacket lay crumpled on the floor. Costa picked it up. The mobile phone was still in the pocket. He stared at the screen in vain. He was deep inside the rock of the Palatine now. There was no chance of a signal. No sign of his gun either, or a soul anywhere nearby.

He stood up, paused for a moment to let the pain at the back of his head subside, then walked around the room. It looked like the kind of place Randolph Kirk would have used, professionally and for his private pleasure too. There were paintings on the walls, old, rough ones, never retouched over the centuries. He stared at the images that, just like at Ostia, ran around the place in a continuous frieze a good metre deep. It was the same theme that he'd seen in the underground chamber by the coast, an initiation ceremony. A young girl, more puzzled than frightened on this occasion, was being led through a crowd of revellers, only some of them human.

As he walked round the room, following the story, he realized this was different somehow. The rape looked more like seduction here. The girl seemed passive, willing even, with bright, knowing eyes and the hint of pleasure in her face. There was a graphic depiction of her coupling with the god, locked in his powerful arms, eyes closed, mouth just open, ecstatic, but this was no longer the final piece in the saga. It appeared midway through the frieze and was followed by some kind of frenzied orgy, in which the girl took part, voluntarily, watching the fights and the lovemaking, the vicious wrestling bouts and the acts of bloody violence around her with a nonchalant sense of detachment. Then, in the last frame, she was the central figure once more. The girl stood in front of the god who was now tethered to a stake, his arms held both by ropes and the grip of two female acolytes, his body shrinking in fear. Now she held a knife which she plunged into his right eye. Blood soaked his dreadlocks. A silent scream rose from his throat. The girl was laughing like a maniac and Costa found himself thinking of Randolph Kirk, slaughtered in his grimy little office by a Maenad much like this one, greedy for vengeance over some unseen, unexplained crime. Had the 'god' failed her, and Barbara too in some mysterious way? Was she now more important than him? Or was this simply the last part of an intrinsically inexplicable drama, the fury in which every participant, man and woman, human and mythical, visited the extremes of their imagination?

The simple answer – that the god, and by implication Kirk and his associates, were exploiters of young women – didn't fit this story. There was, Costa realized, some form of reward on both parts, and some kind of revenge if, for whatever reason, the bargain wasn't kept.

He forced himself to stop examining the pictures. They had a hypnotic, openly erotic quality that drew him in, made it hard to think of anything else. Costa scanned the corners, his eyes becoming more used to the shade. There was a door, dimly visible in the shadows beyond the bed. He walked towards it and touched the surface: old, tough wood. It was locked but as he rattled the handle he heard a sound from the other side: a surprised gasp, not far away. And female.

He thought of the night before and the bright blonde head disappearing into the maw of the cave, that repeated again and again in the photographs that covered the walls of the central chamber. Costa drew himself close to the crevice and tried to peer through. The wood wasn't a perfect fit. There was light on the other side, the same dim, faint luminescence as in his own chamber.

'Suzi—' he whispered through the crack. Someone moved on the far side. He heard her breathing.

'Suzi,' he said again, more loudly. 'My name is Nic Costa. I'm a police officer. Please look at the door. See if you can let me in. Let me help you.'

The person on the other side didn't make a sound. He tried to put himself in her shoes: trapped, lost in this labyrinth, not knowing what to do, or who to trust.

'I talked to your mother,' he said in a normal, controlled voice. 'She's worried about you. This will all work out. Trust me. Please.'

He thought he heard a choked sob. Maybe she wasn't alone. Maybe Mickey Neri was there, holding a knife to her throat, trying to work out what to do with the pair of them. Costa hadn't thought about his own fate for a moment. Now he did, something puzzled him. Why had Mickey let him live at all? If Neri just wanted him out of the way he'd surely be dead, or somewhere far from the heart of what was going on.

'Suzi—' he said for one last time.

There was a sound on the other side of the door: a bolt being drawn back.

Costa made a conscious effort to think like a cop again. He needed a weapon. He needed to know where they were, how the hell they could find a way out of this damp, stinking place.

The door didn't move. He heard footsteps receding on the other side.

'It's OK,' he said. He took hold of the handle, turned it and pushed gingerly. The old wood creaked open. On the other side was a room much like the one he'd woken in: small, almost circular, with paintings round the wall, a double bed with a single light bulb above it, and opposite, in the shadows, another door.

She stood against it with her back to him, hair shining under the wan light, shoulders hunched, crying he guessed, most likely terrified.

Nic Costa walked over and put his hands on her shoulders, unable to take his eyes off that bright, gleaming head of hair.

'Suzi—'

She turned suddenly and thrust her face into his chest, threw her arms around him, clenching his back hard with her hands.

He held the taut, slim body, his head beginning to spin, trying to work out why this felt wrong.

Her mouth worked its way to his neck. Warm, damp

lips brushed his skin, a tongue flickered against day-old bristle.

Automatically, his hand went to her head, felt the soft hair, pushed her gently away.

'Suzi—' he said, then was quiet.

It was as if two people had merged into one. Or as if they had never been quite separate in the first place.

Tears starting to stain her cheeks, her face framed by this bright shock of too-young hair, Miranda Julius looked up at him, pleading, drawing him ever closer.

'I'm sorry, Nic,' she said. 'I didn't want you here. I'm sorry.'

'Don't be,' he whispered, and found his hands roaming her shoulders, holding her tight to him, his lips close to her shining head, his eyes locked on the figures dancing over the walls.

Beyond the glass of Leo Falcone's office the Questura buzzed furiously. For once the rival forces of the DIA and the carabinieri were making an effort to work in tandem, sharing information, scouring the streets for any sign of Emilio Neri. The old hood had gone to ground, and it was clear he had done it well. For all Falcone knew he could be out of the country already. The networks of informers used by all three organizations had come up with a few nuggets of information. They told him what he already suspected: the blast outside the house in the Via Giulia was Neri's own work, a parting gift deliberately timed for the arrival of the police. There would be no return. From this point on Neri would hide out abroad, doubtless somewhere he believed the Italian extradition laws would never reach him.

Vergil Wallis sat opposite wearing his long leather overcoat, a brown travel bag on his lap, black face impassive as a rock, and said, 'I'm glad you made time for me in the middle of all this.'

'You seemed to think it was important,' Falcone replied.

'It is.' Wallis opened the bag and took out a digital camera, turned on the screen, and passed it over the table.

'What the hell's that?' Falcone asked.

'Got thrown over my wall at three this morning,' Wallis said. 'With this.' He held up a mobile phone. 'Started the dogs barking. I'm surprised those people you've got outside never saw who did it.'

Falcone screwed up his eyes at the picture on the little screen. 'They're not ours. That was the DIA's job.'

He picked up the camera. Peroni came and stood behind him then swore softly under his breath. The picture was of Nic Costa unconscious, lying on a bed in an anonymous room.

'This is my fault,' Peroni groaned.

Falcone pressed a button. The next picture was of Miranda Julius, her hair dyed the same bright blonde they all now associated with her daughter, scowling at the lens, tied to a chair. Then a third. The lighting was slightly different this time. More harsh. It looked as if the picture had been taken in different circumstances. The face was that of a young girl, with the same blonde hair, looking vacantly into the camera. She too was tied to a chair, but somewhere else.

'That's the missing girl?' Wallis asked.

'Suzi Julius,' Peroni confirmed. 'We got the pictures her mother gave us. It's her.'

The big black figure folded his coat around him as if it were a second skin. 'There's a message too. Play the last thing you find.'

They did. It was a little video of Mickey Neri staring straight into the lens, looking scared as hell, glancing around him as if someone else was giving the orders. Mickey gulped once then said, in a mock tough voice, 'Vergil, you bring what I want at ten. Use the phone. I'll call you and tell you where to collect at seven. At nine I call and tell you where to deliver. You'll know the way. Don't come with anyone else. Don't fuck with me. Do anything other than this and they're dead.'

'For all we know they're dead already,' Peroni murmured.

'Maybe,' Wallis agreed testily. 'I can't tell you one way or the other. This is none of my business. What am I supposed to be here? Some kind of messenger boy? What's going on, huh? Can you tell me that?'

Falcone scanned through the pictures again. 'Did you get the call at seven?'

'On the dot. Sent me round to some private banker out in Paroli. He was waiting. He'd had a call too. Got this packed. As soon as I saw it I knew I was passing it on to you guys.'

Wallis opened the bag. It was full of brand new banknotes, big denominations, still with the ties around them. 'Half a million euros there.'

'Whose?' Peroni demanded.

'Man said it came from some woman called Miranda Julius. She'd ordered it collected overnight. Little guy was petrified. Can't say I blame him. So why am I expected to act the bagman for this woman's ransom money?'

Peroni glanced at Leo Falcone, checking he wasn't going too far. 'The word is Emilio Neri and his boy have fallen out big time. Over what exactly we don't know. This Julius girl, maybe. That's not Emilio's style. It seems pretty clear Mickey's the one who snatched her in the first place. Now he's got our guy too. And the mother. He could use the money. Maybe he wants to give up the life and open a café or something.'

Wallis glared at both of them. 'I'm sorry to hear that. Really. But I'm still asking the same question. What the hell has it got to do with me?'

'You do remember Mickey?' Falcone asked.

Wallis's dark eyes glittered at them. 'OK. Yeah. I remember him. He was a jerk. Just like his father. That still doesn't explain why he should be putting out a call for me to run errands. I'm not dumb. This little punk wants my hide or something.'

'Your hide?' Peroni asked. 'Mr Wallis. Please. You're big time. This is Mickey Neri we're talking about here. You don't honestly believe he's got the nerve to take on the likes of you, do you?'

Peroni watched the American's face. Pride was such a powerful emotion.

'I don't deal with punks like this,' Wallis said in the end.

'So why are you here?' Falcone wondered.

'Just being a good citizen, that's all. You get one of your guys to take this stuff, go run this errand.'

'Won't work,' Peroni said. 'You heard the man. It's you or nothing.'

'You want my help?' There was a touch of disdain in his expression. 'These women have nothing to do with me. This cop's your problem. You hear what I'm saying? *This is not my business.*'

Falcone held up his hands. 'I agree. Besides we have a policy. We don't give in to ransom demands. Even ones as unusual as this.'

Wallis pulled his coat around him, ready to go. 'Then there's nothing else to discuss. You keep the camera. You keep the money.' But he didn't move. Falcone glanced at Peroni and wondered: were they thinking the same thing? Vergil Wallis wanted to do this run. He liked the idea of giving the cops information, probably because Mickey Neri had virtually signed a confession with that stupid piece of video. But something inside Wallis was nagging him to go through with this idea.

Peroni pushed a piece of paper across the table. 'Mickey Neri—'

'Fuck Mickey Neri,' Wallis interjected.

He put a hand lightly on Vergil Wallis's shoulder and Gianni Peroni was amazed to discover something about himself. He found a certain degree of pleasure in pushing this man around a little. He could, if he tried, start to enjoy it.

'Vergil, Vergil,' he said mildly. 'Calm down now. This is your decision, no one else's.'

Wallis picked up the paper and stared at it, his eye drawn to the fancy stamp of the state lab letterhead sprawled across the top.

'We just want you to be informed. That's all.'

They sat on the bed, Miranda Julius next to him, shivering in his arms, wearing little more than a short tee-shirt, huddled under the old, dull coverlet, staring into his face.

'Where is he?' Costa asked.

'I don't know. My door's locked, like yours. I haven't heard anyone there most of the night.'

She held his wrist, turned it and looked at the watch. It was now just after eight. 'He said he'd be back for me around nine thirty.'

'To do what?'

She shook her head. 'I don't know any more.'

Costa thought about the voice he'd heard the night before. 'It was the man you saw in the picture? Mickey Neri?'

She nodded. 'He phoned me last night, Nic. Said he wanted to talk. Said I had to dye my hair like this so that he'd know me. Not that that makes any sense, of course.' Her face went down, close to his chest. 'I just wasn't thinking.'

He looked at the walls again and knew: this was the place, the scene of the photographs, one room of several in Randolph Kirk's seedy subterranean pleasure palace, each with a bed, each with a history. And in one Eleanor Jamieson had surely died.

She put a hand to his head. 'Are you all right? I heard him hit you. It sounded horrible.'

'I'm fine,' he said, and took her hands, looked hard into her frightened eyes. 'Miranda. We need to work out how to get out of here. I don't know what this guy's up to but it isn't good.'

There were so many threads of possibilities running inside his head. He didn't know which was true, which imagination. Neri on the run, fleeing the evidence left at his accountant's. The bomb outside the old hood's house. How in spite of that he'd pressed Peroni so hard to chase the sighting of Suzi even though his colleagues lay stricken and wounded on the ground around him. Was this a kind of treachery? It seemed the right decision at the time. Just now, though, his head refused to clear sufficiently to understand what had happened afterwards.

She took his hands and looked earnestly into his face. 'Listen to me, Nic. He's desperate somehow. He just wants money.'

'How much?' It wasn't the question he wanted to ask.

'Pretty much everything I have. Not that it matters.' She sighed and looked down at the bed. 'I got the impression that perhaps his plans had changed. To be honest with you I don't care. Suzi's alive. I *saw* her. She was here before he threw me into this dump. I just want her free. I'd give everything I've got for that.'

He tried to remember now: perhaps there were two female voices in the darkness last night, before he was struck down.

'Where is she now?'

'I don't know,' she shrugged. 'This place seems to be full of rooms like this. Perhaps he just likes using them. Perhaps—'

Her face darkened and he knew what she was thinking.

'Perhaps it's not just about the money after all,' she continued. 'I don't care so long as I have her back. I had to make some calls back home to organize the money. Maybe he's keeping her somewhere just to make sure I haven't pulled any tricks. She's collateral. If she's lucky. I'm sorry, Nic. I know I should have called. But—'

Her eyes bore into him, blue, unrepentant. 'I knew

what you'd do. You'd turn this into a cop thing. I couldn't take that risk. And it's just money.'

Costa took the phone out of his jacket and looked at the screen again. It was still dead. He stared around the room trying to think of some way to escape.

'We can't get out, Nic,' she whispered. 'I tried. We're here till he comes back. What kind of place is this?'

Her mouth was so close to his neck he could feel her breath, damp, hot, alive. She was shivering against him.

'A kind of temple, maybe?'

'To what?'

He knew that instinctively. They both did. 'To losing it.'

In spite of everything she was calm now in some way he couldn't quite comprehend. Perhaps it was simply knowing that Suzi was alive.

She shivered violently. His arms went round her. Miranda Julius reached down and took out a small silver pill case from her bag then shook two tiny tablets, sugar-coated and red, into her palm.

'I need these,' she said, shaking. Her eyes closed, her white, perfect neck went back. Costa couldn't stop looking at her, feeling her pain and her need, pinioned to the bed by her agonized beauty.

It happened swiftly. She moved fully into his arms. Her slender hand gripped the hair at the nape of his neck. Her mouth closed on his, soft, wet and enticing. He responded. Their lips joined. Her tongue ran beyond his teeth, her hands beginning to tear at his shirt, firing something red and senseless in his imagination.

He thought he heard her whisper his name, then the tongue returned, probing, hard, insistent, finding the deepness in his throat. There was just the hint of something solid on the tip, something that made him swallow and, in the heat of the moment, scarcely notice the act.

Nic Costa closed his eyes, not thinking, letting her hands do their work, rising when he was bidden, feeling her straddle him, panting, demanding, feeling the heat rise between them, drowning out the doubts in his head.

In the fevered stream of his imagination painted figures watched from the walls, eyes bright, gaping mouths laughing, particles of dead, dry dust coming alive, waiting for the ancient siren song to rise in her throat, waiting for the ecstasy to bind them.

At some point afterwards he closed his eyes and slept. When he woke she was quietly singing a line from an old song, one his father possessed among that ancient pile of vinyl back in the farmhouse off the old Appian Way. He recognized it: Grace Slick fronting Jefferson Airplane, all those years ago. Miranda Julius was softly chanting the same refrain over and over again.

'One pill makes you bigger,' she sang in a low, breathy voice that ran through his head like a dream.

'He's offering me *what?*'

Emilio Neri couldn't believe his ears. Maybe he'd misjudged the kid all along. It was now almost eight thirty. He'd just finished breakfast in the cellar of the safe house on the Aventine hill, after the best solitary night's sleep that he could remember in years. Bruno Bucci made the choice. Neri had forgotten he even owned the place. The radio and TV stations were now blurting out his name as the chief culprit for the previous night's bomb blast. One of the newspapers had even put up a reward for anyone who helped track him down.

None of this worried him. Bucci was a good guy. He'd done his homework. He'd paid the right people, sealed the lips of those who might be tempted to go for the main chance. The Albanian mob reckoned they could spirit Neri out of the country late that afternoon. By midnight he'd be in North Africa. In a couple of days he'd find himself in Capetown, ready for a little holiday, in preparation for the trip across the southern Atlantic to his new home. Once he was beyond his native shores no one could touch him. A long line of money would grease his path all the way, from one understanding state to the next.

But now, as luck would have it, a little temptation had got in the way, and Emilio Neri knew the moment he heard it nothing would induce him to walk away from Mickey's offer.

'Tell me again,' he said. 'Just so I know I'm not dreaming.'

Bucci grimaced, unhappy with the idea from the outset. 'If you forgive him, if you let him and Adele live, you can have Wallis on a plate. He just wants some money, that's all. And some guarantees.'

'Guarantees?' Neri waddled around the room, shaking his head. 'Tell you what. Get him back on the phone. Let me talk to the kid. I'll give him guarantees. Why didn't he call me direct anyway? I'm his father, aren't I?'

Bucci shook his head. 'He won't speak with you, boss. He's pissed off with you. Says you expected Toni Martelli to off him last night. Seems to think that was an insult or something.'

'Yeah,' Neri laughed. 'Maybe it was. But Martelli's dead and he's alive. So where's the insult now? How much does he want?'

'A cut of the action.' Bucci said gloomily. 'Ten per cent of everything going forward.'

Neri slapped Bucci cheerfully around the cheeks. 'Hey, don't look so miserable, Bruno. There's plenty to go round. Be realistic. Nothing's ever fixed in stone now, is it?'

'Whatever you want, boss.' Bruno Bucci said that a lot, Neri thought. It could get annoying.

'Did you know anything about this?' he asked. 'Mickey snatching this girl on the side? Be honest now. I'm not pissed off with you.'

Bucci threw back his big shoulders as if it were some kind of insult. 'No. You'd have been the first to know. He's always up to stuff. Stupid little bastard. Why fuck around with crap like that? What's the point?'

'His dick's the point. Some things never change.'

Bucci sighed and gave Neri a knowing look. 'Stupid—'

'Don't be ungrateful, Bruno. When the word gets around about this nonsense you come out looking good. No one wants a lunatic running things. You get the business. I get retired. And that black bastard Vergil Wallis gets dead, which is a good lesson for anyone who thinks they can fuck with this house in the future. Understand?'

'Sure.' He really didn't look happy. 'Look, boss. We made lots of good plans here. I can get you out of the country, no problem. If we start messing around like this, I don't know—'

Neri smiled. 'You can do it.'

'Why not let me or one of the boys handle Wallis? We can see to him.'

'Yeah,' Neri grinned. 'Mickey and Adele too, huh? You think I'm stupid?'

Bucci was silent. Neri patted him on the shoulder. 'Hey, I'd do the same thing myself. Hell, you *will* do it when I'm out of the way. Let's not fool ourselves otherwise. But I got a score to settle with Vergil Wallis. Got some personal questions I'd like answered too. He whacked that little accountant of mine. He gave all them private papers to the DIA. It's thanks to him I get to retire now. I wanna show him a little gratitude. Understand?'

'I understand. But is it worth the risk?'

'Yes,' Neri snapped. 'It's worth the risk. Besides, with you planning things, there *is* no risk. Am I right?'

Bucci looked at him oddly. There was something going on in his head Neri couldn't see. 'Am I right, Bruno?'

'I never asked you for anything, boss. Let me ask now. Just this one thing. Stick to what we've got. No distractions. Just go and enjoy being retired. I'll look after things.'

Neri would have given up on him then, changed his mind completely. But he was too far down the road and Bucci, he guessed, understood that already. 'I'm still running things right now,' Neri snarled. 'You do the fuck what I say. A man's gotta leave a few memories behind him. They got last night. Now they're gonna get Wallis too. That's my legacy, Bruno. Don't fuck with it.'

Bucci grunted something incomprehensible.

'So when do we wrap this up?' Neri demanded. 'Where?'

'He's gonna call us back.'

Emilio Neri thought about his son. And about Adele.

Maybe this was all her doing. Maybe this was her way of convincing Mickey she could set him up for life. What a pair they'd make. She'd be screwing the chauffeur before Christmas.

'You know there's just one thing I don't understand,' Neri said, more to himself than to Bruno Bucci. 'How the hell has Mickey talked Wallis into walking out into the open like that? After all this time? Is he just getting dumb in his old age or what?'

'Maybe he's thinking of retirement too,' Bucci suggested. 'Maybe he wants to even things out.'

Emilio Neri grinned. 'Oh, he's retiring. That's for sure.'

They clutch each other on the cold, damp bed. His too-bright eyes, the pupils now dilated, dart everywhere, to places he doesn't want to see. She watches, face close to his, her breath on his skin, smiling, thinking.

He looks into her eyes and just at that moment, when she's caught him completely, she says, in a new voice, a low voice that seems as if it should belong to someone else, 'Every good deed needs a witness, Nic. Every crime has to meet with some punishment. Without that—'

He's laughing, can't help himself, can't believe the words coming out of his mouth.

Call the cops, he says. *That's what we're here for.*

She slides her slim, taut body onto his chest. Firm fingers grip him, force his eyes to look into hers. Then she turns his head and he looks once more at the shapes on the walls, writhing, laughing, chattering in some unknown language. He closes his eyes. From somewhere deep inside, somewhere he can't discern, comes a voice, rough and cruel, rumbling up from the guts through a crazy mask's bulbous lips.

It says, *Look you fucker look. You got to in the end.*

No. He knows the word never leaves his throat.

Sounds from beyond the wooden door. People. Events. Real, perhaps. Or memories, shadows of the past seeping into the present.

I think, she says, *there was a girl here once. Years ago, but not so distant we ought to forget. A young girl. Others too. But this girl was special.*

Everyone's special, he murmurs. How?

She was beautiful.

Everyone's beautiful. After a fashion.

The rough voice laughs from behind the hidden mask, a sound filled with scorn.

Hot breath enters his ear, a torrent of words that transform into pictures inside his head. He sees them now, forced into his imagination by what he hears and the pulsing elements roaring through his veins. They both have a stiff schoolgirl stance, backs to him, arms behind, fists clenched. Long blonde hair falls over slim shoulders onto sackcloth robes. A garland of flowers hangs around each too-young neck, a smaller one crowns each shining head. Carnations for love, lilies for death. Their smell fills the room, bright and harsh and cloying, with something else beneath it, a narcotic perfume worming its way into every hidden corner of every head.

One figure turns and he sees Barbara Martelli, now sixteen years younger than the woman he never really knew, long locks down to her waist, smiling face full of warmth, pleased to see someone.

Barbara opens her mouth. No sound emerges. She is a gift. He understands that just by looking at her, the way she stands, the way she beckons, and something in Barbara's face seems to say she's aware of this too.

Her slim arms, tanned, still a little chubby from her youth, reach out, seeking a man's touch and the gift it will bring.

Barbara knows, he thinks. Barbara wants.

Miranda's lips, damp and scorching, move against his ear.

She whispers, whispers, *Look*.

A second figure turns and he feels his heart become stone, feels the air disappear from his lungs.

Eleanor Jamieson stands in front of him, alive and smiling, and Miranda is right. She is more beautiful than any of them, not because of how she looks, but from the simple light that shines from her eyes, the naïve, unworldly light of innocence begging to be dimmed because it burns too brightly for the rest. This is her undoing. Men will see this flame, perhaps women too, and want to suck on its power, steal the life from within it, jealous of its intensity. And she understands none of this. She simply smiles, and beckons.

She doesn't know, fuckhead, the old voice croons. *She doesn't have a clue.*

Eleanor Jamieson opens her perfect mouth and smiles.

Her teeth are the colour of mahogany. Her wide, unseeing eyes are pools of black, as deep and as dead as the fetid Tiber.

In her throat something glitters, silver and gold. A coin to pay the ferryman.

Behind her back something moves in the shadows.

*

Vergil Wallis said nothing for a good five minutes after he read the lab report. At his boss's suggestion, Peroni went out for some coffee and to find out if there was any news. The men who had been combing had found nothing. Mickey Neri seemed remarkably well organized.

He came back, discreetly shook his head behind Wallis's hunched figure at the desk, and placed a cup in front of the American. Wallis had the makings of tears in his eyes. He wiped them away with the back of his hand.

'Sorry,' he said eventually. 'You've got a lot of surprises around here right now.'

'Too many,' Falcone replied. 'You had no idea? You never knew she and Mickey were messing around together?'

This was the moment, Peroni realized. Vergil Wallis could stick to his guns, pretend he had pretty much told them the truth all along and just try to brazen the whole thing out. And if that happened then Nic Costa would be dead, along with the Julius woman and her kid. Everything hung on this old crook's decision.

'No,' Wallis answered dolefully. 'I still can't believe it. You'd never have guessed it from seeing them together. Eleanor was smart. A little naïve. Maybe that was why I indulged her from time to time. But she could have walked into any college she liked. The Neri kid was just an oaf. Worse than his father, if that's possible.'

'Maybe that's what she liked,' Peroni suggested, trying to be reasonable with this man because he understood how essential he was to them. 'I have kids. You get to understand these things. A little anyhow. Sometimes they do the opposite of what you want just because it *is* the opposite of what you want. It doesn't mean you can go blaming yourself for what happens next. That's how people are made.'

Wallis nodded. 'True.'

'So,' Peroni continued. 'Now you know this, how about we stop pretending, huh? We know she didn't go missing just off the cuff. And I got to say, Mr Wallis, you must have realized that all along. So let's cut the crap. We got a little time before your appointment. You tell us. What really happened that day?'

'Really?' There was some bitter amusement in Wallis's face. Peroni didn't like what he was seeing. This man just might help them, but he'd never relinquish control, and never fully divulge anything he didn't think necessary. 'I've no idea. That *is* the truth. I swear to it. If I'd known—'

He didn't finish the sentence.

'You'd have killed him?' Peroni suggested. 'Just for screwing around?'

Wallis nodded. 'The person I was then . . . I would have killed him.'

'And now?'

'Now I live in Rome and read my books,' Vergil Wallis said quietly.

He pulled the overcoat tighter around him. 'A man can drown himself in a few illusions if he likes. Is there anything wrong in that?'

Falcone and Peroni exchanged glances. Then Falcone tried to get things back on track.

'Where did you think Eleanor was going that day?'

'To some kind of party. Neri knew what interested me. Knew what interested her too. They were the same things. When we went on vacation together it was just after Eleanor's birthday. Neri said he wanted to give her a gift. A surprise. Something out of the past. I'd given her Kirk's book as a birthday present. She loved the stupid thing, read it all in a couple of days. So I mentioned this to Neri and said, maybe—'

Wallis paused and sighed. 'The next thing I know Neri's fixed a meeting round at his house. Me and him and the Kirk guy, who's all eyes at the idea he might get paid to throw the party of his dreams. If I'd thought about it maybe the alarm bells would have started ringing. I didn't even know what a Dionysian ceremony was. Maybe that was why the Kirk guy kept looking at me, weird, all the time. I just didn't . . . imagine.'

He hesitated over this last point. 'Eleanor knew, of course. Neri's kid must have set her up for the whole thing.'

'Where was this supposed to happen?' Peroni asked.

'I don't know,' Wallis replied. 'I never asked. I could have gone along if I'd wanted. I didn't.'

'Why not?' Peroni wondered.

Wallis glowered at him. 'Watching some young kids dance around in costume? That's what I thought it was. I'd been in Rome long enough to recognize all the tourist shit they try to sell you. They say it's culture. I thought it was just one more turn around the block. If Eleanor wanted it . . . fine. I'd better things to do with my time.'

Peroni shot Falcone a look that said *unconvinced*. 'Did you drive her there?'

'No. She went off on that little bike of hers. Like I said.'

'You really have no idea where she might have gone?'

'None at all. And that's the truth.'

They waited. Wallis wasn't going to give this up to them easily.

Falcone pressed him. 'It's nine in the morning and she's left for this fancy dress party. Is she wearing the clothes we found her in?'

'She had them in a bag. The Kirk guy sent them along with some other stuff.'

'Then what?' Falcone asked.

Wallis closed his eyes for a moment and Peroni felt his heart skip a beat because this could just be the point where the American thought '*no further*'. 'Then nothing. For hours and hours. And I'm busy. I got people to talk to, calls to make. So I don't think twice about it. Not until the evening and then I think . . . she never said when she'd be back. She went out there and she was so excited she didn't even care about what time it all ended.'

'Then you call Emilio Neri, right?' Peroni could work this through for himself. It was what you did as a father. Not approach the kids direct, even if you could find them. That was wrong. That was *uncool*. You phoned their dads and said, look, man to man . . .

'Eventually, Neri calls me.' Wallis shook his head. 'I never touched dope. Sold plenty. I never thought about it. It wasn't anything that came near me. It never affected anyone I loved, not even back in the old days when I was just some black punk on the street. Dope just existed. It was a utility for us. Like water or electricity.'

'Pretty lucrative utility, Mr Wallis,' Peroni observed. 'Bought you that nice house on the hill.'

'Bought me part of that nice house. Not as much as you think.'

'Does that hurt? Now you realize the kid got burned by dope?'

For a moment Peroni thought Vergil Wallis might take one of those big black fists out of the pocket of his leather overcoat and smack him with it.

'But she wasn't, was she?' Wallis replied calmly. 'Someone cut her throat. Neri said it was dope. He acted like he was furious too. Said he came in on the thing and found the kids had been popping stuff on the side, and even the professor guy never knew it was that bad. He said—'

Vergil Wallis could have been a good actor, Peroni thought. Or maybe he did feel this cut up after all these years.

'There'd been an accident,' Wallis continued. 'Eleanor had overdosed on some bad crack one of the kids – not Mickey – had smuggled into the party. She'd gone into a coma. They'd called a doctor they knew. They'd tried everything. She was dead. Nothing they could do.'

'Then what?'

Wallis stared at his long black hands. He hunched up inside the coat looking as miserable as any man Gianni Peroni had ever seen. 'For an hour or two I went crazy. Went round smashing things. Beating up on anyone I could find. Trying to find someone else to blame.'

'You blame yourself,' Peroni said instantly, and found, against his wishes, some feelings of sympathy rising inside himself. 'That's how it works.'

'That's how it works.'

'But after,' Peroni continued, 'when you stop feeling quite so mad, what do you do? Go to the cops? No. Because you're a crook, Mr Wallis. And crooks don't go to the cops. We'd start asking where that dope came from. We'd start asking all kinds of stuff.'

Wallis nodded and didn't say a word.

Peroni thought about this. 'And those bosses of yours back home wouldn't be none too pleased I guess. All the same, I'd want to see the body. Didn't you want to see the body?'

'Seen a lot of bodies in my time, mister,' Vergil Wallis murmured. 'That's one I didn't want coming back to haunt me at nights. I just told Neri to get on with it. He'd offed the kid he said brought in the dope. Or so he claimed. I just went back into my shell. And I remembered.' The black eyes flashed at both of them. 'I remember well.'

'Dope.' Peroni hated working drugs. Everything got so unpredictable. 'Once you walk into that place it all gets so messy. Who's to say that wasn't what killed her, really? That it wasn't little Mickey out of his head thinking he was the love god come to call? And getting all cut up or something when she says no, and by the by, Mickey, I'm carrying a little present for you?'

Wallis pushed his big fists deeper into the overcoat. 'What is it you want of me? There's nothing I can do to bring her back.'

Peroni bridled at that. 'There are two women and a cop you could help bring back, Mr Wallis.'

'Why me?'

'Mickey Neri says you know the way,' Falcone reminded him. 'Do you?'

'I have no idea what the hell he's talking about. All I can guess is what you can guess. He wants me there for my hide. I'd need a damn good reason to lay it on the line for people I don't even know.'

Falcone glanced at the clock on the wall. It was two minutes to nine. 'You might get to find out who really killed her. Isn't that enough? Isn't that the lure Mickey's really dangling in your face? Also, you get me and half the cops in Rome behind you. We quit chasing bombers, quit chasing street thieves and dope dealers, pimps and murderers, and try to save your lying ass instead. The choice is yours, Mr Wallis. But if I have to pick up any more dead bodies at the end of this, your cosy sweetheart deal with the DIA goes out of the window. I don't see you sitting comfortably in that house of yours on the hill for much longer now. Do you?'

Wallis grimaced. 'Is that a deal you're offering me? Play ball and you stay off my back?'

Peroni was quietly whistling through his teeth, looking livid.

'If that's the way you care to see it,' Falcone replied.

'And you think you're good enough to keep me alive? All the dead bodies I've seen on the news this past couple of days don't give me much in the way of optimism.'

Falcone shrugged. 'Take it or leave it. Either way we're pulling away all those people from your gate. The DIA don't do security. Who do you think's going to guard your back then? Your golf buddies have got to go home some time. Neri's people aren't going away. And they want blood over that accountant, I imagine. Thanks for the gift, by the way.'

Vergil Wallis leaned over the desk and pointed a long black finger in Falcone's direction. 'Listen to me, man. I didn't touch Neri's accountant. I'm retired. OK?'

Then he fell back into his chair and closed his eyes, waiting.

Bang on the minute – Mickey Neri was punctual – the phone rang. The two men watched Vergil Wallis. He waited, just long enough to make them nervous, then picked up the handset.

Wallis hit the button and barked, 'Speak.'

He listened. It didn't last long.

'Well?' Falcone demanded.

Wallis reached inside his coat and pulled out a piece, a silver pistol, nice and shiny, of a kind neither cop recognized. 'You're not thinking of taking this off me now?'

'My,' Peroni observed. 'The things retired people carry around with them these days. Does that get covered by the state pension or what?'

Wallis opened the bag and dropped the gun inside. 'Front steps of San Giovanni. Twenty-five minutes. I want Mr Sweet Talk here to drive. I hear he played boss class once. Don't want any amateurs stepping on my toes.'

Mickey Neri sniffed in the dead air of the caverns and wished he had the courage to walk outside, out into good daylight, away from the mess he was in. That wasn't possible. Adele had made him place the calls. She said they had no choice. They needed money. They needed his father to give them the chance to start again, free of his anger. So they just sat in one of the chambers in this stinking, dark maze, trying not to bitch at one another. Mickey just couldn't work out the geography of the place. Adele walked around as if she knew every last corner, every last twist and turn. It pissed him off. He thought he was going to end up in charge. He was grateful for what she'd done at Toni Martelli's. But he'd have killed the old bastard without her help . . . in the end.

If it worked out now they'd get some money, some

kind of reconciliation, and they would earn the old man's thanks. Mickey knew his father well. Gratitude was one thing that did count with the old man. Emilio had his faults but he had a thing about fairness, a thing that was almost a virtue. If he and Adele could deliver Vergil Wallis's head on a plate, then it was possible – just – that everything else could be forgiven. Or if not forgiven, forgotten. These were, as Adele was swift to point out, changed times. Emilio Neri couldn't go back to being a resident Rome hood, not after felling a bunch of cops with a bomb. His power was failing him. But the cops couldn't touch Mickey with any of this. He could stick around, live off the cream of the estate. With or without Adele in tow – he hadn't decided on that one yet.

It all hinged on Vergil Wallis showing up. Without him, Mickey thought, they were both dead. And that thought didn't leave him any the happier. If he were the big black crook up on the hill, trying to look respectable for all the world, the last thing he'd do would be to run an errand to his worst enemy. It made no sense.

'What if Wallis don't turn up?' he asked.

'He will.'

'Why are you so sure?'

'You don't understand anything, do you?' she snapped. 'These are serious men. Maybe they do end up trying to kill each other. Maybe that would be good for us. But men like this talk, even in the middle of a war. They have to understand how everything lies, if there's some middle ground between them. Wallis wants this settled just as much as Emilio. And also—' She gave him that frank look, the one that went right through him. 'I imagine he wants to know what happened back then. Don't you?'

'Why ask me?' he demanded. 'Never even knew the stuck-up little kid. Never even touched her.'

'No?' She didn't sound convinced.

'No. Anyway, that was years ago. It's time people started thinking about now, not what happened way back.'

She laughed, shook her sleek, perfect hair and gave him the same kind of look his father wore so often. One that said: *don't be so dumb*. 'That's what happens when you get older, Mickey. You don't have so much future ahead of you. It's the past that gets more real.'

'What do you know? You've only got a year or two on me.'

'Guess I grew up more,' she said, watching him reach for his cigarettes. 'Don't light that.'

'Why not?'

'Because if all this goes bad someone's going to be shooting in the dark. Think, for once in your life. It's easier to aim at a smell.'

He swore and threw the pack onto the floor. 'And if it goes well? What then?'

She moved close to him, smiling, and placed a slender hand against his chest, toying with the buttons on his shirt, a gesture he knew was mocking him somehow. 'Then we get to inherit everything. You and me. We can make a couple. Can't we?'

'Yeah.' He could hear the uncertainty in his own voice. He was trying to stay on top of things. It wasn't easy. 'What's the cop doing here now, Adele? And that woman too? What do we do with them?'

She shrugged, playing with his collar. 'You don't have anything to worry about except your old man. Leave the rest of them to me.'

'What? This guy's a cop. If they think I whacked him they'll never leave me alone. I want this shit over when we get out of here. I want to be free of all this crap.'

'Mickey,' she said firmly. 'When I say this isn't your problem, I mean it.'

He tried to laugh but it didn't ring true. 'So you're the boss? You're going to take on Emilio and that Bucci animal all on your own? There's just the two of us. How's that gonna happen?'

She just smiled and it wasn't a smile he recognized. He wasn't sure he really knew this woman any more.

'You don't need to worry about Bruno. I screwed him before I screwed you.'

Mickey Neri suddenly felt dead stupid. 'Really?' He didn't know what to think, except that it offended him. 'That's nice.'

The cold eyes blinked then stared into him. 'Yes. Nice. I did it just the once. That was all it needed. Thanks to that I got a little warning about what was going on in Emilio's sick head when he found out about us last night. Thanks to that I knew enough to get out of the damn house before he blew it to pieces, and to save your pathetic ass. It means we stay alive and Bruno gets to prosper too. That's called diplomacy, Mickey. It's a skill you have to learn. Bruno knows he doesn't have what it takes to run a family. There'd be a war within months and he'd lose. He's a number two. He's smart enough to realize that.'

'That's good,' he said. 'So long as it stays that way he's got nothing to worry about.'

'No.' She was mocking him and he couldn't do a damn thing about it. Not yet anyway.

Some time the previous day Adele had put some blonde stuff on her hair, mixing it over the red. It was more noticeable under the yellow light of the caves. It made her look different. More classy somehow. And younger.

'You coloured your hair,' he said, and reached to stroke it, thinking that maybe there was time to fit something in. Maybe this damp, stinking place in the earth was just the place for it. She could go down on him maybe. They could even stay in this little room and fuck. 'I like it.'

She snatched his hand away. 'I didn't colour it, you moron. This is what it's meant to be like. And don't touch me, Mickey. Not without my say-so.'

He tried to think back over the years. She was right. She did used to be blonde. It just didn't last too long for some reason. 'Why not?'

The green eyes were so hard now, full of something not far from hate. 'You need to learn what "no" means. You might as well start now.'

She hesitated. She looked a little nervous just then and he couldn't work out whether this was good or bad.

'Do you remember what I told you?' she asked. 'Can I rely on you, Mickey?'

'Yeah. Just don't fuck around with me afterwards.'

Her skinny hand came up and touched his cheek. 'No,' she said, smiling.

'Adele?' She was walking out of the room, without another word. '*Adele?*'

She stopped in the shadow of the open door and blew him a kiss.

'You've got to cope with this on your own now, Mickey,' she said. 'I've got other things to do.'

Teresa Lupo went back to her office with Gianni Peroni's words ringing happily in her head. A little praise went a long way. Her thoughts were beginning to clear a little too. The vicious cold virus in her head was in retreat from a bombardment of aspirin, and with its abatement came some clarity. She'd found the change of clothing she kept in the office, showered, and now felt fresh and clean. Her hair was combed and back in the businesslike crop. If she peered in the mirror – which she didn't plan to do – she guessed her eyes wouldn't even be that bloodshot any more. The mood was a touch infectious. Monkboy had recovered some of his composure too when the report from the lab came through. It had confirmed what Teresa, in her heart, already knew. The paternity of the tiny preserved foetus she'd recovered from Eleanor Jamieson's corpse may have been more about morale than closure. No one had any idea where the Neris had fled overnight. But morale mattered. Maybe everyone was still walking in the dark but at least they had a spring in their step.

One thing continued to bug her. She would have saved everyone so much grief if only she'd carried out a conventional autopsy when the body from the bog arrived. This was a lapse in judgement and it bothered her. If she could fail once, she could fail again. How many other oversights lay around her now in this over-crowded haven for the dead? Gianni Peroni's point, brought home with that sudden, unexpected kiss, was a good one. In times like these it was all about priorities, looking closely under a handful of promising stones, not trying to steal a quick glance at everything. She hadn't focused enough. Most of all, she hadn't focused on Professor Randolph Kirk, which was odd given that he represented the sole customer in her career who had fallen into her care, so to speak, within earshot. Everything was about connections. It had been all along. If she could just find the right one it would all fall into place.

Silvio Di Capua wandered in from the corridor. He looked into her smiling face with a frightened devotion that threatened to bring the black clouds of depression straight back.

'Silvio, my man,' she said, her voice still husky from the cold. 'Tell me about the good professor. What news of him?'

'News?' he replied, bemused. 'He got shot. What news do you want?'

'Oh, how he feels about the whole thing. Who he wants to call.'

He did call someone. The memory, which was less than two days old, now seemed shockingly distant. Randolph Kirk called someone and all hell started to break loose straight afterwards. The conventional thinking around this place, she reminded herself, was that Eleanor Jamieson was the Pandora *du jour*. It was her ossified corpse that summoned the four riders from wherever else in the world they'd been, whipping up a little apocalypse for tea.

'Up to a point,' she said to herself.

Monkboy looked a little scared again. 'What?'

'It was Randolph Kirk.' She recalled that disgusting habit he had with his nose. 'Booger Bill. *He* started this crap off. With a little help from me, of course. Bog girl had been out of the ground for two weeks up till then, and nothing whatsoever had happened.'

Silvio Di Capua blinked then performed a polished impersonation of a terrified rabbit. 'Lots of work to do, Teresa. Nice routine stuff. You've already given the boys next door a present to get along with. From what I hear there's plenty more to occupy them besides.'

Her ears pricked up at the scent of gossip. 'Plenty more what?'

He didn't say a word.

She picked up a pair of scissors and snapped them open and shut a couple of times. 'Speak, Silvio, before I am filled with the urge to snip a testicular sac or two.'

He gulped. 'I heard one of the guys talking down the way. He says this mobster's son's straight in the frame now, even without the paternity stuff. Seems he's trying to get himself a little holiday money by holding them to ransom.'

'Them?' She didn't understand. 'He's only got Suzi Julius.'

He swallowed hard. 'Not any more. Seems he's got the mother too.' He hesitated and dropped his voice to a whisper. 'And a cop.'

Something black turned in her head. She advanced on Di Capua still holding the scissors. 'What cop?' she demanded.

'That guy you like,' he said feebly. 'Costa. God knows how. Or where. But they've got a picture of him and the mother tied up somewhere.'

'*Nic?*' she screeched. 'Oh shit. What are we doing—?'

She was looking round the morgue, mentally counting all their options. 'Let's think this through.'

Silvio Di Capua drew himself up to his full height, which was still a good measure below hers, and yelled, '*No!* Don't you get it? I don't want to fucking think this through! It's not why we're here!'

She'd never made him this mad before. Perhaps that was a failing on her part. This newly assertive Silvio Di Capua seemed a little more human somehow.

'And for God's sake, Teresa, stop saying "we".' He calmed down a little now. 'They are cops. We are pathologists. Different jobs. Different buildings. Why don't you get that?'

'Because Nic Costa's my friend.'

'Good for you. He's their friend too, isn't he? Don't they get the chance to be heroes sometimes? While we settle down to a nice routine of cut and stitch and let things run their natural course?'

'Natural course?' Her voice was a touch too loud. She was aware of this but it didn't help somehow. 'Have you been following the events of the last couple of days, Silvio? What the fuck is natural about any of this? Also—'

'*No, no, no* . . .' His head was down, bald scalp shining under the harsh morgue lights, long hair, even more lank than normal, unwashed for days, revolving around his podgy little shoulders.

Monkboy's miserable face rose to greet hers. 'Promise me, Teresa. Promise me you won't go anywhere this time. Promise me you won't set foot outside this place. Falcone's handling this kidnapping crap himself. It involves ransoms and money and surveillance and all those things we know nothing about. Let's stick to what we do for a living, huh? Just for a change. You shouldn't be involved in these things. If you'd been here more we wouldn't be in this shit in the first place.'

'You sound like one of them,' she said.

His flabby cheeks sagged as if they'd been slapped. 'Maybe. But it's true.'

'I know that. It's just—' How did she explain this? There was something irredeemably personal about what had happened two days before. It wasn't just her own near-death. The memory of Randolph Kirk, Booger Bill, nagged at her. He'd died in her presence, his rustling shade had somehow whistled past her, too busy to say goodbye.

After he called someone.

Booger Bill. Mister No-Friends, whose personal habits surely precluded closeness of any kind, except when wearing a mask and dealing with doped-up juveniles.

She looked at Monkboy. 'Didn't you find *anything* useful in Kirk's pockets? An address book or something? A note with some numbers on it?'

'No,' he said sulkily. 'And before you ask – yes, I looked.'

She bunched up her sizeable arms, folded them on her chest and began to walk. 'Everyone's got to write things down from time to time,' she said, moving briskly across the morgue, towards the storage drawers, Monkboy in her wake, whining every inch of the way.

Teresa Lupo found the one with Kirk's name on it and pulled the handle, listening to the familiar sliding noise, steeling her nose for the inevitable rush of chemical odour that always followed.

'What are you doing?' Monkboy moaned. 'We've finished with him. We got a whole load of others standing in line.'

'Well tell them they can wait.'

Randolph Kirk looked pretty much like any other dead person post-autopsy. Stiff, pale and somewhat messed around. Monkboy never was any good with a needle and thread.

She took a long, professional look at the cadaver in front of them, and picked up each dead wrist in turn. 'Has he been washed?'

'Sure!' Monkboy answered. 'And I gave him a manicure and dental floss too. What do *you* think?'

'Just wondered.'

'Wondered what?'

She was starting to get annoyed with him now and didn't mind if it showed. 'Wondered, as it happened, whether he'd got around to scribbling something on his hands or his wrists. Something like a phone number. Disorganized people do that kind of thing. Or am I not supposed to know that? Doesn't it fit the fucking job description?'

'Yes,' he answered mutely. 'Sorry.'

She went back to the desk, retrieved her notes from the previous day and called Regina Morrison, heard the surprise at the end of the line.

'You have the time to call me?' said the dry Edinburgh voice. 'I'm amazed. Things can't be as busy as the newspapers say.'

'Oh but they are,' she snapped. 'Busier, actually. Now can you tell me please, Regina? Did Randolph Kirk keep some kind of personal address book at the college? Did you pick that up on your rounds?'

There was a pause on the end of the line. Teresa had remembered enough to pronounce the woman's name correctly. That wasn't enough, though. She wanted some deference, and right then there just wasn't the time. 'No. So this isn't a social call?'

'What about a pocket diary? Did you see him use something like that? One of those electronic organizers perhaps?'

A long sigh made its way out of the earpiece. 'Clearly you didn't spend enough time in Randolph's company to gain a true picture of the man. That was the most messed-up, technologically challenged disaster of a human being I ever met. I wouldn't trust him in the company of a toaster.'

'Damn. So you're saying he just kept it all in his head?'

'All what? He didn't know anyone.'

But he did. He had to. He made a call and then the crap hit the fan. Except it couldn't be like that. The crap had to be on its way already. All she'd done was accelerate it a touch, speed up the machine a little. Nevertheless, *he made a call*.

She slammed down the phone, aware that Regina Morrison was, to her astonishment, uttering noises that sounded very like an offer of dinner.

'What is wrong with these people?' she wondered out loud.

She walked back over and stared at the corpse of Randolph Kirk, wishing she could wake him up for one minute and ask a few simple questions.

Her head was back in Kirk's office now, watching him work at his nose with that disgusting piece of cloth.

'Booger Bill, Booger Bill,' she whispered to herself, aware that Monkboy looked ready to call in the men from the funny farm at any moment. 'Never in my life have I seen a handkerchief in that condition, not even in the middle of a flu epidemic. Not even—'

Monkboy watched her, petrified. 'You're not leaving this room,' he warned. 'I will lock that door, I will swaddle you in bandages I swear—'

'Oh my God,' she gasped, then foxed him altogether. She was smiling, beatifically.

'Please—' he whined.

'His clothes, Silvio. I want them. Now.'

They are dressed, moving, through the door, out into the cold and the caves, his legs as heavy as lead, detached from his control. She has to help him round this baffling labyrinth of tunnels, stumbling in and out of the yellow pools of light cast by the random bulbs that hang from the ceiling.

Stay in the shadows, he says. *Until I tell you.*

They enter another room and she holds him, keeping them both close to the wall, in the darkness. It's a large chamber, one he remembers, well lit in the centre. He notices now that there is a table at its centre, dusty, with rickety chairs, maybe as many as twelve. An ancient wand – his head searches for the name Teresa Lupo gave it, thyrsus – lies at one end, in front of a chair that is high-backed and grander than the rest. A theatrical mask, with the familiar gaping mouth and dreadlocks, sits next to it, black-eyed, a dead totem, waiting to be reanimated.

The walls are what he recollects best from the night before. Picture upon picture, blonde on blonde, the same shining colour as Miranda's hair now. Suzi Julius and Eleanor Jamieson, young and innocent, laughing for the camera, thinking they'd live forever. They haunt the room like ghostly, incandescent twins, their glittering eyes following everything.

Miranda Julius darts into the light and picks up the thyrsus, waves it in the air. Specks of dust dance in the yellow light. The smell of ancient fennel, faintly sweet, reaches his nostrils.

She replaces the wand, returns and looks at him. There are voices, distant ones. This curling, twisting tangle of caverns could encompass scores of chambers. He tries to think for both of them.

Her hand is on his arm. Her eyes are bright orbs alight in his face.

There is a dark alcove set back from the table. He pulls her further into the shadows and the effort makes his head hurt, his breath comes in snatched pants.

He takes her face in his hands. His head's starting to clear now. He can hear his own voice and it's real.

'Miranda. The best thing we can do is find a way out of here. Find some help and come back for Suzi.'

There's such fear in her face. She embraces him, her hands reach behind his back for something unseen, her head moves to the back of his neck, lips bite hard on the skin there. She's moving, pressing herself now to his lips. She lunges forward, kisses him, thrusts herself into his mouth, probing, probing, feeling the softness. And this time he is certain. A tiny object rides the tip of her long, strong tongue until it reaches the back of his throat. He gags, begins to fall and a voice somewhere in his head sings, *one pill makes you bigger.*

He opens his eyes and sees her lips moving to the words as she holds him, blocking his mouth with his fingers until he swallows.

*

Silvio Di Capua looked at the object on the table, shivered then let out a long, pained groan. It was Randolph Kirk's handkerchief, a piece of once-white pristine fabric now crumpled into a compact ball held tightly together by a random collection of solidified green and grey gloops.

'Don't turn squeamish on me, Silvio,' she said. 'Scalpel?'

'Oh come on,' he complained. 'You want me to find you a surgical mask too?'

Teresa Lupo gave him the extra cold look, the one she saved for special occasions. 'Wouldn't be a bad idea, would it?'

He grumbled and passed her the instrument. 'This is insane. This is the most insane thing I have seen in these recent insane times.'

'Booger Bill wrote those numbers down somewhere,' she insisted. 'It wasn't on the back of his hand. It wasn't on the cuffs of his shirt. And there was more stuff on this damn hankie than mere snotballs. It was only my natural reticence that stopped me remembering this before.'

She could swear he stamped his little feet on the tiles at that. 'Teresa! There's something creepy about this need of yours to please. Even if you're right we shouldn't be doing this. We should be handing it over to forensic.'

'This is human snot, Silvio. *Our* territory.'

'Excuse my pointing this out but we are not looking for snot. Snot we have by the bucket. We are looking for some phone number this weird, dead bastard has thoughtfully written down, hopefully in indelible ink, in between the snot. Which, all things taken into consideration, is both a very strange thing to do and indubitably a job for forensic.'

She found a point of entry and began to ease the fabric, holding down one end with the gloved fingers of her left hand. 'If you'd met Professor Randolph Kirk in the flesh you wouldn't be saying that. You'd think it the most normal thing in the world, as normal as—'

An entire corner of the fabric fell over under the pressure of the blunt side of the blade.

'I did surgery once, Silvio,' she said proudly.

'On a hankie?'

'Adaptability, my man. We live in modern times. Adaptability is everything. Behold . . .'

There were numbers there. Six of them, written in a tiny, cramped hand, mostly so old the ink was blurring into the fabric. One she recognized straight away. It was Regina Morrison's. This really was his address book. She hated to think what the rest were. A dry cleaners? Did Randolph Kirk even grace such an establishment?

But one was more promising. The ink was fresh, the strokes of his spidery hand unblemished. This number had never gone through the wash like the others. Maybe, she thought, written just a day or two before he died.

'Gimme that report,' she ordered.

He clutched the thing to his chest. 'This is not right. Not right at all. We should just pass this information on to the people who need it and let them decide what it's worth. It isn't our job—'

The ferocity of her gaze stopped him dead.

'Silvio, if you tell me one more time what my job is I will, I swear, fire you and fire you good. In case you hadn't noticed, those lovely policemen out there are busy chasing all the big things they like to think of as their prey. People who plant bombs. People who kill and kidnap other people. Were I to walk into their midst bearing a hankie, albeit one of more than minor interest, I would be inviting their ridicule. Who knows? They might even invent a name for me. What do you think? Crazy Teresa? How does that sound, huh?'

He swallowed noisily and said nothing.

'Gimme.'

He passed it over. She scanned the numbers that came with the report Monkboy had purloined from the Questura that same morning, counting off the names.

'Neri's home. Neri's mobile. Mickey's mobile. That office they keep down near the station, Barbara Martelli . . . *shit!*'

'Probably his aromatherapist.'

'Shut up!'

'Teresa! Give it to the cops. They just type it into their computer and up pops a name.'

'You are so naïve,' she hissed. 'So very, very naïve.'

Then her eyes fell on the pad of paper next to his list. Her own notes from the past couple of days, starting from the morning, just forty-eight hours before, when she'd planned to unveil to the world Rome's newest archaeological asset, a two-millennia-old bog body.

'Different lifetime,' she whispered. 'Different—'

She stared at the paper, unable to believe what she saw.

'Teresa?'

There was no mistake. It was impossible but it had to be true, and what it meant for everything was quite beyond her. She needed to see Falcone, immediately, needed to pass the whole damn thing straight over to him, retire to a quiet corner bar somewhere and drown her wildest thoughts in drink.

'Where's the darling inspector?' she asked. 'I am filled with an urgent desire to speak with him.'

'Went out fifteen minutes ago, mob-handed and ready for action. Got tons of people with him. Busy man.'

'Hmm.' Her mind was racing. Nic Costa was out there somewhere, wrapped up deep in all this shit. There was no time for niceties. 'Do you still come to work on that little motorbike, Silvio?'

'Sure but what the fu—' His pale cheeks flared with a sudden rush of blood. '*Oh no, no, no, no, no . . .*'

She gripped him by the collar of his white medical jacket and jerked so hard that his face was just a couple of inches away from hers.

'Gimme the keys now. I've got to talk to Falcone.'

He pulled himself back, folded his podgy arms to give himself a little dignity and displayed as much hurt as his featureless face could manage. 'You want to take my motorbike and catch up with Falcone to talk to him? That's it, isn't it?'

'Yes, Silvio,' she said calmly. 'That's it.'

'OK,' he said very slowly. 'Here's the deal. Do you know what this is?'

She looked at what he was holding and realized he had a point.

'This,' said Silvio Di Capua, 'is what we earthlings call a phone.'

The tunnel ran beneath the Quirinale Palace, cut straight through rock, four hundred metres, built originally for tram cars, now choked by traffic trying to short-cut the hill above. Big tourist coaches were double parked on the Piazza di Spagna side to dump their contents for the short walk to the Trevi Fountain. Construction lorries working on the endless repairs in the Via Nazionale habitually blocked the opposite end. It was, in theory, the easiest way from the Questura to most points east. Falcone had dictated this was the route to take, Peroni with Wallis in front, the cover cars following some discreet distance behind.

Peroni didn't feel at home. He slunk behind the wheel wishing someone else had picked the short straw. This was so far from vice, so distant from the world he knew, he felt like an interloper, just waiting to make some stupid mistake.

They drove straight into the tunnel and hit the jam a third from the end. He banged on the wheel then looked in the mirror. Falcone and the back-up cars were nowhere to be seen. Maybe they'd made it in before the traffic fouled up. Maybe not.

Wallis, mute and expressionless in the passenger seat, took the phone out of his pocket and stared at the little screen. 'Not much use in here.' He tapped the mike wired behind the lapel of his leather coat. 'This isn't either.'

Peroni eyed the man in the adjoining seat and wished he could shake off the idea that something, somewhere was deeply wrong. 'So, Vergil,' he said amicably. 'Here's an opportunity for the both of us. Get this off your chest, man. You can tell me what's really going down here and nobody but the two of us gets to know.'

Wallis peered at him imperiously. 'You're a very suspicious human being. I'm doing you a big favour. A measure of trust wouldn't go amiss.'

Peroni shot him a filthy look. 'Trust. Excuse me, *Mr* Wallis but I don't buy this retirement story. I didn't when that poor bitch Rachele D'Amato spun it for me. I didn't when I met you. Leopards don't change their spots. Crooks don't do the cops favours. Come on. I got a friend involved in this. Level with me.'

Wallis took a deep breath and looked up at the grimy roof of the tunnel. The air in the car was disgusting, just a thin stream of oxygen fighting to get through the clouds of carbon monoxide getting pumped out by the jam around them.

'You know what's up there?'

'Changing the subject? Understandable I guess. Yeah. Mr President in his pretty palace. Don't you just love him? I used to work guard duty at the Quirinale when I wore short pants.'

Wallis gave him a condescending glance. 'Interesting. I meant historically.'

'Oh. Excuse me. I'm Italian. What the hell would I know about history?'

'That's where the Sabines lived. You remember the story? It had rape in it. Gives the thing some modern currency.'

Peroni did remember that story vaguely. It was important. Romulus or Remus, one or the other, stole some women and had to get their act together to clean up afterwards. And out of that mess – out of rape and murder – came Rome. 'They lived up there? I thought they came from miles away. I thought they were like foreigners or something.'

'Up there,' Wallis replied, pointing again. 'But that's an interesting reaction, you know. Maybe we like to deal with bad memories that way. By thinking that the only people who got affected were from some place else, a long way away. It makes everything so much easier.'

'You can say that again.' There was a gap in the traffic out in the daylight ahead. They'd be gone soon. 'You know, I kind of admire you for knowing so much about history and stuff. When you grow up on top of it you tend not to notice things. I still don't understand why, though.'

'Why?' Vergil Wallis shook his head and actually laughed. It was a pleasant sound. It even made Gianni Peroni feel a little less jumpy. 'Because it's Rome. It's where we all came from, in a way. It's about how good things can be. And how bad if we choose to make them that way.'

'Really?' Peroni got ready to kick the car into gear.

'Really.'

'You know,' Wallis said in that low, calm drawl of his. 'I enjoy talking to you. I think that, in different circumstances, we could maybe have a mutually enlightening conversation.'

'Point taken, point taken.' The idiot up ahead was slow to get moving. Peroni fell angrily on the horn. 'All the same, Vergil. I still think you're a lying sonofabitch.'

'That's your privilege. Tell me. Whatever happens now you've got Neri and the kid anyway, haven't you? You know the old man planted that bomb. Now I gave you that camera, you got Mickey too. They're finished whatever.'

'True.' Peroni found his attention split. Between the gap opening up in the traffic ahead and the sudden loop in Wallis's conversation.

'So what if the two of us cut a deal? You just give me a spare thirty minutes dealing with this asshole in my own way. After that I call and you get to come in and do what you want.'

Peroni looked at him and knew at that moment he wasn't driving this black hood anywhere except back to meet Falcone. Something was getting played here he didn't understand.

Wallis put a large, firm hand on his arm. 'Peroni,' he said. 'I got your number, man. I know what happened a couple of months ago.'

'You do?'

Peroni thought about that and wished he'd had more time to go through the details back in the Questura. Nic had gone missing some time before midnight. Vergil Wallis had picked up half a million euros less than eight hours later. What kind of 'private banker' did Miranda Julius use? Who on earth had that kind of money lying around ready to be bundled up in a bag at a moment's notice?

'I heard you got busted down from on high,' Wallis said. 'Why'd you think I picked you for this job? It says two things to me. You're a man who's open to ideas. Plus you could use the cash.'

Peroni noted the growing gap in the traffic ahead and wondered how quickly he could make a U-turn. 'You disappoint me, Vergil. You are a very, very bad judge of character. Best we turn around right now and go through this whole thing again with Inspector Falcone, only in a little more detail and leaving out the lying parts.'

There was enough room, if only the idiot in front would pull forward enough to let him make the turn.

'An honest cop,' Wallis said, nodding his imposing black head. 'Who'd have thought it? I admire that, though. And it's because I do I'm not gonna hit you as hard as I might otherwise.'

Peroni wasn't sure he heard that last one right. He took his foot off the pedal, screwed up his face and said, 'What?'

When he opened his eyes a big black fist was coming towards him, fast, so fast he could do nothing but watch and wait as it crashed straight into his right eye.

It got a little fuzzy after that. Huge hands moved around him. The belt got unbuckled. Vergil Wallis's collar mike got torn off and thrown onto the floor. A big foot came across and kicked open the driver's door. Then a pair of arms came beneath his body and hurled him out of the car.

He fell on the filthy road with a crack, took one breath of the stinking air and started to cough.

The unmarked police car was doing a U-turn into the tunnel, now facing a clear run back into the city, headed anywhere but San Giovanni. And – Gianni Peroni would remember this for a long time he told himself – he'd be damned if the grinning black figure behind the wheel wasn't waving goodbye.

She whispers and, through the chemical fire that rages in his head, he sees.

The thyrsus sits in the same place, now green and vivid, coloured ribbons round its shaft, beneath the bulbous priapic head. The lights are brighter. Men, middle-aged, stiff in their movements, conspiratorial in their shared glances, move beneath them. There are glasses in their hands, brimming with purple wine. A couple smoke, long, hand-made roll-ups that send blue-grey smoke rolling up to the rocky ceiling. They talk among one another: Emilio Neri, the little accountant Vercillo, Randolph Kirk and Toni Martelli, others who are just faces half hidden in the shadows.

Mickey lurks behind them, miserable, uncomfortable, unsure of where he belongs.

They talk and talk and now Nic Costa understands why. These men, powerful men, influential men, are nervous. This is something new for them. An experiment, a break with convention. They look at Randolph Kirk and their eyes say everything: *make this work or else*.

Randolph Kirk knows this. He's more nervous than the rest, almost twitching with anticipation. He speaks but his words are inaudible. He claps his hands and, though they make no sound, the men stop talking and look. A line of young figures gathers at the door. Girls in sackcloth shifts, flowers in their hair, young, young. Some giggle. Some smoke. Their eyes are bright yet hazy. They are, like Randolph Kirk, afraid.

The mood pivots on a breath, a gesture, anything that might break the spell.

One of the initiates, Barbara, young yet knowing, walks forward, expectant, animated. Her hand falls on the mask. Her fingers stroke its ugly features, caress the vile, bulbous nose.

Watch, the chemical screams, a god inside him, so strong it is impossible to fight.

The golden girl lifts the dead, ugly face, looks at each of them in turn and smiles.

They left the house on the Aventine hill just after nine. Bruno Bucci drove. Neri huddled down in the rear with one man either side. Then the Mercedes snaked down the back roads, taking the narrowest it could find, before it emerged in Cerchi, just where the call had dictated.

Not that Emilio Neri needed directions. He'd never forget this place. Too many memories lay behind the scarred earth.

The car pulled onto the pavement. They got out and stood in the shadow of the escarpment that ran into the Tarpeian Rock. The sun was coming up on another fine spring day. If there'd been a little less traffic Neri could have taken a deep breath and believed he would miss Rome.

Bucci looked at him, nodded at the black hole of the cave, behind the broken gate with its ancient city archaeology department notice saying, 'Keep Out'.

'Yeah, yeah,' Neri said and ducked into the darkness. 'I'll handle this on my own. Just make sure he's carrying nothing when he shows, huh?'

'What about Mickey?' Bucci said.

'Mickey?' Neri laughed. 'What about him? He's just a stupid kid. I can handle my own son.'

Neri thought about Bucci again and briefly wondered about his own judgement. 'You think I'm being dumb, don't you?'

Bucci didn't say a thing.

'OK. Don't answer. I got to say, Bruno. I'm being more than fair to you here.'

'Sure. I'd still like to come in with you.'

Was this sentiment? Or just some self-serving show of concern? Neri couldn't decide. Maybe Bucci was right. He could handle Mickey, no problem. But if his son had others in tow . . .

'You heard of anyone going over to Mickey?' he asked.

Bucci laughed out straight. 'Are you kidding? Who'd be fool enough for that?'

Neri nodded at the shadowy mouth of the cave. 'So it's just him in there. And maybe Adele. Do you honestly believe I cannot cope with my own son and a two-timing wife I can slap down with one hand?'

Bucci shuffled on his big feet, uncomfortable.

Neri took that as a yes. 'Just make sure Wallis goes in on his own and he's not carrying anything,' he said. 'I don't share out this pleasure with anyone. Besides. I've been thinking. There's some questions I want to ask, and they're all family. I don't want anyone else listening.'

'Think of me as back-up.'

Neri tapped him on the chest with a single finger, quite hard. 'I was putting men down before you were born, Bruno. Don't get presumptuous. You got the rope and the tape like I asked?'

Bucci nodded and handed them over.

Emilio Neri patted his jacket, felt the butt of the gun there. Then he walked into the darkness, surprised how cold it was, surprised too by how little illumination the bulbs gave.

His memory must have been playing tricks. In the old days everything seemed much brighter.

Leo Falcone watched Peroni dabbing his head next to him in the back seat.

'That's one big black eye on the way,' he said. 'Do you have any idea where Wallis might have gone? Did he say anything?'

'Yeah. First he asked if Neri and his kid were safely in the net anyway, even without this. Then he tried to bribe me to look the other way so he could get a spare thirty minutes with the fat man. I was explaining the problems this posed for my fragile sense of public duty when he whacked me in the face. Said he wasn't hitting me so hard because he admired me. I'm glad I wasn't on the hate list. If he punched like that when he's a fan—'

The radio barked at them. Wallis had dumped the police car in a side road near the Trevi Fountain and disappeared into the tourist masses. Falcone swore and then issued the standard call. Tall black men in flapping leather overcoats weren't that common in Rome. Someone ought to see him.

'Maybe he'll take a cab,' Peroni suggested. 'That guy is as cool as they come. You know what I think? He intended to make that drop all along. And on his own. He just came to us to make sure we got that camera with Mickey on it. Make sure the Neris wind up in the shit whatever.'

Falcone picked up the mike and ordered every man he had to cruise around Cerchi. He told his own driver to get there too. It was the last place Costa had been seen. If they got lucky . . .

It was hard thinking straight. Then his phone went and it got even harder.

'Not now,' he said instantly.

'Yes now,' she yelled at him and Falcone wondered for a moment why he and Teresa Lupo so seldom had a conversation at normal volume. 'Listen to me. I've just been through Kirk's belongings again. I've found some phone numbers. One in particular. The most recent. Maybe the one he called before he died.'

'Maybe?' Falcone roared. 'What the hell use to me is "maybe".'

'He called Miranda Julius,' she said simply. 'At least that's the number on his snotty little handkerchief, as bright and clear as day. She gave me the number when we were in that apartment of hers. Doesn't that sound more than a little interesting? Some time before he died, Randolph Kirk called the mother of the kid we're supposed to think he snatched in the first place.'

Falcone shook his head trying to clear some space for thought then ordered the car to pull into the side of the road. 'What?'

'Her mobile number was there on Kirk's person. There is no mistake about this. And given how disorganized that particular man was I can only think it was there for a very recent reason. You tell me.'

Leo Falcone leaned back into the soft seats of the Alfa saloon and stared out of the window, out at the tourist crowds mingling near the mouth of the tunnel, making their way at a snail's pace to the little square and its overblown fountain. Miranda Julius had given them a picture of Randolph Kirk near the Trevi, staring myopically at her daughter. Or so it appeared.

'Meet me at her apartment,' he said, making a particular effort to keep the volume down. 'I'll send a car.'

'Hey,' said the surprised voice on the other end of the line. 'I'm just a pathologist. I don't want to tread—'

'Be there,' he yelled and cut the call.

Mickey Neri stood with Adele in the shadows, watching his father walk into the big, brightly lit chamber. The old man was grinning at the pictures on the walls, happy as could be, as if they brought back good memories, which was, Mickey knew, ridiculous. Something else must have been making the old man feel this way.

The shadows in this stupid place had such substance. They were places you could hide and feel you didn't really exist as you watched what went on in the light. Mickey Neri knew he would be happy to stay in shadows like this, all the way to one of the several exits she'd talked about, and out into the bright new day. Then Adele gave him a short, damp kiss on the cheek, whispered 'Ciao' and propelled him out into the yellow light.

Neri opened his arms in a welcoming, paternal gesture. 'Son, son—'

Mickey didn't move. Neri took two steps towards him. 'Mickey . . . Why the long face? Are we going to argue about this forever?'

He stood his ground, fearing the presence of the old man.

'I gave you a test, Mickey. What do you do? Not just kill that talkative bastard Martelli but come up with a present for me too? So you've been screwing Adele. What the fuck? If it's gonna happen best it's kept in the family. I don't care. Screwing around's such a little thing for a man of my age.'

He looked around the chamber. 'Jesus, we had some times in here. Where is Adele exactly?'

'Dunno,' Mickey mumbled. 'She said she'd leave us two alone. Catch up with you later.'

The old man gave him a cold smile. 'Yeah. I guess that will happen some time. Except I won't be in Italy much longer so maybe she knows I won't be fixing social appointments for a while. It's always the same with that woman. Adele's in it for herself. Forget that and things just might get dangerous.'

Mickey wanted to kick and scream and yell at the fat, grinning figure in front of him. Neri was behaving as if what happened the previous night was just one of those things. 'Fuck her! You nearly got me killed! Like you wanted it or something.'

Neri took one more step towards him, opened his arms wider, embraced his son, overwhelmed him with his strong, commanding presence. Mickey couldn't remember when they'd last touched like this but he knew that had been a bad time too.

'Don't make so much noise,' the old man whispered. 'You could wake the dead screaming like that.'

'You—'

The big arms enfolded him, buried him in Neri's bulk. 'I've been a lousy father. I know. You've every reason to feel mad at me.'

'Yeah—'

'Quiet,' Neri said. 'I'm talking. I brought you up bad, Mickey. I left you with that bitch of a mother for too long. When you weren't with her I didn't spend the time with you I should.'

'Yeah right—'

'Ssshhh.' Neri put a fat forefinger to his son's lips. 'Listen.'

Mickey pouted and the kid could have been ten years old again. Emilio Neri wanted to laugh out loud.

'There are so many things I never taught you. When it's time for a little honesty for one. People like us need to know that. Sometimes it's the most important thing of all.'

He looked at the photos on the walls, holding on tight to Mickey, turning his head to see. 'She was a good-looking girl, his stepdaughter. Anything you want to tell your old man about her now, huh? And this other one too. All these games on the side. Jesus—'

Mickey's head shook from side to side. 'No. I got nothing to tell you.'

'You think that's what Vergil Wallis is coming all this way to hear? He's not falling for this ransom shit, Mickey. He don't give a damn who you've been messing with now or what you wind up doing with them. He's coming to find out why we lied to him all those years ago. He's looking for answers. When I think about it I got to be honest with myself. Maybe he deserves some.'

His rank, old man's mouth came close to Mickey Neri's face. 'You gonna tell him, son?'

'I didn't do nothing!'

'Mickey, Mickey.' Neri was smiling all the while, loving this. 'You were banging her in Sicily. I may have been a lousy father but I knew that. You banged her so well she was carrying some little bastard for you by the time we came back here. You told me so yourself once I beat it out of you. Remember?'

Mickey didn't look his father in the eye. He'd thought this was all dead and would stay that way.

Neri kept staring at her photo. 'That kid. Lovely as an angel but she was so damn stupid. Stupid as you in a different way. I mean I know why you wouldn't bother with a rubber. I wonder if you use them now with those African whores of yours. But her . . . I guess she just didn't know any better. Tell me now. In Sicily. It was the first time for her, wasn't it?'

'Yeah,' Mickey mumbled.

'So it makes sense. When she told you there was something on the way that made you real worried I guess. I mean Vergil . . . he's not a man to cross now.'

'I told you years ago. I didn't k . . . k . . . k . . .'

It was just like when he was a kid. Even down to the stammer.

'You didn't k . . . k . . . k . . . ?'

'K . . . kill her.'

The old man withdrew his arms and looked sternly at his son. 'Maybe not. But you know something? After all these years I'm not even sure it matters.'

Emilio Neri put his hand gently to the back of his son's head and stroked his soft hair, wishing it wasn't that stupid blonde colour. There were tears in Mickey's eyes.

'Don't cry, son,' Neri said, then brought his head down hard on the table, slamming it onto the old wood, ignoring his screams.

He pulled out the tape and wound it first round his mouth then his eyes. He bound Mickey's wrists, kicked his feet from under him so he landed roughly in the nearest chair and tied him tightly to the back, circling the rope around his chest.

'Plenty of time for crying later.'

Emilio Neri looked at his handiwork.

'*Hear that, Adele?*' he roared into the darkness. 'Just so much time for that later. You listening?'

Two times merge now, and in each he's leading the way, looking, staying close to the walls, in the shadows, Miranda behind, whispering, whispering. Nothing stands between her words and the images in his head. There is a light in one of the side chambers. They steal to the door, peer inside. Something flashes at the back of his imagination. The pictures he saw in Leo Falcone's office rise again in his muddled head, real this time, rolling past his eyes. A fat, white naked shape rolls around on the bed lunging at something only dimly seen beneath him. The air reeks of dope. A spent needle sits by the table. On the floor lies the girl's sackcloth shift and the garlands of flowers, discarded like an old skin, shed for her becoming. The man grunts like a pig. The girl beneath him squeals: pain, he thinks, revulsion. Is this the first time? In a dank underground chamber reeking of stagnant water and mould? In the sweating arms of a middle-aged man who comes bearing flowers and oblivion in a syringe?

Can you see who she is? Miranda asks.

No, he says, not looking.

You have to know, Nic.

He walks on, knowing she's behind, talking, talking, and here is another chamber, deeper into the pulsing vein of rock, the light a little brighter inside. More cries of pain, a young girl's voice, sobbing.

Look, she says.

Costa leans against the dusty wall. His breath comes in snatches. His body feels like a lumpen machine beyond his control. He's stiffening, ashamed of the fact. She sees this, touches him there.

We're only beasts sometimes.

No, he answers. *Only if we allow it.*

Then the old voice sounds, deeper, impossible to ignore, chanting, *Look you fucker look and learn.*

The shape in the shadows is pumping from behind at a girl who straddles the back of a big armchair, face upturned towards them. His arms hold her legs and the memory of a childhood game – *wheelbarrow, wheel-*

barrow, an act so innocent the memory hurts – races into his head.

There are tears in Eleanor Jamieson's eyes. The girl looks at them from across the years, pleading. Two voices burn in Nic Costa's head, one young and innocent, one old and knowledgeable.

The man cranks up his grinding a gear, forcing himself into her with a brutal, punishing force. She screams from the agony. She begs for his intervention.

This is just a dream, kid, no one gets to change the past, grunts the old voice.

Then he hears her screaming . . . *I'll tell I'll tell I'll tell.*

Nothing changes, not even a break in the rhythm of the panting man behind.

The figure forces himself harder into her. The chair leaps forward propelled by his momentum. A face emerges into the light, distorted, ugly. It wears the mask, grunting, grunting.

He tries not to watch but the mask is staring at him, something alive behind those dead black eyes, the old voice rising, laughing, *Look you fucker look.*

And in the corner, in the darkness, something else. Another pair of bright young eyes, hidden, terrified.

Adele Neri walked out into Cerchi the way she had come, through the main entrance, straight to where Neri had left his men. She blinked at the sunlight then brushed down the cobwebs and crap from her black cashmere coat. Bruno Bucci and his men were standing in the shadows next to a 'Keep Out' sign that lay half askew behind some barbed wire marking the site.

She smiled and walked over to him. Bucci nodded.

'Mrs Neri,' he said carefully. The other men watched him like a hawk. 'Is your husband OK in there? I'm a little concerned if you want to know the truth.'

She put a slim hand on his arm. 'Of course he's OK, Bruno. You know him.' She stared at the men, not letting go until they dropped their eyes to the ground. 'You all know him.'

Bucci was trying to make some private contact with his eyes. She didn't play ball. She just lit a cigarette and stared down the big, busy road, watching the traffic.

'He told you what to do, didn't he?' she asked without looking at him. 'Mickey couldn't hurt his old man.'

A taxi drew up a little way along from them. They watched a tall, dark figure get out. He was carrying a leather bag.

'It's not Mickey I'm worried about,' Bucci grumbled.

They watched Vergil Wallis walk slowly towards them, swinging the bag, whistling some old tune, face expressionless, eyes never leaving the mouth of the cave. He came to stand between them, raised his arms high up in the air and said to Bucci, 'Well—?'

A couple of strong hands undid the leather overcoat and went up and down Wallis's chest, then down to his belt, down his trousers. Bucci swore, put a hand around the man's left ankle and came up with a gleaming silver hunting knife. He held the blade up in front of Wallis's face.

'Forget something?' Bucci asked.

'Guess so,' Wallis replied nonchalantly. 'It's these early mornings. I'm getting too old for them.'

Bucci looked at the knife then passed it to one of his minions. 'This has gone far enough, Mr Wallis. Why don't you just walk away? We can pass on the money. We can pass on any messages too. You can count on me to get what you're buying. This . . . disagreement needs to stop now.'

Wallis laughed in his face. 'Wow. I knew Neri was losing it. But so soon? Are you making the decisions already, Bruno?'

The big Italian hood fought to control his temper. 'I'm just trying to draw a line under all this shit.'

Wallis patted him hard on the shoulder. 'Don't bother. You're still new to all this, man.' He nodded towards the rock. 'You don't want to step out of line now, not with him still around. Mr Neri wants to see me. I want to see him. That's all there is to it.'

Bucci shook his head and reached for the leather bag.

Adele got there first and said, 'I can do this.'

She lifted it up to her chest, ran open the big bronze zip and rummaged thoroughly through the contents with her right hand. It took a good minute or more. Then she smiled at Vergil Wallis.

'You got a lot of money there,' she said. 'I hope you think it's worth it.'

'I hope so too,' he murmured and caught the bag as she flung it at him.

Vergil Wallis walked into the darkness. They listened to him whistling and then the sound died altogether.

Adele leaned close to Bruno Bucci, looked up into his big, impassive face and ran a finger down his arm.

'Bruno?' she asked. 'Do you boys really want to hang around here all day?'

*

By the time Teresa Lupo arrived, the door to Miranda Julius's apartment was down, torn from its hinges by the entry team. Men were swarming everywhere, opening drawers, scattering their contents on the floor, looking for anything.

She walked straight into Suzi's room. They hadn't reached there yet. She was glad. It gave her time to think.

There was a sound from the corridor, a gentle cough. She turned to face it and Falcone stood in the doorway looking as grateful as he could manage.

'Thanks for coming,' he said.

'Why am I here?'

Falcone stroked his angular, silver beard and looked as if he were asking himself the same question. 'For luck I guess. Maybe I'm getting superstitious in my old age. We could use some luck.'

'No sign of Nic or Wallis? I heard when I was leaving.'

He shook his head. 'What made you come to this room first? Do you think there's something we should be looking for?'

'No. Nic and I did look, didn't we? It's just—' The conviction had grown in the speeding police car on the way. 'I should have said something when we were here before. This room doesn't feel lived in. Not at all. People leave their mark. If you go into the mother's room you can still feel her presence. There's mess. Chaos. This—'

She took another look to make sure. 'This is for our benefit. Do we really know for sure that Suzi Julius exists?'

Falcone's eyes didn't leave her. 'We've got video of someone getting on that bike. We've got the photos the mother gave us.'

'I know. But apart from that?'

'No.' Falcone sat down on a small cheap chair and looked around the bedroom. 'Maybe that was all for our benefit too. Let's face it. If you wanted to stage something for the police there's no better place than the Campo. We're always around. She'd know she wouldn't have to scream for long. You don't need to be a genius to see there's CCTV there either. It's hanging from the lamp posts.'

Teresa could see he was right. 'But *why?*'

Falcone walked silently back into the big living room. She followed, becoming aware of the roar of traffic from outside.

'Look,' he said, and pointed to a pile of old maps. They were detailed drawings of archaeological digs, all over the city out into the suburbs and beyond. She sifted through the top of the pile. There wasn't one she'd heard of. 'The Julius woman was interested in these places too,' he said. 'How many reasons can there be for that?'

Peroni was bent double over the woman's notebook computer, thrashing at the keyboard. Teresa crouched next to him, unthinkingly put her hand on his shoulder and watched, in amazement, as he hammered the keys, working through the machine.

'How the hell do you know about computers?' she asked.

He stopped for a moment, and stared at her, bemused. His right eye was a puffy red mass, almost closed. He looked awful. 'I got kids, Teresa. Who else is suppose to fix their problems?'

It had never occurred to her how family shaped a man

in such small, unpredictable ways. All her preconceptions about Peroni seemed false.

'Gianni,' she said softly. 'What the hell happened to you? Have you seen a doctor about that?'

He laughed. 'It's a punch in the face, for Christ's sake. Ask me something important. Ask me about her reasons.'

'Which are?' she asked and wondered whether she really wanted to know.

'Good ones,' Peroni replied and pulled up some photos on the computer.

Teresa Lupo watched as he flicked through shot after shot and wished she'd stayed where she belonged, safe in the morgue.

Peroni pointed to one of a contemporary Randolph Kirk standing at the dig in Ostia, clearly unaware someone was furtively taking his picture. The expression on his face was one of puzzlement and perhaps a little fear. 'We've still no idea who she is really. According to the British the only woman of that name with a current passport is sixty-seven years old. Also we found these—'

There was a pile of passports on the table. 'Another British one. American. Canadian. New Zealand. She looks different on every one. Different hair colour. Different style. If you'd given me this back when I was on narcotics and asked me her true profession I'd have said she was a mule. But we just don't know. She's into photography though. This . . .' he picked up the picture of Kirk, ' . . . was the inspiration for the photo she gave us to establish a link between Kirk and Suzi. It never existed. She just took his head from that picture and pasted it into the background of one she had of Suzi at the fountain. *Kirk was never there. Kirk never threatened anyone.*'

'Perhaps,' Falcone said, 'it was the other way round. She was blackmailing Kirk.'

Teresa tried hard to think about Miranda Julius. If it was an act, it was a very good one.

Peroni pulled out an envelope, extracted two prints and she believed there was a glimmer of light in the darkness. These were, it seemed, from the series she had been handed by Regina Morrison. They had the same seamy quality, the same backdrop. The time was sixteen years earlier. In one the young Miranda Julius – or whatever she was really called – stood next to Emilio Neri, a big, innocent smile on her face, a glass of something in her hand. Flowers in her younger, brighter blonde hair, the petals falling down onto that stupid ceremonial shift. Teresa Lupo wanted to pick the thing up and tear it into shreds, unwind the years.

He took out the second print and placed it over the first. Miranda was naked now, pale body lolling back drunkenly on what looked like a cheap, fake Roman couch. Her legs were wound round the large, cloaked body of a man who was pumping away for all he was worth and not getting very far either. It was Beniamino Vercillo, already looking old and past it. Teresa stared into the blank eyes of that young face and tried to imagine what it would be like to be in that room. Maybe they thought Miranda was so out of it she didn't understand what was happening. That if they poured enough booze and dope down these dumb kids they'd forget half of what went on, and think the rest was as much their fault as anyone's. You could work that trick on someone like Barbara Martelli, particularly if you threw in a nice job in the police as a reward. It wasn't like that for Miranda. There was physical pain there. There was resentment, hatred too at having this animal steal your innocence on some cheap couch in a stinking damp cave.

'There are more,' Peroni said, reaching for the prints.

Falcone abruptly put his hand on the envelope. 'Not now.' He looked at her a little slyly. 'So what do you think?'

It didn't require a genius. She smoothed back her dark hair, wondering how bad she looked just then. The work clothes were back on. Her mind was in order. But she still felt out of sorts. 'Miranda, or whoever she was, came back for vengeance. But why wait so long?'

'Because this wasn't just about getting raped by these creeps,' Peroni said. 'One of those girls died and Neri told everyone it was a drug overdose. He told Wallis that too. From what we've seen it must have been a pretty plausible story. Until we fished that body out of the bog.'

There was some logic there, she thought. Just not enough. 'So why doesn't she just kill the bastard? Why go to this trouble?'

Peroni took out a handkerchief and dabbed his damaged eye which was surely leaking something and must have hurt like hell. 'Which bastard would that be?' he wondered. 'Mickey? Maybe. Maybe she's not sure. Maybe she knew all along and was just too scared to say. Until she realizes she can finally prove it and, bingo, it's the first plane to Rome. So one day Barbara picks up the phone and it's Miranda saying, "Hi, guess who's in town and you'll never guess what I heard. Our old initiation girlfriend from the fuck club didn't OD. Some bastard cut her throat and got away with it." Can you imagine

Barbara, even the somewhat crooked Barbara we now know existed, enjoying that?'

Teresa Lupo continued to be amazed by the respect they gave their murderous former colleague. She bent down, removed the handkerchief from him, dabbed gently at the wound. Peroni was right. Nothing was cut. It was just swelling, and some weeping from the bruised eye. She touched the corner of his cheek lightly to remove some of the liquid.

'This would explain why the lovely Barbara wanted to put a bullet in my head too, presumably. You can dab away anything wet here, Gianni, but if you touch any place else I'm confiscating the hankie and sending you to hospital. Understood?'

Peroni wriggled in his tight grey suit, took back the hankie and touched it gingerly on the precise spot. 'Thanks. Be honest with yourself, Teresa. In her shoes, in those circumstances, what did you expect her to do? *Explain?* These were women with a mission. God help anyone who got in their way.'

Falcone bent down and peered into Peroni's damaged face. 'Miranda did kill someone. Beniamino Vercillo. We've got the mask. It was dumped in a bin nearby. It's got blonde hairs on it. I'd put money on them being hers. She had the personal motive. We've got the proof here. But she also wanted to expose those papers and bring Neri down for good. It wasn't enough, all this stuff about the missing girl. We'd got distracted then by Barbara killing Kirk.'

'And me . . . nearly,' she interjected.

'And you,' he agreed. 'All the same she had to keep the pressure up. She identified that hair-band from Ostia which could have belonged to anyone. She identified

Mickey when I doubt he's even been near whoever "Suzi" really is. The rest, I don't know. Maybe it would be hard for her to get to Neri and Mickey. Maybe . . . He'll be OK, won't he?'

Falcone was grasping for ideas in the dark and struggling to find them.

'He'll be fine if he can stop poking it,' she replied. Teresa recalled what Regina Morrison had said about the ritual and the roles each participant would play. 'She's what they made her, Neri and the rest. A Maenad. A woman who's all sweetness and light, a warm bed and anything else you want when times are good. And the banshee from hell when she feels she, or one of the sisterhood, has been wronged. Think of it from Miranda's point of view.' She pointed at the picture, with the figure in the mask humping and grunting away. 'Who would you want to kill? Just this sad bastard?'

'The whole damn lot of them,' Peroni said softly. 'As nastily as possible. I'd want to watch them tear each other apart and dance on their graves afterwards.'

They looked at each other, lost for words. Then a woman officer walked through, smiled briefly at Teresa Lupo, and said, 'We've picked up Neri's lieutenant and a couple of sidekicks. In Cerchi. They're not talking.'

Peroni raised a crooked, bloodied eyebrow. 'Is that so?'

Emilio Neri sat at the head of the old table, smoking a Cohiba, ignoring his son, toying with the black gun he'd owned for years, used so many times it was like another limb. Thick grey cigar fumes curled their way up into the darkness, swirling on some unseen current. He watched

Vergil Wallis walk in. The American was carrying a leather bag on one outstretched arm and had the other high up in the air.

Neri looked him up and down and said, 'You met the guys outside?'

'Yeah. What's his name? Bucci?'

Neri hated this man. He had no business knowing the names of his lieutenants. 'He's a good guy. I trust him. All the same—'

He waved the gun at Wallis. 'Put the bag on the table. Take the coat off. Throw it on the floor. Then stand upright, keep your arms out. Fuck around and I just shoot you now.'

Wallis carefully eased the coat off, let it fall, then held his breath as Neri got up and walked round him, patting in all the right places, making sure.

'You can sit,' the old man said finally, indicating a seat at the table with the gun. Then he went back to the other side and resumed his place next to Mickey. 'Show me the cash. Don't reach inside or anything. Just turn it upside down and let me see.'

Wallis took the bottom of the bag and upended the thing. Bank notes, big denominations, tucked into wads straight from the till, fell onto the table.

Neri gave it a derisory stare. 'So this dumb shit of a son of mine's willing to cause all this anguish for this. What an idiot. I'd have given him more as spending money if he'd asked.'

'Perhaps,' Wallis wondered, 'that was the point. He got tired of asking. He wanted a little independence.'

Neri laughed and cast a brief glance at Mickey. 'That worked, huh?' Then he looked at the pictures plastering the room. 'What is it you think this is buying you, Vergil?

That kid Mickey has stashed somewhere? Don't ask me about it. I don't know no details and I don't want to. He was just playing freelance there. That kind of thing's beneath me, but I guess you know that.'

Wallis frowned. 'I got asked to come. I came.'

'You want justice or something?'

'Or something.'

'OK.'

Neri reached into his pocket, took out a knife, flicked open the blade and placed it on the table. He motioned to Mickey with the gun. 'I'm a fair man. I'm going to let you take him. I got to be honest with you, I nearly did the same myself sixteen years ago. I mean, you got a nice party going, you're thinking everyone's having a good time. Then what happens? Your dumb kid comes in all doped up to the eyeballs, hysterical and weeping, saying look, look, look. Here's my girlfriend, dead as they come, throat cut from ear to ear. And I watch him twitching away like that and I think, let's make it two. Because this worthless piece of shit surely deserves it after what he's done. I don't know about you but I was never into beating up women. I'd kill them if it was necessary. But not out of anger or some weird doped-up pleasure. Also . . .' Neri took a last puff of the cigar then threw it on the floor, ' . . . it spoiled a damn good evening. Had to cover up stuff to make sure you wouldn't hear of it for one thing. Not that I remember the details, to be honest with you. Got to admit I was a little out of things myself.'

He looked for some sign of emotion on Wallis's face. The American sat impassive, with his hands palm down on the table.

'We were all out of it,' Neri continued. 'It was a lapse

of concentration. Dangerous. But, hell, it was a good party anyway. From what I recall I banged three different girls. Adele being the best, which is why we ended up getting hitched in the end. But three! All in one night. Something else.'

He leaned forward, grinning. 'What about you, Vergil? Tell me. Man to man. How many you'd bang, huh?'

She holds his head. Her tongue, chattering, chattering, soaks his cheek in desperate saliva.

What do you see? she says.

Costa's peering down the blackness, half visible as a corridor in front of him, trying to fight the confusion in his mind, trying to think of some way out.

You know what I see, he says.

Miranda takes his head in her hands, forces him to look into her bright eyes. *No, Nic. Not what you know already. When you look into the corner. What do you see?*

In his imagination, formed by her suggestions, he sees her for sure now. A huddled shape, wretched with fear and shame, hiding in the darkness, thinking itself safe.

What's she thinking, Miranda asks.

Tell me.

Her voice starts to break. *She sees, she knows, she never has the guts to tell.*

In the waking dream the figure sobs, bites her hand, trying to stifle the noise.

Who is she, Nic? Who?

*

'You don't want to say. Well I guess it could be boasting.'

Wallis leaned back in his chair looking bored, saying nothing.

'Maybe you don't remember, huh? It's a long time ago. Which was what puzzled me, you see. When all this shit started happening. When we got to know that body was this stepdaughter of yours. I mean a *stepdaughter*. Not like she's your own flesh and blood, is it? You don't have any of your own flesh and blood, do you? Problems down there or something?'

Wallis nodded at Mickey. 'You think I'm jealous?'

Neri laughed and took the point. 'Over this piece of shit? Nah. Who would be? But I know Mickey. He's just a weak, stupid kid, same as he was then. And all this crap got me wondering. Got me trying to remember, which is hard after all this time. And you know one thing I remember?'

Wallis peered at his nails.

'Vergil, Vergil. This is important. This is the fate of your stepdaughter I'm talking about.'

'What do you remember, Emilio?' Wallis snapped.

'Two things now I come to think about it. Once Mickey started blubbing on about how he'd got the stupid kid pregnant I didn't even *ask* why he'd cut her throat. And one other. She just didn't get the game we were supposed to be playing. You said she'd get turned on by that jerk from the university. That we'd all be having fun. And we did, all except her. She didn't want to fuck with anyone but Mickey. I asked, all nice and polite. Tori Martelli did too. And it was all just those flashing eyelashes, and lemme get you another drink, and then what do you know, she's off with Mickey again. Maybe it wasn't her kind of party. Maybe she was like

434

that because – I got to be blunt here – it wasn't the first time for her, like it was for the rest. And that, if you recall, was one of the rules that university guy you found for us laid down. He said bad things would happen otherwise. Maybe he was right. Where *did* you find him by the way? The cops seem to think he was something to do with me. As if—'

Wallis turned his head, listening, trying to work out if there was anyone else present in the pitch black corridors. 'I move in wider circles, Emilio.'

'Oh yeah. You're *educated*. I forgot. Anyway, what does it matter? I promised you could have Mickey. I don't break promises. You can do what you like. But the knife only.'

He slid the blade across the table. Wallis's hand closed on it in an expert, practised grip. Mickey Neri, blind to the game, hung his head and sobbed behind the gag.

'You can do him like he did the girl, Vergil. Only—'

Neri thought about this. 'Let's give the kid a chance to talk first. Only fair—'

Watching the seated man opposite very carefully he got up and tore the tape from Mickey Neri's eyes in one rough sweep then did the same for his mouth. Mickey screamed from the pain, looked across the table at Vergil Wallis holding the knife and the noise died in his mouth.

'Jesus—' he whispered. 'Dad, don't do this to me.'

'Man's got a right to know what happened to his girl,' Neri said severely. 'Best get it off your chest, son. Best do that now before it's too late.'

She's you, he says in a still, dead voice.
   Who?

You.

Miranda takes his pained head, stares at him with two eyes from the present, kisses him, crying, shaking from the release.

He looks at the young Miranda Julius cowering in his imagination. Time has worked such changes on her face, removed so much. No lines. No cares. No jaded acceptance of an imperfect world.

You're beautiful, he says.

A thin, unconvincing laugh now, local, in his own piece of staggering space. Hers.

Only on the outside, Nic. The outside tells you nothing. The outside lies. The only truth lies in your imagination. Forego that and there's nothing but the dark.

Shouts echo through the caverns. Ripples of fear and anxiety – real, not imagined – disturb the wakeful dream inside his head.

He tries to walk and stumbles. The chemical fire is raging unchecked through his head. She holds him. He trembles. He sweats.

There's more, she says.

'I just screwed her,' Mickey bleated. 'That's all. She begged for it. All the time. I got bored if you wanted to know. I wanted to mess around with the others like we were supposed to. She wouldn't let me. It was just, "Mickey, Mickey, Mickey". I said that wasn't the point. She was supposed to mix it. She didn't want to know. She—'

His nervous eyes flickered between the two men.

'She said you was just a bunch of dirty old bastards. She wasn't putting it out for any of you. She just went on about love and stuff. Like the whole world was something special. Even her being knocked up was special and I just wanted her down the clinic, get the thing out. Love? All I did was bang her.'

Wallis watched him, toying with the knife, saying nothing.

'See,' Neri suggested. 'Like I said. The girl just didn't want to play the game. Her choice, I guess. But why come along in the first place?'

Mickey nodded at Wallis ''Cos he made her. It wasn't some birthday present. He thought it'd be good for business. That's what she said.'

Neri cocked his head to one side, thinking about this. 'I find that hard to believe, Mickey. Vergil here is an educated man. He came up with the idea for that party after all. He fixed all that stuff with the robes and the flowers. I just brung the dope and some guys who might be grateful for a chance at some young ass. The girl must have guessed what was coming.'

'*None of them guessed*,' Mickey yelled. 'You were so far out of it you didn't even get that, did you? Him and that professor guy of his just filled them up with so much stuff then put them in a room full of old guys with hardons and bolted the doors. They didn't get any choices. They did what you wanted. Then when it turned bad you thought you could shut them all up with a few promises and that was it.'

Neri stared at Wallis. 'Is that right, Vergil? My memory's not so great after all these years.'

The American shot Mickey a hateful glance. 'That fool was shot full of so much dope—'

Neri nodded. 'I agree there, Mickey. You're just trying to avoid the truth. You knocked up this poor girl when you first met her in Sicily. You fucked her rigid that night we came here. Then what? She told you she was coming to me and Vergil to announce a little shotgun wedding? Or did the dope and the festivities just go a little too far and you woke up one moment with a knife in your hand, and her stone dead?'

'*No!*'

Neri grimaced. 'This is going nowhere. We don't have time to piss around forever. Maybe I should just let Vergil do his thing now.'

Mickey Neri turned on his father, pleading. 'Will you listen, for chrissake? I went outside for a smoke. It was driving me crazy in here. All these old guys screwing everywhere, taking junk like they were twenty years younger. And this place. It's like being dead. In the grave. I was out there maybe an hour. I thought I'd go home but I knew you'd be mad with me. Then I came back, into that room you gave us, and *she was there*. Like you saw. *It wasn't me.*'

Neri's mouth hardened into a tight bloodless line. He looked at his watch and said nothing.

'But it's always the same,' Mickey snapped. 'There's shit around and who do you turn to? Me. You never once asked what happened. You just looked at her, looked at me, then shook your head like you always do. You know how many times I've seen that over the years?'

'The girl was dead, Mickey,' Neri said quietly. 'You were the only one who was with her. I was supposed to be doing business with her stepfather who was just a couple of rooms away, out of his head, playing god or something, fucking everything that moved. If I'd hesitated then, if I'd let him know what had really been going on – you screwing the girl, getting her in the way like that – you'd have been dead anyway. Did you ever stop to think of that?'

Mickey was quiet for a moment, a tiny light of clarity sparking in his head.

'No,' he mumbled.

A part of him is almost sleep, hiding behind closed eyes, listening to what she says. Another *sees*. The god is angry. The girl screams. Fists fly, nails tear. Through the dream he feels the pressure of their shrieking rebound off the damp and rocky veins that enclose them. A strong black arm pumps back and forth. She falls, blood pumping from her perfect lips.

He tears off the mask. A black face, rent by fury, demands obeisance, receives only scorn.

I'll tell I'll tell I'll tell, the girl screeches, furious.

The man moves behind her, raises his arm. Silver flashes in the yellow light. Two eyes glitter, terrified, hidden in the shadows, watching, witnessing.

Then the reverie ends. He opens his eyes and walks towards the voices and the light.

Neri glanced towards the shadows, wondering if it were Adele skulking round there now, then nodded towards Mickey.

'So Vergil. What are you waiting for? Are you going to do him?'

Mickey's head fell down on his chest. He began to sob.

'And then what?' the American demanded. 'You shoot me.'

'Nah. What for? You lost a daughter? I lose a son. You probably find this hard to believe but I never killed someone without a reason. Even those cops outside my house had it coming to them. You? Well, you got me in all manner of trouble with them, but you did me a favour too. You reminded me I was ready for retirement. A man should know when to walk off this stage. You did, didn't you?'

Wallis made a lazy wave with the knife point and said nothing.

'Besides,' Neri continued, 'if I just walk away from this mess and leave you sitting in the middle of it, you're going to have so much explaining to do. Reading about all that from somewhere nice and warm and safe could be real amusing. I might just die laughing.'

'You might,' Wallis said, and allowed himself a smile.

'An eye for an eye then,' Neri said, returning the gesture. 'Just as it should be. We agreed? All this nonsense ends here?'

'Yeah,' Wallis said. 'It ends here.'

Neri looked at him approvingly. 'That's good. You don't mind if I ask one more thing though? Just a tiny detail that bothers me.'

The big American had let go of the knife now. His hands were flat on the table, behind the pile of money, unseen.

'It does?'

'One of my cop friends told me the oddest thing. He said that when they found that poor kid she had a coin in her mouth. Some accident, I thought. Then he looks at me the way you look at me. As if I'm dumb or something. Seems this has some *significance*, Vergil. People used to put it there for a reason. You think

Mickey knew that reason? I didn't. We didn't put it there when we got rid of the body out near the airport. See, we're not *educated*.'

Neri picked up the gun in front of him and angled it halfway across the table. 'Oh, but you are. I guess you'd know what that reason is. Kind of a nice reason my cop friend told me. It says farewell, sorry maybe. That professor of yours would know too. But let's face it. He was just some little pervert you picked up along the way to sort things out for you. He didn't have the spunk to kill someone. Besides, why? If you'd gone in there, on the other hand . . . Maybe not taking no for an answer. Maybe finding out about Mickey's little present. Or wondering how the hell you were going to square screwing her with her mother afterwards.'

Wallis's black eyes burned across at him.

'One thing I do remember, Vergil, and it's so clear it's like yesterday.' Neri nodded at the mask at the head of the table. 'You really liked wearing that stupid thing a lot. And when you wore it you know something? I think you thought you really *were* some kind of god. One who was better than the rest of us. One who could do what he liked to just anybody and never feel the consequences. Which is why you came here really. You're scared that little secret might work its way into the light of day, aren't you? You just want to keep it good and buried, preferably with Mickey's name on instead.'

Neri looked at his son then at Wallis, blinking back the fury. 'You're no god. None of us is. You just fuck up the world pretending. Because of that – because I failed to see it – I've been punishing this poor, dumb son of mine for years.'

He waved the gun at the figure across from him.

'Jesus, Vergil. I wish I had more time with you. I wish I could do this some other way and—'

The explosion burst through the gloom. Emilio Neri found himself flying backwards in his chair, clutching his chest, feeling something turn his guts inside out. He landed on the floor, upright enough to see Wallis's hand emerging from the money pile, clutching a small pistol taped beneath one of the bundles.

'Bruno—' he croaked, through a mouth filling with blood, into the reddening darkness.

The uniformed men lined Bucci and three of his sidekicks against the wall just off the main road. Bucci had that punk look on his face, the one Falcone and Peroni knew so well. The one that said, *you can ask and ask and ask but no one's saying*.

'You got any idea what they were doing?' Falcone asked the uniformed sergeant.

Gianni Peroni had recognized Bucci as the leader straight away. Had gone straight up and pushed his face into his, one bull neck against the other.

'No,' the sergeant replied. 'They were walking by the time we stopped them. I guess they saw us first.'

Falcone walked over to Bucci and said, 'I don't have time to waste on you, sonny. I got a man out there somewhere and if he dies I promise you your life won't be worth living. Neri's old goods here. You stick with him you go down with him. Understood?'

Bucci looked at the other three hoods with him and laughed. 'You hear that? What's this town coming to? When a decent Italian man can't walk down the street without some ugly fucking cop coming and staring in his face?'

'Ugly?' Gianni Peroni asked. 'You calling me ugly? No one ever called me ugly before. I take that as an insult.'

Bucci laughed. His shoulders jerked in that punk way the cops all knew. 'Yeah. Ugly. Ugly as—'

It came so quickly even Falcone didn't expect it. Peroni dabbed his big head forward in a single blow, stomped his bone-hard temples straight into Bucci's nose. The big hood fell backwards onto the wall, blood and snot streaming down his face, gasping for air. Then Peroni butted him again, twice, punched a big fist into his guts, got him on the ground and laid in a flurry of stiff kicks. Bucci writhed there, screaming, bleeding, and Peroni took hold of the man next to him, a skinny-looking jerk in his thirties with mud-green eyes now as big as saucers, grabbed his shoulders, pulled back ready to strike.

'Down the road in some fucking cave, man,' the jerk whined. 'Don't hit me. Please.'

Gianni Peroni didn't wait for anyone else. He was first into the dark stinking mouth of the caverns. In seconds he was fighting to find his bearings under the dull yellow lights that ran through the labyrinth, leading into the blackness.

Mickey Neri whimpered. He'd pissed himself. The hot stream felt like acid against his leg.

'Don't do this, mister. P-p-p-please.'

Wallis stalked him with the knife. The big American

couldn't take his eyes off the mask with its dead eyes watching them.

'Got to,' Wallis murmured, coming round to stand behind the figure strapped in the chair. He reached down, grabbed a hunk of Mickey's hair in his fist, jerked back his head, held the silver blade over the pale throat below.

They watch, hidden in the black corner, and two times collide in Nic Costa's head. What he sees before him now is no god, just a man, bright beneath the single yellow bulb, angling himself behind the screaming shape on the chair, pitiless, determined.

Don't fail me, Nic, she says. *Remember what you are. Don't make me the silent witness twice.*

Her hand grips his and passes something over. Its shape slips beneath his fingers, cold metal, the old, familiar dumb machine.

The powerful black arm rose, . . . *rises.*

A figure strides out of the darkness. Vergil Wallis watches and pauses, surprised. A name slips from his lips, hangs in the air between them. He lowers his gaze, nods at the table.

You got your money, the American says, staring at her too-blonde hair, eyes glittering covetously, remembering. *You know the deal. Get gone.*

Her face is more radiant than anything in the room, shining with a living brightness leeched from the vibrant photos pasted everywhere. She shivers, she shakes, rooted to the spot, afraid but not afraid.

Wallis waves the blade at her. *Take it*.

No movement. Fear and resolution.

I know, she says.

He halts, confused. Her golden head shakes. There are tears in her eyes as, stuttering, she says . . .

I saw, I know, I never had the guts to tell.

He looks at the dead mask on the table and laughs, wondering whether to try it on again for size.

So what's one more? he wonders, then laughs, staring avidly at the shining hair. *Afterwards* . . .

The blade rises, then falls. A red line starts on the white, shining skin.

You got a talent for watching, girl . . . he tries to say into the dark air, but finds himself struggling for the words. Wallis looks beyond her, into the shadows, where fire and thunder are shredding the darkness.

He stares at this black shape there and tries to roar, to find the god inside him. Blood rises in his throat. He falls and, in the smoke and powder stink, Nic Costa finds his consciousness fading too. His head spins, his legs become feeble.

On the ground, sight fading. One last memory.

She bends over the fallen man, opening his bloody lips, still mouthing, still trying to say some single word. A coin glitters briefly between her fingers then is gone.

Another room. Smaller. A pool of grubby light pierces the darkness. Her older voice now talks to him and it is calm, unmoved.

Sweet Nic, sweet Nic. You save yourself. You save me.

No, he says, and hears his own voice rumbling around

the inside of this curling, twisting intestine cut into the rock.

He sits on a chair. She crouches above him, holding his cheeks. Her face fills his vision, becomes all there is to the world.

You have to feed the savage sometimes. It's the only way to keep him in his cage.

Fighting to control his hands, his fingers reach her shoulder, push the fabric of her tee-shirt down.

And hears the old voice, laughing, *you should have looked earlier, kid, call yourself a cop.*

Deep in the flesh, dark blue and old the dreadlocked face grins at him, victorious. His mouth closes on the stained skin, swallows its guttural voice. His teeth bite into her, chewing, licking, sucking the vile blue poison from her pores, takes it into himself, feeling the rush.

Voices down the corridor, voices in his head. He snatches a breath and knows: *this is only the beginning.* The dope is moving higher up the ladder, seizing more territory inside his limitless imagination.

Then, like a lifeline from sanity, a familiar voice rings through the guts of the labyrinth, echoing, distant.

Nic! Nic!

A sound from the old world. The real world.

One pill makes you small, Miranda Julius sings.

Nic!

She bends down to kiss him, tongue darting briefly into the corner of his mouth.

'Don't look for me,' she whispers, then vanishes into the shadows, leaving just the aftertouch of her skin, her presence, glowing in his head.

The light dies. It is dark and cold. He shivers alone.

APRILE

It was late afternoon on the first day of April. They sat in the old courtyard garden of the hospital of San Giovanni enjoying the last of the sun. Peroni bolted down the remains of a panino, balled up the bag and despatched it into a nearby rose bed.

'Nice to have you back, Nic,' he said. 'I never had a partner with acid flashbacks before. What's it like?'

Costa gave him a wry look. 'I'll let you know when it happens.'

'Not yet, huh? Did they ever find out what shit that woman pumped into you?'

His partner's eye had mended but still had a rosy bloom above the eyelid. Given the state of the rest of Peroni's face it didn't look particularly out of place. Peroni was unchanged by events. Nic Costa had stared at himself in the mirror that morning and wondered if anyone would say the same about him. He looked older, more marked by the world. He'd even found a couple of grey hairs above one ear. This went with the odd new territory he seemed to have carved out for himself within the Questura. He wasn't a hero, quite. But when he'd walked down the corridors that afternoon, for the first time since the incident, he realized he was now the kind of man who turned heads.

'If they did,' he said, 'they haven't told me.'

'Drop off a bottle of pee with Teresa,' Peroni declared. 'She'll know. I'm serious. That woman's a genius.'

Costa thought of the role the pathologist had played in the Julius case. Maybe she was too. 'So you never found out who Miranda really was?'

Peroni shook his head. 'We got the "daughter" though. Not that it did us much good. She was a teenage model from Prague. Wanted to break into acting. Seems she was picked out of a portfolio for her looks, paid to come here and "audition". Which meant getting her hair dyed a touch more blonde and her picture taken in a few places. You can guess by who. Oh, and doing that stunt on the motorbike for the benefit of the cameras and any cops who happened to be lurking in the Campo at the time.'

Costa thought about this. 'She didn't know anything about Miranda? She was just picked at random because of how she looked?'

'Sure. Miranda claimed to be a big talent scout from America. How many questions do you think would-be actresses ask in those situations? She got her plane ticket. She got put up in a nice hotel. Then, after performing the "action audition" with the bike, she took a taxi for Fiumicino and flew home. You got to admit it, Miranda did a great job. While we were thinking her daughter was lying drugged in a cave somewhere, making out with Mr Beastie and about to get killed, she was actually back at school strutting around in front of her classmates boasting about her new career in Hollywood. She can't give us a clue who Miranda really is. And you want to know something? I doubt we're ever going to find out.'

Costa wondered how he really felt about that. 'Falcone's letting it drop?'

Peroni hesitated, choosing his words carefully. 'I wouldn't put it quite so crudely. You got to remember, Nic. People like him answer to lots of different bosses. Some of them hold the purse strings and ask about the money. Is it really worth it? Ask yourself. Is it?'

'Six people dead. I would have thought so.'

Peroni took a deep breath. 'That's seven actually if you include Eleanor Jamieson. Not counting those poor bastards outside Neri's.'

Costa shook his head. The death toll there had risen to five in the end, some DIA, some cops. It could so easily have been higher. 'We can't just let this drop.'

His partner sighed. 'Nic. Let's have this conversation once and then leave it to one side forever. Most of this is wrapped up already. We got hard evidence that Mickey Neri accounted for that bastard Toni Martelli, for which he will stand trial once we can get him out of the hospital and into a jacket with sleeves. Barbara Martelli, meanwhile, popped Randolph Kirk to stop him talking to us before disappearing down a hole outside Fiumicino. Thanks to you we know most of the rest too. Wallis killed his own stepdaughter and got to Emilio Neri too, before you had the chance to stop him. This . . .' Peroni patted his knee to emphasize the point, ' . . . is all good news for the statistics, and the people who live above Leo *survive* on statistics. Do you think it possible Crazy Teresa has the hots for me by the way? I've been getting some funny looks from that woman lately.'

'No,' Costa objected. 'What about—?'

'Mr Vercillo? Miranda Julius, or whoever she is, did him. There's forensic on that costume we found, and we got some blood stains on a shirt in the apartment too. So you see the dilemma? Do we really waste public money – big public money in all probability – chasing all over the world for a woman who, let's be honest here, probably did the Italian public at large some very big favours?'

Costa scowled and said nothing.

Peroni sniffed a young rose on the bush next to them, just coming into bloom. 'Summer's on the way, Nic. Let's put all this behind us.'

'I'm trying,' he murmured.

Peroni's hand went to Nic's shoulder and that big ugly face now stared up at his. 'OK. I know. I checked the records. It's the first time you shot a man. And it bugs you. I don't blame you. I never shot anyone in my life.'

Costa looked Peroni straight in the eye. 'Did you ever want to?'

A touch of colour rose in Peroni's face. 'Nic. Stop feeling sorry for yourself. As luck would have it I am going to be by your side somewhat longer than I expected. And I do not intend to sit back and watch you choke trying to swallow this. Do you think either of them, Neri or Wallis, was going to let you walk out of there? You're damn lucky the woman did. Still not sure I get that. What I do know is she filled you up with dope before this happened. If you're looking for someone to blame, blame her.'

Costa carefully removed his partner's arm from his shoulder. 'Don't worry. What bothers me is I'm not that bothered. It wasn't the dope, either. Not all of it anyway. I wanted that man dead. He was a monster.'

Gianni Peroni looked at him and Costa was unsure of his expression. It just may have been shock.

'I'm sorry to hear that, Nic,' he said eventually. 'In a way. A part of me wants to say, "Welcome to the real world, Mr Costa. Where most of us go round having some such thoughts on a daily basis." A part of me hopes you don't catch the same bug everyone else gets. Let's not make a habit of it, huh? It's such an easy way out. Is that a deal?'

'Yeah,' Costa replied, feeling a little embarrassed.

'Good.' His partner was grinning now. It made him look younger and a little scary.

'What do you mean you're sticking around with me?' Costa asked. 'I thought you were going back to pushing a desk in vice.'

Peroni took another look at the single rosebud struggling into bloom on the bush next to them then snipped off the stem with his forefinger and thumb and placed the flower in his jacket pocket. 'You wouldn't believe it. That Bucci bastard, the hood I knocked around good in Cerchi, laid in a complaint about me. Amazing. He may even sue too. Police brutality. First time I ever truly hit a man on the job, *and* he's a murdering goon. What with all the hooker stuff that went down before they wanted to kick me out altogether. But old Leo waded in and started screaming at everyone high and low. At least so I gather. He's not even said so much as a word either way to me.'

Costa tried to decode the expression on Peroni's face. 'Is that good or bad? You staying with me?'

'It's good for me,' Peroni yelled. 'I got a job still, and a partner I can live with. How about you?'

Costa shrugged. 'I may need to think about it for a while.'

'Jesus,' Peroni gasped. 'Will you analyse every last fucking event on the face of this planet until it rolls over and dies? *It is how it is.* Nothing I can do will change things. So why sweat over it?'

Costa chuckled.

'Your sense of humour could do with some improving,' Peroni moaned. 'Country boys like me don't get these finer points.'

'I'm sorry, Gianni. Really I am. What about your wife? How are things going there?'

Peroni looked shifty. 'We met at the weekend. I had to go to a funeral back home. She wanted a reconciliation but . . . You know the one thing I have learned from you people? To recognize that dead means dead. And that marriage is dead. I'll see the kids don't get damaged though, as much as I can.'

His battered face was unreadable. 'A funeral?'

'Yeah. That old cop. The Tuscan amateur plastic surgeon.'

Peroni pointed to his scars. Costa was surprised to discover he was now very used to them. This *was* Gianni Peroni. 'The nice guy who did this to me.'

'You went all the way home for that?' Costa asked, astonished.

Peroni laughed and shook his head. 'Christ, Nic. What a pair of lousy detectives we make. You can't see it any better than I could, not that you had as much time of course. He was my old man. He begat me. Half my genes are his. He . . . oh shit, even now I find it hard to use the f-word. *He was my father*. There. I think my mamma must have thought keeping him sweet was part of the terms and conditions of working behind that bar. Who knows?'

Costa looked at his partner. When he was getting to know Gianni Peroni he'd always thought of him as a rock, impervious to the mundane tragedies of the world. It was, he now realized, such a superficial view.

'When did you find out?' he asked, knowing the answer already.

'Just after Christmas. When they worked out his liver was finally throwing up its hands and surrendering. He wanted to see me one last time. So I went and guess what? It was all about him really, not me. He wanted to explain that when he was remaking my face it was nothing personal. It was just himself he was beating up all along because of how guilty he felt about having fathered a bastard at *all*. So we shed a few tears together, me being the utter fool I am, and yes, maybe twenty-four hours later I break the habit of a lifetime and fall into bed with a Czech hooker because, well, *why not, why the fuck not?*'

Peroni put a big hand over his crooked mouth, thinking. 'You're wrong about Teresa, by the way. I just know it.'

'But—' Costa wanted to ask so many questions.

'Ssshhh,' Peroni interrupted, watching a tall figure stride down the arcade opposite. Then he glanced at Costa. 'What I just said is between the two of us, Nic. No one outside my family knows that little secret. No one else will. You share a little of my private burden. I'll share a little of yours if you want me to, before I go back to my true vocation in life and you become my driver. At which point I doubt I'll talk to you at all, the class war being what it is.'

Costa laughed. 'I can't wait for that day.'

'Good. What's more, now we're back on duty, we both get to share a whole load of old Leo's burden. And that is one big load to bear.'

Falcone was beckoning for them to join him. He looked spruced up and dressed in his Sunday best. In his hands was a fine bouquet of roses and carnations.

'Hospital visits,' Peroni said, getting to his feet and patting the tiny rose in his jacket pocket. 'Don't you love 'em?'

Rachele D'Amato sat upright in her bed in a private room. She wore a white silk shirt, torn up to the right elbow to make room for the cast on her arm, with sheets up to her waist. The fading remains of a livid bruise stained her forehead close to the scalp. Leo Falcone, watched by Costa and Peroni from the door, kissed her gently on the left cheek, presented a small golden box of chocolates then removed some old flowers from the vase by her bed and replaced them with his own.

'Here.' He passed the dead lilies and gladioli to Peroni who grimaced at the things then dumped them in a wastebasket in the corner of the room.

'Flowers,' she said, smiling. 'Chocolates. Oh, Leo. How . . . quaint.'

The three men looked at her and understood the position. Nothing had really changed. She wielded the same control over her emotions. Even a bomb couldn't change Rachele D'Amato.

'You're welcome,' Falcone mumbled.

'Sit, if you like. I thought—' She looked at Costa and Peroni. 'I thought you might have come before. I rather expected you on your own when you did find the time.'

Falcone stayed on his feet. 'I'm sorry. They say you're doing well. A couple of days more—'

She played with the flowers, improving the arrangement. 'Can't wait. I'm bored to death. I want to get back to work.' She hesitated. 'I keep hearing all these stories. So tell me. Will you find this woman?'

'We will,' he nodded.

The firmness of his answer surprised her. 'Really? I heard people were starting to consider it was a waste of time. She's out of the country. You don't know where to start. You don't even know her real name.'

'Don't believe everything you hear.'

She stared at the chair next to the bed until he sat down in it. Then he opened the leather document case he'd brought with him. 'When you go back to work you'll have to deal with this one.'

Falcone threw a photo of the young Adele Neri onto the sheets. She picked up the colour print and looked at it.

'Where did you get this?'

Falcone had lost some of his winter holiday tan. He looked tired and troubled. 'The Julius woman was careless. She must have scanned Kirk's photos into the computer to mess with them or maybe just for safe keeping. She thought she'd wiped the ones she didn't want to fool with. She hadn't. Our computer people managed to recover a few. Quite a lot actually. Adele Neri was on several.'

'Oh.' She stared at the photo then gave it back to him. 'Are you telling me Neri's mob is now in the hands of his widow? These *are* changed times. I know that happens in the south. But in Rome—? It seems wrong somehow.'

'It seems wrong,' he agreed.

'And you think she was involved in what happened? With this in mind?'

'Partly with this in mind. I'm certain of it.'

'Can you *prove* anything?'

He said nothing, watching her open the chocolates, put one in her mouth, smile faintly with pleasure then close the lid.

'Life will be interesting when I get out of this bed,' she said, still chewing.

'Quite,' he replied, then very suddenly, too quickly for her to protest, began to extend the tear in the silk shirt, ripping it up her arm with both hands until he reached the shoulder.

'Leo!'

The three men stared at the pale patch there, round, like the mark of a coin. Or a badge. Skin that was unlike the rest of her, bleached, changed.

'I remembered that,' Falcone said.

'I imagine,' she replied, 'you remember most of me. Oh, Leo. You're not that kind, are you? Lying in bed at night, on your own, just thinking of me? Trying to picture what I looked like when I was there under the sheets with you? Really. Aren't you a little old for that kind of thing?'

Falcone couldn't take his eyes off the white patch of skin. 'It never quite works, does it? I imagine they promise no one will ever notice. The tattoo will just go and you get old skin in its place.' He touched her on the shoulder. 'What you really get is new skin that never ages. Not quite right.'

'It's a birthmark,' she said very patiently. 'I told you, surely.'

Falcone wasn't listening. 'Neri worked so hard to clean this up, to keep you all sweet and silent. He married one of you. Barbara he put in the police. He put you through law college, then into the DIA. And another ran away for some reason. She knew all along Eleanor never died from drugs. She just didn't dare say so. Then, when a body turns up, she decides to put matters right. She comes back to make sure you all know the price of what you'd won.'

Rachele D'Amato was into her second chocolate by now. 'These really are delicious, you know. You don't mind my not sharing them. I am still an invalid. Just. And frankly I always feel good chocolate is wasted on men.'

'So she tells Vergil Wallis who goes along with everything,' he continued. 'Perhaps he bankrolls things. This fake abduction. He leans on Randolph Kirk to cooperate. Never understanding that you know already who killed Eleanor. And it's not just him you want. It's all of them, him included. Him especially.'

She closed the box. 'No more. I've put on enough weight in this place already. I must say, Leo. You *are* entertaining today. Is this how the police intend to pursue investigations in the future? Just guess your way through everything until you find an answer that fits?'

Falcone took no notice. 'Someone had to tell her about Vercillo. Kirk wouldn't know him as anything other than a face at the party. There's no reason to think Wallis could have provided his address. But the DIA—'

'*No reason?*' she laughed. 'Have you actually run these fantasies past a lawyer? Is this what constitutes evidence in the police force these days?'

He shook his head. 'And someone had to drive that bike with the bogus Suzi Julius on the back. You have a licence.'

Rachele D'Amato stared coolly at the three of them. 'I have a licence? My. That's incriminating.'

'It bothered me afterwards. I talked to you that day. You were in a hurry to leave for an appointment. I told you, I checked. There's nothing in your DIA diary to account for that.'

'I told you. I met a man. I'm sorry if that hurts your tender ego.'

'Does he have a name?' Falcone asked.

'He's married. I'm not dragging him into this for your sick curiosity.' She nodded at Costa and Peroni. 'Is that why they're here? Is this a formal interview?'

'Just came along to wish you well, ma'am,' Peroni said with a little bow. 'So pleased to see you're recovering your customary composure so quickly.'

'Jesus,' she murmured. 'That man gets uglier by the day, Leo. Did you have to pick him?'

'And your charm too,' Peroni said with a smile. 'Glad that's returning.'

'There was no man,' Falcone said. 'There never has been. Not even me. What was I for, Rachele? Promotion? Or did you just feed back information to Neri even then?'

'This is ridiculous,' she hissed.

'That's what they did to you,' he continued. 'All of you. Barbara. Miranda Julius. They took away any chance you had of a normal relationship. Perhaps that's what you hated most, even more than the thought that they'd tricked you over Eleanor.'

He threw another photo on the bed. She looked at it. 'And what's this supposed to be?'

'You. Dressed up and ready just like all the others. You were there. Which one was it? Do you remember? Toni Martelli? Wallis? Or did they take turns?'

She flung the picture at him. 'Take this away. Go find something better to do, Leo.'

'It's you,' he insisted. 'They even got you to dye your hair blonde back then. Whose idea was that?'

She was laughing at all of them. 'What are you talking about? Look at this girl! It could be anyone!'

'It's you.'

Rachele D'Amato sighed and leaned back into the pillow. 'Do you think you could convince a court of that? And even if you could, *does it matter*? It's just a picture.'

'What about those people outside Neri's house?' Costa asked. 'Don't their relatives deserve some answers?'

'I was one of them,' she snapped. 'In case you forgot. Neri placed that bomb. Neri's dead. How many answers do you need?'

Peroni sniffed and looked at her. 'What about Barbara Martelli? No feeling there?'

She picked at another chocolate then said, 'I never knew the woman.'

'Rachele,' Falcone said, and heard the note of pleading that had crept into his voice. 'You can't just bury this.'

'It's buried already, Leo. You just don't see it. Ask

yourself a question. Are we living in a better world now? Or a worse one?'

'That's not for the likes of us to decide.'

'No!' she yelled. 'Don't take that line with me. You make those decisions just as much as anyone. If you think you have one piece of hard evidence against me then use it. If not I suggest you keep your mouth shut and try catching a few criminals instead of boxing shadows. Now get out of here. And take these with you!'

She picked up the vase of flowers and launched them against the wall next to Peroni and Costa where they shattered noisily, dispensing water, petals and fragments of pottery everywhere.

It was dark by the time they got outside. Falcone clutched his leather case to his chest, looking lost. Costa shuffled on his feet, hunched up inside his jacket, silent, thinking.

'I know—' Peroni said hopefully. 'Let's get a drink. Something to eat. There's a place near here—'

'Is the wine good?' Falcone asked. 'I don't drink any old shit.'

'Me neither,' Costa grumbled. 'And I don't just want salad.'

'Boys, boys,' Peroni sighed. 'Stick with your old uncle, Gianni. He'll see you right.'

Ten minutes later they were in a tiny bar behind the Colosseum. Falcone sniffed approvingly at an expensive glass of Brunello and some prosciutto crudo. Nic Costa was testing a Tuscan chardonnay and some porcini on crostini. Gianni Peroni had one beer under his belt already, along with some translucent slices of expensive pork *lardo* on a slab of country bread.

'I can give everything I've got to the DIA,' Falcone said to no one in particular. 'Let's see what *that* does for her career.'

'You can, Leo,' Peroni said. 'And by the way, thanks for putting in a word for me.'

The tall inspector rolled back on his seat as if affected by some slight. 'I just did my job. They asked my opinion. I gave it to them.'

Peroni ordered another beer and said, 'For which I'm grateful. Let me offer a thought in return. Do you really think the DIA will appreciate if it we keep this thing on life support? I mean, either they know already, in which case it's their problem. Or they don't and frankly I'm not sure they'll be pleased to have it laid on their plate. I mean. She's good at her job, isn't she? She didn't kill anyone. She didn't do anything except ride a motorbike and hand out some information, not that we can prove any of that. Also, maybe they're aware of some of the people who had their photos taken in that place. Maybe some of them *are* those very people.' He paused. 'Have you thought of that?'

Falcone glowered back at him. 'Are you ever going back to vice?'

Another beer landed on the table. Peroni took a deep swig. 'Who knows? Who the hell knows anything these days? How's your drink? How's the food?'

Falcone sniffed at the wine. 'The Brunello is as good as one might expect for the price. I don't mean that as a criticism. The ham is . . . fine.' He took another sip then nodded with a measure of approval before grumbling, 'And we still don't know that damned woman's name.'

Gianni Peroni sighed and stared at his beer glass.

'A good white,' Costa said, holding his glass up to the light. 'Well-balanced. A little under-chilled.'

It was the colour of old straw under the yellowing candle bulbs of the bar. He took a gulp, larger than normal, and paused over the sudden and unexpected kick of the alcohol.

One pill makes you bigger, she sang, and he wondered, once more, why she'd dyed her hair that night.

He recalls a face now, frightened, furious and dying, under the same light, something glittering in its throat, choking as it tries to speak the same word, over and over again into the echoing darkness.

'We do know her name,' Nic Costa says, mind half recoiling from the memory, half flying towards it like a moth dancing for the candle.

'She told us time and time again.'

And no one else was fool enough to listen, says an old, cruel voice, still locked somewhere at the back of his imagination.

'Her name is Suzi.'

THE SACRED CUT

DAVID HEWSON

MACMILLAN, APRIL 2005

For the first time in decades the Eternal City is paralysed by a blizzard. And a gruesome discovery is made in the Pantheon – one of Rome's most ancient and revered architectural treasures. Covered by soft snow is the body of a woman – her back horribly mutilated . . . Before Nic Costa and Gianni Peroni of the Questura can begin a formal investigation, the US Embassy has brought in its own people, FBI Agents who want the case closed down as quickly and discreetly as possible.

But Costa is determined to find out why the enquiry is so sensitive – and as the FBI grudgingly admits that this corpse is not the first, the mutilations of the woman's body point to Leonardo da Vinci's Vitruvian Man – and to a conspiracy so sinister and buried so deep, that only two people know its true, crazed meaning.

AN EXTRACT FOLLOWS . . .

MERCOLEDI

The two plain clothes cops huddled in the doorway of a closed farmacia in Via del Corso, shivering, teeth chattering, watching Mauro Sandri, the fat little photographer from Milan, fumble with the two big Nikon SLRs dangling round his neck. It was five days before Christmas and for once Rome was enjoying snow, real snow, deep and crisp and even, the kind you normally only saw on the TV when some snap blizzard engulfed those poor miserable bastards living in the north.

It fell from the black sky as a perfect, silky cloud. Thick flakes curled around the gaudy coloured lights of the street decorations in a soft, white embrace. The pavements already owned a crunchy, shoe-deep covering in spite of the milling crowds who had pounded the Corso's black stones a few hours earlier, searching for last-minute presents in the stores.

Nic Costa and Gianni Peroni had read the met briefing before they went on duty that evening. They'd looked at the words 'severe weather warning' and tried to remember what that meant. Floods maybe. Gales that brought down some of the ancient tiles which sat so unsteadily on the rooftops of the centro storico, the warren of streets and alleys in the city's Renaissance quarter where they spent most of their working lives. But this was different. The met men said it would snow and snow and snow. Snow in a way it hadn't for almost twenty years, since the last big freeze in 1985. Only for longer this time, a week or more. And the temperatures would hit new lows too. Maybe it was global warming. Maybe it was just a trick throw of the meteorological dice. Whatever, the world was about to become seriously out of sync for a little while and that knowledge, shared among the two and a half million or more individuals who lived within the boundaries of the Comune di Roma, was both scary and tantalizing. The city was braced for its first white Christmas in living memory and already the consequences of this were beginning to seep into the Roman consciousness. People were preparing to bunk off work for any number of sound and incontrovertible reasons. They'd picked up the throat bug that was creeping through the city. They couldn't take the buses in from the suburbs because, even if they made it through the dangerous, icy streets, who knew if they'd get back in the evening? Life was, for once, just too perilous to do anything but stay at home, or maybe wander down to the local bar and talk about nothing except the weather.

And they were all, librarian and shop assistant, waiter and tour guide, priest and shivering cop, thinking secretly: *This is wonderful.* Because for once Christmas would be a holiday. For once the city would step off the constantly moving escalator of modern life, remember to take a deep breath, close its eyes and sleep a little, all under that gorgeous, ermine coverlet that kept falling in a constant white cloud, turning the black stones of the empty streets to the colour of icing sugar.

Peroni glanced at his partner, an expression Costa now recognized, one that said: *watch this*. Then the big cop from Tuscany walked over and threw an arm around Sandri, squeezing him hard.

'Hey, Mauro,' he growled, and crushed the photographer one more time before letting go. 'Your fingers are frozen stiff. It's pitch dark here with nothing to look at but snow. Why don't you quit taking photos for a while? You must've done a couple of hundred today already. Relax. We could go some place warm. Come on. Even you clever guys could handle a caffè corretto on a night like this.'

The photographer's round, bulbous eyes blinked back at them suspiciously. He flexed his shoulders, maybe to shrug off the cold, maybe to get back some feeling after experiencing Peroni's muscular grip.

'This would be a duty break, right? I can still shoot if I want to?'

Nic Costa listened to Sandri's squeaky northern tones, sighed and put a restraining hand on his partner's arm, worried that Peroni's temper just might take a turn in the wrong direction. The photographer had been doing the rounds of the Questura all month. He was a nice enough guy, an arty type who'd been given some kind of government grant to create a documentary record of the station's work. He'd photographed all manner of people: traffic cops and forensic, the lunatics from the morgue, the paper-monkeys in clerical. Costa had seen some of his work already: a set of moody monochrome prints of the warders working the cells. They weren't half bad. And he had noted the man's steady progress around the station, understanding the greedy, interested gaze Sandri gave him and Peroni every time they crossed his path. Mauro was a photographer. He thought in visual terms, nothing much else in all probability. He must have looked at Nic Costa, small, slight, young, like an athlete who'd somehow quit the track, set him, in his mind, against the big, bulking frame of his partner, more than twenty years older and with an ugly, violently disfigured face no one ever forgot, and felt his shutter finger start to itch.

Gianni Peroni surely knew that too. He was used to sideways glances, for his looks and his history. He'd been inspector in vice for years until, almost a year before, he'd been busted down to the ranks for one simple slip-up, when he'd tasted the goods he was supposed to be investigating. All for a private, internalized reason he'd later shared with one person only, the partner who pounded the street alongside him. That didn't stop an intelligent man, one who could read an expression even on Peroni's battered features, seeing the two of them together and understanding there was a story there. It was inevitable that Sandri would pick them as his subject one day. Inevitable, too, that Gianni Peroni would see it as a challenge to ride the photographer a touch hard along the way.

'You can still shoot, Mauro,' Costa said and caught a glimpse of a resentful twinkle in Peroni's bright, beady eye.

He took his partner's arm again and whispered, 'They're just pictures, Gianni. You know the great thing about pictures?'

'Tell me, Professor,' Peroni murmured, watching

Sandri struggle to work another 35 mm cassette into his Nikon.

'They only show what's on the surface. The rest you make up. You write your own story. You imagine your own beginning and your own ending. They're fiction pretending to be truth.'

Peroni nodded. He wasn't his normal self just then, Costa thought. There were dark, complex thoughts rumbling around deep inside a head that temperamentally liked to avoid such places.

'Maybe. But does this particular fiction have a caffè corretto inside it?'

Costa coughed into a gloved hand and stamped his feet, thinking about the taste of a big slug of grappa hidden inside a double espresso and how little activity there could be on a night such as this, when even the most crooked Roman hoods would surely be thinking of nothing but a warm bed.

'I believe it does,' he answered, and scanned the deserted street, where just a single 62 bus was now struggling down the centreline at a snail's pace, trying to keep from slipping into the gutter.

Costa stepped out from the shelter of the doorway, pulling the collar of his thick black coat up into his neck, shielding his eyes from the blizzard with a frozen hand, then darted into an alley, towards the distant yellow light struggling from the tiny doorway of what he guessed just might be the last bar open in Rome.

There proved to be the only three customers in the tiny café down the alley beyond the Galleria Doria Pamphili, among the dark tangle of ancient streets that ran west towards the Pantheon and Piazza Navona. Now Costa stood with Gianni Peroni at one end of the counter, trying to calm down the big man before something untoward happened. Mauro Sandri was crouched on a stool a good distance away, concentrating hard on polishing the lenses on his damn cameras, not even touching the booze-rich caffè Peroni had bought him before war broke out.

The owner, a tall, skeletal man in his fifties, with a white nylon jacket, scrappy brown moustache and brushed-back greased grey hair, looked at the three of them in turn and declared very firmly, 'Were this up to me, I'd slap the guy around a little, Officer. I mean, you got to have limitations. There's public places and there's private places. If a man can't get a little peace and quiet when he wanders into the pisser and gets his cazzo out, what's this world coming to? That's what I want to know. That and when you people are getting the hell out of here. If you weren't police I'd be closed already. A man don't pay the mortgage selling three coffees in an hour, and I don't see anyone else showing up for this party either.'

He was right. Costa had seen just a couple of figures scurrying through the snow when they trudged to the bar. Now it was just solid white beyond the door. Anyone with sense was, surely, snug at home, swearing not to set foot outside until the blizzard ended and some sunlight turned up to disclose what Rome looked like after an extraordinary night like this.

Gianni Peroni had downed his coffee and added an extra grappa on top, which was unlike the man. He sat hunched on an ancient rickety stool, designed to be as uncomfortable as possible so no one lingered, staring mutely at the bottles behind the bar. It wasn't Sandri's stupid trick with the camera that had caused this. Costa knew that all along. Trying to get a picture of Peroni taking a piss – vérité was what Mauro had called it – was just the final straw that had pushed the big man over the edge.

They'd discussed this already earlier that evening when Costa had quietly asked if everything was OK. It all came out in a rush. What was really bugging Peroni was the fact he wouldn't see his kids this Christmas, for the first time ever.

'I'll get Mauro to apologize,' Costa said now. 'He didn't mean anything, Gianni. You had the measure of the guy straight away. He just does this, all the time. Taking pictures.'

Besides, Costa thought, it could have been quite something too. He could easily imagine a grainy black-and-white shot of Peroni's hulking form, shot from the back, shrinking into the corner of the bar's grubby urinal, looking like an out-take from some fifties shoot in Paris by Cartier-Bresson. Sandri had an eye for a picture. Costa half blamed himself. When Peroni dashed for the toilet door and Sandri's eyes lit up, he should surely have seen what was coming.

'I've bought all the presents, Nic,' Peroni moaned, those piggy eyes twinkling back at him, the scarred face full of guilt and pain. 'How the hell do I get them to Siena now with this shitty weather everywhere? What are they going to think of me, on top of everything else?'

'Phone them. They know what it's like here. They'll understand.'

'They will?' Peroni snapped. 'What the fuck do you know about kids, huh?'

Costa took his hand off Peroni's huge, hunched

shoulder, shrugged and said nothing. Peroni had two children: a girl of thirteen, a boy of eleven. He never seemed to be able to think of them as anything but helpless infants. It was one of the traits Costa admired in his partner. To the world he looked like a bruised, scarred thug, the last kind of man anyone would want to meet on a dark night. And it was all an act. Underneath Peroni was just a straightforward, honest, old-fashioned family man, one who'd stepped out of line once and paid the heaviest price.

'Oh, crap.' Peroni sighed. 'I'm sorry. I didn't mean it. I don't want to lash out at you. I don't even want to lash out at Mauro over there.'

'That's good to know,' Costa replied, then added, 'if there's anything I can do . . .'

'Such as what?' Peroni asked.

'It's an expression, Gianni. It's a way a friend has of saying, "No, I haven't the first idea how I can help, and the truth is I probably can't do a thing. But if I could, I would." Understood?'

A low, croaking snort of semi-amusement escaped Peroni's throat. 'OK, OK. I am contrite. I repent my sins.' His scarred face screwed up with distaste aimed, it seemed to Costa, somewhere deep inside himself. 'Some more than others.'

Then he shot a vicious look at Sandri, huddled over the Nikons. 'I want that film, though. I'm not having my pecker pasted all over the notice board for everyone to see. They told the guy he could follow us around and take pictures. They didn't say he could walk straight after us into the pisser.'

'Mauro says there's really nothing there. People

wouldn't even see it was you. And maybe it's a good picture, Gianni. Think of it.'

The battered face wrinkled into a set expression of scepticism. 'It's a picture of a man taking a piss. Not the Mona Lisa.'

Costa had tried to talk art to Peroni before. It didn't work. Peroni was irretrievably romantic at heart, still stuck on the idea of beauty. Truth came somewhere far behind. And it occurred to Costa too that maybe there was more to the big man's misery then the genuine distress he felt at being separated from his kids. There was also the matter of the relationship he had struck up with Teresa Lupo, the pathologist working at the police morgue. It was meant to be a secret, but secrets never really stayed hidden for long inside the Questura. Peroni was dating the likeable, wayward Teresa and it was common knowledge. When Costa found out, a couple of weeks before, he had thought long and hard about it and had come to the conclusion that they might, just, make a good couple. If Peroni could swallow down his guilt. If Teresa could keep her life straight for long enough to make things work once the initial flush of mad enthusiasm that came with any affair subsided into the routine of everyday existence.

'Gimme a cappuccino,' Costa said to the barman. 'It's going to be a long, cold night out there.'

There was a howl of protest from behind the counter. 'It's nearly twelve, for God's sake. What am I running here? A soup kitchen for cops?'

'Gimme one too,' Sandri said from the other end of the bar, pushing away his cold corretto. 'Get one for all of us. I'm paying.'

Then the photographer walked over, looked Peroni in the eye and placed a 35 mm film cassette in his hand.

'I'm sorry,' he said. 'Really. I shouldn't have done it like that. It's just . . .'

Peroni waited for an explanation. When it didn't come, he asked, 'Just what?'

'I knew you'd have said no. I apologize, OK? I was wrong. But you have to understand this, Peroni. If a man like me had to ask every time he took a photograph, there'd hardly be any pictures in the world. All those ones you remember. All those ones you think are important. They came from some guy with a camera who pointed the stupid thing while no one was really taking any notice and went . . . pop. Improvisation. Speed. That's what this job's all about. Stealing other people's moments.'

Peroni looked him up and down and considered this.

'A little like your job, huh?' Sandri said.

The barman slid three coffees down the counter, spilling milk and foam everywhere.

'Listen, assholes, this is the last,' he snarled. 'Do you think you could possibly just pay for them then go steal a few moments some place else, huh? I'd like to go to bed and count the seven and a bit euros I earned tonight. And I got to open those doors at six thirty tomorrow morning, not that anyone's going to be walking through them.'

Costa had downed one mouthful of hot, milky coffee and foam when the radio went. Peroni was looking at him hungrily as he took the call. They had to get out of the bar, they had to find something to do. If they stayed any longer, they'd never leave.

'Burglar alarm,' Costa said when he'd listened to the

message from the control room. 'The Pantheon. We're the closest.'

'Ooh,' Peroni cooed. 'A burglar alarm. Did you hear that, Mauro? Maybe we've got some wild action after all. Maybe all those bums who hang around there fleecing the tourists are breaking in, looking for somewhere warm to spend the night.'

'Damn stupid thing to do if they are,' Sandri said immediately, looking puzzled.

'In weather like this?' Peroni asked.

'It's got a hole in the roof the size of a swimming pool,' Sandri replied. 'The oculus. Remember? It's going to be as cold in there as it is outside. Colder even. Like a freezer. And nothing to steal either, not unless you can remove a few marble tombs without someone noticing.'

Peroni gave him a friendly slap on the shoulder. Not too hard this time. 'You know for a guy who talks art you're OK really, Mauro. You can take pictures of me all you want. Outside the crapper.' Then he gave Costa a querulous look. 'Are we calling the boss? He sounded desperate.'

Costa wondered about Leo Falcone. He had made a point of insisting he could be easily disturbed. 'For a burglar alarm?'

Peroni nodded. 'Leo doesn't say those things without a reason. He wants out of that place.'

'I guess so.' Costa pulled out his phone as they walked to the door and the white world beyond, feeling somewhat uneasy that Leo Falcone was so reluctant to spend a little leisure time with his superiors. And thinking all the while too about what Mauro Sandri had said.

There was no point in anyone breaking into the Pantheon. None at all.

*

Leo Falcone listened to the drone of men's voices echo around the private room in Al Pompiere, the stiff, old-fashioned first-floor restaurant in the ghetto where, by tradition, they met once a year just before Christmas. Then he looked at their heavy business coats, lined up on the hangers by the wall like black, dead-animal skins, and turned his head towards the window, wishing he was somewhere – anywhere – else.

The snow was now falling in a steady, persistent stream. Falcone took his mind off the dinner for a moment and wondered what the weather meant for the days to come. He liked to work Christmas. Most divorced men did. Those without kids anyway. He'd seen the quick, internal flash of disappointment on Gianni Peroni's face earlier in the week when the new rotas had been posted, and Peroni and Costa had realized they would both be on duty over the holiday. Peroni had hoped to go home to Tuscany for a brief reunion with his estranged family. Falcone had wondered, for a moment, whether he could arrange that. Then he'd checked himself. Peroni was just another cop now. He had to live with the hours just like everyone else. That's what duty was about. That and turning out for an annual dinner with a bunch of faceless grey men from SISDE, the civilian intelligence service, men who never really said what they meant or what, in truth, they wanted.

The seating arrangements were preordained: one cop, one spook, arranged in turn around the white starched cloth and the highly polished silverware. Falcone sat at the window end of the long banqueting table next to Filippo Viale, who now smoked a cigar Land clutched a glass of old chardonnay grappa as clear as water, his second of the evening. Falcone had listened to Viale's quiet, insistent voice throughout the meal, picking at the food: a deep-fried artichoke to start, a plate of *rigatoni con la pajata*, pasta seated beneath calf's intestines sautéed with the mother's milk still inside, then, as secondo a serving of bony lamb scottadito served alongside a head of torsello chicory stuffed with anchovies. It was the kind of food Al Pompiere was known for, and, like his dinner companion, not to Falcone's more modern taste.

Viale had been his point man with the SISDE since Falcone made inspector ten years before. In theory that meant they liaised with one another on an equal basis from time to time, when the two services needed to share information. In reality Falcone couldn't remember a single occasion on which Viale or any other of the grey men, as he thought of them, were ever of real assistance. There'd been plenty of calls from Viale, fishing for information, asking for a favour. Usually Falcone had complied because he knew what the cost of reluctance would be: a call to an appointment upstairs and an icy interrogation from his superiors, asking what the problem was. Before he was promoted, he'd thought the grey men's power was on the wane. That was in the early nineties, when the Cold War was over and terrorism seemed a thing of the past. A time of optimism, as he saw it now, when a younger Falcone, still married, still with some sense of hope, was able to believe the world was becoming a smarter place, one that grew a little wiser, a little more safe, with every passing year.

Then the circle turned again. New enemies, faceless ones with no particular flag to identify them, emerged out of nowhere. While the police and the Carabinieri struggled to hold the fort against a rising swell tide of crime using increasingly meagre and conventional resources, the funding went to the grey men, filling their coffers for operations that never came under any public scrutiny. There was a shift in the moral fulcrum. For some in government the end came to justify the means. This was, Falcone knew, the state of the world he would probably have to work with, for the rest of his professional life. That knowledge didn't make it any easier to bear. Nor was he flattered by the grey men's apparent belief that they saw something in Leo Falcone they wanted.

'Leo,' Viale said quietly, 'I have to ask. I know we've been through this before. But still . . . it puzzles me.'

'I don't want another job.' Falcone sighed, hearing a note of testiness in his voice. 'Can't we just leave it at that?'

They'd been trying to recruit him off and on for a good four years or more. Falcone was never quite certain how genuine Viale's offer was. It was a standard SISDE trick to hold out lures to men in the conventional force. It flattered them, made them feel there could be a future somewhere else if life got too difficult in the Questura.

Viale downed the grappa and ordered another. The waiter, who was handing around a very old-fashioned sponge cake as dessert, took the glass and returned with it filled immediately. Viale was a regular here, Falcone guessed. Maybe he had booked the dinner. Maybe he was the boss. SISDE officers never said much about their rank. By rights Falcone was supposed to be matched against someone near his own position in the hierarchy. He didn't know Viale well. Like so many SISDE officers, the man was infuriatingly anonymous: a dark suit, a pale, nondescript face, a head of black hair, dyed in all probability, and a demeanour that embraced many smiles and not a touch of warmth or humour. Falcone couldn't even put a finger on his age. Viale wasn't the physical type. He was of medium height, slightly built, with a distinct paunch. Yet Falcone felt sure there was something more serious about the man than he allowed. Viale didn't sit behind the same kind of desk as he did, nor did he have to tackle the same, incessant trinity of problems: detection, intelligence and resources. Viale was, somehow, a man who made his own life and there, Leo Falcone thought, was something to envy.

Viale put a slight hand on Falcone's arm and looked directly into his face. There was northern blood in him, Falcone thought. It showed in the flat, emotionless landscape of his anonymous face, and those grey-blue eyes, cold, mirthless.

'No, we can't just leave it at that, Leo. Just say yes now and I can push through the paperwork straight away. You could be sitting behind a new desk before the end of January.'

Falcone laughed and watched the snow again. It made him feel good somehow. It reminded him of his parting words to every man he'd sent out into the city that night, ordering them, for once, to disturb his private time for the slightest reason.

'I'll think about it,' Falcone replied. 'Just like last time.'

Viale cast him a vile glance and muttered a low, obscene curse. He was, Falcone realized, more than a little drunk.

'Don't fuck with me, Leo,' Viale murmured. 'Don't play games.'

'It's always been one of my rules,' Falcone answered

calmly, 'not to fuck with the grey men. It's bad for your career.'

Viale snorted, then casually stuffed a piece of sponge cake into his mouth, despatching crumbs and sugar down the front of his black jacket. 'You think you're above all this, don't you? Sitting there in your grubby little office. Sending out grubby little men to chase people you probably can't put in jail anyway, even if you catch them.'

'It's a job someone's got to do,' Falcone said, then looked at his watch. It was almost midnight. Perhaps it was late enough to make a polite exit without offending anyone except Viale, who was offended enough as it was.

'It's a job?' Viale snarled. 'Jesus Christ, Leo.'

The grey man cast his eyes around the room and shook his head. Falcone did the same. Most of the individuals there were getting stinking drunk. It was tradition. It was Christmas.

Viale barked at the waiter. The man came back with a flask of grappa. Viale clutched it and poured out a couple, just for them, as if no one else in the room existed.

'This is a hundred a bottle and I'm paying,' he muttered, then nodded at the tiny window, now blocked with snow. 'Even you need something warm inside on a night like this.'

Falcone took the glass, sipped at the fiery drink then put it on the table. Spirits had never been his thing.

Viale watched him. 'You don't like joining in, do you? You think you can get through all this shit on your own, so long as your luck holds and you keep getting good marks every time they come to check the statistics.

What's a man like you messing around with that crap for?'

Targets, benchmarks, goals . . . Falcone didn't like the jargon of the modern police force any more than the rest of his colleagues. But unlike most he saw a point behind the paperwork. Everyone needed some kind of standard by which their efforts could be measured internally, and publicly if need be. It was anathema to people like Viale, who could screw up for years and never get found out unless a rare, scrupulous civil servant or politician got on their back. That thought jogged a memory from somewhere, but he couldn't nail it down.

Falcone looked at his watch then pushed the glass away. The raw smell of the spirit was overwhelming. 'Say what you want to say, Filippo. It's late. I want a good night's sleep. With this weather the Questura's going to be short of people tomorrow. Maybe we'll have to help out uniform or traffic. I don't know.'

'Traffic!' Viale snapped. 'Why the hell would you want to waste your time on that?'

'I believe it's something to do with being a public servant,' Falcone replied dryly.

Viale waved the glass of clear liquid at him. 'And I'm not, huh? How do you know?'

'I don't, Filippo. That's the point.' Falcone shifted awkwardly on his seat. He didn't want to upset this man any more than he had already. Viale had influence, power over him perhaps. But he didn't want to prolong this difficult interview either. 'Shouldn't we discuss this some other time? During the day. When we both feel —' he couldn't suppress a glance at the carafe of grappa – 'more ready to talk sense.'

Viale's immobile face flushed. 'I'm amazed you think you have the time.'

Falcone remained silent, waiting for the rest.

'Think about it, Leo. You're forty-eight. Has anyone asked you to sit the commissario interview recently?'

Falcone shrugged. He hadn't even considered promotion of late. Life had been too busy.

Viale provided the answer for him, which was interesting of itself. 'Not in three years. And you haven't even asked. That looks bad.'

'Promotion's not everything,' Falcone replied, knowing his answer sounded feeble. 'Some of the most important people we have are just plain street cops who'll never move up the ladder in their lives, or expect to. Where the hell would we be without them?'

Viale leaned along the table and breathed booze fumes in his face. 'We're not talking about them. We're talking about you. A man who looked like he was going far. And now he's treading water. Worse, he's making bad decisions. Backing the wrong people.'

Falcone bristled. He'd an idea now where this was leading. 'By which you mean . . .?'

'Shit,' the grey man hissed. 'You know damn well. You're getting sentimental in your dotage, Leo. You're looking out for people who don't deserve it. This Peroni idiot for one thing. If it wasn't for you he'd be out of the force now and without a pension. With good reason too. Why'd anyone with any sense stick up for a guy like that?'

Falcone thought carefully before answering. 'They asked my opinion. I gave it. Peroni's a good cop, whatever happened in the past. We can't afford to lose people of that calibre.'

'He's a disaster waiting to happen. Him and that partner of his. Now don't tell me you never stuck up for him. Hell, if it wasn't for you they wouldn't even be working together.'

None of this was SISDE's business. It infuriated Falcone that he was getting a lecture on personnel issues from someone outside the force. He'd be damned if he'd listen to it from anyone inside either. Costa and Peroni were on his team. It was his call who worked with whom.

'These are two lowly cops on the street, Filippo. My problem. Not yours.'

'No. They are two time bombs waiting to destroy what's left of your career. Peroni's going to go off the rails again before long. Mark my word. And the Costa kid . . .' Viale leaned forward and said this quietly, as if it were a condence. 'Come on, Leo. You know who his old man was? That stinking commie who caused us no end of trouble when he was alive.'

Now Falcone recalled the memory that had been eluding him. Some fifteen years earlier Costa's father, an implacably incorrupt Communist politician, had exposed a series of financial misdeeds inside both the civilian and military security services. SISDE in particular came out badly. Heads had rolled as a result. A couple of fall guys even found themselves briefly in jail.

'What on earth has that got to do with the son?' he asked.

'There's trouble in the blood,' Viale muttered. 'People like that have got ideas above their station. Be honest with yourself. You know it as well as I do.'

'These are internal police matters,' Falcone replied

sharply. 'You don't have to concern yourself with our business.'

'I'm concerned with you, Leo. People are taking note. They're starting to wonder. In this business you're either moving up or moving down. No one stands still. Which way do you think you're going right now? Huh?'

He leaned close, wreathed in grappa fumes, to make sure his last point went home. 'Where I am everyone moves up. You know why? This is our world. We own it. We have the money. We have the power. We don't need to go squeaking to a committee of bureaucrats so we can use it. We don't have to worry whether some asshole of an MP is going to start shooting his mouth off in parliament about what we do. Not any more. You're a man who wants results. That's what I like about you. We've got opportunities for someone like you. Ten years down the line you're still going to be employed too. Which, given how things stand . . .'

Viale paused and, with an unsteady hand, poured the remains of Falcone's glass into his.

' . . . isn't the case where you are now. Listen to a friend, Leo. These last few years I've been offering you a job. That's not what's on the table now. I'm throwing you a lifeline. One that could pull you out of all the crap you're swimming in. Before it's too late.'

Falcone's mobile rang. He excused himself, answered it, listening carefully to the familiar voice.

'I'm needed,' he said when the call ended.

Viale's face creased in a drunken sneer, one Falcone found faintly amusing. 'What is it? Some tourist got mugged again down the Colosseum? The Kosovans getting uppity about who rules the hooker trade?'

'Not exactly,' Falcone replied, smiling, getting to his

feet, reaching for his camel-hair coat, wondering whether it really would keep out the cold on such a night. 'It's much more important than that. Excuse me.'

Viale raised his glass. 'Ciao, Leo. You have until the New Year. After that you're on your own.'

They left the car where it was, tyre deep in drifting snow in a blocked dead-end off the Corso, and walked to the Piazza della Minerva through a squally wind. The weather changed by the moment. Briefly, through a clear patch high overhead, a full moon illuminated billowing banks of heavy cloud scudding over the city. The stars shone, bright and brittle in the thin winter air, possessing a piercing clarity that was almost painful.

Then the blizzard returned, and the three men pulled their jackets around their faces and turned the corner into the small square, where the plain, brute cylinder of the Pantheon's rear wall loomed above them, luminous under the night's silver light. It was a sight Nic Costa had never expected to see. The vast hemisphere of the dome, the largest in the world until the twentieth century, so vast that Michelangelo had made the diameter of St Peter's dome half a metre smaller out of respect, was now swathed in snow, cutting an unmistakable semicircle out of the sky, like the meniscus of a gigantic new moon rising above the dark urban horizon.

Costa cast a glance at Bernini's famous elephant in front of the church. The creature was almost unrecognizable. A heavy drift had engulfed the statue and the foot of the diminutive Egyptian obelisk that sat on its midriff. A perfect, miniature mountain rose up from the ground to form a triangular peak, surmounted by the bare needle-like pinnacle of the column, etched with impenetrable hieroglyphs. Sandri fired off some more shots. Peroni watched and shook his head. Then they carried on, walking parallel with the eastern wall of the Pantheon, into the small, rectangular open space of the Piazza della Rotonda.

Costa felt he knew every inch of the pizza. He'd arrested pickpockets working the busy summer crowds who had flocked to see the impossible: an imperial Roman temple unchanged in its essential form over almost twenty centuries. And a sight that, just as important to many, was free, since Hadrian's original shrine to every last god in the heavens had in the seventh century been converted into the consecrated church it still remained. Once Costa had picked up a drunk who'd fallen asleep beneath the spouting mouths of the comical dolphins and fauns of the fountain opposite the temple's massive, colonnaded portico. But long before he became a cop, when he was just a school kid full of awe and passion for the history of his native city, he'd come here whenever he could, just to sit on the steps of the fountain and listen to water trickle from the dolphins' beaks like liquid laughter, just to stare at the way everything changed in the shifting light of the day and the season, feeling two thousand years of bustling history brush up against his face.

Tonight he scarcely recognized the place. The blustering northerly wind was funnelling down the narrow alleys facing the piazza, cascading new and fallen snow straight into the square and the mouth of the Pantheon's portico. Curious organically shaped drifts clung to the fountain. The streams of water from the dolphins' mouths and fauns' were now frozen solid, like lumpen jewels gleaming in the moonlight.

Peroni was scanning the piazza for signs of life. Mauro had his camera out, changing films. Costa approved. This was a rare sight, he thought. It deserved to be recorded.

'Where the hell is everyone, Nic?' Peroni asked. 'I don't even see the bums.'

The poor were with you always. Particularly in a place like this.

'Maybe they're inside already,' Costa said. Or, even better, perhaps the city had discovered hidden reserve of compassion and found space to house them for the night.

'We've got company,' Peroni said, pointing to a figure emerging from behind the western wall of the building.

The man shivered inside a dark uniform, shielding his face against the snow, which seemed to have found some newly energized vigour. He stumbled through the blasts, stared at them hopefully, then asked, 'You the cops?'

Peroni waved his badge. Costa looked around the square again. More people should have been there. Falcone ought to arrive soon too.

'I'm not going inside on my own,' the caretaker said. 'Some of these scum use knives.'

Peroni nodded at the doors. 'Best open them up then.'

The man let loose a dry laugh then looked at Sandri, firing shots right, left and centre. 'Sure, Officer. That's all it takes. Is your man here going to shoot some pictures too? They say you see it just once in a lifetime. Snow coming down like that, straight through the eye.'

'So what are we waiting for?' Peroni asked.

Costa knew the problem. Behind the portico lay the

largest pair of imperial Roman doors in existence. Worked bronze, almost as high as the porch itself, and more than a metre deep. Sometimes, before going on duty, he'd take a coffee in the square in the early morning, watching the Pantheon being prepared for another day's crowds. No one who worked in the building ever approached through the front, not to begin with. The doors opened inwards, their mass being drawn back slowly from behind.

'We need the tradesmen's entrance,' Costa said.

'Precisely.' The man sniffed, then drew back his collar to reveal a gnarled, florid face that looked as if half a bottle of grappa could be wrung out of it. 'All three of you coming?'

Costa looked at Peroni. 'I can handle a couple of street people. Stay here with Mauro. Wait for Falcone.'

'No,' Peroni said, striding towards the shelter of the portico. 'I stay here.'

Costa followed in the caretaker's swift footsteps, walking to the western flank, where they descended some stairs down to what must have been the original level of the city when the Pantheon was built. There was a locked iron gate, then further steps and a long, narrow path, in the shadow of the high modern wall of the adjoining street, to a small, secure door almost at the rear of the building.

'The tradesman's entrance,' the caretaker said icily, then turned a couple of locks and threw it open. Costa stepped into the alcove and waited as the man fumbled with some keys at a second door, which led, he guessed, to the great circular interior, wondering what kind of bum locked the doors behind him.

He listened to the metal tumblers turn.

'After you,' the caretaker said. 'I'll get the lights.'

Nic Costa walked into the darkness and felt the chill of fresh winter air on his face. The night breeze was circling in the vast hemisphere he knew lay before him. And there was another sound too. Of a human being moving: short, anxious steps in the blackness beyond.

He felt his jacket, wondered about the gun. Then the lights of the building burst into life, bringing a sudden harsh sun into the shadows of the vast, airy, artificial universe enclosed beneath the structure's huge dome.

Someone cried out with surprise. A young voice. The noise reverberated around the vast emptiness so quickly it seemed to come from everywhere.

'Will you look at that?' the caretaker said, not even thinking about the intruders any more.

Through the the giant open eye of the oculus came a steady, swirling stream of snow, pirouetting around itself with the perfect, precise symmetry of a strand of human DNA.

It fell in the dead centre of the room, where an inverted, icy funnel was growing, spreading out beyond the central marble ring and rising, at its peak, to a metre or more.

Costa heard movement to his right. A slight, small figure dashed through a brilliant yellow beam cast down by a spotlight near the main altar, then fled into the pool of shadows in a recess on the far side of the building.

'Scum,' the caretaker muttered. 'What are you going to do?'

Costa had been running the options through his mind. Chase some lone, cold, hungry bum through the darkness of Hadrian's holiest of holies? And all for what?

'Open the doors,' he said. 'The main ones.'

Costa was walking towards them already, anxious to enjoy the look of astonishment on the faces of Gianni Peroni and Mauro Sandri when those gigantic bronze shutters were pulled back to reveal this wonder to the world on the other side.

'What?' the caretaker asked, putting a hand on Costa's shoulder until something in the detective's eyes told him this was not a good idea.

'You heard!' Costa snapped, getting angry with the man, wondering what he thought he was protecting here.

There were more keys and some kind of electronic monitor needed attention. Costa got on the mobile and called his partner, just beyond the doors.

'I'm not playing hide and seek in here, Gianni,' he said. 'I think it's just a kid. If he runs, you can get some exercise. Otherwise . . . hell, it's almost Christmas.'

The big man's laugh came back as a double echo, from the phone and, fainter, from beyond the doors. 'You're itching to do Leo's clean-up statistics some good tonight.'

'Just stand back and watch when we open this place.' Then he thought about what Peroni had said. 'Is Falcone there?'

'Walking right across the square. And on the phone too. This isn't a conference call or something?'

Costa heard a low metallic groan and put the phone back in his jacket. The caretaker was heaving at the bronze behemoth on his right, tugging it back on a set of ancient hinges. Costa took hold of the second door and pulled hard at the handle. It moved surprisingly easily.

In the space of a few seconds they had them open.

The night wind rolled straight up the portico and blew snow into their faces. Nic Costa brushed the stinging flakes out of his eyes. Gianni Peroni stood there, transfixed by what he saw. Sandri was a few steps behind him, tense, upright, firing off photos constantly. Falcone had arrived too and seemed to be barking angrily down the phone.

Costa turned round and took another look at the magical scene behind him, snow swirling down from the heavens, as if tethered to a magnetic, twisting beam of light.

The bum was moving in the Pantheon now. Nic Costa no longer cared. He stood back from the door to let the intruder run, break out from this tight, enclosed universe that was the dream of an emperor who had been dead for nearly two millennia.

Then he looked outside again and recognized a different shape – upright and stiff on the steps of the fountain – not quite able to believe what he was seeing, to reconcile it with this bewitching night.

A figure slipped past him, brushing against his jacket. Costa didn't even look. With fumbling fingers he unzipped his coat, felt for his gun in the holster.

'Get down,' he said, still trying to marshal his thoughts, letting the words slip from his mouth so softly he doubted the caretaker even heard. Then he took a deep breath and yelled, as loudly as he could, 'Gianni! Get down for Christ's sake!'

Automatically, without planning the move, he dashed out into the portico and felt the freezing wind bite at his face. Gianni Peroni was still staring into the interior of the Pantheon, face alight with joy, grinning like a kid.

Falcone was getting close to him too, his stern, immobile features for once rapt, captured by the scene inside.

'Get down!' Costa screamed again, waving his hands, waving the small black revolver through the falling cloud of white flakes. '*Now!* The bastard's got a gun.'

He heard the first shot drown out the end of his words. Something small and deadly sang its way through the air. Sparks flew off the column close to the astonished faces of the two cops under the portico. Falcone's arm went out and pushed Peroni down to the stone pavement.

Costa was focused on the man on the steps now. The figure was on his own directly by the fountain, dressed in black from head to foot and wearing one of those idiotic tie-down hats with earpieces that made you look like Mickey Mouse caught in a storm. He was standing in a professional firing position, the Weaver stance, right hand on the trigger, left supporting the gun, feet apart, comfortable as hell in the sort of pose Costa sometimes saw at target-shooting events. The small pistol was aimed, very deliberately, in their direction. A tiny flame lit up the barrel as Costa watched and a muffled crack rolled their way.

Costa scanned the piazza, doing his best to check there was no one else in the vicinity then unleashed two shots towards the figure in the snow. A stream of tiny fires lit up furiously in response, sending more sparks up from old stone that was, at least, some kind of protection for them. For those who were smart enough to take it.

Mauro Sandri was still standing. Maybe it was panic. Maybe it was just second nature. He was flapping around like a wild man, one hand still on the stupid camera, loosing off frames of anything, the Pantheon, the night, the three cops trying to squirm their way out of the firestorm coming at them from the square.

Then he turned, and Costa knew precisely what would happen next. Mauro spun round on his little heels, camera in hand, the motor drive of the Nikon clicking away like a clockwork robot, turned and faced the black figure still upright on the steps.

'Mauro,' Costa said quietly, knowing there was no point.

He was a stride away from the little photographer when the bullets hit. Two. He heard the reports as they left the barrel of the gun. He heard them hit the diminutive black figure on the steps, tear through the fabric of his winter jacket, bite like deadly insects deep into Sandri's body.

The little photographer flew into the air like a man receiving an electric shock then fell in a disfigured heap onto the ground.

'See to him,' Costa yelled at Peroni and Falcone as they scrambled to their feet in the deep, consuming snow. 'This son of a bitch is mine.'

Knowing the idea was pointless, that no one could shoot that well, not even the dark-hearted bastard standing by the frozen dolphins and fauns, Costa let off a bullet all the same, then began to sprint, began to hit his speed, and thought: *At least I can run. Can you?* The figure was folding on himself, turning, like a crow shrinking into a crouch before it half jumped, half fell off a fence. There was fear there as he fled down the steps on the far side of the dolphins and fauns. Costa knew it and the knowledge made him pump harder with his legs, not minding how slippery the centuries-old paving stones were beneath his feet.

He loosed off another shot. The man was fleeing into the corner of the square, trying to find sanctuary in the dark, tangled labyrinth of narrow streets and alleys that lay beyond, in every direction.

And, just as Costa was beginning to digest this thought, the weather joined in. A sudden vicious squall careered straight out of the north, a thick wad of snow deep in its gut. The cruel, cutting ice stung and blinded. His feet gave way. The rugby player in him surfaced from the long dead past, told him there was no option but to roll with the fall, to tumble into the soft, freezing blanket on the ground, because the alternative was to pitch gravity and momentum against the weakness of the human body and snap a tendon or a bone along the way.

It was dark and cold as he fell into the soft, fresh snow, taking the hard stone beneath with his shoulder. For a brief moment the world was a sea of whirling white and sharp, violent pain. Then he was still, feeling himself, checking nothing was broken.

When he got his equilibrium back and forced himself to his feet, the figure in black was gone. Dense clouds of white were falling with an unforgiving force again, burying the man's footprints with every passing second, turning everything into a single, empty shade of nothingness. Costa strode to the corner of the street. He could have gone one of two ways, west down the Via Giustiniani, towards the church of San Luigi dei Francesi, with its Caravaggios and, for Nic Costa, some bitter memories. Or north, into the warren beyond Piazza della Maddalena.

Costa stared at the ground. It looked like a fresh bed sheet, scarcely crumpled, full of secrets, all of them unreachable.

Reluctantly, understanding what he would find, he retraced his steps to the portico. A siren was sounding somewhere in the wintry night. Costa wondered how long it would take the ambulance to make its way through the treacherous streets. Then he saw Gianni Peroni hunched on the flat stone of the portico next to Mauro Sandri's inert form, and knew it didn't really matter.

He walked over, determined to handle this well.

'Hey,' Costa said, placing a hand on his partner's shoulder, then crouching down to peer into those strangely emotional squinty eyes, which were now liquid with cold and a bright inner fury. 'We couldn't have known, Gianni.'

'I will remember to point this out when I break it to his mamma, or his wife or boyfriend or whoever,' Peroni replied bitterly, trying to bite back his rage.

'He must have looked like one of us, I guess. It could have been you. Or me. Or anyone.'

'That's a comforting thought,' Peroni mumbled.

Costa glanced at the dead photographer. Blood, black under the moonlight, was caking in Sandri's open mouth. Two more patches, one on his upper chest, the second in the centre of his abdomen, shone on his jacket. Costa remembered that curious stance the gunman had held while firing at them. It contained some meaning. When they had started to swallow down the bitter bile of their shock, when the investigation proper began, this was a point to note, an item of interest to be pursued.

Peroni patted Sandri's still arm. 'I told him, Nic. I said, "Mauro, you're not going to die. I promise. You're just going to lie there and wait for the medics to come. Then one day you go back to photographing mugs like me, and this time round you can take snaps of my pecker as much as you want. This time round" . . . Oh shit.'

'We'll get the bastard, big man,' Costa said quietly. 'Where's Falcone?'

'Inside,' Peroni said with a slow, deliberate venom. 'Maybe he's enjoying the view.'

A blue flashing beacon began to paint the walls on the far side of the square. Then a second. The cater-wauling of the sirens became so loud that lights came on in apartment windows in the neighbouring streets. Costa got up. There was no point in talking to Peroni when he was in this mood. He had to wait for the storm to pass.

Costa walked through the doors towards the stream of white that fell, still circling around itself, from the vast open eye of the oculus.

The caretaker was in his cabin by the entrance, florid face down into his chest, trying as hard as he could to stay out of everything. Leo Falcone stood by the inverted funnel, which kept growing as it was fed from the sky. Costa remembered studying the Pantheon at school in art class. Here, at the centre of the hall, lay the defining focal point of the building, the axis around which everything was arranged in a precise show of ancient symmetry, both the great hemisphere and the monumental brick cylinder which tethered this imaginary cosmos to the ground.

'The photographer's dead, sir,' Costa said, trying to allow a note of reproach to slip into his voice.

'I know,' Falcone replied without emotion. 'Scene of crime are on the way. And the rest. Do you have any idea where the man in the square went?'

'No.'

Falcone's stony face said everything.

'I'm sorry,' Costa added. 'We came here thinking it was a bunch of bums breaking in to keep warm. It was a burglar alarm, for God's sake.'

'I know,' the inspector said carefully. He walked to the head of the funnel, where it was close to the apse and the altar, pointing due south, directly opposite the portico entrance and the open bronze doors. Costa followed. There Falcone bent down and, with a gloved finger, pointed at the edge of the fresh snow.

Costa's breath caught as he began to understand. A thin line of pigment was running from inside the funnel, out to the edge of the crystals as they tried to turn to water on the marble and porphyry. The stain became paler and paler as it flowed towards the edge but there could be no mistake. Nic Costa knew the colour by now. It was blood.

'I've done this once already,' Falcone said, pulling out a handkerchief from his coat. 'Damn snow.'

Slowly, with the same care Costa had seen Teresa Lupo use in such situations, Falcone swept at the funnel with light, brushing strokes.

Costa stood back and watched, wishing he were somewhere else. The head of a woman was emerging from beneath the soft, white sheet of ice. An attractive woman with a large, sensual mouth, wide open dark green eyes, and a face which was neither young nor old, a full, frank, intelligent face that wore an expression of intense shock so vivid it seemed to border on outrage.

Falcone briefly touched her long jet black hair, then turned to watch the snow coming down and the way it was beginning to bury her anew.

'Don't lay a finger on a thing,' Falcone said. 'I shouldn't have done as much as I did.'

'No, sir,' Costa whispered, his head reeling.

'Well?' Falcone didn't even seem put out by this. It was as if everything was as normal, just another everyday event that the cold, distant inspector could take in his stride.

'Well what?' Costa snapped back.

'Well how about you sit down on that chair over there and write down every last thing you remember. You're a witness here, Costa. Interview yourself. And don't skip the awkward questions.'